Praise for Penny Vincenzi's

⊰ THE BEST OF TIMES ⊱

"Gripping, heartbreaking and exciting. . . . An exhilarating read." —*Woman & Home*

"Vincenzi is at her absolute best when describing the mores, manners and manors of the affluent middle classes, and here she serves up more fabulous gardens, riverside homes, privately educated children and dramatically-exposed affairs with dirty women than you can shake a stick at. Classic Vincenzi." —*Daily Mail*

"Sweeping, dramatic, [and] surprising."
—*Bookreporter*

"The charm of *The Best of Times* lies in the chain reactions that occur after the crash, as if things always happen for a reason, and that much good can come from great tragedy."
—*Las Vegas Review-Journal*

"You won't want to put down *The Best of Times* until you've turned over the last page."
—*The Coventry Telegraph*

"Enthralling and heartbreaking."
—*The Daily Mirror*

PENNY VINCENZI

❦ THE BEST OF TIMES ❦

Penny Vincenzi is the author of several major best-sellers, including *Sheer Abandon*. Before becoming a novelist, she worked as a journalist for *Vogue*, *Tattler*, and *Cosmopolitan*. She lives in London.

THE BEST OF TIMES

A Novel

PENNY VINCENZI

ANCHOR BOOKS

A DIVISION OF RANDOM HOUSE, INC.

NEW YORK

FIRST ANCHOR BOOKS EDITION, JUNE 2010

Copyright © 2009 by Penny Vincenzi

The Library of Congress has cataloged the Doubleday edition
as follows:
Vincenzi, Penny.
The best of times / by Penny Vincenzi.—1st ed.
p. cm.
1. Life changing events—Fiction.
2. Traffic accidents—Fiction. I. Title.
PR6072.I525B47 2009
823'.914—dc22   2008053916

Anchor ISBN: 978-0-7679-3085-7

www.anchorbooks.com

Printed in the United States of America
10 9 8 7 6 5 4 3 2 1

For Emily and Claudia,

with much love.

For saving the plot, the book,

and their mother's sanity.

❖ THE BEST OF TIMES ❖

A Time Near to Now

It happened just before four p.m. after a brief thundery shower. The Friday traffic had packed the M4 in both directions, heavy enough to hold cars in the fast lane just within the speed limit, light enough to keep all three lanes moving. Viewed on the CCTV cameras, everything looked orderly and under control.

At one minute to four, a lorry travelling eastwards swerved suddenly, and then accelerated towards the central median, cutting through it with lethal force, and then turned in on itself, its trailer twisting and half rearing before falling onto its side, slithering along the road into the oncoming traffic and finally coming to a halt just short of the hard shoulder. It burst open, not only the doors, but the roof and sides, discharging its burden of freezers, fridges, washing machines, dryers, some tossed into the air with the force, some skidding and sliding along the motorway, a great tide of deadly flotsam, hitting cars and coaches in its path.

A minibus driving westwards in the fast lane became impacted in the undercarriage of the lorry; a Golf GTI immediately behind it swung sideways and rammed into one of the lorry's wheels. A vast, unyielding dam of vehicles braking, swerving, skidding was formed, growing by the moment.

On the eastbound side of the carriageway, the cars immediately behind the lorry smashed into it and one another; one hit the central median with such force it became embedded in it, and the dozen or so after that, with an advantage of two or three seconds' warning, skidded into one another relentlessly but comparatively harmlessly, like bumper cars in a fairground.

The freezers and refrigerators continued on their journey with enormous force; one car hitting them head-on made a hundred-and-eighty-degree turn, and was struck by an oncoming motorbike; another shot sideways and hit the central median.

Up and down on the road, then, stillness formed, and a strange semi-silence overtook the road, engines stopped, horns hushed, but replaced by other, hideous sounds, of human screaming and canine barking, and through it all the absolutely incongruous noise of music from car radios.

And then a hundred mobiles, in hands that were able to hold them, called the police, the ambulance service, called home. And even as they did so, the chaos spread out its great tentacles, reaching far, far down the road in both directions so that hundreds were unable to escape from it.

Within the space of thirty or forty seconds, chance, that absolutely irresistible force, had taken its capricious hold on the time and the place. It had disrupted the present, distorted the future, replaced order with chaos, confidence with fear, and control with impotence. Lives were ended for some, changed forever for others; and a most powerful game of consequences was set in train.

Part One

BEFORE

Laura Gilliatt often said—while reaching for the nearest bit of wood—that her life was simply too good to be true. And indeed, the casual observer—and quite a beady-eyed one—would have been hard-pressed not to agree with her. She was married to a husband she adored, Jonathan Gilliatt, the distinguished gynaecologist and obstetrician, and had three extremely attractive and charming children, with a career of her own as an interior designer, just demanding enough to save her from any possible boredom, but not so much that she could not set it aside when required, by any domestic crisis, large or small, such as the necessity to attend an important dinner with her husband or the nativity play of one of her children.

The family owned two beautiful houses, one on the Thames at Chiswick, a second in the Dordogne; they also had a time-share in a ski chalet in Meribel. Jonathan earned a great deal of money from his private practice at St. Anne's, an extremely expensive hospital just off Harley Street, but he was also a highly respected NHS consultant, heading up the obstetric unit at St. Andrews, Bayswater. He was passionately opposed to the modern trend for elective caesareans, both in his private practice and the NHS; in his opinion they were a direct result of the compensation culture. Babies were meant to be pushed gently into the world by their mothers, he said, not yanked abruptly out. He was, inevitably, on the receiving end of a great deal of criticism for this in the more vocally feminist branches of the media.

The beady-eyed observer would also have noted that he was deeply in love with his wife, while enjoying the adoration of his patients; and that his son, Charlie, and his daughters, Daisy and

Lily—his two little flowers, as he called them—all thought he was absolutely wonderful.

In his wife he had an absolute treasure, as he often told not only her but the world in general; for as well as being beautiful, Laura was sunny natured and sweet tempered, and indeed, this same observer, studying her quite intently as she went through her days, would have been hard-pressed to catch her in any worse humour than mild irritation or even in raising her voice. If this did happen, it was usually prompted by some bad behaviour on the part of her children, such as Charlie, who was eleven, sneaking into the loo with his Nintendo when he had had his hour's ration for the day, or Lily and Daisy, who were nine and seven, persuading the au pair that their mother had agreed that they could watch *High School Musical* for the umpteenth time until well after they were supposed to be in bed.

The Gilliatts had been married for thirteen years. "Lucky, lucky years," Jonathan said, presenting Laura with a Tiffany eternity ring on the morning of their anniversary. "I know it's not a special anniversary, darling, but you deserve it, and it comes with all my love."

Laura was so overcome with emotion that she burst into tears and then smiled through them as she looked at the lovely thing on her finger; and after that, having consulted the clock on their bedroom fireplace, she decided she should express her gratitude to Jonathan, not only for the ring but for the thirteen happy years, in a rather practical way, with the result that she got seriously behind in her school run schedule and all three children were clearly going to be late for school.

Laura had been nineteen and still a virgin when she had met Jonathan: "Probably the last in London," she said. This was not due to any particular moral rectitude, but because until him, she had honestly never fancied anyone enough to want to go to bed with him. She fancied Jonathan quite enough and found the whole experience "absolutely lovely," she told him. They were married a year later.

"I do hope I'm going to cope with being Mrs. Gilliatt, quite an important career," she said just a little anxiously a few days before the wedding; and, "Of course you will," he told her. "You fit the job description perfectly. And you'll grow into it beautifully."

As indeed she had, taking her duties very seriously; she loved cooking and entertaining, and had discovered a certain flair for interior design. When they had been married a year, and their own lovely house was finished to both their satisfaction, she asked Jonathan if he would mind if she took a course and perhaps dabbled in it professionally.

"Of course not, darling, lovely idea. As long as I don't come second to any difficult clients."

Laura promised him he wouldn't; and he never had. And neither, as the babies arrived, in neat two-year intervals, did they; for many years, until Daisy was at school, she simply devoted herself to them, and was perfectly happy. She did have to work quite hard at reassuring Jonathan that he still came absolutely first in her life, and was slightly surprised at his impatience and near-jealousy created by the demands of the children. Clearly her mother had been right, she reflected—all men were children at heart. For the first few years, therefore, she employed a full-time nanny; for the demands of Jonathan's professional life on her time were considerable, and he liked her to be totally available to him.

But when Daisy went to school, she began quite tentatively to work. She had a particular flair for colour, for using the unexpected, and she was beginning to earn a small reputation. But it all remained little more than a pleasingly rewarding hobby, very much what she did in her spare time: which was not actually in very large supply.

But that was how Jonathan liked it; and therefore she liked it too.

· · ·

Spring that year had been especially lovely; it arrived early and stayed late, perfect green-and-gold days, so that as early as April, Laura was setting the outside table for lunch every Saturday and Sunday, and as May wore on, she and Jonathan would eat dinner outside as well, and watch the soft dusk settle over the garden, listening to the sounds of the river in the background, the hooting of tugs, the partying pleasure boats, the raw cries of the gulls.

"How lucky we are," she said maybe a hundred times, smiling at Jonathan across the table, and he would raise his glass to her and reach for her hand and tell her he loved her.

. . .

But now it was midsummer and the rain had arrived: day after relentless day it fell from dark grey skies. Barbecues and summer parties were being cancelled, floaty summer dresses put away, the shops holding what they called end-of-season sales, and a stampede began for flights to Majorca and Ibiza for long weekends in the sun.

For the Gilliatts there was no such stampede; Laura was packing, as she did every year, for their annual pilgrimage to the lovely golden-stone farmhouse in the Dordogne, where the sun would shine down unstintingly on them, heating the water in the pool, ripening the grapes on the veranda vine, and warming the stones on the terrace so that the lizards might siesta in the afternoons along with their landlords.

"And thank goodness for it," she said. "Poor Serena is so dreading the holidays, keeping the boys amused all those weeks, well, months really . . ."

Jonathan said just slightly shortly that he had thought the Edwardses were off to some ten-star hotel in Nice, not to mention the week they would spend with the Gilliatts on the way down; Laura said, well, that was true, but it still added up to just over three weeks, and that left six or even seven in London.

Jonathan said that most of his NHS patients would not regard that as too much of a hardship, given the three and a half weeks of luxury sunshine; he was less fond of Mark and Serena Edwards than Laura was. Mark was a public relations consultant for a big city firm, oversmooth and charming, but Serena was Laura's best friend and, in Jonathan's view, made Laura the repository of just too many confidences and secrets.

Jonathan was not able, of course, to spend nine weeks in the Dordogne; he took as much of his annual leave as he could and, for the rest of the time, flew out each Friday afternoon to Toulouse and back each Monday.

And so, as she read reports of what appeared to be almost continuous rain in England, and indeed listened to friends in England complaining about it and telling her how lucky she was not to be there, Laura savoured the long golden days even more than usual, and even more than usual counted her own multiple blessings.

. . .

Linda Di-Marcello was aware that she also was fairly fortunate, which meant that, given her line of work, she was doing very well indeed. Linda ran a theatrical agency, and as she often said, her role was a complex one. She was, in almost equal parts, nanny, therapist, and hustler; it was both exhausting and stressful, and she threatened repeatedly to give it up and do something quite different. "Something really undemanding, like brain surgery," she would say with a smile. But she knew she never would; she loved it all too much.

The agency's name was actually Di-Marcello and Carr; Francis Carr was her nonsleeping partner, as he put it, a gay banker who adored her, had faith in her, and had put up the money for the agency, in return for "absolutely no involvement and forty per cent of the profits."

So far it had worked very well.

She was thirty-six, an acknowledged beauty, with dark red hair, dark brown eyes, and a deep, Marlene Dietrich–style voice, and she had been to drama school herself before deciding she really couldn't hack the long, long slog into nonstardom and that she rather liked the idea of agenting. She had had the agency for five years; before that she had worked for several of the established organisations before setting out on her own. And she had proved to have a talent for it; she could look at an apparently plain, shy girl and see her shining on the screen; at a charmless, ungracious lout and know he could play Noel Coward.

She didn't have many big stars on her books—yet. She had Thea Campbell, who had just won a BAFTA for her Jo in the new BBC version of *Little Women,* and Dougal Marriott, who had just been cast as the grown-up Billy in the sequel to *Billy Elliot,* and three or four more who were almost as successful, but she had a big battery of middle-rankers, mostly picked out by her from the drama schools, almost all of whom were carving out good careers for themselves. But her younger clients particularly found it hard to face reality; they were inevitably disappointed with the slow progress, and while most of them did part-time jobs in bars and restaurants or worked as runners for the TV companies, a handful were emotionally needy, impatient, and at worst disparaging of the work Linda could get them.

"You know," she said irritably to Francis Carr, "I long to tell these kids that thousands and thousands of young people can do what they can do and do it superbly well; they need an awful lot of luck and star quality to stand out. And most of them don't have those things. They're an ungrateful bunch on the whole, you know; nothing's ever good enough for them."

Francis said that the same could be said of his clients, who never felt their money was invested quite well enough or that he gave any of them quite enough of his attention. "It's human nature, Linda, fact of working life."

"I suppose so. I'm obviously making a big fuss about nothing. And when somebody does take off and I know I've been a key part of that, it's a great feeling."

"Well, exactly. Has anyone taken off recently?"

"Not exactly. It's all been a bit run-of-the-mill this summer. If you can call it summer indeed . . . Probably that's what's getting to me."

"I don't think so," he said with a grin. "You're always complaining about it."

"Am I? God, how depressing for you. Sorry, Francis. I'll try to be a bit more positive in future."

. . .

Linda lived in a mansion apartment just off Baker Street: large and luxurious, expensively furnished—in a mix of antique and contemporary—and absolutely immaculate. Her office—a sleek, modern suite near Charlotte Street—was equally so. Linda was a perfectionist in every aspect of her life. She was, by any standards, a hugely successful woman. And yet she quite often felt she was actually a failure.

She was lonely, and however much she told herself that she was lucky, that she had a far better life now, happily single rather than unhappily married, she didn't really believe it. No amount of looking at the rows of designer clothes she was able to buy, at her collections of art deco figures and lamps, at her growing gallery of modern paintings properly made up for it. She would have given all of it—well, most of it, anyway—not to be alone, not to be lonely.

She *did* have a social life—by most people's standards a glamorous one. But it wasn't quite the sort she wanted. Of course, *Sex and the City* had made singledom fashionable, which helped. Nobody had to sit at home staring at the cat anymore; you could lift the phone, call girlfriends or man friends, propose any kind of outing. You could do what you liked, when you liked it. During the week it was fine: she often worked late, and there were theatres and film screenings to go to; and she made sure her weekends were fully booked weeks or even months ahead. She did a lot of quick trips—flips, as she called them—to Paris, Milan, Rome, usually with one of her single girlfriends to visit galleries and shop; she was a Friend of Covent Garden, of Sadler's Wells and the RSC. It would certainly take a fairly remarkable man to deliver so indulgent a lifestyle.

But . . . it wasn't actually what she wanted; it was cool and demanding, and somehow self-conscious, when she yearned for warmth and ease. She wondered if perhaps she should have given Mr. Di-Marcello another chance instead of throwing him out of the house at the first discovery of his first affair.

But she knew, deep down, that she shouldn't; it *would* have been only the first one; he was about as monogamous as a tomcat. But the divorce had hurt horribly, and had been followed by a second bad relationship, with another charmer who had been seeing another girl almost before he had moved into Linda's apartment. She had an eye for a rotter, Linda often thought gloomily.

She didn't exactly want domesticity, she didn't want children, and she certainly didn't want to take on a man with a ready-made family, as so many of her friends seemed to be doing; but she did want someone to share things with, pleasures and anxieties, jokes and conversations—and, of course, her bed.

Nor did she meet that many men she fancied; the world she moved in contained an exceptionally large number of gay men, and still more addicts of one kind or another: "The London branch of the AA is incredibly A-list," as a young actress had astutely remarked (and indeed the meetings were regarded as an excellent opportunity for networking).

"I want a solicitor," she wailed to her friends. "I want a bank manager; I want an accountant." And they would tell her that she wanted no such thing, and of course they were right in one way and quite wrong in another, for what were accountants and bank managers and solicitors but synonyms for reliable and sensible and loyal?

The fact was, she no longer felt free; she felt lonely, no longer self-sufficient, but insecure. What was the matter with her? Was it such a big thing to ask? Not just to fall but to be in love. Wholeheartedly, wondrously, thunderously, orgasmically in love. It did seem to be. She really couldn't see how it was ever going to happen again.

. . .

"Only five weeks to the wedding. I absolutely can't believe it."

Barney Fraser looked at his fiancée, in all her absurd prettiness and sweetness, and sighed.

"I think I can," he said.

"Barney! That doesn't sound very . . . positive. Aren't you looking forward to it?"

"Yes," he said quickly, "yes, of course I am."

"It's the speech, isn't it? But you'll be fine; I know you will. It's all going to be wonderful. If it stops raining, that is. Pity it's not September; that's usually more reliable, much better than the summer, actually. Wouldn't you say?"

"What? I mean, no. I mean—"

"Barney, you're not listening to me. Are you?"

"Sorry, Amanda. I was . . . well, I was thinking about something else. I'm very sorry."

Actually he wasn't. He was thinking about the wedding; he thought about it more and more. Well, not the wedding. More the marriage.

"What?"

"Oh—just work. Sorry. More wine?"

"Yes, please."

He grinned at her and refilled her glass; there was nothing he could really say about his misgivings over the wedding. It was too late and it wouldn't help. It wasn't his wedding, for God's sake, that he had misgivings about; it was Toby's, and Toby was old enough to look after himself.

And Amanda was so thrilled at being maid of honour, and the bride was one of her very best friends. And when she and Barney got married the following spring, Tamara would be *her* maid of honour. And Toby would be Barney's best man.

Toby wasn't just one of Barney's best friends; he was absolutely his best friend, had been ever since prep school, when they had lain in their small beds the first night, side by side, smiling gallantly, refusing to admit either of them felt remotely homesick. And the friendship had never faltered, intensified, Barney always thought, by the fact that they were both only children, and were soon spending time with each other over the holidays as well as the term. They had stayed cheerfully together right through prep school and Harrow; then after the separation of universities, Toby at Durham, Barney at Bristol, the delight of discovering that they were both applying for jobs in the city and managed to end up not at the same investment bank—that would have been too much of a cliché—but at closely neighbouring establishments either side of Bishopsgate.

Toby was just the best: clever, funny, cool, and just plain old-fashioned nice. Barney didn't like to think of their friendship in terms of love—these days if you said you were terribly fond of another bloke, people presumed you were gay. But he *did* love him, and admired him and enjoyed his company more than that of anyone else in the world—except Amanda, obviously. Not that you could compare how you felt for your best friend and your fiancée: it was totally different. What was great was that despite their both being engaged and setting up home and all that sort of thing, they were still able to see an enormous amount of each other.

And the two girls were great friends; both worked in the city as well. It was very neat: Amanda in human resources at Toby's bank, Tamara on the French desk at Barney's. There was no reason they should all not remain friends for the rest of their lives.

Barney didn't just think that Tamara wasn't good enough for Toby—no, he *knew*. OK, she was gorgeous and sexy and clever, and their flat in Limehouse was absolutely sensational, more to Barney's taste, if he was honest, than the house he and Amanda had bought in Clapham. It was a bit . . . well, a bit too fussy, full of clever ideas that Amanda had found in the house magazines and copied, without considering whether it all worked together properly. But still, she was great and he loved her, of course, and not having much of a visual sense himself, he just accepted it all. There were more important things in life than decor.

Amanda was solid gold, through and through; Tamara, he felt, was composed of some rather questionable nickel under her lovely skin. She was selfish, she was spoilt—first by her doting parents, and now, of course, by Toby—extremely possessive, dismissive of Toby's feelings, given to putting him down, albeit with her rather sparky humour, when it suited her. Toby really loved Tamara; he told Barney so repeatedly, almost too repeatedly, Barney thought sometimes. He had been an angel over the buildup to the wedding, agreeing to everything she wanted, even their honeymoon in the Maldives when Barney knew that sort of place bored him. But, "It's her wedding," he would say easily, apparently unaware of the irony of it: that it was his too.

And with the stag do—a long weekend in New York—only a fortnight away, it was really much too late to do or say anything about it at all.

Barney just remained uneasy about it, and couldn't discuss it with anyone. Not even Amanda. Actually, least of all with Amanda. That was a bit worrying too.

CHAPTER 2

Well, she'd done it now; there could be no turning back. Mary took a deep breath, turned away from the letter box, and walked home through the pouring rain, hoping and praying that she had done the right thing. In four or five days, the letter would arrive in New York, at Russell Mackenzie's undoubtedly grand apartment, bearing the news that yes, she thought it would be lovely if he came to England and they met once again, after all these long, long years.

More than sixty years since they'd said good-bye, she and Russell; she'd stood in his arms at Liverpool Street station, surrounded by dozens of other couples, the girls all crying, the soldiers in their khaki uniforms holding them close. It was almost unbearable, and when finally she had to let him go, it was as if some part of her had been wrenched off, and she'd stood watching him walking down the platform, climbing into the train, waving to her one last time, and she'd gone home and run up to her room and cried all night and wanted to die. Literally. She had loved him so much, and he had loved her too. She knew he had; it wasn't just that he'd told her so—he'd asked her to marry him, for goodness' sake. But it had been too frightening, too unimaginable to go away, all those miles away from everyone she knew and loved. And anyway, she was spoken for, engaged, even if she didn't have a ring on her finger: engaged to Donald, sweet, gentle Donald, who was coming home to her to make her his wife.

She had been wonderfully surprised when Russell continued to write to her; he had done so almost as soon as he arrived back in the States.

"I want us still to be friends, Mary," he had said. "I can't face life totally without you, even if I can't be with you."

She had agreed to that, of course: what harm in letters? Nobody could object to that, think it was wrong. And the letters had flown back and forth across the Atlantic ever since.

He had sent pictures: first of himself and his very grand-looking parents and their very grand-looking house, and later, as time passed and wounds healed and lives inevitably progressed, of his bride, Nancy; and she had written of her marriage to Donald and sent pictures of the two of them on their wedding day, and of the little house they had bought in Croydon. And later still, they exchanged news and photographs of their babies, her two and Russell's three, and sent Christmas and birthday cards to each other. Donald had never known; she had seen no reason to tell him. He wouldn't have believed that Russell had been only a friend, and he would have been quite right not to believe it either.

The letters arrived about once a month, usually after Donald had gone to work. If one did happen to arrive on a Saturday, and he saw it, she would say it was from her American pen-friend. Which was true, she told herself. He was. In a way.

Russell's stories of splendid houses and Cadillacs and swimming pools were clearly true; his parents were rich, with an apartment in New York and a house somewhere called Southampton, full of big houses, and people played polo there and sailed on the ocean in their yachts. He and Nancy spent every weekend at the Southampton house.

It had been a happy marriage, as far as Mary could make out; as hers to Donald had been. But Nancy had died when she was only fifty-two, of cancer, and Russell had married again, to a woman called Margaret. Mary had been absurdly comforted when Russell told her it was only so the family had a mother figure.

Donald had died on his seventy-fifth birthday, had had a heart attack while the house was full of his beloved family. He had been a wonderful husband; he had never made much money, had worked away perfectly happily at his job in an insurance company, and had no ambitions to change it.

As long as he could come home every night to Mary and the children, he said, and knew he could pay all the bills, he was content.

She had kept all Russell's letters, and photographs, safely hidden in her underwear drawer, tucked into an empty packet of sanitary towels; Donald would no more look in there than fly to the moon. And every so often, she would get them out and relive it all, the wonderful, passionate romance that had led to a lifetime of secret happiness.

And then last year, Russell had written to tell her that Margaret had died. "She was a very loving wife and mother and I hope I made her happy," he wrote. "And now we are both alone, and I wonder how you would feel if at last we were reunited? I've been thinking of making a trip to England and we could meet."

He had been over occasionally on business—she knew that—but of course they had never met.

Mary's initial reaction had been panic; what would he actually think, confronted by the extremely ordinary old lady she had become? He was so clearly used to sophistication, to a great deal of money, to fine birds in very fine feathers; she was indeed his "Little London Sparrow," the name he had given to her all those years ago. And all right, she lived in a very nice house on the outskirts of Bristol, where she and Donald had moved when he had retired, to be near their beloved daughter, Christine, and her family, and she had a few nice clothes, and she had kept her figure; she was still slim, so if she did get dressed up she looked all right. But her very best outfits came from Debenhams, the everyday ones from Marks & Spencer; her hair was grey, of course, and a rather dull grey at that, not the dazzling white she had hoped to inherit from her mother; and she had very little to talk about: her most exciting outings were to the cinema, or playing whist or canasta with her friends. And Russell spent a lot of his life at things called "benefits," which seemed to cover all sorts of exciting events: theatrical, musical, even sporting. Whatever would they talk about?

But he had rejected her argument that they might spoil everything if they met again now—"What's to spoil? Only memories and no one can hurt them"—and gradually persuaded her that a rendezvous would be at worst very interesting and fun, and friendship "at best wonderful."

"I want to see you again, my very dear Little Sparrow. Fate has kept us apart; let's see if we can't cheat her while there is still time."

It hadn't been fate at all, as far as Mary could see; it had been her own implacable resolve. But gradually she came round to feeling that she would greatly regret it for whatever was left of her life if she refused.

And so she had written to tell him so, and that he should go ahead and make the arrangement for his visit—"ideally at the end of August."

Which was only a few weeks away.

. . .

On that same morning, Linda received a phone call from an independent production company; they were casting a new six-parter for Channel Four, a family-based psychological thriller.

"Very meaty, very raw. We need a young black girl. Obviously pretty, but cool as well, properly streetwise. First casting in three or four weeks' time. If you've got anyone, e-mail a CV and some shots."

Linda did have someone, and she sent her details over straightaway.

She'd had Georgia Linley on her books for just over a year, and she was beginning to think it was a year too many. OK, she was gorgeous and very, very talented; Linda had picked her out from a large cast at an end-of-year production at her drama school, put her through her paces, and taken her on. Since then it had been an uphill struggle. Georgia had not only been something of a star at college, and hated the crash down into bit parts and commercials; she was also extremely impatient and volatile. After every failed audition, she would turn up at the agency and weep endlessly, bewailing her own lack of talent combined with her bad luck, and Linda's inability to help her or even understand the idiocy and blindness of the casting director she had just been to see. Linda was initially patient and was very fond of her, but a year on and she actually dreaded her phone calls.

Of course, Georgia had problems—"issues," as the dreadful expression went—about her colour, about the fact she was adopted, about her hugely successful, brilliant brother. But as Linda had tried to persuade her many times, none of those things were exactly professional drawbacks.

"There are dozens of successful black actors these days—"

"Oh, really? Like who?"

And, of course, there weren't. There was Adrian Lester and there was Sophie Okonedo and Chiwete Ejiofor . . . and after that the list tailed to a halt. Dancers, yes, singers, yes, but not actors. She had tried to persuade Georgia to go for some chorus parts in musicals, but she wouldn't hear of it.

"I'm a lousy dancer, Linda, and you know it."

"Georgia, you're not! Maybe not Covent Garden standards, but extremely good, and you've got an excellent singing voice, and it'd be great experience; you'd almost certainly have got a part in *Chicago,* or that revival of *Hair,* or—"

"Which folded after about three days. Anyway, I don't want to be a dancer. I want to act. OK?"

She still lived at home, in Cardiff, with her adoptive parents. Her father was a lecturer at Cardiff University, her mother a social worker:

charming, slightly hippie middle-class folk, unsure how to manage the ambitions of the beautiful and brilliant cuckoos in their nest. Their other child, Michael, also black, blacker than Georgia, who was actually mixed-race—a fact that added to her neuroses—was five years older than she was, a barrister, doing well in a London chambers; he had gone to Cambridge and was acknowledged as extraordinarily clever.

Well, maybe this production would be Georgia's big chance, Linda thought; and much more likely it would not. She decided not to tell Georgia about it yet; she couldn't face the unbearable disappointment if the production company never even wanted to see her.

. . .

People—nonmedical people, that was—always reacted the same way when they heard what Emma did: "You don't look like a doctor," they said, in slightly accusatory tones, and she would ask them politely what they thought a doctor did look like; but of course she knew perfectly well what they meant. Most doctors didn't look like her, blue eyed and blond and absurdly pretty, with long and extremely good legs. And she had learnt quite early on in her career that she might have been taken more seriously had her appearance been more on the . . . well, on the earnest side. Now that she was a houseman, she wore longer skirts—well, on the knee anyway—and tied her hair back in a ponytail, and obviously didn't wear much makeup; but she still looked more like a nurse in a Carry On film than the consultant obstetrician she was planning to become.

She was a senior houseman now, working at St. Marks Swindon, the new state-of-the-art hospital opened by the health secretary earlier that year. She knew she was very lucky to be there; it was not only superbly designed and multiple-disciplined, with extremely high-calibre and highly qualified staff; it was just near enough to London, where she had first trained, for her to see her friends.

She was really enjoying accidents and emergency—A&E; apart from obstetrics, it was her favourite department so far. It was so different every day; there was always something happening, and yes, you did have to cope with some awful things from time to time—major car accidents and heart attacks and terrible domestic accidents, burns and scalds—but a lot of the time it was quite mundane. And the whole A&E experience was very bonding; you shared so much, day after day; you worked together, sometimes under huge pressure, but it had a culture and a language all its own, and you made very good friends there, lasting relationships. And you felt you really were doing something, making people better, mending them there and then, which sounded a bit sentimental if you tried to put it into words, but it was the reason she had gone into medicine, for God's sake, and it was far more satisfying than orthopaedics, for example, seeing people with terribly painful hips and backs and knowing it would be months before anyone could do anything for them at all, and then it wouldn't be you.

She had been three of the statutory four months now in A&E, as senior house officer, and she was really dreading moving on. Especially as her next department would be dermatology, which didn't appeal to her at all. She had even considered, very briefly, becoming an A&E consultant, like Alex Pritchard, her present boss, but he had told her it was a mug's game and that she'd never make any money.

"Not many private patients come into A&E, and as we all know that's where the money is."

"Money isn't everything, though, is it?" Emma had said.

"Perhaps you could try telling my wife that," he'd said, and scowled; she never knew whether he was going to scowl or smile at her. He was a great untidy bear of a man, with a shock of black hair, and beetling eyebrows to match, and very deep-set brown eyes that peered lugubriously out at the world. Emma adored him, though there were more scowls than smiles at the moment—he was reputedly going through a very unpleasant divorce. But he was immensely supportive of her, praised her good work while not hesitating to criticise the bad, and when she removed a healthy appendix unnecessarily, having put down the symptoms of IBS to acute appendicitis, he told her he had done exactly the same thing when he had been a junior surgeon.

"You just have to remember everyone makes mistakes; the only thing is, doctors bury theirs," he said cheerfully as he found her sobbing in the sluice, "and that woman is far from being buried. Although with her weight and her diet she probably soon will be. Now dry your eyes and we'll go and see her and her appalling husband together . . ."

But obstetrics had remained her first love, and the following summer, she would start applying for a registrarship.

. . .

Emma was twenty-eight and, as well as her exceptional looks, was possessed of an extremely happy, outgoing personality. She had grown up in Colchester, where her father had worked for a finance company and her mother was a secretary at the junior school that Emma and her brother and sister had all attended before going on to the local comprehensive. It had been a very happy childhood, Emma often said, lots of fun, treats, and friends, "but Dad was very ambitious for us, quite old-fashioned; we were all encouraged to work hard and aim high."

Which Emma, by far the cleverest of the three, was certainly doing; a Cambridge place followed by a Cambridge First. In medicine, a subject acknowledged as very tough, she was about as high as anyone could have hoped for. She had never thought for more than five minutes that she might have preferred to do something else. She loved medicine; it was as simple as that. She enjoyed—almost—every day, found the life hugely satisfying and absorbing, and remained extremely ambitious.

. . .

Emma looked at her watch: three o'clock. It was Friday and it seemed to be going on forever. She was on the eight-a.m.-to-six-p.m. shift, and it had been one of the slow days. Tomorrow she was going to London and out with her boyfriend. She'd been going out with him for only three months, and he was the first she had had who wasn't a medic. She'd met him in a bar in London; she'd been with a crowd of friends from uni, and one of them, a lawyer, had worked with him briefly.

His name was Luke Spencer, and he worked for a management consultancy called Pullman. He earned what seemed to her an enormous amount of money and worked tremendously long days—almost as long as hers, but then, while she went home exhausted and slumped in front of the television, Luke and his colleagues went out for dinners at hugely expensive restaurants like Gordon Ramsay and Petrus and extremely trendy clubs like Bungalow 8 and Boujis and Mahiki. Occasionally Emma and other WAGs, as Luke insisted on calling them, rather to Emma's irritation, were invited along on these evenings. The first time Luke had taken her to Boujis, Emma had practically burst with excitement, half expecting to see Prince Harry every time she turned round. How Luke and his friends got on the guest list there she couldn't imagine.

She liked being with Luke; he was cool and fun and funny, and he threw his money around, which was rather nice; he hardly ever expected her to pay for herself, and he wore really great clothes, dark suits and pink shirts and silk ties done in a really big loose knot. He took all that very seriously. He wouldn't be in his suit today, she reflected, because it was Friday, which was dress-down day, and they all wore chinos or even jeans. Not any old jeans, obviously, not Gap or Levi's, but Ralph Lauren or Dolce & Gabbana, and shirts open at the neck, and brown brogues. Dressing down or indeed up on any day was not something that figured large in Emma's life.

She wasn't at all sure if she was actually in love with Luke—although she had decided she would really like to be—and she was even less sure if he was in love with her; but it was very early days, and they had a lot of fun together, and she always looked forward enormously to seeing him. He was very generous, always tried to take her somewhere really nice. The other thing that was really sweet and that had surprised her was how much he respected her work.

"It must be absolutely terrifying," he said, "life and death in your hands. And surgery: cutting people open, how scary is that?"

She said it wasn't that scary—"What not even the first time?"— and she explained that you arrived at the first time so slowly and so well supervised, you were hardly aware at all it actually was the first time.

She was certainly looking forward to seeing him; they were going to have quite a bit of time together, not just Saturday night, but the whole of Sunday and Sunday night as well; she didn't have to be back at the hospital till ten on Monday morning.

So she'd be able to stay in his flat for two nights, which was a really cool studio apartment; and obviously that meant they'd be having sex, quite a lot of sex. Luke was good at sex, inventive and very, very energetic, but also surprisingly considerate and eager to please, Emma thought, smiling to herself as she looked at the text he'd sent her that morning: *Hi, babe. Really looking 4ward 2 tonite. I mean really. Got some news. Take care Luke xxx.*

She wondered what the news was: probably something to do with work. It usually was. Anyway, only seven more hours . . . There'd been a few kids with broken bones, a couple of concussions, and a boy of seventeen with severe stomach pains. It turned out he'd drunk two bottles of vodka, three of wine, and a great many beers over the past twenty-four hours, celebrating his A levels, and seemed surprised there could have been a connection. And then there were a few of the regulars. All A&E departments had them, Alex Pritchard had explained to Emma on her first day, the Worried Well, as they were known, who came in literally hundreds of times, over and over again, with the same pains in their legs or their arms, the same breathlessness, the same agonising headaches. Most of those were seen by the resident GP in A&E, who knew them and dispatched them fairly kindly; Emma felt initially that she would dispatch them rather more unkindly, seeing as they were wasting NHS time and resources, but she was told that medicine wasn't like that.

"Especially not these days," Pritchard said. "They'd be suing us, given half the chance. Bloody nonsense," he added. It had been one of his scowling days.

Anyway, she might not look like a doctor, Emma thought, but she was certainly beginning to feel like one. And even sound like one, or so Luke had told her last time he'd had a bad hangover and she'd been very brisk indeed about the folly of his own personal cure: that of the hair of the dog.

"You've poisoned yourself, Luke, and swallowing more of it isn't going to do any good at all. It's such nonsense, and it's so obvious. The only cure is time, and lots of water for the dehydration."

He hadn't liked that at all; knowing things, being right about them, was his department.

"If I want a medical opinion, I'll get it for myself when I'm ready," he said in a rare demonstration of ill humour. "I don't want it doled out in my own home, thank you very much, Emma."

And he poured himself a large Bloody Mary and proceeded to drink it with his breakfast eggs and bacon.

Alex Pritchard, who adored Emma, and had never met Luke, but had heard more than he would have wished about him, and referred to him privately as the oik, would have interpreted this as proof, were it needed, of his extremely inferior intelligence.

❖ CHAPTER 3 ❖

The thing most occupying Laura's time and attention as the long summer holidays drew near to their close was Jonathan's surprise birthday party; he was forty in early October and had said several times that he didn't want any big festivities.

"In the first place, I'll feel more like mourning than celebrating, and in the second I find those big-birthday parties awfully self-conscious. So no, darling, let's just have a lovely family evening, Much easier for you too, no stress, all right?"

Laura agreed with her fingers only slightly crossed behind her back, for what she had planned was very close to a family evening, just a dozen or so couples, their very best friends, and the children, of course. She was sure Jonathan would enjoy that and would actually have regretted not having a party of any kind; and so far the preparations were going rather well. Before their return from France, she had already organised caterers; Serena Edwards had been enrolled as her helpmeet with the flowers and decorations (it was most happily a Saturday, when Jonathan was on call), and Mark, Serena's husband, was compiling a playlist and organising and storing the wine. Everyone invited could come; and Mark and Serena had also been enrolled as decoys, and had invited them both for a drink before dispatching them home again for dinner with the family. All the children were in on the secret and thought it was tremendously exciting.

. . .

Would she recognise him? Well, of course she would. From the pictures. Only people did look different from their photographs, and Russell had clearly selected his with great care over the years.

The day was nearly here; only two and a half weeks to go. And after they had met at Heathrow—and for some reason she had insisted on that; it was neutral territory—they would travel together to London, where he had booked rooms at the Dorchester—"two rooms, dearest Mary, have no fear; I know what a nice girl you are!"— for two days, while they got to know each other again: "And after that, if you really don't like me you can go home to Bristol and I shall go home to New York and no harm done."

She still thought much harm might be done, but she was too excited to care.

She had told no one. She didn't want to be teased about it, or regarded as a foolish old lady; she had simply told her daughter, Christine, and a couple of friends that she was going to London to meet an old friend she'd known in the war. Which was absolutely true.

But she had bought a couple of very nice outfits from Jaeger—Jaeger, her!—where the girl had been so helpful, had picked out a navy knitted suit with white trim and a very simple long-sleeved black dress; and then, greatly daring, she had asked Karen, the only young stylist at her hairdressing salon, if anything could be done to make her hair look a bit more interesting.

"Well, we can't do much about the colour, my love," Karen had said, studying Mary intently in the mirror, her own magenta-and-white-striped fringe falling into her eye, "although we could put a rinse on to make it a bit blonder-looking. Or some lowlights," she added, rising to the undoubted challenge, "and I do think you could wear it a bit smoother—like this," she said, putting a photograph of Honor Blackman in the current *HELLO!* in front of Mary.

Mary heard herself agreeing to this; after all, Honor Blackman was almost as old as she was. "You going to meet someone special, then, when you go away?" Karen said, as she started leafing through the magazine for more inspiration.

"Oh, no, of course not," said Mary, "just an old friend, but she's rather . . . rather smart, you know?"

"Mary, you'll look smart as anything when I've finished with you," said Karen. "Now let me gown you up and we'll start with the colour. Very gently, then if you like it, we can push it a bit. When's the trip?"

"Oh—not for another two weeks," Mary said.

"Well, that's perfect. We can sort something out, see how you like it, and then keep improving it."

"And if I don't?"

"You can go back to your own style, no problem."

"Bless her," Karen said, smiling after Mary as she walked out after the first session. "That took real courage, but you know, she looks five years younger already."

They had met on a bus, Mary and Russell; he was on a forty-eight-hour pass and wanted to take a look at Westminster Abbey: "Where England's kings and greatest men are buried," it said in his booklet.

"Instructions for American Servicemen in Britain, 1942" it was called, and all servicemen had been given a copy on departing for Europe. It had produced a lot of cynical comments on the troopship, with its warning that Hitler's propaganda chiefs saw as their major duty "to separate Britain and America and spread distrust between them. If he can do that," the booklet went sternly on, "his chance of winning might return."

To this end, there were many and disparate warnings: not to use American slang, lest offence might be given—"*bloody* is one of their worst swear words"; not to show off or brag—"American wages and American soldiers' pay are the highest in the world, and the British 'tommy' is apt to be specially touchy about the difference between his wages and ours." And that the British had "age not size—they don't have the 'biggest of' many things as we do."

It had warned too of warm beer, and of making fun of British accents, but most relevantly, to Russell, of the British reserve. Soldiers should not invade the Brits' privacy, which they valued very highly; and they should certainly not expect any English person on a bus or train to strike up a conversation with them . . .

. . .

The bus he was on made its way down Regent Street, stopping halfway. Several people got on, and Russell realised a girl was standing up next to him; he scrambled to his feet, doffed his cap, and said, "Do sit down, ma'am." She had smiled at him—she was very pretty, small and neat, with brown curly hair and big blue eyes—and she thanked him, and promptly immersed herself in a letter she pulled out of her pocket.

The bus had stopped again at Piccadilly Circus. "See that?" said one old man to another, pointing out of the window. "They took Eros away. Case Jerry 'it 'im."

"Good riddance to 'im, I'd say," said a woman sitting behind, and they all cackled with laughter.

The bus continued round Trafalgar Square, and Russell craned his neck to see Nelson's Column: he wondered if Jerry might not hit that as well. They turned up Whitehall; about halfway along, a great wall of sandbags stood at what one of the old men obligingly informed the entire bus was the entrance to Downing Street. "Keeping Mr. Churchill safe, please God." There was a general murmur of agreement.

Everyone seemed very cheerful; looking not just at his fellow passengers, but the people in the street, briskly striding men, pretty girls with peroxided hair, Russell thought how amazing it was, given that thousands of British civilians had already been killed in this war and London was being pounded nightly by bombs, that the city could look so normal. OK, a bit shabby and unpainted, and everyone was carrying the ubiquitous gas mask in its case, but on this lovely clear spring day there was a palpable optimism in the air.

The bus stopped and the woman conductor shouted, "Westminster Abbey." Russell was on the pavement before he realised the girl he had given his seat to had got out too, and was looking at him with amusement in her blue eyes.

"Are you going into the abbey?" she asked.

"Yes, ma'am."

"You know," she said, "we do speak to strangers. Sometimes. When they're very kind and give us seats on the bus, for instance. I bet you've been told we never speak to anyone."

"We were, ma'am, yes."

"Well, we do. As you can see. Or rather hear. Now, that's the abbey to your left—see? And behind you, the Houses of Parliament. All right? The abbey's very beautiful. Now, have a good time, Mr. . . . Mr. . . . ."

"Mackenzie. Thank you, ma'am. Thank you very much."

Her amusement at what he had been told about her countrymen had made them friends in some odd way; it suddenly seemed less impertinent to ask her if she was in a great hurry; and she said not a great hurry, no, and he said if she had just a few minutes, maybe she could come into the abbey with him, show him the really important things, like where the kings and queens were crowned.

She said she did have a few minutes—"only about ten, though"—and together they entered the vast space.

She showed him where Poets' Corner was; she pointed out the famous coronation stone under the coronation chair, and then directed him to the vaults where he could see the tombs of the famous, going right back to 1066.

"I've never been down there myself; I'd love to go. You know Shakespeare is buried here, and Samuel Johnson and Chaucer—"

"Chaucer? You're kidding me."

She giggled again, her big blue eyes dancing.

"I never thought anyone actually said that."

"What?"

" 'You're kidding me.' It's like we're supposed to say, 'Damn fine show,' and, 'Cheers, old chap.' I've never heard anyone saying that either, but maybe they do."

"Maybe," he said. He felt slightly bewildered by her now, almost bewitched.

"Now, look, I really have to get back to work—I work in a bank just along the road, and I'll be late."

"What . . ." Could he ask her this? Could he appear possibly intrusive but . . . well, surely not rude . . . and say, "What time do you finish?" He risked it. She didn't seem to mind.

"Well—at five. But then I really do have to be getting home, because of the blackout and the bombs and so on—"

"Yes, of course. Well—maybe another time. Miss . . . Miss . . ."

"Miss Jennings. Mary Jennings. Yes. Another time."

And then, because he knew it was now or never, that he hadn't got another forty-eight for ages, he said: "If you'd accompany me around all those people's graves for half an hour or so, I could . . . I could see you home. Through the blackout. If that would help."

"You couldn't, Mr. Mackenzie. I live a long way out of London. Place called Ealing. You'd never find your way back again."

"I could!" he said, stung. "Of course I could. I found my way here from the States, didn't I?"

"I rather thought the United States Army did that for you. Sorry, I don't mean to sound rude. Where are you stationed?"

"Oh—in Middlesex." He divided the two words, made it sound faintly exotic. "Northolt."

"Well, that's not too far away from Ealing, as a matter of fact. Few more stops on the tube."

"Well, what do you know?"

"Goodness, there you go again," she said, giggling.

"What do you mean?"

"Saying, 'what do you know?' It's so . . . so funny to hear it. It's such a cliché somehow. I didn't mean to sound rude, to offend you."

"That's OK. But . . . maybe in the cause of further cementing Anglo-American relations, you could agree to meet me. Just for half an hour."

"Maybe I could. In the cause of Anglo-American relations." She smiled back at him. "Well . . . all right. I'll meet you here at ten past five. Anyway—better go now. Bye."

And she was gone, with a quick sweet smile, half running, her brown curls flying in the spring breeze.

And so it began: their romance. Which now—most wonderfully, it seemed—might not be over . . .

. . .

Patrick Connell was tired and fed up; he'd stopped for a break on the motorway, and was drinking some filthy coffee—why couldn't someone provide some decent stuff for lorry drivers? They'd make a fortune.

Life on the road wasn't a lot of fun these days, and you didn't make the money either, because you were allowed to work only forty-eight hours a week, and that included rest periods and traffic jams, and the traffic just got worse and worse . . .

And so did the sleep problem.

It was turning into a daytime nightmare. It started earlier and earlier in the day, a dreadful, heavy sleepiness that he knew made him a danger. Even when he slept well and set out early, it could catch him halfway through the morning; he would feel his head beginning its inexorable slide into confusion, force himself to concentrate, turn up the radio, eat sweets: nothing really licked it.

He'd actually gone to the doctor the week before—without telling Maeve, of course; she was such a worrier—to see if he could give him anything for it. The doctor had been sympathetic, but couldn't. "If I give you pep pills, Mr. Connell, you'll only get a kickback later, won't be able to sleep that night, and that won't help you, will it? Sounds like you need to change your job, do something quite different. Have you thought about that?"

With which unhelpful advice Patrick had found himself dismissed; he had continued to take his Pro Plus and drink Red Bull and eat sweets and struggle on somehow.

Everyone thought lorry drivers could do whatever speed they liked; everyone was wrong. The lorry itself saw to that: a governor in the fuel pump that allowed exactly the amount of fuel through to do the legal fifty-six mph and no more. Some of the foreign drivers removed the fuse, or adjusted the pump, but Patrick wouldn't have dreamed of doing that. Not worth it. You got caught, you lost your licence. And anyway, then there was the tachograph fixed in your cab that told it all: how many hours you'd done, how long you'd stopped, whether you'd speeded at all. So you literally got stuck in some god-awful place, unable to leave because your hours were up. And they could be up simply because of being stuck in traffic, not because you'd made any progress.

What he longed for more than anything right this minute was a shower and a shave and a change of clothes. Life on the road didn't do a lot for your personal hygiene. On the English roads, anyway; it was better in Europe. Like the food. And the coffee . . .

CHAPTER 4

"What a perfect summer it's been," said Jonathan, smiling at Laura, raising his glass of Sauvignon to her; and, "Yes," she said, "indeed it has. And it's even nice here now. For our return."

"I thought maybe in future we could spend Easter in France, as well as the summer," he said.

"Well . . . well, that would be lovely, except—"

"Except what?"

"Well . . . the thing is, Jonathan, the children are growing up so fast, they've got lives of their own now, and they want to be with their friends."

"They can be with their friends the rest of the year," he said, sounding mildly irritable.

"I know, but . . ." Her voice trailed off. How to explain that a remote, albeit beautiful farmhouse for weeks at a time wasn't going to be quite enough for children approaching adolescence? She'd hoped Jonathan would realise that for himself, but he didn't seem to.

He had a very strong controlling streak: everything had to be done his way, and she could see that already Charlie was beginning to kick against it. And, of course, the girls, while wonderfully sweet and biddable at the moment, would inevitably reach the same point. But it hadn't happened yet; and Laura was quite adept at ignoring difficulties. She had even considered having another baby, in order to ensure that at least some of the family remained small and compliant; but babies weren't that compliant, and Jonathan found them difficult anyway. Probably best to enjoy the near perfection of the present.

"Oh, now, I hope this is all right, darling," he said. " I'm going to have to be away next Thursday night. Big conference in Birmingham: old medical student chum's gone over into the pharmaceutical business; he seemed to think if I spoke he'd get a better attendance rate."

"Well, of course he would," she said, smiling at him. "You're such a draw these days at these things, such a big name—I was so proud of you at that conference in Boston. That was fun; I loved being there with you. Maybe I should come next week . . ."

"Oh, darling, I hardly think Birmingham could compare with Boston. Not worth you packing your bag, even—"

"I wouldn't mind," she said, "if you'd like me to come."

"Darling, don't even think about it. I thought you had enough to do next week, what with getting the children fitted up for school and seeing that madwoman in Wiltshire about doing her house up for Christmas. What an absurd idea! Paying someone to put up a few garlands and fairy lights . . ."

"Jonathan," said Laura, almost hurt, "not everyone has the time to do it for themselves. Or the . . . well, the ideas. That's what I'm for."

"Of course. I'm sorry, sweetheart, stupid of me. And you'll make it look so lovely. Do you have any ideas about it yet? I'd love to hear them; you know I would . . ."

He did that sometimes: professed interest in what she did. It was only professing—he didn't really care if the Wiltshire house was decked out with barbed wire—but it was very sweet. He was very sweet . . . She was very, very lucky.

. . .

Georgia knew virtually every word of every character already. Linda was right: this was a fantastic part. The series was a thriller about a grandmother who vanished from the family home without a trace. She could have just wandered off, she could have met with an accident, she could have been murdered. The part Georgia was up for was the granddaughter, Rose, very close to her grandmother, angry at the way her dad belittled and bullied her, convinced he had something to do with her disappearance. The more she read it, the more excited about it she became; she could really develop the character as she went along. She couldn't think of anything else.

The first audition was a week from Friday; it was at the casting director's office, and there would be loads of girls there, anywhere up to twenty or thirty. Tough as that was, Georgia didn't mind the first audition as much as the later ones: it was less tense; the chance of getting the part seemed really rather remote; it was possible to relax just slightly. But it was still hideous.

The first thing that always struck her was how many girls there were, all looking rather like her. Which was logical, but always seemed surprising. And her next reaction was invariably that they were all much prettier than her.

Then there were all the awkward little conversations, the longest with the girl immediately ahead—*Oh, hi, how are you, what have you been doing, love the dress/boots/hair.* And then the long wait while she did her bit, and came out smiling, or looking really tense. And then they called you in and it began. At this stage, it was usually just you and the casting director, who would read a scene with you. With the camcorder running, of course. And then you waited—and waited. The first callback came within a day or two; if it didn't, forget it. And if it did come, that audition was much scarier: you knew they liked you; the pressure was on. And there were still five or seven or even eight of you. All, it seemed, better actors than you. You just felt sick for days and days, waiting. And quite often for a big part—like this one—there was a third call, with the choice whittled down to maybe two of you. That was really agony.

But . . . it would all be worth it if she got this part. She'd be on her way at last. And Linda did seem to think she had a real chance.

"You can act. You look perfect. And you've certainly got plenty of attitude, which is what they're looking for. D'you want to come up the night before, stay with me?"

"No," Georgia said quickly, "no, it's really kind, but I'll get the coach from Cardiff first thing."

She didn't like staying with Linda; she was nice, she was really fond of her, but her flat was so bloody perfect, Georgia was scared to move in case she made it untidy or knocked something over. The audition wasn't till three thirty: she could get to London in loads of time.

"Fine," said Linda. "As long as you're not late."

"Linda! As if I would be, opportunity like this. Do you really think I've a chance—"

"Georgia, I really think so, yes. But there are lots of other girls. What do you think of the script?"

"I think it's great."

"Me too. And directed by Bryn Merrick. It should be superb."

It was all absolutely amazing, really. She might actually be getting a part in a brilliant, high-profile Channel Four series, directed by one of the most award-winning people in the business. She might . . .

Georgia went back to her lines.

. . .

"Not long now, Toby," said Barney.

"No. Absolutely not."

There was a silence. The stag weekend had been a great success: they'd done all the touristy things in New York, Barney had managed to organise a Marilyn Monroe strip-o-gram for Toby, and they'd got some pretty good pictures of her—only Toby had got into one hell of a sweat over that and made them all swear to make sure Tamara never found out, or saw the pictures.

Tamara's hen weekend didn't sound exactly great; Amanda was very loyal about it, but even she admitted that an alcohol-free weekend at a spa retreat near Madrid, however wonderful the treatments, and however grand the clientele, ran out of fun.

Several of the girls suggested at least one trip into town, maybe for a meal or a bit of clubbing, but Tamara had said slightly coolly that of course they should do whatever they liked, but for her the concept of the whole weekend had been a luxurious detox, and she didn't want to undo all the benefits for one night of what, after all, they did all the time in London.

And as the date of the wedding drew nearer she had become increasingly possessive of Toby, disturbing client evenings with endless phone calls, relentlessly e-mailing him about absurdly detailed arrangements, and even arriving at his desk in the middle of the morning with a handful of ties for his consideration; Amanda had struggled to explain this to Barney.

"I know it's all a bit much, and she seems so cool and self-contained, but she's actually a mass of insecurities. She's absolutely terrified something's going to go wrong, and she only feels better when Toby's actually with her."

Barney didn't trust himself to speak.

. . .

Emma wasn't sure how she felt about Luke's news. Which was that he was going to Milan for six months. Seconded—that was the word—to some car manufacturers, called Becella: "They are the greatest cars in the world, you know. I'd have one while I was there."

"Goodness."

"Yeah. It really is a fantastic opportunity, Emma. I'm well chuffed."

She had said it sounded great, yes, really wonderful, congratulations—while wondering if actually he was getting around to saying he thought they should stop seeing each other now, before he left—and then he said he knew she'd be pleased, and of course there'd be loads of trips back home—"every other weekend, actually, or they're pretty good about flying people out. So you could come over whenever you wanted."

Not finished then, which made smiling and seeming pleased easier—but how often did she have a whole weekend in which to go to Milan, for God's sake? She'd thought at last she'd found the perfect boyfriend, settled in London, always around, and now he was going off for at least six months. It was . . . well, not very nice.

But no worse than that. Which probably meant she wasn't actually in love with him. She wasn't sure how she felt about that either.

. . .

It had been a particularly happy weekend. Jonathan had been relaxed and not even on call, which meant Laura could relax too, and at breakfast he had offered each of the children a treat of their choice. He did that occasionally: loved the conspicuous spoiling and role-playing of the perfect father.

"But it has to be in London—no point struggling out; the roads'll be jammed. London's great in August; my treat is going to be—"

"You're not a child," said Daisy.

"I'm still allowed a treat. It's a ride in the Eye, so we can have a look at everything. We haven't been on it for ages. Any objections?"

"We'll never get on," said Laura.

"We will. I've bought tickets."

"Oh, Jonathan, how lovely. When for?"

"Tomorrow morning. Eleven o'clock. And they're VIP tickets, so absolutely no queuing. Now, then, what would Mummy's treat be?"

"Um . . . a picnic. Which I didn't have to prepare. In . . . let me see, Kew Gardens."

"That's easy. We'll make the picnic, won't we, kids? Lunchtime today, Laura?"

"Yes, please."

They had their picnic; Lily's wish was a rowboat on the river; and then they all went for supper on the terrace at Browns in Richmond, watching the sun set on the water.

"It's so lovely," said Daisy. "It's *all* so lovely, I feel so happy, I don't really want a treat."

"That's very sweet, darling," said Laura, "and very grown-up of you. But how about you and I go shopping, just for a little while, in

Covent Garden tomorrow, after the Eye? We could get one of those lockets you liked so much, from that jewellery stall. You too, Lily, if you want to come. Otherwise, Daddy can take you and Charlie to watch the buskers. Or on the roundabout."

"I'll come," said Lily.

Charlie's wish was a ride on the bungee jumps just beside the Eye, and after their ride they watched him soaring skywards, laughing, his skinny legs pretending to run, his brown hair shining in the sun, while they drank hot chocolate with whipped cream on top.

And then, after the shopping excursion, they went home for a late lunch in the garden, cold chicken salad and strawberry meringues, and then for a walk along the river, all holding hands.

I'm so happy, Laura thought, *so happy and lucky. I wish these years could last forever . . .*

CHAPTER 5

This was even worse, Patrick thought, than the week before. He had left London on Wednesday morning and now it was Thursday afternoon, and the night drive he had planned to get him home for Friday morning had been scuppered by a five-hour queue at the warehouse for loading up and a stroppy manager, with the words they all dreaded: "We're closing, mate."

Useless to argue, although Patrick tried to point out that it was only four thirty, with half an hour to closing; the man was unmoved. "I can't get all that on board in half an hour; come back in the morning."

Well, nothing else for it; he'd just have to bite the bullet and call Maeve; and then get some food and start looking for somewhere to spend the night.

And—wouldn't you just know it—the weather was getting hotter and hotter.

. . .

This time tomorrow, Mary thought, she would be with Russell. She felt alternately terribly excited and terribly nervous. But now, actually, the excitement was winning. Her greatest fear—that they would be complete strangers, with nothing to say to each other—seemed suddenly unlikely. It wasn't as if they hadn't been in contact all these years. And how odd that was, she thought, their two lives and lifestyles being so utterly different. But then they always had been; there had been nothing actually in common—unless you counted the war. Which had, of course, bound people very tightly together by its shared ideals and hopes, dangers and fears. Russell and she, growing up thousands of miles apart, in totally different cultures, had found each other through that war, found each other and loved each other; at no other time and in no other way could such a meeting and consequent relationship have taken place. And it was one of the things that had convinced Mary that their lives together could not be shared, that when the war was gone, much of the structure of their relationship would be gone too, the differences between them increased a thousandfold.

But now . . . well, now they had their past to bind them: the wonderful bridge between any two people, however different, who had raised children; seen grandchildren born and partners die; lost the strength and physical beauty of their youth; faced old age and loneliness; and shared, inevitably, the broader ideals of love, of loyalty and family, and wished to pass the importance of those things on to the generations that followed them, their own small piece of immortality.

All these things Mary thought that night as she lay in bed, unable to sleep and looking forward only just slightly anxiously to tomorrow.

. . .

What was she doing here? Georgia wondered. What? She must be totally, utterly, absolutely mad. Out clubbing in Bath with Esme and Esme's up-himself boyfriend, drinking cocktails that she couldn't afford, when she should be at home in bed in Cardiff, her alarm set for seven, giving her plenty of time to get to the coach station and take the ten-o'clock to London. *Shit, shit, shit.* It had seemed such a good idea at the time: an evening with Esme in her parents' house; she'd even thought she might run through some of her scenes with Esme—it would help with the awful nerves—and then she could get the coach in the morning from Bath. Her mother hadn't tried to stop her, just told her to be sensible and not miss the coach—as if she would; and then Georgia'd arrived and Esme was all stressed out because of the boyfriend, who she thought was about to dump her, so that when he called and asked Esme to meet him in town at some bar or other, Esme had acted like it was God himself, and insisted Georgia go too—"Honestly, Georgia, it'll only be an hour or so; then we can come back and you can get to bed. I can't go alone; I just can't." So she had gone, and how stupid had that been? Because now it was almost two, and no prospect of leaving, and she had no money for a cab, and the boyfriend kept saying he'd get them home.

What would Linda say, if she knew? The chance of Georgia's life and she was risking throwing it all away . . . Well, she'd just have to get up early somehow, get some money out of the hole in the wall, and then sleep on the coach. She'd drink loads of water now—and anyway, none of them had any money left for cocktails, thank goodness—and just demand they leave. Only—God, where was Esme now? She'd been on the dance floor a minute ago, with thingy's tongue down her throat, and now she'd vanished, must have gone outside—oh, God, oh God, what was she doing here, why had she come . . . ?

. . .

"God, it's hot." Toby pushed his damp hair back off his forehead. "Might take a dip. Fancy one, Barney?"

"Sounds good."

They were in the garden of Toby's parents' house; Toby had asked Barney to stay there with him the night before the wedding. "Stop me running away," he said with a grin. But there had been something in his voice, a slight catch. He'd been a bit odd altogether, actually, all evening: quiet, edgy, jumping whenever the phone rang. He'd left twice to take calls on his mobile. "Tamara," he'd said both times when he came back.

Carol Weston had served a delicious dinner for the four of them—poached salmon followed by raspberries and cream—which they had eaten outside, burning copious candles to keep the insects at bay; Ray Weston had served some very nice chilled Muscadet, and proposed the toast to "the perfect couple. That's you and Toby, Barney," he said, smiling, and they had sat there, chatting easily until it was dark, reminiscing. But then Toby became increasingly silent, almost morose, and Carol and Ray went in to bed, with strict instructions to them both from Carol not to be late.

"We don't want any hitches tomorrow, any hungover grooms."

"Oh, for Christ's sake!" Toby said, and then swiftly, apologetically, "Sorry, Mum. But do give me a bit of credit. We'll just have a couple of quiet ones and then bed, Barney, eh?"

"Absolutely."

They climbed out of the pool and sat, briefly cool, on the terrace at the back of the house.

"Quiet one then?" Toby said and, "Yes, great," said Barney. He'd expected Toby to fetch more wine; was a little alarmed when he saw him come out of the house with a bottle of whisky and some tumblers.

"Tobes! You heard what your mum said."

"Oh, don't you start. There's no nightcap like scotch. Neat scotch. Want some?"

Barney nodded.

"That's better," Toby said, taking a large gulp, then leaning back in his chair, studying his glass.

"Better? You're not nervous, are you?"

"Well—a bit. Inevitable, really. Lesser men than me have run away."

"Tobes. You wouldn't."

"Of course not. What, from a girl like Tamara? God, I'm lucky. So lucky."

A second whisky followed the first; a silence; then Toby said, quite suddenly: "I've . . . well, I've got a bit of a problem, Barney. Actually. Been a bit of an idiot."

"How? In what way?"

"I . . . Oh, shit, I should have told you ages ago. Well, weeks ago, anyway."

He was staring into the darkness, his hands twisting.

"Toby, what is it; what have you done?"

"I've . . . well, I've made a complete fool of myself. With some girl."

Barney stared at him in total silence for a moment, then said, "Fuck!"

"Well, exactly that. Yes. I . . . well, I got incredibly drunk one night with some friends round here. Anyway, we went to a club near Cirencester, and this girl was there. On a hen night. She lives in the next village, actually. Dead sexy, works for some local builder, you know the sort of thing."

"Think so," said Barney. He was feeling rather sick.

"Anyway, I . . . well, I screwed her. I . . . gave her a lift home, in a cab. Well, it seemed a good idea at the time. When we got back to her place, she said why didn't I come in for a nightcap, her parents were away for the night, and—well, one thing led to another."

"Toby, you lunatic!"

"I know, I know. Anyway, I felt pretty bad in the morning, obviously, hoped she'd see it my way, just a bit of fooling around—she didn't."

"Oh, Tobes—"

"She knew where I lived, or rather where my parents lived,

became a complete pest, always calling me, at work as well, on my mobile, actually turned up here once or twice. I . . . well, I tried to get rid of her, but it didn't work. She got quite unpleasant, started accusing me of treating her like a tart—"

"Well—"

"I know, I know. God, what wouldn't I give to have that time over again. Anyway, next thing is, last week she calls, says she's pregnant."

"Shit!"

"I tried to call her bluff, but . . . well, unfortunately, I . . . well, I left all that sort of thing to her; she said she was on the pill—"

"You idiot," said Barney, "you total idiot."

"I know. I *know*. I can't explain it. I've never done anyting like that. Ever. Well, you'd know if I had. No secrets from you, Barney. I s'pose . . . I suppose it was a combination of last-fling time, nerves about . . . well, about being married—"

"You mean to Tamara?" said Barney quietly.

"Yes. At rock bottom. I do love her—but she's quite high-maintenance. Bit of a daunting prospect. Anyway—that's not an excuse. I . . . well, it was an appalling thing to do. I know that."

"So—what's happened?" It seemed best to stick to practicalities.

"I told her to have a test, all that sort of thing. Anyway, she'd gone all quiet. I thought it was OK, but . . . well, anyway, she called me tonight. That was what those calls were. She wants some money. So she can have a termination. She wants to have it done properly, as she puts it. At a private hospital."

"Well, tell her she can't."

"Barney, I'm in no position to talk to her like that. Even if none of it's true, I daren't risk it. You know what Tamara's like—"

"Well—yes. I do. But—"

"Anyway, she wants a couple of grand."

"Blimey."

"Moreover she wants it tomorrow morning. In cash."

Barney felt sick, oddly scared himself.

"You can't give in to that sort of thing," he said finally.

"Barney, I have to. Otherwise, she's threatened to come to the church. It wouldn't look good if she turned up at my smart society wedding, as she called it, would it?"

"No," said Barney, after a pause, "no, it wouldn't be great."

"So—I've got to give her a grand in the morning. In cash. Which I don't happen to have about me. Do you?"

"Nope. Got about a hundred, but—"

"I'll have to go to a bank, get it out. The most I can get on my card is four hundred quid."

"I can get that too. But—"

"No, no, Barney, it's my problem. And then I'll have to take it to her. To her parents' house, fifteen, twenty minutes away. So—"

"Toby, you do realise it may not stop at this, don't you? That's the whole thing about blackmail."

"Yeah, but whatever she does next, I'll be married, the wedding'll be safely over, Tamara won't have to be confronted by it—literally. I'll deal with it somehow. Anyway, I've got a feeling she'll back off. Meanwhile—busy morning."

"Yeah. Well, look, surely I can deal with that. I can get the money; I can take it to her—"

"No, that's just too complicated. I'll do it. I should be back here by ten thirty, eleven, latest. Then I'll just change and we can go. We might be a bit late for the ushers' lunch, but that won't matter."

"We need to leave by eleven, really, for that, mate."

"Well, maybe we'll have to drive faster. Oh, God. What a total fucking idiot I've been. Let's have another of those, Barney. Then we'd better turn in. Busy day tomorrow."

He nodded at the whisky bottle; Barney poured the drinks out, his hand shaking slightly, wondering how he could possibly have got Toby so wrong. He'd have trusted him with his life, always regarded himself as the slightly wild card. And now . . .

. . .

Laura was just drifting off to sleep when the phone rang.

"Darling?"

"Oh, Jonathan, hello. How did it go?"

"Oh—pretty well, I think. Yes. Jack seemed pretty pleased."

"I bet he was. I bet you were wonderful."

"Hardly. Anyway, you're all right, are you?"

"I'm absolutely fine, darling. Just a bit hot. But we got all the uniforms, then I took them out to supper—"

"Let me guess. T.G.I.'s."

"Correct."

"God, I don't know how you can face those places."

"Well, the children love them. And I love the children."

"So do I. But . . . well, you're a saint. They're lucky to have you. I'm lucky to have you."

"And I'm lucky to have you."

"Well—as long as everything's OK. Night, darling. I'll be home tomorrow, around six, going straight up to St. Anne's from here."

"Fine. Love you."

"Love you too."

. . .

That was done then: very unlikely now that she would call him again.

Jonathan walked into the foyer of the Bristol Meridien, so nicely anonymous, so filled with pleasurable associations.

He checked in and went up to his room, had scarcely pushed the door open when she walked out to greet him, stark naked, holding out a glass of champagne.

"You're very late," she said. "What kept you?"

CHAPTER 6

When all else failed, Georgia prayed. Not because she believed in God, exactly, but because He did seem, on the whole, to be very good about listening to her and letting her have what she wanted. Which meant, she supposed, that she really ought to believe in Him a bit more, and be a bit more grateful.

Well, if He answered this particular prayer in an even half-positive manner (she promised both herself and Him), she would make a much, much greater effort not just to believe in Him, but to behave in a way more appropriate to the belief. Because He most definitely would deserve it.

What she was going to ask of Him today, she thought, eyes screwed up, fists clenched in absolute concentration, was not actually that difficult to grant. She wanted a car: a car driven by someone else, on its way to London, and with a spare seat. And actually, since she was standing just above the approach road to the M4, it would not be a miracle on the scale of the loaves and fishes. All God had to do, in fact, was point her out, perhaps nudge the driver into thinking some company would not go amiss, and He'd be free to get on with whatever other tasks were on His mind.

After half an hour, her arm aching, her bare legs drenched in dust, it began to seem that God had better things to do that morning.

At this rate she just wasn't going to make it. She had to be there, actually at the audition, by three; it was already twelve, and her father always said you had to allow two and a half hours minimum from the Severn Bridge. And that was when you knew exactly where you were going; she had to find some obscure place in the middle of London, and get herself tarted up before she could present herself to the snooty cow—they were always snooty—in reception. She was almost thinking of giving up. Of going home again, telling her mother that she had missed not just the early coach but the later one and that it was absolutely, yes, her own fault. Only actually it wouldn't be that easy to get home again; she'd need another lift just to get back to Cardiff; she might as well carry on, get to London anyway.

God, she was so stupid. Why hadn't she stayed safely at home in Cardiff and gone to bed early, so she'd have heard her phone when it went off? Only she wouldn't have had to; her mother would have made sure she was awake and driven her to the coach station in plenty of time. But it had been after two when they got home, and her phone had failed totally to wake her until almost nine. Esme's mum had been very sympathetic, but she didn't have a car; Georgia'd gone out in a panic to find a cash machine and catch the next coach, only it spat her card out, and she couldn't get any money. Her only hope now was the train; she'd gone back to Esme's in tears, hoping to beg some money from her, but she didn't have any either. She'd hoped the boyfriend, who'd stayed over, might lend her the money, but he was clearly tight as well as a complete wanker. In the end, he did offer to take her to the M4 in his car and drop her there so she could hitch a lift.

And here she was, on the side of the road, praying . . .

. . .

Maeve Connell had also been calling upon the Almighty—not for help, but to be her witness in an ultimatum to her husband.

"I swear before God, Patrick Connell, you don't get home in time for my mother's birthday dinner and it's the last meal that'll be cooked for you in this house. Because I'll have gone, left you for good. I'm sick of it—sick to the death of looking after the kids alone, and sleeping alone, and coping alone, and I don't want to hear any excuses about how we'll soon have a great house and a fine car. So is that clear, Patrick, because if it isn't I'll say it all again, just so there's no doubt in your mind whatsoever . . ."

Patrick had told her it was quite clear, and that of course he'd be back in Kilburn, and in good time for the birthday dinner. "And I have a great gift for your mother as well; just wait till you see it. So kiss the boys for me and tell them I'll see them tonight. Now I have to go, or I'll get pulled over for using the phone and then I'll never arrive in time. Bye, darling. See you later."

He snapped off his mobile, pulled over into the middle lane, and moved up to the fifty-six miles an hour that was his top speed.

He was dead tired. But he should be home by seven at this rate. If only it wasn't quite so hot . . .

. . .

Georgia looked at her watch again. Twelve fifteen now; it was hopeless, completely hopeless. She gave up praying, gave up smiling at every car that came along, gave up hope, sank onto the grass verge by the lay-by, buried her head in her arms, and started to cry.

. . .

Rick Thompson was in a foul mood.

He was supposed to be getting home early; he'd got up at bloody dawn to finish a job in Stroud—some silly cow had decided at the beginning of the week she wanted the fence he'd put up for her painted white instead of stained brown, and it had meant an extra day and a half's work. He wouldn't have minded so much—it was all work, after all, all money—but she liked to chat, and it was, well, boring, mostly about her husband who was away "on business, in Japan actually," and his views on life in general and how he liked her garden to look in particular. When she was through with that, she moved on to her children, who were all very musical, especially her eldest . . .

Anyway, he'd finished that morning in record time, mostly because she'd gone to Waitrose in Cirencester—"I know it's a bit of a trek, and terribly wrong of me, environmentally, but it's just so much better quality"—and he was waiting for her to get back so he could hand her the invoice, when his boss phoned and said he wanted him to pick up a load of timber from a yard outside Stroud and drop it off with him before the end of the day.

Since the boss lived outside Marlow and Rick lived in Reading, this was not too great an imposition, but the yard had been closed when he got there, bit of paper pinned on the door saying, "Back by one thirty," but it was nearer two when the lumber yard guy arrived.

"Sorry, mate, got caught up with something."

"Yeah, well," Rick said, his face assuming the expression that sent his wife diving for cover, "some of us like to get home before midnight, specially on a Friday, OK? Let's have it, PDQ."

There was still some wood from the last job lying around in the bottom of his van; the man suggested he clear it out before putting his new timber in.

"Yeah, well, I'll leave it with you, then; you can dispose of it for me."

"Oh, no," said the man, looking at the assortment of dusty, split planks, some of them still stuck with rusty nails, "you dispose of your own rubbish, mate. Sign here, please."

Swearing under his breath, Rick signed, and then found the back doors of the van no longer shut properly.

"This is all I need. Got any rope? I'll have to tie the fucking doors together."

"You ought to tie those old planks down, mate. Not have them rattling around like that."

"Look," said Rick, "when I need your advice, I'll ask for it. Right now I don't, all right?"

And he pulled out of the yard, with Rudi, the black German shepherd dog that was his constant companion, on the passenger seat. He turned along the A46 in the direction of the M4, cursing the heat, his own misfortune in not having a van with air-conditioning, and the fact that his windscreen wash was almost empty.

And that he couldn't now be in Reading much before four.

. . .

Patrick saw her as he stood in the queue at the tea stall; she was only a few yards away, her face tear streaked, clutching a mug of tea. Gorgeous, she was, black, no more than twenty, wearing a very short denim skirt and then those funny boots they all seemed to like: sheepskin, not ideal for a hot August day, but then that was fashion for you. She was small and quite thin, but she had very good boobs, nicely emphasized by a pink low-cut T-shirt, and her wild black hair was pulled back into a ponytail on one side.

He picked up his own tea and a couple of bottles of water and went over to her.

"Not a serious problem, I hope?"

"Who said there was a problem at all?" she said. "I'm just waiting for someone."

Her voice was surprisingly posh; he was surprised. Then he chided himself for being classist or racist or whatever such a reaction might be labelled. Soon, he reflected, you wouldn't be able to say anything at all without upsetting someone.

"Your friend late, then?"

"I'm—" she said, and then stopped, smiled reluctantly. "I'm not waiting for anyone, really. I'm just hoping to get a lift back to Cardiff. You're not . . . not going that way?"

"No, sorry, my love. Going to London."

"Oh, God," she said, and her huge eyes filled with tears again, "if only I'd met you just half an hour earlier. I was trying to get there."

"Any particular reason?"

"Well—yes. Yes, I had an appointment."

"Important, was it?"

"Terribly," she said, and started to cry in earnest again.

"Come on," he said, sitting down on a bench, indicating to her to join him. "Tell me all about it."

.   .   .

"Linda, I've got Georgia on line three—"

"Georgia," Linda said, picking it up, "what is it? Are you in London yet?"

"Linda, don't be angry, please, please don't. I've . . . well, I've had a difficult day so far, and . . . and, well, I'm on the M4."

"The M4! God in heaven, whereabouts on the M4?"

"Um—almost in Gloucestershire. The Bath turnoff."

"Georgia," said Linda, trying to keep her voice under control, "do you know what you've just done? I worked so hard to get you that audition. I lied; I practically bribed. What am I going to tell them? I hope you realise this damages me and my reputation as much as it does yours. Rather more so, actually, since you don't have one. Now get off this line and out of my life. I—"

"Linda, please. Please listen to me. I'm so, so sorry, I know everything you say is true, and I don't deserve any more of your help or kindness. But . . . it really wasn't my fault. Really. I was staying with a friend in Bath and—"

"I don't want to hear this."

"But isn't there anything you could tell them? That will just make them wait a couple of hours for me? They're seeing lots of girls; couldn't you ask if I could be last? I know I can be there by five thirty . . ."

There was a long silence; then Linda said, "I don't know, Georgia. I don't know."

"But you've got to talk to them anyway, tell them I'm not coming. Wouldn't it be better for both of us if you told them I had a tummy bug or something? Please, please?"

Another silence; then Linda said, "Well, I'll consider it. Are you on your mobile?"

"Um, no, someone else's. Mine had—had just died."

"Oh, for Christ's sake. Give me the number. And if you don't hear from me, don't be surprised."

"No, no, all right. Thank you, Linda. Thank you so, so much."

. . .

Georgia switched off the mobile and handed it back to Patrick rather shakily.

"I think she's going to try. You were right: it was worth calling her.

So . . . can we go, please? I mean, will you take me? I'd be grateful for the rest of my life . . ."

. . .

He had to finish it: absolutely had to. For the sake of a few dizzy days and nights of novelty, the absolute adrenaline rush of danger, he was at serious risk of losing everything he had.

He looked across at her as they drove along, this raw, sexy, not even very beautiful young thing, only twelve years older, dear God, than his son, and saw his life, its perfect edifice, being rocked to its foundations.

It wasn't even as if there was anything wrong with his marriage. It was perfect; Laura was the perfect wife, caring, loving, beautiful . . . Everyone told him so, told him how lucky he was, and he was. It was just that . . . well, it was all a bit predictable. Their conversations, their social lives, their family lives, their sex lives. Especially their sex lives. He supposed that was what had actually led him into this heady, dangerous situation . . . Laura knew sex was important, she wanted to please him, she claimed he pleased her, she never refused him; but she never initiated it, never suggested anything, never wanted it moved out of the bedroom . . . He felt every time that she had ticked the experience off, seen yet another duty done. Which had been the charm of Abi, of course; with her demands, her inventiveness, her risk taking. Sex was at the centre of her.

And what kind of bastard set those things before love, before loyalty, before family happiness . . . ?

His sort of bastard, it seemed . . .

Initially he had tried to excuse himself, to tell himself it was only a one-night stand, or at the very most, the briefest fling, purely sex, that it would revitalise his marriage, make him more aware of the treasure he possessed.

But Abi was more than a fling; he felt increasingly addicted to her. She seemed to be completely amoral: she had lost count, she once told him, of how many men she had slept with; she drank too much; she did a lot of drugs. She was the sort of woman indeed that he despised and disliked, and what he was doing with her, he had no real idea—except that he was having fantastic sex with her. And finding a huge and dangerous excitement in his life.

He had met her only two months before, when he had been (genuinely) at a medical conference. The conference organiser, one of the big pharmaceutical companies, had wanted some photographs taken of the speakers and people at the dinner; the photographer had been an annoying little chap with a nasal whine, but his assistant, following him round with a notebook to record the names of subjects, and a second camera, had been . . . well, she had been amazing. She was dark, tall, and very skinny, with incredible legs. Her long hair was pulled back in a half-undone ponytail; her black silky dress was extremely short and, although quite high necked, clung to a braless bosom. Jonathan could see it was braless because her nipples stood out so clearly. She wore very high-heeled black boots with silver heels, very large silver earrings, and quite a lot of makeup, particularly on her eyes, which were huge and dark, and her lips, which were full and sensual.

As she bent down to speak to Jonathan to ask his name, her perfume, rich and raw, surrounded him, confusing him.

"Sorry about this," she said, "but it's my job. Do you mind telling me how you spell Gilliatt?"

He spelt it for her, smiling. "Don't apologise. You make a nice change from all the other obstetricians."

"Good." She smiled at him, stood up, and walked away.

He sat and stared after her, suddenly unable to think about anything else. She walked . . . How did she walk? Rhythmically, leaning back just a little, her hips thrust forward; it was a master class (or mistress class? he wondered rather wildly) in visual temptation.

As dessert was served, he saw her working a table in the far corner of the room. He excused himself from the male midwife beside him (now waxing lyrical about womb music) and headed for the gents'; on his way back he spotted her working another table, went over to her.

"Hello again."

"Hello, Mr. Gilliatt."

She had a very slow smile; it was extraordinarily seductive.

"I . . . wondered if you had a business card. I . . . well, I speak at a lot of these conferences and very often they want pictures, for the local press and so on. It's . . . always useful to have a name up one's sleeve."

"Yes, of course. That's great; I'm supposed to hand them out, so you've just won me some brownie points from my boss. That's his number and this is mine—Abi's my name. Abi Scott."

"Thank you very much, Abi. Nice to have met you. Maybe we'll meet again."

"Maybe," she said. With another slow smile.

He went back to the table and engaged very cheerfully in a heated debate on induction, fingering Abi's card and telling himself that he would pass it to his secretary at St. Anne's the next day.

He stayed the night at the hotel; he had strange, feverish dreams, and woke to an appalling headache. He showered and dressed and scooped up Abi Scott's card, along with his keys and his wallet, which were lying on the bedside table, stared at it for a moment, then sat down again and, before he could think at all, rang her number . . .

They had an absurd conversation, both of them knowing exactly what it was actually about, while dissembling furiously.

He'd like a copy of a couple of the pictures for his wife (important to get that in—*Why, Gilliatt, why?*); could she perhaps e-mail them to him? She could do better than that: they had prints ready—she could drop them off at the hotel; it was only round the corner from her office. That would be extremely kind. Yes, she could be over in half an hour.

She'd been waiting in the foyer when he came down, leaning on the reception desk, fiddling with a long strand of her dark hair; she was wearing the tightest jeans he'd ever seen—they were like denim tights, for God's sake—with the same silver-heeled boots worn over them, and a black leather jacket. Her perfume hit him with a thud as he neared her, held out his hand.

"Good morning."

"Good morning," she said. "Nice to see you again, Mr. Gilliatt."

Her eyes moved over his face, rested briefly on his mouth. She smiled again, and the invitation in the smile was unmistakable.

"Maybe I could buy you a coffee," he said, the words apparently leaving his mouth entirely unpremeditated, unplanned. "To thank you for bringing the pictures."

"That'd be . . . yeah, that'd be great."

. . .

"So," he said as they settled at a table, "do you live in Bristol?"

"I do, yes. But I come from Devon. Born in Plymouth."

"Oh, really? How interesting. I come from Devon, too. I was born in Exeter." God, he must sound ridiculous to her. Pathetic. "So . . . what were you doing before you worked for Mr. . . . . Mr. . . . ."

"Levine. Stripping," she said briefly.

"Really?" He could hear himself struggling to sound unsurprised, unshocked.

She laughed out loud.

"Not really. Although it wasn't a hundred miles from that. I was an underwear model. I worked for some cruddy local photographer who specialised in it. Publicity, you know. It meant having representatives from the manufacturers at the sessions. They liked to adjust the bras, that sort of thing. It was gross. What I do now is quite civilised."

"Yes, I see."

There was a silence; then he said, "Well, I should be getting along, really. Back to London. Back to the real world."

"OK," was all she said.

Right, Gilliatt. It's still OK. You're still safe. Go and have a cold shower and get off to London. But—

"I'll be down here again in a couple of weeks, another conference, in Bath. Staying here, though. Maybe we could have a drink."

"Yeah," she said with the slow, watchful smile, "yeah, that'd be great."

And that had been that really.

. . .

That had been two months ago; since then he had thought about her obsessively, all the time. He longed to be with her, and not just for sex. He found her intriguing, almost frightening, so unlike anyone he had ever known. She excited him, she shocked him, and while he did not imagine himself remotely in love with her, he was certainly in her thrall.

She made him run appalling risks; she would stop suddenly as they walked through a dark street, force him into a doorway, pull him into her; she brought cocaine to the hotel rooms where they met, and made a great play of laying out the lines while the room service meals or drink were wheeled in; she called him on his mobile when she knew he was at home, claiming to be a patient, refusing to get off the line until he had made some arrangement to see her.

The terror of it all made his adrenaline run high; the comedown was fearsome. She had become his personal, addictive drug; he needed her more and more.

But the fear had perversely given him courage; he was resolved that this had been the last time—had begun to try to tell her so as they ate breakfast in bed this final morning. It had all been wonderful, he said, really wonderful, but perhaps the time had come to—

"To what?" she said, looking at him sideways, picking up a croissant, dipping it in her coffee.

"Well, to . . . to draw a line."

"What sort of a line? I'm afraid we used all mine last night."

"Abi, please don't be . . . don't be . . . difficult. I think you know what I mean. We have to finish this."

"What on earth for, when we're having such a great time? Or did

I miss something last night? Were you trying to get away from me, escape into another room or—"

"Of course I wasn't trying to get away from you. Don't be ridiculous."

"Well, then, Jonathan, I don't get it. Now come on, let's get rid of this tray and have one last glorious fuck. Then I'll leave you in peace. For now. Oh, no, not quite—I forgot I want a lift to London. Presume that's OK?"

"Of course it's not OK. I can't possibly drive you into London. Someone might see me—us; you know the rules."

"Oh, yes, the rules. It's all right, Jonathan. Don't look so frightened; I'm not proposing a visit to your very lovely home in Chiswick. I want to do some shopping, meet up with a girlfriend, maybe go to a movie."

"Oh—right," he said, "but still—maybe I could drop you at the station; you could get the train—"

"I don't like trains. And I don't really think it's very likely that out of the millions of people in London this afternoon we're going to be spotted by one of your chums. No, I'd prefer you to drop me . . . well, Harley Street would be fine; how'd that be?"

"Abi, I am not taking you to Harley Street."

"Why not? I like it there. I've been there before, remember?"

He did remember—remembered her coming to his rooms, claiming she was a patient, pulling him into her on the examination bed; he still felt sick just thinking about it. Sick and . . . amazing.

"Well, you can't come today. Someone might recognize you. Abi . . ." He took a deep breath. "I really do want to talk."

"We can talk in the car. Waste of time talking. Now come on, what can I do to interest you . . ."

She turned him on his back, began toying with his cock with her tongue. He struggled briefly, then gave himself up to the pleasure of her. It could be the last time . . . He would take her to London and they would talk in the car. He would retreat from the madness and rebuild his life. It would be tough, and he would miss what she did for him, but a few weeks from now it would seem like a dream. A disturbing, dangerous dream. And it would be over, with no great harm done—to him or Laura or the children or his marriage . . .

The possibility of his harming Abi never occurred to him. And if it had he would have dismissed it utterly. She really was not his concern.

CHAPTER 7

Linda had made the phone call. She told the casting director that Georgia had been up all night with food poisoning, but that she was struggling to get to London just the same; however, there was no way she'd be there by three. It would be more like five.

The casting director said that since Georgia would hardly be at her best and they were seeing three more girls the next day, then she could come along in the morning.

"At—let's see—ten thirty?"

Linda thanked her not too effusively—she didn't want to appear grovelling—and tried to ring Georgia back on the number she had given her. It was on message; Linda said could Georgia ring her immediately and get to her office in London as fast as she could. That way she could keep her literally under lock and key until she delivered her personally to the audition in the morning . . .

. . .

"So is it films you're looking to get into?"

She was a nice kid, Patrick thought, very appreciative, sitting up there beside him, doling out his sandwiches and his jelly babies, his chosen sweets on the road, so sweet your blood sugar level—and thus your concentration—went up just looking at them.

"It's what everyone wants, actually," said Georgia. "Actors might say they just want to play Hamlet at the National, but really and truly they all want to be big names in films and TV."

"I'll look forward to your first premiere," said Patrick, grinning at her.

"Well, I'll certainly invite you. I'd never have made it, if it wasn't for you."

"I've enjoyed the company." He added, "And that's the truth. But we're not there yet. Mind if I put the radio on?"

. . .

It was eleven thirty; Toby had still not returned.

What the fuck was he doing? Barney wondered, pacing the house desperately.

They'd all had breakfast together—Toby had said it was important to appear normal, and anyway, no point getting to the bank before it opened at nine thirty. After which he set off, telling his parents some cock-and-bull story—or so it seemed to Barney—about having to collect some currency from the bank.

"But, Toby, no one gets currency from the bank anymore; that's what plastic's for," his father said.

"Not in the Maldives; no cash machines where we're going, and I can fill the car up at the same time. I meant to do it yesterday, but I forgot."

Toby had always got himself—and very often both of them—out of scrapes at school by lying; Barney had always been awed by how accomplished at it he was. It was very rare for him not to get away with things: in no small part because he was a successful boy, very good at games and bright, and the staff therefore liked him and were inclined to believe him anyway.

The Westons left at about ten thirty; they had a couple of things to pick up on the way, they said, before meeting their friends.

It was after twelve before Toby got back.

"Barney, I'm so sorry. She wasn't there—no one was; she made me go to her office—"

"Couldn't you have left it at the house?"

"No, she said she wanted it in her hands. Even then, I had to wait there for about ten minutes as well."

"Yeah, all right, all right. Go and get changed, for Christ's sake. We're supposed to be having lunch with the ushers at one."

"Well . . . we'll have to cut it. Barney, the wedding's not till four thirty. We'll be fine . . ."

"OK," said Barney reluctantly, "I'll call them. Now, please. Hurry up."

. . .

Toby, clearly shaken, was a long time in the shower; then he couldn't find the Paul Smith socks he had bought, the only ones fine enough to make his new, stiff bridegroom shoes comfortable.

"Tobes, mate, we've got to go. And I'd better drive; you look bloody awful."

"Yes, OK, OK. Oh—shit. I still haven't filled the car up."

"Toby! For Christ's sake. Well, come on. Let's go. Back way?"

"No, let's nip along the M4. It's only one junction, and we can fill up at the service station."

"Toby, it's Friday. Motorway's not entirely the best idea—do we really have to get fuel?"

"We really have to. It's bloody nearly empty. Anyway, we'll be heading towards London, not out of it. It'll be fine. Much quicker anyway than all those country lanes. We could just as easily get stuck behind a tractor—"

Barney was about to say that you could always get round a tractor if it was absolutely necessary, but Toby suddenly said he needed the lavatory. He disappeared for almost five minutes, came out looking very shaken.

"Sorry, Barney. Just been sick. Nerves, I suppose. Still don't feel great. In fact—" he disappeared again.

Well, at least there'd be plenty of lavatories at the service station . . .

. . .

Georgia had discovered a message from Linda on Patrick's phone. She looked at him, smiling radiantly.

"She doesn't exactly say it's all right, but she still wants me to get to London, so I think it must be, don't you?"

"So tell me about yourself," he said. And she did.

How she had wanted to be an actor all her life; how she had been the star of all the school productions, especially as Juliet. "Some of those bitches there said, 'Oh, you can't have a black Juliet,' but our drama teacher was a complete legend, and she said of course you could; it was no stranger than all those white actors playing Othello." And how she had then won a place at NAD, as she called her drama school, the National Academy of Drama, and how she had been spotted by Linda at the end-of-term performance.

"I'd like to be able to say the rest is history," she said, biting into an apple, "but I can't. If I get this thing today, well, it's my big chance; it really is."

She told him she'd been adopted when she had been a baby. "My birth mother was only fourteen and she couldn't keep me—well, didn't want to, more like it—so Mum and Dad took me on. They gave me a really happy childhood; I felt really safe and loved, had lots of nice things, went to a good school, you know? I think I was a bit of a disappointment to them, though. My mum dreamed of me being a teacher. God. I couldn't do that. No patience. Not with little kids, anyway."

Patrick agreed that you did indeed need a lot of patience with little kids. "I have three boys all under eight; life isn't exactly peaceful."

"I bet it's not. Your wife must get quite . . . tired. What's her name?"

"Maeve."

"Maeve, that's pretty. Does she work at all?"

"What, with three kids? She does not, although nothing makes her more annoyed than when people ask her that. 'What do you think I do all day?' she says. 'My nails?' "

"Oh, sorry. Stupid of me. I should know; I get all that sort of shit as well."

"What sort of shit would that be?" said Patrick, amused.

"Oh, people saying things like, 'How lovely for you to live in Roath Park.' That's the really middle-class bit of Cardiff where our house is. Or, 'Wasn't it lucky for you that Jack and Bea adopted you?' What they mean is, 'How lovely for you to have been adopted by white, middle-class people, instead of dragged down by your black birth mother.' Well, it is in a way, but it's bloody hard as well."

"And why should that be?"

"Well, if you're black, you're black," said Georgia slowly, "and it feels odd to be all the time with white people. You have no idea what it was like, as I got to four or five, to go to a kids' party and be the only black face there. You feel . . . I don't know . . . terribly on your own. And a bit bewildered . . . as if you shouldn't be there, not really. Can you imagine that?"

"I . . . think I can, yes."

"Thing is, you're only there because your own mum and your real family have failed you and someone's conscience meant you got rescued. And you feel you ought to be grateful all the time, and you really resent that. It got better as I grew up, because Cardiff's a pretty mixed community and there were lots of black and Asian kids in my school. But then I thought, Well, what does that say for my relationship with my mum and dad, if I don't feel good with the people they know and like?"

"Did you ever go and find your birth mother?"

"Yes," said Georgia flatly, "but it didn't work."

"And did that upset you?"

"Yes, of course. Well, at first. Then I just sort of . . . pushed her back where she'd been all my life. Nowhere." She looked at Patrick and smiled. "I never usually talk about all this stuff till I've known someone for ages, and not always then. You must have some kind of magic, makes people talk."

"I'm just naturally nosy, I suppose. We're doing well, you know, Georgia. You'll be there by five, the rate we're going. Here, your phone's charged. Best take it; don't want you leaving it behind. Oh, Jesus, these people . . ."

A van had cut them off, overtaking from the inside; Patrick had to brake quite sharply.

"That was hideous," said Georgia, adding, "White van driver, are they really all bad?"

"Most . . ."

Something had fallen on the floor. Georgia bent down to pick it up; it was a small box.

"What's this?"

"Oh, now take a look; I'd be glad of a woman's opinion. It's a present for my mother-in-law, for her birthday. Her fiftieth. We're having a bit of a celebration tonight; it's one of the reasons I have to press on."

Georgia opened the box; it was a very pretty watch on a silver bracelet.

"It's lovely, Patrick. I do like watches. My last boyfriend had bought me a beautiful one the very night I decided to dump him. I had to make him take it back; it nearly killed me."

"So, why did you dump him? Or is that just one nosy question too many?"

"No. He was just . . . boring."

"Well," said Patrick firmly, "you did the right thing. Even if you did have to give up the watch. Maeve and I, now, we drive each other mad sometimes, but we're never bored. Now just keep hold of that watch, would you? I should have stowed it away a bit better than that."

"I'll put it into my bag—it'll be safe there—and give it to you when I get out."

"Fine. Don't go running off with it, will you?"

"Don't be silly; of course I won't."

· · ·

"Oh, Jesus. Oh, dear sweet Christ, it's the fucking police. Right behind us. Jesus, that's all we need."

Barney pulled over, guided by the relentless blue light onto the hard shoulder, wound down the window.

"Afternoon, sir."

"Good afternoon, Officer."

"Perhaps you'd be kind enough to get out of the car, sir. Do you have any idea the speed you were doing then?"

"Er—not quite. No."

"Ninety-eight, sir. Little above the speed limit."

"Yes, yes, I'm sorry, Officer. I . . . well, I was in rather a hurry."

"I could see that." A half smile crossed his face. It wasn't a very kind smile. "Going to a wedding, are you?"

"Er, yes. Yes, I am. I'm the best man. My friend here is the bride-groom."

Surely, surely they'd get some points for sympathy.

"Could I see your licence, sir?"

"Yes. Yes, of course. Toby, could you give it to me, please? It's in my wallet. I put it in the glove compartment."

He passed it over; the cop looked at it carefully.

"So you are Barnaby John Fraser? This is your licence? And it's your own car?"

"No, it belongs to Toby here. Mr. Weston."

"But clearly you are insured to drive it, sir. I'll just take down the details, sir. I see you live in London."

"Yes, that's correct. But we were staying with Mr. Weston's parents in Elcombe."

"And the wedding is?"

"In Marlborough. Well, just outside."

"So why did you come up to the motorway, sir, I wonder . . . see-ing Elcombe is on the south side as well."

"Well . . . we thought . . . roads all windy and narrow, we thought the motorway would be a better bet."

He knew why the policeman was keeping him talking: so he could smell his breath, see if he'd been drinking.

"Well, you could have made a mistake there, sir. Now I'm afraid I shall have to Breathalyze you."

"But I haven't had anything to drink."

"Regulations, sir. We have to do it. Won't take long." And then, as Barney handed him back the tube, "What time is the wedding, sir?"

"Four thirty."

"In Marlborough? That's cutting it a little bit fine. Right, well, there's no alcohol registered in this. You'd better be on your way, then. Good luck. You will be hearing from us, of course."

They'd be watching them, Barney thought. Even though they were going ahead, he couldn't risk overtaking them. Buggers. Total buggers. God, the petrol was low. Well, they were nearly at the service station. And it was still only just after three. OK, ten past. Should still be all right . . .

"Bastards," Toby said, pushing his hair back as they swung onto the motorway. "Think we should call someone?"

" 'Fraid so, mate, yeah. Who, though? Tamara? Her ma?"

"Jesus, no!" Toby turned white. "Whoever you called about the lunch."

"Pete. Well, you'd better do it. Get it over."

"OK. Christ, I'm sweating. Shit, Barney, how did this bloody well happen? Fine best man you've turned out to be."

He thought Toby was joking, and then realised he wasn't. Not entirely.

· · ·

Just after three Jack Bryant pulled onto the motorway. He'd been looking forward to today for some time; he was driving up to Scotland for a bit of grouse shooting with some chums, which would be great fun, and moreover, he was able to drive up in the E-Type. She really needed a good run.

The E-Type was his pride and joy: bright red, not a scratch on her—well, not anymore there wasn't—soft top, the works. She went like the bloody wind too, hundred and twenty easy, not that you could do that often these days.

He'd bought her after his last divorce: three years ago. He'd always wanted one, and after the handout he'd had to give his ex-wife, he felt he deserved something for himself.

Hard to believe he and the car were roughly the same age—well, he was a good bit older, truth to tell.

Jack had fallen on slightly hard times; he'd made a fair bit of money out of the first property boom, but not sufficient to keep him for the rest of his life, or support his ambition to lead the life of a country gentleman. He wasn't a country gentleman, of course—he was a grammar-school boy made good—but he had a lot of friends who were, and though he now lived rather modestly in Fulham, he was to be found most weekends in the country; he was useful, as a single, socially acceptable man always is, and besides, it was impossible not to like him—he was so good-natured, so energetic, such a fund of good stories.

He had been in Bristol for a couple of days staying with friends; hence his presence on the M4 that afternoon. And while there, had had the E-Type overhauled by a very good mechanic he knew, and then had given her the final once-over himself. Well, you couldn't be too careful with these old ladies, and it was a long way.

. . .

Mary was feeling a bit sleepy. It was the heat, of course; and the fact that she'd been awake most of the night. With excitement. She might have a little nap—it couldn't do any harm, and it would make the journey seem shorter. The driver would tell her when they were nearly there, so that she could comb her hair and so on—not that there wouldn't be lots of time when they arrived. The plane wasn't due till six, and the taxi company had advised allowing an extra hour just in case. Mary had allowed an extra two.

"So, how are we doing?" she said.

"Fine, love." Her driver, who had told her to call him Colin, was very nice, she thought. And middle-aged, so almost certainly a better driver. It would have been awful if he'd been one of those tough young ones, with a shaven head. "An hour and a half at the most from here. Even if the traffic snarls up a bit nearer London."

"Is that likely?" said Mary anxiously.

"If I knew that, my love, I'd be a rich man. That's what every motorist wants: to know how the traffic is going to be, whether there'll be an accident, that sort of thing."

"An accident! Oh, dear, I hadn't thought of that . . ."

"Look, Mrs. Bristow, we're in the inside lane, as you requested, doing a nice steady sixty-five. Not much chance of an accident happening to us. And even if there was an accident, the speed I'm going and us being right next to the hard shoulder, there'd be no way it would affect us."

"Do you think so?"

"I know so, my love. Look, why don't you have a little sleep. We'll be there then before you know it."

Mary settled herself peacefully in the corner. It had got very dark suddenly. Maybe it was going to rain; it was close enough for thunder. He was right, her nice driver: they would indeed be there before she knew it. And then she'd see Russell and . . . and . . .

Mary drifted into sleep smiling.

Thank Christ for that, Colin Sharp thought, put his foot down hard, and pulled over into the middle lane.

. . .

"Maybe we'd better have that chat now?" said Abi as they swung onto the M4.

They were in his new car: a Saab. He had had it only a week, and was still not entirely comfortable with it. The car itself was fine, but

· 68 ·

the sound system was slightly faulty, and the hands-free phone didn't work at all.

Abi had turned on Radio 1: very loudly. He turned it down; she turned it up again.

"Abi, I can't think against that sort of noise. Let alone talk."

"You're showing your age, Jonathan."

But she turned it off and picked up his phone from the dash-board, started fiddling with it.

"Abi, put that back."

"Why? I was going to take a photograph of you. You look so sweet. All stern and distant. So different from an hour ago. There. That's great. Now I want to check if you got that text I sent you—"

"What text?"

"While you were in the shower. Yes, here it is; you can look at it later. It's a very nice text."

"Abi, put that back, please. Now."

"OK." She shrugged.

"He took a deep breath. "Abi, I think it's time we . . . we stopped this."

"Stopped what?"

"Our . . . this . . . this relationship."

"Why?" The question sounded very aggressive.

"Well, I think it's run its course. I've been feeling increasingly . . . unhappy about it. It's great—you've been great—but I think we should say good-bye before . . . well, before we regret it—"

"I'm not regretting it, Jonathan."

"Abi, I . . . Look, you don't understand."

"I think I do," she said, and her eyes were very hard. "You've had your fun and now you're getting windy. The excitement isn't quite enough anymore, so I'm supposed to let you just walk away into the sunset, am I? Just because you're feeling a bit flaky."

"Well, you can't have imagined there was any kind of future in it."

"I might have done," she said. "You came on pretty strong to me. As I recall."

"You didn't exactly hold back yourself either. As I recall."

Her voice was very tense, very angry. "You've got a fucking nerve, Jonathan Gilliatt. For weeks I've been providing sex on demand—"

"I seem to remember you doing quite a lot of the demanding."

She ignored this. "Now I'm just to fuck off, leave you to go back to perfect little wifey, pretend I was never there. Well, I just might not do that, Jonathan. Sorry, but none of this strikes me as quite . . . fair."

She was right: given how zealously he had pursued her, it wasn't fair.

"Well, I'm sorry. But, Abi, you must see it can't go on forever. It's not . . . not realistic."

"I don't see, no. And what if I'd prefer it to continue? Had you thought of that?"

He felt a stab of absolute panic.

"I . . . well, I—"

"You hadn't, had you. You thought because I was easy meat, what I felt or thought didn't matter; you thought that I'd just go quietly, say, 'Yes, Jonathan, no Jonathan, three bags full, Jonathan, good-bye and amen.' Well, I'm not going to. I don't see why I should. Actually."

He glanced at her; she was white, her features taut with rage.

"Look—are you saying you want money or something? Because if you do—"

"No, I don't want any fucking money. That's a filthy thing to say. What do you think I am, Jonathan? You're scared, aren't you now? That I'm going to turn into some kind of bunny boiler?"

"No," he said, realising this was exactly what he was afraid of, "of course not." And then, looking at the clock on the dashboard: "This traffic's horribly heavy. I'm going to be late. We need some fuel too. I'll have to call; we'll go to the next service station."

"Who are you going to call, your wife?"

"No, my rooms in Harley Street. I've got a clinic at four."

He pulled in at the service station; while he filled the car, he called St. Anne's. His secretary sounded brisk. "You have quite a big clinic,

Mr. Gilliatt; do you want me to ask people to wait, or shall I just reschedule?"

"Get them to wait if they will. I should be there by four thirty, five at the latest. I'm so sorry."

"Oh, and Mr. Gilliatt, your wife called. Asked if I'd heard from you; apparently she's called you a couple of times. Shall I call her, explain or—"

"Yes, that'd be great, Jane. Hard for me to talk; my car phone isn't working properly. Thanks."

He felt odd, confused; the conversations with Abi had scared him, and at the same time had thrown all his emotions into sharp focus: the longing to finish it, to be safe again—and, absurdly, the misery of losing her.

She got out of the car as he approached it.

"Where are you going?"

"To the toilet. That OK? Or do I have to get permission?"

"Abi, I'm in a desperate hurry."

"Well, so am I. To get to the toilet."

He felt like hitting her.

"Oh, for Christ's sake. Well, get a move on."

He sat fuming, half tempted to drive off and leave her. But he was scared of what she might do. He was scared of what she might do anyway.

Might be an idea to call Laura, in case she called him. He dialled the house; it went straight to the answering machine. The same happened with her mobile.

"Laura, darling, it's me. Just to let you know I'm on my way, bit late. Don't call me, will you; the hands-free's not working properly. I'll call you when I can."

He saw Abi coming back, her face stormy, obviously gearing up for a fight . . .

CHAPTER 8

Mary woke up feeling uncomfortable. It was her bladder, not strong at the best of times, and when she was under stress, distinctly weak. She would never get to Heathrow without going to the toilet; she'd have to ask Colin to stop at the next service station and hope he wouldn't mind. Donald had got irritated when she was constantly asking him to stop on journeys.

But she was paying Colin, she told herself; he'd have no business being irritated. She was sure Russell would have said that. She had a quick worry about whether Russell would get irritated with her constant need for the toilet, and then, after about another few minutes, took a deep breath and said, "Colin, I wonder if you'd mind very much pulling in at the next service station? I need to go to the ladies'."

Colin said he wouldn't mind at all, and in fact he could do with a break himself; he'd got through his bottle of water already and they were only about halfway there.

"It's this heat. All right if we just go to the fuel section? Takes so long if you have to park up in services."

"Of course. And I'll get you the water, Colin. Unless you want to . . . to get out yourself, that is."

"No, no, Mary, that's fine. Bladder of steel I've got. Yes, if you would, couple of bottles and maybe some chewing gum? I like to chew when I'm driving; helps my concentration."

Mary hoped that didn't mean his concentration was flagging. She'd seen some very alarming driving since she'd woken up: cars speeding, motorbikes weaving in and out of the traffic, lorries sitting horribly close behind cars—all with foreign number plates, she noticed—and just now, a white van sitting on their tail, flashing furiously into Colin's mirror before suddenly accelerating into a very small space alongside them and then shooting into the outside lane against a background of furious hooting.

"What very unpleasant behaviour," she said. "My husband always said that bad driving was really little more than bad manners. Would you agree with that, Colin?"

"I certainly would. Right, here we are, Mary. Doesn't look too busy, considering; shouldn't hold us up much."

"I do hope not," said Mary.

. . .

"So—what do these things do for you then?" asked Georgia, helping herself to a handful of jelly babies.

"Wreck my teeth. Make me feel sick. Keep me awake, mostly . . ."

"How? I'd have thought coffee would be better."

"I'm practically immune to coffee, Georgia. These are the thing, pure sugar. Don't you eat them all, now."

"I won't."

"In fact, I'm surprised to see you eating sweets at all. You're so skinny."

"I'm incredibly lucky. I just don't seem to put on weight. Other girls are really jealous of me. They have to work at it so hard, hardly eat at all, some of them, exist on cigarettes and lettuce. I would say at least half the girls in the business have an eating disorder. It comes from casting directors and agents and so on going on and on at you— 'You must keep the weight down, you've put on some weight.' So you see how lucky I am."

"I do indeed."

She was silent for a while, munching the sweets; then she said, "You can see a lot from up here, can't you? It's amazing, almost like flying."

"It is indeed. And you can see a lot of what's going on in the other vehicles as well as you pass them. I find that the greatest temptation, to peer into people's cars and their lives."

"Well, why don't you?"

"Because I'm busy keeping my eye on the road, that's why."

"Well, I'll do it for you for now. Oh, now, here comes a coach driver up beside us. He looks well bored, all those old grannies sleeping. S'pose they've been on some tour or other—oh, God, that looks like a real nightmare. Poor bloke."

"Who's that then?" said Patrick.

"A bridegroom. All done up in his monkey suit, top hat on the backseat, and another beside him, best man, I s'pose. They look well stressed. Late, I s'pose. Too much last night, probably. They're coming up *so* fast . . . God, how awful. Late for your own wedding . . . Hope the cops don't stop them. How are we doing?"

"Pretty well. Reckon you might make it yet."

. . .

"Mate, I need the toilet; can you do the petrol?"

"Sure. How're you feeling?"

"Not great. But I'll make out. Could do without this gut rot, though."

Barney resisted the temptation to point out that it was stress rotting Toby's guts, not some malign fate. He still felt very shocked and confused by Toby's revelations. Toby, on the other hand, seemed much better, more normal; it was as if, having dealt with the situation as best he could, he could set it all aside and return to his role as model bridegroom. He didn't seem the Toby Barney knew anymore; it was almost scary.

Barney filled up the car, and then thought that he might take a look at the tyres. He'd felt the car pulling a bit. The way they were driving, they needed twenty/twenty wheels.

"For God's sake, what are you doing now?"

Toby had reappeared.

"I want to check the tyres," said Barney. "The front offside's a tad soft. Look, you go and pay, and get some more water, will you? Time you've done that I'll be through."

"OK."

. . .

Toby went back into the building. He grabbed two bottles of water, and found himself behind an old lady in the queue. There were three people in front of her—Jesus, this was taking forever. He looked at his watch. It was OK. It was fine. Hours yet. Well, an hour . . .

As he stood there, trying to keep calm, his phone rang.

"Toby Weston."

"Where are you, you little shit?"

It was Tamara's father. Who doted on her to an absurd degree, who clearly considered Toby to be a most unworthy contender for her hand . . .

"I'm . . . we're just on the motorway now, George. Should be with you quite soon."

"And what the fuck are you doing on the motorway?"

"Well, I—Sorry, I did phone Pete; you obviously didn't get the message. Be there in no time. Just filled up, want to check the tyre pressures—"

"The tyre pressures. What the fuck are you doing checking tyre pressures? An hour before your wedding, for Christ's sake."

"Yes, George, I know, but one's a bit down—"

"Look, you just forget the fucking tyres. You get over here right now. This is the biggest day of my daughter's life and I'm not having it wrecked for her. Now, you listen to me: I don't care if the tyre's right down on its rim; you just fucking well get here, you understand?"

The phone went dead.

Toby looked at the queue of people in front of him—now down to two, one nice-looking girl and the old lady—and said, easing his way forward, "Look, can I go first, do you mind? Emergency, must get away—"

The girl stood aside at once; the old lady gave him the sort of look that he could remember his grandmother giving him when he was naughty and said, "I do mind, yes, as a matter of fact. We're all trying to get somewhere important, and I have a plane to meet. You must wait your turn, like everyone else. I'm sorry."

And then she spent an inordinate amount of time counting out the exact money for her purchases.

The other queues were all longer; Toby just had to wait.

. . .

Mary felt mildly remorseful, watching him haring towards a car parked up by the air line. And more so when she realised he was wearing the striped trousers and braces of a wedding guest. That hadn't actually been very kind of her, and neither was it in character. But he had been rather arrogant. If he'd asked nicely she might have felt differently. Although . . . she knew why she'd reacted like that, really. It was because she was on edge herself . . .

. . .

"Barney, come on, come on, we have to get the fuck out of here. Just get in, for God's sake. I'll drive . . ."

Toby threw himself into the driver's seat, slammed the door.

"But—"

"I said get in. Look, I'm off. You can stay here if you want to."

Barney got in, telling himself you could only die once. And sending up the closest thing he knew to a prayer that it wouldn't be today . . .

. . .

Laura frowned when she heard Jonathan's message. It was all very well, him telling her not to call in that rather high-handed way, but she needed to know when he would be back. He did obsess over the mobile business; he could surely take a quick call—it would be over in a second. She'd just give him maybe another fifteen minutes and then . . .

. . .

"Give me some more of those jelly babies, would you?"

Georgia looked at Patrick; his eyes were fixed on the road, oddly unblinking. Was he sleepy? She felt sleepy herself, thundering along, the road shimmering in the heat haze. And was it her imagination—was it getting darker; were they losing the sun—

"We're running into a storm," Patrick said, wide-awake suddenly. "Dear God, will you look at that—"

And, in an odd yellow blackness, great sheets of rain came beating down on the road, turning it to glass and then seeming to wrap around them, crash after crash of thunder; and then the rain turned to hail, the stones hitting the windscreen, vying with the thunder for noise, whiting out the road markings.

She looked anxiously at Patrick, and his face was tense, his hands on the steering wheel white knuckled; all she could see of the approaching cars were their headlights, some on full beam, an endless procession, and in front of them nothing but spray—thick, impenetrable spray, only half pierced by the long red of the brake lights.

And then it was over as fast as it had begun; they ran out of it into brilliant sunshine, the thunder gone too, and the sky a sweet, clear blue.

"Wow," she said, "that was kind of . . . scary."

. . .

"So . . ." said Abi. They had driven through the darkness of the thunder and the hail; the sun was shining again. "So . . . what do you want me to do?"

Relief flooded him. She was going to be all right after all; she'd just been making a point.

"Well . . . nothing, I suppose. Just . . . just—"

"Go quietly. Is that it?"

"I . . . suppose so. Yes. If you put it like that."

"I can't think of any other way to put it, Jonathan. You want out. If I don't, that's my problem. You have a marriage to look after. And I only have me. Poor little old me." She sighed.

He felt a pang of remorse and irritation in equal proportions. He hadn't behaved entirely well. He could see that. But . . . she was hardly in a vulnerable position. She was financially self-sufficient; she had a flat; she had a good job, a car; she was young, sexy, tough—she didn't exactly need him. As Laura did . . .

"Abi, I'm sorry. I shall miss you. But . . . I don't really have any alternative. Our relationship can't go anywhere. And it's very wrong. You must see that."

"Well, why start it then?" Her voice was ugly, harsh.

"I . . ." He felt very tired suddenly, unable to deal with her arguments. The late night, the drive down from Birmingham, the lack of sleep, the stress of the journey, the shock of the storm: it all combined to confuse him. He slowed the car down.

"What are you doing?"

"Moving into the slow lane."

He moved behind a red E-Type—lovely old car, he thought, surprised that he could notice it even, given his turmoil—then eased himself into a large space in the slow lane in front of an old Škoda.

"You know it's bloody unfair," she said, lighting a cigarette.

"Abi, I said not in the car."

"Yes, I know you did. It's all totally unfair, Jonathan. What do you think I am, some kind of automaton? Didn't you ever think that I might have taken what you were doing just a little bit seriously? When you sent me flowers and bought me expensive dinners and the odd bit of costly stuff? Did you see doing all that as a substitute for just paying for me, the price of the sex?"

"Don't be ridiculous. You know perfectly well I'm very . . . very"—*careful, Jonathan, don't start claiming affection, could be very dangerous*—"very concerned for you."

"Oh, really? Well, I don't think I do know that, actually. I think that because you're rich and successful and you've got a wife who believes every filthy fucking lie you tell her, you can spend nights away in pricey hotels, get your sexual pleasure that way, rather than a quick screw with a tart. Well, it sucks, Jonathan. It's filthy and I think your wife ought to know what a filthy slob she's married to; I think you should have to deal with that and her. And I think maybe I should tell her."

"Abi, don't be absurd. What good would that do?"

"Quite a lot—in the long run. Not to you, or to me, but to her and any other poor bitch whom you might fancy fucking in the future."

"You wouldn't dare."

"Of course I'd dare. What have I got to lose? Nothing at all."

"But . . . but . . ." He found he was pleading with her. "But, Abi, you couldn't do that; you'd hurt her so much."

"No, Jonathan, it's you who's hurt her. Not me. So—"

Jonathan's mobile rang sharply; he shouldn't—he was driving—but he was in the slow lane, going very slowly . . . He picked it up, looked at it. It was Laura. Without thinking, wanting only to reassure her, and to somehow be safe with her, he pressed the button.

"Hello, darling—"

"Darling!" Abi was shouting, her face ugly with rage. "How can you do that, you rotten bastard? How can you talk like that? Give me that phone . . ."

"Hello! Hello, Jonathan, is that you?" Laura's voice was faint, crackly. "Jonathan, what's—"

. . .

The traffic was very thick; a huge lorry was alongside them, travelling at the same speed, the red car in front pulling ahead now—nice, that old Jag; he'd love something like that—the one behind too close on their tail, really, all of them part of a great orderly mass of power, riding the highway in the dazzling sun: he took it in with some strange detachment, trying to think, absurdly, what to say . . .

And then . . .

. . .

"Jonathan, be careful, look out, the lorry, what's happening to it—"

"Patrick, look out, look out, what's happening, what is it, be careful, look out—oh God—"

· · ·

"Shit! Fuck! Jesus Christ."
"Toby, stop, hold it, for Christ's sake, hold it."

Part Two

THE ACCIDENT

William Grainger always said his life was totally changed in one moment: the moment when he stood, awestruck, in the field high above the side of the motorway, looking down onto it. He'd gone out to check on the heifers they'd moved that morning from the field on the other side of the farm. Usually they were untroubled by the traffic; occasionally they became nervous.

This lot seemed untroubled. They walked over to him with their swinging walk, hoping he was food; when they realised he was not, that he had brought nothing for them, they stopped and turned away, an untidy, disappointed, good-natured crowd. One of them had lifted her tail and discharged a mass of cow shit on his boots; a protest, he'd thought, cursing her, pushing his feet through the dry grass to try to get rid of the worst. And then, as he looked down at the road, shimmering in the heat haze, the air brilliantly clear again after the brief thunderstorm, he saw it and knew even as he watched that he would never forget it: all in a sickening slow motion, a lorry suddenly swerving sharply to the right, cutting across the fast lane and then failing to stop, bursting through the central median, its trailer sinking onto its side, like some great dying beast, and then discharging the deadly flotsam of its load—whatever it was; he couldn't really see—tossed into the air and continuing on its journey into the advancing traffic. A minibus travelling westwards in the fast lane became impacted in the undercarriage of the lorry; and a black Golf immediately behind that swung sideways and rammed into one of the lorry's wheels. A silver BMW behind the lorry, apparently out of control, spinning, twisting, across the road, coming finally to rest, rammed into the car in front of it. Cars began to swerve and skid into one another, like bumper cars in a fairground; one hit the central median; another made a small, odd leap and landed on the hard shoulder; it all went on, seemingly unstoppable in both directions of the road.

William stood, frozen with horror now, hearing the scene as well as watching it—the dreadful noise, blaring horns, and crunching metal and raw, dreadful shouting and screaming—and aware too of the dreadfully dangerous smell of burning rubber.

Instinct told him to go down to the road; common sense told him not to. He could be of no use, would add to the chaos; he reached in the pocket of his jeans for his mobile, remembered he had left it in the tractor on the other side of the fence, and started to run, waving his arms at the scene in a futile gesture, as if anyone seeing him would have understood what he was going to do.

CHAPTER 10

For just a second, Jonathan was tempted to drive on, remove himself from the horror and the carnage, get to London swiftly and safely, rid himself of Abi. If he went on, he had a chance of disentangling his life; if he stayed, he had none.

He stopped the car and left his former life forever . . .

The car immediately ahead of him was driving steadily on as if nothing had happened; other cars coming from behind him were slewing into one another, gradually coming to a halt. Jonathan sat, fighting for breath, leaning on the steering wheel, recovering from the shock, hauling himself under control together with the car; the road ahead emptied now as the traffic went on forwards, vanishing into the haze of the heat, caught up in the doctrine of the motorway, of pushing on, of getting there, of never looking back, not getting involved, leaving him behind: and he would have given in that moment all he had to be one of them . . .

He opened the door, slowly and very cautiously, started to get out, and then found his legs wouldn't hold him; he felt sick and dizzy and sat down again, his head dropping weakly onto the steering wheel.

He looked at Abi; she was green-white, staring at him, her eyes huge with fright: there was an ugly gash on the side of her head. "What happened?" she said. "I don't understand."

"I'm not sure," he said. "I couldn't see; the lorry seemed to lose control. Your head all right?"

She felt the gash, looked at the blood on her hand. "Yes, I think so. I've got some tissues somewhere; I'll just—"

"Give me my mobile."

"I can't find it—I dropped it."

"Well, give me yours then."

He took it, dialled 999. Asked for the police and gave them the whereabouts.

"Yes, thank you, we've got that one," the voice said. "Several people calling in. They'll be there in ten minutes."

Jonathan looked at the great mass of traffic gathering, stretching in both directions. "I hope so," he said. "It's pretty bad." And then watched, disbelieving, as first one car, then another and then another, moved onto the westbound hard shoulder, accelerating and driving away.

"Stupid fucking bastards," he said; and then got out of the car and began to walk slowly, almost against his will, towards the lorry.

. . .

It was a hideous sight. A minibus had gone straight into it, under its wheels, and had crumpled up like so much paper, and from it he could hear the hideous sound of children screaming; a Golf, desperate to avoid it, had first turned, then skidded a hundred and eighty degrees into the traffic in the middle lane; a larger car—a big Ford—had managed to miss it, but driven into the barrier and swung round before it stopped, facing the wrong way . . . A man was climbing out of it, shaking his head oddly, as if to rid it of what he had just seen and done; his windscreen was shattered, and blood was running down his face.

Jonathan realised the Golf's engine was still running; turning it off seemed suddenly the most urgent thing. He scrambled over the barrier, ran to the car. The window had shattered with the impact, as had the windscreen. Jonathan looked down and into it: at a girl, or all he could see of her, a mass of long blond hair and blood, a bare brown arm with a white watch—odd how one noticed these things—flung out towards the windscreen as if warding it off; and yes, the engine still switched on. Jonathan reached in, turned the key, and then very gently lifted the arm, felt for the pulse. And found nothing.

He straightened up and found himself staring into the shocked, puzzled eyes of the driver of the Ford, and simply nodded at him, confirming the girl's death, unable to speak.

"Oh, God," said the man, staring round him at the carnage, "what did it . . . How did it happen?"

"Christ knows. You OK?"

"Seem to be. Yeah. Can't think how. Arm hurts a bit."

Jonathan looked at his arm; it was hanging oddly.

"Looks like it's broken. I'll check it later."

They stood there for a moment, looking up at the lorry from the driver's side; the cab was astonishingly intact. They walked round it, and as they reached the near side, they saw the door was open, and a girl was standing on the step. She jumped to the ground.

"You OK?" said Jonathan, and then, "You weren't in there, were you?"

She stared at them both, her expression totally blank, then shook her head, turned her back on them, and vomited rather neatly onto the road. She was very young, and very pretty, Jonathan noticed; after a moment she walked, slowly but quite steadily, towards the hard shoulder, where she sat down and put her head in her arms.

"Shocked," said Jonathan, "but she seems OK. Extraordinary."

"She can't have been in there, can she? Or climbed up to have a look?"

"God knows. Look—I'm going up into the cab. Make sure the engine's turned off there. It could explode any moment."

Oddly, he didn't feel frightened, wasn't aware of being brave; just knew it had to be done.

. . .

Constable Robbie Macyntyre had been dreading his first big crash. He just didn't know how he would deal with it. He wasn't exactly squeamish, and of course they had spelt out to them in training that things like severed limbs and worse were inevitable and shown them DVDs. It wasn't that; more the thought of people in terrible pain, crying out, begging for help.

The first calls had come in five minutes ago; hundreds more would follow. Already two cars had left the depot, and he was in the third, with his colleague Greg Dixon. Robbie was intensely grateful that this was not Greg's first big crash, or even his hundred and first. "Been doing this for ten years," he'd said to Robbie when he joined the unit. "Got pretty bloody used to it. *Bloody* being the word, if you get my meaning."

As far as they had been able to establish, the congestion on the road was already severe in both directions.

The main priority now, apart from clearing a way for the emergency services to get through, was to garner information and communicate it to the control room: how many casualties, how many ambulances would be required, whether the fire brigade would be needed to cut people out.

Robbie kept remembering his superintendent's words: *Gridlock on the motorway takes seconds: you'll have a mile tailback inside a minute.*

One of the main problems subsequent to a crash, he'd been told—although it didn't sound as if it would be today—was rubbernecking. "You can get an incident entirely on one carriageway and the traffic comes to a standstill on the other," Greg Dixon said. "Just because people slow down, even crash into the car in front at times, just to have a gawp. Good old Joe Public."

He didn't take a very rosy view of Joe Public; Robbie was swiftly coming to realise why.

. . .

Jonathan slithered down from the lorry's cab; the Ford driver was still there.

"OK?"

"Yes, the engine was off. Hell of a mess up there. Windscreen's shattered, blood everywhere. Poor bugger driving it's not too good, though."

"I bet he's not. Is he . . . alive?"

"Just. Maybe not for long."

"Should we get him out?"

"Christ, no." He glanced over at the hard shoulder. "That girl OK?"

"She's disappeared," said the man. "She was still sitting on the hard shoulder last time I looked. Nobody with her. But she's not there now."

"Wandered down the road, I suppose. She seemed very shocked. Oh, well. She's the least of our worries, I have to say . . ."

A man was walking towards them, holding a small boy by the hand; he was crying and saying, "Mummy . . . Mummy . . ."

"Is he all right?" Jonathan said.

"He's all right," said the man, and he spoke so casually it was as if he was discussing the weather. "His mother's not, though."

He nodded in the direction of a large black car behind him; its windscreen was shattered and there was a woman lying on the road; she had clearly come through the windscreen.

"She just undid her belt, just for a second," the man said, "to give the little fellow a drink. And she . . . she . . ."

He shook his head, turned away from them.

"I'm a doctor," said Jonathan gently. "Would you like me to come and see her?" He knew it would be futile, but it needed to be done.

The man nodded. "If you wouldn't mind."

The man with the broken arm looked after them.

"Poor bugger," he said, "poor, poor bugger."

. . .

Emma had just finished eating a rather dodgy BLT when the news came through: of a major crash on the M4, of a jackknifed lorry, a crushed minibus, road blocked in both directions, almost certain fatalities. And by some grisly coincidence, there was a second accident farther down the road, a continental truck with a blowout had slewed across the exit road of the next junction. Nobody was hurt there, but there was a mass of traffic behind it, and an obvious route for the emergency services to the crash, travelling the wrong way up the motorway, was temporarily, at least, out of the question.

She half ran into A&E and put in the trauma calls, the special unmistakable *bleep,* summoning people to A&E, removing them from their day-to-day work and rosters; she would need, she reckoned, an orthopaedist, a cardio thoracic surgeon, two general surgeons, two anaesthetists, a general surgical registrar, and ATL—hospital shorthand for advanced trauma and life support. Plus at least ten nurses.

They stood together in A&E. a group of people, some of whom knew one another only slightly, working as they did in totally different departments of the hospital, others who were in daily contact. There was a minute of formalities, of handshaking, name giving.

Alex Pritchard appeared; half an hour earlier he'd waved to her across reception, off on a clear weekend.

"Thought I'd better come back, see if I could be useful."

Apart from the surgical registrar and Alex, there was just one other properly familiar face: Mark Collins, a young orthopaedic registrar she'd worked with a few months earlier on a ghastly multiple motorbike crash. He had been great then, calm and tireless.

"Hi, Emma. This sounds like a big one. Worse than the bikers, I fear. OK. Who's going to be team leader?"

That had surprised Emma, on her first big incident. Somehow she'd thought everyone would just know what to do anyway. But it was essential, she had discovered, to establish a chain of control—for order and swift delegation, and to cut through the chaos and any panic; the first thing ambulance crews always asked on arrival was, "Who's team leader?"

"You, Alex?" she said now to Pritchard.

"OK. All right with everyone? What news, Emma?"

"Well, it's pretty bad. Jackknifed lorry, trailer on its side, driver trapped, several cars, minibus—three lanes blocked, in both directions, several fatalities. And someone just rang to say people are driving down the hard shoulder in the westward direction, so the road could be impassable pretty soon."

"Is the driver of the truck alive?"

"So far. Amazingly, there's a doctor right on the scene. He rang to report that the bloke was completely trapped, steering column embedded in his chest, just about conscious, pulse very weak, but definitely alive—Excuse me." Her phone had rung—it was the first of the ambulances. "Hi. Yes. We have a full team ready. Good luck."

. . .

Jonathan had turned his attention to the minibus; the driver's door was jammed shut, but the one at the rear opened fairly easily. There were eight small boys inside, all miraculously unhurt, but the driver was dead, hideously so. He was about to climb in when he heard Abi's voice: "Jonathan, what can I do?"

She was still white, but very calm; he felt a reluctant thud of admiration for her.

"Help me get these chaps out. Don't look at the front."

She undid their seat belts, took their small hands, led them, talking encouragingly, shepherding them past the worst of it, trying to distract them from the girl in the Golf. They were dazed, obedient with shock, all white faced and shaking, many of them weeping: but astonishingly unhurt.

There was another man in the van, neatly strapped into his seat, as the boys had all been; he was staring in front of him, also unhurt, but apparently reluctant to leave the van. Jonathan urged him out onto the grass verge, where he sat down obediently, then buried his head in his arms. Post-traumatic shock, Jonathan decided, and felt at once sympathy and a totally unreasonable irritability. He could have done with some help with these poor little buggers from someone who knew them.

. . .

"Tobes," said Barney. "Tobes, are you OK?"

He felt odd, disoriented; his ears seemed to be blocked, sound muffled. He shook his head and looked sideways out of the window, the fog of shock clearing, and saw a surreal landscape of cars, many, like them, come to rest against fridges and washing machines, others at a right angle to the crash barrier, some facing completely the wrong way. At first, as he looked, the landscape was quite still; then, like some gradually speeded-up film, it came to life as people began to climb out of cars, peer into others, clearly fearful of what they might see, talked on their mobiles, approached one another, united as survivors, members of a blessedly elite club.

And then he realised that there had been no answer from Toby, not even a groan or a grunt, and turned very slowly to look at him, frightened beyond anything.

He was lying over the steering wheel, one arm holding it, his face turned to Barney, apart from a flow of blood down his face from a head wound, utterly still. And then Barney realised that there was a far worse injury to Toby than his head; the car below the steering wheel was crumpled, collapsed inwards, and Toby's right leg below the knee appeared crushed by the interior of the car. There was a great deal of blood flowing from it.

Slow with terror, he reached for Toby's wrist, pushed up the new white cuff, felt for his pulse. And for an age he sat there, looking at him, just waiting for something to happen, for him to move, make a noise, groan even, for Christ's sake. But . . . there was nothing.

"Oh, Tobes," he said aloud, his thumb moving first gently, then desperately up and down Toby's wrist. "Tobes, don't, please . . . You can't—shit, where is it—oh, God—"

And then he started to weep.

. . .

"There you are," Jonathan said to the last little boy, settling him on the grass verge. "You're fine. What's your name?"

"Shaun," he said, and then, "I'm ever so thirsty."

"I'll get you . . ." said Jonathan, and then realised he couldn't get him a drink; he and Abi between them had finished the one bottle of water he'd had in the car. And Christ, it was hot; he could have done with another litre of the stuff himself.

"I'll see what I can do," he said, reflecting with a sort of detached surprise on the fact that here, on a three-lane motorway in the twenty-first century in one of the most highly developed countries in the world, a thirsty child in blistering heat could not have a drink, and probably would not be able to for some considerable time.

He could hear a phone ringing somewhere, and wondered where it was; by the time he'd realised it was his own it had stopped. He was obviously not functioning as well as he might be; he'd better be careful.

Abi had briefly disappeared; he looked round for her, saw her scrambling over the barrier. He called her name; she turned round, scowled at him, and continued down the bank, out of sight. Where was the silly bitch going; what was she doing?

He looked rather vaguely for the girl in the cab; there was no sign of her either. Maybe Abi had seen her; maybe that was where she was going . . .

He looked at the missed call register; it had been Laura. Again. She must be very worried, but he couldn't ring her back yet; he didn't have the strength either to talk to her or even begin to think about what he might say. The extent of his own predicament was beginning to hit him: being on the wrong motorway, in very much the wrong company. How was he going to explain that, for Christ's sake? But he was unable even to think about it yet . . .

His phone rang again. "Police," said the voice. "We're probably about half a mile from you. From your description, it sounds like the truck driver'll need cutting free. Would you confirm that, sir?"

"Absolutely, yes," said Jonathan.

"Thanks. We'll be there as soon as we can."

. . .

Abi had reappeared.

"Where the fuck have you been?"

"I needed to pee," she said. "And don't talk to me like that. None of this is my fault."

"I hope you're not implying it's mine."

"Well, you were on the phone," she said. "Police might not like that. If they knew."

"Oh, for fuck's sake!" he said. But he suddenly felt extremely sick.

. . .

Mary bit her lip with the pain and saw Colin turning round, his face white, but apparently perfectly all right; and then she looked out of the window and saw a scene of unimaginable chaos, right across to the other side of the motorway: cars shunted into one another, people walking and even running about, and huge white objects all over the road. As she turned round with huge and painful difficulty, she saw a large red car, half-embedded in the back of them.

Colin opened the door and climbed out and walked round to it; she heard him say, "Jesus," and then, "Jesus Christ," and then, "You all right, mate?" and then saw him come to the front of the car and lean onto the bonnet, shaking his head, his eyes closed.

Emma turned back to the group. "Apparently the road on the west-ward side is completely blocked. Some moron on the hard shoulder has broken down way ahead, and the police cars can't get through at all at the moment. Going to be tough. And our doctor says the lorry driver is in a bad way, that it's a neuro job. He's impaled on the steer-ing column, pulse fairly steady, but really slow, about forty. Injuries mainly internal, no visible haemorrhage, severe bruising on the left temple, almost certainly concussed."

"Poor bastard'll need fluids, morphine," said Alex, "and it's going to take so bloody long. We should get HEMS on the case."

HEMS—the Helicopter Emergency Service—was called out far more than Emma would have expected: not just to bad traffic acci-dents, but to people stranded climbing, sailing. She had a secret yearn-ing to be able to join them one day.

The phone rang again and Alex answered it.

"The doctor says there's a young girl in a GTI dead, plus one other woman—and so is the driver of the minibus. Apparently there's a load of kids on board."

"Any of them dead?"

"Nope."

Emma fought down an absurd rush of sorrow for the girl in the GTI.

. . .

William Grainger had returned to the vantage point at the top of his field, having called the police. He couldn't do anything else, really, couldn't ignore what was going on down there, couldn't get on with any of the things that had seemed so important an hour ago. There might be something he could do when the police and ambulances arrived—although at the moment there seemed little chance of that. On the great curve of road stretching away from him backwards towards London, the traffic was solid, all three lanes motionless;

and cars that had tried to escape via the hard shoulder were at a complete standstill as well. *And serves them right,* William thought. What kind of a selfish idiot would block that, the route so essential to the emergency services? Even as he watched, a procession came in sight, breakdown trucks preceded by police cars and followed by ambulances, coming towards him; they had obviously closed the road altogether from the next junction, reversed the normal flow of traffic.

His phone rang. "Mr. Grainger? Police here. Where are you now? As related to the accident."

"Where I was when it happened."

"How's it looking from where you are?"

"Pretty . . . pretty bad . . ."

"Many people walking about?"

"Yeah, quite a lot now."

"How would you feel about a helicopter landing in that field? An air ambulance?"

"Well, the cows wouldn't like it. I'd have to get them moved. Otherwise, fine, of course. Just let me know."

"OK. Could we ask you to move them anyway, as a precaution? Straightaway, if you'd be so kind. Might make a bit of a mess."

"That's perfectly all right," said William. He switched off his phone, looked down at the chaos below him, increasing now, farther back in the road, perhaps two, three hundred metres or so away, as more and more people left their cars, some on mobiles, shouting into them, some with dogs on leads, barking furiously, others with small children, many of them crying, carrying them to the grass verge, all talking to one another.

Better get the cows shifted fast.

CHAPTER 11

"No, he's alive."

Barney had never heard anything as wonderful as those words spoken by this really great bloke who'd put his head in the window as Barney sat there, helplessly still holding Toby's wrist, said he was a doctor, and could he help?

"But he's in a lot of trouble from that leg, I'd say, possibly his pelvis as well, and he's probably concussed. But—"

"Shit," Toby said suddenly. "Fuck. Holy shit."

"There you are. Very much alive. He should be OK. I've certainly seen worse."

"You OK, Tobes?" said Barney

"It hurts," Toby said. "My leg hurts. You all right?"

"I'm fine."

"What happened?"

"Lorry went out of control. We hit another car."

"Oh, I see." His eyes had closed again, at what clearly was to him an acceptable explanation; he seemed to have drifted away again.

"What should we do?" Barney was trying not to panic, but it was difficult. "Would it be better if we got him out? He might be cooler."

"No, the best thing is to get him into the hospital. And we shouldn't move him, and it certainly isn't cooler outside, unfortunately."

"So . . . I can't help?"

"We can try to stop that leg bleeding. Tie something round it, make a tourniquet. Got anything we can use?"

"My shirt?" said Barney, tearing off his wedding waistcoat, ripping off the shirt.

"Good man. Now if we can just rip it into strips—that's the way—and then I can . . . Yes, pass it to me . . . There—sorry, old chap," he said as Toby yelled in pain. "Now what you can do is keep an eye on his pulse. Not difficult. If it starts to drop dramatically, just come and find me. I won't be far away. Try to keep him awake, distract him if you can from the pain, just keep talking to him, tell him medical help's on its way."

"But how do we get the medical help?" asked Barney, his voice desperate. "The traffic's totally solid—"

"Emergency vehicles are on their way, and the ambulances are being diverted down this wrong side of the motorway. Should be here quite soon. From a large and very good new hospital near Swindon."

"So . . . so could you make sure they deal with Toby first?"

"It's not my decision. But I will point out to them that he has serious injuries and probably needs blood urgently."

"Why do you think the air bag didn't work? Neither of them did."

"No idea. Maybe because of the angle the car was struck." He smiled almost cheerfully at Barney. "Jonathan Gilliatt. Nice to have met you. Albeit under rather unhappy circumstances." He paused. "From the look of you, I'd say you were on the way to a wedding."

"Yeah," said Barney.

"Jesus! Look, I'll come back and check on you a bit later." His phone rang. "Hello. Oh, good. Great. Look, we have a seriously injured man in a car over on the eastbound side, up against the safety barrier, just short of the truck. Car embedded in another. Silver BMW. Pulse not bad, but probably concussed, and a very nasty leg injury. I've put a tourniquet on, but he'll need blood urgently, so if you can get that message through to someone . . . Thanks.

"I'm going farther down the line now," Gilliatt said. "See if there's anything else I can do." He put the mobile back in his pocket, smiled at Barney. "They should be here pretty soon. You heard what I said to them. Just let me know if they don't find you, OK? Give me your phone; I'll put my number in it for you—"

. . .

Jonathan was just setting off back through the chaos when a wild-eyed man grabbed his shoulder from behind.

"I believe you're a doctor. It's my wife. Could you have a look at her? Please? She's in the car, just here."

It was a Volvo, the car the wedding boys had struck from the rear.

"She's . . . well, she's pregnant. She's having stomach pains, and I'm terrified she's going into labour."

"How pregnant?"

"Seven and a half months."

"OK. Let's have a look at her."

The girl was doubled up over her stomach in the front seat, her face contorted with pain. Jonathan waited, saw the pain clearly pass, saw her relax.

"Hello," he said. "I'm a doctor. An obstetrician, actually. So you've come to the right place."

She tried to smile.

"How long have you been having the contractions?"

"Oh . . . about . . . I don't know. Fifteen, twenty minutes."

"But they're quite strong?"

"Yes."

"And how often?"

"Every few minutes, it feels like."

"Can I feel your tummy? Just put the seat back; that's right. Lean back; try to relax. Now, then—"

As he felt her tummy, it tautened; the girl gasped, bit her lip, threw her head back. No doubt about it.

"Look," he said gently, picking up her wrist, taking her pulse, "I do think that, yes, you are in labour. Brought on by the shock, I expect."

"And the blow from behind, surely," said the man.

"I'm sure. Your necks are OK, are they? No whiplash?"

"No, thank God."

"Well, look. There's not a lot I can do. The contractions are frequent, but they're quite short. I don't think she's going to give birth imminently. But—"

"Oh, God." The girl started to cry. "This is so scary. It hurts so much, and it's much too early!"

Jonathan sat in the driver's seat; then he took the girl's hand and started talking to her very gently.

"Now, look, the first thing is to try to relax. I know it's easy for me to say, but it really will help. Have you been to antenatal classes, done any breathing techniques?"

"Yes. But—"

"Well, do them. For all you're worth. It will help you and help your baby. Now, let's get you more comfortable. That seat go any lower?"

"Yes," said the man.

"Good. The next thing is, seven and a half months isn't so terribly premature. Providing we can get you to the hospital, the baby will have an extremely good chance. Promise. Now, ambulances are coming, and I'll ring ahead and tell them about you. They can have an obstetric team ready. Oh—here comes another one," he said, seeing the girl tense, her eyes widen with fear. "Do your breathing! Go on. That's it. Nice and slow. Better?"

She nodded feebly.

"Good girl. Now, you just keep that up. And I'll come back in a little while, check on you. I'll give my number to your husband. Here." He reached for the man's phone. "Now, you just concentrate on what I've told you, and it's my opinion you'll have that baby in a nice delivery room at the hospital. OK?"

"OK," said the girl. She looked much calmer.

"Good girl." Jonathan smiled at her, got out of the car. "Try not to worry too much. Tough little things, babies. I should know."

· · ·

The helicopter was approaching; William could hear it, although he couldn't see it. He looked at his watch: five fifteen. That poor bloke in the cab, probably dead by now, if he hadn't been when he'd crashed. And the minibus behind, half buried in it. No one could have survived that, surely.

He could see the helicopter approaching now, see the trees

bending in its path. William waved both arms furiously; the helicopter began to circle its way down towards him, then dropped dramatically onto the top of the field. The blades slowed; a man got out, waved at William, followed by another. William ran over to them.

"Hi!" he said.

"Hi. Thanks for this. Couldn't have managed without you. The fire brigade should be here soon; they're being sent down the carriageway from the other direction as soon as the road's sufficiently clear. We're almost certainly going to need them. Now, we'll get down there, see what's what. Thanks again for your help."

"Can I go down? With some water, maybe? People are going to be terribly thirsty, I thought. This heat."

"Good idea. But stay on the verge; don't get in the way of the emergency vehicles."

"Of course I won't," said William. What did they think he was? Some kind of an idiot?

People did seem to have a very low opinion of farmers' intelligence. It was one of the many distressing things about being one.

. . .

"What do you mean, he's not coming? Of course he's coming; he can't not come; it's . . . well, it's . . . Of course he'll come. Just got . . . got held up. That's all."

"Tamara," said her father, "he's not coming. He's got caught up in some ghastly crash on the M4. Barney just phoned."

"Barney! Well, Barney's an idiot. Let me have your phone, Daddy; let me call him back. There must be some way he could come, cut across country or something—we can keep the church for a couple of hours, just do everything later; yes, that'll be all right; that's what we should do—"

"No, my darling, it won't be all right. I'm terribly, terribly sorry, but Toby's . . . well, Toby's been hurt—quite badly hurt, I'm afraid.

He's concussed, and one of his legs is injured, and there's a possibility he's got some internal injuries as well. Apparently the car hit a load of freezers or something—Barney wasn't making a lot of sense."

"Freezers! Oh, now I know it's a joke. How could a car hit a freezer? Here, give me your phone—"

"Tamara, it's not a joke," said her mother, "or an excuse. Toby's badly hurt, and they're waiting for an ambulance now to take him to the hospital."

"No," said Tamara, pushing back her veil and biting her fist. Tears were rising in her huge eyes. "No, that's impossible; he was fine this morning, fine early this afternoon, even. Barney must have made a mistake; he's— Oh, God!"

And she sat down on the front pew in the little church all bedecked with white roses, buried her head in her hands, and began to sob. And the vicar, standing quietly at the altar, asking for God's help both to comfort her and to save the life of her young fiancé, who was clearly in grave danger of losing it, looked at this beautiful girl, her veiled head drooped in despair, her bouquet flung onto the church floor, cheated of the greatest day in her life, and thought it was a very long time since he had seen anything quite so poignantly sad.

. . .

"Excuse me. Someone said you were a doctor?"

"Yes," said Jonathan shortly, "I am."

"My girlfriend's just . . . well, she keeps being terribly sick. She's in a bad way. I wonder if you could—"

. . .

"I understand you're a doctor."

"Yes, that's correct. But—"

"A lady here . . . we're rather afraid she's having a heart attack. She has angina; I wonder if you could—"

Jesus, Jonathan thought, exhausted now, desperate for some reprieve—what would they all have done if he hadn't been there . . . ?

. . .

"Miss. Miss, can you help me, miss?"

Abi felt terribly sick; she would have given anything for a drink of water, but felt that if anyone should be thirsty, anyone should suffer, she should.

She tried to smile at the little boy.

"What's the matter?"

His eyes were big and scared as he looked at her.

"I think I'm going to have an asthma attack, miss, and I haven't got no inhaler with me. It was in me"—he paused, clearly breathless—"in me rucksack, miss.

"Oh, Oh, I see."

"And I'm ever so thirsty, miss."

"Me too, miss," said the boy next to him, and then another and another.

"Well, look, I haven't got any water, I'm afraid. But I can go and ask in some of the other cars. Now, you, Master Asthma . . ."

The little boy managed to smile at her.

"Yes, miss?"

"I can't do anything about your inhaler yet. I'm sorry. But when Jon—the doctor—comes back next time—he's the man who got you out of the bus—I'll see if he might have one."

"All right, miss. But me chest feels well tight. I get it really bad, sometimes have to go to the hospital." And he burst into tears.

"Oh, don't be scared," Abi said, and she sat down beside him, put her arms round him. "Very soon now the ambulances will be here and they'll have inhalers, I'm sure. So you've just got to hang on a bit longer. What's your name?"

"Shaun, miss."

"Right, Shaun. Well, do you know when I was your age, I had asthma. If I got an attack and I didn't have my inhaler, I used to do breathing exercises. Shall we try? Not too deep, just nice, even, slow breaths. That's right. I'll do it with you. While I'm counting. Ready—"

Shaun fixed his large blue eyes trustingly on her and, after about ten breaths, said, sounding more breathless still, "It's not helping, miss. I'm that wheezy." And he started to cry again.

"Oh, God." Abi looked round. The heat was awful, the sun relentless, and the air close and stifling. There was an odd smell, at once sickly and sour; they might not have been outside at all, and indeed the air itself was thick, hazy, cloudy with traffic fumes. This wouldn't be helping. She saw Jonathan walking towards them, waved at him to come over.

"You haven't got an inhaler with you, have you? For asthma?"

"No, of course not," he said tersely. "I'm not a walking pharmacy."

"No. No, I realise that. But Shaun here's getting an asthma attack, and I wondered . . . I just thought you might—"

"Well, you thought wrong, and I have more serious concerns than a bloody asthma attack. The driver's bleeding to death in that truck, and the bloody medics—Oh, here they are, thank Christ—this way, please, quickly."

"I can't help it, miss," said Shaun. "Why was he cross?"

"He's just very . . . very worried," said Abi, looking after Jonathan as he directed the ambulance men towards the truck. "He's not cross."

"My mum always says that about my dad, when he gets cross," said another of the little boys. "Says he's upset, not to take no notice."

There was a general chorus of recognition at this scenario; Abi looked at them and smiled for the first time. Distracting them was clearly the best thing she could do.

"Why don't you all tell me your names?" she said. "Just first names. I'm called Abi, short for Abigail."

"That's a nice name," said Shaun carefully. His breathing was very quick and shallow, and speaking was clearly difficult.

They all told her their names, then where they lived, what they liked doing, what their mums were called. Almost cheerful. And then—

"I'm so thirsty, miss. I got to have a drink; can you get us one, miss?"

The others all joined in. A couple were crying, saying they'd never felt so thirsty, not ever. Abi looked round desperately. She felt like crying herself. Had any of this been Jonathan's fault? He'd been on the phone; had he lost control? Had she distracted him? *Abi, don't, don't go down there.* It had been an accident, that was all, a terrible, awful accident. *Concentrate on water, water* . . . How on earth was she going to find some water?

· · ·

William was working his way down the field, skirting round a small spinney of young trees, carrying his containers, when he saw her: a young girl, very pretty, very dark, with wild black hair, stumbling along just above the ditch. She was crying silently.

"Hello, can I help? Are you involved in the crash; is someone with you hurt?"

She stared at him, her dark eyes filled with panic; then she shook her head and moved on, trying to run away from him through the long, uneven grass.

William shrugged and continued on his journey. She seemed all right—not hurt, anyway. He could see more pressing claims on his attention. Odd, though; but then, this was a very odd day.

· · ·

The little boys' distress and thirst were growing. Abi began to feel panicky. She mustn't panic; it would be fatal—it would spread. She saw a woman walking towards her with a golden retriever, and pointed him out to the boys by way of distraction; they crowded round, stroking him, asking the woman what his name was.

"Jasper."

"That's me brother's name," said Shaun. "My mum's boyfriend says it's a poof's name."

"Oh, really?" said Abi, smiling at the woman. She didn't smile back; indeed, she glared at Shaun. "I don't suppose you've got any water?" Abi said. "By any amazing chance?"

"If I had any I'd give it to this poor fellow," the woman said firmly. "He's beside himself. We're going to try in the woods."

"OK," said Abi carefully, "fine."

"But I need a drink!" One of the biggest boys was getting angry now. "I really, really need one. I'll die if I don't. We all will."

"No, you won't," said Abi. "People can live for quite a long time without water; you'd be surprised. However thirsty you are."

"But, miss—"

How on earth could she get them a drink? How could normal life have disappeared so swiftly?

And then: "Need any help?" said a voice. And like some kind of divine visitation came a man, very tanned, with brown, rather shaggy hair, wearing baggy—and filthy—jeans, a checked shirt that had clearly left the shop many years earlier, and some very heavy dusty boots. And he was carrying—yes, he was actually carrying two very large plastic containers. Containing—

"Oh, my God!" said Abi. "Water! How amazing. Can't be true."

"It certainly is. Was last time I looked, anyway." He grinned at her; he had the widest, sweetest grin she had ever seen. She smiled back.

"And I've even got some paper cups. Here, kids. Careful, one at a time—you'll knock it over if you're not careful. That's better." He held out a cup to Abi. "You want some?"

"No, no," she said, "they really need it."

"So do you, by the look of you. That's a horrible cut on your head. How did you do that?"

"Oh, I hit it as we stopped. It was pretty sudden."

"Yeah? It looks nasty. Here, take a cup. Let me—"

"Could I have some of that? For the dog; he's desperate. I've got a container—here, look."

It was the woman Abi had approached earlier.

"Oh, I don't think so," said the young man. "There're a lot of people here in terrible need. Sorry about the dog, but he'll be OK. Get him into the shade; I would— Hello, young chap," he said to a toddler clinging to his father's hand. "Need some water? Here we are."

He stood there on the roadside doling out his precious water, cup by cup, firmly refusing second comers.

"Just for now it's got to be one cup per person Not fair otherwise. Only person who can have two is Shaun here, because he's not very well."

"Where did you come from, then?" said Abi, looking at him in a kind of wonder.

"I live in a farm, just behind the hill there. The chopper's on our land. I saw it happen, actually." His voice was very quiet, rather slow, surprisingly posh. You didn't expect farmers to be posh. "I was standing up there with the cows, just moved them, and there it was, everything breaking up. Or seeming to be."

"Yes? So what . . . what happened exactly? Do you think?"

"Well, the lorry just swerved, really hard, and went through the barrier. No apparent reason. And then the load just . . . well, it was as if it had burst, came out of the doors at the back, the sides, out the top even—did you see any of it?"

"Not—not really. I . . . We were just ahead of the . . . of it all."

"Scary, isn't it? Terrible things, accidents. One minute everything's perfectly fine, under control, the next . . . well, it's not. Lives ruined, all these people hurt through no fault of their own. Through nobody's fault, really."

"Yes. Terrible." She smiled at him and sipped the water, the cool, wonderful water. She ought to get some to Jonathan, really.

Mary looked across at Colin; he was sitting on the bonnet of the car, lighting yet another cigarette. That was his sixth since the accident. Not that it mattered, and it was probably helping him, but she wished she could do something so simple that would make her feel better. She felt terrible, sick and exhausted, her neck and her head very painful. Colin had found her some painkillers, but they hadn't really taken the edge off the pain.

The people in the car behind, Janet and John Brown, which had rammed into her, were being very kind too. The driver, a man, had hurt his wrist very badly, but apart from that they were fine.

They had produced a rug from the car, some picnic chairs and a thermos, sat Mary down, given her a cup of tea. Which had been very welcome, but if she'd thought a bit longer, she would have refused it. It had gone straight through her . . .

She looked at her watch: nearly five. Just an hour until Russell's plane landed. Obviously now she couldn't possibly get there. What would he think; what could she do . . . ? *Keep calm, Mary, keep calm.*

. . .

She was desperate now to go to the lavatory. She wondered if she could enlist Janet Brown's help, ask her to hold up the blanket, perhaps, but decided she didn't know her well enough.

Her bladder stabbed at her; it was agony. And something else stabbed at her: the horribly familiar sense of squeezing pressure on her chest that signalled an attack of angina.

She felt absolutely terrified suddenly. For her nitrate spray was in the crumpled boot of the car . . .

Mary began to cry.

CHAPTER 12

Gradually order was being restored: two fire crews were still working on their grim tasks, but most of the casualties had been driven away in ambulances. Robbie followed Greg as he strode amongst the wreckage on the motorway, alternately talking into his radio, informing the AA and the RAC and local radio stations, taking witnesses' names and addresses, waving their cars over for inspection, and talking to the people who were stranded.

Mostly they wanted to know when they might get away; whether they could move their cars, whether the police could help with water and, as the time wore on, food.

One woman started shouting at them, demanding water; but on the whole they were pretty calm and cooperative. Greg was calm too, reassuring them that it shouldn't be too much longer now before they could start clearing the cars, directing them to the police car that had arrived with a huge supply of water, offering the use of his and Robbie's mobiles where essential.

Their task now that the worst was over—although the poor sod in the lorry was still being cut free—was to keep the scene as far as possible intact until the investigation unit arrived. Measurements and photographs had to be taken, a plan of the scene, complete with details of the debris, the exact location and direction of skid marks. Only when that was completed would they begin to get the cars out. Fortunately, the road into London was more or less clear now, but two lanes were still being used for the emergency services. There were a few cars on the hard shoulder, the doctor's—great bloke he was, fantastic help—and a rather nice middle-aged couple who'd walked back about two hundred yards: the only ones who had stopped—incredible it was, really—to see if they could do anything.

There'd been a drama with some girl who'd gone into labour. Robbie had been told to stay with her and the husband until they were safely on their way. He hadn't liked that too much. She'd been in considerable pain, alternately moaning and panting like a dog.

"I don't want to have it here," she said, gripping her husband's hand. "I'm so scared."

"No need for that," Robbie said, hoping it was true. "And listen—I think . . . yes, I can hear it now, an ambulance, here it comes now . . . I'll just flag it down, make sure it stops . . . yes. Good. Right. Over here, quickly, please," he called to the two paramedics, one a girl. "The lady's here, in this car."

As he said afterwards to his girlfriend, he'd never been quite so terrified in his entire life, not even when that young thug came at him with his knife.

"Thought she was going to have it then and there."

The girlfriend said briskly that policemen were always delivering babies. There'd been a story in the *Daily Mail* only last week, and she was sure he'd have been perfectly all right. Robbie was sure he wouldn't.

. . .

"Jonathan? Jonathan, thank God, at last—wherever are you; where have you been?"

Laura's voice was unusually harsh; he winced at the thought of how much harsher it would become.

"I'm on the M4, darling. Sorry not to have got in touch before."

"The M4? What on earth are you doing on the M4? Everyone's been so worried. I rang the clinic, but they hadn't heard from you since early afternoon, and then when I did ring you this afternoon I heard your voice, and then it was just—just an awful noise and then nothing—are you saying that wasn't you?"

"Laura, there's been a very bad crash on the motorway," said Jonathan, struggling to keep his voice level, finding it—illogically—hard to believe that she didn't know. "Really bad—I got caught up in it; lorry driver went through the barrier. At least three people killed, I'm afraid—"

"Oh, my God, Jonathan, how ghastly. Are you all right?"

"Yes, I'm fine. But I've been doing what I could. Obviously."

"Yes, of course. I understand. But . . . well, I wish you'd phoned, darling, I've been so worried."

"I'm sorry. Somehow, with all that's going on, didn't think of it. Lot of badly injured people, one chap practically bleeding to death, old lady having a suspected heart attack; I really didn't have time to chat."

"No. No, of course not. How horrible for you, darling. I'm so sorry. You must be exhausted. When do you think you might get away?"

"I . . . don't know. Fairly soon now, I think. Most of the casualties are on their way to the hospital, although the poor bugger in the lorry is being cut out by the fire brigade . . . Look—sorry, darling, got to go. The police are waiting to speak to me . . ."

. . .

"Come with me! Please! You gotta come with me."

Shaun gripped Abi's hand. He was still wheezing, fighting for breath.

She looked at the ambulance driver.

"Can I?"

"Yeah, s'pose so. Might be a long wait at the other end, though. Come on, now, mate," he said to Shaun, "you're not trying. Use that inhaler properly, deep breaths, that's right."

The man in charge of the boys was already gone to St. Marks; he'd remained very shocked, staring silently ahead of him, shaking violently from time to time. He had a suspected concussion. Abi and William had liaised over the welfare of the children; he would wait with them until they had all been taken safely away.

"OK," she said now. "Well, William, this looks like good-bye. Thanks for everything. You've been great."

"It was nothing. Wish I could have done more. Bye, Shaun."

. . .

William watched her as she climbed into the back of the ambulance.

Right," he said, sitting down on the grass again, next to the other boys. "We've just got to wait now. Shouldn't be too long. Anyone know any good songs?"

It wasn't until all the boys had been driven safely off by the Highways Agency that he found Abi's mobile in the pocket of his jeans, and remembered her asking him to take it while she led the boys one by one down the bank to pee.

CHAPTER 13

Time had become irrelevant. Emma supposed she felt tired, supposed she felt upset, even; but she was not actually aware of it. She worked like an automaton, conscious only of the superb organisation that was directing everyone's efforts. If Alex had told her to clean all the toilets she would have done it without question.

Ambulances arrived; people were brought in, were assessed and directed to the relevant station, and then on to theatre and, where necessary, intensive care. For much of the time she moved from station to station, seeing patients, trying to reassure them, administering painkillers, putting in cannulas and then intravenous drips and blood, taking blood tests, listening to chests, organising X-rays. The X-rays were portable, brought up to the beds, the machines moving round the patients, Dalek like; many people had fractures, and the simpler ones she set herself, having checked with the orthopaedic registrar— wonderful, calm, even funny Mark Collins—and she sewed up lacerations too, and butterfly-clipped minor head wounds.

Many of the cases were fairly mundane: broken ribs, fractured wrists; some more serious, mostly head injuries. There was a girl in premature labour—Emma held her hand, timing her contractions as they waited for a midwife to collect her, checking that there was someone still free to set up an epidural, soothing the wild-eyed husband. Emma was spared almost entirely her greatest dread: badly injured children; for the most part they had survived in the astonishing security of their seat belts. One small boy had a concussion, another a broken leg; a very young baby was badly dehydrated, but for the most part, they grinned at her cheerfully as she checked bumps and bruises, enjoying the excitement and drama, intrigued by her stethoscope, asking her endless questions.

A middle-aged man in considerable pain was frantic that his wife should not be contacted: "She has a heart condition; I don't want her panicking."

He proved to have several fractured ribs, one of which had punctured his lung. "Nothing we can't fix pretty quickly. You can go home tomorrow; tell your wife you've got in a fight," said Emma cheerfully, setting up a chest drain.

"Oh, bless you," he said, patting her hand, and then, "You don't look like a doctor, you know."

"I do know," she said.

One case was particularly poignant: a young man was stretchered in, covered in blood, his equally blood-soaked friend walking beside him.

"They were on their way to the injured guy's wedding," Mark told her when she met him outside the theatre. "How cruel is that?"

"Bad as he looks?"

"Not sure. Head injury fairly superficial, but horrible mess, that leg—we're not sure yet if we can fix it. Going to try to pin it, but it's extremely complex . . ."

. . .

Russell looked at his watch; he kept looking at it, willing it to stay still, stop making it later, stop Mary failing him. But it was moving relentlessly on, ignoring his bewilderment and his unhappiness: Seven forty-five, it said now. A whole sixty minutes late. An hour. Surely,

surely she'd have got a message to him if she'd been held up some-where. Surely it couldn't be that difficult . . .

He'd come through to arrivals at a half run, he'd been so excited, his heart thudding as he pulled his flight bag behind him. The rest of his luggage had been FedExed to the hotel.

Although he'd instructed her to wait at the Hertz desk, he'd still wondered if she mightn't walk over to where everyone else was wait-ing, leaning on the barrier. He scanned the row of people: scruffy, for the most part, generally young, lots of children sitting on their father's shoulders, pulling on their mothers' hands, people holding banners saying things like, *Welcome Home, Mum* and the rows of dark-suited drivers, with their signs neatly filled with people's names. He had been met all over the world by such people; automatically he scanned the boards now . . . But there was no neat, smiling white-haired lady, waving as she had been in the wildest of his wildest dreams, calling out, "Russell! Over here!"

Mary had written in her last letter that there'd be no risk of bad holdups, because she'd be travelling against the traffic.

"And I shall allow lots of time, Russell; you can be sure of that. Was I ever late for you?"

And she wasn't; somehow she had always been on time, working her way briskly across London, hopping from bus to bus, often walk-ing if the traffic was bad. Well, she had been, once, terribly late—two and a half hours—but she had turned up safely just the same, had run into the bar where he'd agreed to meet her, flushed and flustered. "The siren went off, Russell; I had to go down to the tube and wait for the all-clear. I'm so sorry."

It had been his last night before being moved to a new base; he wouldn't be able to stay long, he warned her, but she'd said she'd get away from work early specially.

"I might not see you again for . . . for a long time. I mean, you never know. I don't want to waste our last evening together, Russell, not seeing you.

"I'm so, so glad you were still here," she said, smiling as he kissed her, and he said of course he was still there; he'd have waited for her for all night if need be, risked getting into every kind of trouble.

As he would now. And this had been only an hour . . .

. . .

The lorry driver had been brought in by helicopter, Alex told Emma, the last casualty to arrive, and taken straight to the theatre. His chances were not rated very high. She had expected him to be old, but apparently he was in his early thirties, with a young family.

"He fielded most of the steering column," said Alex, "poor chap. You name it, he's got it: fractured ribs and sternum, tension pneumothorax, contusions of his heart, and then a few more minor things"—he grinned at her—"ruptured spleen, some liver injury. They've worked wonders on him, though. He's very much alive. At the moment. Amazing the punishment the human body can take."

"And . . . spinal injuries?"

"Not established yet. Poor bugger. Wife's on the way, apparently."

"I hope someone's with her," said Emma. "She'll be terrified." And then suddenly she found she had to sit down.

"God," she said, "it's ten o'clock. How did that happen?"

"Tired?"

"A bit. Any idea at all yet what caused this?"

"Not yet. But the lorry was at the front of it all, went through the barrier. Could have been him, fell asleep, skidded, whatever."

"Well, if it was, he's been well punished for it," said Emma soberly.

. . .

Abi and Shaun were still waiting in A&E. They'd arrived almost two hours ago, and Abi was beginning to feel as if they might be there forever.

The relief of reaching St. Marks had been intense. It was a vast, pristine building, gleaming in the evening sun, only four storeys high, but Abi felt suddenly nervous. What on earth might be going on in there? Maybe they could wait outside. She felt she had seen enough blood and guts for one day—literally.

It was very noisy, ambulance sirens cutting endlessly through the air, and a lot of shouting. Ambulances were pulling up constantly, porters running out with wheeled stretchers, nurses following them.

"Right, my love, follow me; let's get you registered."

Abi took a deep breath and braced herself for a scene like something out of *ER*.

But inside it more closely resembled Waterloo station in rush hour than *ER*: a huge room with a large raised desk by the entrance with three women sitting at it, and an electronic sign that said, *Welcome to St. Marks. Approximate waiting time from arrival is now five hours, fifteen minutes.* This changed even as she watched it to five hours, thirty minutes. People were crammed onto chairs, standing three deep at the desk, pestering for information any nurse reckless enough to appear. Children were crying, running about, being shouted at; mobiles were ringing constantly, despite stern written instructions not use them, and the three women at the desk were astonishingly calm as they fielded questions, issued directions (mostly to sit down and wait), put out calls for people to go for assessment, and handed out admission forms to newcomers.

A small corner with a low green fence round it—marked, *Children's Play Area*—was empty of both children and toys; there were several battered model animals and Thomas the Tank Engines being fought over in various parts of the room.

Bureaucracy took over; Abi was handed a form to fill in and had to leave most of it blank, having no idea who Shaun's next of kin was, apart from its being clearly his mother, nor his address, nor even his religion. She elicited such information from Shaun as she could, but it was patchy. She sat down obediently with Shaun—having taken him, wildly protesting, into the ladies' when he wanted to pee—and played Hangman and Join the Dots with him until he slumped into an exhausted stupor.

A white-faced young woman next to her, with a small girl on her lap, sat staring at the door; she looked as if she was about to cry. Abi smiled at her.

"You OK?"

"Not really. I'm worried out of my wits. My other little girl's out there somewhere with her dad; she's been hurt and they're waiting for an ambulance."

"I'm sorry," said Abi. "Is she badly injured?"

"Not according to him, but he wouldn't know bad if it hit him in the eye. He says it's just a banged head, but that could be anything, couldn't it? He'd been to collect her from her nan's; they were late leaving. I said to him, if he'd been on time for once in his life, she'd be home tucked up safely in bed by now, but no, he had to go and check on a job he was doing first."

"That's the thing about accidents, though, isn't it?" said Abi. "It's all bits of chance and fate, muddled up together. I'm sure she won't be long; there are so many ambulances out there, and they've cleared a way right through the traffic, apparently."

A man with his arm in a makeshift sling was sitting staring into space, grey faced, opposite Abi; he started chatting to her, clearly glad of the distraction.

"Car hit one of the fridges. Front's pretty well stove in. The wife's coming to get me, but we live in Manchester, so bit of a way." He shifted, winced. "Glad to get this set—"

A nurse appeared, called out, "Brian Timpson."

He stood up. "Well, nice talking to you. See you later."

Almost immediately his place was taken by a hard-faced young man carrying a notebook; he'd been talking to several people, she'd noticed, some had been more receptive than others. "Hi," he said, "Bob Mason, *Daily Sketch*. Wonder if you'd mind if I chatted to you for a bit. You were out there in the crash, I take it?"

Rage shot through Abi.

"I was," she said coldly, "and I'd mind very much if you chatted to me, actually. Just piss off, will you?"

"OK, OK," he said, "sorry to have troubled you."

Every so often she wondered vaguely what Jonathan was doing, what complex lies he might be telling Laura; that was as far as her curiosity—or indeed her emotions—extended towards him. He seemed to belong in an entirely different point in her life; the accident had, in some strange way, restructured everything.

She was just considering moving into a corner seat, where she might be able to doze, at least, only it would mean waking Shaun, when a young man, looking deeply distressed, walked dazedly in, slumped down in the chair next to her, and put his head in his hands. He was naked from the waist up and his trousers were held up with red braces. Poor bloke had obviously had a very tough time. She could scarcely believe it when the reporter sat down on his other side and said, "Hi. Bob Mason, *Daily Sketch*. Mind if I talk to you? I'm just—"

The man lifted his head out of his hands, stared at him for moment; then he said, "Yes, I bloody well do."

"Parasites," she said, as Mason walked away. "They shouldn't be allowed in."

He said nothing, stood up still looking dazed, and walked over to the watercooler, filled a cup of water for himself.

As he stood drinking it, a nurse appeared in the doorway. "Mr. Fraser? Yes, the doctor will talk to you now."

Mr. Fraser half ran out of the room.

"Such a sad story," said a middle-aged woman sitting opposite her. "He was here much earlier; he was on his way to be best man at a wedding. The bridegroom's been very badly hurt."

"God," said Abi, "that's so terrible."

She felt freshly shocked; fate was certainly having a field day.

. . .

Linda was beginning to feel extremely worried. Something quite serious must have happened to Georgia. She'd been so upbeat, so grateful to Linda for rescheduling her audition. And suddenly . . . she appeared to have vanished. Linda had tried ringing her twice, but her phone was on voice mail. That was unlike her, too—Georgia never missed an opportunity to chatter. And it was well into the evening. But Georgia didn't have to be anywhere until the morning; there was plenty of time. *Get a life, Linda, for God's sake.*

She tried Georgia's phone just once more and then started clearing her desk preparatory to leaving it. Linda could no more have left an uncleared desk than she would have left home in a crumpled skirt or shoes in need of heeling.

But Georgia was still not picking up.

• • •

Abi was half-asleep, her head lolling onto Shaun's, when she was jerked awake by a voice saying, "Shaun! Shaun, where are you?" And he sat up, rubbing his eyes, and then shot off towards the direction of a pallid, overweight young woman, yelling, "Mum, mum," and pushed himself into her slightly reluctant arms.

She was accompanied by two other small children and an equally overweight older woman whom Abi assumed was her mother; they all came over to Abi, who started to tell Shaun's mother how brave he'd been and how proud of him she should be.

She stared at her rather blankly and then said, "You're all right, are you?" to Shaun, interrupting the little speech.

"I think he's OK," Abi said rather tentatively. "He had an asthma attack, as I expect you know, but he's been checked over by the doctor here and given some Ventolin, and all he needs now is you, I should think."

"Yeah, well, thanks. Who can I ask about him?" The girl sounded hostile.

"Well, I'm not sure," Abi said. "They're pretty busy, as you can see. I suppose the women over there on the desk would be best. But a doctor did return him to me saying he was fine—"

"Yeah, well, I want to hear it from them," she said. "What's he doing with you, anyway?"

"Well, I was involved in the crash," Abi said. "I was with a friend and we weren't hurt, and he got the boys out of the minibus and left me in charge of them while he went to see if there was anything else he could do. And then when the ambulance came for . . . for your little boy, he wanted me to go with him. So I did. We'd become friends by then, hadn't we, Shaun?"

Shaun nodded, tentatively putting out his hand again, into hers.

"Oh, yeah. Well—thanks anyway." His mother spoke begrudgingly, looking Abi up and down, clearly taking in her tight trousers and her spike-heeled boots. "Give over, Shaun; don't hang on to me like that—I can't hardly breathe."

Abi felt a rush of rage. "He's had a horrible time, you know. Really horrible. the . . . the driver of the minibus was . . . well, he didn't survive, and I think Shaun needs lots of reassurance, you know?"

"Mum, it was horrible," Shaun said. "Mr. Douglas, he was killed; he was all covered with blood and—"

"I don't really want to hear," said the girl. "Just try not to think about it, Shaun; that's the best thing. Come on, say good-bye to the lady and let's go and try to find a doctor, make sure you're all right."

"Bye, Abi," Shaun said. "Thanks for looking after me and the singing; I liked the singing."

"Singing!" said the girl as they moved off. "What on earth you been singing for? Whose daft idea was that? Come on, and you, Mum, over here . . ."

Shaun was led away, and Abi wearily walked over to the desk.

"Any chance of a taxi to the nearest station, would you think?" she said.

"You could try," said one of the women. "Don't rate your chances."

She handed Abi a few cards; Abi rummaged in her bag for her phone. It wasn't there.

· · ·

"How are you feeling now?" The nurse smiled into Mary's eyes. "Bit better?"

"Yes. A little. Very tired, that's the worst thing. So tired . . ."

"Well, that's quite usual, considering what you've been through. They'll be taking you to the theatre in a minute."

"The theatre? I don't need surgery; I haven't been injured."

"Of course not, dear. But they're going to have a look at that heart of yours; it's not working too well just at the moment. Dr. Phillips wants to be quite sure."

"Who's Dr. Phillips? And what isn't he sure about?"

"He's one of the cardiologists. He'll be along in a minute, and you can ask him yourself."

"Honestly," said Mary, "I'm fine. I keep telling you. And I have to get out of here; I'm so worried."

"Now, why are you worried? Your family have been notified; they're all fine; they're on their way—"

"No, not my family. I was meant to be meeting an old friend at the airport, and . . . oh, dear. He'll still be waiting. Can we get a message to him somehow, please—"

"I'm sure we can. Do you have a number for him, a mobile, perhaps?"

"No, I don't," said Mary, and started to cry. "I lost it in the crash. I was supposed to be meeting him at the Hertz desk, at Heathrow."

"And then where were you going? Home?"

"No, no, to a hotel. The Dorchester."

"Well, maybe we could call there."

"Oh, that would be very kind. Would you?" Mary gave the nurse Russell's name.

"Of course. Straightaway. Now you try to have a little rest. Just until Dr. Phillips comes."

She bustled away, and Mary relaxed a little.

Unfortunately, as the nurse reached the nursing station a new patient arrived from the theatre, after which yet another elderly lady was brought straight up from A&E, deeply distressed; Mary's call was first postponed and then forgotten.

. . .

"Emma, why don't you go home? Everyone's done, either on the wards or in ITU."

"I want to check on the baby, the preemie one, caught in the crash, see if it's OK."

She made her way to maternity. The baby was a lusty four-pound boy, in an incubator, but the prognosis was excellent.

The father was sitting by his wife's bed, holding her hand; she was asleep.

"Thank you so much," he said, smiling up at Emma. "You really helped her down there. I'm so grateful."

"It was nothing. I'm sorry I couldn't have stayed with her longer; obstetrics is my specialty. Or will be. But I'm on A and E at the moment, and there was rather a lot to do. Well, take care of both of them."

"I will . . ."

In the corridor, she saw a young man and a middle-aged couple standing looking very distressed.

"Hi," she said. "Can I help; are you looking for someone?"

"Our son," said the woman. "He was in that accident today, you know—"

"I do know," said Emma, "I work in A and E."

"Oh, my goodness. Well, perhaps you know what's happened to him. We were told he'd been taken to the theatre, but that was hours ago, and now we've been sent up here . . . Oh, dear . . ."

She started to cry; Emma put her hand on her arm.

"Tell me his name, and I'll see what I can find out for you. Everyone's been so busy today."

"Of course. We appreciate that," said the man. "Weston's his name, Toby Weston."

"Right. Look, there's a waiting room down there; it's got a coffee machine, and you'll be more comfortable. I'll get back to you as soon as I possibly can, hopefully in a few minutes."

The ward sister was very brisk; she was clearly exhausted.

"He's only just been brought here . . . Holding his own, that's all I can say. No chest injuries, and his neck's OK. CT scan showed that. And quite a mild concussion, but that leg is a mess. The main danger is infection. I don't need to tell you that. He's on a morphine drip, pretty out of it, poor lad. Tell them his condition's serious but stable; that's always a good one. Don't want to get their hopes up too much; don't want to scare them."

"Thanks, Sister. I'm going home now, but I'll tell the Westons what you said. Can they see him? They seem very sensible."

"Maybe in an hour or so, for a few minutes."

. . .

The young man was standing in the doorway of the waiting room when Emma went back; he was rather curiously dressed, in slightly baggy striped trousers with braces hanging down and a T-shirt. He was white faced and looked completely exhausted.

"Hi," he said. "What . . . that is, any news?"

"Well . . . he's stable. Serious, but stable. And if he's stable then he's coping. But still quite ill. So what happened? Were you there?"

"I was in the car with him," he said. "We were going to his wedding."

"That was you, was it? How awful. I'm so sorry."

"Yes. Look, I'd better go and tell his parents. They're in a terrible state."

"I'll come and tell them if you like," she said. "People always prefer to hear from doctors directly."

She went in, smiling her professional smile.

"Hello, again. Well, the news isn't too bad. He is seriously ill, lost a lot of blood, and the wound to his leg is quite extensive, but he is stable."

"Oh, thank God," said the man. He blew his nose rather hard. "There you are, darling, what did I tell you?"

"Can we see him?" asked Mrs. Weston.

"Well . . . not yet. Sister says she'd rather you waited for another hour or so. Then you can see him, but only for a few minutes. And he may not be properly awake even then. Oh, and I should warn you, they've fitted his leg with an external fixator: that's a sort of cagelike frame outside the leg, with pins going through to the bone. It may look a bit alarming, but don't worry."

"We don't mind," said Mrs. Weston, wiping her eyes. "We don't mind anything. We just want to see him. Thank you so much . . . er—"

"Dr. King," said Emma, smiling.

"You don't look old enough to be a doctor," said Mr. Weston.

Emma smiled at him determinedly; that was the variation of not looking like one. It usually came from older men.

" 'Fraid I am," she said. "Anyway, I'm leaving now. I'm off duty tomorrow, but I'll be back on Sunday and I'll see how he is then. Try not to worry. It sounds like he should be OK."

"Thank you so much," said Mrs. Weston.

"I think I might come down with you," said the young man, "if that's all right. I . . . well, I could do with a bit of fresh air. I won't be long," he said to the Westons.

"You take your time, Barney. We're not going anywhere."

"What I could really do with," he said to Emma once they were in the lift, "is a fag. I expect you think that's terrible."

"Of course I don't. I still smoke myself occasionally. When I'm out."

"Yeah?" He grinned at her. "Well . . . I plan to give up one day. Very soon."

"Great. Right now I should think you need one. So what happened? Or don't you want to talk about it?"

"I . . . don't have that clear an idea," he said. "This lorry suddenly swerved in front of us. Went right through the barrier. And we . . . we had a . . . a blowout. I think. Trying to stop. And then . . . well, then it's all a bit of a blur. We finished up embedded in another car. I don't know why I didn't catch it as well. I . . . Oh, shit sorry." His voice quavered; he dashed his hand across his eyes. "It was pretty bloody scary. The whole thing."

They had reached the ground floor; she ushered him to the main door; he stood leaning against the glass, taking deep breaths.

"Look—sit down here for a bit. You're obviously pretty shattered."

"Yeah. I feel a bit . . . sick actually. Sorry. I—"

He bolted for some bushes, was gone for a while, came back looking shamefaced.

"I'm so sorry," he said, sinking down beside her on the steps. "Not very cool."

"Don't be silly. I'll get you some water; stay there."

When she came back, he still had his head in his hands.

"Thanks," he said, "you're very kind."

"All part of the service."

"What sort of a doctor are you, then?"

"I'm going to be a surgeon, I hope. An obstetric surgeon."

"Sounds very impressive. Did you see Tobes when he arrived?"

"I did, yes, but only very briefly. It's been a nightmare day."

"I bet." He held out his hand. "Barney Fraser."

"Hi, Barney. Were you going to be the best man?"

"Yup. I was."

"How's the bride; how's she coping?"

"Pretty badly, I think," said Barney. His tone was dismissive. "She's too upset to come tonight, apparently."

"I see. Well, I'd better go. I'm quite . . . tired."

"I bet you are. Thanks so much, Dr. King."

"Emma, actually. Bye, then, Barney. Good luck. And . . . I know it's nothing to do with me, but you should take it easy for a couple of days. You've had an awful shock. Don't expect to just feel fine because it's over."

Thinking about him as she drove her car out of the hospital, she reflected that he was really rather good-looking, with his spiky brown hair and sort of hazel eyes with darker flecks in them and that gorgeous smile. She wondered if he had a girlfriend; and then mentally slapped herself. *Emma, you're obsessed. You've got a perfectly good boy-friend of your own. Get a grip.*

* * *

Linda was just going to bed when she decided she couldn't ignore the fact any longer that Georgia might have been caught up in the crash that had filled the evening news.

With some reluctance and a strong feeling of dread, she called the Linley household, bracing herself for the worst.

"Bea, I'm sorry to call so late. Linda Di-Marcello here. I won-der . . . if you've heard from Georgia."

"Oh, hello, Linda. Yes, she's arrived home safely. Bit weary. And very disappointed she didn't get the part, of course. But I've told her there's always another time, and I'm sure you'd say the same. She's asleep, but I'll tell her you called. It's very kind of you, thank you so much."

* * *

Georgia was lying under the covers, her pillow over her face to smother the sound of her weeping. It was a terrible thing she'd done: so terrible. And how was she ever going to put it right?

Part Three

NEXT

CHAPTER 14

"Where are you going now?"

Laura tried to keep the exasperation out of her voice, but it was difficult. Jonathan had hardly spoken to her since he had come in, just after nine the night before.

He had walked in, white faced, his eyes dark with exhaustion, dropped his overnight bag on the hall floor, and stood there, as if he didn't know where he was.

"Hello," he said rather vaguely. "Sorry to be so late."

"Don't apologise, Jonathan. Come in and sit down; tell me all about it. What would you like, tea, scotch, water . . . ?"

"Water'd be great. Thanks, darling. But could you bring it through to the study? I really need to check my e-mails."

"What, now?" she said, surprise making her stupid.

"Yes, now," he said. "Sorry, but it's important. I've been out all day and I don't know what's going on at the clinic—or the hospital."

"But I want to know all about it, what happened."

"Laura, I really don't want to talk about it. Not yet, anyway. I'm all in."

His voice shook slightly; she told herself he had had a day of such horror that few people would be able even to imagine it, and that she must be patient.

She took a bottle from the fridge in the kitchen, and when she walked into the study, Jonathan was sitting staring blankly out of the window. The sun was setting, a great red ball etched out of the brilliant turquoise sky.

"Lovely sunset," she said, setting the water down.

"What? Thanks, darling."

"I said, lovely sunset."

"Yes, very lovely. I'll be finished soon, Laura. I'll come and find you, all right?"

"All right. I'll be in the kitchen, waiting to have supper with you."

"Darling, I don't want any supper. I still feel sick."

"But, Jonathan, you haven't eaten—or have you; did you get something at the hospital?"

"What hospital?"

"The hospital handling the casualties."

"What on earth makes you think I'd go there?"

"Well . . . I just thought you might. As you'd been helping the . . . the crash victims."

"Christ, no. Plenty of people to do that, once they got there."

"I see. Well . . . what have you been doing all this time then?"

"All what time?"

"Jonathan, it's after nine. You called me at five, five thirty. Said the ambulances were coming. Did you stay on after that, helping there? Or were you talking to the police or something?"

"Laura, what is this, an inquisition? I finally got under way at about seven. They had to check my car—"

"Your car? Why?"

"Oh, to make sure it's mechanically sound, brakes OK and so on. Apparently it's standard procedure these days, if you're involved in a crash."

"I thought you weren't involved?"

"Laura, I was there, for Christ's sake. And then the traffic was still appalling. And I gave some bloke a lift. Young chap, got caught in it all, desperate to get to London, almost in tears, missed some crucial meeting. I dropped him off in the Cromwell Road. There were a lot of people like that, lives just thrown into the air. Thanks for the water. I'll see you later."

At ten thirty he was still in the study. She knocked rather nervously; he was sitting staring at his laptop screen.

"Are you nearly through? I'd like to go to bed soon."

"Well, go to bed. I'll be up later."

"I want to be with you. I'd rather wait."

"Well, I'd rather you didn't. Laura, you just go ahead. I'll be a while yet."

Finally at eleven she had gone up to bed herself, and stayed awake a long time, thinking that any moment he'd appear, saying, "Sorry, darling, sorry, sorry, sorry," as he so often did when he knew he'd kept her waiting. But at midnight he had still not appeared and she finally fell asleep.

And now here he was, wearing his cycling clothes, for heaven's sake, at seven in the morning.

"I'm going for a bike ride," he said in answer to her question. "Try to clear my head. I've got my morning round to do at the clinic. I'll see you after that."

"Breakfast?"

"I still don't feel very hungry."

"Jonathan, you must eat."

"I'm not one of the children, Laura; I can decide for myself when I need food."

"Oh, please yourself," she said, allowing irritation to break through for the first time. "And don't forget we're going to lunch with the Edwardses."

"I really don't think I could face a barbecue today," he said. "I feel absolutely shattered, I've got a clinic to do, and it's going to be bloody hot again."

"Well, I think you're going to have to face it," she said. "It's Serena's birthday; there are several couples going, and—"

"If there are several couples, would it really matter if I wasn't there?"

"Yes, it would. She's my best friend and she'd be very hurt. Oh, just go out on your bloody bike, Jonathan. I'll see you later."

"OK," he said, and he was gone.

"He's being really weird," said Charlie. He had come down the stairs and heard most of the conversation.

"Just a bit." She went into the kitchen with Charlie and started doing the scrambled eggs he loved; she felt confused and upset. She needed to talk to Jonathan, needed him to tell her about it; and while they were about it, she needed to know why he had been on the M4 and not the M40. She tried to crush the notion that he was avoiding her because he didn't want to tell her.

. . .

Russell woke horribly early; he hurt all over. Not just his heart, which felt physically sore, but his head, his stomach, his limbs. It was as if he had been beaten up.

He got up, walked over to the window, and opened the curtains. It was going to be another lovely day; at a little before six, the sun was shearing down through the trees; the sky was the slightly hazy blue that spoke of staying power. Russell sighed heavily and turned away; he would have looked for rain, for greyness, for cold: the weather of disappointment.

What had happened to Mary? How could she have failed him like this? Why hadn't she somehow got a message to him? He had told her where they would be staying: at the Dorchester, the American home away from home. Even if she hadn't been able to send a message to him at the airport, she could have surely have rung there.

He had arrived at the desk there breathless, convinced she had been delayed, somehow, and had gone straight there, looking round wildly in reception on his way, half expecting to see her there, small and neat and smiling; only to be told that no, so sorry, there was no message, and no one had arrived asking for him either. And he had gone up to his room and ordered a martini and then another and sat in a chair, staring at the telephone, and after a while he began to weep, as he had not since he had been a young soldier leaving England on his way home at the end of the war, sitting in the lavatory in the troop train, thinking of Mary and wondering how he was going to get through the next eighty years or whatever without her.

And then, slowly but very surely, he started to get cross.

Russell was a very nice person, kind, caring, and for the most part thoughtful. But he was rich and successful; and like all rich and successful people, he was spoilt. All his life, from his earliest childhood, he had had everything he wanted: the toys, the outings, the fun. And, as he grew up, the girls.

Losing Mary had been the worst and greatest shock of his life; but once he had begun to recover from that and was returned to the world he knew, that of money and worldly success, he forgot any lessons he might have learned from her. He worked hard, to be sure, but for considerable rewards. He lived in both style and comfort—first one wife and then another ran his home and did what they were told—his children were brought up in awe of him, and his reputation as one of New York's most generous philanthropists assured him further admiration. And now, in the senior compartment, as he called it, of a gilded life, he was rarely crossed, never criticised, and had his every demand almost instantly met.

He was finding the present situation extremely difficult. Whatever it was that had happened to Mary, this was the twenty-first century, for heaven's sake. Even if she was unwell, she could have rung the hotel, or got word to him somehow. Or somebody could. It showed a lack of consideration as well as courtesy. He had gone to enormous trouble to make everything perfect for her; had anticipated her every need, answered her every question in advance. He had given her all the numbers: the hotel, his mobile . . .

Sorrow turned to self-pity turned to resentment turned to outrage. Mary had, not to put too fine a point on it, stood him up.

And now the damn sun had the nerve to shine . . .

.   .   .

"Mrs. Connell, are you all right?"

Maeve struggled to sit up; she had been asleep on the sofa in the ITU corridor.

A doctor was looking down at her; he had a lot of dark hair and very kind dark eyes. He looked about forty-five, possibly more; that was reassuring. Maeve felt that doctors should be old.

Certainly well into middle age.

"Yes, I'm fine," she said, "thank you."

"I'm Dr. Pritchard. I admitted your husband last night. I'm the A and E consultant. Specialist doctors and surgeons have been looking after him, but I wanted to come and see how he was doing, say hello. And to see how you were."

"Never mind how I am—what about Patrick?"

Dr. Pritchard was silent. *That's it,* she thought, *he's died, he's gone, and they've sent this person with his kind eyes to tell me.* He was probably specially trained, maybe even chosen for those eyes . . .

"He's died, hasn't he?" she said.

But: "No, he's holding on. It's amazing, but he is. He must be very strong, Mrs. Connell."

"I s'pose he is, yes. I don't know why; all he ever does is sit in that cab. So—"

"But he is still dangerously ill, I'm afraid. There were abdominal and chest injuries; his spleen is ruptured; we've had to remove one of his kidneys and part of his large intestine. None of which is necessarily fatal. And he'd lost a lot of blood, of course, but that's fairly easily dealt with. He also had some injury to his heart: contusions, we call them—that is, blood collecting in a sac round it—but we put a needle in and drained it."

"And . . . is he conscious?"

"Semi. Actually, we decided to keep him asleep last night, to make sure he was stable. Lot of drugs, of course, going round his system. He has a tube in his trachea—his throat—and he's on a ventilator; it's doing his breathing for him."

"It sounds so dreadful," she said.

"I know. But we would hope to extubate him quite soon now—"

"What does that mean?"

"Turn off the anaesthetic drugs and wean him off the ventilator. Take out the tube. He'll start to breathe on his own and wake up. And then, of course, he'll be given plenty of painkillers. He'll be pretty out of it for a day or two."

"When can I see him?"

"Oh, fairly soon. But you have to be prepared for a shock, Mrs. Connell. His face and hands are cut, his head is swollen and a bit out of shape, and there are all these tubes coming in and out of him. Not the prettiest sight, I'm afraid. And he'll be very confused, but he'll want to talk; people always do."

"You're very kind," said Maeve, and meant it. People said the NHS was falling apart these days, but as far as she could see it was absolutely wonderful. Fancy a busy doctor finding the time to talk to her like this . . .

. . .

Time was actually not a problem for Alex Pritchard that day. He should have been at home—he was not officially on duty—but he had come in partly to check on the condition of the more serious victims of the crash, partly to get out of the house, the lovely big Edwardian house where he and Samantha had lived for fifteen years and raised two children. He felt sad and outraged that it was to be sold, and the proceeds were to buy another more than adequate house, as far as he could see, for Sam and the children and a rather inadequate flat for him. He was to lose the children he loved so much, apart from every other weekend; he was to lose quite a large proportion of his income; he was going to be extremely lonely—and all so that Sam could pursue her own life and her new relationship. OK, he hadn't been the greatest husband; he'd been bad tempered and difficult, and absent a lot of the time, and yes, Sam had to bear the brunt of running the house, caring for the children, going to parents' evenings and nativity plays on her own, all that stuff; but did he really deserve this . . . exile?

Yes, he had had an affair, albeit a brief one, born of retaliation rather than desire, and how happy for Sam that he had, for her lawyer had been able to add it to the sins of omission and absenteeism that had lost him his family.

It was doomed to failure from the beginning, his marriage—he could see that now—to the lovely Sam, ten years younger than he, with her social ambition and her need for admiration. She had never understood the whole medical thing, the claims of the job, the loyalty to the patients, and never bothered to try either.

Why was he always late, why did a crisis at the hospital take precedence over a dinner party, why should she give up her time and energy to hospital causes? Why then was she so happy with the lifestyle his large salary brought her?

He had been beguiled by her, had thought he was marrying a princess, when beneath her lovely face and body was a self-seeking ugly sister.

Well, he had learnt his lesson and very painfully; and if he ever had another relationship it would be with someone who understood his career and the life it led him into, someone who was not concerned with her own life and her own ambitions. Only he never would have another relationship; he never would have the stomach for it.

He looked back at Mrs. Connell as he walked away and wondered how on earth she was going to cope with what lay ahead of her. For he had not told her that there was possible damage to her husband's spinal cord. It was more than possible that he would be paralysed, a helpless cripple, wheelchair-bound, and how would she care for him, in addition to three young children?

. . .

Dianne Thompson looked across the breakfast table at her husband.

"This sounds like an awful pileup yesterday, Rick. On the M4. Did you see anything of it at all?"

"No. Why should I have?"

"Because you were on the bloody road, that's why. Around the time. Four o'clock, it says here."

"Course I wasn't. I was delivering the stuff to that snooty cow in Marlowe by four."

"Oh, OK. What if you'd been a bit later, though? Doesn't bear thinking about."

"Yeah, well, I wasn't."

"Says here a lorry went right through the central median and the driver's in intensive care, still unconscious, he was, last night. At least three dead, it says, and loads of serious injuries. It's enough to make you think you'll never get in a car again."

"Yeah, well, some of us have to."

"I know, babe, I know. Part of why your job's so stressful, isn't it? Was the traffic very heavy then, when you was driving up?"

"Not specially, no. Oh, I don't know. Can we stop this, Dianne, talk about something a bit more cheerful?"

· · ·

"Tamara, are you ready, darling? Daddy's got the car in the front of the house."

"Yes, coming, Mummy, just finding my shoes."

They had to be the right shoes; it seemed important. Wearing the right clothes altogether was important. Toby was probably a bit down in the dumps today, and it would cheer him up to see her looking really great. A lot of girls might not have bothered about it, specially having been robbed of their wedding day, but Tamara was not being beaten by a little something like that. There could be another wedding day, and they would be able to start planning it that very morning. She had her diary with her so that they could choose another date, at least.

She felt extremely proud of herself, being so strong about the whole thing. She could think of at least half a dozen friends who would have been completely destroyed by it. Of course, she had been dreadfully upset yesterday, and there was no way she could have gone to the hospital last night; she'd looked appalling, her eyes all piggy and her skin blotchy with crying, and she'd felt completely and utterly drained by it.

But today . . . well, today was quite different. She felt really refreshed, and able to cope with it all.

She finally settled on a pair of white patent high-heeled mules, which went with the red shift she had decided to wear—it was one of Toby's favourites; he said she was his own personal lady in red in it—and ran downstairs barefoot, holding them in her hand.

. . .

"It was so awful," she said later, sobbing in her father's arms in the car park. "I thought he'd be sitting up in his pyjamas, you know, and I could give him the strawberries and everything, and he was just lying there, looking all pinched and white, and there were lots of drips and things, and one of them was blood, and goodness knows what the others all were, and then he had this cage thing over his leg, with sort of pins going through his skin—it made me feel quite sick, actually—and he turned his head just very slowly and said my name, but he could hardly get that out, and he tried to smile, Daddy, but he couldn't quite manage it, and then his eyes closed again, and he tried to give me his hand, but it sort of flopped before it reached me. And it was so upsetting I just started to cry. And then some beastly nurse said that if I'd like to wait outside, the doctor was coming to see him, and I said couldn't I stay, and she said no, she didn't think that was a very good idea—that's the NHS for you, treating everyone like idiots—and I had to wait outside for ages, and then when the doctor came out I nabbed him, said how was Toby, and he said not very well, but he'd be back in a couple of hours and he'd have a better idea then. He seemed to think I could just wait. So I went back in to Toby and he just seemed totally out of it. And then the nurse came back and said she was sorry, but that was enough for now, and if I liked I could come back this afternoon. I'm just so . . . so disappointed and upset, Daddy, and so worried; he's obviously much worse than anyone was letting on last night."

"Oh, darling, try not to worry too much." Gerald Richmond

passed her his handkerchief. "Come on, blow your nose. You've been so brave up to now; you've just got to keep it up a bit longer. Shall we go and have a nice lunch somewhere and then come back this afternoon? Would you like that?"

"Yes. No. Oh, I don't know. I mean honestly, Daddy, if you'd seen him, you'd have wondered if there was any point in my going. It was quite . . . scary. He hardly seemed to be there."

"Well . . . if the nurse told you to go back and the doctor's been to see him, I'd have thought it was worth it. I'll come with you, if you like. Just to hold your hand. As Toby can't." He smiled at her. "Come on, poppet, dry your eyes. We'll go to the Bear, have a really good lunch, and then come back and see how he is. I'm sure he'll pick up very quickly; he's young and very fit."

"Yes. All right. Thanks, Daddy, I expect you're right. Oh, now look at me!" she said, half laughing as she studied herself in the mirror. "My mascara's all run, and I don't have any makeup with me. Maybe we could buy some stuff in Marlborough after we've had lunch."

"Of course we can. You're being very brave, darling. I'm so proud of you."

"Thanks, Daddy. I don't feel very brave. Oh, it's all so sad. Pretty cruel, fate, isn't it? Why did it have to happen yesterday? And to me?"

❧ CHAPTER 15 ❧

Abi was in the gym; she felt absolutely dreadful, sick and exhausted, aching in every limb—and seriously stressed. She'd rung her phone repeatedly, in the hope someone would have it and answer it, but it remained stubbornly switched off.

Clearly she needed to speak to Jonathan; the police had told her they would want a statement from her, as she had been in the forefront of the crash, and she presumed they had said the same thing to him.

The thought most frightening her was an odd, almost shadowy anxiety that she had in some way contributed to it. Jonathan had been on the phone—and she had been shouting at him, swearing at him, even; she'd provided a pretty serious distraction. And she and Jonathan had been right beside the lorry; suppose he'd swerved, made the lorry swerve too? It didn't bear thinking about. And they'd surely be required to recount very precisely what they had seen. And if all she could tell them was that it was a blur, that she couldn't really remember, they wouldn't be very impressed. They might even think she was covering something up.

And then—she presumed—Jonathan would require her to go along with whatever story he planned to tell Laura: the reason for being on the wrong motorway, and her presence in the car. It was extremely unlikely, she felt sure, to be the bald truth; and that shifted the balance of power between them just a little. Yesterday, Laura could have been kept in ignorance of Abi's existence—unless Abi herself confronted her with it. Today, she almost certainly could not. So if he wanted Abi to go along with any lie he might concoct, she held quite a few more cards than she had done; and that was, actually, rather pleasing.

Abi was not vindictive; in spite of her threat to Jonathan of confronting Laura, she actually had no intention of doing so. Rather perversely, she was on Laura's side. She didn't admire her; indeed she viewed her—and other wives like her—with something near contempt: for their dependency, their willingness to do what they were told and be what they were bidden.

Kept women, Abi regarded them as: lacking in courage, personal ambition, and self-worth. She had no wish to join their ranks; she would not consider moving into a large house, wearing expensive clothes, and driving a flashy car if it wasn't due at least in some large part to her own efforts. She wanted her own stake in life, not one bought by simpering at dinner parties and providing sex on demand.

Just the same, she felt that they did deserve better than being cheated on. She despised Jonathan for what he was doing to Laura: he was the real wrongdoer, in her eyes, the villain of the piece, playing with Laura's happiness and love, and that of his children. It was he, and not Laura, who deserved to be punished.

But to punish Jonathan would be to punish Laura too, and not to be contemplated in the normal run of things. This run, however, was not normal . . .

. . .

"How're you feeling, mate?" Barney smiled determinedly at Toby.

Toby opened his eyes with an obvious effort, said, "Cheers, Barney," and managed a rather feeble smile. He closed his eyes again, grimaced, tried to shift his position. "Christ, this leg hurts."

"The nurse said you were on morphine; thought that'd fix it."

"I am. I certainly know when it's wearing off, but it still doesn't kill it. I've got a sort of pump thing; I can give it to myself, but it knows when you've had enough, so you can't OD, unfortunately." He tried to smile again.

"I hear you've had lots of visitors."

"Yeah, Mum and Dad. And Tamara, of course. She's been such a brick, so good about cancelling the wedding. Didn't complain at all."

"Really?"

"Yeah. She wanted to set another date, but I just wasn't up to it. She seemed a bit disappointed about that, but . . . maybe tomorrow."

"Well, no rush, eh?"

"No, s'pose not. But it would make her feel better, she said."

The thought of Tamara pestering Toby in his hospital bed about another date for the wedding made Barney feel slightly sick.

"How's the food?" he said after a pause.

"Don't know. I'm just getting stuff through these things." He indicated the various drips and lines.

"Amanda sent some grapes. Here. But if you can't eat them—"

"Thanks. How is Amanda?"

"She's fine," said Barney. "She says she'll come in with me tomorrow if you like, if you don't have too many visitors."

"Yeah, course. Well, let's see. Give her my love."

He was clearly exhausted and certainly in no condition to talk about the things Barney was worrying about. More than worrying. He was haunted by them.

He patted Toby on the hand, told him he'd be back later, and went down to the main entrance, where Amanda was waiting for him.

"How is he?"

"Not good. In a lot of pain. Poor old Tobes."

"Oh, dear," said Amanda, "it's just so, so sad. And so unfair."

Her blue eyes filled with tears; Barney put his arm round her.

"He'll be all right," he said. "Promise. Come on, let's start driving back, maybe have something to eat on the way?"

As they started going down the steps, Emma came running up them; she smiled.

"Hi. Nice to see you. How's the patient today? I haven't been up there yet, but I was planning to check."

"Oh—not too good. Seems in a lot of pain."

"Try not to worry," she said. "It's almost the worst day, this. Lot of trauma: medical trauma, I mean, swelling, bruising coming out." She smiled at Amanda, held out her hand. "I'm Emma King. One of the A and E doctors. I met your . . . Mr. Fraser . . . on Friday night, when he was leaving your friend's ward."

"I heard you'd all been wonderful," said Amanda, taking the hand. "Thank you so much. I'm Amanda, Barney's fiancée."

"Well . . . you know. We do our best."

And they stood there in the sunlight shaking hands: two pretty girls with blond hair and blue eyes, worlds apart in education, class, lifestyle, and aspiration, slightly wary of each other without having the faintest idea why.

There was a silence; then Emma said, "Well, I mustn't hold you up. And I will go and see . . . Toby, was it? As soon as I can. Try not to worry. Bye now."

"Bye," said Amanda. "Come on, Barney, we must go too."

. . .

So he did have a girlfriend, Emma thought, looking after them as they walked towards the cars; and what a suitable one. And she had a boyfriend, didn't she? So . . . why was she even concerned about Barney? She wasn't. She so wasn't. And she was *so* late. She must go . . .

. . .

Mary sat in her bed in the cardiac ward, feeling physically better, but increasingly agitated about Russell, begging to be allowed to go home.

They kept saying no, that she had to stay another forty-eight hours, that Dr. Phillips was very pleased with her, but he wanted to keep an eye on her.

She'd had what they told her was a cardiac catheterisation the night before. "It measures the pressure actually inside your heart's chambers," Dr. Phillips had said. "Nothing to worry about; we just want to make quite sure everything's OK."

It had sounded rather alarming, but they had gone into her heart through an artery in her leg, and although she was a bit sore, she felt fine. And it had been established that her heart was still doing a pretty good job.

"So why can't I go home?" she said, and they said, well, she was in her eighties, it had all been a considerable trauma for her, and she needed to be kept under observation. And indeed to rest.

The last thing Mary felt she could do was rest. She supposed that once Russell had got the message, he would simply wait until she got in touch with him. Just the same, she needed to know that he had got it; and she could do that only by telephoning his hotel. But she didn't have the number; that was also in her address book in her suitcase. Well, she could find out the number from directory enquiries.

"Can I get up, go down the corridor?" she asked the nurse. "Use the telephone?" But she was told perhaps tomorrow, not today. "But we can bring the phone to you, Mary; that's no problem."

"Oh, that's very kind. Thank you so much."

And all might yet have been well had not Mary's daughter, Christine, and her husband, Gerry, arrived at that moment.

"There, now," the nurse said, "they'll make your phone call for you, Mary."

"What phone call is that, Mum?" asked Christine, setting down the cyclamen plant she had brought.

"Oh, to a friend of mine. It's not important. Don't worry; I can do it when you've gone."

She still couldn't face telling Christine about Russell, not if everything was going to go wrong now. She'd look even more foolish.

And she submitted to an inquisition about the crash that was so long and detailed that she became exhausted; and one of the nurses noticed and said that she thought Christine and Gerry should leave her to rest. After which she was finally able to make her phone call; and was told that Mr. Mackenzie had checked out of the Dorchester a couple of hours earlier.

. . .

Jonathan had got extremely drunk at the barbecue. He was surprised by how drunk he was; he hadn't actually consumed that much—a couple of beers, two or three glasses of wine—but by the time everyone was on the tiramisu, he could hardly stand.

It was Charlie who noticed, Charlie who put his arm round his shoulders, asked him if he was OK, Charlie who brought him the bottle of mineral water that he forced into himself before knowing the absolute humiliation of throwing up on the path as he ran desperately for the lavatory.

. . .

"Darling! Oh, darling, how awful . . ." Laura's face and voice showed nothing but concern. "Serena, I'm so sorry; I think it's delayed reaction from yesterday. It must have been such a horrible experience for him—and the heat, of course; he really doesn't do heat very well . . ."

And, grateful for the excuse, dimly aware that Mark Edwards was hosing down the path even as Laura helped him into the house, terrified he was going to vomit again, he bolted into the Edwardses' cloakroom and sat there for a long time, holding his head and wondering how on earth he was going to get through the next days and weeks—and possibly even years.

For the dawning of the day had made him realise that he was in a fairly appalling mess. To start with, he was going to have to explain to Laura why he had been on the M4 at all, rather than the M40, and moreover with a woman, a young and attractive woman—although maybe Laura would not have to know that—for whose presence he would have to provide an acceptable explanation.

There was also the uncomfortable fact that at the time of the crash he had been on the phone, and the police might well take the view that that made him at the very least not entirely blameless, and that they should investigate his version of events rather more closely than they might have done. Of course, it had not been dangerous, and the moment he had realised the trouble they were in, he had quite literally dropped the phone—but then again, they might not accept his word for that. And maybe—just maybe—it had meant his reactions were not as sharp as they should have been; maybe he'd swerved in his turn into the lorry . . .

Forcing himself to relive the whole thing in painstaking detail, over and over again, he had decided that, at least, was not even remotely possible; but the police might well not agree. And there would be a lot of close questioning: and of Abi as well. He was, in fact, in what was known as a terrible bind.

. . .

William was having a difficult day. The cowman, returned from his day off, had pointed out a couple of cows looking off-colour: "Could be bluetongue; let's hope not."

William agreed they should hope; it was not in the language of farming, with its day-after-day routine of problems, some huge—like foot-and-mouth or TB—some smaller—like mastitis, or the delivery of a sickly calf—to express emotion verbally. But if the cows had blue-tongue, it would be pretty disastrous. They would survive because they had to, and because there was, actually, no alternative. All their money, all their assets, their entire future was invested in these acres of Gloucestershire; they might own the land, two thousand acres of it, they might be rich on paper, but it was of doubtful value if farming as an industry failed.

Right at the moment, though, farming was having one of its rare ups rather than downs; the price of milk had risen, along with everything else; there were reports of a coming food crisis, of a world shortage of wheat and rice, a higher demand for dairy products—which was improving the outrageous, profit-leeching price of milk—and food prices too were higher than they had been for years. But costs were still very high, the price of fuel was eye-watering, and the farm overdraft was still way over the agreed limit.

And they were under siege from the Greens, constantly and rigorously inspected by people who seemed to know almost nothing about the realities of farming, but who would ruthlessly cut subsidies if a new and entirely necessary building entailed cutting down trees or cropping hedges. The government urged them all to diversify, which William was absolutely in favour of, except that diversification inevitably led to more people, more construction, more waste products. Which led to more complaints from the Greens.

And then his parents were very opposed to change. His proposal to jack up the commercial shoot business had fallen on very stony ground; his father loathed seeing what he called the city boys tramping over his land, in charge of guns many of them were scarcely qualified to use. It was a miracle, he said, none had been injured.

And then just before lunch today, hours before he'd been expecting them, his parents had arrived back from their holiday, and his father had been heavily critical about the state of the yard and the fact that the cows had not been moved to the other field, despite his instructions; and his mother was full of complaints about the state of the house.

William explained about the crash and the helicopter in the field, and said he'd move the cows that afternoon, and even managed to apologise to his mother for the mess she had returned to. Which he did have to admit was rather bad; but he'd been out on the farm from six every day, grabbed some increasingly stale bread and cheese at lunchtime, and come in at dusk to feed himself from some tins from the store cupboard.

"I don't know what you're going to do when I retire," his father said, as he had at least fifty-two times a year for the past five years; William longed to tell him that his life would be a great deal easier if he could run the farm on his own, using his methods, streamlining costs as he saw fit, instead of its being one huge, unworkable compromise. But as far as he could see, his father would never retire; he was sixty-two now, and the farm was still his life.

He knew he should have a serious confrontation with his father on the subject of modernisation, but he shrank from pointing out the unpleasant fact that he was growing old and out of touch. Time, he told himself, would solve the problem, along with the related one of his living at the age of thirty-four in his parents' house, his domestic life entirely in the care of his mother. It had its bright side, obviously: there was always a meal on the table, and his washing was done. But on the other hand, he found still being told to hang up his coat and take his boots off and clean up the bathroom after himself quite trying. He should be married by now, he knew, but somehow he'd never found anyone who both knew about farming and whom he fancied— and who would put up with living in a house where time had stood more or less still since the 1950s.

And besides, he really didn't have the time to find her . . .

And all through this long, predictably difficult day, he kept returning to the one before, so literally nightmarish in recollection, hardly credible at this point. He kept seeing it all, again and again, almost detachedly now—like something on television or in a film, or even in a radio play, for the noises had been as vivid and horrifying as the sights. He remembered feeling the same way about the events of 9/11: he had sat watching the screen, fascinated as much as appalled, and actually thinking what a fantastic film it was, how brilliant a notion. But it had been real, of course; and yesterday had been real—the deaths and the pain and the grief and the moment-by-moment awareness of seeing lives wrecked and ruined. He had seen so much and yet so little of the actual crash; from his grandstand view he had focussed, in appalled fascination, on the lorry, but that had been all. With a gun to his head he could have told no more details, no possible further causes; the police would be requiring a statement, he knew—he was a key witness, given his viewpoint—but he feared he would be a disappointment to them. He felt increasingly distressed by some memories, all still so vivid: the girl in the Golf lifted tenderly out, as if that was important; the hideous sight inside the minibus, the young father weeping over his dead wife; and he was comforted by others, by his ability to provide a safe landing for the helicopter, by the astonishing gratitude of people when he gave them water, by the easing of the misery of the small boys as they formed an attachment to that girl, that tough, brave girl, so gentle with the little boys . . .

He was just washing his hands in the kitchen before sitting down to the meal his mother had organised when he saw her mobile lying on the windowsill by the sink; he had left it there the night before, intending to do something about it, but then had gone to sleep in front of the TV and forgotten all about it. Probably the best thing was to trawl through the numbers, see if he could find one he could ring. Most of the names obviously meant nothing to him; he had looked for "Mum" and "Dad" and even "work" and "office" and found nothing. And then he saw "Jonathan" and remembered that was the name of the chap she'd been with; it was a start, anyway.

He walked over to the back door and stood looking at the yard, thinking about Abi as he called the number: her amazing legs and her huge dark eyes with all those eyelashes—bit like the cows' eyelashes, he thought, that long and curly—and her dark hair hanging down her back. She'd been nice, really nice, and very, very sexy; not the sort of girl who'd find him interesting, though, and hardly likely to fit into his life.

A woman's voice answered the phone: a pretty, light voice. "Hello?"

"Oh, good afternoon," William said. "I'm very sorry to bother you, but I think you might know someone called Abi . . ."

❧ CHAPTER 16 ❧

Luke was waiting for Emma in the Butler's Wharf Chop House, just below Tower Bridge; she was late. Unlike her, that—very unlike her. He'd tried her mobile, but it seemed to be dead; he hoped she was OK.

She'd been a bit funny when he'd told her about Milan. He'd been surprised; he'd thought she'd see it as an opportunity. Lots of girls would, having a boyfriend working in Milan, with all-expense-paid trips over there whenever she fancied them. Milan was one of the shopping capitals of the world, for God's sake.

Of course, she'd miss him; and he'd miss her. But . . . it was such a brilliant opportunity for him. Anyway, he was planning to make her feel really good later, with what he'd bought her. There was no way she wouldn't be pleased with that . . .

He ordered another Americano, went over and got a paper from the rack by the door. The front-page news was a bit boring: Afghanistan. He turned to the inside page and saw a bird's-eye view picture of a pileup on the motorway. He was about to give that a miss too when he read, "almost all the casualties were taken to St. Marks, the new state-of-the-art hospital in Swindon, where medical staff worked tirelessly all afternoon and through the night."

"Blimey," said Luke, and folded the paper, starting to read it intently.

"Hi, Luke."

It was Emma, smiling, but pale and tired-looking. She was wearing jeans and a T-shirt and had no makeup on; she usually made more effort. Still . . .

"Hi, babe." He kissed her. "Come and sit down."

"Thanks. I'll have one of those, please." She indicated the coffee.

"I've just been reading about the crash. So that's why you didn't ring me last night. It was obviously a big one. Says here it was the worst this summer. God, Emma . . ."

He sat looking at her in silence; she smiled.

"You look rather . . . impressed."

"I feel it. Definitely. Yeah. My little Emma, involved in a thing like that. Were you actually . . . you know . . . doing things? Operating and so on?"

"Of course I was! What did you think I was doing, reading a magazine?"

"No," he said, "no, of course not. It just sounds . . . so bad."

"It was so bad. It was awful. Lots of casualties, loads of injuries, people's lives wrecked forever. Anyway—sorry not to have rung you."

"That's all right, babe; I can see why now. You look tired."

"Thanks," she said. "That's exactly what I need to hear."

"Well, you do. You can't help it. I'm sorry for you."

"Well, good."

She looked at him, and the great blue eyes filled with tears; she dashed them away, smiled determinedly at him.

"Sorry. Got to me a bit. You know, I might like a drink."

"Course. What d'you fancy?"

"Oh . . . glass of white wine. I'll just . . . just go to the toilet. See you in a bit."

Luke looked after her thoughtfully; she seemed in a very odd state.

"Tell you what," he said when she came back, "why don't you go back to the flat, have a kip before tonight? I've got us a table at Alain Ducasse at the Dorchester; you want to be able to enjoy that, and I've got something to do this afternoon—thought we could do it together, but I can manage . . ."

Emma stared at him. Such thoughtfulness was not quite his style. Then she leaned forward and kissed him.

"Oh, Luke," she said, "you're so sweet. And you're right: I am very tired. That'd be lovely. I'd really appreciate it. Thank you."

. . .

Talking to Abi had become a priority—before the police started taking statements. They had to get their story straight: why they'd been together, and on the M4, what they'd seen, how they thought it might have happened. And Laura was going to have to know; important the story was watertight for her too. He'd been working on it: Abi was just a colleague, from the conference; he'd never met her before, just giving her a lift to . . . where? Maybe not London, maybe just Reading, somewhere like that.

He'd tried to raise her the night before, had walked down the road away from the house, praying Laura wouldn't see him. There had been no reply, her phone clearly switched off. He didn't leave a message: too risky. And again this morning, while he'd been out on his bike; still no reply. It was now six p.m. and he was beginning to feel frantic. Maybe he should e-mail her; she had a laptop in that little flat of hers, supplied by the office, as there was so much weekend work; but her housemate, Sylvie, might see it. He'd met her once, hadn't liked her at all. He wouldn't trust her an inch. Just the same, he had to talk to Abi soon . . .

Patrick always said afterwards that the worst thing, in a way, was not knowing what he could and couldn't remember. Going through the barrier, certainly; calling on God to keep the trailer from jackknifing— He'd failed him there, all right—and then a long, long confusion, a swirling mass of pain and fear, and a complete inability to move. He seemed to be in some kind of a vice, and every time he struggled to get out of it, the pain got worse. It was unimaginably dreadful, that pain, like a great beast tearing at him; after a while it seemed better to stay in the vice without struggling And then after a long time, there seemed to be people with him, one trying to get at his hand, saying, "This'll help you, mate; just hold on," and he wondered how his hand could be of any use when his whole body had been rendered useless. And then he had swum off somewhere, where the pain was removed from him, although he could still feel it in some strange way; and then there was a long blank when nothing seemed to happen at all. He remembered some angel smiling down at him, holding his hand, an angel with long blond hair and huge blue eyes. She'd said he was just going into the theatre, and he'd wondered why on earth anyone should think he was up to watching a play in the state he was in; after that he couldn't remember anything much at all, and he certainly couldn't have told you how much time had passed, but he seemed to be surfacing somehow into something very uncomfortable—and then as he opened his eyes to see what it looked like, there was Maeve, smiling at him.

"Sweet Jesus," she said, and, "No, no, darling," he said, "not Jesus, no, it's me, Patrick."

And then he felt completely exhausted and went back to sleep for quite a long time.

. . .

Russell sat in the departure lounge at Heathrow waiting for his flight to be called. He could hardly believe this was happening, instead of his being in London with Mary, as they had planned, revisiting old, half-remembered places, lunching with Mary, then driving out to Bray for dinner at the Waterside Inn with Mary—God, he must cancel the table. He felt wounded as well as angry, and he wanted the reassurance of home. The more he thought about Mary and what might or might not have happened to her, the more he felt convinced that she had just not tried hard enough to contact him—and that hurt.

He stayed at the Dorchester until lunchtime, still hoping she would contact him, had called her home several times, but there had been no reply. He left a couple of messages, giving his mobile number, but his phone remained stubbornly silent.

They had brought him the *Times* with his breakfast, but after he had read the front and the city pages, he phoned down and demanded the *Wall Street Journal.* It was the only paper he ever read. The young man who brought it asked him if he would like him to switch the television on, but Russell told him sharply that if he wanted to watch it, he was quite capable of switching it on himself.

Russell was an enthusiastic user of technology: of his laptop and his iPhone. However, he was not a television watcher; he hated its banality, its obsession with trivia. He preferred the radio, and most of all he loved the BBC World Service. He and Mary had discovered that they both listened to it when they couldn't sleep, and although their nights only partly overlapped, he still liked to think of her lying there, listening to the same voices, the same news reports. It brought her closer . . .

Well, he had obviously been keener on that closeness than she had . . .

The car journey, once they were on the M4 extension, had been swift. "Bit different from yesterday, sir," the driver said. "Traffic held up for hours, it was. I gave up, just went home—there was no way you could get through."

"Really?" said Russell, getting his iPhone out of his attaché case and rather ostentatiously fitting the earbuds into his ears. He would listen to music. He had no intention of getting involved in a conversation about traffic, for God's sake . . .

*   *   *

He checked in, went to duty-free and bought himself a couple more books, and then moved up to the first-class lounge. He walked through the seating area, passing the TV screens on his way. He glanced at them: an earnest girl was saying something about Prince William and Harry and some concert they had just put on and how marvellous it had been. He moved off. As he did so, he half heard something about an accident the day before and that someone or other was still in intensive care. Not guaranteed to take his mind off his troubles; he moved into the computer area and called up his e-mails. There were three: two from his secretary, one from a colleague. He'd tried very hard to persuade Mary to have e-mail, but she'd resisted. "I like getting letters," she said, "and if it's urgent you can telephone me."

It might have helped . . . he wasn't sure how, but it might . . . Dear God, this was painful.

An hour passed while he wrote e-mails and looked at the online edition of the *Journal*; then he decided to get a whisky. That might ease the pain.

He walked out to the bar; they had only one whisky, and that was a blend.

"I'm not drinking that rubbish," he said. "I want a single-malt. What is this, economy or something? Just give me a club soda."

He went and sat down near the screens, so that he could see the latest on his flight. No delays; they should be in the air in thirty minutes. And he could shake the soil of bloody England off his feet. He should never have come back, never.

The flight was called; he walked to the departure bay slowly; there seemed to be a delay.

"For God's sake, what is the matter with this airline?"

"Sorry, Mr. Mackenzie. If you just wait over there, shouldn't be more than a few minutes."

He sat down, sighed heavily. This was what he hated most about flying: sitting helplessly, life at least temporarily out of his control . . .

The man sitting next to him was reading a newspaper; he had it fully open, knocked Russell's arm as he tried to fold it over.

"Sorry, mate."

The man turned to his companion, a pasty, overweight creature in a tracksuit.

"Shocking thing, that crash yesterday," he said. "Thank God we wasn't trying to get a flight last night. Says here seven miles, both directions. Hundreds of people missed their planes. Three people killed . . ."

Russell stood up. All anyone seemed to be interested in today were car crashes . . .

"Would rows A to G please commence boarding immediately. First- and club-class passengers may also board at their convenience."

Better check his phone for the last time; not that there was anyone he wanted to hear from . . .

There was one message on it. Left that day, half an hour earlier. A number he didn't recognise . . .

"Hello, is that Mr. Mackenzie?" It was an English voice. "Mr. Mackenzie, you left a message on my mother's answering machine. Mrs. Mary Bristow. I'm afraid she's in the hospital—she was involved in a traffic accident yesterday. We only heard ourselves quite late last night. Anyway, if you want to ring me back, my number is—"

A series of clicks went off in Russell's brain. *Holdups for miles . . . serious traffic accident . . . in intensive care . . . hundreds missed their flights.*

So there had been a reason: a perfectly good reason. And he had been too blind, too arrogant, too self-centred to try to find it. And Mary, his little Mary, was lying in a hospital, possibly dangerously ill . . .

. . .

Abi's flat was in a rather unlovely outpost of Bristol; she'd bought it eighteen months earlier, on the strength of her new job. She loved it; it was in a small purpose-built block, fairly recently built. It had two bedrooms, one of which was let to her best friend, Sylvie, to help pay the mortgage; a very cool galley kitchen, with white cupboards and black work surfaces; a studio living room with floor-to-ceiling windows; and a bathroom that, as Sylvie said, was too small to swing a kitten in, much less hold a bath, but which served its purpose perfectly adequately.

She had furnished it slowly, through the year, refusing to put any old rubbish in it that she didn't like; the Bristol branch of IKEA had served her well. The room she was most proud of was the living room, with its white blinds, white carpet—no one was allowed in with their shoes on—and two black corner sofas. She'd talked a photographer mate into giving her a very nice set of black-and-white prints of pictures he'd taken in New York, and had them framed by one of the suppliers at work; it all looked seriously classy. Her latest acquisition was a plasma TV, not too huge, but big enough to feel you weren't missing anything watching a film on DVD rather than in the cinema.

She was actually watching *Notting Hill* for the umpteenth time, having got back from the gym exhausted but feeling slightly better, and wondering if she could face any lunch, when she decided to ring her phone once more.

"Hello?" said a voice.

"Oh . . . oh, my God . . . it's William, isn't it?"

"Yes, it is. And that's Abi? I was hoping you'd ring."

"So—you've got my phone?"

"Yes, you gave it to me to hold yesterday. I'd put it down and forgotten all about it, only just found it again."

"Fantastic. I thought I must have dropped it on the road or something. It was such a terrible day, and—"

"Certainly was. How are you feeling?"

"Oh . . . you know. Bit . . . out of it. Look, could I come and get it, do you think? I'm really missing it. Tell me where you are, and I'll drive over."

.   .   .

"Hello, Linda."

"Hello, Georgia. How are you?"

"OK. Why shouldn't I be?"

"Well . . . I could be forgiven for wondering. Don't you think? First I have to change the time of your audition; then I wait for hours for you to arrive, and you don't return any of my calls. Then I hear that you're back at home and you've told your mother you didn't get the part. What's going on?"

"Nothing's going on."

"Well . . . why didn't you come to the audition?"

A silence: then: "I lost my nerve. I was scared, OK? Really scared. I'm sorry, Linda. Very sorry. I got stage fright."

"They're very disappointed. They really thought you'd be ideal."

"Yeah? Well, they'll have to get over it."

"That is an extraordinarily stupid attitude, Georgia. Not the way to get on."

"Maybe I don't want to get on."

"Well, in that case, you won't be needing me any longer." Linda struggled to keep her temper. "This kind of thing does me no good at all. I mean that, Georgia. If you're not worried about your future, I'm certainly worried about mine."

"Yes." The voice had changed, become more subdued. "Yes, I know. I'm sorry, Linda."

"Well, look. When you feel ready to talk about it some more, call me."

"Yes, OK."

Another silence. It was tempting to just put the phone down, but Linda was fond enough of Georgia and worried enough about her not to.

"There were several articles in the papers today about the crash on the M4," she said.

Silence: then: "Oh, really?"

"Yes. It certainly sounded very bad. Very bad indeed. Several people killed, and some poor lorry driver in intensive care."

"Oh. Yes, I see." Another silence. "But . . . is he all right? Did it say?" Her voice shook slightly.

"He's alive. But not very well. Obviously."

"Did it . . . did it give his name?"

"No, they never do until they're sure the close relatives have been informed. Why?"

"Oh . . . no reason," Georgia said uncertainly. "Did it . . . did it say what caused it?"

"No. The police are investigating it apparently. So . . . you didn't see anything of it at all, then?"

"No. No, of course I didn't. Why are you asking me all this? Just leave me alone, Linda, will you? Please!"

. . .

It hadn't been easy to find William's farm; she was hopeless at reading maps. In the end, Abi found herself driving through the scene of the accident and then turning back on herself, via the next junction. That had been hideous. The crash barrier was still broken, the central median ploughed up; there were areas taped off on both sides of the road, a lane closed, police cars parked on the hard shoulder, and several men, two in uniform, studying photographs. A sense of déjà vu flooded Abi; she went back there, in that moment, to the noise and the chaos, the broken cars, the crumpled minibus, people shouting and groaning, children crying . . .

When she reached the turnoff, she pulled onto the grass verge at the top of it and sat there, her arms resting on her steering wheel, her head buried in them, wondering how she was going to live with that memory for the rest of her life.

She drove on, missed the turn William had instructed her to

take—"It's got a cattle sign about a hundred yards down it"—found herself in a village, and stopped an old chap who was wandering down the street looking at the paper.

Who was able to direct her, with amazing ease, to the Graingers' farm—"Just after the church take a left, looks like a track, and go up to the end and there it'll be straight in front of you."

And there indeed it was, settled just slightly down from the track, quite a big squarish house, with a yard to the left of it and several cars parked on it, including a totally dilapidated pickup truck, one newish-looking Land Rover, and a couple of tractors. After hesitating for a while, she parked her car next to the Land Rover and knocked on the door.

William was in the milking parlour, his mother said, adding graciously that Abi could wait if she liked, or go up there.

As Abi hadn't the faintest idea where the milking parlour was, or indeed what it was—it sounded rather like something in a cartoon, with all the cows lounging around on sofas—she decided on the waiting.

She'd dressed quite carefully for the occasion in jeans and a T-shirt and some new red Converse trainers; she didn't want William to think she was some townie airhead, tottering through his farmyard in three-inch heels. She smiled at Mrs. Grainger, who managed what might have passed for a smile in return; she was not in the least what Abi would have expected William's mother to be like, not a cosy lady in a cotton pinny, making bread, but a rather smart, upper-crust woman with well-cut hair, wearing dated but clearly expensive trousers, a checked shirt, and a pair of brown leather loafers.

"Come through to the drawing room." She led Abi through the hall and into a rather dark room lined with books and paintings and gestured towards a sofa. "Do sit down. Can I offer you something, a sherry perhaps . . . ?"

Abi shook her head. "No, I'm fine, thanks. I'll just wait."

Abi sat down and folded her hands in her lap in what she hoped was a ladylike manner and smiled apologetically at Mrs. Grainger.

"I'm so sorry if I'm being a nuisance," she said.

"You're not, of course. But you must excuse me. We've been away and there's rather a lot to do."

"Of course."

When she had gone, Abi stood up and wandered round the room; the walls were covered in extremely faded brocade paper, the carpet was a sort of very large rug, set down on flagstones, and threadbare in places. What looked like the remnants of about a hundred fires, a vast heap of ash and burnt-out logs, lay in the grate, and there were no curtains at the tall windows, just wooden shutters.

The furniture was all clearly very old and rather mismatched: a round polished table in quite a light colour, and then a chest so dark it was almost black. There were two deeply comfortable-looking armchairs, but the sofa was stiff and button backed. Several portraits hung on the walls, mostly of men, clearly going back a century or two, although there were two of women, both rather pretty, one in a low-waisted, narrow ankle-length dress, and one in what looked like a rather elaborate nightie. She wondered if they were William's ancestors. Somehow the sweet-faced, untidy bloke she had met yesterday didn't seem to fit in here. But clearly she was wrong.

She looked out of the window now; as far as she could see were fields, fields and hills and trees. She wondered if it all belonged to the Graingers and decided, if it did, they must be very rich.

After about twenty minutes, she got bored and, purely by way of a diversion, decided to go in search of a loo.

As she crossed the hall, looking tentatively at the doors, Mrs. Grainger appeared.

"Can I help you?"

"I was wondering if I could use your toilet?" said Abi apologetically.

A slightly pained expression settled on Mrs. Grainger's face.

"Of course. Follow me."

She led the way upstairs and across a landing; then, "The lavatory is there," she said, pointing down a corridor and emphasizing the word rather pointedly. *Silly cow,* Abi thought.

As she made her way back downstairs, William appeared. He was filthy, his face grimy and sweat-studded, his hair awry with shoots of grass in it, and, as an extra accessory, an enormous cobweb slung from one of his ears to his shoulder. Abi smiled and then, as she studied him, giggled slightly.

"Hello," he said. "Sorry, I didn't realise you'd arrived." And then, as she continued to smile at him, added, "What's so funny?"

"Oh—nothing. Sorry. You've got . . . Here, let me . . ." She stepped forward, reached up, and pulled the cobweb from his ear.

"Well, it's very nice to see you," William said, smiling his amazing, life-changing smile.

Abi smiled back and thought how wonderful it was to see him and then—driven by some compulsion entirely outside her control—reached forward and kissed him on the cheek just as his mother came into the hall.

. . .

"I'm not sure my mother knew what to make of that," he said, grinning, handing her the large gin and tonic she had asked for in the pub, "you kissing me then."

"Yes, I'm sorry," she said. "I don't quite know what came over me. It's been such a sh—horrible day, two days, and then suddenly there you were and everything seemed so much better and I just wanted to let you know that. Sorry."

"No, no, don't apologise," he said. "It's fine; doesn't matter if she liked it or not, and I certainly did." He smiled again, indicated the drink. "That all right for you? Got enough ice?"

"Oh—yes, thank you. Plenty. It's very nice."

"Good." He took several large gulps of beer and then set the glass down again. "That's better. Bad day for me too. Lost a calf this afternoon—"

"Oh, no," said Abi. "Where—should we go and look for it?"

And then felt stupid when he said, half laughing, "Not lost like that; she was born dead, breech; got the cord round her neck. Dad and I were tugging for over an hour, but she came out limp as you like; we couldn't get more than two breaths out of her. Heifer calf too, much more of a loss. Then we couldn't get the old tractor started—that's how I got so filthy, rummaging in the barn for a jump lead—and Dad, he tends to take it out on me, that sort of thing. So it was really good to see you there and to have something take my mind off all that stuff. How were my directions?"

"Rubbish," she said, grinning, and then, rummaging for her cigarettes, said, "Could we go outside? I really need one of these."

"Course . . . Want another drink?"

"Oh—no, thank you. I have to drive back, and I felt really, really bad on the road again down there. I—"

"I know what you mean. Bit heavy, wasn't it? Come on, let's go outside. Want some orange juice or something?"

. . .

He came out with the orange juice, and another pint for himself; she smoked a cigarette and then another

"Sure you won't have one?"

"No," he said, "I never got the hang of them. I did try to like them once, when I was at college, but they just made me feel sick."

"And where was college?"

"Oh, Cirencester," he said, clearly expecting her to know what Cirencester was. "I went there straight from school."

"And . . . where was school?"

"Eton," he said, with much the same intonation. Abi decided it was time to go.

. . .

As she dropped him off at the bottom of the track he said: "Thanks for coming. I should have come to meet you halfway. It's terrible when you lose your phone, isn't it? I'm always doing it, and I don't suppose mine's nearly as important as yours. I did ring a number on yours, by the way, but whoever answered it wasn't very helpful."

"And who was that?" said Abi.

"Oh—that chap you were at the crash with. Jonathan. I scrolled through looking for a name I might recognise, and saw his."

The evening seemed to have got even hotter.

"And . . . ?"

"I got a woman. His wife, maybe? I tried to explain, said I'd been at the crash, and that you'd given it to me while you saw to some kids. I asked her if her husband was a doctor, just to satisfy myself I'd got the right bloke. Anyway, she just rang off, very abrupt she was."

"Oh, really?" said Abi. "I wonder why . . ."

CHAPTER 17

Jonathan was drifting in and out of a painful, dehydrated sleep when Laura came in and sat down on the bed.

"How are you, darling?"

"Oh . . . bit better. Yes. I'm so sorry, Laura. Embarrassing you like that."

"It's all right. You've had such a terrible time. I just felt very sorry for you."

"Oh, darling . . ." He reached out, took her hand. "I'm so lucky to have you."

"Well, I'm glad you think so," she said. She drew her hand away after a moment, pushed her hair back. "Would you like anything? Some more water, chamomile tea, something like that?"

"Water, yes, please. With ice in it."

She came back with a big jug, set it down, smiled at him again.

"Kids all right? Not too ashamed of their father?"

"Don't think so. You mustn't worry about it."

"Well, it was pretty . . . unattractive."

She was silent, then shrugged. It was distant, cool, unlike her. A tiny spiral of something—not fear, more unease, ice-cold unease—began to work its way into Jonathan's stomach.

"Jonathan," she said, "can you tell me just one thing? I still don't understand why you were on the M4. Not the M40."

"Oh," he said, and was astonished at the ease with which it came out, "cutting down there can actually be quite a good idea on a Friday afternoon. Rather than sticking on the M40, which is a horrible road. Always get a buildup of traffic towards the M25. So it didn't seem as silly as it sounds. But it was a big mistake. As it turned out."

"Yes. It certainly was. But . . . all's well that ends well, I suppose. For you, anyway. I'll leave you in peace, darling. See you later."

She left the room, closed the door behind her. Jonathan suddenly felt very frightened indeed. He absolutely must speak to Abi—and as soon as possible.

. . .

"Jonathan? Jonathan, we need to talk—"

"It's good to hear from you. But I'm a bit tied up at the moment. I'll call you back later. Everything OK with you?"

Obviously she was there—there or near.

"Yes, fine," she said. "But—"

"Fine. I'll speak to you first thing in the morning, or later this evening, maybe? We can discuss the prognosis then. Well, thanks for ringing. Bye, now . . ."

It was clearly not the occasion to tell him that William had spoken to Laura. Pity. For all sorts of reasons. Not least that she really was rather looking forward to it.

. . .

"Mrs. Connell, hello. Your husband is doing very well, you know. Very well indeed, holding his own magnificently." It was Dr. Pritchard again. Maeve managed somehow to smile at him. "Now, the staff nurse says she thinks you should go home for twenty-four hours, and I agree with her; you look completely exhausted. He's in very good hands, you know."

"Yes, of course," said Maeve. "I do know that. But—"

"Got a car here?"

"Well, no. My friend brought me in yesterday, and she's gone home now, obviously. My mother's coming tomorrow, so I could maybe go home with her."

"How about the train?"

"Well . . ." She hesitated, and then started to cry. She hadn't cried before, not once, but somehow these minor problems of getting home, not being able to afford the train, seemed to be defeating her. "The thing is, I haven't got . . . got much money—on me, that is . . ."

He looked at her in silence for a moment, and then said, "Mrs. Connell—Maeve; do you mind if I call you Maeve?"

She shook her head helplessly.

"Maeve, I've got to pop out for half an hour, go into town. I'll take you to the station if you like. And if you're short on cash, I can lend you twenty quid, if that would help—"

"I couldn't possibly—"

"Now, why ever not? You can pay me back whenever you next see me. Come on, now, dry your eyes, and I'll be back for you in about ten minutes. Don't argue; I insist. And don't worry about your husband; he's not very well, of course, but he's more or less off the danger list; he's a walking miracle . . ."

· · ·

Jack Bryant settled into a wonderfully comfortable, battered old chair in what Hugh Mackintosh called his study, but which would have contained most of his Fulham flat. It was a glorious evening; the view of the moors was ravishing, the colours just turning autumnal. He was clearly in for a very good few days.

"Another gin, Jack?" Mackintosh picked up the bottle, waved it at him.

He was one of Jack's oldest friends; they'd had a hell of a time together in the sixties: Annabel's and a different dolly bird every night, and he'd taught Jack to shoot as well. Good chap.

Jack grinned, held out his glass. "Yes, thanks."

"You must be tired. Hell of a drive. Even in that car of yours."

"It was fine. Enjoyed it. Lovely to give the old girl a bit of a run. And, of course, I stopped in York last night."

"You didn't get caught up in that crash yesterday then, on the M4? We thought it might have delayed you."

"No, bloody lucky. Must have missed it by inches. I read it was at four p.m. I can't have been clear of that spot by more than five minutes. If that."

"Christ. You must have a guardian angel of some sort."

"Doubt it. Anything angelic gave up on me years ago, as you know, but it sounds ghastly."

"Well, I'll leave you to get settled in. Expect you'd like a bath before dinner. No rush, down here for drinks at seven thirty. Moira's dying to see you."

· · ·

Luke grinned at Emma.

"You look great, babe. I really like the dress."

She'd known he would; it was black, low-cut, very short. What she thought of as a bloke's dress.

They were in a cab now, on their way to the restaurant. Her sleep had done Emma good; she felt relaxed and happy. And . . . pretty sexy, actually.

A uniformed doorman was standing outside the Dorchester; he whisked open the taxi door, stood respectfully aside while they got out.

Now, this was what posh places should be like, Emma thought.

Those cool bars were all very well, but if you were going to spend loads of money, you surely wanted a bit of service. She smiled happily at Luke, allowed the doorman to usher them through the revolving door, stood looking round the lobby. It was wonderfully luxurious, huge urns of flowers, deep sofas, smiling staff everywhere.

"The restaurant, please," Luke was saying. "Alain Ducasse."

"Certainly, sir. This way, please."

"Luke," hissed Emma, "I just want to go to the loo. You go on. I'll follow in a minute."

"Oh . . . OK. Yes. Good idea."

The ladies' was extremely luxurious. A woman was waiting by the basin when she came out, holding a towel. She stood patiently while Emma washed her hands, then handed it to her, and then took it and threw it into a basket. Emma half expected her to come and help her comb her hair and put her lip gloss on for her.

She walked back into the lobby, looked around for someone to tell her where the restaurant was, and then heard the words, "St. Marks Hospital, Swindon," spoken in an American accent. "Yes. On . . . let me see, yes, Agatha Ward. Can you confirm they'll arrive first thing in the morning? I'll wait."

He stood there, tapping his fingers on the concierge's desk: a tall, white-haired man, with Paul Newman blue eyes and a neat white moustache, quite elderly, but standing ramrod straight, wearing a suit that looked as if it had only just left the tailor's.

The girl at the desk looked up at him from her phone.

"Yes, that's all fine, Mr. Mackenzie."

"Good, good. And I'll want a car to take me there, to visit my friend, first thing. I'd like to be there by . . . let me see, nine . . ."

This was too much for Emma; she walked over to the desk.

"Do forgive me for interfering," she said, "but I'm a doctor at St. Marks. I'm really sorry, but you won't be allowed in at nine. Ten thirty is the earliest."

The man looked at her; at first she thought he was going to be cross. Then he smiled, a slow, sweet smile.

"That is so extremely good of you," he said, "and I will indeed forgive you for interfering. Thank you so much. Make that an hour and a half later then," he said to the desk, and then, turning away, taking Emma's arm, he said, "I wonder if you'd be kind enough to give me news of a patient there. A Mrs. Bristow, Mrs. Mary Bristow. She was involved in the crash on the freeway yesterday . . ."

Clearly he moved in a world where hospitals were small and exclusive, Emma thought, and where any doctor would recognise any patient's name.

"I'm sorry," she said, "but there are around fifteen hundred patients there at any given time. I was on duty in A and E yesterday when people were arriving. I'm afraid I don't remember a Mrs. Bristow. Was she . . . was she an elderly lady?"

"A little elderly," he said with another sweet smile. "May I say, incidentally, you don't look old enough to be a doctor."

Emma smiled back. "Well, trust me, I am. Anyway, I assume, since you're going to see her tomorrow, that Mrs. Bristow isn't too seriously ill."

"Well, you know, I don't believe so. They didn't tell me much when I phoned. Except that she was comfortable . . ."

"And that you could go and see her?"

"Oh, yes. And her daughter—I spoke to her—she said she didn't seem too bad. But . . . I don't suppose you could get any more details for me? Now, I mean, I really am most concerned."

"Well, I . . . I'll see what I can do. Only . . . well, I'm supposed to be having dinner with my boyfriend."

"Oh, my dear young lady, the last thing I would want to do is stand in the path of true love . . . Forget it; I'm sure she's absolutely fine."

"No, no, it's perfectly all right. I'll just go and tell him, and then I'll call them, OK? Could you possibly show me the way to the restaurant?" she said to the girl behind the desk. "Oh—no, it's all right; here's my boyfriend now."

Luke was irritable, and more so when she said she'd be five more minutes. Even when she explained.

"I didn't realise you were on call," he said.

"Luke—"

The old gentleman stepped forward, held out his hand to Luke.

"Russell Mackenzie. I am so very sorry to intrude on your evening. But I am extremely worried about a friend in the hospital, and this enchanting young lady of yours has offered to help."

"Oh, fine," said Luke, slightly grudgingly. "I'll be at the table, Emma."

"Oh, dear," said Russell Mackenzie, "I'm afraid he's a little annoyed."

"He'll get over it," said Emma. "He's very good natured. Now, then, let's see what we can do—I can't promise anything, but . . ."

Five minutes later she smiled at Russell.

"She's much, much better. She has angina, apparently, and had an attack at the scene of the crash, and they did an exploratory investigation under anaesthetic. They thought she'd probably had a minor heart attack. But she's doing well. And yes, you can see her tomorrow."

" I cannot thank you enough," said Russell, "and now you'd better get along to that young man of yours. That fortunate young man."

. . .

"OK," said Jonathan, "this is what we say. Our relationship is purely professional; you're a colleague—"

"A colleague? How could I be a colleague? I'm not a doctor."

"Of course you're not a doctor. You take photographs at conferences. Or rather, your boss does. So you were there at the conference in Birmingham. You came up by train from Bristol that morning."

"Jonathan, they can check that."

"Why the fuck should they want to check it? There's no reason for them not to believe us; it's got nothing to do with the accident. All they'll want to know is what we saw, and not why we were there together. It's irrelevant. I was giving you a lift to London, or maybe not London, possibly Reading, what do you think?"

"Whatever," said Abi. She felt close to tears, without being sure why.

"OK, Reading then. Don't forget."

"What was I going to Reading for?"

"To visit friends. For the weekend."

"Jonathan, this is getting so complicated. You don't think it might be better to tell the truth?"

"Abi, no. For Christ's sake. Do you want to—" He stopped.

"Do I want to what, Jonathan? Oh, I get it. This is about your marriage, isn't it? About being caught with your pants down—literally."

"I . . . To a degree, yes. Of course. I don't want Laura hurt—"

"Maybe you should have thought of that earlier."

"Oh, Christ." She could almost hear him struggling to keep calm. "Abi, please—look, we're far more likely to get into trouble over this if there is any indication that we were having an affair."

"I don't see why we should get into trouble at all. We weren't doing anything wrong. Oh—except that you were on the phone, of course." She couldn't resist that.

"Yes, well, hopefully that won't come to light." His voice was very cold. "I would say there's no need to actually mention it. Unless they ask, of course. Is that . . . I mean, would you agree with me?"

"Why should I lie to the police on your behalf?"

"I'm not asking you to lie, simply not to mention it."

She didn't answer. She could almost hear him sweating. It was very, very pleasant.

"Abi?" he said. "Can I have your agreement to that?"

"Well . . . let's see what happens, shall we?"

"No, Abi, I need to know that you agree."

"I don't see why. If they ask, they ask. Look, you were in no way responsible for that crash, Jonathan. The lorry went into a skid; it couldn't stop, went through the barrier . . . We just happened to be there. We didn't hit anything. Or cause anyone to hit anything. And then you did your Dr. Wonderful act. What's for them to be suspicious about?"

"Nothing. Of course. It's just that . . . well, it is a bit of a blur, and I can't help feeling anxious about it. I'm not sure why. I'm glad you don't."

"No," she said, aware that she was not being strictly truthful, "I don't. And I really, really don't like the idea of lying to the police."

There was a very long silence; then he said, "I need you to do this, Abi."

"So you said. I, on the other hand, don't need to do it. Funny, that."

Another shorter silence. She'd got him now, got him shitting himself.

Then: "Abi, I think you do need to do it. Actually."

"Oh, why?"

"Because I don't think you'd want the police to know about your little habit, do you?"

She felt the floor literally heave under her. He couldn't have said that; he couldn't. She had a friend who'd got caught with drugs in her flat; she'd got a suspended sentence and a big fine. She'd lose her job, she might even go to prison . . .

"I can't believe you're saying this," she said, amazed that her voice sounded so steady, "or thinking it. Anyway, I seem to remember you enjoying the odd snort."

"You might have trouble proving that. You provided it. Rather visibly, I seem to remember, on one or two occasions. And who do you think they'd believe, you or me?"

She threw her head back, stared at the ceiling, tears stinging her eyes, as much from shock as fear. This was a man who'd told her he cared about her, who'd sought her out, told her she was one of the best things in his life . . .

"Don't worry, Abi. Of course I won't say anything to the police.

Or to your boss. As long as you do what I ask. All right? Just stick to the story; it won't be difficult. Clever girl like you."

"Screw you, Jonathan Gilliatt. Screw you to hell!"

"So . . . does that mean I have your agreement?"

Even if the police didn't believe him, they would check her out, her friends, work, Sylvie, everyone.

"Yes, you do," she said. "Fuck you."

"Right. Good. Well, that's that. I think. The less we communicate the better. at the moment. Don't ring me."

"Don't worry, I won't."

"Good. And don't forget: keep it simple."

She cut him off.

Bastard. Absolute bastard. How could she have been taken in by him?

But . . . God. If he did . . . Not that she kept any, ever. She simply bought it when she wanted it. Which wasn't very often. Even so . . .

Abi suddenly felt very sick; she made the bathroom only just in time. Afterwards she stood in the shower for what felt like hours, then came out and lay down on the bed.

Later, trying to calm her whirling, heaving fear, she thought that there was no way she was going to tell Jonathan that William had called and spoken to Laura. Let him dig his own grave on that one. Funny that Laura hadn't mentioned it yet. She was obviously cooler than Abi had realised. Waiting for Jonathan to trip himself up. Clever, really. Very clever. Perhaps she had misjudged her.

. . .

"Emma. There's something really important I want to say . . ."

"Yes, Luke?"

"The thing is, I haven't said it before, because I wasn't sure. I've never said it to anyone, matter of fact . . ."

She put her fork down. This was . . . well, very . . . well . . .

"I . . . I love you, babe. I really do."

"Oh, Luke . . ." She felt tears in her eyes: joyful, wonderful tears.

"Hey," he said, "hey, the idea was to make you happy."

"Sorry. I am. Terribly." She hoped her mascara wasn't running.

"Thing is, it's taken me a while to realise, but I was talking to Mum the other night, and . . ."

He was worryingly devoted to his mum; any girlfriend was in danger of taking second place.

"Yes?"

"And she said it was obvious to her—she'd never heard me talk like that before—and she said I should tell you . . ."

Good old mum; if she'd walked in then, Emma would have hugged her. She must stop thinking harsh things about her.

"Oh, Luke . . ."

"Yeah. So . . . well, that's about it, really."

She was silent, realised he was looking slightly embarrassed, less his usual confident self.

"That's wonderful," she said, "absolutely wonderful."

"Good. Now, there is something else . . ." He raised his fingers, signalled to the waiter.

"Could you bring that package over, please? The one I asked you to keep at the desk?"

"Certainly, sir."

She sat in an agony of suspense. Package? What would be in a package? A . . . a . . . *No, Emma, not that. Surely not that. Not yet, not—*

The waiter put the package down in front of Luke; it was blue, that glorious, soft turquoise blue, with that wonderful, wonderful white ribbon—Tiffany! A package from Tiffany. What came from Tiffany? Well, lots of things, but—

Luke handed it to her. "Go on," he said. "Open it."

Her hands shaking, she untied the bow; inside the bag was a box. A quite small box. With another white ribbon.

She undid the second bow, took the lid off the box, pulled out the small blue pouch. What was it; what could it be, if not—

"Oh, Luke, that's so lovely! Wonderful. Oh, Luke. Oh, my God!"

She was fighting to keep her voice enthusiastic, not to betray the sliver of disappointment that . . . well, that was undeniably there. *Emma, Emma, he loves you; that's enough—anything else would be too much now; don't be ridiculous.* And how could any girl be disappointed, getting a gold Paloma Picasso heart on a chain—and not just plain gold, but the one with a diamond set in it. God, it must have cost a fortune; he must really, really care about her. Never mind it wasn't a ring; it was absolutely gorgeous . . .

"I love it," she said, smiling, leaning over to kiss him. "I really love it; thank you so much, Luke. Here, help me put it on . . ."

"Good. I thought you'd like it. Now you have to wear that all the time, Emma, OK, so you think of me all the time. Even when I'm away."

"Of course I will," she said, and she was crying now. "I promise, Luke, I really do. I couldn't bear to take it off anyway, not ever . . . Oh, dear, I must go to the loo again; my makeup'll be all smudgy and . . ."

It wasn't until she had repaired her makeup, put on some more perfume, combed her hair, and admired the necklace that she realised she hadn't told Luke that she loved him too. Well, plenty of time for that later. Maybe when they were in bed . . .

CHAPTER 18

Mary had begun to despair by Saturday evening of ever hearing from Russell again, as the hours went by with no word, no message of any sort . . . She found it extremely painful that he had apparently made no effort to find her; it seemed to display a lack of true devotion. The crash had been in all the papers, and you had only to turn on the news on that first morning to see graphic pictures of the pileup, the lorry straddling the motorway, the ambulances and police cars and the helicopter. How could Russell have missed all that?

And then the nurse had come over to her bed, with the message, at six o'clock.

"From a gentleman, Mary; he sounded like an American. He said to give you his . . . his special love. He was called Mr. Mackenzie. That mean anything to you?"

"Oh, yes," said Mary, "oh, my goodness, it does."

"And he's coming to see you in the morning."

And Mary had flown up into some unreachable, untouchable place of happiness and felt she would never, ever come down again.

. . .

And then on Sunday morning the flowers arrived: a vast bouquet of red roses.

"My word," the nurse said, "St. Valentine's Day's come late this year. I don't know what I'm going to put them in, Mary; I haven't got a vase big enough for half of them."

"You don't have to," said Mary. "Look, they're in water already. Can I . . . can I have the card, please?"

"For my beloved Little Sparrow," it said. "Get very well, very soon. Russell."

Mary burst into tears.

. . .

And then there he was, walking across the ward, smiling, his brilliant blue eyes fixed on her, and he really didn't look so very different, still so handsome and so slim and tall, and the years rolled away, and they were young again, standing together in Parliament Square, and she had known she was falling in love; and it was all she could do not to leap out of bed and run into his arms.

Only it wasn't necessary, for he half ran to her instead, and when he reached her he took her hand and kissed it, and she simply felt warm and safe and absolutely happy. This was love, then, as they had known it all those years ago; and they had much to do, in whatever time was left to them, to see to it and nurture it and allow it to come into its own.

. . .

The police, or rather the CIU, called Jonathan on Sunday to discuss when they might talk to him.

"Just a quick call, Mr. Gilliatt, to arrange a time; the sooner the better, while it's all still fresh in your mind."

"Yes, of course. Although I should tell you a lot of it is rather a blur."

"That's all right, sir. Just tell us what you can and we'll worry about the rest."

They'd settled finally on Tuesday evening, at six thirty.

He'd slept horribly badly again, and he was sitting in the conservatory just before supper, trying to read the Sunday papers, when Laura walked in with a bottle of white wine and a bowl of olives.

Her voice was at its sweetest; the coolness of the past twenty-four hours or so seemed to have passed.

"I thought we'd earned this," she said, smiling at him. "Well, I certainly have. Bit of a day, with the children and so on."

"Yes, I'm sorry, darling; been no use to you at all. I'm feeling much better now; I'll be back on course tomorrow."

"Good."

"Um . . ." This was it; he had to do it—had to broach the subject of the police interview . . . "Just one thing, darling. The police are coming here on Tuesday evening. To talk to me about the accident. About six thirty. Will you be around?"

"Of course. In fact, I'd like to sit in on it, if you don't mind."

A thud of fear hit him.

"Well, darling, I don't mind, of course. But they might feel differently. Protocol and all that."

"I can't see why. Anyway, if they don't want me there, they can tell me and I'll go away. When you say talk to you, what exactly does that mean?"

"Well, I presume they're gathering evidence about how it happened exactly, what I saw—"

"Yes, I see. And how do you think it happened?"

The coolness had returned.

"Well . . . it's so hard to say. Everyone was driving in a very orderly way; no one was speeding. And then suddenly, out of the blue, this lorry swerved and I suppose skidded, and went through the barrier. It had just rained, of course, and—"

"I see. So where were you in all this? In front of him, at his side?"

"Laura, what is this, a rehearsal for Tuesday?"

"Don't be ridiculous; I could have lost you! Of course I want to know everything."

"Sorry, yes, of course you do. Well, I was more or less beside the lorry. On the inside lane. There was an old car immediately in front of me, which presumably just drove on, and in front of the lorry a sports car of some kind, an E-Type, I think, that disappeared too. There really was no apparent reason for the lorry to do what it did. I thought he might have had a blowout, but I looked and his tyres were all intact. Anyway, I found myself—and that was what it was like, finding myself; I certainly don't remember getting there—stopped at an angle on the hard shoulder. About a hundred yards ahead of him, I suppose. It was all bloody scary."

"Of course. Terrifying. And then you involved yourself, helping all those people. That was so good of you, Jonathan; they were lucky you were there."

"Well, one does one's bit. I think I helped, yes. Hope so. Er . . . Laura . . . there is one thing I hadn't told you before—silly, really, so unimportant, but it might come out in this interview thing."

"And what's that?"

"Well, I . . . wasn't alone in the car."

He was sweating.

"Had you given someone a lift?"

"Well, sort of. Someone I met at the conference. A woman. Very nice, needed a lift to Reading, had a problem with her car . . ." He must remember to tell Abi that; God, it was getting so complicated.

"Well, that was kind of you. Maybe another reason to cut down to the M4. If she had to get to Reading . . ."

"No, no, I mentioned it, that I'd decided to go that way, at the end of the morning session, and she asked me if I could give her a lift."

"I see. She was a doctor, was she?"

"No, no, she worked for the PR company. Who were covering the conference. She . . . worked with a photographer, got everyone's names and details, that sort of thing. Anyway, it's just that she was in the car, and of course when the police were taking names and addresses, they took hers, so . . . yes, she's bound to be mentioned. I just thought I should tell you, so you wouldn't be . . . be . . . well . . . surprised, that's all. Especially if you're going to be sitting in on the interview. Which I would love, actually. Not the nicest thing to have to recall in great detail."

"No. Well, that's very considerate of you, darling. Thank you for telling me." She leaned back in her chair, took a sip of wine, smiled at him very sweetly. He allowed himself to relax just slightly.

"Tell me, Jonathan. Would that have been . . . Abi? By any chance? Was that this woman's name?"

. . .

It would have helped, of course, if he hadn't spilt his wine. He was very aware of Laura watching him while he mopped rather ineffectually at the tray with his handkerchief and the paper napkins she had brought out, and that she had that new, cool, slightly distant expression on her face. Finally he sat back in his chair and managed to smile at her.

"Sorry, darling. What a mess."

"You could say that," she said, and there was an edge to her voice that was unmissable.

"Anyway . . . yes, Abi, that was her name. Abi Scott. How . . . how did you know that?"

"A very nice young man rang up, said he'd been there on Friday, and that this . . . Abi . . . had given him her phone to look after. I'm not sure why. She went off without it, and yours was one of the names on it, so he rang. He said none of the other names meant anything to him, but he did recognise yours because she'd been with you, had mentioned you. He was very charming, and very diffident about bothering me and so on."

"Yes, I see. Well, that was nice of him. Er . . . when did he call?"

"Yesterday afternoon. While you were asleep."

"You should have told me."

"Oh, darling, I didn't want to wake you up. And then I forgot. Till now."

She smiled again, the smile sickly sweet now.

"So . . . the only thing I wondered was, Jonathan, why was your name in her phone? Since you'd only just met her."

"Oh" he said, thinking fast, "oh, I was moving around from car to car, she was doing other things, we didn't want to lose contact with each other, so I put my number in her phone. I did the same for several people, a girl who'd gone into premature labour—that reminds me, I must call the hospital, see if the baby's all right—and a nice young chap, best man to the bridegroom, the one whose leg was crushed . . ."

"I see," she said, and then with a half sigh, "Oh, Jonathan! This had better be true. Otherwise, I can't quite think what I might do. Except that I'd want to be sure you wouldn't like it."

And she got up and stalked out of the conservatory; when he followed her a few minutes later she was nowhere to be seen.

CHAPTER 19

Linda's initial reaction was to say no; she didn't want to risk her reputation again, and Georgia simply didn't deserve it.

But after two double espressos, she decided that Georgia was still
her client and that she owed it to her—professionally—to put the
proposal to her. She called Georgia's mobile; it was switched off. Not
even taking messages. She tried the landline. Bea Linley answered.

"Oh—Linda. Hello. Nice to hear from you. Georgia's . . . well,
she's gone out."

"OK." Linda could hear the controlled exasperation in her own
voice. "Ask her to call me, would you, Bea? As soon as she gets in. It's
important."

"Yes, of course. Is it about that part? Are they reconsidering her?"

"Something like that."

"Oh, Linda, that's wonderful. She's been so upset ever since she
got back. Won't eat, keeps crying. I'll get her to call you the minute
she gets in. Thank you, Linda. She's a very lucky girl."

"She certainly is," said Linda, "very lucky indeed. Bye, Bea."

"Mum! I can't! I told you to say I was out."

"I did," said Bea, "and I really don't think she believed me for a
moment. Anyway, you're to ring her immediately."

"I'm not going to."

Bea didn't easily lose her temper, but she lost it now.

"Georgia, I think it's time you took a hard look at yourself. You're
not a child; you're twenty-two years old. Your father and I have been
very patient; we've supported you in every sense of the word all your
life, never put any sort of time limit on it. You've taken that completely for granted—our faith in you as well as the practical help. And
now, with what sounds like a real chance of actually getting a part, you

just turn your back on it without a word of explanation to me, or to Linda. It's absolutely dreadful and I feel quite ashamed of you. Now, I'm going out to work—it's clearly escaped your notice that most of us have to do that—and when I get back, I either want to know you've arranged to go for this audition, or you can forget the whole wretched acting nonsense and go and find yourself a proper job. Your time's up, Georgia. It's your decision."

. . .

Barney was sitting at his desk, trying to pretend it was any old Monday, when the police phoned. They would like to interview him about the crash; when would he be available?

"Oh—whenever it suits you," Barney said, fighting down the fear that seemed quite literally to slither up from his stomach and take possession of his head several times each day. "Yes, course."

"We could call round to your home, sir. If that suited you. More pleasant perhaps than a police station, but it's up to you . . ."

"No, home sounds good. Around seven? Er . . . can you give me an idea of the sort of things you'll be asking? So that I can be prepared, brush up on my memory a bit."

"Oh—we're just looking to get all the information we can, sir. Everything you can remember of the crash. You are, of course, a prime witness. Now, there will be two of us—I'm Sergeant Freeman and I shall be accompanied by Constable Rowe."

"Very good, Sergeant. Thank you."

. . .

Barney was feeling very odd altogether. He was terribly worried about Toby, of course, but he hadn't yet got over the shock of his behaviour: that he had been capable of such a thing with that girl. And then there was the business of the tyre: OK, they hadn't caused the accident, but they had had a blowout. And driven into the car in front and caused the girl to go into labour. It seemed very possible to Barney that the soft tyre could have contributed—or even caused that. He should have insisted on checking it, made Toby wait somehow . . . And was he supposed to mention the tyre to the police? He really needed to discuss it with Toby—who was in no state to discuss anything with anybody.

He was having trouble sleeping, having feverish dreams, and waking, sweating, several times each night, with a terrible sense of fear.

God, he felt a mess . . .

. . .

She had no idea how she was going to get through it. But anything was better than being alone in her room just . . . thinking about it. Being alone with the memory. And the terror. She must stop hiding, running away. And nobody knew what she had done, after all. She hadn't thought of that in her initial blind panic. Except Patrick, of course. Patrick, who had been so kind to her.

And it looked like he was getting better, according to the papers.

Just take it a day at a time, Georgia. One day and then the next. And then, one day, possibly quite soon even, she would go and see Patrick in the hospital. She would. She really would. But . . . not today. It was going to be quite hard enough just getting up to London and doing the audition. After that she'd see. One day at a time. That was what she had to do. One day at a time.

. . .

Mary suddenly felt very restless; she had been stuck in this ward for too long. She longed to go for a little walk, just round the hospital, and wondered if they'd let her. Probably not. Best not to ask, perhaps, just slip out while no one was looking.

Feeling rather as if she'd escaped from prison, Mary made for the lift. She had no idea where she was going; just to be out of the ward was pleasure enough.

The lift was full of people. They all seemed to be going to the ground floor; Mary thought she might as well go there too. She wandered round the foyer for a bit, looking at all the fortunate people who could go out into the street at will without getting permission or signing forms, and then saw a Costa café outlet; it looked rather cheerful and normal, and she was tempted to go in, but there really wasn't anything she wanted. She decided to go back to the lift, and on her way, she passed a sign to ICU; she knew what that meant: intensive care. Presumably that was where the lorry driver lay, poor man. As she stood there, looking down the corridor, a young woman, clearly absolutely exhausted, walked towards her, her eyes blank and unseeing, and then passed on and into the café, where she sat down at one of the tables, slumped over her handbag.

Without stopping to think, Mary followed her and sat down opposite her.

"Hello," she said, and smiled at her encouragingly. "You can tell me to go away if you want, but you look to me as if you could do with some company."

The woman stared at her, then shook her head.

"Can I get you a cup of tea then?"

"No . . . that is . . . well, yes. Thank you. Good and strong. With sugar."

She was obviously far too exhausted and distressed to wonder why a strange old lady in a dressing gown might be bothering with her; Mary went over to the counter, paid for the cup of water and tea bag, and carried it over to the table, together with several minicartons of milk and packs of sugar.

"There you are. I should leave the bag in for a bit longer."

"Thank you for that. I will." She looked at Mary, then managed a very faint smile. "Are you a patient here, then?"

"I am indeed. Only until the end of the week, thank God. Then I'm going home."

"Well, you're a lucky woman." She had an Irish accent and was young and rather pretty, Mary thought, in spite of the exhaustion . . . She dunked the tea bag up and down in the cup, then fished it out and added the milk. "That's great. Thank you."

"That's all right. You look terribly tired."

"I am. I feel I've been here forever. My . . . my husband's in intensive care."

"Oh, how terribly worrying for you. Has he had surgery?"

"He has indeed. A great deal. But that's only the beginning." And she started to cry, then looked back at Mary and said, "I'm sorry."

"Don't be silly," said Mary, rummaging in her dressing gown pocket for a tissue. "Do you want to tell me about it?"

. . .

"Mr. Fraser? Sergeant Freeman, CIU. And this is Constable Rowe."

"How do you do?" said Barney. "Come into the sitting room. This is my fiancée, Amanda Baring."

"How do you do, Sergeant," said Amanda. "I was wondering . . . is there any reason why I shouldn't sit in on the interview? I wasn't there, of course. But I thought it would be nicer for Barney if I was with him while you talk to him. I promise not to interrupt or anything, but . . ."

She smiled at Sergeant Freeman, who smiled slightly foolishly back.

"That's perfectly all right," he said, "if that's what you want."

"It is. Thank you. Now, can I get you a cup of tea?"

"That would be very welcome," said Sergeant Freeman.

"Certainly would," said Constable Rowe.

They were an odd pair, Barney thought; Freeman was thin, almost gaunt, while Rowe was plump and rosy, and looked like an Enid Blyton policeman. They settled side by side on the sofa, and Freeman took out a large pad of paper and a pencil. Barney half expected him to lick it . . .

"Before we start, sir, how is Mr. Weston?" Freeman asked.

"Not very well, I'm afraid. A bit better in himself today, but his leg was very badly mashed up."

"I'm very sorry to hear that, sir. Now, I realise he was driving, but it's your recollection, interpretation of events that's important . . ."

They began with the basics: name, address, profession, when and why he had been on the M4 that afternoon.

"The wedding was at four thirty, which would mean that by leaving when you did, you were cutting things a bit fine."

"Yes, it was rather . . . late," said Barney.

"Any particular reason?"

"Er . . . yes. Mr. Weston was . . . was unwell. He had a stomach upset."

"Would that be a euphemism for a hangover, sir? Forgive the assumption, but—"

"No," said Barney firmly. "He did have a few drinks the night before, but I do assure you, as we didn't leave until around lunchtime the following day, he would have been absolutely fine. No, he was extremely sick several times during the morning."

"And could you tell us exactly how much he drank, sir? Very important, as I'm sure you'll appreciate."

Barney fought down his irritation; he really hadn't expected this. "I suppose . . . maybe half a bottle of wine with dinner, certainly no more—and a couple of glasses of whisky afterwards."

"Were you also drinking, sir?"

"Well, yes."

"So what else did you do in the evening? After dinner?"

"Oh . . . we swam in the pool. Talked. Played some music."

"Now, let's get on to the journey. Why did you choose the M4 route?"

"The other way involves endless back roads and narrow lanes, and we needed to get some petrol. We thought it would be easier to go to the service station, fill up there. The tank was practically dry."

"Forgive me for saying so, sir, but I'd have thought that would be part of the best man's duties to get that sort of thing done in good time."

"Well, I assumed Toby would have done it. He'd been at the house all the day before," said Barney. He felt edgy suddenly and under threat. "But I should have checked; you're right. Er . . . is that really relevant?"

"Probably not, sir, no. Now . . . his parents, as I understand it, were at the house? When did they leave?"

"Oh . . . about ten thirty. They were having lunch with friends in Marlborough."

"Weren't they worried about their son's condition?"

"We . . . managed to keep it from them. They would have been very worried."

"I see. And when you left the house, who was driving the car?"

"I was."

"So . . . you stopped at the service station and filled up the tank. Did anything of note happen on your way there?"

"Yes, we were stopped by the police."

"For speeding?"

"Yes. And, of course, that made us later. Much later."

"Presumably you were Breathalyzed then, sir?"

"Yes, of course." He was beginning to feel beleaguered. "And it was absolutely fine."

"Right. Well, we can check on that, of course. May I ask what speed you were travelling when you were stopped?"

"Er . . . ninety-eight," said Barney with an apologetic look at Amanda.

"A little over the speed limit, sir. Well, we don't need to waste time on that now." He made a separate note. "And then you proceeded on your way? To the service station?"

"Yes, that's right."

"And . . . you filled up with fuel. Anything else?"

This was it. No need to mention it, though. Completely irrelevant. Red herring.

"No, nothing else."

"You didn't need oil, or windscreen wash?"

"No, we didn't. And then we went on our way."

"And were you still driving?"

"Well . . . no," said Barney. "Toby took over."

"Why was that?"

"He just wanted to. I think he felt less stressed if he was behind the wheel."

"I see. And presumably you were going more slowly by then."

"Yes, of course. No more than seventy-five, eighty, max."

"Right. So . . . were you aware of any other cars at this point, or indeed earlier, driving erratically ahead, overtaking you . . . ?"

"Yes, there was one," said Barney slowly. "It was a white van, and he was going like the clappers—tailgating, flashing, weaving in and out of the traffic, behaving extremely dangerously. He certainly deserved to be stopped. As much as, if not more than, we did."

"I see. I don't suppose you were aware of any markings on the van, any name of the firm . . . ?"

"No. Sorry."

"That's all right. Someone else might have seen it. Now, tell me what happened next. Take your time."

"We were just driving along in the outside lane. The traffic was quite heavy, and everyone was driving very steadily. Actually rather slowly. There'd just been a storm, and the road was still wet. Anyway, quite suddenly, it seemed, the lorry just lost control."

"You were beside it? Behind it?"

"Behind it. But in the outside lane. There was a Volvo Estate in front of us, more or less even with it. Anyway, he veered over to the right, towards the central median, and just . . . well, went through it. Stopped finally on the westbound side, jackknifed, total chaos. Toby slammed on the brakes, obviously, but we had a blowout. I've never known anything like it; it was absolutely terrifying. The car was all over the place; it was as if the steering just didn't work. Or the brakes. We seemed to be swinging about on the road, and then somehow, Toby got it back under control, and it—well, it went into the Volvo. Which had managed to stop. It was so odd; it seemed to happen so slowly, as if we had all the time in the world. I know people always say that. So weird."

"Indeed. Now, were you aware of hitting anything, however small, that may have caused the blowout?"

"No," said Barney, "we weren't. But there could very easily have been something."

"Well, again, Forensics are doing a full report on your car; they may come up with something. Of the tyre being cut in some way."

"But surely . . . the tyre was in bits. How could they see anything at all?"

"You'd be surprised what they can see, sir. Anyway, you impacted with the Volvo. Then what happened?"

"We just went on and on into the Volvo's rear. We hit it on Toby's . . . on the off side; it crushed the bonnet and drove the steering column down into his leg. He was bloody lucky it wasn't worse, I suppose."

"Indeed, sir. Are you all right?"

"Yes. Yes, thanks."

But he wasn't; he could feel his eyes filling with tears. Amanda came over to him and took his hand. He looked at Freeman.

"Sorry. All a bit vivid."

"I'm sure. Anyway, I'm going to go over this with you now, and then prepare a statement, and you can sign it if you're happy with it. Shouldn't take too long."

Going over it meant a gruelling trawl through the whole thing again. It seemed, quite literally, endless.

. . .

"God," said Amanda when they'd gone, "they're very thorough, aren't they? All those questions about how much you'd drunk, who was driving. You don't think Toby was over the limit, do you?"

"Absolutely not," said Barney impatiently. He felt absolutely exhausted, drained of emotion, and the last thing he wanted was further questioning. "He'd had the same as me, I swear to you—really not much at all—and it was fifteen, sixteen hours later, for God's sake, and when I was Breathalyzed, when they stopped us, I was fine."

"Yes, of course. But . . . there is one thing I still don't understand. Haven't from the beginning. I mean, why did you leave so late? It does seem awfully stupid."

"I told you. Tobes was in a bad way."

"Oh, yes I see," said Amanda.

But she didn't sound altogether convinced.

. . .

"Nice young chap," said Constable Rowe as they drove through the crowded streets of Clapham, "and what bad luck. And for the bridegroom, imagine missing your own wedding like that . . ."

Sergeant Freeman said he knew several people who might have wished to miss their own weddings, and said that they should examine the CCTV footage at the service stations as soon as possible.

"With what in mind, exactly?"

"To make sure everything happened exactly as he said . . ."

CHAPTER 20

"Shit," said Jonathan aloud, and his eyes filled unaccountably with tears. He was sitting at his desk in his tiny room at St. Andrews, ostensibly going through his notes for the next patient; the day had seemed interminable, everything everyone said to him meaningless.

He must speak to Abi before the police interview, absolutely must. And he really needed to know what Laura was going to do or say during the interview; even the mildest indication that she was suspicious of the relationship might lead to further questioning. And then there was the small matter of the phone call . . .

He went out into the hospital grounds, armed with his mobile, and dialled Abi's number. "Abi, it's Jonathan. Please call me. There are various things we need to discuss most urgently. Anytime in the next three or four hours."

He realised he didn't even know if the police had been on to her yet. Christ, it was getting worse by the minute . . .

.   .   .

It was only when the police rang and said they would like to interview her about the crash that Abi decided, in her own interest, she had better let Jonathan off the hook. She was eating a sandwich at her desk when the call came through; the call did rather destroy her appetite.

.   .   .

His voice was terse, impatient.

"I wish you'd got back to me sooner. You must have got my messages."

"You're not the only busy person in the world, Jonathan. I have a life too, you know. I can't just take phone calls in the middle of jobs. I realise they're not as important, my jobs, as chatting up mothers-to-be, but . . ."

"Oh, just stop it," he said. "Look, have the police been on to you?"

"Yes. They're coming to see me on Thursday."

"Right. Well there's one new thing for you to remember. You had a problem with your car; that's why you didn't have it with you at the conference. Can you remember that?"

"I'll try."

"Abi, please, this isn't some silly game; it's very important."

"What, so Laura doesn't find out about me, do you mean?"

"Well, so that she doesn't know the truth about you. She's insisting on sitting in on the interview; it's essential we get the details right.

Look, you've got it all, haven't you? The lift to Reading, the car, all that stuff. And . . . probably best not to mention the phone call. Which wasn't a phone call, in the strict sense of the word. I answered it and then threw the bloody thing on the floor."

"Oh, for Christ's sake. Is there anything else you'd like me to say? Like you weren't there at all, I just happened to be driving your car? Lying to the police is a crime, you know, Jonathan. I looked it up on the Internet. You're inciting me to commit a crime. And actually committing one yourself. That's called blackmail."

There was a silence; then he said, "I think you're in danger of making a very big mistake, Abi. I could, if required, get witnesses, you know. Employees at hotels, for a start. I seem to remember you rather enjoyed impressing them with your little demos . . ."

She felt sick again. Very sick.

"All right, Jonathan," she said. "I've got it." And then, because she couldn't resist it, she added, "I think."

Two could play at this game . . .

· · ·

How was she doing this? Georgia wondered. When she'd spent the past three days crying and quite literally wishing she was dead. She'd been in bits only half an hour earlier, holding Linda's hand, shaking with nerves, and feeling terribly sick.

And now, suddenly, she felt fine, cool, self-confident, and upbeat.

It was always like that; all actors knew about Dr. Stage. Dr. Stage could mend a sprained ankle so its owner could dance, could heal laryngitis so a voice could fill a theatre; he could cure migraine, gastric flu and asthma, stanch tears and heal grief, summon strength and banish pain. Not forever, not even for very long, but long enough for the show to go on. And he was working very hard on Georgia's behalf at that moment.

She walked into the casting director's room, smiling radiantly at the people watching her from behind their table. She was surprised—

and pleased—that there were three of them; she'd been expecting just the casting director. Every moment was important now, she knew; the camcorder was running already, filming the way she looked, moved, talked, smiled.

"Hi, Georgia. I'm Tony; I'm the casting director. This is Bryn, the director, and you know Sue, my assistant."

"Yes, I do. Hi. Thank you so much for letting me come today. I'm really sorry about last week."

"That's OK. So, what are you doing at the moment, what have you been up to?"

"Oh . . . lots of things. Episode of *The Bill,* episode of *Casualty,* two episodes of *Hollyoaks,* bit of modelling to make ends meet." She grinned at them.

"Who was the modelling for? TV?"

"Yes, one for a car commercial, one for a new chocolate, and a fashion shoot for *Glamour.*"

It didn't add up to a row of beans, and they would know it; the scenes for *The Bill* and *Casualty* had been tiny, *Hollyoaks* only a bit bigger; she'd been in a crowd scene in the car commercial, maybe slightly more of a presence selling the chocolates, one of three girls eating as suggestively as the client felt they could get away with. And fashion shoots—well, she might just as well have not mentioned it. Except that it did mean she looked all right. But they could see that for themselves . . .

Then the standard questions they always asked: would she shave her head if she was asked, did she have any tattoos anywhere on her body, would she take all her clothes off, do a nude scene. Georgia told them she'd shave her head and take her clothes off all in one scene if they asked; no tattoos, though, so if they were looking for them . . . They laughed; then there was a silence. They were going to tell her to go away, not bother, she thought, panic rising, but: "Well, from those scenes we sent you, Georgia, would you like to do scene ten? With a bit of a Brummie accent, maybe. Sue will read the dad."

"Sure."

That was lucky: scene ten was her favourite. She walked towards Sue, stood with her legs slightly apart, her hands on her hips.

"Dad," she said, "can I have a word . . . ?"

By the time she finished the scene she felt quite emotional; and she could tell they'd liked it. They sat looking at her in silence, the casting director smiling.

"OK, Georgia," he said. "Now could you do it again, please, without the accent. Just in your normal voice."

It wasn't quite as good, and she was more nervous, but they still smiled at her when she'd finished.

"Thank you, Georgia. That was great. Thank you very much. We'll be in touch. Shouldn't be too long. Few days, probably."

"Fine. Thank you."

She allowed herself to tell Linda she thought it had gone well; she felt she owed her that.

And she'd been really great, not reproached her at all, not asked her any more questions about the crash. Not that she would have answered her if she had. Indeed she didn't think she would be able to. The only way she could cope now was pretending it had never happened. Or rather that she hadn't been there. That seemed to be working quite well.

. . .

Jonathan sat down facing them, fighting a rising panic and a fear that he might actually vomit.

"Right, Mr. Gilliatt. Perhaps first we could establish exactly what you were doing on the M4 that afternoon, sir? Just so we're fully in the picture, you understand?"

Right in the deep end, then. He smiled at them carefully. He didn't look at Laura; that would seem anxious. She mustn't think he was anxious. About any of it.

"I was driving back from a pharmaceutical conference: I'd been speaking at a dinner the night before. At the Birmingham International Hotel."

"So why the M4, sir; why not the M40?"

A sudden and very vivid image came to him of where he had gone on the way and what had happened there. It was disturbing; he crushed it.

"It was Friday afternoon; the M5-to-M4 route may be longer, but it's often less congested."

"And you left Birmingham when, exactly, sir?"

"Oh . . . late morning."

"Right. So you cut down onto the M4 and reached it at what time?"

"Well, it must have taken a couple of hours. I'm not absolutely sure."

"That's perfectly all right. Not important. And then you drove straight on towards London?"

"Yes."

"Did you stop at all?"

"Yes, for some petrol. At Leigh Delamere."

"Fine. So that would have been about what time?"

"Well, I suppose about two thirty."

"And you were alone, were you? In the car?"

He felt Laura stiffen, from right across the room. "I had a young lady with me. Abi Scott. She was at the conference in a business capacity, but she'd been having trouble with her car; she'd come up by train, and I offered her a lift to Reading. She was spending the weekend there."

"I see. Ah, yes, Abi Scott. We'll be interviewing her as well."

"Anyway, it was a purely professional relationship. I'd never met her before."

He was aware of Freeman glancing up for a moment, seeming about to ask something, then returning to his task.

"Right, sir. So . . . were you in a hurry to get to London?"

"A little. Yes. I had a clinic at four thirty at St. Anne's."

"Which is where, sir?"

"Just off Harley Street."

"I see," said Freeman. "Well, sounds quite a tight time frame to me. I imagine you were driving fairly fast? In the outside lane, perhaps?"

"Well, not at all, no. The traffic was very heavy; there were a couple of minor holdups . . ."

"So your hunch was a wrong one?"

"I'm sorry?"

"About it being quicker on the M4."

"Yes, it was a mistake. A bigger one than I knew." He smiled at them and then at Laura. Her face was expressionless; she didn't smile back.

"So . . . just before the crash, you were driving along . . . in which lane, sir?"

"Oh—the inside lane."

"Why would that have been, sir? If you were short of time?"

"Well, I had a bad headache. The traffic was very heavy in all three lanes; then there'd been a thunderstorm, of course, which was very disconcerting. It was hard to see for a bit, and then a lot of water on the road. Very dangerous."

"And what time was that, would you have said?"

"About three forty-five, I suppose."

"Yes. Well, we can check that. So would you say that it was the storm that decided you to move over?"

"No, it was a number of factors. Maybe it was the deciding one. Anyway, then the storm was over as fast as it had begun."

"Right. So, at what point were you first aware of the lorry?"

"Oh . . . I don't know. Around the same time."

"And were you driving along level with it? Behind it?"

"More or less level. Yes."

"Any other traffic that you can recall, sir? In your immediate vicinity, that is, just prior to the accident? No bad driving that comes to mind, nothing that could have cut across the lorry's path, perhaps?"

What did that mean? Was he suggesting it might have been him? His own fears came back, reinforced by the questioning. Had it been him, confused by the row with Abi, the phone ringing; had he lost concentration, veered in front of the lorry in some way? No! Surely, surely he'd remember if he had. God, it was frightening.

"No," he said firmly, "nothing like that. Everyone was driving rather well, as a matter of fact. I do remember a rather fine old E-Type in front of the lorry, but he was driving perfectly safely. Pulling ahead steadily, but certainly not speeding."

"And the vehicle ahead of you?"

"Oh . . . it was a large station wagon of some kind. Again, driving very steadily."

It went on and on: could he pinpoint where he had first noticed the lorry, had he been driving erratically, cutting in and out of lanes? Then, suddenly:

"Did you have the radio on, sir?"

"Yes. Briefly, although not just prior to the crash. Miss Scott had switched it on, but I found it distracting, asked her to turn it off again."

"I see. So you were just . . . talking?"

"Yes. Chatting, you know."

Just chatting. While he tried to end the relationship, while she threatened to go and see Laura . . .

"And I presume you weren't using a phone?"

Shit. Here it came. He managed to prevaricate.

"The in-car system in my car wasn't working properly, and I had my ordinary mobile with me. I called my secretary at the clinic from the service station. To say I might be late."

"And did anyone call you?"

"I did," said Laura suddenly.

"At what time would that have been, Mrs. Gilliatt?"

They weren't going to like this.

"Oh, I don't know. Two or three times. He just didn't answer. I was frantic with worry. Then finally I got through."

"And what time was that?"

A long silence. Very long. Her eyes met his very steadily. He remembered an expression about your entrails withering or something. His were doing exactly that.

"It was around four, I think," she said finally. Reluctantly.

"And what happened?"

"Well, it was answered. He said . . . well, he said, 'Hello.' "

"And? Was that all?"

"Absolutely. Then there was an awful noise and then it was switched off. Well, it went silent, at least."

"Did you switch it off, Mr. Gilliatt?"

"Well, no. Not consciously. I just flung it down; the lorry was already skidding—"

"Skidding?"

"Well, swerving. Whatever. I was scared by then by what was happening. Switching the bloody phone off was the last thing on my mind. Maybe Miss Scott did it. I honestly don't know. I keep telling you, it's all a bit confused."

"Of course." Sergeant Freeman's voice was soothing. "It's entirely to be expected. Right, sir. Could we perhaps now concentrate on the actual crash? What was the first thing you were aware of, the first sign that something untoward was clearly happening?"

"I'd say the first thing I was aware of was the lorry swerving violently away from us, and I couldn't see why. It seemed to be out of control. I . . . well, I just put my brakes on and made for the hard shoulder. Managed to stop there. Incredibly lucky. I was the very last car to get through, so to speak, before the road was blocked off."

"So you stopped?"

"Yes. I . . . well, I just sat there for a moment or two, wondering what the hell had happened. And then I got out, and all the fridges and freezers and so on were spilling all over the place; it was almost surreal. And I looked back and saw this dreadful sight: the lorry, ploughed across the other side of the road, all this, this stuff everywhere, and cars just skidding, swerving, driving endlessly into one another . . ." He paused, smiled feebly across at Laura, then said, "It was all extremely . . . traumatic."

"Of course, sir. It must have been dreadful."

He waited respectfully for a moment. Then: "Now . . . if we can carry on from there, sir. What did you do next?"

Jonathan suddenly felt an odd release of tension; now that the memories were clear, unconfused, he found he could give a straightforward account; it was acutely painful reliving his genuine emotion at the death of the girl in the Golf, the young mother, the carnage of the minibus, the horror in the lorry driver's cab . . . but it was easier.

Freeman paused in his note taking, looked at him, and smiled.

"You acted very courageously, sir, by all accounts. Climbing up into the cab to switch the engine off. Most commendable."

"Well, I'm sure anyone would have done the same."

"I'm afraid you're wrong there, sir. Now, could we ask you about a girl by the lorry?"

"A girl—what girl?" He stared at him stupidly. Then, "Good God. I really had forgotten about her. Yes, of course. You know, because she just disappeared . . . I assumed . . . well, I imagined someone was looking after her, or . . . How stupid . . ."

He was genuinely embarrassed, discomfited; he could see Laura was staring at him. Another mysterious girl. Did this put him in an even worse light?

"That's perfectly all right, sir. You had a great deal on your mind."

"You could say that. Yes, I was standing with another chap; he wasn't badly hurt, just a broken arm, I think."

"Mr. Blake. It was him who told us how you climbed up into the lorry. And he said this young lady just appeared out of the van."

"Yes. Yes, she did. Well, she was actually standing on the step; I can't think she'd have climbed in to have a look. She was obviously very shocked; she vomited, didn't say anything, and then just went over to the hard shoulder and sat down on the ground, but she clearly wasn't hurt. I was too concerned about the lorry bursting into flames to pay her much attention, but when I got down on the ground again, she seemed to have disappeared. I intended to have a look for her later, but there really were more serious things to worry about. She might have turned up at the hospital; I really have no idea."

"Could you describe her?"

"Yes. She was very young, pretty, black, or certainly dark skinned; I think she was wearing a dress of some sort, and then a pair of boots. Suede boots with a sort of fur or sheepskin lining. I did notice the boots because it seemed so extraordinary on such a hot day . . ."

"UGG boots," said Laura. "They all wear them, the girls. However hot it is. Our daughters are pestering me for some."

"Right, well, thank you, Mr. Gilliatt." And then: "Now, the young lady, sir. Miss Scott. What happened to her? She wasn't hurt, I take it?"

"Well, she did cut her head. On the dashboard, as we stopped. It wasn't serious, bit of a gash. She was fine."

"And you drove on to London, I believe? After the injured had all been taken to the hospital?"

"Yes, I did."

"And Miss Scott?"

"Well, she was looking after some small boys. And she went back to the hospital in the ambulance with one of them, apparently. He had an asthma attack."

"And have you heard from her since?"

"Just that she's OK. She called to let me know—as I said, our relationship was entirely professional."

"Indeed. Fine. Well, I think that's all for now, sir. We may have to ask some more questions later."

"I really don't think I can possibly tell you anything else. I'm sorry."

"No, no, sir. It's just that if any other evidence came up, we might want to check it with you. Given that you were at the very front of the crash, one of our prime witnesses, so to speak. But you've been most helpful. Thank you very much."

· · ·

When they'd gone, he looked at Laura.

"God. Bit of an ordeal. Think I might like a drink. How about you?"

"No. No, thank you. Sorry if I dropped you in it with the phone business, but I just think it's best to be completely honest."

"Of course it is. Sure you don't want a drink?"

"Quite sure." A pause; then: "I hope you're being completely honest with me, Jonathan."

"What do you mean?" It was all he could think of to say.

"You know what I mean. About Abi Scott."

"What about her?"

"Oh, Jonathan, please! I'm not a complete cretin. You're somehow on the wrong motorway, with a strange woman whom you didn't even mention when we spoke earlier, for whom you were going to make a large detour when you were already late for your clinic. It doesn't quite add up. To me."

"Well, it should," he said. Lightly. Determined not to sound self-righteous. Or even ruffled.

"Really?"

"Really."

"What does she do, this girl? Tell me again."

"She works for a commercial photographer. Who was at the dinner, taking photographs. She helps him, gets people's names and so on. To send the photos to. She's very nice," he added. "She'd be very amused if she could hear this conversation."

"I don't see why. Is she married? Living with anyone?"

"Laura, I haven't the faintest idea!"

"Oh, really? All those hours in the car together. She must have told you something about herself."

"Well, she did say she had a boyfriend. Darling, this isn't like you. Please! Let's go and see the kids; I need a bit of distraction after all that. It wasn't the best hour of my life."

There was a long silence; then: "Yes, all right," she said. "They're watching TV."

He followed her through to the den; he felt sick and shaky. Not just because of the police interrogation, or even hers. But because there was a new darkness between them, created not just by Laura's discovery of Abi's existence, but by her clear unwillingness to accept his explanation. Lovely, lovely, trusting Laura. That was the really disturbing thing.

CHAPTER 21

It was much scarier, the second recall. All actors knew that. Far more hung on it. You had more to lose; you were higher up; you had farther to fall. The pressure was really on . . .

"I don't know if I can face it," Georgia said. "I've been feeling so terrible all the way up on the train. I thought I was going to be sick twice. I spent most of the journey in the loo."

Linda struggled to keep her voice level.

"Well, I'm sorry," she said. Georgia couldn't be pregnant, could she? That would explain a great deal. "I know how tough it is at this stage. Just the same, you're clearly in with a very fighting chance. Try to be positive, Georgia."

"I am trying," said Georgia. "It's just that I'm so tired. I can't sleep for stressing about it, and what if I don't get it, then what? I'm terrified, Linda, absolutely terrified . . ."

Linda felt a strong desire to slap her.

"Well, you don't have to go," she said. "There are three other girls, all still in the race. Just give up now, why don't you?"

Georgia stared at her. "Of course I'm not going to give up," she said, her voice throbbing with outrage. "That's a ridiculous thing to say." And then she suddenly sat down in the chair opposite Linda's desk and started to cry.

Linda pushed a contract to the back of her desk. There had to be more than this part. There had to be.

"You can't go on like this, Georgia; you'll have a nervous breakdown. What is wrong?"

Georgia looked at her, and there was something like terror in her great brown eyes. She took a deep breath and then said, "Well, it's . . . That is . . ."

"Yes?"

"Well, you see, I . . ."

And then she drew back, as if from some deep physical danger—literally shifted her body in the chair. "No, I'm sorry, Linda, really sorry. I'm being silly. I've just got my period; I feel like shit."

She wasn't pregnant then. That was something.

"OK. You going to be all right on your own?"

"Of course I am. Promise. I'll see you later."

She seemed OK. Just going a bit over-the-top emotionally. Nothing new there, then.

. . .

"That looks like a lot of paperwork." Constable Rowe smiled at Sergeant Freeman; he didn't smile back.

"It is. It's Forensics' report on the crash."

"Oh, yes. I thought you'd read it."

"I have read it," said Freeman coldly. "I like to keep referring back to it. As our investigations go on. Certain things fall into place. Or don't. And the loose wheel nut they found on the road. Where the hell does that fit in?"

"Surely it came off one of the other cars in the collision?"

"No, Rowe, it didn't. We would know that from the examination of those cars."

"Obviously, yes. And . . . not off the lorry?"

"Not off the lorry."

"Well . . . perhaps it isn't very important. Maybe it had been in the road a long time."

"I doubt that very much," said Freeman, "and so does Forensics. The devil's in the details in this game, Rowe; I've told you before. This is a detail. We just have to find out how important it is."

"Or how much of the devil is in it, I suppose," said Rowe.

"Yes, Rowe. Precisely."

. . .

At last, Mary was allowed to go home. The next day, anyway. A whole week after the accident. And even now, not exactly home—they said it was too soon for her to be on her own, but to stay with Christine. Which wasn't ideal, of course, but it was a lot better than still being in the hospital. And she got on pretty well with Christine, always had . . . although she sometimes felt, absurdly, rather nervous of her. She had inherited her father's build, rather than her mother's, and his rather heavy features, rather than her mother's sparkly prettiness.

She was wonderfully capable, ran her home along almost military lines, but she was also judgmental, very strict with her family, easily made impatient. And she was deeply conventional. So how would she react to her mother's news?

It seemed to Mary quite likely that she would be shocked, and if not shocked, disapproving. It was quite a difficult situation for any daughter: to discover that her mother had been corresponding with a man—of whose existence neither she nor her father had any knowledge—for sixty years. And that they had been—finally—reunited.

Russell came in to see her every single day, and every day, each meeting had been happier and more wonderful than the last. Any doubts that she might have had had fled, leaving her at once excited and at peace about him and his part in the rest of her life. The only thing that was unthinkable now was not being together. After sixty years of separation she and Russell were going to be married. They had been given this priceless treasure, this second life; they must nurture it and honour it and savour the happiness it so clearly contained.

Russell had continued to stay at the Dorchester; Mary had suggested he move to a hotel nearer Swindon, but he was absurdly nervous, it seemed, of anywhere other than the West End of London, had had this deep conviction that the only proper place to be was an expensive, upper-class one. She had teased him about it a lot; she could see she probably would again.

"So when I'm home in Bristol, will you still insist on staying there?" she had said, and, "No," he had said; he was investigating a hotel between Bristol and Bath that sounded pretty decent . . .

"Only pretty decent, Russell? You sure that's good enough?"

He had been fretting over the hospital too, saying he would rather she was in a private one, but she had told him that was ridiculous; this really was a very good place.

They'd had to arrange the times of his visits quite carefully, so that they didn't coincide with Christine's. He said he couldn't see the problem with that; he couldn't wait to meet Mary's children, both of them; but Mary told him she thought it might be a bit of a shock for them, particularly for Christine, who had adored her father, and she wanted her to be well prepared before being confronted by a totally strange man who would, after all, become her stepfather. It would be a hard thing for a woman of almost sixty to understand.

But now they would be alone together all day and every day, for a while, and she could tell Christine all about it. And hopefully Christine would be really happy about it. Hopefully . . .

· · ·

"Abi?" It was William's calm, deep voice. "Abi, it's William here. I've just had the police on the phone—got to give them an interview, wondered if they'd approached you as well."

"Oh, William," said Abi, thinking it would be worth going through any number of police interviews to have William discussing them with her. "William, it's great to hear from you. Yes, they have. In fact, it's tonight; I am so not looking forward to it."

"Oh, it'll be all right," he said easily. "You were just a witness, that's all; nothing to worry about. All you've got to do is give them a straightforward account of it."

She wondered, What on earth would William say if he knew about the real her . . . ? "When are they seeing you, then?"

"Tomorrow morning. I can't say I'm looking forward to it either; my father'll be getting involved, probably, telling them the field's been ruined with their helicopter."

There was a long silence, then he said: "Look. I was wondering. How would you like to have a drink tomorrow night? We can have a chat, compare notes."

"William, that'd be great. Really." Was this for real? Was he actually asking her out? God . . .

"OK. It's a date. Where should we meet, Bristol, I s'pose?"

"Well, that'd be nice. Long drive for you, though. And then you won't be able to drink much."

"Oh, I'm not a big drinker anyway. Tell me where we can meet. You can show me a few of the bright lights over there; how would that be?"

"Great," said Abi. "Really great."

"Good." He sounded slightly surprised himself. "And meanwhile, don't worry about the interview. All you've got to do is tell the truth." If only it was as simple as that; if only she hadn't got to lie and lie, and remember so many crucial things . . . "It's no big deal. What about your friend the doctor; I expect they're seeing him as well?"

"Yes, I believe so," said Abi, and then: "He's not a friend, William, just a business connection. I thought I'd told you, I'd never met him before Friday. He gave me a lift from the conference . . ." This was quite good; she could rehearse her lines.

"Oh, OK. Well, it'll be interesting to see what they do want to know. Anyway, I'll see you tomorrow night."

She sat thinking about him for a bit after ringing off: sitting there on the tractor, looking tanned and so bloody fit, with those lovely kind, sort of hazelish eyes . . .

Oh, God. What was she doing fancying a farmer, of all things? And a posh farmer at that. What was she doing seeing him? Where was the sense in that? She should be distancing herself from everyone and everything to do with the crash, not going out with them. She was bound to give the game away, slip up . . .

She had been genuinely hurt as well as angered by Jonathan's rejection of her; she had not, of course, ever imagined their affair had any real future, but somehow he had beguiled her—with his generosity, his enjoyment of her company as well as her body, his apparently genuine interest in her—into thinking he did actually care about her as a person. And how stupid had that been? Of course he hadn't. He was like all the rest of them. He had wanted what he could get out of her, and beyond that—nothing.

Abi took a very dim view of men—not unnaturally, considering what she had endured at their hands. She was aware of being something of a walking cliché: knocked about by her mother's first boyfriend, after her own father had walked out, seduced by the second, and then forced to listen to his lies that she had seduced him. Which had resulted in her being thrown out of the house at the age of fifteen. There had been a long parade of boyfriends, a few of them permanent. By the time she was twenty-one, Abi had turned into the sort of person she really didn't like—without being able to see what she could have done about it.

She couldn't suddenly become marriage material now; she couldn't wipe out her rather desperate past. No one was going to look after her; she had to do it herself, and part of that seemed to be taking her sexual pleasure where she could, rather as men did. Only it was all right for men. Even married ones like Jonathan. It was all very unfair.

The reports in the Sunday papers had been awful: the lorry driver, who she now knew was called Patrick Connell, "very seriously injured and still in intensive care"; Toby Weston, the bridegroom (the media had latched on to that story in a big way), still "heavily sedated," his leg with its multiple fractures a "grave cause for concern"; and there were several photographs of the families of people who had died, and of the blond girl in the Golf, taken on some beach the previous year, laughing, holding the hand of her boyfriend. And there were a lot of annoying stories about Jonathan, his courage, and how hard he had worked, how calm he was and how skilful. Although—annoying as they were—they were true. It was one of the reasons she didn't actually want to drop him in the shit.

. . .

What was he getting into? William wondered. It was insane, absolutely ridiculous. But . . . so what? Who said relationships had to be sensible? Wasn't that the whole point, that relationships couldn't necessarily be called to order, that an attraction was uncontrollable and could, if followed, lead to some very pleasant chaos? William would have welcomed a bit of chaos into his life just now. He was too young to be settled into total predictability, too old to have to conform to his parents' lifestyle. He wanted an adventure—and if not an adventure, at least an excursion to adventure's perimeter. And Abi had seemed to be leading him towards one, beckoning him with her long, magenta fingernails, luring him with her dark, knowing eyes. OK, she could clearly be troublesome, but God, she was a living, breathing master class in sexiness.

So . . . what was wrong with that? Absolutely nothing at all. In fact, it looked rather the reverse.

William put the tractor into gear and sent it up the hill feeling suddenly pretty bloody good.

. . .

Maeve had been sitting with Patrick for some time, and was beginning to think rather longingly of the coffee shop for what had become her supper, a latte and a cookie, and thinking also that on her way back she'd pop up and see her new friend Mary.

She was absolutely dreading Mary's going home. She was so wonderfully comforting and cheering, and filled with common sense. Maeve had told her about the dreadful possibility of Patrick's being paralysed: "It will be so unbearable for him; he's so active, so strong; he loves haring about; he can carry two of the boys and run at the same time. How will he cope with sitting in a chair for the rest of his life?"

"He will because he'll have to," Mary said. "You love him so much, and he loves you so much, and you know, Maeve, it's a wonderful thing, love. They say faith can move mountains, but to my mind so can love. But you don't know; he may recover completely—they can do such wonderful things these days . . ."

Maeve had thought Patrick was getting more with it, as she put it, day by day. It might be a long time before he came home, and the very least he had to face was major abdominal surgery, but he was still alive, which a week ago had seemed far too much to hope for. She was saying all this to Patrick when he reached out for her hand and squeezed it very tightly, and said, "Maeve—I'm beginning to remember."

"Remember . . . what?" she said, and there was a band round her chest as tight as his hand round hers.

"The accident. What happened. How it happened. It was hot. Terribly hot. The sun was so bright. And I was so tired, Maeve. So tired . . ."

"Oh, Patrick . . ." She'd been terrified of this ever since she'd heard about it, certainly since she'd known he was going to live. She wanted to stop him, to shut him up, to keep him—and her—safe from the memories. But . . .

"I was eating jelly babies, you know, and they weren't working. I can remember eating them, lots of them, handfuls, I could feel my head going, you know? The fuzzing, I've told you about the fuzzing."

"Yes, Patrick, you have."

He had: the feeling his brain was getting confused, not working for him.

"I went to the doctor about it, you know, but he couldn't help. That's all I can remember. The fuzzing—and then blankness."

"Yes, but Patrick, darling, that was when you blacked out. Lost consciousness. Not went to sleep. Went unconscious. Of course you can't remember."

"I think . . . well, I think I can. And Maeve . . . I think there was someone else in the cab."

"Someone else? What do you mean?"

"I don't know. I just seem to remember . . . remember . . . there was someone else there."

"But, Patrick, how could there have been? There was no one with you when they found you, and where could they have gone . . ."

"I know. But I still think . . . Oh, I'm so afraid, Maeve. So afraid I must have . . . must have . . . gone . . . gone to . . ."

And then he stopped talking and tears squeezed slowly and painfully from his eyes, rolled down his cheeks, large, childlike tears. And Maeve, still clutching his hand, stroking it, trying to comfort him, thought that if he had gone to sleep, if he had caused that awful, dreadful crash, for which he had been punished, and was still being punished so horribly, then she was to blame as well: for hassling him, hurrying him home, when perhaps another hour or two of rest would have made all the difference. All the difference in the world—and for some people, indeed, the difference between life and death.

* * *

"Dr. King? Emma?"

Emma turned to see who had called her and saw Barney Fraser, Toby Weston's friend.

"I thought it was you. How are you?"

He was looking different. She couldn't think why, then realised he was in his city togs: sharp suit (although the jacket was slung over his shoulder), formal shirt (pink check, *really* suited him), tie even (although hanging loose round his neck).

"Good."

"I'm on my way to the café, get a shot of caffeine before I go back to town. You?"

"I'm in search of caffeine, too."

"OK . . . we could go together."

He smiled at her. God, he had a wonderful smile. God, he was so gorgeous . . . *Stop it, Emma. He's taken. And so are you . . . now.*

"OK. Mustn't be long, though."

They went into the café; she grabbed a Diet Coke, and then joined him at the coffee counter, ordered an Americano.

"Snap. Same as me. I actually wanted a double espresso, but they're not great at coffee-speak here. Can you sit down for five minutes? Or do you have to rush back?"

"Well, five minutes."

"Cool."

"So, have you been visiting Toby?"

"Yes, I have."

"Driven all the way down from London?"

"No, I came on the train. I'm about to call a cab; there's a notice about them in the main reception. How's the service this time of night?"

"Not bad. Not great. How . . . how is Toby?"

She knew he wasn't very well; she'd talked to Mark Collins about him the day before. He had been running recurrent fevers from Sunday night, and complaining of feeling generally unwell. Today he even seemed confused.

"It points to infection, I'm afraid," Mark had said. "We've upped the antibiotics and we're going to take him to the theatre tomorrow and do a washout. And the end of this road—the bad end, anyway— well, you know what it is as well as I do."

Amputation, Emma thought, wincing: what a terrifying prospect for a bloke of thirty. She hoped Barney didn't realise that, at least.

"How is he?" she said again. As if she didn't know.

"Not great. They did some washout thing today."

"Well," she said carefully, "that should do some good . . ."

"And if it doesn't, he'll lose the leg, right?"

She was shocked.

"Nobody here told you that, did they?"

"No, no, I rang a mate who's a medic."

"Oh. Oh, I see. Well, without knowing Toby's case—"

"Emma, it's OK. I've taken it on board. It's hideous, but—"

"But it really would be a last resort. And I'm sure—well, I hope—he's miles from that. I . . . I hope you haven't told his parents this."

"No, of course I haven't. I'm not a total retard."

"Sorry. It's just . . . well, we have to be so careful about that sort of thing."

"I'm sure. No, it's fine; I haven't told anyone. Except Amanda, that is."

Amanda. The preppy, perfect girlfriend. Correction, the preppy, perfect fiancée.

"How did Toby seem in himself?"

"Oh, bit out of it, actually. When . . . when will they know if it's worked?"

"Oh, not for several more days. Um . . . what about his fiancée; has she been down much?"

"I'm not sure. She's still at home with her parents, getting over her cancelled wedding."

His voice sounded bitter; Emma looked at him sharply. He interpreted the look, said, "Sorry, shouldn't have said that."

"You can say what you like to me, Barney. But . . . well, it must be pretty awful for her, worrying about Toby, and she wouldn't be human if she wasn't upset about the wedding . . ."

"Of course."

"What do you all do?" she said with a glance at her watch.

"Oh, Tobes and I are those wicked banker people. You know, earn as much as the budget of a small country. If you believe the press, that is."

"And Amanda, what does she do?"

"She's in HR. In the same bank as Tobes. And Tamara, she's on the French desk at my firm. Yeah, so it's all a bit incestuous, really. Tamara is seriously cool. You should see their apartment—talk about retro."

"I probably wouldn't appreciate it," said Emma, laughing. "I'm still at the furnished-flat stage myself."

"Yeah? How long will you be here, do you think? Moving on, up to London or whatever?"

"I have no idea where I'll be. But I want, eventually, to go into obstetrics. At the moment I'm just a general surgeon. Doing my four months' stint down here, in A and E, which I do love."

"You're a surgeon? You mean you actually . . . well—"

"Cut people up? Yes, I do." She laughed. "Don't look so horrified."

"Not horrified. Just seriously impressed. I mean, you don't look old enough—well, hardly—to be a doctor at all, and—"

"Oh, don't," she said. "If I had a pound for every time I'm told that . . . I think I'll put it on my tombstone: 'She didn't look old enough . . .' Barney, I really must go. It's been lovely talking to you, but God knows what's happening down there." She nodded in the direction of A&E. "Look, I'll pop up and see Toby tomorrow. If you think he'd like that."

"Emma, anyone out of short trousers would like being visited by you. Actually, even if they were in short trousers. Thank you so much. And for your time. Really cheered me up."

"It was a pleasure. Honestly."

She held out her hand; he took it, then rather hesitantly bent down and kissed her cheek.

"Pleasure for me too. Honestly. Thank you again. For all your help, not just this evening."

And then he was gone, hurrying out of the café, pulling on his jacket.

Emma walked rather slowly back to A&E, then sat down at the doctor's station and said, "Shit."

And Barney, settling into the corner of a cab, on his way to the station, said, "Fuck."

For much the same reason.

❖ CHAPTER 22 ❖

It had gone pretty well, Abi thought. They'd questioned her closely, but she hadn't let them rattle her.

She'd been pretty stressed by a panicky phone call from Jonathan very early that morning, telling her more things that she must and must not say. Like the time they left the conference in Birmingham—that she must be vague, say between eleven thirty and twelve, that they'd been held up at the service station, and—change of information—he had now told them Laura had called his mobile at four. "Well, she told them, actually. But she said she only heard me saying hello and then it all went blank. Just say it rang and I answered it and hurled it on the floor when the lorry started to swerve. It might not even come up. Did you switch the phone off, incidentally? I didn't, and—"

"Yes, I did."

"Fine. Well, I think that's everything. Bye, then."

She didn't answer. She felt very bleak suddenly, bleak and alone. He hadn't even said "good luck." *Bastard.* God, how she hated him.

Anyway, she'd said what he'd told her: about their relationship, about her car not starting so she'd gone by train to the conference, and then all the stuff about the accident—a relief to be able to relax and just speak the truth for a bit—and then she'd told them how marvellous Jonathan had been afterwards. Which had been true as well.

She said they'd hardly spoken since then, just that she'd reassured him that she was safely home . . .

She was actually quite pleased with herself, felt high with relief. And at least it was over. The very worst was over . . .

And now she had her evening with William to look forward to . . .

. . .

"Well, what did you think of that, then?" Freeman closed his notebook, filed Abi's statement carefully, and turned to Constable Rowe.

"Oh, she seemed rather nice," said Rowe. "Very, very sexy."

"Indeed. Any man would be tempted by her. Even a man with a beautiful wife . . . You didn't think her story was in any way suspicious?"

"No. It tallied exactly with Dr. Gilliatt's."

"Too exactly, I'd say. Almost word for word. Like 'it was a purely professional relationship.' Why did they both have to tell us that, do you think? It's not relevant. And about her car not starting—she just volunteered that; we didn't ask her. It was all a bit . . . pat. Something's starting to smell a bit here; something's not quite right . . ."

"Yes, but why should they be lying?"

"Well, in his case, his whole marriage hangs on it. For her . . . well, maybe she thinks if she goes along with him he'll carry on with the relationship. She probably gets some pretty good perks out of it; these girls do, you know: expensive little trips abroad, for instance, staying in the best hotels, jewellery—"

"What's it got to do with the crash? Doesn't mean they're guilty of anything else."

"No, of course not. He might have been—almost certainly was, I'd say—screwing her into the ground. That doesn't mean he's guilty of dangerous driving, or of causing that crash. But maybe he was partly to blame. Maybe she was. Maybe he was driving dangerously; maybe she was distracting him. I wouldn't be totally surprised if he slewed out into the road, in front of the lorry. In the absence of any other explanation for it suddenly swerving—"

"The driver could have gone to sleep."

"He could. He could also have had to swerve. Anyway, we've got Gilliatt's measure now. We can take other things he says with a pinch of salt. We'll tuck this into our back teeth and keep it there. All right?"

"Yes, all right," said Constable Rowe.

Freeman smiled for the first time that day. "That's why this game is such fun, in its own peculiar way. I think we have to go back in, ask a few more questions. And we must take a very close look at the CCTV footage at the service station, see what we can pick up there . . . Also her firm—what's it called? Oh, yes, Conferphoto—check whether they did actually cover this conference."

"Should I check with her firm or the conference organisers?"

"The organisers. We don't want her rattled, thinking we're on to her. We don't want to rattle either of them in any way. You know what they say, Rowe: give them enough rope and they'll hang themselves."

. . .

"Poor Mr. Connell." Jo Wales walked into the nurses' room on HDU. The police had become very pressing about questioning Patrick, and reluctantly his doctors had agreed. Jo had sat in on the interview, and her conviction that it was too soon had strengthened with every moment.

"Did they upset him?" Her colleague, Stephanie Hitchens, who had also nursed Patrick, had been equally against the interview.

"Yes, they did. I nearly stopped it twice—sorry, Maria," she said to the Spanish cleaner whose path she was obstructing. "Anyway, he recovered himself each time. So I let them have their fifteen minutes."

"Are we any the wiser?"

"Oh, not really. Still going on about going to sleep, remembering getting drowsy, eating his jelly babies—in tears once. That's when I asked them to go, but he said he was all right, wanted to finish. And he said he thought there might have been someone in the cab with him."

"Really? Seems very unlikely. I mean, where could such a person have gone?"

"Well, exactly. But of course the police got very interested in it, started questioning him more closely—he got very upset."

"Poor Patrick. There he is, the sweetest man, having to cope with all this horror. I'll pop along and chat with him for a bit."

Maria, whose English was much better than most people in the hospital realised, finished her desultory floor wiping and set off for the lift. That would give her something to tell the journalist who had been pestering her for information for the past few days. And she should get that fifty pounds he had promised her . . .

. . .

Jack Bryant had had a good week. He'd bagged over a hundred brace of grouse, eaten some excellent meals, and furthered his acquaintance with Margo Farthringoe most satisfactorily. She was fifty-one, modestly good-looking, extremely sexy, and a very good shot. She was also newly separated from Gordon Farthringoe, who was disporting himself around town with a fine example of twenty-two-year-old arm candy. Margo and Jack had enjoyed a great deal together that week, and arranged to meet in London in the near future.

Jack was loading up the boot of the E-Type with as much grouse as he could decently take away with him when he thought he should give the car the once-over. She wasn't as young as she had been, and she needed a lot of TLC. Everything seemed fine: except that she seemed to have lost a wheel nut. Bit of a bugger.

He had no idea where he might have lost it, decided it would be foolhardy to try to drive back down the M1 without it, and embarked on a quest for a new one. It took most of the day; the border country was not rich in specialist garages. His irritation was considerably eased, however, by the offer of a further night at the Mackintoshes', and a further foray into the arms of Mrs. Farthringoe.

. . .

Linda went over to her fridge and took out one of the minibottles of champagne she kept there for such moments. She poured herself a glass, savoured it for a moment, then lifted the phone, dialled Georgia's mobile number.

"Darling, it's good news. I mean *really* good news. They want you."

"Oh . . . God. Oh, God, Linda, that is so . . . so cool!"

God, thought Linda, *that word. That inadequate, all-purpose word.*

"I know. It's lovely. Many, many congratulations. I'm totally thrilled. What are you doing now?"

"I'm in Topshop. Oxford Circus. With a friend. I'm staying with her."

"Well, want to come over, have a glass of bubbly? You can bring the friend."

"Can I? Linda, we'd really love that; thanks so much. Can we come over right now? We'll be about thirty minutes."

"Great. I'll get the glasses out."

"Cool!"

. . .

"So . . . how was it?" William said.

He had driven to Bristol to meet Abi in a state of considerable emotional turmoil; he felt anxious and excited in just about equal measure, alternately wishing he had obeyed his innate instinct that he shouldn't see her again and wondering why on earth he hadn't invited her out sooner. She was so bloody sexy, and seemed really nice too, much nicer than you'd have thought a girl like her would be, and seemed (only seemed, he was sure) to like him too.

Of course, a relationship between them was a pretty futile idea; she obviously lived life very much in the fast lane (an unfortunate choice of words, he thought, smiling to himself), and his was . . . well, from her point of view, anyway, pretty much in the very slow one.

And as for what his mother would have to say . . . the whole thing was pointless, and this must be a one-off evening, dedicated—as he had said when he called her—to discussing their respective interviews with the police.

But then . . . he'd walked into the bar she'd suggested, and she had waved at him, walked over to meet him, kissed him hello—her perfume was incredibly powerful, musky and sweet—taken his hand, and led him back to her table. He had said he mustn't drink, that he had to drive; three beers later, his head was swimming a bit and he was wondering rather anxiously how he was going to get home. Maybe if they had a meal—a large meal—and he drank only water he'd sober up sufficiently.

He would not have drunk so much had he not found himself so relaxed; he might have expected to find someone like her hard to talk to, but she was easily chatty and funny, and she had a talent for listening too, asking him endless questions about the farm, about his life, about his parents, even, and displaying what seemed a genuine interest in the answers.

And he had slowly become aware that one of her long legs was pressing against his, that she was leaning closer to him, that she was studying his mouth as he talked; the combination of all these things, together with the three beers and the heady cloud of her perfume, was making him feel physically dizzy . . . surely, surely she couldn't fancy him . . . ?

"Oh, it was OK. I think," she said now. "I'm glad it's over. But they were very nice. You?"

"Oh, I think it was OK. Wonder if we had the same ones? I had Sergeant Freeman and Constable Rowe, his sidekick."

"Yes, the same."

. . .

God, he was so . . . so gorgeous. She would never have believed she would find herself fancying someone like him: so public-school, so straight-down-the-line, so old-style polite. He actually came round to push in her chair, for God's sake, stood up when she went to the toilet and again when she came back.

She felt like . . . well, she felt like someone completely different. The sort of person who'd grown up used to that sort of thing herself. It was like being stroked, or eating chocolates, or lying in the sun; it was soothing, warming, totally pleasing.

And he was so incredibly good-looking. He could have been a model, if he'd wanted. OK, his haircut was a bit dated, but it suited him. It was great hair. That wonderful rich, conker brown and then sort of blond streaks.

He had no idea how attractive he was. He was a bit like a child, completely unself-conscious; she looked at him now, sitting in the bar, his long legs stretched out in front of him, his shirtsleeves pushed up to the elbows, showing his brown arms—so brown, they were, covered in thick blond hair—grinning at her, talking about the farm, about how much he loved it in spite of everything, loved being out-of-doors all the time, about the satisfaction of it, of harvesting the wheat, of rearing healthy animals.

"My brother's an accountant, one of those city types. Now, that's an awful existence, pushing money around, helping rich people stay as rich as they can. It's a mean, selfish little life."

She was surprised by how articulate he was; somehow she'd always imagined farmers would be the strong, silent type. When he moved on to the supermarkets and how they screwed the farmers into the ground, ruined the small ones, she began to care about them too, enjoying listening to his deep, rich voice—and yes, it was a bit posh, and she didn't usually like posh, but it was his. So she liked it.

"Sorry, Abi; you mustn't let me bore you. You probably want to talk about our respective interviews with the police."

"You're not boring me," she said, "and I don't want to. Plenty of time for that."

"Fine. Look, I've had far too much to drink. Can we find somewhere to eat and let me buy you dinner? I need to consume about five thousand calories even to start to mop it all up. We could talk about the interviews then. Or . . . maybe you've got other plans?"

Abi said no—no, she hadn't, and dinner would be great.

He suggested Browns; he would know Browns, she thought; it was made for people like him. She didn't often go there; it was . . . well, full of people like him. Which tonight seemed pretty good.

"So, come on," he said when they had ordered—a large steak for him, a crab salad for her. "What about you? Tell me about your job, tell me about your family, tell me what you like doing."

She had an almost irresistible urge to tell him what she really liked doing and how much she'd like to do it with him, but suppressed it and gave him as sanitised a version as she could of her life, her friends, her job. She cut out the lingerie modelling, the drugs, and—obviously—most of her boyfriends. Especially the last one.

"So . . . no one serious at the moment?"

"No."

"I can't think why not."

He looked so genuinely baffled she wanted to kiss him. She did kiss him. Only on the cheek, but . . .

"What was that for?" he said, grinning at her.

"For wondering why I hadn't got a serious boyfriend. I wish . . ."

"But why not? I really can't imagine."

"Because they're mostly rubbish, that's why. The men I meet. Spoilt. Up on themselves. Waste of space."

"Well, that's pretty damning," he said, laughing. "You must have met a particularly bad lot. I feel I should make an apology for my sex. No, seriously. You've obviously been very hurt by . . . by someone."

"Yes, lots," she said, and then the person who had hurt her the most and the most recently swam before her eyes, and the magic was gone, albeit briefly, and she felt suddenly and dreadfully sad.

"Well, I'm sorry," he said. He was clearly much too much of a gentleman to ask her about it; and she could hardly tell him. So they sat in silence for a moment or two, and then he said, "Look, I should be getting back quite soon and we've still not talked about our interviews. So . . . how was yours? Really? Was it as awful as you expected?"

"No. No, it was fine. They were very nice. Much less scary than I expected. Yours?"

"Also very nice. Very thorough. They went into absolutely everything. Who I talked to, all that sort of thing. They even asked about you."

"Me! What did they ask about me, for heaven's sake?"

"Oh, well, I told them how great you were, helping the little boys. How you went to the hospital with one of them. And then they asked me if I knew anything about your relationship with the doctor bloke."

"My relationship with . . . But I don't . . . That is, why should they ask you that?"

"No idea. Well, first they asked what happened to your car, why it wasn't still on the motorway, and I said you'd been with the doctor in his. And then they asked me if I knew anything about your relationship with him. I said absolutely nothing, except that it was a professional one, that you'd been at a conference together."

"Oh. Right."

"Oh, and I said he seemed pretty tense, was shouting at you at one point."

"Well, he was. Quite true."

Did it matter, their knowing that? Not really. And William had said all the right things: that her relationship with Jonathan was only professional. But . . . why were they interested? It was a bit worrying.

"Anyway, that was about it, really. Ah, here's the bill. No, no, I insist"—as she fumbled for her cards—"don't be silly. Look, can I drop you anywhere?"

God, he was such a fucking gentleman; most men, after buying you three cocktails and dinner, would expect to be well into your knickers.

"No, it's OK; I'll get a cab."

"Oh, now, that's ridiculous. I'll just drive you home."

Maybe he did want to. It seemed crazy not to find out.

They went out to the street, and as they walked to his car, she put her arm through his, and he looked down at her and smiled in that . . . God, that sort of . . . sort of charming way, and then he said, "Come in, hop in."

Abi hopped.

It was a ten-minute drive; as they parked outside the block on her bleak, narrow street, she said, hoping she sounded like the nice girl he seemed to imagine she was, "Would you like to come in for a coffee?"

"I'd love to, but I really mustn't. My ghastly brother's coming down tomorrow—"

"What, the accountant?"

"That's the one. God, I must be boring. Banging on about my family."

"William," said Abi, reaching up to kiss his cheek, "you couldn't ever be boring. I could listen to you all"—she had been going to say "all night" but amended it hastily to—"all day. Even talking about your cows. Your girls, as you call them."

He did; she had found that unbelievably sweet.

"Really?" She was sure if it had been light, she would have seen him blushing. He did blush; became discomfited quite easily. He wasn't exactly shy, but he was quite . . . bashful. The other thing he did was giggle. He had a wonderful laugh, a booming, roaring laugh, but he also, when suddenly amused, giggled uncontrollably and infectiously.

"So why is he coming? Your brother? Family party?"

"No, no. It's business. Potentially difficult, actually. Which is why I want to have a clear head."

"Why? In what way?"

"Oh, Abi, I've bored you enough."

"No, you haven't. Come on in and tell me about it."

She knew Sylvie was out—for the night. They'd be quite . . . undisturbed.

He said nothing, just got out of the car, came round, and opened the door for her. This was just . . . ridiculous She felt she was in a fifties movie or something. She got out, smiling, trying to be graceful and ladylike, and promptly tripped on a jutting paving stone and fell forwards.

His arms went out to catch her and, having caught her, somehow went round her; and she stood there, held by him, looking up at him, and he was looking down at her, and then slowly, rather tentatively, he bent his head and started to kiss her. And having started, continued, and it was the most fantastic kiss, hard and probing and quite slow at the same time; and she felt herself responding in the most unladylike way, meeting his tongue with hers, feeling the kiss working, moving downwards, the sensation warm and invasive, rippling out in a series of ever bigger sensations, and she pushed her hips against him, felt him responding; and then suddenly he drew back, stopped kissing her, just looked down at her, half smiling, half-embarrassed, and she said, "Why?"

And he said, "Abi, I'm sorry, I—"

"Sorry?" she said, and then, "Fuck sorry, William; just do it again, or come in, or—"

But, "No," he said, "I mustn't. Honestly, Abi, I'd love to, I really would, but we hardly know each other."

And that made her laugh, rather weakly, leaning against him and pulling his head down and kissing him, quite differently now, on the cheek, on his nose.

"You really are special," she said, "so, so special. Promise me one thing: let's do it again, very soon."

"What, drinks, dinner—"

"Yes, if you want. Drinks, dinner, kiss, and then see what happens next. OK?"

He was silent, looking down at her very seriously, and . . . *God,* she thought, *I've gone too far, acted like a tart*; and then he smiled, almost embarrassed, and said, "Yeah, well, that'd be great. Absolutely great. I'll ring you, OK?"

"You'd better," she said, releasing herself from him, grinning at him, walking towards the front door of her block. "And if you don't, I'll ring you. I haven't been very well brought up, you see. That's what I do, ring blokes I fancy. Night, William—thanks for a great evening."

"No," he said, "no, thank you. It's been terrific. You're very special too, Abi. I hope you know that."

And he drove off slowly, and she stood there looking after him, and then went inside and got into bed, and lay there wide-awake, still excited, still hardly touching reality, wondering how soon she might see him again and whether that time she would be able to persuade him into bed with her. Even though . . . what was it he'd said? Oh, yes, even though they hardly knew each other. Incredible that people still thought like that. Absolutely incredible . . .

. . .

And William drove home rather slowly, playing his favourite Bruce Springsteen CD, and wondering if it was even remotely possible that a girl as sexy and funny and fun as Abi could possibly enjoy being with him, and whether she'd meant it when she'd said she'd like to go out with him again.

CHAPTER 23

Laura wanted to believe Jonathan more than anything on earth. About Abi Scott. Her whole life and happiness hung on it. Because if it wasn't true, if he'd been having an affair with her—with anyone— then there was no way she could stay with him. She had always felt that trust was absolutely synonymous with love. However wonderful Jonathan was, however good their marriage was, however perfect their life, if he'd betrayed her, she couldn't possibly go on with it. How could you go to sleep beside a man, wake up with him, live in his house, bring up his children, if he had lied to you, if all those "I love you"s, all those "I couldn't live without you"s, had been said to someone else?

If he had made love to someone else, known her body intimately, caressed her, entered her, made her come, then how could you possibly stay with him, accept those lies, forgive them—and him? How would you ever believe him again if he said he was working late, on a business trip, dining with colleagues? Suspicion would poison every smile, every kiss, every caress; would distort pleasure, wreck contentment, ruin memory. That was the worst thing, perhaps: that you would remember all the most precious times—the commitment to stay together forever, the arrival of the babies, the sweetly charged intimacies of marriage—and know it had all been a sham, see it as distorted, ugly, cruelly changed.

She was trying—so hard—to get it back, the happiness and the trust. But until she knew for sure, she was failing. And becoming obsessed with the need to know . . .

• • •

"Now, this is interesting," said Freeman. They were examining CCTV footage. "Here we have our best man standing in the queue for the tyre gauge."

"What's wrong with that?" said Rowe.

"Nothing. It's the responsible thing to do—especially if you're thinking of driving rather fast. But the point is, Mr. Fraser told us he hadn't done anything at the service station except get fuel."

"Well, I expect he just didn't mention it. Forgot."

"Rowe, you don't forget things like that. Especially when x minutes later your tyre bursts and contributes to a major accident. No, I think we should perhaps talk to Mr. Fraser again. Ask him about it. Or—which might be cleverer—talk to the bridegroom. Get a separate account."

"You can't do that yet," said Rowe. "He's very unwell. I thought they said he might be having major surgery on Monday."

"Mr. Connell is also very unwell. We learnt quite a lot from him."

"That's true. Although it was pretty muddled. All that stuff about feeling sleepy and eating jelly babies. And the second person in the van."

"I've told you before, Rowe, the devil's in the details in this game." If he said that once more, Rowe thought, he'd thump him. "The very fact that he was talking about jelly babies, not just chocolate, could be important. If he can be precise about his sweets, then we can take more notice of the rest of his testimony.

"Now, it could be his confusion, this second person in the van. But put together with—what—three reports now about this mysterious girl at the scene of the crash, I think it bears a very close look indeed." He paused. "You know, Rowe, I'm wondering if we can get the media interested in this one. We'd get more eyewitnesses to what actually happened. And in particular, who else might have seen this girl, and a second person in the lorry—who, of course, are not necessarily one and the same. I think I'll talk to the PR department first thing Monday. See if they can get it on the news."

"So how would we go about it?"

"Oh, we—or the PR people—contact one of their researchers, give them the story, make it sound as interesting as we can; after that it's up to them. Bit of a beauty contest, really—"

"I wonder if they ever found that missing dog," said Rowe suddenly, "the golden retriever. That would be the sort of thing they'd like . . ."

There was a silence; then Freeman said, slightly grudgingly, "It could be, yes. Why don't you check it out, Rowe?"

. . .

Georgia was beginning to feel she had two heads. Or two selves. It was very odd. There was the Georgia who had just got a part in a prestigious TV series, who was feeling pretty pleased with herself; and there was the other Georgia, who was scared and miserable and ashamed of herself, who didn't remotely know what to do to make things better. Or rather who did know, but seemed to entirely lack the courage to do it.

She could be walking through Cardiff, going to meet a friend, listening to her iPod, and looking in the windows of Topshop, and without warning the terror would be there, the terror and the awful despair. She would stand still, shaking, feeling she would never move again, trying to set aside the memories and the guilt, and then she would have to call the friend, plead illness, and go home again, creeping under her duvet, crying, sometimes for hours at time.

And then, equally without reason, it would go again, and she would find herself able to say, Well, was it really so bad, what she had done? And no one need ever know, and one day, yes, one day she would go and see Patrick—who was, after all, still alive—and say she was sorry . . .

Only . . . she knew she couldn't. She really, really couldn't.

. . .

"Wednesday's the big day now," said Toby. He had rung Barney at work; his voice was painfully cheerful.

"Yeah? For . . . what?"

As if he didn't know.

"Oh—this final washout thing. If they don't think it's working then—"

"Well, then, they'll try again," said Barney.

"Mate, they won't," said Toby.

"Course they will. They're not going to give up on you."

"No. Just take the leg off. Or some of it."

"Oh, Tobes. Of . . . of course they're not. Whatever makes you think that?"

"Because the fucking doctor told me so. He was very nice, very positive, said he was fairly confident that it would be OK, but we had to face the fact it might not be. I'll have to sign a consent thing, apparently, before I go down. Shit, Barney, I'm scared."

There was a silence; then Barney said, "So . . . have you told Tamara?"

"Oh, no, no. I thought it would upset her too much."

"Well, that's very brave of you," Barney said carefully. "What about your parents?"

"No, I haven't told them either. Poor old Mum, she's upset enough as it is."

"Well . . ." Barney sought wildly round for something to say that might help. "Well . . . tell you what, Tobes: would you like me to come down on Wednesday? Be there when it's done? Not in the operating theatre, of course—don't think I could cope with that—but I'll spend the time beforehand with you, be there when you come back. With two good legs, obviously."

"Shit, Barney, you are the best. Would you really? Yeah, that'd be great. They said it'd be the afternoon probably. I was thinking what a ghastly long day it would be. But . . . you'll be—"

"I'll be there . . ."

Sometime, when Toby felt better, Barney thought, they should discuss the little matter of the tyre. Just so that they were saying the same thing. If anyone asked Toby. Which they probably wouldn't . . .

<h2>CHAPTER 24</h2>

Patrick was in the grip of a horror and fear that had a physical presence, that were invading him as surely as the pain had done on the day of the accident. Somehow talking to the police had made it worse, had made him more certain that he had gone to sleep; just hearing his own voice, describing it, made it seem impossible that there had been another explanation. He had killed all those people, ruined all those lives; it was his fault; he had blood on his hands as surely as if he had taken a gun and shot them all.

And not being able to remember anything made it worse, rendered him completely out of control. They'd told him it would come back, his memory, but the more he tried to remember, the more difficult it got; it was like trying to see through a fog that was thickening by the day. Even the other person in the van seemed to be disappearing into that fog. And even if someone had been there, he had still been at the wheel . . .

The horror never left him; he lay for hours just wrestling with it, woke to it, slept his drugged sleep with it, dreamed of it. There was no room for anything else: for hope, for calm—just the horror rendering it ugly and even obscene. It was all going to go on until he died; there was no escape anywhere. He reflected on all the skill and care that were going into his recovery, or his possible recovery, and there seemed no point, absolutely no point at all in any of it. He wished it would stop altogether; he wished he could stop.

And then in a moment of revelation, it came to him that actually, if he really wanted that, he could.

. . .

"You look tired, Mum; why don't you go through and watch TV. Gerry'll help me clear away, won't you, Gerry?"

"Oh . . . no," said Mary. Her heart thumped uncomfortably. "Look . . . I'd like to talk to you both about something. The thing is . . . well, look, dears, this may come as . . . well, as a bit of a surprise to you, but you know I was on my way to London last week? The day of the crash? I wasn't entirely honest about the reason. I was going to meet someone."

"Yes, you said . . . A friend."

"Indeed. But he was a little more than a friend."

"He? Mum, what have you been up to?"

Christine's eyes were dancing.

"Well, the person I went to meet was an American gentleman. Called Russell Mackenzie."

"Good heavens! And—"

"Well, and we met a very long time ago. During the war. He was a GI and we . . . well, we became very fond of each other."

"What, you had an affair, you mean?"

"Certainly not," said Mary. "Not in the way you mean. We didn't do that sort of thing in those days. Well, I didn't, anyway."

"But . . . you were in love with him?"

"Yes," said Mary. "Very much."

"Gosh, how romantic. Weren't you tempted to marry him, go out there after the war, be a GI bride or whatever?"

"No. I wasn't. I had promised to marry your father; we were unofficially engaged. He was in a prisoner-of-war camp. As you know."

"But . . . you still had an affair—all right, a relationship—with this chap?"

"Yes, I did. But he knew there was no future in it, that I was going to marry your father."

"But he carried on . . . chasing you? And you let him?"

"Well . . . yes. I know it's hard for you to understand, but it was wartime; things were very different."

"Of course. Anyway, he went back to the States?"

"Yes, and married someone else in due course, and I married your father. But . . . we kept in touch. We wrote . . . regularly. All through the years. We remained very . . . close. In an odd way."

"How regularly? A few times a year?"

It was best to be truthful. This was too important not to be. "No, we wrote at least once a month."

"Once a month! Did Dad know?"

"No, he had no idea. I knew it would . . . upset him. That he wouldn't understand."

"I'm not sure I do either." Christine's face was suddenly flushed.

"You're telling me you were so involved with this man you wrote to him every month, for years and years and years, right through your marriage, but it didn't affect your feelings for Dad?"

"Yes, that's right."

"But, Mum, it must have done. I couldn't deceive Gerry like that."

"It wasn't exactly deceit, dear."

"Mum, it was. Did he tell his wife? This Russell person?"

"No, he didn't."

"Well, it sounds pretty unbelievable. I mean that all you did was write. Did he ever come over; did you meet him without Dad knowing?"

"No, Christine, I didn't. I wouldn't have done that."

"Well, go on." She was looking almost hostile now. "What happened next in this romantic story?"

"Chris!" Gerry was looking very uncomfortable. "Don't get upset."

"Well, I am upset. I suddenly discover there's been another man in my mother's life that my father didn't know about—if Dad had found out, Mum, don't you think he'd have been upset?"

"Yes, I do. Which was why I never told him."

"Well, then. It was wrong. Anyway, go on."

Mary felt like crying; this was exactly what she had feared.

"Well, now, you see, Russell's wife has died, and . . . he's come over to see me, and we . . . well, we still feel very fond of each other."

"Has he been to the hospital?"

"Yes, he has."

"But you didn't tell me?"

"No, dear."

"You were obviously feeling guilty about it. That proves it, as far as I'm concerned. He was there, in your marriage to Dad, even if Dad didn't know. I think it's really, really bad."

"Chris. Easy! Your mum's done nothing wrong."

"Well, I'm sorry, but that's a matter of opinion. Anyway, what happens next? I hope he's not coming here."

"Not if you don't want him to."

"I don't."

"But I would like you to meet him."

"I don't want to meet him."

"But, Christine, we are planning to spend a lot of time together. A lot. I know you'd like him if you only met him."

"I don't want to like him. And what does 'a lot' mean? I hope you're not planning to set up house with him or something?"

"Chris!" said Gerry.

Mary met her daughter's eyes steadily. She had hoped to take it gently, to let Chris meet Russell, get to know him, but—

"Actually," she said, "we are hoping to . . . well, to get married. We feel very strongly that we've spent enough time apart."

"Oh, please spare me. You've been reading too many Mills and Boon books, Mum. You've not been apart from this man; you've been married to Dad. Whom you were supposed to love. Poor old Dad! He must be turning in his grave."

"Chris," said Gerry, "I think we've had enough of this conversation. You're really upsetting your mother."

"Good. She's upset me. And I don't know what Timothy's going to say. Oh, I'm going to go and do the clearing up. I'll see you both in the morning."

Mary felt dreadful. Russell had been wrong: he'd said Christine would understand, would be happy for her. Now what could she do? Everything was spoilt suddenly; she felt guilty and ashamed, instead of happy and excited.

She went to bed and lay thinking about Donald, and that he would actually have minded very much if he had known, and feeling, for the very first time, that she had betrayed him.

. . .

"I know it's awful of me," said Tamara, slipping her arm through Barney's as they walked towards the lift, "but I'm beginning to feel just the tiniest bit selfish about all this. I mean, I haven't said one word to Tobes, obviously, and he can't help what's happened, but . . ."

Her voice trailed away; Barney felt a wave of rage so violent he actually wanted to hit her, instead of taking her for a drink, as she had persuaded him to do. She had come back to work at the beginning of the week—"Well, I was so bored, and fed up, working suddenly looked like quite fun by comparison"—and had appeared by his desk after lunch, suggesting that they should go for a drink after work.

And so here he was, up on the forty-second floor of Vertigo with her, and faced by at least an hour of her phony distress—well, he supposed the distress was genuine; it was just over the wrong cause . . .

"Yes," she said, sipping thoughtfully at her champagne, "like I was saying, Barney, I just can't help it; I feel really, really bad."

"About Toby, you mean?"

"Well, yes, obviously, poor angel."

"How do you think he's doing?" said Barney, desperate to postpone the moment when she would clearly expect sympathy. "With his leg, I mean?"

"Oh, darling, I don't know. The doctors don't seem to know what to think about it—between you and me I wonder if they know what they're doing half the time—but Toby seems to think they're marvellous, and his parents do too. I mean, I'd have insisted he went private, but it's not up to me, of course. Apparently they've made inquiries and been told he couldn't be anywhere better . . ."

"Yes, that's what he told me on Sunday, how good it was—Amanda and I went down—"

"Barney, you're so sweet and good to go and see him so often. I can't tell you how much he appreciates it."

"Well, he is my best friend, after all."

"I know, but it's such a long way—"

"It is, yes. I'm surprised you came back up here, actually, Tamara, when you could visit him so easily from your parents' house—"

"Well, as I say, I was getting very depressed. Being there kept me thinking about the wedding, you know? It wouldn't be so bad if we'd been able to settle on another date, but we can't even do that."

He was silent.

"Anyway, he so understands, bless him, that I need to get back to work. And of course I'll be there every weekend."

"Right."

"But like I was saying, it's all beginning to hit me now. And I wouldn't point the tiniest finger of blame in your direction. Not the tiniest." There was a silence; then she said suddenly, "Except . . . why were you so late, Barney? I'd quite like to know. Seeing it cost me my wedding."

Barney felt his stomach lurch.

"Tamara, it was the crash that cost you your wedding."

"No, it wasn't. It was because you left so late. If you'd left in time, you'd have been there hours before the crash. I mean, you were going to have lunch with the ushers, weren't you?"

"Yes. Well . . . the thing is, Tamara . . . I . . . He . . . that is . . . Toby wasn't very well. He kept throwing up. All morning. We really couldn't set out before. It was impossible."

"Oh. Oh, I see . . . Poor old Tobes. Something he ate, I s'pose. Or a bug. I mean, you wouldn't have let him get drunk, obviously, it wouldn't have been a hangover."

"No, of course not," said Barney.

"He didn't actually mention any of that . . . Well, thank you for telling me. I feel better now."

"Good," said Barney. He found he was sweating. The champagne was wonderfully cold; he drank down half the glass gratefully.

"Anyway, obviously I'm not going to raise it with Toby, or anything like that. He's feeling guilty enough, poor darling."

"Guilty?" said Barney. He was genuinely shocked.

"Yes, course. Barney, of course he's feeling guilty. I mean, of course he shouldn't, and I did tell him that, but . . . well, he does; he can't help it. I mean, wouldn't you? If it had been yours and Amanda's wedding?"

"I don't think so," said Barney, "no." He couldn't take any more of this. "Anyway, Tamara, I must go. I—" His phone rang. "Excuse me. It's Amanda. Hi, darling. You all right?"

"I'm fine, Barney. But . . . Carol Weston's been on the phone, wants to talk to you. Some bad-ish news about Toby's leg, I'm afraid. I think she'd like you to ring her. And are you going to be late? Because if you are—"

"No," said Barney. "No, I'm leaving right now."

CHAPTER 25

Georgia was sitting in the kitchen in Cardiff, grazing through the newspaper, and wondering if she should get a job in a bar for the next two or three weeks until *Moving Away* went into production. (It was one of the good days.)

"Oh, my God!" She thought she might be about to throw up.

She stood up, staring at the paper, open at a page of minor news items, the largest of which read, "Mystery on the Motorway" and continued with a story of a "so far unconfirmed report" that the lorry driver who had crashed through a barrier on the M4 the previous week, causing a seven-mile tailback in both directions and killing several people, had spoken of a second and unidentified person in his cab who had subsequently vanished.

"This is the first indication that there might have been a passenger in the cab. The police refuse to confirm or deny it, and there have been no further reports. If such a person does exist, then he or she could clearly have valuable information that would go a long way towards establishing the original cause of the crash, something police are very eager to settle.

"Although many of the injured are recovering in the hospital and some have returned home, there is still anxiety over the fate of Toby Weston, the young bridegroom who sustained serious injuries in the pileup, and never reached his wedding. The bride, Tamara Lloyd, told our reporter she was 'absolutely distraught with worry.'

"The crash, which is still being investigated by the police, was one of the worst in years.

"There have been several calls recently for lorry drivers' hours to be more strictly regulated. While British drivers adhere strictly, for the most part, to the rules, drivers from the continent often drive twice as many miles in a week, and break the speed limit for heavy vehicles. This can lead to acute tiredness and dangerous driving. The lorry driver in question was British . . ."

. . .

"Very carefully written," said Freeman to Rowe, when it was brought to his attention. "Plenty of suggestion that the crash was caused by dangerous driving on the part of the driver, without actually saying so. Nothing we could actually object to."

"It's disgraceful," said Rowe, "hardly going to make the poor sod feel better, is it?"

"No," said Freeman, "but it'll probably make the TV people more interested in our case."

"The PR people were more interested in the dog," said Rowe.

. . .

Toby was very low: two days to go. He'd rung Barney in the office; Barney had decided to go down that evening. He found him sitting in bed, pale and morose.

"I'm shit scared," Toby said.

Tears formed in his eyes, rolled slowly down his face; Barney reached out and gripped his hand.

"Oh, Tobes. You'll be all right. I know you will."

"I don't. Oh, God. Barney, what am I going to do; how am I going to face it? It's so fucking unfair. Just five more minutes and we'd have been OK. We should have left earlier, shouldn't we? Tamara keeps saying that."

"Oh, really?" *Cow. Bitch. How helpful. How totally helpful* . . .

"Still, you did your best, I know."

"Yeah, I did. And, Toby, we couldn't have left much earlier."

"We couldn't?"

"No. Course not."

"Why?"

"Toby, you had to go and see that girl—"

Toby suddenly looked different: wary, almost suspicious.

"Barney, that so didn't happen. You do know that, don't you?"

"Yes. Yes, its OK, Toby; don't worry, mate. " He drew his finger across his throat, grinned at him determinedly. "Your secret's safe with me."

"It's not funny," said Toby. "Not a joke. OK?"

"Yes, OK."

"Just . . . didn't happen."

"No, all right." Barney began to feel mildly resentful. What did Toby think he was going to do, tell Tamara, his parents?

"But, Tobes, there is something else. The tyre. You remember?"

"What tyre?"

"The one that blew."

"Oh . . . yes."

"I didn't . . . well, I didn't say—to the police, that is—about its being soft."

"Was it?"

"You know it was. And we didn't put any air in; you didn't want to wait—"

"Oh . . . Christ, no. We don't want to tell them that. Start looking for trouble—"

"No. Good. Well, I just thought . . . they're bound to interview you when you're out of here. Important we're singing from the same song sheet."

"Yeah, OK. Pretty obvious, I'd have thought."

"Right." He felt irritated suddenly, almost angry. He'd been making himself sick with worry over this whole business, and Toby was treating him with something close to arrogance.

Suddenly he couldn't bear it any longer.

"Look, Toby, I must go. Got to get back. But I will be here on Wednesday. Promise."

"Yeah, I know. Oh, Barney . . . you're . . . well, you're all right, you know that?"

He reached across the bed and shook Barney's hand; the sheer stiff-upper-lipness of the gesture made them both grin, slightly embarrassed.

"Right. See you then. You won't be here much longer. We'll have a party, Tobes, biggest fucking party ever, when you get out of here. We'll have you dancing on the tables . . ."

. . .

Barney felt very upset as he left the hospital, almost physically dizzy at the horror of what might lie ahead, and—he had to be honest with himself—Toby's behaviour. Of course, he was ill and scared shitless, but he didn't have to treat him like some kind of wanker who was going to sell him down the river. He sat down suddenly on the steps, trying to pull himself together, fumbling in his pockets for his cigarettes.

And then: "Barney?"

She was standing above him, her huge eyes concerned; she had no makeup on, and she looked absurdly younger than ever. And absurdly lovely . . .

"Oh—hello, Emma."

"You OK?"

"Yes. No. Well—just left Toby. He's . . . he's . . . well, got to have this final washout thing on Wednesday. And they've told him he might . . . might lose his leg. Or part of it."

"Oh, Barney. Oh, I'm so sorry."

She sat down beside him abruptly, her blue eyes full of sympathy.

"But . . . it's not certain, is it? They're still hopeful?"

"Toby doesn't seem very hopeful. Anyway, I'm going to come down again on Wednesday. Be with him. Before and so on. And . . . and after."

"That'll help him a lot."

"Really?"

"Well, yes. Positive support is really important on these occasions. What about his fiancée?"

"Oh, she doesn't know." He was unable to disguise the contempt in his voice. "Toby says it would upset her."

"Oh, I see."

"I feel like shit," he said suddenly.

"I'm sure you do. You're so fond of Toby, and—"

"No, no. More than that. I feel awful a lot of the time. About the accident. About us having that blowout, hitting the other car, that girl and her baby, all those people killed, Toby's leg—and look at me, not a scratch. Doesn't seem right."

"Lots of people feel like that," she said. "It's the whole thing about people dying, you getting off without a scratch. It's very common."

"Really?"

"Really. It wasn't your fault, Barney, any of it. You can't start thinking that."

"I have started thinking it, though," he said, "I think it all the time. It's . . . well, it's horrible."

"Maybe you should talk to someone about it. Someone who could help."

She looked at him, her eyes so full of sympathy and concern he felt suddenly better.

"Oh . . . no, thanks. I'm sorry, Emma. I hate that sort of stuff."

"What stuff?"

"Oh, you know, what I call *Guardian* stuff. Counselling, all that crap. I'm fine, honestly. I'll just have a fag; that'll cure me."

She laughed.

"Look, I've got to go now. But I'm here on Wednesday. On duty. Come and find me in A and E while he's . . . well, in the theatre. If I'm not too busy, we could have a coffee or something, pass the time. If that'd be a help at all."

Barney looked at her; her expression was sweetly earnest. Seemingly unable to help himself, he leaned forward and kissed her on the cheek.

"That is so, so kind of you, Emma," he said, "and of course it would be a help. Thank you."

"Good, it's a date then. Look, I've got to go. I'm late already." She smiled at him, jumped up, half ran across the car park. Of course. She was off to meet the boyfriend, no doubt. *Lucky bastard. Lucky, lucky bastard.*

CHAPTER 26

"There's a letter for you, Mum."

Christine smiled at her briefly, but it was a polite, rather cool smile, the one she had been using ever since Mary had told her about Russell.

Mary had phoned Russell the day after their conversation, when Christine was out, to explain; he had been surprisingly agreeable about it, had said he was sure she'd come round in a day or two. As the two became three and then four, he was growing impatient. And it was so hard to talk to him at all; she had to wait for the phone until Christine was out. Well, only another week, and then she'd be in her own home; and she had booked a cab to take her over to the hotel on Saturday, when Christine would be out for the day and wouldn't know. But the long-term prognosis was not good.

She took the letter from Christine—it was written in that unmistakable American handwriting—and went upstairs with it. "My darling Little Sparrow," the letter began. "How hard this new separation is . . ."

. . .

That afternoon, Maeve walked quietly into Patrick's room; he was sitting staring straight ahead of him; he had become very pale and thin in his two weeks' incarceration.

"Hello, Patrick."

He scarcely looked at her, just sighed and said, "Hello, Maeve."

"How are you today?"

"I'm how you'd think," he said, and his voice was heavy. "I am sick of being here in this bed. I'm in pain, I can't sleep, I'm going to be here for the rest of my life, and no doubt people would say I deserve all of that, and I would say it of myself. I'm a murderer; I killed all those people—"

"Patrick, hush." She went over to the bed, put her arms round him, kissed his cheek. "Patrick, you don't know that. You have to try to keep faith with yourself; something else might have happened . . . You can't remember—"

"I remember enough," he said, "enough to know I was desperate for sleep, biting my own fists, counting backwards from a thousand—"

"You don't . . . you don't remember this other person being there with you? It's not . . . not clearing at all?"

"No," he said, his voice bitter. "If anything it's going farther away. I'm beginning to think it was some kind of hallucination, wishful thinking . . ." He reached for a tissue, blew his nose, wiped his eyes. "How are the boys?"

"They're fine. They want to come and see you so much. Callum has done you a fine picture, look, and Liam says I have to give you fifty kisses—shall I bring them in tomorrow, Patrick? Mum says she'll drive us all down."

"I don't want to see them," he said. "I want them to forget about me."

"Forget about you? And what sort of a child will forget his own father? As fine a one as you? And why should he?"

"If the father is a killer, if he's been responsible for the deaths of many people, he's better forgotten, Maeve. I wish only one thing now: that I had been killed myself, that I had died in that cab—"

"Patrick Connell, will you just shut up now?"

The seemingly endless strain and exhaustion finally defeated Maeve; she felt angry with him, angry not for what he had done—or not done—but for his willingness to give in, to turn his back on the children.

"How dare you talk like that, how dare you, when the finest doctors in this hospital have worked so hard to save you, when your own children cry every night, they want to see you so much, when I feel so tired I could just lie down on that floor and sleep for all eternity myself. But I can't, Patrick, because someone has to keep going. Someone has to see after the children, and visit you every day, and work so hard to cheer you, and—"

He turned his head to look at her, and his expression was quite blank, his eyes dull and disinterested.

"You don't have to come," he said. "It would be much better if you didn't."

Maeve straightened up, looked at him very briefly, and then picked up her bag and walked out of the room.

. . .

Russell's letter had been to tell Mary that she wasn't to worry about him; they had the rest of their lives together, after all, but to concentrate her efforts on making her peace with her daughter.

"That really is the most important thing right now. How extraordinary this all is! I've started to worry about my children's reactions as well. Maybe we should run away together to Gretna Green and get married with just a couple of witnesses. But it's not what I want, of course: I want all our friends and family there; I want everyone to watch us being married, you becoming Mary Mackenzie. After all these years."

But Mary could see that both their families might find this a little difficult. And she was sure Russell's rather grand family would look down on her. What had seemed incredibly romantic and exciting suddenly was turning into a depressing mess.

· · ·

When Toby went down to the theatre, Barney headed in the direction of Cirencester. He parked in the centre of the town, sat down on a seat, and smoked a couple of cigarettes, and suddenly found himself consumed with anxiety, a fear that was so physical he actually shook, over what might be happening to Toby right this minute. How would he manage with only half a leg? What would he do when he couldn't swim or run or play tennis or ski? How would he be able to cope with the social life of work, the rowdy drinking, the late-night dining, the clubbing, when he had to be helped in and out of places, relying on friends, on kindness, permanently grateful, always different from the rest. Of course, they would give him prostheses—people managed wonderfully well with such things, and Toby would try with all the courage he had to do the same. But at the end of the day, he would no longer be the Toby he had been, impatiently fit and fast; he would be a different, less independent creature, robbed of being physically confident, and—Barney knew—slightly ashamed, literally, of himself. And what of Tamara; what would she make of him, no longer her perfect, wonderfully handsome fiancé, but someone she would certainly see as second-rate, second choice? Give her six months, present her with a different and perfect young man, and it was horrible to contemplate how quickly she would back off, making ugly, feeble excuses . . .

Barney wrenched his mind off Tamara and looked at his watch, which had advanced terrifyingly far, and drove very fast back to the hospital.

. . .

He was in such a state of terror as he parked his car that he misjudged the size of the space available to him and hit the wing mirror of a horribly new-looking Audi TT in the next bay. Barney knew about those Audis; fixing it would cost several hundred pounds. Well, it hardly compared with a shattered leg. He scribbled a note and left it on the windscreen.

He looked at his watch: one fifteen. *Shit.* Toby would probably be out of the theatre now. Conscious and needing him. Fine friend he'd turned out. He ran across the car park, and then, unable to contemplate hearing the bad news on his own, made for A&E and Emma. It was deserted, apart from a woman with a wailing baby and an elderly man with an arm in a sling. He looked over at the reception desk; there was only one woman on duty, and she was chatting to a nurse about some event in the department that had taken place earlier in the day. He walked over and waited politely for what felt like ten minutes; then, driven beyond endurance, said, "Excuse me . . ."

"Yes?" said the woman coldly.

"I wondered if I could see Dr. King. Dr. Emma King?"

"What would it be concerning?"

"A patient," he said. "Toby Weston."

"Well, there's no one of that name here."

"No," said Barney, slightly desperately, "no, he's on Men's Surgical. He's in—been to—the theatre this morning."

"Well, that's nothing to do with Dr. King. Who told you to ask for her?"

"She did," said Barney firmly. "When I saw her earlier today." As Toby was being taken down to the theatre . . .

"Well, I can't think why."

"I could explain," said Barney, "but . . ." He looked at the clock. *Shit*. One twenty-five. "Look," he said, "couldn't you just page Dr. King or something, tell her I'm here? She is expecting me. Please. It really is very important."

The woman sighed and started tapping at her computer keys.

"Barney! Hi!" It was Emma. Barney had never seen her without a lift of his heart; at that moment he felt he could have taken off through the hospital roof. "I wondered where you were. Come with me. It's fine, Pat; he's a friend."

Emma led him through the doors at the back of the waiting area, and then along a corridor into a small office.

"I'll ring up to the theatre now."

Emma dialled a number; waited. And waited. Hours seemed to pass. Barney felt he was about to throw up.

"They're obviously frantic," she said, "just not answering. Look—let's go up there. Come on."

She led the way on what seemed to Barney an endless journey: into lifts, along corridors, through doors, through more doors. Looking at his watch as she stopped in front of a door marked, Medical Personnel Only, he was amazed to see it was only five minutes since she'd appeared in A&E.

"Wait there," she said, and knocked on the door. A nurse dressed in scrubs appeared; she looked rather coldly at Emma.

"Yes?" she said.

"Sorry," said Emma, "Dr. King, from A and E. I'm . . . well, I wondered if you had any news of a patient. Toby Weston."

"Oh, him. Not yet, no," said the nurse. "He's only just out of theatre. Still under. Shouldn't be long. Wait out there." She glared at Barney. "I'll give you a shout."

That was it, then: nearly three hours in surgery. Emma had said that if the news was good he'd be back in an hour or so. It must have gone horribly wrong. There could be no other explanation. Toby had lost his leg. And his old life with it. And if Barney'd got him onto that road just a bit earlier, none of it would have happened; they'd never have got into that bloody accident; it was his fault. Tamara had been right in that, at least . . .

He looked at Emma; she had blurred, and he realised he was crying. *Stop it, Fraser, not for you to blub. Get a grip.*

He turned away; he felt a hand slide into his. A cool, small hand.

"Barney. Don't give up yet. They've been terribly busy; they might have had to delay it. Or—"

"Or they didn't. Or his leg's gone. How could it take this long, Emma, how could it possibly . . . ?"

"I . . . don't know. But . . . well, this isn't an exact science; they're not building a car."

They were both silent; he realised he was still holding her hand. He looked down at it, and then at her, smiled slightly awkwardly.

"Thank you for doing all this, Emma. It's very good of you."

"It's my pleasure. Honestly. Well . . ." She smiled suddenly, that brilliant, light-the-day-up smile. "Well, I hope it is. I mean, I hope it will be."

"If . . . that is . . . if they do . . . you know—"

"Amputate?" she said gently. It was somehow good hearing it spoken, confronted like that.

"Yeah. If they do, who'll tell him? The doctor, the nurses—"

"They will tell him very carefully. They're quite . . . gentle these days. The surgeon in charge is a friend of mine. He's—"

"What, you know the guy who's doing this?"

"Well, yes."

"Oh, for fuck's sake." For some reason this had made him angry. "Why the fuck won't he tell you, at least? That is so arrogant. What sort of rules do you people live by?"

She stared at him; she flushed.

"Barney, you don't quite understand. It's—"

"You're too damn right I don't. Here we are sweating our guts out, no one having the decency to come out of that door and tell us what's happening, and you say the person doing this to Toby is a friend of yours. Rum sort of friend, that's all I can say."

She shrugged, turned away; he had clearly upset her. Well, that was fine. She—The door opened suddenly, and the nurse came out.

"Dr. King," she said, "can you come in a minute?"

Well, that was definitely it. He knew now. It was the worst. He felt sick, then as if he might cry again; he turned away from the door, stared down the corridor, wondering how . . . what—

"Barney."

He turned. Emma was standing looking at him; she was flushed, looked close to tears herself.

"Yeah?" he said, aware he sounded hostile still.

And then he realised she was smiling and, yes, almost crying at the same time, and then she said, in a voice that was clearly struggling not to shake, "Barney, Toby's fine. The leg's good; it's beginning to heal. He's . . . well, he's only just coming round properly now. Mark—that's the surgeon—says you can see him, just for a moment. Want to come in?"

"Oh, shit," said Barney, "oh, for fuck's sake. Oh, Emma. Emma, I'm so sorry; I didn't mean anything I just said. Here . . ."

And suddenly, he was hugging her, and she was smiling up at him and hugging him back, and then she took his hand again and led him through the door and into a small room where Toby lay on a high, hard bed, struggling to smile through the confusion of his anaesthetic.

"Hello, you old fucker," said Barney. "You really put us through it this morning, didn't you?" And then he couldn't say any more, because he really did start to cry, tears running down his face; and he realised both Emma and the nurse were smiling at him, and he pulled out his handkerchief and blew his nose very hard and said, "Well done, mate. Bloody well done."

CHAPTER 27

Freeman and Rowe had been to interview Mary Bristow that day; expecting a dotty old lady, they had found themselves confronted by a razor-clear mind, and an extremely lucid account of what she had seen of the accident and, indeed, the road that day.

"Some terrible driving. Two or three lorries cutting in and out of the slow lane, moving in front of people. I have to say they were all foreign number plates. I found that reassuring, in a way. At least our drivers seem to know how to behave."

"Any more particular cases of bad driving that you recall?"

"Well, I did notice several white vans; they're supposed to be the worst, aren't they? Anyway, one did particularly strike me; he'd been sitting very close behind us, and then shot past, and I noticed that he didn't even have his back doors properly fastened. They were just held together with a bit of rope; it seemed very unwise."

"Indeed. Did you notice any writing or anything like that on his van?"

"There were three letters on one of the back doors, obviously part of a name, but not in sequence. If you see what I mean. That is to say, not a complete word or name. The rest had come off. It wasn't at all a well-looked-after vehicle."

"And can you remember what the letters were?"

"I can, as a matter of fact."

These old parties: amazing, thought Freeman. He supposed it was surviving the blitz or something . . .

"Yes," she said, "they were W-D-T. In that order. I remember because we used to play a game with the children, making up words from car number plates. I'm sure you know the sort of thing. I mean B and T and W would obviously be Bristow. Although proper names were not allowed, of course."

"Of course," said Freeman. He was beginning to feel rather confused himself.

"So, yes, I still do it rather automatically. Ah, WDT, I thought—War Department. We used to get countless letters from them, or rather my husband did; they figured rather large in our lives at the time. I don't suppose it's much help, but—"

"It could be a help, Mrs. Bristow. I don't suppose you were playing the same game with the number plate?"

"Oh—no. I'm so sorry. Not his. Some of the others, but—"

"Well, never mind. And at what point in the journey did you see this van? Shortly before the crash, or—"

"It was a good fifteen minutes before. And he was going very fast. He would have been well ahead—unless he stopped, of course, but it was after the service station; I do know that."

"So you stopped at the service station—that would have been what time?"

"Oh, about three fifteen. We moved off in less than ten minutes. My driver—and I would like to stress that he drove quite beautifully, in the inside lane at my request, all the way—needed some chewing gum and I offered to buy it for him, as I needed to . . . well, to go to the ladies'. I . . ." She hesitated. "I feel a little guilty now. About something I did."

"Oh, yes? I'm sure it wasn't too bad."

"Well, I hope not. A young man—who I now know was the poor bridegroom, and of course he was wearing the striped trousers and so on, although not his tailcoat—he was in a terrible hurry, and he asked if he could go ahead of everyone in the queue. I'm afraid I . . . well, I wouldn't let him. I said he should wait his turn, that we were all in a hurry for various reasons. I do hope that didn't affect the course of events at all. It must have delayed him, perhaps made him drive too fast. One is so aware of how tiny things can lead to greater ones. What is that called, something about butterflies . . ."

"The butterfly effect," said Rowe. "Apparently a butterfly can flap its wings in the jungle somewhere and cause a hurricane three days later . . ."

"Perhaps we should move on," said Sergeant Freeman. "Can you give us your account of what you saw of the collision?"

"Well, this is where I really am going to disappoint you. I fell asleep, you see, and woke up as we stopped and the car behind drove into us. It was very shocking, and of course if we hadn't been in the inside lane, it could have been very much more serious . . ."

She was silent for a moment; her eyes filled with tears.

"Take your time," Freeman said gently. "Just tell us what you remember."

She proceeded to describe with great lucidity the position of her car related to all the others near her, and to the lorry, and what she had observed.

. . .

"Pity all our witnesses aren't that clear in their accounts," said Rowe, as they drove away.

"Indeed. Those letters might be a help. I'm certainly beginning to want to talk to that van driver. Maybe we could get him mentioned on the TV programme as well."

. . .

Oh, my God. Oh, my God . . .

Just as well God hadn't answered that particular prayer, then. The one about the read-through being cancelled. They still hadn't finally cast the grandmother's friend and wanted her to do a read-through with the two they were down to, and she'd tried to tell Linda she couldn't do it. But Linda had told her to get a grip, and thank goodness she had or she'd never have set eyes on . . . on Him. Not God, but still worthy of a capital letter. The most unbelievably gorgeous bloke she'd seen for . . . well, she'd ever seen . . .

Who was he; what was he doing here . . . ?

And he was actually—*God*—actually walking towards her, smiling at her, saying, "Georgia?"

"Yes," she said, and her voice sounded odd, slightly squeaky.

"Thought so. I'm Merlin. I'm the second assistant director on *Moving Away*. So we'll be seeing quite a lot of each other, once shooting starts."

"Great!" Not the cleverest answer. But what could you say that was cool, but still friendly, in response to such a discovery? A discovery that you'd be working with someone who looked like a dollop of Orlando Bloom, a smidgeon of Johnny Depp, maybe even a sliver of Pete Doherty at his most savoury? Tall, he was, and very thin, with almost black spiky hair and dark, dark brown eyes and a rather narrow face, and really great clothes: tight black jeans and combat boots and a white collarless shirt . . .

"Great," she said again, rather feebly.

"Yeah, it looks like it'll be fun. Casting director's been raving about *you*."

Hmm. Bit of a luvvie. But then . . . what was wrong with that? They were in the luvvie profession, weren't they? Her included. In which case . . .

"Thank you," she said, and smiled. He smiled back. He had absolutely perfect teeth. "I'm pretty excited about it, I can tell you. Still pinching myself about getting it."

"Have you worked with Bryn before?"

"No."

"I have. He's a great director. And he makes it fun too. Anyway, come on over, Georgia; everyone's here."

He steered her towards a group chatting together like lifelong friends. She recognised some of them—Tony, the casting director; Bryn Merrick, the director, of course; but not a rather scarily efficient-looking person called Trish, who was the producer—and smiled politely, moving round the group shaking hands, smiling nervously, saying how thrilled she was to be part of the production. She felt very shaky, partly because of being with all these brilliant people, partly because Merlin was . . . touching her. Even if it was only on her shoulder. Well, you had to start somewhere . . .

"Right, Georgia. A word . . ." Tony, the casting director, drew her aside. "Now, we've got two actresses reading for Marje. Both very talented, both very suitable—it would be very helpful in our decision to see how you relate to each of them. I expect Linda's explained."

"Yes, she has."

"So we want you to read the same scene, first with Barbara, who's already here, and then do a bit of improvisation with her—and then Anna is coming in later. Same thing with her. Oh, and by the way, Davina—you know she's playing your mum—is coming in around lunchtime; she's got a meeting with the executive producer, and she specially wanted to meet you. So if you can hang around for a while—"

"Yes, of course," said Georgia. "No problem at all."

. . .

The first read-through was fine; she liked Barbara very much—she was funny and fun, and put her at her ease. But somehow when they did the improvisation it became more difficult. Barbara made Georgia feel rather insipid and too low-key for her own part. She did her best, but it was a struggle.

"Marvellous," said Tony as they finished, "thank you both. God, this is going to be difficult. Barbara, thank you so much for coming in. You like our Rose, then?"

"Very much," said Barbara. "We'll have fun, won't we, Rose?"

Georgia said she thought they would and Barbara left.

"Right," said Sue, "coffee, I think. Anna's coming in at twelve—Merlin, could you get that organised, darling?"

How wonderful, Georgia thought, to be old enough and sophisticated enough to be able to call everyone darling. Especially Merlin . . .

. . .

Anna didn't look so right, Georgia thought; she was rather beautiful in a hippie sort of way, with silvery blond wavy hair and intensely blue eyes, and was surely much too young for the part; but she was a marvellous actor. Georgia was amazed at the way she simply put on ten years with the first line she spoke. And she was surprised to find how she could relate to her in the improvisation, far better than with the overjolly Barbara.

Tony said all the same things again: a lot of marvellouses and thank-yous and how difficult it was going to be making a choice. Anna left. The four of them went into another room and Merlin grinned at Georgia.

"Well done. You were awfully good. Honestly."

"I don't know about that."

"No, you were. Tough decision now, I'd say."

"Yes, I should think so."

Why couldn't she say something witty and incisive, for God's sake?

. . .

They all emerged smiling; she was terrified they might ask her which of the two she had felt more comfortable with, but they just told her how well she'd done and thanked her again.

"Now, Davina's been held up for a couple of hours, Georgia. It's up to you, of course, but if you'd like to meet her, she'll be here about three. Can you find something to do till then?"

Georgia said she'd go shopping and headed for Topshop.

. . .

She got back on the dot of three, to be told Davina now wouldn't be there till four.

"Drink?" said Merlin.

"Oh—yes, thank you. Diet Coke if you've got one."

"There's white wine."

"No, honestly, I'd prefer the Coke."

"OK," he said with his amazing smile. "I'll follow your example."

Now he'd think she was a killjoy as well as boring.

· · ·

"Sorry about the wait," Merlin said suddenly. "I'm sure if you wanted to go, it'd be fine."

"Well . . . do you think I should?"

"No, no, I'm sure she meant it about wanting to meet you. But if you've got something important going on, I know she'd understand. She really is great."

"Honestly, it's fine. I don't have anything to do this evening."

She shouldn't have said that; what kind of loser had nothing to do on a Friday night?

"Wish I didn't."

No doubt he had to go out clubbing with some glamorous actress.

"My parents' silver wedding party."

"Oh, really? Where is it?"

"Elena's L'Etoile. They've got the private room upstairs."

"Oh . . . great," she said, hoping she'd sound as if she knew all about the private room at Elena's L'Etoile.

· · ·

Davina turned up at five, when almost everyone had gone except Merlin. He was clearly an important ingredient in all this, Georgia thought. Well . . . good. Davina was an absolutely dazzling black woman, with a wonderful wide grin showing big perfect teeth, her fountain of black hair braided.

She kissed Georgia, said how much she was looking forward to being her mum for a bit. "Bryn says you're a real find," she added.

"Now, do we know who's doing Marje yet, Merlin?"

Merlin said he didn't.

"Go and find out, darling. I've got my fingers crossed for Anna; she's such fun, and such wonderful stories."

Merlin went off obediently; Georgia smiled at her.

"I love your hair," she said tentatively into the slightly long silence, and then felt silly; but Davina smiled and said, "Well, I'm hoping everyone will; it's taken me four days."

"Do you do it yourself?" asked Georgia.

"Of course. I enjoy it; it's therapy. Hard on the arms, but—"

Bryn came into the room.

"Davina, my darling, how totally gorgeous you look. Come on into my office; meet Mariella. Georgia, you were great today. And I hope Davina'll be pleased to hear Anna's cast as Marje. She related very well to Georgia here."

"That's marvellous. Georgia, I'd have loved to chat a bit longer, but I've got to go after this. Got a train to catch to Paris."

Georgia thought how glamorous that sounded, and indeed how wonderful all the rest of the day had been, and then of her own train going to Cardiff, and suddenly felt the nightmare closing in again. She didn't want the day to end; she really didn't . . . She wondered what Linda was doing and if she'd have left the office yet. She might be able to go and see her—she was pretty near—and she could tell her about her day. It would keep the glamour going a bit longer . . .

. . .

Linda was delighted to hear from her; she told her to hurry round to the office and they could have a glass of wine to celebrate what had obviously been a successful day.

. . .

Mary was up in her room at six o'clock; she had just had a bath and was lying on her bed, in her dressing gown and slippers, before getting dressed again for supper. She liked to do that; it gave Christine the run of the kitchen, and helped ease the general tension. Which was still not easing much. She had spent much of the day reading another letter from Russell, over and over again. It was the most wonderful letter, four pages of it, telling her how much he loved her and was missing her and how he had been wondering where they should live.

"It will be difficult deciding; we will both want to be in our own countries. Right now I'm thinking we might split the year and do six months in each—buy two houses. Or maybe three months and then a change. You have a rival, I'm afraid—I have fallen in love with Bath and the surrounding countryside—and I know you will love many places in the States. That way we can each see as much or as little of our respective families as we and they wish."

The thought of having two homes made Mary feel quite dizzy.

She was just getting the letter out of her bag to read it yet again when Christine called up the stairs.

"Quick, Mum, they've just trailed an item about the crash. Come on, hurry up or you'll miss it. And do be careful on the stairs in those slippers."

She sounded more her old self, seeing Mary as some sort of elderly child. Well, it was better than being an adulteress . . .

. . .

Linda decided to watch the news while she waited for Georgia. She felt she needed a glass of wine; she was just pouring it when a familiar, a horribly familiar scene presented itself . . .

. . .

The children were all in bed when Maeve arrived home, still deeply upset at Patrick's behaviour. Her mother told her to go and sit down in the front room while she made some tea. She brought it in on a tray, together with some biscuits and the remains of a box of chocolates, and then joined Maeve and suggested they watch TV for a bit.

"Put your feet up, darlin'; it'll do you good. This'll soon be over, the news, and then we can watch—Oh, my God. Maeve, do you see what they're doing . . ."

For there on the screen was some old footage from the crash: the horrible, horrible footage of Patrick's lorry, the trailer lying on its side, and the cars scattered about it like toys, and then there was a quick rundown about it, when it had been, how many people had been involved . . .

· · ·

"But two weeks later, there is some good news. The lorry driver is recovering well and is expected to be out of intensive care in a few more days; the baby boy born prematurely is thriving and is going home this weekend; and the famous golden retriever who was lost in the chaos turned up at a farm and has been reunited with her owner. In fact, you can see Bella for yourselves in a couple of minutes; we have her in the studio with one very happy owner. But before we do that, there is one rather more serious matter. The police are still gathering evidence on events leading up to the crash and would be interested in hearing from anyone who may have seen something they feel is relevant that afternoon: a car or van possibly driving erratically— or perhaps some debris on the road . . .

"All calls would be treated as confidential. They are particularly interested in a young girl who—"

"Oh, my God," said Maeve. "Oh, my dear Lord."

· · ·

"Laura, put the telly on quickly. Channel Eight, the news. Don't ask; just do it . . ."

· · ·

". . . a young girl who was seen by several people at the scene and is thought to have been possibly travelling in the lorry, and who has not yet come forward . . ."

· · ·

"Hi, Linda, I brought you a bottle of—Oh, my God, what's that about . . . ? Oh, my God . . ."

"So if you know anything of this girl, or you think you know where she might be, please do get in touch with the police—in confidence. They do stress that there is no suggestion of anything suspicious, merely that in a crash as big as this one, there must be no stone left unturned in the subsequent investigation. And now, as promised, we have Bella and her owner, Jenny Smith, from Northamptonshire . . ."

. . .

"Oh, Mother Mary and all the saints," said Maeve.

. . .

"Oh, I do hope Maeve is watching," said Mary.

. . .

"How extraordinary," said Laura.

. . .

Georgia made an odd sound; Linda looked at her. She was absolutely ashen, her hand clasped over her mouth. She suddenly sat down, as if her legs wouldn't hold her any longer, her eyes still fixed on the screen.

"Georgia," said Linda very gently. "Georgia, was that . . . you?"

CHAPTER 28

The story had come out haltingly, punctuated with much weeping and sheer blind terror at what she had done—and concealed—through two long, dreadful weeks.

She had quite simply panicked: Linda had tried to tell her that it was not so unusual, not so terrible a thing to do. But Georgia would have none of it: "It was horrible, awful. He'd been so kind to me, and there he was unconscious, with God knows what injuries, and did I try to help? No, I just ran. It was disgusting of me, Linda; I'm so, so ashamed. But somehow the longer I left it, the worse it seemed. And do you know what my very first thought was? After we'd crashed? That I'd miss the audition. Can you imagine anything as awful as that?"

"You were in shock; it brings about some very strange behaviour."

She had felt dazed at first, she said, not sure what she was doing, and, "I felt very sick and dizzy. Two men by the lorry asked me if I was all right and I couldn't speak to them; I threw up right there in front of them; it was horrible. And then I had to sit down for a bit. Everyone was much too busy looking after people who were really hurt to bother about me. After that I climbed over the barrier, by the hard shoulder, and slithered down the bank and started running. All I could think of was getting away; does that sound crazy?"

Linda shook her head. "Not at all."

"There were all these cars crashed into one another, and huge white things everywhere. I didn't know what they were then, but of course they were Patrick's load, fridges and freezers and stuff. I just turned my back on it all and ran—towards Cardiff. That was all I wanted: to get home. I found a sort of track thing and followed that, and when I couldn't run anymore I walked, on and on. Every yard I went, I felt less frightened; I was farther away from it all; I felt . . . safer. How weird was that? I cut up into that bloke's land, that farmer guy who was just on the TV, and then on to a village, and then I hitched a lift in a car going to Bristol.

"The driver said he'd been avoiding the M4, that there'd been a terrible crash, miles and miles of tailback, and I had to pretend to be surprised. Oh, God . . ."

In Bristol she had eventually managed to get a lift in a lorry going to Cardiff. "I was scared of being in another one; I thought he might crash too—"

"And . . . tell me, do you think Patrick went to sleep?"

"No! Of course he didn't go to sleep. It wasn't his fault in any way at all. In fact . . ." She paused, gathered her breath, then said in a desperate shaky tone, "In fact, if it was anyone's fault it was probably mine."

· · ·

Shaking, clinging to Linda's hand, she rang the programme help line, who said they'd get the police to call her.

"Pretty soon, they said . . . Linda, I feel sick. I feel so awful. What will they think of me; what will they do to me? I'm disgusting; I deserve to be . . . to be put away somewhere. Oh, dear. Can I have another cigarette?"

It was a measure of her distress and of Linda's intense sympathy with that distress that Linda had actually agreed to let her smoke. She loathed not just smoking, but smokers. To allow Georgia to smoke in her flat was akin to handing round glasses of wine at an AA meeting.

It was she who took the call; she passed the phone to Georgia.

"It's a Sergeant Freeman."

"Thanks. Hello. Yes, this is Georgia Linley. Yes, I did. Of course. Yes, I think I can help. I'll . . . I'll ask . . . Um, Linda, they want us to meet them at some police station in the morning. They're going to ring back with the exact address. Is that OK? . . . Yes? Hello. Yes, that's fine. Thank you. What? No, it's not my mum; it's my agent. No, I'm fine, thank you. I'll be there in the morning."

She put the phone down and looked at Linda, her face somehow gaunt, her dark eyes red with weeping, her small, pretty nose running; she wiped it on the back of her hand. She looked about six.

"You will come with me, won't you?" she said with a tremor in her voice.

Linda held out her arms and said, "Of course I will. Come here, you."

And Georgia went to sit next to her on the sofa, resting her head on Linda's shoulder, and said, "I couldn't do all this without you, you know."

"Well, I'm glad to have helped."

"You have. So, so much." Another sniff, then: "You'd be a great mum, you know. You really should, before it's too late . . ."

"Well . . . thanks," said Linda.

. . .

The police were very kind, very gentle with her.

She sat, her teeth chattering with fright at first, but still telling her story perfectly lucidly, up to the point of the actual crash.

"We were just going along very steadily, chatting. Patrick was absolutely fine, not going fast at all, driving really carefully in the middle lane. We'd been through a storm—that was quite scary; it got very dark, and he slowed down a bit, said the water on the road was dangerous after the heat. But the sun was out again; it had stopped raining. And then—suddenly—there was this great crack of noise and we couldn't see. Not at all. It wasn't dark, just everything blurred. It was like being blind. It was so, so frightening, because the windscreen was just . . . well, you know, impossible to see through. And Patrick just . . . well, slammed on the brakes and then swerved, quite sharply, and he was hooting and shouting—"

"Shouting? What was he shouting?"

"Oh, things like, 'For the love of God,' and, 'Jesus'—well, he is Irish," she said with the ghost of a smile. "And then the lorry just wouldn't stop; it went on and on—it seemed for hours I couldn't see anything, except out of the side window, and I could see we were going completely across the middle of the road, with the traffic on the other side coming towards us. It was weird; it all happened so slowly. And then . . . then we stopped. And I felt a sort of violent lurch as the trailer went, and there was this horrible noise and . . . Oh, dear, sorry." She started to cry.

"Now, now," said Sergeant Freeman, "no need for tears; you've been most helpful—your account is quite invaluable. With the lorry driver unable to remember anything much, this is the first really lucid account we've had. So, what did you think had happened? To cause it?"

"Well, the windscreen shattered. There wasn't a hole in it; the glass just had all these weird patterns all over it, making it impossible to see."

"Something hit it, perhaps? Maybe that was the crack you heard."

"Yes, but what could it have been?"

"That's for us to find out. You can stop worrying about it now."

"You're being so kind," she said. "You must be so . . . so shocked at me, by what I did."

"Miss Linley," Freeman said, "if you saw one percent of what we do, you'd understand that we're not very easily shocked. Isn't that right, Constable?"

"Absolutely right," said Constable Rowe.

"You might be shocked at this, though," she said, in a voice so low it was almost inaudible. "I think . . . well, I think some of it . . . could . . . could have been my fault. You see, I . . . well, I dropped a can of drink. As we swerved. On the floor. It was rolling around. I think . . . it might have interfered with Patrick's—Mr. Connell's—brakes. And if I hadn't done that, maybe he could have stopped. I mean . . . oh, God—"

"Miss Linley," said Sergeant Freeman, "we will of course put this into our report. But I really don't think you should worry about it too much. The brakes in those things are huge, very powerful, and power-assisted. One small can of drink rolling around would not have had the slightest effect. What would you say, Constable?"

Constable Rowe smiled at Georgia and said yes, indeed, he would say the same thing.

He found himself very moved by Georgia's distress. She hardly looked old enough to be out in the world at all, let alone hitching lifts in lorries.

"Really?"

"Really. I hope that makes you feel better."

"It does. A bit." But she was still looking very uncertain.

"So . . . you would say the whole accident was caused by this shattering of the windscreen? By Mr. Connell being unable to see? Not because of any other cars? Please think very carefully, Miss Linley; it's very important. Very important indeed."

"Oh—definitely, yes. Suddenly, he had to drive without being able to see. It was like he was blindfolded. That was the only reason, I'm sure."

"Well, that's pretty clear. Now, let's just talk about the other cars, Miss Linley. Did you notice any in particular?"

"Oh . . . a few. You notice everything from up there. I was talking to Patrick, describing things to him; he asked me to, said it helped ward off what he called the monster."

Sergeant Freeman looked up sharply.

"What monster would that be?"

"Well . . . being sleepy. He said it was like a sticky monster in his head. But"—she looked at them—"but he was not, I swear to you, not remotely near going to sleep; you really do have to believe me—"

"It's all right," said Freeman, and despite the soothing words, Linda thought that she could detect a slight change in his expression. "That's absolutely fine. Now, go on; tell us about the other cars."

"Well, there was a lovely car in front. A sports car, maybe an old one, bright red, amazing. By the time of the actual crash, he'd gone. But he was driving very nicely, not speeding."

"Right. How far ahead was he, would you say? When the windscreen went?"

"I'm not sure. Impossible to say. I mean, I could still see him quite clearly—"

"Could you read the registration number? I mean, was it near enough for you to read it?"

"I . . . don't think so. He was pulling ahead quite fast. I s'pose about fifty metres, something like that?"

"Right. What about a dark blue Saab? Did you notice that?"

"Oh—yes. They were beside us. Just before it happened. Well, a bit behind—you can't see anything when the car's right beside you. I noticed it in the mirror, and I was interested because it was such a nice car, and there was a man and a woman in it, and they seemed to be quarrelling—she was waving her arms about and stuff. And then—" She stopped. "Look, I don't want to get anyone into trouble—"

"Don't worry about that. Tell us what you saw."

"Well . . . he did seem to be on a mobile. But then . . . I heard the crack and Patrick hooting and shouting and . . . well, I've told you the rest."

"You have indeed. So, there was no question of their driving in any way dangerously? Pulling out in front of the lorry, for instance?"

"No, no, not at all."

"Right. Well, you've been very helpful, Miss Linley, very helpful indeed. And try not to worry about that drink can. I really think you can put your mind at rest, although we will put it into the report, of course. One last thing—did you notice a white van at all, with the back doors just tied shut? On the road that afternoon? At any stage?"

"I certainly did. He was driving like a maniac. But he couldn't have had anything to do with it; he passed us doing about ninety ages before the crash."

"You didn't notice any writing on it? Any logos of any kind?"

"No, I'm sorry. Nothing. Nothing at all."

"Was he alone in the van?"

"No. Well, he had a big dog sitting beside him."

"Well, I really cannot tell you how helpful you've been, Miss Linley. You've given us an invaluable account, and the information on the other cars is most helpful as well."

Soon after that, having read her statement and signed it, she was told she was free to go.

. . .

"Poor Mr. Connell will be pleased, won't he?" said Constable Rowe. "S'pose you'll be letting him know."

"Yes, of course."

"Today?"

"No, Monday morning will do perfectly well."

"Yes, of course," said Constable Rowe hastily, and then added, "I was wondering: might the windscreen have been shattered by that wheel nut?"

"Very unlikely," said Freeman, "very unlikely indeed."

. . .

"Hi, William. It's Abi."

"Abi! Oh, my God. Yes. Hello."

"Hello, William. What kind of a reception is that?"

"I . . . Oh, sorry. Yes. It's wonderful to hear from you."

"Hope so." She laughed. That laugh. That—almost—dirty laugh. "I did warn you I'd ring if you didn't. Anyway . . . I thought it might be good if we went out tomorrow night. What do you think?"

"Well . . . well . . . yes. Of course. It'd be great. Fantastic. Yeah. Er . . . tonight'd be better. Well, sooner."

She laughed again. "I've got to go out with some mates tonight, William. A friend's going to Australia for a year. I'd ask you along, but I don't think you'd enjoy it too much."

"OK, then. Tomorrow it is."

"Good. I thought I'd come over to you, save you the trek. We could meet in the pub you took me to."

"Are you sure?"

"Yes, of course I'm sure. Eightish?"

"Eightish," he said. "Yes. Great. Well . . . thanks for calling."

He rang off and punched the air.

. . .

Patrick felt very tired; it had been a long, wakeful night without his sleeping pills, and a painful one too. The temptation at one point to raid his horde, to take at least one of them, was intense; then he thought he would simply be prolonging the agony—literally. He had calculated that by tonight he would have enough; he would take them after he had been settled for the night. And then—oblivion. No more remorse, no more pain, no more of being a burden on everyone. He was actually looking forward to it; he knew it was a mortal sin, knew he should have absolution, was afraid in his very darkest moments of going to hell. He had thought of asking for the priest, but it seemed dangerous; he might be tempted to confess, or even to talk of his absolute wretchedness, his sense of being abandoned by God, as well as everyone else, and the hospital priest was a clever, sensitive soul; he might well become aware of Patrick's despair and the danger of it. So he must do it alone, must say his own prayers, ask for God's forgiveness himself, and then . . . leave. He could manage; he was afraid, but not as afraid as he was of continuing to live with this awful, terrifying misery and guilt.

. . .

Georgia hadn't realised at first that there was anything in the papers about her. It was only when she and Linda were having lunch that Linda passed her the *Mail,* looking rather grim.

"Sorry, darling. But you ought to see this."

It was only a small item, on an inside page, mostly conjecture: illustrated by yet another picture of the crash and headed, "Mystery Girl of the M4." But it was enough to upset her considerably: to see her behaviour described for the millions of people who bought the *Daily Mail* to read about. And no doubt there would be millions of other people reading it in other papers.

"Try not to worry too much. It's not that interesting."

"I can think of lots of people who would think so. If they knew it was me. Like everyone in the new series, for a start. What on earth will they make of me, Linda? They'll be so shocked to find I'm not the nice little girl they thought, just a rotten, cowardly wimp. And they'll realise it was all lies about the audition as well, that I wasn't ill at all, oh, God . . ."

She started to cry again. And Linda, looking at her, felt very much afraid that she might be right.

As for what the press might make of it, if they knew the mystery girl was an about-to-be-high-profile young actress . . . well, Linda was rather familiar with the press; she felt this was a story that might run and run.

"Georgia, darling, don't cry. You've been so brave today."

"Yeah, and so cowardly for all those other days. Linda, I've been wondering—do you think I ought to go and see Patrick? Or at least get in touch with his wife? I mean, she might have seen the programme. She must be so worried; she must be wondering who or where the . . . the girl—well, me—where she is."

"Well . . . it would be the right thing to do."

A silence, then: "Maybe I will. I'm absolutely shit scared, and he'd be within his rights to spit in my face, but I feel he ought to know what I've told the police. He might be feeling terrible, with all these stories in the papers about him going to sleep, don't you think?"

"Pretty terrible, yes. Well, it would be very brave."

She really thought so; in a way that would take more courage even than going to the police.

"Maybe . . . maybe tomorrow. I'll go to the hospital. Linda— would you come with me?"

"Of course I will . . ."

. . .

"You all right, then, Patrick?" Jo Wales smiled at him. She was just going off duty.

"Yes, I'm fine." His voice was flat.

"I heard the family came to see you today."

"They did, yes."

"And were they pleased to see you?"

She knew he hadn't seen them, but she felt a chat might help.

"No. No, I sent them away."

"Patrick, why did you do that? Your wife said they were so excited."

"Yes, well, I didn't feel up to it."

"Oh, I see. Yes, well, maybe tomorrow."

"No, I don't think so."

She looked at him thoughtfully. His face was oddly expressionless, his eyes blank.

"Are you feeling OK, Patrick?"

"I'm feeling how you'd think I might be feeling," he said. It was an aggressive statement, delivered in an aggressive tone. It was unlike him.

"Well . . . I'm sorry. Is the pain very bad?"

"It's not great."

"Next week's surgery should help quite a lot. With your tummy. Is that the worst?"

"It hurts everywhere. Except my legs, and what wouldn't I give to have some pain there as well."

Jo smiled at him gently, put her hand on his shoulder.

"You will. You must have faith."

"Faith I've lost, along with everything else."

"Well, let's see. In time, I promise you, things will be better."

He shrugged.

"Is . . . is there anything you'd like to watch on TV tonight? There's quite a lot on, a good film—"

"No, I don't want to watch anything," he said. "I'm very tired. I just want to be quiet, be left alone."

"All right. Well, I hope you have a good night, Patrick, at least."

She walked out of his room, stood in the corridor for a moment, then went to find Sister Green, on duty that night on the ward. An extra sleeping pill would probably not be a bad idea. Just for tonight.

. . .

Alex really didn't want to go home. That made him feel miserable. And angry. Not only had Sam ended their marriage; she had virtually rendered him homeless. Well, deprived him of a place he wanted to be, where he was welcome.

Their bedroom had long since ceased to be in any way his, and the small spare room was unwelcoming. Sam and the children occupied the kitchen and the family room in the evening, and if he walked into it, even the children looked awkward, forced to confront his discomfort. He still had his study, of course, but it was very much a study, occupied by his desk and computer and files and books, not somewhere he could sit back and relax.

Anyway, he had no stomach for staking any claims over personal space tonight; he would rather stay at the hospital. He'd brought in his pyjamas and wash things. He had a room there, with a bed; he could get some food at the café and then go to bed, read himself into a stupor and hope no major accidents or traumas might disturb him. He wasn't on call; if they did want him, he could tell them to get stuffed. In fact, that was precisely what he would do. He could even drink a glass of wine. He would drink a glass of wine. Or two. Or even three . . .

. . .

Patrick had asked to be settled for the night early. Sue Brown, the young nurse who was looking after him, brought him his hot drink and his drugs, and said if he wanted anything to ring for her.

"But hopefully you'll have a lovely sleep, Patrick, and feel much better in the morning."

When she had gone, he made his preparations very carefully. He felt calm, not frightened at all. He wrote a letter to Maeve, telling her how much he loved her and how this way would be much better for both her and the boys. He thanked her for being a wonderful wife and told her that the boys had the best mother in the whole wide world. He signed it, "All my love, my darling Maeve, Patrick."

He wrote a separate letter to the boys, telling them how much he loved them and how sorry he was to have sent them away that day. "Be good for your mummy; Liam, you will be the man in the family now, so you must look after her. And remember me always as I used to be, not as I am now. Your very loving Daddy."

Then he wrote another note for "whom it may concern," asking not to be resuscitated if there was any question of it.

And then he wrote a note to Alex Pritchard, thanking him for all his kindness both to him and to Maeve, and telling him how much he had helped both of them in the first awful, early days. "All doctors should be like you, Dr. Pritchard," he finished, signing it off, "yours with gratitude, Patrick Connell."

He propped all the letters up on his bedside unit, and then he lay back on his pillows to rest.

The sun was setting by then; he could see the sky from his window. It was ravishing, a stormy red streaked with black, with great slanting shafts of light pushing through the clouds: a child's-Bible sky. He lay there quietly, watching it blaze and fade, and then he reached into his bedside cupboard for his rosary and said his prayers. He asked God for his forgiveness for what he was about to do, committing a mortal sin, and he asked Him, too, to forgive him for the dreadful carnage he had wrought on the motorway. He felt that if God was a good and loving God, He would understand his anguish and find it in His heart to forgive him.

He asked Him to comfort and care for Maeve and the boys, and then he recited the twenty-third psalm. He would indeed be walking through the valley of the shadow of death; he would need God's rod and staff to comfort him. He prayed again that he would not be denied it. And then finally he said a Hail Mary and the Lord's Prayer and made the sign of the cross.

As he did so he discovered that he was weeping, and discovered, too, that he was not really surprised. The life that had seemed so promising, so happy, so filled with delight and family pleasure and a wife he loved and who loved him, was gone forever, destroyed by his own carelessness and arrogance. He would not see that life again; it was lost to him, and he did not deserve it. He had caused immense misery to many, many people; he had robbed a child of his mother, a mother of her child. He had read the papers, read the interviews, in spite of the efforts of the hospital staff to keep them from him. He had read about the sense of utter loss and desolation and anger felt by the people whose lives he had destroyed; it seemed absolutely wrong, a reversal of the proper order of things, that he should be still alive. He would die, and it would be a reparation of sorts, would perhaps show some of those poor, unhappy people how sorry he was for what he had done to them. He hoped someone would tell them.

And then he sat for a while longer, his head bowed, holding his rosary, reflecting on what he was about to do, and preparing himself for the moment when it became reality.

CHAPTER 29

He knew he'd never be able to forgive himself. Never. It was so true what they said: Everyone made mistakes, but doctors buried theirs.

He could never remember feeling so remorseful. How could it have happened? How could a man, a desperately ill man, confined to his hospital bed and, moreover, under intensive medical scrutiny, have managed to store up enough drugs to kill himself? And, more important, how could he, Alex Pritchard, have failed so totally to recognise the depths of that man's despair? He felt shocked at the failure of the hospital and its systems and, perhaps worst of all, ashamed of himself, that he could have been so bloody obsessed with his own problems that he hadn't noticed what was going on under his own nose.

. . .

He'd met Maeve in reception at three a.m.; she was white and wild eyed.

"Hello, Maeve."

"Dr. Pritchard! It's good to see you. How is he?"

"He's . . . he's doing OK, we think. There was concern about his kidney, his one remaining one, you know, but it seems to be coping, with the help of the drugs. He's not completely out of the woods yet, but we're hopeful."

"Oh . . . Dr. Pritchard, thank you. Thank you so much."

"No thanks due to me," he said, and meant it.

. . .

Nurse Sue Brown, checking on her patients just after ten, had found them all peacefully asleep. Even poor Patrick Connell.

The other nurse was not at the desk; Sue had settled down to do the reports—and then remembered she'd been instructed by the sister to give Mr. Connell an extra sleeping pill that night. Which she had, of course; she'd counted them out very carefully, and had then fetched him some extra water, as he'd asked, and when she got back, he'd taken them all. But she wasn't sure what that brought his total dosage to. She'd need his notes to do that, and they were in his room. Just for a moment she was tempted to leave it and fill it in in the morning. But no, it was too important.

She opened the door very cautiously. Thunderous snores greeted her. He seemed very firmly asleep. *Good.* She fished the notes out of the pocket at the bottom of his bed, and was just leaving the room again when she realised he was lying rather oddly, slumped onto his right side. She moved over to the bed, to see if she could ease him into a more comfortable position without disturbing him too much, and saw the neat pile of notes on his bedside unit.

The top one was addressed to "my boys." That was good. He'd sent them away today, she'd heard; he was probably telling them how sorry he was and how much he'd like to see them soon. As she leaned over him, starting to ease his pillows into a more supportive position, she knocked the pile of letters onto the floor. She bent down to pick them up and saw that there was one addressed to Dr. Pritchard. That was . . . well, it was odd. Why write to one of the doctors? And then she saw another—"To whom it may concern"—and her heart began to beat uncomfortably hard.

She looked at Patrick again, and then reached out for his hand to take his pulse. It was cold, and the pulse was very slow. Very slow indeed . . .

Sue Brown half ran from the room and set off the alarm. It was the early hours before it could be pronounced with any certainty that Patrick was going, probably, to be all right.

. . .

Alex, in ICU, had realised for the first time perhaps how wretched and impotent it felt to be on the sidelines there. But at least he was able to comfort Maeve; he had sat with her in the relatives' room, fetching her tea, which she didn't drink, talking in platitudes, even holding her hand while she wept and berated herself for not being more under-standing and sensitive to Patrick's depression.

"How could I have got cross with him, Dr. Pritchard?" she said, wiping her eyes, "yesterday and on Friday, telling him to pull himself together, not to be so selfish. How could I have done that?"

"You've been under a dreadful strain, Maeve," he said, "and been so brave and loyal. How many people would have done that awful journey every day, uncomplaining?"

What he would have given for a wife like Maeve. Even a bit like Maeve . . .

. . .

The journalist from the *Daily Sketch* was woken by his mobile ringing at seven a.m. It was Maria, the hospital cleaner. She was talking very quietly and very fast. He had to ask her to repeat herself twice before he worked out what she was saying.

"Mr. Connell, he try to kill self. Last night. He all right now. You meet me dinnertime. And for last time. And bring my money, OK?"

. . .

Maureen Hall, the receptionist at the main entrance of St. Marks, took an immediate dislike to Linda. She was so bloody sure of herself, standing there as if she owned the place, in the middle of a busy Sunday afternoon, not an auburn hair out of place, demanding to see Mr. Patrick Connell . . .

"I'm sorry," she said to Linda, "you can't see him. He's in ICU—the high dependency unit—and can't have any visitors."

"In that case, I wonder if I could see the doctor in charge of his case, please."

"I'm afraid that won't be possible," said Maureen Hall disdainfully. "Our doctors are all very busy, not available for consultation in that way."

"I see. Well, it is very important that I—this young lady and I—see someone who is caring for him."

Maureen Hall looked at the young lady; she was very young indeed, and looked terrified, standing behind the woman, chewing her nails.

"Well, the only thing I can suggest is that you talk to Patient Liaison. They may be able to help you. What name shall I say?"

"Di-Marcello, Linda Di-Marcello."

"Right." Maureen tapped on her computer keyboard with her long nails; a silence ensued; then she said, "I've got a Miss de Marshall here; she wants to see someone about Mr. Patrick Connell. Yes. No, I know that, but she's very insistent. Can she come up; maybe you can explain? Thanks, Chris."

She turned to Linda.

"You can go and see the patient liaison people if you like. Second floor. The lift's over there. It's signposted when you get up there. Sorry, madam," she said with exaggerated politeness to the woman standing behind Linda and Georgia in the queue. "Sorry to have kept you so long."

"Cow," hissed Linda to Georgia. Even that didn't make poor Georgia smile.

. . .

"I can't tell you how important it is that we see the doctor or doctors responsible for Mr. Connell," Linda said. They were now in Patient Liaison. "This young lady was with him on the day of the crash—you do know about the crash, don't you. Miss . . . ?"

"Mrs. Patel. Yes, of course I do. But Mr. Connell is extremely ill. As I explained to you. It would be quite impossible for you to see him."

"Yes, but—" Linda stopped. She felt so exasperated, words temporarily deserted her. She looked at Georgia. Who had suddenly stopped looking frightened. And was leaning on the desk, half shouting at Mrs. Patel.

"If he's extremely ill, he needs to know what I can tell him. It's really, really important. It could make him feel much better. Now, we're not going to go away. We're going to stay here as long as it takes, making a nuisance of ourselves. So you really might just as well be helpful, instead of obstructive. I mean, what about his wife? Is she here? Could we see her? Or could you tell us where she lives, so that we could talk to her . . . ? Just do something, for God's sake."

Linda felt like clapping.

"Just a moment, please—I will go and make some enquiries." Mrs. Patel got up and walked out of the room.

. . .

Alex had showered and changed his shirt and was on his way back to Maeve. Patrick was increasingly alert and increasingly angry, apparently, demanding to know why his instructions had been ignored, refusing to see anyone, even Maeve. She would need his support.

He picked up his beeper, informing the staff on reception that he would be back shortly, and made his way to the lifts. There were two people waiting there: a rather glamorous red-haired woman, exactly the type he most disliked, and a very pretty black girl who looked as if she might be about to run away. As they got in, the woman took the girl's hand and held it. The girl half smiled at her, then resumed her petrified expression, staring at her feet. Presumably someone up there they were worried about. He managed to smile at them. The woman smiled rather briefly back.

There was one other person in the lift with them: a tall young man with curly brown hair dressed in jeans and a denim shirt. He wore a very anxious expression and didn't look at any of them.

As the lift stopped, Alex stood back and allowed the two women off first; the redhead gave him a slightly cool nod. The young man followed, then stood studying a file he was holding, scribbling notes on various pieces of paper and peering out of the window that faced the lift. Obviously something to do with the planning department, Alex thought. Bloody nuisance, all of them.

The two women stood there, clearly puzzled as to where they should go; slightly to Alex's surprise, Maeve Connell appeared, hurried towards them.

"Hello," she said to them, "I'm Mrs. Connell. It's so good of you to come. Oh, Dr. Pritchard, hello. Have you come to see Patrick?"

"No, I've come to see you. I hear good news now—to a degree—of Patrick . . ."

"You could call it that, I suppose. But he . . . Oh, dear . . . I don't know what do. Anyway, these two ladies may be able to help."

She looked anxiously first at Alex, then at them; Linda smiled encouragingly at her.

"Do please go ahead; talk to the doctor. We'll wait."

She had a nice voice, Alex thought; the only thing he could find to like about her. It was very low and husky.

"No, no, Maeve, you talk to the ladies. If you want me, you can get any of the nurses to page me."

"All right, Dr. Pritchard. Thank you so much. He is the kindest man on God's earth," she said, ushering Linda and Georgia along the corridor. "I don't know what I'd have done without him these past two weeks."

"Is he in charge of your husband?" said Linda.

"No, he's the A and E consultant. But he did admit Patrick, and kept a very close eye for a few days, until . . . well . . ."

. . .

"So . . . Mrs. Connell . . ." Georgia's voice was tentative as they sat down in the relatives' room. "How actually is Patrick?"

"Maeve, please. Well . . . he was getting better. But of course he has a very long way to go. He's paralysed from the waist down—"

"Paralysed!" Georgia's great dark eyes filled with horror. "Oh, no, no—"

"I'm afraid so. The neurosurgeon is hopeful that it's temporary, but of course it's hard for Patrick to believe that. He's had to have a lot of surgery and will have more. And he's very depressed, of course. He . . . well, he took an overdose last night, but they found him in time."

"Oh, Mrs. Connell. Maeve. If only . . . I mean, if . . . if I'd known! I was in the cab with him when it happened," Georgia said, and her voice was very strong suddenly, no longer frightened or tentative at all. "He gave me a lift; he was terribly kind to me. And I was there when . . . when he crashed."

"So . . . did . . . did you see what happened?" said Maeve, so quietly Georgia could hardly hear her.

"Yes, I did. Everything."

"Because, you see . . . he thinks . . . that is, he is convinced . . . that it was his fault. That he went to sleep. That is what is so terrible. That's all he can remember—being sleepy. Even though most of the reports talk of another car going out of control in front of him."

"Oh, dear God. Maeve, I can tell you, with absolute certainty, that he did not go to sleep. No way. We were chatting; he was fine. Right up to the very last moment. I don't know how far all the enquiries have got, or what Patrick or you think, but I can tell you, absolutely for certain, that it wasn't Patrick's fault. Not in the very least."

. . .

"Patrick . . . it's me, Maeve. How are you feeling now?"

"How you'd expect. Dreadful." And he did look it, back on all the machines and drips, propped up on high on the ICU bed, grey-white, his skin somehow transparent, his eyes sunken in his thin face. "Maeve, I keep telling you, stop coming here, for the love of God. Just leave me in peace."

"I know, Patrick, but . . . but I have some news for you. Some very important news. You . . . you know you said you thought you could remember someone in the van with you? Just before the crash? Well . . . she's here. She's come to see you. A young girl, name of Georgia."

"I don't care. I don't want to see anyone. There's no point—"

"Patrick, there is. It's going to make all the difference, because she says she saw what happened."

"She saw me going to sleep? Is that what she saw?"

"No, no, Patrick that's exactly what she didn't see. She says—Will you see her Patrick, please? Just for a moment."

"Maeve, I'm too tired for girls with fairy stories. Why should I believe what she says? She'd have come before if it was true. I just wanted an end to it; they've robbed me of that. Now leave me be, will you?"

He closed his eyes; Maeve left the room and made her way along to Linda and Georgia.

"He . . . oh, God, he says he doesn't want to see you. He says how can he believe you were there; why . . . Oh, it was good of you to come, both of you, but I'm afraid there was no point. Not with Patrick, anyway. Maybe if you talked to the police again . . ." She looked utterly defeated, her eyes swimming with tears. She tried to smile and failed totally; her mouth trembled and she bit her lip.

"Oh, dear. Oh, this is dreadful. Um . . . Maeve . . ." Georgia started rummaging in her bag. "Maeve, do you think this might make a difference? Here . . ."

She put a small box into Maeve's hand.

"It's a watch. It was a birthday present for your mother. Patrick showed it to me, and then he gave it to me to look after. I've had it all this time."

Maeve took the box, opened it; a small watch lay inside. It was very pretty indeed, set in a diamanté bracelet. She sat staring at it for a moment, then said, "I'll take it in to him. Thank you, Georgia. Thank you so much."

· · ·

Five minutes later she came out again, smiling, her small, tearstained face radiant.

"He remembered it! Could you come in with me? Would that be all right?"

"Of course it would," said Georgia. "It'd be absolutely all right."

· · ·

Alex Pritchard decided to go home. A tedious day with nothing to do in A&E was beginning to look even worse than trying to find a corner he could call his own at home. He'd just go up and make sure Maeve was all right and then leave.

He went into the relatives' room and found the red-haired woman sitting alone, talking into her mobile. She looked up at him, half smiled, and went on talking.

"Just tell them tomorrow that you haven't had any formal voice training, but you can sing well enough for the chorus. Yes, I'm pretty sure. You can put them on to me, if you like. Yes, of course. I'll be in the office. Now if you want me again this afternoon, just ring my mobile. Sure. Ciao."

She rang off and was clearly ready to make another call; it annoyed Alex. There were several notices in the room asking people not to use mobile phones.

"Sorry," he said, making a conscious effort to sound polite, "but you really are asked not to use your mobile on hospital premises."

"Oh, I know," she said. "I also know that it's a load of nonsense. It can't really interfere with equipment; it's just so you don't have patients rabbiting on all day in the wards. Which I completely sympathise with."

"Oh, you do?"

"Yes." She smiled at him. It was a very nice smile. Didn't make up for a considerable arrogance, though. He didn't smile back.

"I'm afraid you're wrong," he said. "If everyone used their mobiles on hospital premises, especially an area like this, where we have extremely sensitive equipment, it would be very bad, so please stop using it. Or go outside."

"I . . ." She stared at him, then stood up, switching off her mobile. "Then I shall go outside. This is a very important call, actually, to Georgia's mother. She wants to know where she is."

"And Georgia is . . . ?"

"The girl who's with me. I'm her agent. Look, we're wasting time. Or rather *you're* wasting *my* time. Good afternoon."

She stalked off down the corridor. He looked after her. She had rather good legs. And an arrogant walk. She was a very arrogant woman altogether. He hoped this would be his last encounter with her.

As he stood there, Maeve and the girl came out of ICU; Maeve's face was literally shining. Georgia was swollen eyed and tearstained.

"Oh, Dr. Pritchard," said Maeve, clasping his hand. "I'm so glad you're here. Patrick's so much better, so much happier. Georgia here really has turned things round. Bless her heart!"

She smiled radiantly at Georgia, who managed a very watery, wobbly smile back.

"Yes, Georgia saw everything that happened, Dr. Pritchard. She was up in the cab of the lorry; Patrick was giving her a lift to London. And it wasn't Patrick's fault at all; something hit the windscreen and shattered it, so he couldn't see. Georgia has told him again and again that he was as good as blinded; there was nothing he could do. Now, isn't that the most wonderful news? And he's sitting in there, just . . . just happy."

"Maeve, I'm so pleased for you. And good for you, Georgia, for coming forward."

"Not . . . not really," said Georgia. "I mean, I . . . well, I should have done it earlier."

"What matters is that you did it at all," said Maeve. "When I think of the state Patrick was in . . ."

"Exactly," said Georgia. "I've just been a total wimp right from the beginning. I feel so ashamed of myself. But I have told the police everything now, so maybe . . ."

"Well done," he said. "That doesn't sound too wimpy to me. No doubt they'll be along to talk to Patrick again. I'd better warn the patient liaison people, Maeve. They may well have been on to them already."

"Um . . . do you know where Linda, my . . . my agent, went?" said Georgia, looking around. "I thought she was going to wait here."

"Ah . . ." Alex Pritchard looked rather uncomfortable. "She's . . . she's gone outside. My fault, I'm afraid. She wanted to make some calls and I . . . I suggested she did it outside the hospital. Look, why don't I take you down to the café, and you can wait there for . . . for Miss . . . Miss . . ."

"Di-Marcello," said Georgia. "But she won't know we're there—"

"I'll tell the people up here to redirect her when she gets back."

"Oh, OK. That'd be very kind. Sorry, we're taking up a lot of your time."

Alex was disproportionately touched by this. Here was this girl, not much older than his own daughter from the look of her, actually aware that people other than her had pressures on their time. Extraordinary.

"That's perfectly all right," he said, and guided them towards the lift. "And Maeve, I'll wager Patrick wants to see those boys of yours now. Am I right?"

"You are indeed, Dr. Pritchard. He said to bring them tomorrow, to take them out of school."

"Excellent."

He smiled at her; he was obviously very fond of her, Georgia thought. What an amazingly nice man.

. . .

Linda was walking up the broad hospital steps, finishing a call when she saw him walking towards her. She scowled at him, rather exaggeratedly switching her phone off.

"Don't worry," she said, "I've finished. I'll just go up and collect Georgia; then we'll be out of your hospital for good."

"Well, she's in the café. That's what I was coming to tell you. I didn't want you to go on a wild-goose chase."

"Oh." She stared at him, clearly surprised. "Well, that's very . . . kind of you."

"No, no. The hospital is vast; you can lose someone very easily."

"I could always have called her, you know," said Linda, "on my mobile. Had you not been around, of course." She looked at him, and then smiled. "Sorry. That was a cheap shot. I shouldn't have been using the phone. I do know that. I apologise if I was rude. It's been a bit of a weekend. No excuse, but . . ."

"I can imagine. And I apologise in turn. It's been a bit of a one here too. Complete nightmare."

"Really?"

He looked different suddenly: shaken and less sure of himself. He was actually rather . . . rather attractive, she thought. In a wild sort of way.

"Yes. I can't go into details, but . . . well, suffice it to say I haven't had much sleep."

"Isn't that the norm, in your profession?"

"In my discipline, certainly."

"Your discipline?"

"Yes, I'm the A and E consultant. Pretty unpredictable lot of patients."

He smiled at her. He had an extraordinary smile; it had a fierce quality, and Linda felt slightly disoriented by it.

"Anyway, let me escort you to the café, make sure you and Georgia are safely reunited."

"I'm sure you've got better things to do."

"Right now, I don't think I have," he said, "as a matter of fact."

. . .

Georgia was drinking her coffee when a young man in a denim shirt sat down at her table.

"I . . . wonder if you'd mind if I joined you."

"What . . . ? Oh, no, course not, go ahead."

She'd thought he meant just to sit and read or something; but he smiled rather determinedly at her.

"I . . . that is, was it you in the lift an hour or so ago? Going up to ICU?"

"Might have been. I mean, I have been up there, yes."

God. She hoped he wasn't trying to chat her up. She looked at him. No, he was probably worried about someone.

"Do you have a relative up there?" she said.

"No, no. Not up there. You?"

"Oh . . . no. Just a friend."

"Not Mr. Connell?"

"How do you know about Mr. Connell?"

"Oh . . . most people do. In the hospital."

"Really? Well I . . . I don't."

"Is that right? I thought I saw you with Mrs. Connell."

"You must have imagined it. Look . . . who are you? Are you something to do with the hospital? Or . . ."

"I suppose I'd better come clean," he said. "I'm a reporter. *Daily Sketch.*" He held out his hand. "And you are . . . ?"

Georgia stood up. She wasn't prepared at all for what she did next; it was as if she was watching someone else.

"You can just fuck off," she said, and her voice was very loud. "Fuck right off, away from me, away from the hospital, away from Patrick Connell. You are totally disgusting, writing lies about people, implying things you don't know are even remotely true."

She half ran out of the café.

All the other customers sat transfixed, staring first after her and then at Osborne, who stood up, trying to look as if he was in control of the situation, and then hurried out after her and into the car park, where both his car and his laptop were waiting.

Part Four

MOVING ON

CHAPTER 30

All she'd done was sigh. And it had been a very small, quiet sigh . . . she'd thought. That nobody could possibly have heard. But that's what had done it. Had launched her into this dangerously stupid, totally wrong, and wonderfully right-feeling thing where every day, every minute was amazing and shiny, where everyone, however dull or unpleasant, seemed charming and amusing, where every task, however disagreeable or onerous, seemed engaging and fascinating. Where she felt calm and cool one moment, and dizzy and sparkly the next; where she looked in the mirror and smiled at herself; where she relived every conversation, every memory, every confidence, every sweet, small discovery, and yet still they seemed fresh and important and worthy of further examination still. Where she was, in a word . . . or rather two . . . in love. Absolutely, unquestioningly, and for the time being, at least, most joyfully in love. And able to see that what she had felt for Luke had not been love at all; it had been finite, reasonable, entirely suitable in every way. How she felt about Barney was infinite, unreasonable, and entirely unsuitable; and it was the most important and defining thing that had ever happened to her.

. . .

He'd said he ought to go that afternoon, once he had seen Toby and knew he was all right. And he'd told Emma that he really should get back to London; there was some really important client coming in the next day, demanding to see the whole team, and Barney had work to do before then. Emma nodded and said yes, of course, and that she'd keep an eye on Toby but she was sure he'd be fine and would probably go home in a few more days.

From which viewpoint—one from which she and Barney would never see each other again—everything looked suddenly rather bleak. Which was ridiculous, because he had Amanda and she had Luke and . . .

"Yes, I see," said Barney. "Well, that's excellent news. Good. Thank you again, Emma. Couldn't have got through the day without you."

"Of course you could," she said, smiling.

And, "No," he said, "no, I couldn't. Not any of it, actually." And he bent and kissed her lightly on the cheek and said, "Bye, then," and turned away; and that was when she'd sighed and he'd heard it and turned back to her and there was a brief silence, and then he said, "Emma, could I . . . that is, well, could I buy you a drink? Just to say thank-you for all your help and support today. And all the other days. I'd like to, very much. But if you're working, of course, or you've got something else on . . ."

"No," she said, "no, no, I'm not. Working. Not after six, anyway. And I haven't got anything on. No."

"So . . . does that mean yes?"

"Yes. I mean, it does mean yes. Thank you. That'd be great. Yes."

And wondered if he realised as clearly as she did what he had asked and what she was saying yes to.

. . .

They had had a drink in a pub she had suggested. It was a lovely evening; they sat outside and chatted. Slightly awkwardly. Quite awkwardly, actually. Both knowing why. She should have said no. She shouldn't have sighed.

After a bit he said he should go; and she said she should go; and they got back into Barney's car and drove back to the hospital, so that Emma could pick up her car.

"Well," she said, "that was very nice, Barney. Thank you. And . . . don't worry about Toby anymore."

And she smiled and she certainly didn't sigh. Mistake, the whole going-for-a-drink thing. Big mistake.

. . .

Barney remembered the next few moments for the rest of his life. Watching her smile, open the door, swing one long leg out of it. And feeling a rush of sheer and shocking panic. She was going, the moment was passing, the day was over, the excuse almost gone. Well . . . good. He was engaged, she was . . . well, probably nearly engaged. What was he doing even thinking what he was thinking?

He put out his hand onto her arm. Her thin, brown arm. Which was warm and felt . . . well, felt wonderful. She looked at him, startled; then down at his hand and then back at his face. Her eyes, those huge blue eyes, meeting his. It was fatal, awful.

"Don't go," he said.

"But, Barney . . ."

"Please don't go. I don't want you to go."

And then, very quietly: "I don't want to go either."

He put the car in gear, drove very fast out of the car park, down the road, towards Cirencester. He knew the whole area extremely well. Knew where there were lanes, quiet lanes, with gateways into fields where you could stop. And park. And turn to someone. And kiss them. Over and over again. And feel them kissing you back.

. . .

Later he said, "I knew, you know; I knew the minute I saw you."

"Me too. 'There he is,' I thought, 'there's the One.' "

"And then what did you think?"

"I thought, 'Oh shit.' I said, 'Oh shit.' "

"I thought the same. I thought, 'There she is.' And then I thought, 'Oh, fuck.' I said, 'Oh, fuck.' "

"Because it's rubbish, isn't it? All that?"

"Course it is."

"I mean, I've got Luke."

"And I've got Amanda. I'm engaged to Amanda. Who's . . ."

"Who's beautiful. And so nice, I can tell."

"Beautiful and so nice. But I don't seem to love her. Not like I thought I did."

"And then there's Luke. Who's such a dude and so nice. But I don't seem to love him either. So . . . what do we do?"

"Explore it a bit," said Barney. "We have to; it's the only thing to do."

. . .

They did; they explored each other. But quickly. One long evening, talking, talking, talking. One long night, making love, hardly sleeping, in Emma's flat. One long day, walking, talking, kissing, worrying; another evening talking, and one hurried, wonderfully awful fuck in a room at the hospital.

Like all lovers, they developed jokes, codes, secrets.

"Thanks for calling" meant "I can't talk now"; "Maybe tomorrow" meant "I miss you"; "My pleasure" meant "I love you."

And every time, every meeting led them nearer to being sure that this relationship, shared between them, was the one that mattered, and the other ones could not go on; and almost equally sure that they wanted to spend the rest of their lives together.

. . .

What must it be like to be one of these people? Freeman thought, looking at the obvious trappings of wealth, on display even here, in this hospital cubicle: the laptop, the iPod, the silver-framed photographs by his bed, the huge plate of grapes, the box of chocolates from Fortnum & Mason, the pile of new hardbacks . . .

To know that if you wanted something you could almost certainly have it? To have gone to the best schools, the best universities, to have no doubt travelled widely, to drive the best cars, to wear the best clothes?

Pretty bloody good, he supposed (having known little of any of those things), but did it make you happy? Did it create a conscience? Or did it make you arrogant, ruthless, greedy for more?

"Sergeant Freeman, do sit down."

He gestured at the chair by his bed.

"Glad you're feeling better, sir. And that your leg is mending."

"Not as glad as I am. Still bloody painful, though, I can tell you. I should be home in another day or two. Thank God. Er . . . I thought there were going to be two of you?"

"There are, sir. Constable Rowe is on his way. Shouldn't be more than a few minutes. Ah, here he is now."

They went through the formalities, the reasons for choosing the M4, the exact location of the church, the late departure . . . "I wasn't too well—seemed to have picked up a stomach bug, kept throwing up. All you need on your wedding day!"

"Not a hangover then, sir?"

"Lord, no, we hardly had anything the night before. Well, Barney had a few; I simply wasn't feeling up to it."

He was cheerfully up-front about being stopped by the police:

"Barney was driving, of course, going a hell of a lick, but then, we were very late. If we hadn't been stopped, we'd have made it in time. Still . . . even bridegrooms aren't above the law, I suppose, Sergeant?"

"Indeed not, sir. But . . . you did also have to stop for petrol, I believe?"

"Yes, we did. And I . . . well, I had to go to the loo again."

"But . . . you didn't need anything else, no oil, anything like that?"

"No, no, just the fuel."

"Although . . . the CCTV shows you in a queue for the air line."

"Ah, yes. Yes, we did . . . That is, we were . . . there."

"Were you worried about the tyres, sir? Did you have any reason to think they needed checking?"

"No, no, in fact, they were new tyres. I was just being careful."

"Very wise. So you didn't think one might be soft, something like that? Which could, of course, have contributed to the blowout."

"No, nothing like that. I just thought we should check them."

"Even though you were so late?"

"Well . . . yes."

"I see. Well . . . we may be mistaken, but again, according to the CCTV, you drove away . . . apparently . . . without doing so."

He was a good actor; he didn't look remotely rattled.

"Ah. Well . . . well, maybe we did. I . . . I went in to pay for the fuel, you see. It was all a bit of a blur. We were pretty stressed out, as you can imagine."

"Indeed. But . . . try to remember, sir, it could be important."

"Yes, I suppose it could. Yes. Look, I . . . I don't want to get anyone into trouble. The thing is . . . Barney . . . you know my best man, Barney Fraser? Did he . . . did he explain about what happened?"

"Not as far as I can recall, sir, no."

"Ah. Well, actually, you see, I . . . I did want to check the tyres. As I said. But he was so worried about how late we were . . . Well, it was his main duty, after all, to get me to the church on time . . . Anyway, he said there wasn't time to check them, that we couldn't wait, that they'd be fine, persuaded me to carry on . . ."

. . .

"Perhaps you didn't see the latest report from Forensics?" said Constable Rowe as they drove down the lane. "The one that came in last week, while you were away, about the fragment of tyre with the nail in it?"

"Oh, yes," said Freeman. "I saw it. Very interesting."

"But . . . if that was the cause of the blowout, as Forensics seems to think, what was all that about whether or not he checked the tyre pressures?"

"There have to be some perks in this job, Rowe," said Freeman, "and seeing little shits like that squirm is one of them."

It was a great pity, as Linda Di-Marcello remarked, that Georgia looked like she did and did what she did. The tabloids all tracked her down, and there were two or three nightmare days when the story ran in most of them. Her hauntingly lovely little face, with its great dark eyes and wayward cloud of hair, sat above the caption, "M4 Mystery Girl," or in some cases, "M4 Mystery Girl Found," and then informed the reader not only that the mystery girl in the lorry was Georgia Linley from Cardiff, but that she was an actress who had just won a part in a new Channel Four drama and that she was on her way to her audition in London when the crash occurred.

There was a quote from Georgia, composed by Linda with damage limitation in mind, saying how sorry she was for any problems she might have caused, that she was unable to answer any questions about the crash because it was still under police investigation, that she had visited Patrick Connell in the hospital several times, that he was recovering well, and his wife and she had become great friends. All of which, as Linda also remarked, was true.

Just the same, it was acutely unpleasant for Georgia, and she continued to feel ashamed of herself, and, most of all, dreadfully anxious about starting work on *Moving Away*, and about how badly the other members of the production team might think of her.

. . .

Jonathan still felt he was living in a nightmare.

Even a call from that old goat Freeman, telling him that there was evidence that the crash appeared to have been due in large part to the lorry sustaining a shattered windscreen—why couldn't these people speak proper English?—but that they were still gathering evidence, failed to make him feel much better. If they were still gathering evidence, then it could even now be seen as important that he'd been on the phone, and God knew where that could land him.

He looked back on his old life—years ago, as it seemed, rather than weeks—with its easy, pleasant patterns, with something near dis-belief. He was often depressed, frequently nervous, his professional confidence shaken, his smooth charm roughened by weariness and self-doubt.

The whole household seemed on tenterhooks, no one easy, even the children; Charlie was edgy, less trustful, almost wary of him, the little girls awkward and fractious. Taking their emotional cues from their mother, he supposed, without realising it.

Laura had moved away from him; she was oddly self-contained, less hostile, but far from warm. They were sharing the marital bed once more, but it was as if she had drawn a barrier down it, holding him from her by sheer force of will. He felt she was biding her time, waiting for something to happen—she knew not what, only that she would recognise its significance and therefore whether or not their marriage was still viable.

And he could see that the danger of that something, while as yet nameless and formless, was still extremely real.

. . .

Abi had never been so happy. Day after day it went on, like some won-derful, long, golden summer. An absurd, sweet happiness, born of this absurd, sweet love affair. Absurd and so extremely unsuitable. For both of them . . .

It had begun in earnest that night in the farm office. Adjacent to the lambing shed.

Not many people had sex in farm offices adjacent to a lambing shed. Or not many people she knew, anyway. Well, nobody she knew. Maybe they did in the country. Life was certainly different there.

They'd met in the pub and he'd suggested they go to another one a couple of miles away: "Too many people here I know."

"Are you ashamed to be seen with me, William?" she'd said.

And he'd blushed and said, "Of course not," in tones of such hor-ror that she'd laughed. "It's just that we'll be . . . well, you know, interrupted all the time." And they'd driven to the other one in the Land Rover, and she'd had two vodkas and he'd had two beers and it had straightaway begun to get out of hand. Or rather she'd got out of hand. She just couldn't stand it, sitting there, looking at him, with those bloody great feet of his, and his ridiculously sexy mouth . . . and she'd savoured that mouth now that she knew what it could do . . . and his eyes moving over her, looking at her cleavage and her legs . . . and she'd shifted her chair nearer him, and pushed one of her legs up against his, just because she wanted to touch him, even through those ridiculous trousers he'd worn—what were they called, cavalry twill or something? Really grossly old-fashioned—and then he'd said would she like another drink, and she'd said, "No, William, not really, thank you very much," and he'd looked a bit nonplussed, and she'd said, "I tell you what I would like, William," and he'd said, "What's that?" looking slightly nervous, and she'd said, "I'd like to go out to the car," and they'd sat in it and snogged rather deliciously for a while, and then she'd said . . . after he'd made it clear he wanted what she wanted, every bit as much, possibly even more, "I'd like to go back to your house. To your room," and he'd been so horrified it had been quite funny.

"Abi, we can't do that. I'm sorry. We just can't. You've met my parents; can you really imagine them sitting calmly watching TV if they thought . . . if they knew . . . we were . . . Well, it just doesn't happen. Honestly, if I tried, I'd be so . . . so . . . well, I wouldn't be able to do it."

She decided not to ask him what he'd done in the past, simply said, "Well, we have to find somewhere, William. I'd suggest going back to mine, but I don't think I can wait that long . . ."

That was when he'd suggested the office.

It hadn't been too bad, the office. It was away from the house, quite far away; they'd gone in his car down a long track, to part of what he called the lambing shed. Which was hardly a shed, but a huge building that could have housed half a dozen families. They went into it; the office was at the far end, a surprisingly clean, warm pair of rooms . . . "This is my bit, mine and Dad's; the other's for the farm secretary. She—"

"William, I don't want to know about the farm secretary . . . Oh, God, can we just get on with it?"

He started to kiss her: that incredible style of kissing he had, slow and hard and sort of thoughtful; and while he did so, she managed to pull her dress off: all she was wearing under it was a pair of pants.

And then he'd started kissing her breasts in the same way, and then she'd pushed him down onto a sort of large couch thing, and . . . well, then it had all been totally incredible.

It seemed to go on for hours, wonderful, wild, noisy hours, as he worked on her body, made its sensations rise and fall, ease and tauten, as he moved slowly, then fast, then slowly again, pushed her to the edge, then pulled her back, as she felt everything with her head and her heart as well as her body, as he invaded every aspect of her, every capacity for pleasure she had, as she came, yelling with triumph, and then again and then, yes, yet again.

. . .

And now, nearly two weeks later, it was . . . well, it was absolutely great. They alternated between her place and one of the empty holiday cottages on the farm . . . He said he hadn't thought of them before, and they were certainly more comfortable than the farm office. She didn't mind William's insistence that they only use candles in case his mother or the cowman who lived quite near them noticed the lights on and came to investigate; it seemed rather romantic. They cooked Ready Meals, usually curry, on the time-warp electric stoves, and drank some very indifferent wine and then had a lot of wonderful sex. She didn't even mind the drive home at some point in the night; in fact, she rather liked it: the roads were clear, and she could play the radio and sing loudly along with it, and think about William and how sweet and funny he was and how much she loved being with him, and not just for the sex. Her only fear, and it was truly dark and dreadful, was that William would find out what she was really like.

CHAPTER 31

Incredibly pushy, what that woman had done: calling the hospital, asking for his secretary, leaving a message, and then calling again before he'd even begun to think what to do about it. And then just . . . asking him out. No excuses, no, "I wanted to hear more about the Connells," or, "I wondered if Georgia had helped as much as we hoped." Simply, "This is Linda Di-Marcello here."

He'd been completely taken aback just hearing from her.

"It was very nice meeting you on Sunday. I've been hearing so much about you from Georgia. Well, from Maeve Connell, really. And I wondered if you'd like to go to a show one night. I get tickets for pretty well everything, and I don't know what sort of thing you like, but there's a new musical previewing, based on *The Canterbury Tales,* supposed to be good, or there's yet another *Macbeth;* take your pick. Oh, and what sounds huge fun at Sadler's Wells if you like dance, sort of flamenco crossed with tap."

"Well, I . . . That's very kind. I'm not . . . well, I don't like dance. Not too keen on Shakespeare . . ."

"Fine. *Canterbury Tales* then. The tickets are for Saturday week. Any good? And then we could have a meal afterwards."

"I'm not . . . sure. I'll have to check my rota. Can I . . . can I get back to you?"

"Of course." She gave him her office number. He rang off sweating.

It was Francis who'd dared her to do it. She'd been telling him how the day had gone, how difficult Georgia had found it, how sweetly grateful Maeve had been, how much she thought they'd helped. And then threw in a little anecdote about Alex and how they'd had a spat over the phone and then made up in the car park.

"He turned out to be quite . . . quite sweet. Apparently he's going through a hideous divorce, Georgia informed me. She got all the goss from Maeve Connell."

"Really?"

"Yes. Well, I'd be on the wife's side, I think. He's clearly very arrogant. Sexy, though. Nice smile. Which, of course, isn't enough to keep a marriage together. I should know."

"Sexy, eh? Your type?"

"No, of course not. Well . . . maybe. Dark and brooding."

"Maybe you should ask him out."

"Oh, don't be so ridiculous, Francis."

"Why is it so ridiculous? Or is this not the woman who sat and moaned through an entire evening that she was lonely and longed for a man?"

"Not very seriously."

"I'd say pretty seriously. Actually." There was a pause; then he said, "I dare you, Linda. To ask him out. What have you got to lose?"

"My dignity."

"What's so great about dignity? Doesn't warm the other side of the bed. Go on. You ask him out; I'll pay for everything when we go to Bilbao."

"Really? First-class, five-star?"

"Yup. Promise."

She was silent, considering this; then she said, "All right. You're on. I'll ask him. Is that all I have to do?"

"Well . . . and take him out if he says yes."

"He won't say yes."

. . .

It was Amy who'd made him accept. Dared him to accept. He got home that night and found her watching *Sex and the City* instead of doing her homework, and switched the TV off. She glared at him.

"First Mum, now you."

"Where is Mum?"

"She's gone out with Larry." She avoided his eyes. Both she and Adam adored both their parents, patently found the breakup painful. "He looked so ridiculous; he's such a medallion man. They were going to some concert or other. Duran Duran. I mean, please. Good thing you don't go out on dates, Dad."

"And how do you know I don't?"

"Well . . . you're too old. For a start. I mean, much older than Mum."

He was stung. "Not that much. Thanks, Amy. And actually, and just for your information, I was asked on a date today."

"What? An actual date? Not some medical lecture?"

"An actual date."

"By?"

"By some woman I met."

"How long have you known her?"

"I don't, really. We only met a few days ago."

"Dad! Dad, that is . . . what's her name? What's she do?"

"Her name is Linda Martello. Something like that. And she's a theatrical agent."

"God! No kidding. Is she as old as you?"

"No. Not quite."

"Good-looking?"

"Yes, I would say so."

"And she's asked you out?"

"Yes. To some play and then to dinner."

"That is so cool. Are you going?"

"No, of course not."

"Why not?"

"Well . . . because . . . because I don't particularly like her. I'd have nothing to say to her."

Amy sat studying him; then she said, "I dare you. I dare you to go out with her. She sounds really cool. And she could be a big help in my career on the stage. And it might be fun. Your life is so not fun. I really think you should."

"Amy . . ."

"If you don't, I'll tell Miss Jackson. And she'll tell the whole hospital."

"You wouldn't!"

She laughed. "No, probably I wouldn't, but I do think you should go. I'd like you to. Go on, Dad; live dangerously."

. . .

They met outside the theatre: arrived at exactly the same time, exactly fifteen minutes before curtain-up. Not a lot of time to talk, to run out of talk, the awkwardness kept at bay by the various rituals: drink, programmes, settling into seats.

Very good seats. Maybe it was going to be all right.

. . .

The musical was terrible; Linda said, as the curtain came down on the first act, that there was no reason they should stay.

"Honestly. I don't mind. I'm not enjoying it, and if you're not either, where's the point?"

He agreed there was none and they went to the restaurant. She had booked it: Joe Allen, in Covent Garden. Alex, while appalled by the noise, did manage to absorb the fact that it offered the opposite of a romantic atmosphere, so at least she had spared him that. Their table wasn't ready, as they were so early, so they sat at the bar. And tried to talk. It was difficult; they had very little in common, no knowledge of each other's worlds. She told him one of her best friends was married to a surgeon; he told her his daughter wanted to be an actress. There was a silence. She apologised for the play; he said he hoped the management or whoever had given her the tickets wouldn't notice their empty seats. There was another silence.

"So . . . how many actors and actresses do you have on your books, then?" he said.

"Actors. No such thing as actresses anymore. I mean, you don't have doctoresses, do you?"

"No, indeed. So . . . how many actors?" He stressed the second syllable, sounding slightly derisive.

"About two hundred."

"That sounds like quite a lot."

"It is quite a lot."

Another silence, a very long one. Then she suddenly said, "Look . . . this was probably a bad idea. This evening. I'm sorry."

"No, no, not at all. Very nice idea."

"Same as the play, really. If you'd rather go, I won't mind. I mean, there doesn't seem a lot of point."

. . .

He looked at her; she really was . . . what? Not pretty. Features too strong. Beautiful? No, not really. But . . . arresting. The amazing auburn hair, and the dark eyes. She had a wonderful figure: tall, slim, good bosom, fantastic legs. And very nice clothes. She was wearing a black dress, quite low-cut but not embarrassingly so, and a bright emerald green shawl. And emerald green shoes, with very high heels. It was a shame, really, that she was so . . . well, a bit harsh. Very direct, very opinionated. And he hadn't liked being corrected over the actor business. Not charming.

. . .

She looked at him; he really was . . . what? Not handsome. Features too irregular. But . . . attractive. Sexy. The wild dark hair, the probing dark eyes. Surprisingly nice clothes: that dark navy jacket . . . really well cut, and the blue-on-white stripes of the shirt really suited him.

"Well . . . look," he said, "it's been very nice. Really, I've enjoyed meeting you. I appreciate your asking me out. But . . . well, I'm on call tomorrow. So maybe not dinner. If it's all the same to you."

"Absolutely," she said.

She smiled at him, totally in control. She was a very cool customer. Much too cool for him. And hadn't he sworn never to get involved again with someone who didn't understand the medical profession? Not that he was going to get involved.

"Well . . . we've ordered this." She gestured at the bottle of wine. "May as well finish it."

"Good idea."

She looked at him as he picked up his glass. What a disaster. Well. She'd done it. Never would again, though. Bloody Francis. What a thing to make her do. *So* not her.

Suddenly she wanted to tell him. It really wouldn't matter. They would never meet again. And she didn't want him to think she was what she wasn't.

"I want to tell you something," she said. "I only asked you out because I was dared to. It's not the sort of thing I usually do. Honestly. I couldn't have you going away thinking I was some kind of hard-as-nails ball breaker."

"You were dared?"

"Yes. 'Fraid so."

"That's really very funny," he said, and started to laugh. "Because I was dared to accept. It's not the sort of thing I usually do either."

"Oh, God!" She was laughing now. "Who dared you?"

"My daughter. She told me I should get a life. Who dared you?"

"My business partner. He told me more or less the same thing. And I thought . . . what have I got to lose?"

"I thought the same. And . . ."

"Miss Di-Marcello, your table is ready."

"Oh. Oh, well . . . we don't really—"

"Oh, come on," he said, "let's eat. I dare you!"

CHAPTER 32

She'd hoped, very much, that things were about to be better. The TV programme had definitely had an effect on Christine; it had made her realise what a lucky escape her mother had had. Seeing the size of the crash—again—realising how easily Mary could have been just a few cars farther forward, or even hit by one of the freezers, had sobered her. She was quiet during supper, and when Mary had said good night to her, later, she had kissed her and said, "Night, Mum. Thank goodness you were where you were—on the road, I mean."

Mary felt more cheerful than she had for a week as she got herself ready for bed.

She had switched on the radio and turned the light out; she was too tired to read, and she liked being lulled to sleep by the well-bred voices of the World Service announcers. But it wasn't quite time for the World Service, and there was a programme on Radio Two about popular music over the past sixty years. Starting inevitably with the war. And equally inevitably with Vera Lynn, singing "White Cliffs of Dover."

The hours she'd spent listening to that song. On her gramophone. The gramophone Russell had bought her, as a parting present. She'd been worried her mother would want to know where it had come from and had invented a woman at work who didn't want it anymore.

"But they're expensive things, Mary. I'm surprised she didn't want to sell it."

"Oh, she's got a lot of money, Mum."

"Even so. Well, you'd better look after it."

As if she wouldn't: the very last present Russell ever gave her, before going off to Normandy. He'd given her other more personal things, the brooch—that had been easier to explain: she'd said she'd spotted it in the Red Cross jumble sale, and her mother would never know that his eye was a real diamond—and of course all the usual things that the GIs had been able to afford that the British troops couldn't—like nylons and perfume. And the gramophone record (together with the sheet music) of Vera Lynn singing what she always thought of as the bluebird song.

She'd played it over and over and over again, until it had become too scratched to hear it any longer, and of course it was always on the wireless too, the song that had seen so many romances started—and had kept them alive through the long years of separation. Whenever it was played, when she was with Donald again, married to Donald, but most of all when she was coping with her unhappiness at saying good-bye to Russell, it was him she thought of, whom she could almost feel beside her again, dashing, handsome Russell, with his perfect manners, dancing with her. He'd been a wonderful dancer, not born with two left feet like poor Donald—they had fox-trotted and waltzed, him holding her very close and telling her how lovely she was. They had even jitterbugged together in dance halls like the Lyceum and places like the Café Royal and, most wonderfully of all, Mary had thought, at the Royal Opera House, Covent Garden. It had been closed for ballet and opera performances but, rather surprisingly, was the scene every afternoon for tea dances. They had only gone there once, for Mary was working, but she had been given the afternoon off and met Russell in the Strand, at Lyons Corner House and they had walked together through Covent Garden Market and gone in the wonderful great doors of the Opera House; she had felt like a queen herself.

She had never gone again, never thought of going to a performance there in the years since; it was terribly expensive. But every so often when she was near it, in the Strand or on Waterloo Bridge, she would make a detour and stand outside, looking up at it, and the years would roll away and she would feel Russell's hand pulling her up the steps and into the red-and-gilt foyer and hear his voice saying, "come along, my lovely Little Sparrow, come and dance with me . . ."

She lay there in the darkness that night, listening to it and smiling. It seemed a very good sign.

But it wasn't too much of one, because in the morning, when she said casually at breakfast that Russell had asked if she would like to take Gerry and Christine to his hotel for lunch the next day so that they could meet, Christine's rather pale face had gone very pink and she said she was sorry, but she didn't feel she could.

"All right, dear," said Mary, trying to sound calm, "we'll leave it for a little while longer. Maybe next weekend?"

"Mum," said Christine, "you don't understand. I really don't want to meet this man. I'd feel terribly disloyal to Dad. I know you don't see it like that, but I can't help it. You're going home in a few days and then you can see him whenever you want to, but meanwhile, please respect my feelings and just . . . well, leave me out of it."

That had been too much for Mary; she had gone up to her room and cried. After a while, there was a knock on the door and Gerry came in. He was clearly very embarrassed.

"I'm sorry, Mary. Very sorry. I think it's . . . well, very nice that you've got this . . . this friend, and I can't see Chris's problem. But you know what she's like, and she did adore her dad. I'm sure she'll come round."

"I hope so," said Mary.

She blew her nose and thanked Gerry for being so understanding and tried to cheer herself up with the thought that at least she could spend the next day with Russell, and that the following week she'd be home and she could see him whenever she liked. But she felt dreadfully sad.

It got better, of course—much better—when she was in her own home, where she had been now for the past week. In fact, in most ways, it had been, well . . . perfectly happy. Russell came over every day in the car, or he sent the car for her and she was driven over to Bath; his hotel was absolutely beautiful, and they would wander round the grounds arm in arm, talking, laughing, remembering one minute, looking forward the next.

And Russell had fallen in love with the beautiful countryside around Bath and the lovely houses that lay within it, and now, he said, he meant to show her one, one that he thought she would really like;

she had thought he meant something like a National Trust property, perhaps, that they could look around and have lunch in.

So she dressed with particular care, put on the Jaeger suit, the fateful Jaeger suit; Russell was waiting for her on the doorstep and got in beside her, said they could have coffee later, and told Ted, the driver, to go "to the house near Tadwick we saw last night," and they drove along in silence for about half an hour, Russell's blue eyes shining as he looked out of the window. Mary could feel his excitement; it was like being with a child on Christmas Eve.

It was a perfect autumn day, golden and cobweb-hung, mists still lying in the small valleys; they were climbing slightly now, and then Russell said "Close your eyes." She did so obediently, felt the car turn off, slow down, stop. "Open them," he said, and she did, and saw a narrow lane curving down just a little to the left, with great chestnut trees overhanging it, and at the bottom, there it was: a house, a grey stone house, quite low, just two storeys, with a grey slate roof, tall windows and a wide, white front door, complete with fanlight and overhung with wisteria. At the right-hand end it bowed out into what Mary would have described—not knowing any architectural terms— as an extra bit, and which Russell—who seemed strong on architectural terms—described as a friendship. They drove down towards the house; Ted pulled outside the front door and they got out.

It was very quiet, very still, the only sound wood pigeons, and somewhere behind the house the wonderfully real, reassuring sound of a lawn mower.

"It's lovely," she said. "Does it belong to a friend of yours?"

"You could say so. Knock on the door; let's see if we can go in."

The door had a lion's-head knocker; it was so heavy, Mary could hardly lift it.

She heard footsteps, heard the door being unbolted, watched it open, found herself looking at a grey-haired woman wearing a white apron. She smiled at them.

"Good morning, Mr. Mackenzie."

"Good morning, Mrs. Salter. This is Mrs. Bristow. She'd like to see the house, if that's OK."

"Of course. Come in, Mrs. Bristow."

The hall was big and square, with a slate floor; a wide, curving staircase rose from it, with a tall window on the turn. There was a drawing room, with tall windows and wooden shutters and a huge stone fireplace with a wonderful-smelling wood fire burning; there was a dining room, with another stone fireplace and French windows opening onto a terrace overhung with a rose-bearing pergola; there was a kitchen, with a vast wooden table and a dark green Aga; there was another smaller, very pretty room lined with books; and an even smaller one fitted out with coat hooks and boot racks. Upstairs were the bedrooms, some bigger, some smaller, two bathrooms with large, rather elderly-looking claw-footed baths and two rather thronelike lavatories, set in mahogany bench seats; after a while Mary ran out of polite, appreciative things to say and just smiled. It was an easy house to smile in; it contained an atmosphere of peace and happiness.

Finally, Mrs. Salter said she expected they would like some coffee and that, now the sun had come out, it might be nicer if they had it in the morning room . . . This turned out to be the book-lined one. "And would you like some biscuits or something, Mrs. Bristow? I've just made a lemon drizzle cake."

Mary said coffee would be lovely and there was nothing she liked more than lemon drizzle cake. Russell ushered her into the morning room and she sat down in one of the deep armchairs by the fireplace and looked at him.

"Like it?" he said.

"I absolutely love it. It's beautiful. The sort of house you see in illustrations in old books. But . . . whose is it?"

"I'm so glad you feel like that. I thought you probably would, but one can never be sure." He paused. "And if you really like it, Little Sparrow, then"—he paused, smiled at her, blew her a kiss across the room—"then it's yours."

. . .

"Is that Emma? The Emma? The Dr. King Emma?"

"It is indeed. And is that Barney? The Barney? The banker Barney?"

This was another code; there was another Emma at the hospital who worked in A&E reception, and the Barney had grown out of that.

"It is indeed. How are you; what have you been doing?"

"Um . . . let me see. Stitched up a little boy's foot; set an old lady's arm; given an old man an enema . . ."

"All right, all right, too much information. When can I see you?"

"Um . . . I've got Thursday off. And Friday, actually. All day."

"Friday all day? Jesus. There's a temptation."

She waited. Then he said, "OK. I can swing the afternoon. I'll be down around . . . oh, I don't know, two."

"Call me when you're near."

"I will. And you think of something we can do . . ."

"Barney! So much."

"OK, OK, but where to do it."

"Er . . . my bed?"

"You're on. Oh, God. I mustn't even start thinking about it. Bye, the Emma."

"Bye, the Barney!"

. . .

"You are extremely inconvenient, you know," he said to her now, as they sat in her lumpy, dishevelled bed in her dingy bedroom, having had some extremely wonderful sex, and drinking the champagne he had produced from his laptop bag.

"I'm sorry."

"That's all right. But there I was, thinking I'd got it all sussed, that I knew where I was going, and how and when, and then along came you, and just blew it all up in the air."

"Is there anything I can do to make myself less inconvenient?" she said.

"No, I'm afraid not. It's the fact of you that's inconvenient. Not you. You are . . . well, you're pretty convenient. In yourself."

"Yeah?"

"Yeah. You suit me absolutely perfectly. You couldn't possibly be even point nought nought nought per cent better for me."

"Nor you for me."

"You're worth it all," he said, suddenly very serious, "all the chaos, all the problems we're going to have. In fact, if you were more convenient, I probably wouldn't realise the worth of you nearly so well. I'd just think, 'Yeah, well, she's a bit of all right; I'd like a bit of that,' and you'd just be easy. Pure pleasure. Which you are, of course, anyway, but kind of . . . well, inconveniently. I love you, Emma, so much."

"I love you, too, Barney. So, so much."

"Hey, you put an extra *so* in."

"Well . . . how I feel needs an extra *so*."

"You mean, you reckon you love me more than I love you? Emma, I love you more than anything I could ever imagine, more than anything else in the world."

"And I love you more than more than anything else in the world."

"I like that," he said, smiling at her, looking like a delighted child. "I like that very much indeed."

. . .

They delighted each other in every possible way. Each found the way the other looked, smiled, talked, thought, absolutely pleasing. Sex for Emma was different with Barney, moving from pure, heady pleasure to something more thoughtful, more emotionally grounded. And she for Barney was an astonishing delight: inventive, fun, tireless.

They both closed their minds—with enormous difficulty—to the thought of the other sex, with the Others. It was something that would end: with the resolution of things.

Which was drawing nearer, meeting by meeting, day by day.

And yet was being held off for a little longer—by Barney, at least, and with Emma's understanding. He had known Amanda for years, had lived with her for over a year; their backgrounds were identical—they had lived the same sort of lives with the same sort of people and, when they met, had found countless friends in common. It was a charmed, closed circle that Emma found herself confronted by; Amanda was protected not only by her relationship with Barney, but by the conventions and mores of its members. Barney would be rejecting not only Amanda, but a large and powerful tribe; it would take great certainty as well as great courage to do so.

He felt in possession of both; but he was still aware of the huge and devastating effect it would have, not only on Amanda and not only on their personal life, but on his professional status and confidence as well.

It would not be easy—in any way at all.

CHAPTER 33

"Is that Georgia?"

"Oh . . . yes. Yes, it is."

"Georgia, this is Merlin Gerard."

"Who?"

"Merlin Gerard. Second assistant to Bryn Merrick on—"

"Oh, Merlin, I'm sorry. Yes, of course, I . . . I was miles away."

God. How embarrassing. He must think she was totally brain-dead.

"Look, wardrobe have asked me to get in touch. They want a day with you asap. How are you fixed for Monday. Is that OK?"

"Yes, fine."

"Good. If you could be at the Charlotte Street office at . . . nine thirty?"

"Yes, nine thirty's fine."

She'd have to get a very early train. She really must sort out somewhere in London to live.

"I'll tell them. Thanks, Georgia. And I'll see you—maybe—next Monday."

"Might you not be there?"

She shouldn't have said that. It sounded soppy.

"Possibly not. We're out looking at houses with the set designer. For filming in. We've got a short list of three."

"Did you actually find them?" There seemed no end to his talents. And importance.

"No, course not," he said, sounding amused, "the location manager does that sort of thing."

She put the phone down feeling terrible. Not just because she'd been so pathetic with Merlin, but because it was actually going to start happening now. She'd got to face them, start working with them, and they'd all know she was the awful, cowardly, pathetic girl who'd run away from the crash. They'd probably all been discussing it, calling one another, saying, "Did you see those stories in the paper? She seemed such a nice girl, and all the time . . ." Oh, God.

She'd been to see Patrick twice more and felt she was doing something for him now, at least. The second time she'd gone, a very nice old lady had arrived; she was called Mary and seemed to know both Patrick and Maeve quite well.

"I was in the crash as well, you see," she said, "and I was brought here for a few days. I met Maeve and we became good friends."

Patrick had gone to sleep, and she'd suggested to Mary that they go and have a coffee together. Mary had seemed incredibly pleased by this, and they'd had a really good chat; she told Georgia that Maeve had told her all about her, and how kind she was being visiting Patrick, "And how brave you were, coming forward . . ."

"Hardly brave," Georgia had said. "I waited a fortnight." But Mary said nonsense, it was coming forward at all that mattered, and that moreover, it was very nice to see a young person giving up her time to visit someone in the hospital.

Georgia had really liked her; she was so pretty, in an old-lady sort of way, and very sparkly, and seemed really interested in Georgia's acting, which Maeve had also told her about: wanted to know all about the series and how it was going. She obviously had a lot of money; she'd had a huge car and a driver waiting for her, and she'd insisted on dropping Georgia off at the station.

"It's been lovely talking to you," she said, kissing Georgia good-bye. "I do so enjoy young people. Thank you for your time, my dear."

She obviously saw shared time as a rare and precious gift; and how sad was that? Georgia thought.

. . .

It had happened—inevitably. Mrs. Grainger had arrived at cottage number one just as Abi had removed every stitch of clothing, apart from her high heels, and was dancing in front of William. Who was sitting on the sofa, wearing a shirt but nothing else—they had actually been playing Abi's version of Strip Jack Naked—and grinning at her happily.

Abi always said later that Mrs. Grainger must have known she was going to find her son inside, doing something unsuitable; if she had actually feared intruders or squatters, as she said, she would have brought Mr. Grainger, complete with shotgun, with her.

In the event, she simply opened the front door, put all the downstairs lights on, and walked into the sitting room; seeing her face (as Abi also said) was almost worth all that followed: the complex mingling of embarrassment, shock, and grim disapproval.

"Ah, William," was all she said; and the worst thing for Abi was his immediate reaction. He went very white, reached for his trousers, and started pulling them frantically on; Abi stood staring at him for a moment before sitting down on the sofa and pulling her dress around her shoulders, at least covering her breasts, on which Mrs. Grainger's attention seemed to be focused.

"I'm sorry, Mother," said William. (*What for, for God's sake?* Abi wondered. *For having, at the age of thirty-four, a sex life?*)

"Yes," Mrs. Grainger said, turning her gaze on him now. "Yes, well, it was rather alarming, realising there was someone in here. I didn't know what to think. You should have told us you intended to use it."

Abi giggled; she just couldn't help it. What was he meant to tell them? "Please, Mother, I intend to use cottage number one this evening for some sexual activity. I hope that's all right." Mrs. Grainger gave her a very cold look, William a desperate one.

"Sorry," she said hastily.

"Right. Well, please lock up carefully when you leave."

And she stalked out.

"Oh, Lord," said William.

"William," said Abi. "William, I know it's embarrassing, but you haven't committed a crime. You're having fun. And at least with a girl. Think if I'd been a boy. Or a cow."

"Abi, please!" said William. "It isn't funny."

"Yes, it is. It's terribly funny." And then she realised how genuinely anguished he was and sat down, took his hand. "Come on. What's so bad? The worst is that she's seen me for what she clearly feared I am: no end of a hussy, leading her little boy astray. She'll get over it."

He shook her hand off.

"No, Abi. You don't understand. She won't. It wasn't very . . . kind to her."

"What on earth does that mean? What was unkind? You weren't laughing at her."

"You were," he said, very quietly.

She stared at him. "William, I can't believe you said that."

"Sorry. But . . . but it's true. She would have been very . . . very upset by that."

· 313 ·

"Well, she shouldn't have been. What planet is she living on, for God's sake?"

"Abi, please. Don't be so . . . so harsh."

"Oh, for God's sake. This is absurd." She stood up, started dressing. "I'm not listening to any more of this rubbish. If anyone's harsh, it's her. And arrogant. Where's her sense of humour; where are her good manners, for God's sake?"

"Good manners?"

"Yes. What she should have done was apologised for embarrassing us, me. Not made us both feel like we were in some kind of a porn show."

"We were, as far as she was concerned," said William. "You don't understand."

"No, I clearly don't. And if this is how your lot behave, I'm glad I'm not one of them."

"What do you mean, my lot?"

"You posh lot. What about thinking of me, William, how I felt— what about defending me? I'm not surprised you're still on your own; that's all I can say." She picked up her bag. "I'm off. Cheers. Hope you don't get your bottom smacked. Or maybe that's how she gets her kicks. And you." She was crying now, aware that she was beginning to show William the real Abi, not in that moment caring.

"Abi! Don't talk like that, please!"

"I'll talk how I like. You should try doing the same; you might find your life got a bit better."

And she walked out of the cottage, slamming the door behind her.

. . .

Laura had bought Jonathan a really nice birthday present: he collected antique medical instruments, and she had found an old otoscope in a beautiful leather case, lined with blue silk. She gave it to him the night before his birthday, and he was terribly touched and pleased.

"I'm just thankful you haven't got anything elaborate planned for tomorrow, darling," he said when he had thanked her, and she had said (while crossing her fingers and touching the headboard at the same time), no, just dinner with the Edwardses, as she'd told him.

"Pity we can't be with the kids, really," he said. "I do like them to share in our birthdays." And she said yes, but they were having the big family party next day, with her parents, Jonathan's mother, and various cousins, and the children would be very much part of that.

"Not sure I feel quite up to that either," he said with a grin, and then, kissing her very gently, "I do love you, Laura. You're far too good for me. I couldn't bear any of this without you."

And somehow the ice that had been holding her heart had softened, and she had returned the kiss, and then he had turned the light out, and his hands had been on her, and she hadn't felt anything but tenderness, and he was very gentle, very sweetly insistent, and she had felt herself moving to and with him; and when she came, trembling with the long, long release, she wept. And heard something from him that was half way between a sob and a sigh, and realised that there were his tears on her face as well as her own.

. . .

Abi really had expected William to call—to say he was sorry, that he could see her point of view, at least, to say he wanted to see her. But he didn't.

And she was going to miss him . . . horribly. Because although she wasn't sure if she actually loved him, she loved being with him. And now she'd blown it. *Fuck, fuck, fuck.*

. . .

Jonathan found himself working on the morning of his birthday, at St. Anne's; he was only on call, but at ten o'clock one of his mothers went into premature labour and he had to go in.

"Ladies shouldn't have babies on your birthday, Daddy," Daisy said indignantly.

"I know, sweetheart, but as you'll find out for yourself one day, babies don't always arrive very conveniently. I'll try not to be long."

They were all excited. Once Jonathan and Laura had left for supper with the Edwardses, the children—and Helga—were to move into action: admit the caterers and the florist, explain where everything had to go . . . and then receive the guests as they arrived, show them where to hide (in the darkened conservatory). Helga was to telephone the Edwards house at eight, and ask Jonathan and Laura to come home, to say that there had been a power cut and she didn't know what to do (thus explaining the unlit house when they arrived).

It was hard to see what might go wrong.

. . .

Abi was driving back from Bristol when her phone rang. At last! William! She pulled into a side road, took the call. Dear William. How sweet he was.

"Abi? This is Jonathan."

It was made much worse by his not being William, by being thrown back into a different, uglier life; it really hurt her, shocked her even.

"Yes?"

"I just wanted to make sure you'd heard about the lorry driver. That his windscreen had been shattered. That's why he veered across the road. So there won't be any charges of any kind."

"Yes. Yes, the police did tell me."

"Good. So that draws the line very neatly, I think. It's over. The whole ghastly nightmare."

"I don't suppose the lorry driver thinks that. Or the man whose wife was killed. That is such a typical thing for you to say. 'I'm all right, so everything's all right.' Pure bloody Jonathan Gilliatt."

There was a pause; then he said, "That was an extraordinarily unpleasant remark."

"Oh, really? Maybe you don't inspire pleasant conversation, Jonathan. How's Laura?"

"Laura is fine."

"Did you ever . . . ever have to confess about me?"

"That's nothing to do with you."

"I think it might be, actually," she said, rage and pain rising up to hit her. Here he was, doing it again, putting her in the box marked, "Rubbish," set well apart from his real life, as no doubt he saw it, with his perfect wife and perfect family.

"What on earth do you mean by that?"

He sounded wary. *Well, good.*

"I mean that of course it's to do with me. I'd quite like to know, actually, if she knows about us. Or if you've managed to sweep me under the carpet, pretend I never existed. I'm not sure why, actually, but it matters to me, where I stand in Laura's life now."

"And what's it to you one way or the other?"

"If you can't see that, Jonathan, then you really are even more stupid than I thought," she said, wondering why he could still hurt her so much. "Because she ought to know there's something rotten in her marriage, that it's not quite the perfect thing she imagines, that she's got it, and you, horribly, horribly wrong, poor cow."

"Abi," he said, and the venom in his voice quite frightened her, "you have no right to talk about Laura and my marriage."

"Well, I think I do, actually. You dragged me into it. You had everything—perfect bloody life, with a wife and children—and still you chose to fuck around with me. Not my idea, Jonathan. Yours. And then . . . then you have the fucking nerve to tell me your marriage is nothing to do with me."

"It isn't," he said. "My marriage is mine, mine and Laura's . . ."

"And pretty unsatisfactory, I'd say, judging by your behaviour."

"How dare you say that to me?"

"I dare because it's true."

"It is not true."

"Well, I think Laura might see it rather differently."

"Abi," he said, "you even think about coming near me and my family, and you'll regret it horribly."

"Of course I'm not coming near you and your family. Why should I?"

"Because you're rotten enough. Disturbed enough even, I'd say. You have considerable problems, Abi. Personality problems. Maybe you should take a look at yourself, rather than throwing accusations at other people. Anyway, I have to go. I had intended to have a perfectly pleasant conversation, reassuring you that you had nothing more to worry about. You've made it very unpleasant, predictably enough. Pity."

And the phone went dead.

. . .

Abi sat there for quite a long time, staring at her phone; she no longer felt angry, just rather tired and drained. And then the pain began. It was awful, the worst she could ever remember. She had never liked herself; in that moment, she loathed herself. She kept hearing Jonathan's voice telling her she had personality problems, that she was rotten, possibly even disturbed, and she found herself agreeing with him. She was indeed absolutely rotten; she was amoral, promiscuous, dishonest. And all right, he had pursued her, but she had at no time refused him; she had encouraged him, enjoyed him, despised his wife, dismissed his family. She was a completely worthless person; she had no right to expect decent treatment from anybody.

She had been conducting a relationship with a man who was quite simply good, transparently nice and kind and honest; how could she have possibly thought that could work? That he could want to be with her if he knew even a little about what she was really like?

She deserved never to see him again. She never would see him again. She didn't deserve him. She deserved rotten people, rotten like her. Rotten like Jonathan.

He'd strung her along very nicely. But . . . God, she had let him. That was one of the most humiliating things. Allowed herself to believe him when he told her she was special, hugely intelligent, that he enjoyed her company quite apart from the sex.

She'd been hurt by a great many men, but Jonathan had won the game easily. He had demanded a great deal of her—and not only since the crash—and had given her no support, shown her no concern, offered her not a shred of kindness, merely bullied and threatened her. And had abandoned her totally, without pity or thought.

She hated him beyond anything . . .

. . .

William had spent a wretched day. He had shot into the kitchen at breakfast time, grabbed some bacon and a slice of bread and made himself a sandwich, filled a thermos with coffee, and headed out for the farthest point he could: East Wood, a six-acre spinney. He was felling some of the younger trees; it was exhausting and noisy, and made thought fairly impossible. He didn't want to think. It hurt too much.

. . .

Abi made her decision almost without realising it. She felt more positive suddenly, and that she needed to see this thing finished. Properly, formally, unarguably finished.

She dialled his number. It was on voice mail. His smooth, actory tones told her that he couldn't answer her call just at the moment, but that if she left a message he would get back to her as soon as possible.

Abi shut him off; she wasn't going to leave a message—she was sick of leaving messages that he didn't respond to. But the clinic—in bloody Harley Street, where he had all those bloody pampered princesses worshipping the ground he walked on—now, she might do a little mischief there. He might even be there; she knew he was often on call on Saturdays . . .

She dialled the number, asked to be put through to him.

"I'm so sorry; Mr. Gilliatt has left for the day. Can one of the other doctors help you?"

Resisting a temptation to say, only if they were up to Mr. Gilliatt's standard on text sex, she asked if they knew where he was . . .

"I'm afraid not. He's not in tomorrow. Perhaps you could ring on Monday?"

As the day wore on, William thought increasingly about Abi. And with increasing remorse. She was right—in a way. His mother had behaved quite . . . well, quite inconsiderately. Unkindly even. She couldn't actually have thought they were burglars or intruders . . . Burglars and intruders didn't normally light candles.

And having discovered it was him, him and a girl, the tactful thing would have been to say something noncommittal and withdraw. He wasn't sixteen; he was thirty-four. Did she really think he was going to get married before he had any kind of a relationship?

Yes, perhaps he should have warned her—and his father, of course—that he was using the cottage occasionally; maybe he should have gone further, asked their permission. Except that they would have wanted to know why, and how could he have told them?

Not for the first time, William became aware of the absurdity of his domestic situation; not for the first time did he wonder what on earth he could do about it. And then it came to him that perhaps he could move into cottage number one, or number two or number three. Make his home there. So that he could claim some independence, privacy, grow up at last. It seemed not unreasonable. He worked on the farm for a very modest income; he could surely claim the cottage as being some kind of a perk. He would ask them that evening; the thought quite cheered him up.

. . .

She decided to ring first. She didn't want to waste a long journey. He didn't know she had the landline number, would probably change it if he did.

The phone didn't ring for long; then: "Hello?" It was a little girl's voice: one of his flowers. God, that always made her want to throw up.

"Is that Daisy? Or Lily?"

"It's Daisy."

"Hello, Daisy. Is your daddy there?"

"No, he's gone out. But he will be back soon."

"Are you sure about that?"

"Yes. Quite sure. It's his birthday. We're doing a surprise party for him. Mummy's bringing him back here at about eight o'clock."

"Oh, really? How lovely. Wish I'd been invited. Well . . . never mind. Bye, Daisy."

"Good-bye."

Such a beautifully expensive, posh little voice. Well, lucky Daisy. She'd been born with a silver spoon in her mouth, all right; and it had stayed there. Like Lily and the beloved Charlie. Jonathan was so proud of Charlie. He never seemed to think she might not want to hear about him. Or about the girls. *So sensitive, aren't you, Jonathan?*

The more she thought about him—being given this party by his family, a lavish affair, no doubt, no expense spared—the more she wanted to throw up. Or kill him. Or both. There he'd be, smiling that awful smooth smile of his, receiving gifts and kisses and compliments, everyone wishing him well, and no one, no one at all, certainly not Laura, knowing what a complete shit he was. He'd managed to lie his way out of everything: how did he do it, the bastard?

Well, not tonight, he wouldn't.

"Sorry, Jonathan," she said quite cheerfully as she dressed for the occasion, in some new leather jeans and a very low-cut black top—well, it was a party, after all—"but you'd better make the most of the next two hours. Because after that . . . bingo!"

Not since Sleeping Beauty's christening was a guest going to wreak so much havoc at a family gathering.

. . .

It didn't go terribly well. His parents said they would of course consider his request, but the cottages were a valuable source of income, and they couldn't quite see how he imagined making the money up.

Abi was right: it suddenly seemed to him they were arrogant, his parents, in their attitude towards him; it was appalling that he should have nowhere he could call his own, other than a bedroom in their house. The fact that it had never occurred to him to demand such a thing was irrelevant.

He began to feel he owed Abi an apology: on his mother's behalf as well as his own. Her initial amusement had been . . . actually . . . rather generous. And typical of her. She was generous. And warm and funny and . . . well, really very kind.

He should tell her so. He went out immediately after supper, drove to the pub, and sat in the car park, calling her. He hadn't expected her to be sitting at home, waiting for him, but he did leave a message saying he was sorry that she had been embarrassed, sorry that he hadn't been more considerate, and asking her to call him. He added that he missed her and really wanted to see her. And went into the pub to get drunk and hope for her call.

. . .

Christ, what a nightmare. What a complete bloody nightmare. When he'd been hanging on to his sanity—just—getting through it day by agonising day, longing only for peace and quiet, and here he was, confronted by what seemed like a hundred people, all laughing and joking and slapping him on the back, telling him what a great guy he was, and Laura hanging on his arm, kissing him and everyone else, saying wasn't it great everyone had come, wasn't he wonderful, who would have thought he was *so* old . . .

The conversation with Abi had upset him badly, and made him nervous. And somewhere, in some deep, well-buried place, he felt a stab of something close to remorse. It was true what she'd said: he had instigated their affair, had walked out of the Garden of Eden for no other reason than that he had felt in need of some new, exotically flavoured fruit. And was Abi really so rotten? Not really. She'd had a raw deal from life; he'd taken advantage of that, used it, enjoyed flattering her, flashing his money around, taking her to expensive hotels, buying her expensive jewellery. And in return she had given him the excitement, the sense of sexual self-esteem that Laura had failed to do.

Christ, what a mess. And here he was, trapped in this farce of an evening. Which somehow encapsulated his whole life. The fantasy that was marriage to Laura, and the reality that Abi had confronted him with.

. . .

No call yet. Well, what could he expect? She would be out somewhere. She was probably still very hurt and upset. It surprised him sometimes how sensitive she actually was; she wasn't really the toughie she seemed.

He'd never forgotten how she'd gone off to the hospital with Shaun that day, for instance. And she was absolutely ridiculous about animals, fussing over a kitten in the street she'd thought had been abandoned, and getting quite worked up when he'd told her he'd just sent a couple of bull calves to the abattoir. He didn't want to lose her. He really didn't.

He texted her, to tell her that she should listen to her messages, in case she hadn't realised there was one; and then in a sudden rash rush of courage, composed another saying, "I love you." He sat looking at it for a while before he sent it, slightly surprised that he could be telling her that, making sure he meant it, and wasn't just trying to make her feel better. But he did mean it; he did love her, and he desperately didn't want to lose her; he pressed "send" and then decided to go home before he was too drunk to drive even the half mile to the farm gates.

. . .

She had wondered how she would get in, whether someone would demand an invitation or something, but the front door was not locked; it pushed open easily. She stood in the hall; it was empty, but she could hear music and people laughing. A large gilt mirror hung on the wall; she went over to it, replenished her lip gloss and her perfume, combed her hair. She wanted to look as good as possible for her entrance . . .

As she stood there, a little girl appeared behind her: an absurdly beautiful little girl, about nine years old, with long blond curly hair, wearing a white lace-trimmed dress and silver shoes. "Hello," she said, "I'm Lily. Have you come to the party? You're late."

"I know," Abi said, smiling at her. "I'm sorry."

"That's all right. They're just serving the food now. Do come in," she added graciously.

Abi took a glass of champagne from a tray and stood in the doorway, looking into a huge room, golden, it seemed, lit with dozens of candles, and filled with great urns of white flowers. People stood in groups, smiling, beautifully dressed people, holding glasses of champagne, and by the fireplace stood Jonathan, and next to him, leaning against him, smiling up at him, was . . . well, she supposed Laura. Lovely, she was, quite small, with a fall of blond hair and dressed in something truly amazing, layers of pale, pale cream chiffon and lace. On the other side of Jonathan were two almost identical little girls and a boy—Charlie, of course, very handsome, with smooth brown hair, dressed in jeans and a blue shirt, already nearly as tall as his mother. It was all unbearably perfect—the light, the music, the display of family togetherness—and Abi really couldn't bear it.

She started to move across the room. Jonathan still hadn't seen her, was holding up his hand; Laura was tapping on her glass; Jonathan was saying, "This is not a speech, promise, promise," and everyone laughed and called out, "Good thing too," and, "Why not?" and, "Better not be . . ."

. . .

He saw her standing there, an entirely dark presence in her black clothes, her eyes glittering, infinitely dangerous; and he was so terrified, he literally could neither move nor speak. He saw Laura look at him more sharply, puzzled at his sudden silence, and then follow his gaze towards Abi; felt her stiffen, heard her intake of breath. In his worst, his wildest nightmares, he could not have imagined this invasion of his family and his home, and in front of all their friends, this confrontation with the awful, ugly truth of her and what he had done. What might she do, or say, how could he stop her . . . ?

. . .

She stepped forward, right up to him, and said, "Hello, Jonathan. What a very lovely occasion. I thought I'd add my good wishes to everyone else's. That's what you deserve. Happy birthday," she added, and leaned up and kissed him on the lips. "You must be Laura," she said, turning to her, and she could hear a distinct graciousness in her own voice. "I'm Abi . . . I'm not sure if Jonathan's told you about me. I'm so sorry I can't stop."

And she turned and walked out again, and he stood staring after her, noticing, absurdly, that she was wearing the same high silver-heeled boots that she had had on the day of the crash.

CHAPTER 34

Illogical things, emotions. She would have expected to feel rage, pain, humiliation; all she felt in those first few minutes was embarrassment. That all their friends should have been there, should have come with such generosity and genuine goodwill to Jonathan's party, and they had been forced to witness this extraordinary thing. It seemed so wrong somehow. Rude. Churlish.

In half an hour they were all gone, embarrassed, not mentioning the intruder—for so Abi had seemed—not properly meeting her eyes, just saying they would go and leave them in peace, very sweetly and charmingly to be sure, kissing her, shaking Jonathan rather awkwardly by the hand, and then the room was empty, horribly empty, the candles and flowers and abandoned champagne glasses the only signs that there had been a party there at all.

She directed the waiters to clear the room, and then dismissed them, told Helga to start putting away the food, load up the dishwasher.

The children were upset, the girls baffled, Lily in tears of disappointment, Charlie clearly troubled and with at least half an idea of what Abi's visit had all been about . . . and she took them up to the playroom, told them not to worry, everything was fine, and that she'd be up in a minute to help them get to bed. And then went back downstairs.

She realised now—of course—that she had never believed any of Jonathan's explanations about Abi. She felt ashamed of allowing herself to pretend. She had let herself down. Been weak, cowardly, feebly female. She should have faced him down on that very first explanation, told him not to insult her, instead of playing the sweet, simple, loyal little wife. Well, not anymore she wasn't. Rage—and outrage—were growing in her, making her strong.

Jonathan was sitting in a chair now, his eyes fixed on her, watching like a terrified child as she moved around—blowing out candles, collecting the remaining glasses. When finally she was done, and faced him across the room, he said, "Darling, I'm so sorry, so, so sorry she did that."

"She!" Laura said. "Jonathan, she didn't do that. You did."

"But, Laura—"

"Jonathan, just stop it, please. I don't want to hear anything from you. You can do what you like; I really don't care."

"How . . . how are the children?" he said.

"The girls simply didn't understand at all, just thought she was another guest, but they're disappointed that the party never really happened. Charlie's clearly got a better idea. He asked who . . . who she was. Of course. Well, they all did."

"Oh, Christ," he said, "dear sweet Christ. What . . . what did you tell them?"

"I said she was a lady from work whom I'd never met—getting rather close to your story, isn't it, Jonathan—and that she had another party to go to, and that was why she couldn't stay. The girls seemed to accept that; Charlie, I'm not so sure. He's old enough to see that she wasn't too much like all our other friends."

He was silent. Then: "I'm sorry, Laura," he said again.

"For what? Doing it, having the relationship at all? Lying to me? Getting caught? Bad luck, wasn't it, being involved in the crash that day? I wonder if it would still be going on if you hadn't. Well, she's very . . . sexy. I can see that. Which I do realise I'm not. And probably rather good fun. Wives tend to be dull."

"Please—"

"And young, of course. I suppose she wasn't the first. Not that it makes much difference."

"She was the first. I swear. And the last."

"Yes, well, she's definitely that."

"Of course." There was a slight—very slight—look of hope in his eyes.

Laura crushed it swiftly.

"Yes. Because that's it, Jonathan. Absolutely it. Our marriage is over. As of now."

"Darling, you can't—"

"Don't 'darling' me. And I can. I've always said there were two things I wouldn't be able to bear. One was anything bad—really bad—happening to one of the children. The other was you being unfaithful to me."

"But, Laura—"

"I just can't cope with it, Jonathan. It's not the humiliation, although that's quite . . . hard. It's not the pain . . . not exactly. It's the death of trust. I'd never be able to believe you again, and I could never, ever again let you near me. I'd always be wondering if you'd been . . .

been making love to someone else. I mean . . . how . . ." Her voice broke; she hesitated, then went on: "How long has it been going on? Months? Years?"

"A couple of months. That's all. And I was about to finish it; I swear to you. That's the awful irony of the whole thing. I'd told her in the car that day that it had to end, that I didn't want to go on with it anymore. I'd been regretting it so much, Laura, hating myself for it . . ."

"Oh, really? And what's that supposed to make me feel? Grateful? Reassured? I keep thinking back, you know," she said, "to all the times you must have been with her. Going to hotels . . . I presume. Or does she have a little pad somewhere? No, don't answer that. I don't want to know. Ringing me last thing, like you always do, making sure I'm safely settled. Telling me you . . . you . . . Oh, God, you are disgusting, Jonathan. I wish I need never see you again. And all that stuff, lying to the police, in front of me . . ."

"But, Laura, you can't, you really can't throw away thirteen years of happiness and a good marriage because of one . . . one indiscretion."

"It wasn't a good marriage," she said. "I know that now. And the happiness wasn't very soundly based. So I can quite easily throw it away, as you call it. I'm going to bed. Good night."

. . .

Abi just could not stop crying. She had started as she drove out onto the Chiswick roundabout, and she had finally pulled into a motel somewhere near Reading, blinded by her tears, fearing that she would crash the car. She had had enough of car crashes . . .

She flung herself down on the bed and cried for quite a lot longer. How could she have done that? Of all the wicked, awful things in her past, that had undoubtedly been the worst. The cruellest and the worst. Jonathan deserved cruelty, but Laura didn't. It wasn't her fault that he was such a one hundred per cent, A1 shit; she didn't deserve to have her beautiful straight little nose rubbed in it; she should have been left to her illusions.

And Charlie too, that handsome boy . . . The little girls had been simply baffled, but he had been upset, his face crumpling into confusion as he stared up at his father and then back at her, some instinct clearly wondering, half comprehending even, who she was . . . what she was.

She had destroyed them that evening, wrecked their happiness, surely and mercilessly; she should be destroyed herself, put down painfully, punished most horribly for her crime: and it was a crime—there could be no doubt of it—worse, far worse, than anything Jonathan had done to her.

She was a totally bad person; there was nothing to redeem her.

She lay there fully clothed, staring up at the ceiling, smoking cigarette after cigarette; somewhere towards dawn, she fell into an aching, troubled sleep.

. . .

At about the same time, William awoke, his head raging. He reached for his phone; looked at it hopefully. There was no message, no text. Where was she; what was she doing? Was she ill? Had she hurt herself? Surely nobody, however angry or upset they were, could ignore the kind of messages he had been sending. He would just try, once more, sending a text; he couldn't ring her at this sort of time. If he didn't hear then, he might even go down and see her. He had to make her realise how he felt somehow.

He wrote, rather sadly now, "Abi, please get in touch. I'm sorry and I love you," and sent it, and, because he knew he wouldn't be able to go back to sleep, got dressed and walked out to the top of the field where he had first seen the crash that day, and stood looking down and thinking about it, and how it had totally changed his life, and willing his phone to ring.

. . .

Abi called at seven, sounding exhausted and ill.

She thanked William for his messages and said it had been lovely to get them, and then said she was very sorry, but she really didn't want to see him anymore, that it had to be over.

William said was it about his mother, and she said no, it was nothing to do with his mother; it was all to do with her, that she really couldn't have any more to do with him, and she wished him well.

"I'm just not your sort of person, William. That's all. I'm so sorry. Good-bye."

. . .

It was a long time since William had cried. The last time had been when his grandfather, whom he had really loved, had died. He had felt then as if a very large and important part of him had gone too. He had the same feeling now, and he stood there, staring down at the place where he had first seen Abi, thinking about her, and how much he did, without doubt, love her, and he began to cry very quietly and bitterly.

CHAPTER 35

Georgia sat on the train back to Cardiff, thinking how she really must find somewhere to live in London. Shooting was starting in a matter of weeks; she could hardly commute. But somehow, she still felt so unsure of herself that the prospect of looking at a load of grotty bedsits or flat-shares seemed impossible.

And the day had been totally shit, trailing round with the costume girl, Sasha. Georgia had started by giving her opinion on the clothes, which ones she thought were cool and would suit her, but had then shut up as she realised they weren't going to agree about any of them, and in fact the worse she thought she looked in something, the more

Sasha liked it, saying withering things like, "You have to look at yourself in character, you know, Georgia; it's Rose we're dressing, not you."

And then they'd got back to the offices and Merlin had been there, and although he'd been really friendly for about five seconds, he then went into a huddle with Sasha in the corner about locations and how the first assistant really didn't seem to have the right idea at all, and Merlin could see Bryn wasn't going to like any of the five short-listed houses; and then Sasha had said she'd had a shitty day too, and why didn't they go and have a drink. Leaving Georgia alone with Mo, the third assistant director, who was plump and rosy and smiling and looked more as if she should be working at a nursery school than an ego-ridden industry like television, and who was very sweet but clearly wasn't going to risk sympathising with her too much when her own job was dependent on pleasing everyone; and then worst of all, Bryn Merrick arrived and was very short with her, just nodded and said, "Hi," and asked Mo where the fuck Merlin was, and when Mo said she didn't know, he'd glared at Georgia as if it was her fault.

"I seem to be working with a group of total layabouts," he said, and stalked out again.

Georgia had left then and called Linda, hoping for a bit of encouragement and reassurance, and possible suggestions of whom she might share a flat with, but Linda had left early to go to one of the drama school productions.

She decided to cut her losses and go home, feeling like Cinderella limping her way bewilderedly back from the ball.

. . .

Abi saw William's car the moment she turned into her street. Her first instinct was to drive away again; indeed, she'd slowed down and was looking for somewhere to turn round when he waved out of the window and then, as she sat there, transfixed with horror, opened the door and got out, stood waiting for her. This was unbearable; this was unendurable; telling him she didn't want to see him anymore over the phone was one thing; being confronted by him, in all his great and terrible niceness, that was something else altogether. She pulled in behind him, got out of her car, walked up to him, tried to smile.

"Hello, William. William, I did say—"

"I know. But I wanted to be sure you were sure. That's all."

"I am sure."

"But . . . why? I don't understand. I really don't. Is it my mother?"

"Of course not. I could perfectly well deal with your mother."

"I wish you would," he said, and couldn't help smiling. She smiled back.

"Please, Abi. I need to know why you . . . well, why you didn't want to . . . to see me anymore. I meant it . . . what I said in my text," he added, and it was so awful, seeing the honesty and the hurt and the hope mingled in equal parts in his brown eyes, that she had to look away.

"I . . . I know, William. And it was great to . . . to know that. Really great."

"But . . . you don't . . . love me? Is that it?"

"William, I don't think I'm capable of loving anyone. I'm awful. Totally awful."

"Abi, you're not, of course you're not."

"No, it's true. If you knew what I did on Saturday alone . . . well, you wouldn't be here."

"What was that, then? What did you do that was so bad?"

"Oh . . . just killed off a little family. A happy little family."

"Killed it?"

"Oh, not literally. I just . . . just totally destroyed it."

She wasn't sure how much she'd been going to tell him. Suddenly she knew. Everything. And she told him, in all its ugly detail, why he could not possibly continue to love her . . .

CHAPTER 36

"So . . . where would you like to get married, then? Where shall we have our wedding? I imagine you'll want it somewhere in England. The bride's prerogative, choosing the venue."

"Well . . . yes. I suppose so. I mean, yes, of course."

"In a church?"

"Oh, of course."

"And then perhaps the reception could be at the house."

"Oh, Russell, that's a lovely idea."

The house—the beautiful house that Russell was buying for them—was actually called Tadwick House; Mary said that sounded much too grand for her, and he had promptly rechristened it Sparrow's Nest.

"But only for our private use; local people don't like the names of houses being changed."

"Nor does the post office," said Mary, smiling. Thinking of how Donald had insisted on renaming their last house, and what a lot of trouble it had caused with the post office. It was in a cul-de-sac called Horseshoe Bend, and right in the middle of the curve. "I want to call it the End House," he had said, "for it is, in one way, the end, the farthest point of the street. And this is our last house, where we shall live to the end of our days. So . . . what could be better?"

Mary had thought that rather gloomy and said so; and Donald had said why, had she never heard of happy endings, "which is what the story of Mary and Donald certainly has."

She recounted this to Russell now; he smiled.

"I like that. You know, I can see Donald was a remarkable person. I know I would have liked him very much."

"You would," said Mary, and it was true. It was one of the things that made her happiest about marrying Russell; he would have liked Donald, and Donald would have liked him. Donald would have recognised him as a good man, into whose care he could entrust his beloved Mary. Which made it all the more sad that Christine had set herself so firmly against him.

The rest of the family were much easier; Timothy, her grandson, said it was really cool and he'd be dancing at her wedding all night; when could he meet Russell and would Russell like to be an investor in the IT company he was planning to set up?

"Only joking, Gran. But I would like to meet him . . . I really would. He sounds great."

Gerry too had expressed—rather awkwardly—a desire to meet Russell, and had said again how sorry he was Christine was being difficult. And Douglas, Donald's pride and joy, the son he had longed for, born eight long years—and several miscarriages—after Christine, had written from Toronto to say how very happy he was to hear about Russell and that he would be over at Christmas, if not before, and couldn't wait to meet him then.

"The kids think it's really cool too," he had written. "Don't worry about Chris"—for Mary had felt bound to warn him about Christine's reaction—"she'll come round."

. . .

They agreed on a December wedding: "so we can spend Christmas together legally," Russell said.

She had received two very sweet letters from his daughters, Coral and Pearl, saying how delighted they were that their father had found her again, what a romantic story it was, and how they longed to meet her. Of course, Mary thought, it must be easier for them; they had learnt to accept and live with Russell's second wife from comparatively early ages. His son had written a slightly stiffer note, but there was no doubt of its friendliness.

"But I want to show you Connecticut," Russell said, "where I think we should have our American house."

When Mary asked him if he was going to sell the apartment, he had looked at her in astonishment.

"No, no, of course not; we'll need a New York base, and I think you'll be happy with it. If you're not then we'll find another. So . . . I'll book a flight around the beginning of November. That way you can experience Thanksgiving, and both girls have expressed a wish to have you there."

Mary said she wouldn't have much time to organise a wedding if they were going to be in America until the beginning of December; Russell said nonsense, they could do most of it before they went.

Three homes. A new family. A wedding. It was all rather hard to take in.

· · ·

William had been desperately hurt and shocked by Abi's confession: almost unendurably. At first, he had been slightly numbed; then, as the days passed and the truth clarified, the pain worsened until it hurt so much he could hardly stand it. It wasn't just that she'd lied to him so relentlessly about Jonathan, and that she'd been sleeping with Jonathan, and God only knew how many other men before him.

It was that he'd allowed himself to think she'd enjoyed being with him as much as he enjoyed being with her; and she hadn't. Of course she hadn't.

She'd just been spending time with him until someone more suitable came along. Abi clearly wanted excitement; she wanted some flashy bloke with plenty of money who could show her a good time, take her to expensive hotels and restaurants and on expensive holidays, not some dull farmer who smelled of cow shit.

And he didn't want someone like her, either, did he? He wanted someone he could trust, who would treat him and his life carefully, someone straightforward whom he understood, not a baffling enigma straight out of a bad TV series, who slept around, and took her sexual pleasures like a cat.

He felt sick, listless, and, perhaps worst of all, foolish. How Abi must have seen him coming; probably imagined he was rich, that he would make a good meal ticket for a while. He couldn't see that he would ever feel any better . . .

. . .

Jack Bryant was exactly the sort of person Sergeant Freeman most disliked. Loud, over-the-top posh accent, old-school tie—not that he recognized that one, and he knew most of them, it was a little hobby of his—signet ring, slicked-back hair, highly polished brogues: he was a caricature.

It had not actually been very hard to find him. The motoring division confirmed the wheel nut came from an E-Type; there were several reports of a red E-Type on the road that afternoon—immediately in front of the lorry, according to Georgia; and she had been quite sure it had been a personalized number plate. They had checked with various E-Type associations and clubs, and after that it was a simple matter of trawling through the personalized registrations—the DVLA were always very helpful—and making phone calls. The whole thing had been one day's work.

However, Freeman was disappointed to discover he couldn't fault him. Bryant was very articulate, had excellent recall, and was eager to help: yes, he had indeed lost a wheel nut, hadn't actually discovered it until a week later, when he was checking his car prior to leaving his friends in Scotland. He'd had no idea when it had come off. "But I did check the whole car over very, very carefully, Sergeant, two days before; my mechanic will confirm that. And I gave it a personal check that morning—tyres, oil, all that sort of thing—and I did actually check the wheel nuts myself. Gave them a final go with the old spanner, just to be on the safe side."

"The irony of it is," said Paul Johns from Forensics, "you can over-tighten those things. The thread goes. What a bloody tragedy. But if it's true what he says, absolutely not his fault."

. . .

Barney and Emma had had a lovely evening at the Stafford Hotel. They always did. There were guilt and anxiety folded into it, into all of it, but time together was still astonishingly sweet.

"We have to tell them. Don't we?"

He hadn't said that before—confronted their situation, what it actually meant. She'd been waiting—not too impatiently, for it was he who must act, his life that must so totally change, he who must be surer than sure about the two of them.

"I love you, Emma. I . . ." His voice shook slightly. "I don't love Amanda. I thought I did, of course, but it was an illusion. I am fond of her beyond anything; I hate to make her unhappy, but I can't marry her. And when she knows, she won't want it either. So . . . I will tell her very soon. I hate these lies, hate living them day after day. It's awful."

"Do you think she knows? Suspects . . . anything?"

"I don't know. Would you?"

"I would, I think. Yes."

"Ah. Well, then. Within the next few days."

"Oh, Barney."

"Oh, Emma. What about you?"

"He really, really won't mind that much. He'll think he does, but he won't. He's quite . . . quite thick-skinned." And then added, anxious not to blacken Luke, who had seemed so recently everything she wanted, "But so lovely in so many ways."

He nodded, looking at her rather solemnly.

"Like you."

"What, thick?"

"No. Lovely in so many ways. I love you, Emma. So much."

"I love you, Barney. So much."

. . .

They left the Stafford soon after ten: Emma to go back to Swindon, Barney to go home to Amanda.

They walked out of the restaurant hand in hand; they had kissed hello, and during the course of the evening had kissed again from time to time, albeit in a very seemly manner, usually because one of them had said something that particularly delighted the other.

No one could have possibly complained about their behaviour; it had been modest, well mannered, and really rather charming.

No one, that is, who was unaware of a relationship either of them might have been conducting with another party altogether.

But as they walked out through the foyer, smiling at each other, Barney failed to recognise that among a rather noisy party of eight, arriving for a posttheatre supper, were Gerard and Jess Richmond. Tamara's parents. And following them, out of a second taxi, together with a couple of other friends, Tamara herself.

CHAPTER 37

"Barney, hi. This is Tamara. I thought we might have a little drink this evening. My treat. No, just the two of us. What? Oh, no, Barney, I think you could spare half an hour. It really is quite important. Great. How about One Aldwych? Well, I know it's a bit of a trek, but maybe better than right on our own doorstep. You know what they say . . . ? Only joking . . ."

Patrick woke early on Thursday morning. Early for him, that was, which meant before six. He had slept badly, which he usually did now they were weaning him off the sleeping pills. They were the worst hours, those early ones, when the depression that he could hold off— just—during the day hung around him like a shroud, when the fears that he would never progress beyond the stage he was at now, bedridden and helpless, never going home, never being together with Maeve and the boys again, never making love to Maeve again—that was one of the worst—those fears were at their strongest, their most dangerous. He had moved himself away—with his own willpower, and the help of the hospital priest—from thoughts of suicide; but the alternative, this death-in-life, seemed little better.

He looked out of the window at the blackness. Where had God been when he'd needed Him so badly? Looking the other way, it seemed. Well, that would have been Maeve's explanation . . .

He sighed; he was thirsty and hot. Maybe he could get the dear little night nurse, the one who had found him that night and of whom he had grown rather fond, to make him a cup of tea. He rang the bell.

. . .

Sue Brown made him a cup of tea, and promised to be back soon, but she had to sort out a couple more patients; it was after seven when she got back to Patrick.

"Right, Patrick, let's get this job done, shall we? Then you can have your breakfast. I'll start with your catheter and then give you a nice wash. Let's see . . . right . . ."

Sue Brown was intent on her task; she didn't hear the slight intake of breath from the patient as she pulled on the catheter, but as she started to insert a fresh one, there was another. Followed by, "What are you doing there, Sue, putting a bit of barbed wire in?"

She looked at him; then, afraid even to ask the question, she said, "Patrick, am I hurting you?"

"Not hurting, no. But it's not exactly comfortable . . ."

Sue Brown closed her eyes, briefly. This was—well, it might be—acutely important.

She withdrew the catheter again, laid it gently on the tray, and said, "Patrick, I seem to have forgotten something. I'll be back in one minute, all right?"

Jo Wales was drinking a very bitter cup of coffee, thinking that really a hospital that had cost over a billion to build might have spent an extra five hundred on a decent coffee machine, when Sue Brown walked in. Or, to be more accurate, seemed to explode into the space in front of her.

"Jo . . . Jo, I don't know what to do. Could you come with me, please?"

"What to do about what, Sue?"

"It's Patrick Connell. He . . . well, I was just changing his catheter and he said it was uncomfortable. The catheter. When I tried to insert it. Was it a piece of barbed wire, he said."

Jo stared at her; her heart thumped uncomfortably.

"Oh, my God," she said. "God, Sue, that is exactly, exactly what we've all been waiting for. Let me come in to him straightaway. But . . . nothing must be said to him yet. All right?"

"Of course not," said Sue Brown, half indignantly. "That's exactly why I'm here, not saying anything to him; I wanted your opinion."

And thus it was that five minutes later, Jo Wales smiled radiantly at Sue Brown across Patrick's bed, having received the same rather plaintive response as she too tried to insert the catheter, and then at Patrick himself, and said, very gently, "Patrick, I think we might have some rather good news here. I'm going to call Dr. Osborne straightaway."

Never, as Patrick said to her, after Dr. Osborne had come up to see him personally and first peered at and then prodded it, had his modestly sized willy caused so much excitement.

. . .

"So . . . Barney, what would you like? Cocktail? Beer? Or should we push the boat out, have a glass of champagne? Drink to both our forthcoming nuptials?"

"I'll have a beer, please," said Barney.

"OK. And I think I'll have something nonalcoholic, actually. I want to keep a clear head."

"Fine."

"Right . . . so . . ." She paused while she gave the order, settled back in her chair. She smiled at him, crossed her long legs rather deliberately. She was wearing a red dress and black, very high-heeled shoes; she looked . . . what? Slightly dangerous.

"So . . . what do you want to talk about?" he said.

"Well . . . I don't know if Toby's told you, but we've got a new date. Next May."

"He hasn't, no. I haven't seen him for a bit. Now that he's home . . ."

"Ah, yes. So you're not hotfooting it down to the hospital every few days. What a good friend you were, Barney. How very . . . unselfish of you that was."

He shrugged. "I didn't mind. He's my best friend. He . . . needed me."

"Of course. Well, I hope you're not implying I didn't do my bit?"

"No, of course not, Tamara. Anyway, May sounds fine. Bit of a way ahead, but . . ."

"I know. But apart from anything else, it's a summer wedding dress. Well, you have to think of these things. What about you, Barney; when are you and Amanda going to do it?"

"Oh, next year maybe. We haven't really finalised it yet . . ."

"Just as well, perhaps." She smiled at him oversweetly. The drinks arrived. "Oh, thanks," she said to the waiter. "Got any olives? Great."

"Tamara," said Barney, "what did you mean by 'just as well'?"

"Ah. Yes. Well, you know . . ."

"No, I don't know. You'll have to explain. I'm a simple sort of chap."

"Oh, Barney, I've decided you're rather complex. Actually."

"Because . . . ?"

"Well, because you seem to be able to conduct two relationships at once. Not the act of a simple chap, surely."

The noise around them seemed to intensify; and yet they seemed oddly isolated, set apart from the rest, just the two of them, staring at each other over this dangerous, deadly conversation.

"I saw you, Barney; that's the thing. Leaving the Stafford the other night. With the pretty little doctor person. It does rather explain your devoted presence at the hospital, day after day . . ."

"This is a disgusting conversation," said Barney.

"I don't think so. If anything's disgusting, it's you. Playing around, cheating on just about the sweetest girl you could find anywhere."

"Have you discussed this with Toby?"

"No, I haven't discussed it with anyone. Yet. I wanted to get your version of it."

"You're not going to get any version of anything out of me, Tamara. I have no intention of discussing my personal life with you."

"Well, I think you might have to. Unless we start with discussing something else."

"And what's that?"

"Starting with the reason you and Toby left so late for the wedding that day. I still haven't had a satisfactory explanation out of either of you. I really want to know that, Barney. And if you don't tell me, I'm going straight to Amanda. Before you have a chance to work up any kind of an explanation."

"I've told you. Toby was ill. He kept being sick."

"And why was he being sick?"

"I suppose he had some bug. I don't know."

"His parents didn't mention it."

"They didn't know. We—specially Toby—didn't want to worry them."

She crossed and uncrossed her legs, began to fiddle with her necklace. It was a complex affair, a mass of small charms on a long silver chain.

"This just so doesn't ring true, you know, Barney."

"Look, why don't you ask Toby?"

"I have. He says much the same. That he must have eaten something. But you and his parents were fine. Now, I know you were stopped by the police, and that must have held you up a good twenty or thirty minutes. But then you went to a service station. What the fuck for? Making you even later."

"Toby needed the toilet. Again."

"No, Barney, he could have thrown up out of the car window if you were that late. I'm sorry. None of this works. I'm going to have to talk to Amanda. This evening, I should think."

She was looking very complacent now, half smiling at him; she was clearly enjoying the conversation.

"No!" he said, knowing she must recognise his panic, trying to disguise it. "No, Tamara, not this evening. Look, I don't want anyone—anyone—talking to Amanda except me. Which is not to say there's anything to talk about. But please . . . if you don't believe me about the wedding day, ask Toby yourself. Ask him to confirm the story."

She looked at him, her eyes gimlet-hard, her mouth set. Then she said, "All right. I'll give you twenty-four hours."

"And will you talk to Toby?"

"Yes, I most certainly will. Right. Well, it's been a fun evening, hasn't it? Bye, Barney."

And she stalked out of the bar on her impossibly perfect legs, pulling her cloud of hair up into a tight ponytail as she went. It was an oddly pugilistic gesture.

CHAPTER 38

"Linda? Alex."

"Oh . . . Alex. Hello." She did have a great voice: husky and sexy and expressive. "Saturday was great, Alex."

"I thought so too."

He was in the car, about to drive home; he smiled into the darkness, feeling a rush of pleasure, partly from hearing her voice, partly from remembering Saturday himself.

They'd gone to the theatre to see *Chicago*; it had been at his suggestion. She'd said she couldn't believe he hadn't seen it, which he'd found mildly irritating—not everyone could spend every other evening in the theatre—but then she said she'd be more than happy to sit through it for the third time. They then went out to dinner, and talked so much and for so long that he really had missed his last train home.

"Damn," he said, "I'll have to get a cab. If I can. Or stay in a hotel. If I can find one."

"Or . . . stay with me," she said, and then added, a gleam in her dark brown eyes, "if you dare."

And when he'd got flustered she'd laughed and said, "Alex, I'm not compromising you. I have a very nice spare room, and you're very welcome to it. Don't start talking about taxis and hotels; it's ridiculous."

And so he'd gone back to her incredibly smart flat, the sort of place he hated, full of aggressively stylish, uncomfortable-looking modern furniture—although she did have two wonderfully large and lush white sofas—and a lot of ridiculous and incomprehensible paintings and rather absurd ornaments.

"What would you like to drink?"

"Brandy?"

"Sounds good to me."

She returned with a tray, poured him a very large brandy.

"Thanks." He suddenly felt awkward; a silence formed. He looked round the room, the perfect room, looking for something to say. "It's all extremely . . . tidy," he said.

"I *am* extremely tidy. Too tidy, people tell me. It means I'm anally retentive, a control freak, all that sort of stuff. What about you?"

"I'm very untidy. So does that make me not a control freak?"

"Possibly. What do you think?"

"I don't know, Linda. I don't feel I know what I am anymore."

"That's a very sad remark," she said, and her eyes were thoughtful as she looked at him.

"I'm afraid I've become a bit of a sad person. In the modern sense as well. My daughter constantly upbraids me for being sad."

"What . . . as in the get-a-life sense?"

"That's the one."

"I don't think that matters. Much more important if you're actually not . . . not happy."

"I'm not," he said abruptly. "I would say I'm quite unhappy. Have been for years."

"Alex, that's dreadful."

"Oh, I love my work. I love my kids. But . . . it isn't very nice, living with someone who finds you totally wanting. Knowing they wish you weren't there."

"This is your wife, I presume."

"It is. My about-to-be-ex-wife. We're trying to sort out accommodation. It's very difficult. I think I told you . . . we've sold the house, only a matter of time."

"Do you think you'll feel better then?"

"I hope so. I'll miss the kids horribly."

"But you'll still see them, I imagine."

"Obviously. But that's not quite the same thing as living with them. And I worry about them, how they'll cope."

"Well . . . I don't know them or anything about them. But living in a miserable household can't be doing them any good either."

Her tone was brisk, almost abrasive; it annoyed him.

"I didn't say the household was miserable; I said I was."

"But, Alex, if they have an ounce of sensitivity, they must know that. And it should worry them. I just think if they care about you and their mother they'll see it's for the best. And deal with it."

"I don't think you can know many teenagers," he said. "And I don't think you really know what you're talking about. That's a very simplistic view."

She stared at him, and flushed suddenly; it was endearing, the first sign he had seen of any crack in her self-confidence.

"Sorry," she said.

He was silent; he felt depressed and defensive, a shadow over the evening. The silence grew.

Then, "I'm sorry, Alex," she said suddenly, surprising him, "if I upset you. And of course I don't know what I'm talking about." She smiled at him rather awkwardly. "I'm just terribly bossy. I can't help it. Well, I suppose I could, if I really tried, but by the time I realise I'm doing it, it's too late. I'll stop now. I just . . . well, I just didn't like the idea of you being unhappy all the time."

"That's very kind of you," he said, "but I think I know how to look after myself."

He could hear himself, pompous, a bit stiff.

"Right," she said, clearly edgy herself, "how about some coffee? And brandy?"

"That'd be very nice," he said. He didn't really want it, but to have turned that away as well as her apology would have seemed very aggressive.

She disappeared, and he leafed rather nervously through a coffee table book on art deco in the cinema. This might have been a mistake. The whole thing might have been a mistake.

"Well," she said on her return, "let's start again. What shall we talk about; what would be safe? You choose a subject."

"I'd rather not."

"Why?"

"Well to be honest," he said, "I'm still a bit nervous of boring you."

"Boring me! Why? I find you not remotely boring; I promise you that."

"I'll try to believe you. I mean . . . you do lead this rather glamorous life. In theatres and so on. And I spend mine . . ."

"Yes. How do you spend yours; what do you do? Day by day, I mean? Tell me."

"Oh, staring into people's orifices. Patching them up. Not the orifices, the people. Dealing with overdoses, cardiac arrests, stab wounds, even the occasional death on site, so to speak. I mean, I love it and it's fascinating, but it can hardly compete with first nights and talent spotting, can it?"

"Alex, I spend about ten per cent of my time at first nights. The rest is hard graft, talking to a load of rather pretentious people, trying to persuade them mediocre actors are wonderful and wonderful ones are worth hiring. And nannying actors, nursing their egos, making sure they get to auditions, listening to them whining, sorting out their money."

"Bit like being a parent."

"Possibly. But . . . I think I might prefer the orifices."

"You wouldn't," he said, and laughed. "Believe me. Not very nice things, orifices. Well, not the ones who land up in Casualty."

"Tell me," she said, "do you really get people coming in with golf balls up their bums, things like that?"

" 'Fraid so. And people get up to the most extraordinary things with vacuum cleaner hoses."

"You're kidding! Now, that really *is* sad."

She leant forward to top up his brandy; he found himself studying her cleavage. She noticed and grinned at him.

"Sorry," he said.

"Don't be. I don't mind. I'd wear polo necks if I did."

"Promise me," he said, laughing, "you'll never come out with me wearing a polo neck. That would make me very sad indeed."

"It's a promise."

"Well, that is . . . if you do come out with me again. I hope I'm not being presumptuous."

"Oh, Alex," she said, and her voice was impatient, "of course you're not being presumptuous. You shouldn't put yourself down so much. You're a very attractive, sexy man. Get used to the idea. If you ask me out, I'll come. There you are; that's another promise. Oh, God. I'm being bossy again, aren't I? What about your wife, is she bossy?"

"Not . . . not exactly. She just does what she wants. But . . . lots of wives do that."

"Do they? I wouldn't know. Most of my friends aren't wives, you see."

No, he thought, *they wouldn't be. You don't move in a married world; you don't know about marriage. Not really.*

"So . . . lots of fights?"

"Not really. I don't fight."

She looked at him thoughtfully. "I'm surprised. I'd have thought you'd be rather good in a fight. You're quite . . . quite powerful, aren't you? Emotionally."

"Linda, you hardly know me."

"I realise that. But . . . I can rather see you roaring and raging away."

"I think you're letting your imagination run away with you," he said, edgy again. "I don't do much roaring and raging. Not at home, anyway."

"Ah. How about work? From what I could see that day in the hospital, you were quite . . . fierce. I bet you're one of those terrible men who takes everything out on their colleagues." She smiled at him, lay back on the cushions. "Am I right?"

"That's a dreadful thing to say," he said. He didn't smile back.

"Oh, Alex, I was only joking. Look, this conversation's going nowhere. Let's go to bed, shall we?"

"Fine." He stood up. And then added, "Maybe I should try to get a cab after all."

"That really is ridiculous," she said. "Why, for God's sake?"

"Because I don't seem to feel very comfortable here."

"Oh, please," she said. "You should stop being so sorry for yourself, Alex. It's very dangerous. You're not the only person who's had a bad marriage; other people go through it and out the other side. Even other people with kids."

He stared at her, suddenly angry. "I don't think you're exactly an expert on the subject," he said. "By your own admission, you haven't done too well yourself."

"Oh, do shut up," she said wearily. "Good night, Alex. There's a towel on your bed. And a spare toothbrush on the chest of drawers. The bathroom's down the corridor. Just . . . let yourself out quietly in the morning, will you?"

It was the reference to the toothbrush that did it. He suddenly felt rather stricken at his rudeness, and thought that whatever else, she had been very generous, not to mention thoughtful. Not many people kept spare toothbrushes for unexpected guests.

"I'm . . . sorry," he said stiffly, "if I was rude. You've been very . . . very hospitable. I shall be glad of the toothbrush. Thank you. Good night."

He turned away, and heard the unmistakable sound of a giggle.

"That was the most ridiculous little speech," she said, "but thank you for it. I'm glad you think I'm hospitable, at least. I seem to have one virtue."

Alex turned; she was shaking with silent laughter, biting her lip, her lovely face alive as she looked at him.

"I'm sorry," she said, "if I've hurt your feelings. I truly didn't mean to. It was . . . well, it was seeing you doing your Heathcliff number. All brooding and wounded."

"I was not doing a number," he said. And then he grinned back, albeit reluctantly.

"Yes, you were. You are Heathcliff. To the life. Don't look so cross. Heathcliff was very sexy as well as brooding. Come on, let's go to bed friends, shall we?" She walked over to him, lifted her face to his, reached up, and kissed him—very lightly on the mouth. But it was enough.

Five minutes later they were in her bed.

. . .

"Saturday was lovely," she said now. "Very lovely. Thank you."

"I thought so too. When . . . ?"

"Oh, as soon as possible, I'd think," she said, "if that doesn't sound too bossy. Of course."

"Well . . . it does, quite. But I'll try to ignore that. How about the weekend?"

"Maybe . . . Friday running over into Saturday? Or does that sound bossy?"

"Very bossy. But . . . I think I can handle it."

"I'll book somewhere, shall I?"

"No," he said, "I'll bloody book. I do know how to. Bye, Linda."

"Bye, Alex."

He started the car and drove home quite fast, smiling at the prospect of the weekend and of her. She might be . . . well, she was difficult. But she just made him feel as if he mattered. It was a very good sensation.

. . .

The note lay on the hall table when Barney got in.

"Sorry, darling, tried to ring you, but your phone was switched off. Left a message, but in case you didn't get it, I've gone to see that Keira Knightley film with Nicola. Hope that's OK, knew you'd hate it. Lots of salady stuff in fridge, back about ten. Love you."

Oh, God, Barney thought. *Oh, shit.* Well, it bought him some time.

Maybe he should do it tonight. It wasn't fair on Amanda, the lying. The cheating wasn't fair either, but it was the lying that was so awful. Pretending all the time, smiling at her when he didn't feel like smiling, saying he loved her when she'd said she loved him, because that really was the only thing to say.

Returning her kisses, pretending he was too tired for sex; it was all horrible. When she knew, she'd hate that, hate thinking that was what he'd been doing.

Yes, he would, he'd tell Amanda tonight. Get it over.

He poured himself a beer, sat there thinking about her, about Amanda, his Amanda, whom he had once thought he loved . . .

The landline rang sharply, cutting into his thoughts. Who could that be, who used the landline anymore, except parents, of course . . . ?

He picked it up.

· · ·

Amanda arrived home two hours later. He heard the taxi door slam, heard her pretty, light voice saying, "Thank you so much, good night."

He sat there thinking of what he must tell her, feeling like an executioner, waiting to do his dreadful deed.

She came in, smiling, kissed him, said, "Hello, darling, it was such a lovely film; I really think you might have liked it. Barney, what is it, what's the matter?"

And: "I'm sorry, Amanda," he said, "so, so sorry. It's . . . it's bad news, I'm afraid. It's your father, Amanda, he's . . . Oh God, I'm so sorry; he's had a heart attack; he's . . . well, he's dead."

And then he stood there, holding her as she sobbed and shook with grief, and thought how cruel, how doubly cruel was fate, mostly to her, of course, robbing her of her beloved father, but also in a small part to him, robbing him for the foreseeable future, of the chance to set his life straight and to do the right thing and be with the person he really loved.

And hating himself for finding room even to think it.

CHAPTER 39

"Toby?"

"Yes, Tamara."

"Toby, I really want to talk to you about something."

"Darling, if it's the date, next May's fine by me."

"Good. But it's not. It's about the wedding: the one that didn't happen."

"Ye-es?"

"Toby, I really need to know . . . why did you leave so late? You've waffled away about your being ill and the police stopping you and then the crash. The fact remains, you should have left literally hours earlier. Why didn't you?"

"Well . . . Look, do we really have to do this?"

"Yes, we really do. Because however much I try to believe all that stuff about your being ill, I somehow can't. And if you weren't ill and you didn't leave in time, there was clearly some other very good reason. What was it, Toby; I really have to know."

Toby looked at her, took a large sip of the wine he was drinking, and sat up very straight in his chair.

"Well, I suppose I'd better tell you. I've been hoping it wouldn't have to come out . . ."

"What wouldn't have to come out?"

"It was . . . well, it was Barney, Tamara, I'm afraid. He . . . well, he got terribly drunk the night before the wedding. I tried to stop him, but he kept saying it was my last night of freedom and we should enjoy it. He must have drunk the best part of two bottles of wine and at least half a bottle of whisky. Honestly, he could hardly walk. I got him to bed somehow. And then in the morning . . . well, you can imagine the state he was in. Kept throwing up, completely unfit to drive, of course . . . I just had to sit it out. And . . . adding insult to injury, if you like, he'd forgotten to fill the car up with petrol. Which actually was why we came on the motorway, nearest petrol station. I could have killed him . . . if he hadn't been my best friend. So . . . there you have it. I'm sorry, darling, really I am. But . . . *non mea culpa.*"

"And why the fuck didn't you tell me before? Instead of fobbing me off with this stomach bug nonsense?"

"Oh, Tamara, how could I? He's my best buddy. I couldn't rat on him, could I?"

"Quite easily, I'd have thought. To make me feel better about the whole thing. Who's more important to you, Toby, Barney or me? Seems like it's Barney."

"Darling, of course it's not. I mean, what good would it have done, splitting on him? And don't, please don't tell him I told you. He'd be so . . . so horrified. He feels quite bad enough as it is. Let's just put it behind us, eh? Next May, you'll be Mrs. Toby Weston and this whole thing'll be like a bad dream . . ."

. . .

"Now, Maeve, please don't laugh, but I would be very honoured if you would be my bridesmaid."

Mary's face was rather pink as she looked at Maeve across the table in the café: the same café that had provided so fateful a meeting place two months earlier. She had come in to see Patrick, alerted of the wonderful news of his recovery by Maeve.

"It's like a miracle, Mary, every day a little more sensation. He can feel almost the whole of one foot now, and the toes of the other. I can't believe it, and he is so happy. And . . . oh, Mary, I'd love to be your bridesmaid; it would be the greatest honour, but what about your daughter—isn't that her place?"

"I'm afraid Christine will want to play a very minor role," she said, "if she comes at all. I just keep hoping she'll come round. There's nothing I can say that will make things better, but my son seems delighted . . . They're all coming over from Canada, for the wedding, and my son-in-law, Gerry, he's very happy about it, and my grandson too. Timothy wants to give me away; I was very touched by that."

"Well, that's wonderful. Very well, but if Christine changes her mind, you must tell me at once, and I'll resign the offer. Now, what are you going to wear, will it be white?"

"Well . . . it will. Do you think that's terribly foolish?"

"Of course it's not foolish; it's delightful. You'll look beautiful, Mary."

"It's a two-piece, quite a straight skirt and a beaded jacket, very pretty. And I'm going to carry just a very small bunch of flowers . . . I thought white roses; what do you think?"

"I'd say pink would be better," said Maeve thoughtfully. "White will hardly show up against your dress. And . . . what in your hair?"

"Oh, a long veil, of course," said Mary, and they both started to laugh: two women, joyfully engrossed as they went about the centuries-old female business of planning a wedding, and it was of no consequence whatsoever that the bride was three times the age of her bridesmaid and her bridegroom four times the age of the man who was to give her away.

. . .

Anything might happen now, Emma thought: it was all horribly dangerous. Tamara might tell Amanda . . . although Barney had told her that he didn't think she would.

"I told her, if she did, I would personally wring her neck. I think she believed me, and I think she'll keep her mouth shut. God, she's a cow. God, I dislike her."

Tamara did sound like a cow, but Emma actually thought that if Toby was really the wonderful person Barney said, then he wouldn't be about to marry someone who was absolutely the reverse.

Emma felt very bad about Amanda herself; but the great fear that was consuming her now was that with Barney being so necessarily close to Amanda, supporting her, comforting her, helping her through the awful days and their awful demands—her mother was in bits, he said—he might find himself drawn back irrevocably into their relationship. Grief was a powerful weapon; Amanda would not only be expecting Barney's presence one hundred per cent in her life; she had an absolute right to it . . .

"Woodentops."

The voice was perky. It sounded more suited to the children's TV programme than a firm of carpenters.

"Good morning. This is the Collision Investigation Unit of the Avon Valley Police."

"Oh, yes?" Slightly less perky.

"We're looking to contact the driver of one of your vans . . ."

"We have several; I'd need more details, please? Driver's name, number of car . . ."

"I don't have either, I'm afraid. But one of your vans was seen driving up the M4 on the afternoon of August twenty-second. Towards London. Is that any help to you?"

"Let me see . . ."

There was a silence; Freeman could hear computer keys clicking in the background. Then: "That would probably be Mr. Thompson. I'm not sure; you'd need to speak to him; as I said, we do have several vans and—"

"Is Mr. Thompson there?"

"No, but I can contact him for you."

"Perhaps you'd ask him to give me a call. Just a routine enquiry, tell him. The number is . . ."

. . .

"Rick, you been speeding again? Had the police on about you. You'd better not lose your licence; you'll be out of a job if you do. Now, it was you, wasn't it, on the M4 afternoon of August twenty-second? Yes, I thought so . . ."

. . .

Shit. How had they traced him? Not that it mattered; he hadn't done anything wrong. He'd been miles ahead of that accident, anyway. Probably thought he could just provide some information. Bloody police, always harassing the poor bloody motorist . . .

By the time he phoned them, Rick had worked himself up into a state of extremely righteous indignation.

. . .

"Is that the Emma?"

God. She'd forgotten how lovely it was just to hear his voice.

"Hi, Barney. The Barney. Yes, it is. How . . . how are things?"

"Bit tough. Yes. How are you?"

"I'm fine. Yes, really fine. Missing you, but . . ."

"Missing you too. So much. It was the funeral today. That was grim. Amanda was incredibly upset."

"Of course."

"But being terribly brave, wonderful with her mum."

She wasn't sure she wanted to hear all this.

"We're staying down here tonight"—she didn't like that *we*; it conjured up images she could hardly bear—"and then I'm going back in the morning."

"Right."

"Amanda's probably coming up in a day or two. She's had a lot of time off work already."

"Yes, I'm sure."

"Emma . . . I don't . . . that is, I can't . . . not until . . ."

"Barney, it's OK. You don't even have to say it. Just take your time. I understand."

"I love you, Emma."

"I . . ." But she couldn't even finish. She choked on the words. And rang off without saying good-bye.

. . .

The second day of rehearsals Georgia arrived early—early enough for coffee alone with Merlin—and she began to feel more comfortable with everyone. Davina told her she was doing great, and Anna was there, rehearsing a scene with Georgia and the grandmother. Anna was wonderful to work with, easy, encouraging . . . and managed to give her character a humour that lifted her scenes beautifully, and which Georgia found herself responding to. Best of all, at the end of the day, Merlin said, "We could have a drink this evening, if you've got time." Georgia was able to find the time.

They went to a pub down the street. Even walking into it with him was amazing; she felt everyone must be looking at them, and thinking how good-looking he was, and what a cool couple they made.

"So . . . things better today? You were very tense yesterday."

"Much better, thank you."

"Anna is great, isn't she? She has a fascinating history. Ask her to tell you sometime."

"Oh . . . OK. So"—this seemed a good opening—"so what about you, Merlin, have you worked on loads of productions?"

"Not that many. Incredibly lucky to be in this one. Bryn is the greatest; you learn such a lot from someone like him."

"And . . . did you go to drama school?"

"Yeah, LAMDA, did their two-year stage management course. Haven't been working that long—I'm still only twenty-six—and the money's rubbish, of course, but who cares? I have to live at home still. But I'm pretty well self-contained, and they don't bother me much."

"So . . . where is home?" said Georgia, encouraged that at least he didn't seem to have a live-in girlfriend.

"Oh . . . Hampstead. Up by the Heath. Pretty nice. Sometimes, early in the morning, you can believe it's actually the country. Birds carrying on and all that sort of thing. Mummy swims in the ponds every day . . ."

"Really?" said Georgia, hoping she sounded as if she knew what the ponds were.

"Yes. She's cool. We get on pretty well."

"And your dad? Does he swim too?"

"Oh . . . not Pa, no. He's a bit of a wimp. Although he does cycle into the college in the summer. If it's not raining, that is."

"The college?"

"Yeah. He's a lecturer at London University. In political history."

"Goodness. He must be very clever."

"He is. God, Georgia, it's been such fun, but I must go. Got to get up to Kensington. I'm going on the tube; how about you?"

"Oh . . . yes, me too. To Baker Street."

"Let's go together then."

He must like her a bit, to want to travel on the tube with her. Just a bit.

. . .

He wasn't in the next day, but she got chatting to Mo and, by careful casual questioning, found out a bit more about Merlin.

"He's a sweetheart," Mo said, "and looking like that . . . God. He ought to be a real brat, but he isn't. Well, not much of one."

"It sounds as if his parents are quite . . . rich," said Georgia.

"Well . . . quite. But they're incredibly socialist as well. Both fully paid up members of the Labour Party. Mama runs this secondhand bookshop in Hampstead, and sells loads of political books and does fund-raising and stuff."

"But . . . Merlin sounds very . . . well, very posh. I thought he must have gone to Eton or somewhere."

"God, no. Holland Park Comp. Where he was bullied terribly, actually beaten up several times, because a group of really rough kids decided he was gay, but the parents didn't care. Their principles were much more important. Poor old Merlin. Anyway, he's all right now. Everyone loves him."

"He's not, though . . . is he?" said Georgia, trying not to sound anxious.

"Not what? Oh, gay, No, of course not. Very red-blooded indeed, our Merlin."

"He's been so, so nice to me," Georgia said.

"Yes, well, he is really . . . nice. But . . ." Mo looked at her, and she thought she was about to say something, but then Bryn Merrick arrived, looking petulant, and demanded freshly ground coffee. And then Davina wanted to run through a scene with Georgia, and whatever it was, was never said.

Part Five

NEXT

CHAPTER 41

William was walking out of a pub in Bristol, quite early in the evening, when he saw Abi. He'd avoided the place as much as he could recently, but an old friend from Cirencester days had asked him to be best man at his wedding and had invited him and his ushers to discuss the demands and requirements of their roles.

He tried very hard to get into the spirit of the thing, downed a couple of beers and laughed at some pretty unfunny jokes about the role of the best man and agreed that the Hunt Ball of the previous week had been terrific, although actually he'd reached a peak of misery there. Gyrating to the pounding rhythms of the Whippersnappers, he'd looked round at all the other gyrators, some young, some older, but with the identical DNA of the foxhunting classes, cheerful, foolhardy, blinkered folk, clinging to their beleaguered lifestyle, and wondered how he was going to live among them for the rest of his life.

Abi was walking along, laden with bags; Christmas shopping, he supposed. She was wearing black as always: black leather coat, knee-length black boots, black furry hat. And dark glasses. In the dark. Why did she do that? She saw him, briefly pretended she hadn't, then half smiled and said, "Hello."

"Hello, Abi. How are you?"

"I'm fine. You?"

"Oh . . . yes. Fine, thanks."

He felt awful, wondering if he was going to throw up or pass out.

"Been Christmas shopping?"

"Yeah. God, it's awful out there. Pandemonium."

"Where's your car?"

"Oh . . . just along there. In the car park. What are you doing here?"

"Mate of mine's getting married; he's asked me to be best man. We were just getting together with the ushers."

"Really? When's the wedding?"

"In April."

"Lambing time."

"No, not for us. We do early lambing."

"Oh, of course you do. In the lambing shed . . ." She looked at him and smiled. "See how much I've remembered? Well I guess I wouldn't have forgotten that."

Oh, God, God, she shouldn't have said that. It had been all right till then; he'd been fine, totally fine, about to move on, say cheers. But the lambing shed . . .

"My car's down there, too," he said. "Let me help you with your bags."

"Oh . . . OK. Thanks."

There was no tension, no uneasy silence as they walked; she asked him how he was, what he'd been doing, what was the main activity on the farm in the winter. He'd forgotten how interested she was in everything, and how much he enjoyed the interest. It was extraordinary—extraordinary and extraordinarily pleasing.

Her car was on the ground floor; he realised that he'd been hoping it would be a longer trip, that they'd have to go up in the lift, that the encounter might continue as long as possible.

She opened the boot. "Thanks, William. That's really kind of you."

He put the bags in; she shut the boot, turned to look at him. He caught the strong, heady scent he remembered; he felt a bit dizzy.

"It was so nice to see you," she said. "I've often thought how nice it would be. Just to . . . well . . . say good-bye more happily. But it didn't seem very likely. I mean, those sorts of things only happen in films, don't they? And books? What are the chances of William

· 364 ·

Grainger, farmer, and Abi Scott, photographer's assistant, actually bumping into each other, on the off chance? One in millions. Billions, probably." She leaned up, gave him a kiss on the cheek. "Bye, William. Once again, I'm so sorry."

"What for?" he said, and in that moment he genuinely couldn't think why she should be apologising.

"Me being me. Right, then . . ." She turned, walked to the door, opened it. "Take care. Oh, and happy Christmas."

She got in, slammed the door, started the engine. William stood there, mute, helpless, unable to do or say anything. She was there, not in his memory, not in his imagination, but for real. Funny and fun and sexy and interested. Interesting and absolutely on his side. And now she was going . . . again. Leaving him to his new—or rather old—life, blank, monotone, nothing to look forward to as he spread slurry in the cold, did the hated paperwork.

She put the car into gear, wound down the window, blew him another kiss. "Bye," she said again.

She moved forward; he jumped out of the way, managed to smile. The car moved slowly off. She was going, leaving him again, and that had to be right, had to be the only thing. He should just be glad—as she had said—that they could say good-bye more happily. There was absolutely no alternative. None whatsoever.

. . .

Barney couldn't believe how much it would hurt: losing Toby. Sometimes he thought it was even worse than losing Emma. At least he could have gone and talked about Emma to Toby, the one person in the world—he had thought—he could trust, talk to about anything. You couldn't admit to being that foolish to many people.

It was like discovering the Rolex Oyster you'd been given for your twenty-first by your parents was a cheap fake. Toby, his best friend, whom he'd have trusted with his life, had turned out to be a cheap fake himself. He still couldn't quite believe it. Or, worse, that he'd been so stupid and that Toby had pulled the wool over his eyes for so long. That hurt too. He also felt incredibly angry quite a lot of the time: angry with Toby, angry with himself, angry with Tamara.

He knew he'd never forget as long as he lived that night she came round and ranted and railed at him; he'd thought that she'd finally had a nervous breakdown because of her cancelled wedding.

But then as she calmed down and he managed to get her to tell him just what it exactly was he was supposed to have done, and as the hideous realisation dawned, he felt so terrible he thought he was actually going to be sick.

"Well," she said, "what have you got to say, Barney, did you really think you could get away with it, all that crap?"

There had seemed no point at that moment in telling her it was Toby who was giving her the crap, Toby who was lying; it was Toby who must be confronted. He simply said he was very sorry she was so upset, that there was obviously a terrible misunderstanding and he would do his very best to sort it out. She had left, after hurling a few more insults at him; she was so clearly genuinely upset that Barney had actually felt quite sorry for her.

Toby had lied, of course; Barney had arrived at the house the following evening, had told the Westons he was going to take him out for a drink, and then parked a mile down the road and confronted him.

"Mate, she's crazy. She must have misunderstood what I said to her."

"No," said Barney, "she didn't misunderstand. She was very, very clear about what you told her. In fact, she repeated it almost word for word. I'd repeat it back to you, if you like, only I don't think I could face hearing any more lies. I don't know why you did it, Toby. I'm baffled."

"I don't understand myself," said Toby, and his voice was rather quiet suddenly. "I've just had so much to cope with, with the accident and the leg and so on, and it was just . . . easier to tell her that. I'm sorry . . . I still feel pretty rotten, Barney, in pain a lot of the time, can't sleep . . ."

"Oh, my heart bleeds for you," said Barney. "I can cope with your not telling Tamara the truth . . . obviously. I wouldn't either. But not lying to her about me. It's hideous, Toby. Any other little fibs I need to know about, just so I don't get any more nasty surprises? If not I'll be off."

"I . . ." Toby seemed about to say something, then stopped. "No, no, Barney, of course not."

"Good. Don't see what's 'of course' about it. Actually."

"Barney, I'm . . . well, I'm sorry. Very sorry."

"Yeah, OK. I'll drop you back. You'll have to think of some story to give your mother. Why do I think you'll be able to manage that?"

He had been so upset he'd actually cried after he dropped Toby outside his house, parked his car at the end of the road and sobbed like a small boy. Then he'd driven very slowly and carefully back to London.

He got home at midnight, sat down, and got very drunk on whisky, grateful only that Amanda wasn't there; he felt betrayed not just by Toby but by life itself. It just wasn't fucking fair.

When Emma phoned two weeks later to tell him that she'd been doing a lot of thinking and she really couldn't see how they could possibly have a future together, or not one based on making Amanda, whom he obviously still loved so much, deeply unhappy, and not to argue and not to try to see her, he found he was hardly even surprised.

Wretched, wounded, shocked, but not surprised.

. . .

"Right," said Freeman. He tapped the pile of papers on his desk. "Ready to go, I think. Dozens of interviews, hundreds of hours. But none of it warrants going to the CPS, in my opinion. No real charge against anyone here . . ."

"Not even our friend Mr. Thompson?"

"No chance. Nasty bit of work, and undoubtedly he contributed to the blowout, but you could never charge him."

"Well, maybe he'll be a bit more careful in future."

"Maybe. For a bit. Then it'll be two fingers to us all and he'll be off again. I'd like to see him fined, at least. But . . . I'd say we simply have an inquest situation here."

Constable Rowe felt quite sorry for him; he looked as if he was about to burst into tears.

. . .

Interviewed at a police station, Rick had been defiant, truculent; yes, he'd had a load of wood on board; that was his job. No, he hadn't been driving dangerously.

"And . . . this wood, Mr. Thompson. Was it properly stowed in your van?"

"Yes, course it was."

"And it was new wood, was it?"

"Yeah."

"It had no nails in it, for instance?"

"Course not."

"Right. Well, perhaps you could explain why several witnesses saw the back doors of your van tied together with some rope?"

"I might have tied some rope round the handles. Nothing wrong with that, is there? Doesn't mean it wasn't properly fastened."

"So you're quite sure that some pieces of wood, with nails in them, could not have fallen out of the van onto the road?"

"Yeah, quite sure. I told you, it was new wood."

. . .

The man from the wood yard near Stroud had remembered Rick very clearly.

Particularly his request that he should dispose of the old timber for him, and that he had refused. And that Thompson had then asked for a length of rope to tie the doors together, which had been insufficient to do the job properly.

Rick was told he would be called as a witness at any trial or inquest on the crash.

"Oh, what! I wasn't anywhere near the bloody crash."

"People have died, Mr. Thompson," Freeman said. "Proper explanations for that have to be found. You could certainly be judged to have played a part in the collision that caused it. You'll be hearing from us in the fullness of time."

. . .

"I think I should move out for a bit," said Jonathan. "This isn't getting us anywhere."

He had walked into Laura's studio, where she was struggling to work; it was late; the children were all in bed and asleep.

"What isn't getting us anywhere?"

"Well . . . drifting along like this. With you obviously unable to bear the sight of me."

"Are you surprised by that?"

"No, Laura. But we can't go on like this for the next forty years or whatever."

"Believe me, I don't want to. I'm just . . . trying to decide what's best. For all of us."

"I presume by that you mean the children," he said, "rather than me and you."

"Well . . . me as well. But mainly them, yes."

"Right. Well, I think rather than go on living in this poisonous atmosphere—"

"I hope you're not implying I'm creating the poisonous atmosphere?"

"Well . . . to a degree, you are. Obviously with some justification, but . . ."

"Jonathan, I can't believe you said that. I haven't done anything.

I'm not doing anything. Just trying to . . . to cope with what you've done. You've betrayed me totally, Jonathan, lied and lied to me, broken every promise, all your marriage vows."

"Laura, I've said so many times I'm sorry, desperately sorry; I would give everything I have for it not to have happened . . ."

"Oh, I don't think so. Your precious career, your doting staff, your adoring patients? And if you're that desperate about it, why didn't you realise how wrong it was, what damage you were doing to us and our marriage? No, you must have felt you had some kind of right to it, to her. And in that case, then either you're rotten through and through, which actually I don't think you are, or there's something wanting in our relationship. So don't try to explain, because I don't think I could bear it."

She could see she had shocked him: not by what she had said, but that she had said it at all. This was not the Laura he knew, berating him; this was not his gentle, softly spoken wife. But then, she thought, he was not the Jonathan she had known, not the loving, loyal husband and father, who had the family at the very centre of his being. They were moving far and fast from their old selves, and there was no knowing where and how far apart they would end up.

"Well . . . in that case, I'll go," he said. "There's no point in my staying. I really can't see it's of any benefit to the children. I'll arrange to see them at weekends and so on. And then we can decide what to do next."

"Yes. All right."

She felt sick suddenly.

"I think I'll go to bed," she said, and walked over to the door. There was a scuffle on the stairs; she looked up and saw Charlie staring down at her, his face white, with two brilliant spots of colour forming on his cheeks. He had obviously heard every word.

* * *

Georgia was still slightly surprised to find herself living with a friend of Merlin's . . . well, not actually living with him, obviously, but in a room in his house in Paddington. She had imagined herself living in a flat with a load of girls, or men and girls, sharing everything, eating together, going around together, not virtually on her own, having to budget and cook for herself and get herself up and out in the morning. It had all been a bit of a shock at first. But there simply hadn't been an option.

It had all begun with a row with Linda, with whom she'd been staying; Linda was being really odd. Far less interested in Georgia than she used to be, demanding, critical, making a fuss about stupid things like a couple of cups left unwashed, or music being played too loudly, and nagging endlessly about finding a place of her own.

She'd looked at about a hundred—well, at least ten—room- and flat-shares one Monday morning, and they were all horrible. She'd just never expected it to be so hard. And then she'd gone in to work in the afternoon and Bryn Merrick had actually shouted at her when she kept getting a scene wrong, and she'd half run out of the hall at six and arrived back at Linda's flat in floods of tears. To find Linda not there; she'd spent a miserable evening on her own until Linda came in at nine o'clock in a foul mood, all because some contract had been cancelled and she'd been with lawyers all evening.

Georgia managed to express sympathy, and to make Linda a cup of tea; but then once Linda had settled on the sofa and reached for the TV remote, she said, "Linda, I need to talk to you."

"Georgia, must it be now?"

"Well . . . yes. If you don't mind."

"And if I do?"

"I'd still like it."

"Oh all right. " Linda put the remote down, folded her arms, and looked at her. "What is it?"

"It's . . . well, Linda, I'm finding it all so hard. The series, the rehearsals, all of it. Mostly Bryn Merrick. He just doesn't like me, and that makes me nervous. You know I still feel . . . bad about the accident, and I'm still so aware of what they must think of me. And today I totally blew a scene, and everyone was so . . . so, like, hostile to me, and I cried all the way home. I wondered if you could help, have a word with Bryn or something, or even if I should just resign or something, let them get someone else for Rose . . ."

She had never seen Linda totally lose it. Which was what happened then. She put down her cup, stood up and folded her arms, and confronted her across the room.

"Georgia, I'm finding something hard too, and I'll tell you what it is. You. You and your self-obsessed, pathetic attitude. You get this part, this amazing opportunity, and ever since the very beginning you've whinged about it. I can tell you I wouldn't like you either if I was on that production. It is of no interest to them whatsoever that you've had a traumatic time and you're suffering from survivor blame or whatever it's called; although I'm sure initially they were very sympathetic. You're been hired to do a job. Grow up. Life's tough. Get used to it. And find yourself somewhere to live in the process."

And then she turned and walked out of the room and into her own and slammed the door shut.

. . .

Georgia didn't go to bed at all that night. She sat in the big comfy chair in her room, fully clothed, in a state of shock. She kept hearing what Linda had said, replayed it over and over again in her head, trying to make sense of it, trying to believe that Linda could have been so horrible to her; but as the night wore on, a small, sneaky voice began to tell her that there might, actually, be at least something in what she had said. She still felt Linda had been totally out of order and she should have seen that it was support that Georgia needed, not a bollocking, but as long as she could get out of the flat and in somewhere else . . . Someone had suggested the YMCA, which Georgia had been horrified by at the time, but it would be better than hanging around crowding Linda's space.

At six o'clock, she got up and packed, wrote a note telling Linda she wouldn't be getting in her way any longer, and called a cab and went to the church hall where rehearsals took place. She knew the cleaners came at six, but she hadn't bargained on Merlin being there.

"Heavy night?" he said sympathetically, and, "No," she said, "not in that way," and started to cry.

Merlin was wonderful; he found her a box of Kleenex and sat down beside her, put his arm round her, and asked her to tell him what the matter was.

Which, having recovered from the considerable shock of finding herself where she had dreamed for the past four weeks—in close physical contact with Merlin Gerard, which suddenly wasn't particularly exciting, but just cosy and comforting—she did.

All of it.

He really was very sweet: he said he could imagine how terrible she must have felt about the crash, and he'd really felt for her . . . "so vile, the tabloids," but he told her no one else had really taken it in at all.

"They all really like you, Georgia. Davina's always saying what a sweetheart you are, and I know Bryn can be awkward, but he's a perfectionist, and he's not remotely regretting casting you. You're doing really well. You're very talented, you know; you should believe in yourself a bit more."

Georgia sniffed. "I don't feel very talented. I don't feel talented at all."

"Well, you are. Now, look, I really have to get on; I came in early to catch up on some stuff, and if Mo finds me sitting here having a goss with you she'll get very sniffy. But . . . what are you doing this evening?"

"Nothing," said Georgia, trying very hard to believe this was actually happening. "Probably trying to find a park bench."

"Why? Oh, yeah, Linda's thrown you out. I'm sure she didn't mean it. But it would be nice to have somewhere of your own. Anyway, I think I can probably help. Hang around if you finish before me and then we'll go for a drink and I'll tell you about it."

He gave her a quick kiss and disappeared into the kitchen; Georgia went through the rest of the day in a trance.

. . .

Merlin's help came in the form of his friend Jazz, whom he'd been at school with; Jazz helped his dad with his building business and what he called his property empire, which was the ownership of two large, crumbling houses the wrong end of the Portobello Road.

"They're divided into bed-sits," Merlin said, "and there's usually at least a couple looking for occupants. I'll give him a call."

Jazz said he did have one, and if Merlin would bring Georgia round in an hour or so, he'd show it to her.

. . .

Jazz was fun: she liked him. He was taller than Merlin, and heavily built, with close-cropped black hair and almost black eyes; he kept punching Merlin on the arm and calling him his old mate; he also argued with him a lot, mocked his job, and told him more than once that he was a bloody great poof.

"Pardon my French," he said, grinning, seeing Georgia's face, "just a joke—got stuck with it at school, didn't you, mate? I thought so meself for a bit, used to stand with me back to the wall when he was around, but don't you worry, my love; nothing fairylike about our Merl. OK, let's go and have a look at this accommodation, shall we?"

. . .

It was pretty grim, right at the top of the house, one of two converted attics, and very cold. It had a gas ring and a sink behind a curtain, and a money-in-the-slot electric meter, and the bathroom was a floor down, not dirty exactly, but grubby, freezing cold, with stains in the bath and a suspicious wetness round the base of the loo. It was all a bit smelly.

But it had brilliant views, through a rather sweet little dormer window . . . and she loved the way the ceiling sloped almost to the floor on two sides. And it would be hers. Her very own home. She said she'd take it.

"Right-o," said Jazz, "it's yours. Next door's some bloke who works for a charity, real do-gooder. Won't cause you no trouble. Anyone does, you just let me know. But we don't take none of your rough types; they're mostly a nice crowd, lotta females—you'll be fine."

And she was.

She replaced the filthy curtain that shielded the kitchen with a bamboo screen and bought some thick blinds at IKEA, and a gorgeous white furry throw for her bed and another for the lumpy armchair, which she supposed was what made the rooms officially bed-sits . . . and she bought a convector heater, which ate money, but even so, she was cold a lot of the time.

Nonetheless, she loved it; it was hers, her very own home that she was paying for; she felt independent and pleased with herself, and that kept her going through the very tough times she continued to have on the series.

. . .

She had also formed a hugely supportive friendship with Anna.

Anna had had a great life; she had trained as a classical singer, fallen in love with a jazz pianist called Sim Foster, and ran away with him. Georgia could see how it had happened; she was astonishingly glamorous and sexy out of makeup and looked far younger than her sixty years. She said she loved character roles: "The less I'm like myself the better I like it."

Her parents had lived in Surrey, and were completely horrified that their beloved daughter should be living with what they called a coloured man and not even married, touring the world with him, singing jazz for fifteen years . . .

"He was fantastic, Georgia, not first division, but definitely top of the second. I adored him, and I adored the life we led, all those wonderful smoky bars—God, how I miss smoky bars—we even played New Orleans."

They had been quite successful, if not exactly Cleo Laine and Johnny Dankworth: "But we put out the odd album, did quite a bit of TV."

Sim had died—"Well, he killed himself, really, just one too many cocaine cocktails"—and she had come home and had to make a new life for herself and their daughter, Lila.

"She was only four. I couldn't support her on the road, so I started doing modelling, mumsy stuff for the catalogues, and some commercials, and one thing led to another, and I got lucky and started acting. Twenty years later, here I am."

Lila was at college training to be a musician: "She can play a mean clarinet, I tell you. You remind me of her, Georgia."

Lila turned up on the set to collect her mother one night; she was very pretty, huge fun; Georgia was flattered by the comparison.

Anna had done a lot to help Georgia over her nerves. "I know what it's like, and it was worse for me; I was a novice at forty, not twenty. You think it won't be easy, of course, but you got the part, for God's sake, so you must be OK, but everyone else belongs to this club with its own language and customs, and you're on the outside, fighting to get in."

They were actually filming now, and she found it much easier in some ways. She recognised that her problems were due to inexperience, not everyone being against her, and she felt more self-confident as a result.

And the others were actually very nice to her . . . even Bryn Merrick had taken time out to go through certain scenes with her.

She had had a rather emotional reunion with Linda, where Georgia cried a lot and Linda cried a bit, and Linda told her how proud of her she was and that Bryn Merrick had called her personally to say how well Georgia was working out and how he knew it must be difficult for her. And Linda was clearly impressed by all that she had done.

She even apologised for her behaviour the night she had lost her temper.

"I'm sorry, Georgia; it was wrong of me."

"That's OK," said Georgia, giving her a hug. "I'd probably still be here if you hadn't." None of it would have happened, of course, without Merlin; Georgia felt she owed him everything. And said so, and even offered to cook him supper on her gas ring to show him her gratitude.

Merlin refused; she was disappointed, but not really surprised. He moved in such exalted circles, was always mentioning famous writers and artists and even the odd Labour politician who'd been to dinner with his parents. How could he be expected to enjoy chilli (her only culinary accomplishment) cooked in a bed-sit? But he continued to be really friendly, to ask her to go for drinks after work, to pass on any compliments.

The weather had been a big factor in the shooting; because it was winter, there were many days when they had to move inside and change scenes at a moment's notice. This necessitated wardrobe changes as well as everything else and was a nightmare for continuity.

But in the end they ran out of indoor scenes, and one very cold November morning Georgia had to run down the street wearing a vest and shorts, buy an ice cream, and stand licking it while she chatted to a woman on a flower stall about her granny; the sun was brilliant, but not exactly warm, and kept going in, and she had to do it five times because, in spite of Merlin's best efforts, cars kept coming across the shot. It was the sort of day guaranteed to produce one of Bryn's hissy fits . . . although as she said to Merlin in the pub, he'd had "a thick coat on and a scarf and gloves, for God's sake."

She remained puzzled by Merlin's attitude to her. He was so sweet, so attentive, and he really didn't seem to have a regular girlfriend, so she couldn't help being hopeful . . .

CHAPTER 42

"Alex, are you going to this wedding on Saturday?"

"I am indeed. I'm told by Maeve that if I don't, she'll never forgive me. I feel a bit of a fraud; I've never done anything for Mrs. Bristow, except chatted to her once or twice, but she said the hospital had been so fantastic to her, looked after her so well, and she wanted to have some representatives there. Plus the Connells are going to be there in force, apparently, Patrick's first outing, and she said she knew what a lot I'd done for him."

"I've been asked too."

"Really? How very nice."

"Yes. I had a sweet note from Mr. Mackenzie saying it was a small token of his gratitude for helping him to find Mary that day."

"I didn't know you did."

"Well . . . I didn't really. Bit of a long story. You don't want to hear it."

"Yes, I do."

"Well, you're not going to." Emma sighed. "Anyway, maybe we could go together?"

"That would be delightful. I think the whole thing will be delightful. We can feel fraudulent together. You're . . . you're all right, are you, Emma?"

"Yes, thank you, I'm fine."

"Good. You look a bit tired, that's all; I wondered if—"

"Alex, I'm fine."

"Good."

. . .

But she wasn't fine; she felt absolutely terrible. She hurt all over—physically, somehow, as well as emotionally. It was extraordinary. Her skin felt tender and her eyes were permanently sore, and she felt utterly weary, as if her bones were somehow twice their proper weight. When she allowed herself actually to think about Barney, she wanted to cry; and even when she managed not to think about him, the awful sadness was still there, oppressing her. She couldn't imagine ever feeling properly happy again.

She had written to Luke, telling him she was very sorry, but she felt it was wrong of her to let him go on thinking she cared about him as she had. She had enclosed the necklace. He had called her, clearly very upset, had asked her to take time to think, to reconsider; he said he could not imagine life without her, that he needed her. "It's not easy, this job, Emma, tougher than I'd thought; I've been really banking on coming home and seeing you at the weekends. Or like I said, getting you out here. It's a really cool city; we could have a great time."

But she stood firm, told him she was sorry, but she couldn't see how it could possibly work out between them, and she liked him and admired him far too much to let him think she loved him when she didn't.

She had been all right in the beginning, when Barney had told her about Amanda and that they must wait awhile. It had seemed the kind—indeed the only right—thing to do. But as time went by, she became increasingly anxious; she was in love with a man who, however much he said he loved her in return, was clearly deeply and tenderly concerned for someone else. Someone whom, until he had met Emma, he had wanted to spend the rest of his life with. And someone who, for whatever reason, had become his first priority once more. And the more she thought of herself dislodging that person, the more impossible it seemed; how could a brief affair, a flash of desire, replace that long, long time of being together?

It was a daydream, an acutely tempting fantasy: not for her—she had no doubt of the reality of her love for Barney—but for him. She should leave him to be with his Amanda, not be singing her siren song to him, luring him onto the rocks of a cancelled marriage.

For a few days, the very rightness of what she had done buoyed her up; she felt stronger, braver, a better person altogether. And then the misery set in, and she knew she had been right. For Barney had not argued, had not fought for her; he had been quiet, gentle, very sad, while seeming to accept absolutely what she said.

It was over; and it was horrible. And . . . while knowing such a thought was foolish and she should disabuse herself of it, she really could not imagine ever feeling properly happy again.

. . .

"Barney . . ."

He was working late; it was quiet on the floor. She was standing by his desk, seeming to have appeared out of nowhere. He hadn't seen her since their last confrontation—surprising in a way, he supposed, since they were in the same building . . . but then, the building contained at least five thousand of them.

He looked at her warily. She was looking rather unfamiliar, slightly nervous, her face pale, her lips unglossed, her hair hanging straight onto her shoulders. Tamara undone. This must be serious.

"Hello, Tamara."

"Barney, this is . . . well, it's hard for me to say . . . Barney, I'm sorry."

If she had disappeared into a pall of smoke, leaving only her shoes and bag on the floor, like the Wicked Witch in *The Wizard of Oz,* he could not have been more astonished. He hadn't thought *sorry* was a word in Tamara's lexicon.

"I . . . I shouldn't have done that."

"Done what, Tamara?"

"Shouted at you. Accused you of . . . well, of what I did. The thing is, I know now Toby was lying to me. It wasn't you who made him late. I went to see him last night. We had a long conversation. Basically, it's over, Barney. We're not . . . not having a wedding. It's him who's the shit. Not you. I know that now."

"I see . . ." said Barney.

"Yes. I began to think and I thought . . . well, I realised that *you* were driving when you were stopped by the police. And they'd have Breathalyzed you."

"They did."

"And if you'd been as drunk as Toby said, you would still probably have been over the limit. So I said that to Toby and started really asking questions. And he . . . well, he suddenly gave in."

"Really?"

"Yes. He told me everything. About . . . well, all of it, the other girl, everything. I said . . . well, you can imagine, I expect."

"Think so."

"I just told him I never wanted to see him again. And left."

"Right . . ."

"The other thing is, I don't know how things are with you and Amanda now, but she says you've been fantastic over all this, that she'd never have got through it without you. So . . . well, I promise you I'll never say anything to her, ever."

"Thank you."

"Right. Well, I must go now. Night, Barney."

"Good night, Tamara."

He didn't feel anything much, except very tired.

. . .

Charlie was being completely impossible. He was cold and insolent to his father and completely uncooperative with Laura, refusing to join the girls for meals, and locking himself away in his room playing with his Game Boy, or painting the Warhammer models that were his new passion, sometimes late into the night. If Laura came in and told him to turn the light off and go to bed he shrugged and didn't even answer. If she turned the light out, he would simply wait until she had gone downstairs and then turn it on again. He did the minimum amount of homework, and when his work came back with low marks he simply shrugged. He refused a part in the Christmas play and didn't turn up for soccer practice.

When Jonathan and Laura went in for a parents' evening, his year tutor showed them the reports he had from all his teachers, and they were horrified. The charming, high-achieving Charlie was suddenly being labelled lazy, uncooperative, and even disruptive.

"Er . . ." David Richards looked awkward. "I wondered . . . is there some problem that we don't know about? All boys get a bit like this towards puberty, but this has been so sudden and such a great change, I feel there must be a rather more immediate explanation."

"Well—" said Laura.

"No," said Jonathan, "no problems at all. I'll talk to him. Clearly it can't go on."

• • •

"Yes, clearly it can't go on," she said, glaring at him across the table of the restaurant where they had agreed they should talk, safe from Charlie's sharp ears. "But I don't see how we're going to stop him. He's just so horribly upset and it's his way of telling us so."

"Fine."

"What do you mean, fine?"

"I mean, of course he's upset. Unfortunately there's not a lot we can do about that. And yes, I know it's my fault. But if we can make him see that he's damaging his own chances, then I think he may start behaving a bit better."

"I hope so," said Laura.

She didn't think it was actually very likely.

• • •

"Fuck you!" said Charlie. "Fuck you, talking to me like that."

"Charlie, don't you dare swear at me!"

"I'll swear at you if I want to. You're awful. Horrible. Doing that to Mum, sleeping with that girl. How could you, how could you when Mum's so . . . so good to you."

"I know she is, Charlie, and I'm deeply ashamed of myself. Terribly, terribly sorry, and so sorry too that you had to find out."

"Yeah, well, if you're so sorry you might have thought a bit harder before you did anything so disgusting."

"Charlie . . . if you could just listen to me for a while. I'm not asking you to understand—"

"Yeah? Sounds like it to me."

"No, I'm not. All I'm saying is I'm desperately sorry, and I would ask you to—"

"To what? Forgive you, I suppose. For wrecking our family, ruining Mum's life. How am I supposed to forgive that?"

"I wasn't going to say forgive, Charlie. Just to beg you not to ruin your own life, your own chances by behaving as you are. I may have made a mess of mine, but you have everything ahead of you. Don't—"

"I don't care if I get expelled; I don't care if I end up in prison. I can't have the only thing I want, which is our family back like it used to be, and you've taken that away from all of us forever. I wish you weren't my father; I wish . . ."

Jonathan walked out of the room and into his study. When she went in much later, to tell him how distraught Charlie still was, Laura could see that he too had been weeping.

. . .

Abi thought she would never forgive herself for what she had done that night to Jonathan: or rather, not to Jonathan, who had deserved every ghastly moment of it, but to his family, who had not. She had contemplated every kind of restitution, from writing to Laura to apologise to seeking out the children and telling them their father was a wonderful man and she was simply a very nasty, angry patient of his and she had been very cross with him. She was afraid none of it would work. The harm had been done; she could not undo it. She could only hope that it had not been too great. Especially to the children.

She was obviously a bad person to be able to do such a thing; she had to learn to live with that.

But seeing William again had upset her badly. She hadn't forgotten—of course—how great he was, how truly nice and good. But being confronted by him again had reminded her horribly vividly. She felt several miles back in the recovery process.

But . . . at least she'd ensured he couldn't entertain any foolish fantasies about her. She'd made quite sure of that. It hadn't been exactly easy, but she'd done it. By telling him how rotten she was, what she was capable of.

She had not allowed him to think for one moment that it wasn't really so bad, that it was maybe not her fault, that her early life excused—to an extent—her behaviour. She had actually told him that dreadful night that she didn't really buy all the crap about people being bad because bad things had happened to them. He had looked at her with those great brown eyes and half laughed and said, "Abi, how can you possibly say such a thing? Of course that's right; of course people are influenced by how life's treated them."

She'd said it just felt like a cop-out to her, but she'd been finishing with him then; it hadn't mattered what she'd said or what he'd believed. She'd been too distraught to care.

She had been beginning to feel better, to rebuild her life. She was looking for a new job, was thinking she might perhaps move into party planning, as it was called . . . well, it would be better than party wrecking . . . She knew she'd be good at it, and it looked like fun. (She'd told William about that, actually, and he'd said that it sounded great. God, he was so nice to talk to; he really, really listened and thought about what you'd said . . .)

Well, she'd advance down the recovery road again, no doubt. If life had taught her anything, it had taught her that. And the fact that she still missed William, really missed him . . . well, she should regard all that as some kind of a penance for the wrong she had done, not only to Laura and her children, but to William himself.

. . .

William had been equally upset by their meeting. It had been great in a way . . . they'd almost become friends once more. But it had made him miss her horribly all over again; he felt like a reformed alcoholic who had had the fatal, dangerous last sip, and he was back in the misery of his addiction.

It was true, of course, what she said: she was not the person he'd thought; in fact—to be brutal about it—she fell extremely short of the person he had thought, and it would be very hard ever to quite trust her again.

But then, she had been honest with him in the end, brutally honest; she had not spared herself; she had not taken the liar's way out and continued to deceive him. And that had been brave. She was brave: immensely so. It was a quality in her that William liked and admired. She wasn't just tough—she was cheerfully so; she didn't whinge about things—she just got on with them. And he missed her . . . horribly. And so he thought, Why not see her again? Without any illusions? The attraction had still been there; what she did for him hadn't changed. Why couldn't he live with the bad, enjoy the good, the sexy, the totally unsuitable, which was—he knew—so much part of the pleasure of her?

He swung from decision to decision, backwards and forwards, as he went about the farm and fed the cows—now in their winter quarters—and mended fences and hedges and drilled for winter wheat and delivered calves and checked on the drives and the birds with the gamekeeper, and changed his mind almost hourly.

What he needed, William thought as he lay most unusually sleepless in his extremely uncomfortable bed, was some kind of a sign that would make up his mind for him. Only . . . what was Abi practically bumping into him, quite equally fancy-free, and clearly pleased to see him, but a sign? Was he really likely to get another one? Almost certainly not.

CHAPTER 43

The one sadness hanging over Mary's wedding day was that Christine refused even to consider sharing her mother's happiness.

"I'm sorry, Mum," she said when Mary asked her. "I can't. It feels wrong, disloyal to Dad. And please don't ask me again, because I can't change my mind. I'm not being difficult; I just feel very . . . uneasy about it."

Gerry was coming, and her son, Douglas, had arrived from Canada with his wife, Maureen, and their two children. Timothy would take her down the aisle, and that would make up—almost— for Christine's absence; they had always had a very special close relationship, she and Timothy. He had always adored her, asking her to all his birthday parties—except the teenage ones, of course— demanded she was outside the school gates after his first day, invited her to all the interminable football matches he played in and the school plays, and, after he had left home, visited her at least once a fortnight demanding the cottage pie she made, he said, so much bet-ter than anyone else.

So there they would all be, and Russell's children had taken her to their hearts, especially his son, Morton; and the girls, Coral and Pearl, were very sweet and kind.

She would be surrounded tomorrow with friends, some old, some new; it would be a wonderful day. But still . . . it hurt that Christine would not come, and more, that Christine knew it hurt, and even so was not persuaded.

They had been to New York, and she had had the most wonderful time; she had met a lot of Russell's friends and attended so many wel-come dinners and cocktail parties she became exhausted and had to go to bed for two days; but she had also been shown the sights, had gone up the Empire State and looked down in awe on the dazzling fairyland that was the city far below, drunk cocktails in the Rainbow Room, done the Circle Line tour, shopped in Saks and Bloomingdale's, and taken a horse-and-carriage ride in Central Park.

But she had gone home at her insistence to her own dear house in Bristol until the wedding; she contemplated its sale with deep misery, but then Russell had had the idea of giving it to Timothy. "It's so tough these days for kids, trying to get a foot on the property ladder, and when they can't get a mortgage for love nor money. Try him out; see what he says."

Timothy had said only one word when she told him, and that four-lettered; he had then gone bright red and said, "Sorry, Gran, sorry, sorry, but that is just so . . . so cool; you are just absolutely the best."

Christine had been a bit funny about that too, said it wasn't good for young people to have things made too easy for them, but Gerry said if anyone had made things a bit easier for him when he'd been young, he might have progressed a bit farther than he had.

Douglas and Maureen and their daughters were staying in the house with her; and Douglas would drive her over to Tadwick Church next day. Russell had moved into Tadwick House, and his three children were staying there; they had said they would go to hotels, but Mary had begged them to use the house. "I hate to think of it not lived in; it will be wonderful to have you there. And besides, it will be nice for Mrs. Salter to have something to do other than wait hand and foot on Russell. So bad for him anyway."

"But, Mary, dear, he's ruined already," Pearl said, and Coral agreed.

"You have to blame Grandma Mackenzie; she thought he was the nearest thing to an angel on this earth."

"Heaven help us all," Mary said, "if we get up there and find it inhabited by people like your father!" And then added hastily that actually of course it would be very nice. You couldn't be too careful with stepchildren: even if they were sixty . . .

. . .

It was a perfect December morning: bright and golden, with frost spangling the hedges and meadows and a sky that was brilliantly clear and blue.

The guests started to arrive at eleven thirty. Russell was deeply touched by how many people, some of them quite elderly, as he remarked to the girls—while clearly and blissfully unaware that this description could be equally applied to him—had accepted and made the really quite long journey to Somerset, England, as they all called it. Mary's friends—also quite large in number; there was no doubt they were good, healthy stock, their generation—followed them in, and the organist began to play, the lovely echoing, rounded sound soaring through the little church. Russell felt a dangerous lump in his throat, and gripped Morton's hand suddenly.

. . .

Alex felt rather proud to be arriving with not one but two extremely pretty women; he had confessed to Emma that he and Linda had become "just friends, nothing more, seen each other for a meal once or twice." Given that he flushed to the roots of his hair as he said it, and failed to meet Emma's eyes, she guessed that the relationship might be just slightly more meaningful than that, but she nodded politely and said how nice that must be.

Linda had suggested she meet them at the hospital; they proceeded in her Mercedes . . . "I'm sorry, Alex, but I'm just not prepared to sit in that bone shaker of yours." The Mercedes was very low-slung and swayed about a lot, and by the time they arrived in Tadwick, Emma, who had obviously been relegated to the back, was feeling extremely sick and had to stand in the lane breathing deeply for five minutes before she trusted herself to go into the church. She was wearing an off-the-shoulder red dress, with a white stole wrapped around her, and high-heeled red shoes, and her long legs were golden and bare. What was it about the young? Alex wondered. What extra, if short-lived gene did they possess that they didn't feel the cold?

Linda was looking staggeringly beautiful in a pale grey silk suit with an ankle-length skirt; she had extraordinarily good ankles, Alex thought, studying them as she walked ahead of him down the aisle, and then as he settled into the pew, found himself thinking rather unsuitably carnal thoughts about the rest of her legs, and tried to concentrate on the organ music instead.

Dear old chap, the bridegroom looked; he had not met him before. He was tall, as far as Alex could make out, and he sat ramrod straight in the pew, occasionally running a hand through his thick white hair and staring fixedly ahead of him; presumably the chap beside him—well into his sixties—was his son. And how wonderful it was, Alex thought, that love could flower so sweetly and so late, that two really very old people could be celebrating their marriage in a spirit of such determination.

And these people coming in now, walking to the front of the church, they must be Mary's family, a grey-haired, rather portly man and a very pretty young girl. And another man, slimmer and fitter-looking, together with a woman in a rather chic yellow coat and brown fur hat, and two girls in trouser suits with very high heels and a lot of makeup.

There was a flurry at the back of the church, and three little boys appeared, all dressed identically in tuxedos; fine-looking little chaps, with dark, curly hair and brilliant blue eyes, flanking a wheelchair in which sat Patrick Connell—also with the dark hair and the blue eyes—dressed in a very smart suit, smiling broadly and pushed by Georgia. Patrick had made such progress, Alex thought; it really was a little less than a miracle: he could sit up properly now, no longer belted tightly into the chair, and his legs in their perfectly pressed trousers were beginning to look larger somehow, and as if they knew how to work and walk, and less at variance with his heavy shoulders and broad chest.

Georgia looked amazing in a brilliant green dress—also bare shouldered—with a green feather arrangement in her wild hair. Linda was sporting similar headwear; they were known as fascinators, she had informed Alex on the way down.

Georgia urged the three little boys into a pew at the back and, after a whispered conversation with Patrick, inserted herself between them, clearly with a view to minimising talking and giggling; Patrick was beside them in the aisle.

. . .

This was a great day, Patrick thought, for all of them, and thought how far he had travelled from that darkest of the dark days all those months ago, and how impossible it would have seemed then that he could have been attending a wedding, dressed up to the nines, his conscience clear and his physical outlook so good . . . He was interrupted in this reverie by a change of pace and tune from the organ and a rustle of excitement from the opening door, and saw that the bride was standing on the porch, on the arm of a handsome young chap positively beaming with pride, and behind them, dressed in the palest, softest pink chiffon dress, his beloved, beautiful Maeve.

. . .

She should be here, Gerry thought, Christine really, really should be here. What demon had possessed her that she had been able to resent her mother's new happiness so deeply; and worse, to be unable to suppress it or at the least conceal it? He was ashamed of her, and he wasn't sure how he was going to cope with those emotions in the days ahead. He—

"Stand up, Gerry," hissed Lorraine, Tim's girlfriend—very nice to have on his arm that day. What did they call girls like her? Oh, yes, arm candy. "They're here."

. . .

Russell was afraid for a moment that he was going to pass out, so strong was the wave of emotion that passed through him then. The sound of the organ, the opening of the door, the knowledge that she was walking towards him down the aisle at last, after a wait of more than sixty years . . . it was an experience of such intensity that the light in the church seemed to fade a little, the sound of the organ to diminish, and all that existed for him was her, walking slowly towards him, then standing beside him, smiling up at him, his Mary, his adored and adorable Sparrow, her eyes as brilliant and blue as they had been then, her mouth as soft and sweetly smiling, and her hands shaking a little as she handed over her bouquet to Maeve.

· · ·

And Mary, looking up at him, saw the young Russell again, whom she had loved so very much, whom she had never forgotten and never failed. She had feared she might cry, make a fool of herself at this moment, as she put it; but she felt steadfast and strong, purely and intensely happy.

· · ·

This was how it should be, Linda thought; this was love she was looking at, true love, not the counterfeit version she had known, and wondered if it was what she felt for the man beside her, who had suddenly and unaccountably gripped her hand.

· · ·

This was how I thought it was, Alex thought, *and do I dare even to think I've found it now?*

· · ·

This is what I thought we had, Emma thought, *and what I've lost, and will I ever find it again?,* and first one large tear and then another fell onto her prayer book, and for a while she saw everything spangled with tears.

· · ·

Mary reached up suddenly and kissed Russell, and the gesture was so sweet, so spontaneous, that a small fragment of applause started from somewhere near the back of the church and spread round it, and Mary

· 391 ·

turned to acknowledge it, smiling, and thought as she did so that she saw the door begin to open; and then turned back to the vicar as he bade them all welcome and prepared to embark on the lovely, familiar words. (While omitting, as they had agreed, those that might appear somewhat ludicrous, about the procreation of children, and carnal lusts and appetites.)

But then something truly wonderful happened: as the vicar began to speak, the door at the back did indeed open—everyone heard it and turned to look—and through it, with no expression on her face whatsoever except one of absolute determination, came Christine, bareheaded, wearing the old mackintosh in which she walked the dogs and some really quite sturdy boots, and Mary, catching sight of her, provided one of the most beautiful moments of the day, for her small face fragmented into joy and she left Russell and walked back up the aisle and put her arms round her daughter, her beloved, brave, difficult daughter, and kissed her, and then led her by the hand to her place in the front pew, next to Gerry. Who, in turn, put his own arm round her and gave her a kiss.

The service proceeded without any further departure from convention; Tim gave her away with his eyes suspiciously bright; Russell beamed throughout, until it was his turn to make his vows, and then as he said, "Thereto I give thee my troth," his strong voice cracked and two great tears rolled down his handsome old face; and as Mary promised to love, cherish, and obey, a giggle rose unbidden in her voice, and it was more than a moment before she could compose herself once more.

And then, having uttered his final solemn exhortation that no man must put them asunder, the vicar pronounced them man and wife and told Russell he might kiss the bride; and Mary was not only kissed but held so tightly and so fervently that it seemed Russell was afraid, even now that she had been pronounced his, of losing her again. The bells began to peal; Mary turned, took Russell's arm, and walked slowly down the aisle, smiling into the dozens of flashing cameras that had most assuredly not been a feature at her first wedding, waving at people, blowing kisses, and hugging the small boys who scrambled over their father and rushed from their pew to greet her.

"I've been to a great many weddings," Maeve confided to Tim, who was walking her down the aisle, "but never in my entire life one more beautiful than this."

❧ CHAPTER 44 ❧

The concert had been Anna's idea. Georgia had been talking to her in the pub one night, trying to explain how bad she still sometimes felt about the crash—"and not just about Patrick, the lorry driver, although there he is, three little kids to keep and no job, really—there are other people who are still really hurting. That man whose wife was killed, with a little boy, he's had to give up his job to look after him, and several other people who have lost their livelihoods, no fault of their own, like one girl who can't walk, and she was a dance teacher, or who've had breakdowns, and I just feel so bad about them—here I am having a great time now, and it's not fair. Is it?"

Anna had agreed it wasn't fair. "But it absolutely wasn't your fault, Georgia; you have to see that."

"I know it wasn't my fault—well, except for deserting Patrick—but that doesn't stop me feeling terrible. I just wish there was something I could do."

"Like what?"

"Well, I don't know. Help. Really help. In a practical way."

"What . . . like raise some money, maybe? Help them at least financially? Don't look at me like that. Quite small things can help a lot. I did a gig for a concert, just a small one, that provides special bikes that physically disabled children can control. It means they can hare about like other kids. But . . . it's only an idea."

"I'm not looking at you like anything. Except in admiration. That . . . well, that could be a really great thing to do. D'you think I could?"

"With a lot of help, yes, I'm sure you could."

Georgia felt as if a light had gone on in her head, shining into the dark, ugly memories and the rotting guilt, slowly but steadily shrinking them away. She could do something—actually do something to help all those people. It wouldn't bring anyone back; it wouldn't restore damaged muscles or bones or nervous systems; but it would be so, so much better than nothing.

She decided to talk to Linda about it.

. . .

Linda was cautiously enthusiastic; she thought it was a great idea . . . "But you really have to do it properly, Georgia. Think long and hard before you get into it, because it could turn into a monster. If you're going to set up a charity, then you have to get it registered, appoint some trustees . . . I know that sounds like a lot of work and rather daunting, but people will be much more willing to help if it sounds official and not like a lot of kids raising a bit of money for fun. And it's got to be done well. The venue alone will be a nightmare to find and fund, and you'll have to scale everything to it. No use getting the Stones to agree to play and then offering them a rehearsal hall in Staines. Sorry, I don't mean to discourage you. I just don't want you getting into something you can't cope with."

Georgia said she was sure she could cope with it, and that she didn't actually envisage getting the Stones; but a few enquiries revealed the extent of the venue problem. Hiring anywhere at all was hugely expensive and would wipe out any profit at a stroke; something radical was clearly required.

Linda said she'd sound a few people out, that she knew quite a lot of musicians, and maybe Georgia might even consider having a couple of dramatic items in the programme. The few people she'd sounded were cautiously interested; Georgia didn't want to ask anyone yet on *Moving Away*—she had enough to cope with there—but it would be worth a try when it was over; Merlin, she was sure, knew a lot of people in the music business.

She could see it was all going to take a long time; it needed intensive long-term planning. But an optimism had gripped her; she felt absolutely certain something would turn up—in fact, she said this so often that Anna had nicknamed her Mrs. Micawber . . .

. . .

The other person she talked to about it was Emma; she and Emma had seriously bonded at Mary's wedding, got quite drunk and danced together. Emma said she thought it was a great idea. She agreed with Linda that it might be better to raise the money specifically for the hospital; she said she didn't think she'd be much use herself, but when Georgia said she was forming a committee and that she was hoping Alex would come on it, she told Georgia to count her in: "Only if you think I could help, of course. I've . . . well, I've got a bit of spare time at the moment, so I could write letters for you, stuff like that, if you like. My mum works for a school, and she's always being asked to go on fund-raising committees. Only small local ones, of course, but the principle's pretty much the same. She might have some ideas."

Georgia said she was beginning to think quite small and local herself: "It's hopeless thinking we can do something big in London; it'll cost squillions, and we'd never get the sort of people we'd need. I mean, the crash was local, and the hospital's local, and people are bound to remember it. And there must be places in Swindon, for instance—it's not that small—or Reading, maybe. Anyway, it's early days. The great thing is to keep trucking, as Dr. Pritchard calls it . . . I'm going to start writing letters."

. . .

She and Emma were both very intrigued by the relationship between Linda and Alex, which had become extremely obvious after Mary's wedding.

"It's a match made in heaven, really," said Georgia. "I mean, Linda's so lonely and needy . . ."

"Is she? She doesn't come across lonely and needy . . ."

"No, but that's her whole problem. Ballsy women, especially good-looking ones, just scare men off. Anyway, then there's Dr. Pritchard, also lonely, you say . . ."

"Well, pretty miserable a lot of the time. His wife is an ace cow. She's literally turfed him out of the house, sold it more or less over his head, as far as I can make out. He's had to move into some cruddy flat in Swindon; it's so not fair. They've got some nice kids, though. Like fourteen, fifteen, that sort of age. How'd Linda be with kids, do you think?"

"Mmm . . . she's been pretty cool to me. We've had a few fights, but we've always worked it out."

"Yes, but you're twenty-two," said Emma. "And she's not having a relationship with your dad. Well, we'll have to hope for the best. I love Alex, I really do; he's such a sweetheart—all bark and really no bite at all. And he does seem much happier these days. I shall be very sad to leave him."

"Which is when?"

"Oh . . . January, February time. Depends what I can get."

"You'd better not go to some hospital in Scotland or something," said Georgia. "Not until after the concert, anyway."

"Right now Scotland looks quite appealing," said Emma with a sigh. "Far away from London as possible, that's what I want."

She didn't tell Georgia why, and Georgia didn't ask. She could see something was hurting Emma a lot, and equally that she didn't want to talk about it. Which usually meant in Georgia's experience that she'd been dumped. Men were such idiots. Who'd dump someone as lovely as Emma?

. . .

The days when Alex mooded around, as Emma put it, and shouted were the days when he was undergoing severe anxieties over his relationship with Linda. She was gorgeous, she was sexy, she seemed really to care about him; on the other hand he had vowed he would not enter another relationship with anyone who didn't totally understand the demands of his career and profession. Linda might understand them, but she was hardly going to give them priority. If it came to a conflict between a first night or a major audition, and a dinner with other doctors and their wives, the dinner would not win. They had already had a couple of run-ins over a South African trip, funded by a pharmaceutical company, which she'd persuaded him to accept. Having promised to be totally accommodating with the spousal programme—"I cannot believe there are things called that"—she had said there was no way she was going to go on a boat trip to Robben Island—where Nelson Mandela had been imprisoned—without him, or go on what she called an obscene trip to one of the townships.

"Patronising, utterly ghastly, I wouldn't even contemplate it."

"I seem to remember your saying that the tourist trade benefited the country."

"I'm sure it does. I just don't think sitting in an air-conditioned car and looking graciously around a series of shantytowns benefits the inhabitants very much. I'm not going to go, Alex, and that's all there is to it."

"Linda, you seem to be embarking on this trip in a rather different spirit from what you'd promised. I really don't think it's viable on this basis, and I don't see how we can go."

"Alex, that's crap."

"It is not crap. I said I didn't like any of it in principle, that I never had, and you talked me round . . ."

"I did not talk you round!"

"Oh, really? I seem to remember a lot of talk about how it wouldn't help anyone, my sulking in Swindon, while someone else went in my place . . ."

"I do dislike the way you play back everything I say to you. All right, then let's not go. Let's not do anything nice. You jut sit in your bed-sit and contemplate your navel."

"I think I'd prefer to do that than see you alienating everyone on the trip. Not just your hosts, but the other wives."

"I'll be delighted to alienate the other wives. If they're the sort of people who enjoy a lot of patronising garbage by way of a meal ticket . . ."

He'd left at that, without another word, too angry for twenty-four hours even to return her dozen or so missed calls. Finally she'd texted him:

VV sorry, totally wrong on this, need bottom smacked. xxx

Alex had replied that he would perform the smacking in person that Saturday; it had all blown over; she had meekly agreed to do everything on the spousal programme—"even the shopping trip"— but it had left him worried. Not just about the trip, but about Linda's whole attitude. He was beginning to be afraid that she wasn't going to be a supportive consort; the whole incident had illustrated that.

And what about the children; how was she going to cope with them? He needed a proper base, a real home, and a decent setup, in order to be able to claim their time and attention to any degree. Not to be haring up to Marylebone at every available opportunity to see a mistress who was hardly likely to welcome him with two inevitably awkward children in tow. A mistress, moreover, who would not in two dozen years consider moving to Swindon . . .

It couldn't work; it was impossible—and the fact that he enjoyed her so much and for so much of the time was depressing in itself.

. . .

Dear Mr. Grainger,

I hope you don't mind my writing to you out of the blue, but a friend suggested that you might be able to help in some way, however small.

I'm hoping you will get this safely and that I've got the right address; I looked up Grainger in the directory and your farm was definitely in the right place: if you see what I mean!

My name is Georgia Linley, and I'm the girl you met wandering round your property on the day of the M4 crash last August. You were very kind to me, and I hope I wasn't rude!

I know you were incredibly helpful to everybody that day—allowed the air ambulance to land on your field, and brought water for people to drink, and did all sorts of other kind things—so I'm hoping you'll feel sufficiently interested to read on!

I am trying to organise a fund-raising concert in aid of the crash victims and their families, many of whom are still in considerable difficulties. I have the support of several people at St. Marks Hospital in Swindon, where the injured were all taken; I could let you have names there, if you're wanting to check my credentials.

Patrick Connell and his family have all become good friends of mine. He was the lorry driver who was at the forefront of the crash, and who had given me a lift that day. He was very badly injured, and can't work at the moment; he's just an example of one of the many deserving causes.

We are setting up a charity, in order to make sure that everything is done properly and in a businesslike way. If you log onto crashconcert.linley.com you can check that as well.

Several musicians have already expressed an interest—nobody very grand yet, I'm afraid—but until we have a venue, we can't get a great deal further, and that is proving the biggest obstacle so far.

I wondered if you would be willing to contribute anything, however small, to our setting-up fund; and in due course, obviously, to bring as many people to the concert as possible.

We're also looking for a sponsor: any suggestions in that area would be hugely helpful.

Yours sincerely,
Georgia Linley (Ms.)

William sat staring at the letter, concerned not so much with helping Ms. Linley, who sounded rather engaging, and whom he remembered as being extremely pretty, or even with the unfortunate crash victims, who were undoubtedly a very good cause, but wondering if this was a second enormous nudge on the part of the Almighty in the direction of his reestablishing a relationship with Abi. If so, then he should surely respond—before the Almighty gave up on him altogether.

. . .

Abi had been at work when he rang.

"Hello, Abi. You all right?"

"Yes. Yes, I'm fine, thanks. You?"

"Absolutely fine. Abi, I've had an idea. Well, I've had a letter, actually."

"Well . . . which? Or is it a letter with an idea?"

"Um . . . bit of both."

"Hmm. Hard to guess this one, William. Film, book, play . . ."

"What?"

"Charades. Didn't you ever play charades?"

"Few times. Yes, I see what you mean. Well . . . what's the sign for concert?"

"There isn't one. William, do spit it out. Please."

William spat it out.

. . .

Three days later, Georgia arrived in the location house, breathless and flushed. "Is Merlin here? Or Anna?"

"Anna's in Makeup," said Mo. "Don't know where Merlin is."

Georgia hared up the stairs to the bedroom that doubled as Makeup.

"Anna, Anna, listen to this; it's amazing, totally amazing. I think we've got our venue!"

CHAPTER 45

The letters arrived after Christmas. Their presence would be required as witnesses at an inquest on February 19 into the deaths of Sarah Tomkins, Jennifer Marks, and Edward Barnes which occurred on August 22, on the M4 motorway. Details of the time and place of the inquest were also given; and the letter was signed by the coroner's officer.

"Well, thank God it didn't come before Christmas," said Maeve. "It would have cast a bit of a blight. Not that you've got anything to worry about. But still . . . good to have it over. A line drawn."

Patrick nodded; he actually felt he had quite a lot to worry about, however much he'd been reassured that the accident had in no way been his fault. The fact remained that his lorry had gone sprawling across the motorway, bursting through the crash barrier, and the result had been three deaths and dozens of injuries, some of them major. Every time he thought about the inquest, he felt the old, panicky fear . . .

· · ·

Abi found the thought of the inquest pretty scary also; she had, after all, lied to the police, albeit about nothing to do with the crash, and she still had nightmares about them charging her in connection with drug offences. She had actually taken legal advice on this; the solicitor had told her that since she had not been in possession of any drugs, either at the time the police talked to her or later, they were extremely unlikely to press charges.

Nevertheless she was a major witness; she would have to stand in the dock or whatever they had at inquests and swear to tell the truth, the whole truth, and nothing but the bloody truth, and it could well transpire that she had lied the first time around, and in front of all those people. It was a complete nightmare.

But at least Christmas was over. Abi hated Christmas usually; she had a few misfit friends, equally at odds with their families, and they would spend the day together, drinking mostly, although they'd cobble a meal together—Christmas odds and sods from M&S and Tesco—and pull some crackers, and even occasionally play charades before the evening really disintegrated, but she was always hugely relieved when it, and its insistence that everyone was part of one great big, happy family, was over.

The best thing that had happened all Christmas was a text from William that she'd got on Christmas night: *Happy Xmas, hope it's a good one, mine isn't. William x.* She struggled not to read too much into it, not to presume his wasn't good because he wasn't with her, and that the kiss was simply what anyone would put at the end of a text on Christmas Day; but the fact remained that he'd been thinking of her enough to send it. She texted back, *Happy one to u2, not bad, thanx, gd 2 hear from you. Abi,* and after that a kiss also. She'd put *gt* at first instead of *gd,* but that looked a bit keen.

And now, astonishingly, she was seeing quite a bit of him, albeit on a completely platonic basis . . .

She was extremely excited about Georgia's concert. It had been her idea that it should be held at the farm, festival-style. She had actually suggested something similar to William once before, when he had been talking about diversifications and moneymaking schemes; and he had been surprisingly receptive to the idea then. It really hadn't been too difficult—amazingly easy, in fact—to repersuade him.

It was very scary—on a professional basis—and she wasn't even sure they would be able to pull it off; but if they did . . . she could launch her party-planning career on the back of it. And see lots of William in the bargain.

The first meeting about the concert had been . . . well, it had been extraordinary. An absolutely violent tangle of emotions. She'd expected the tangle, of course, had expected it to be awkward, had expected it to be painful seeing William; in fact, she'd been so scared the few days before she'd almost decided to pull out of the whole

thing, to put Georgia—and him—in touch with a fri
party planner. But she didn't.

They'd agreed to meet in a pub in Bristol on a Satu
Abi had arrived far too early and had spent at least fift
the loo to avoid sitting waiting for them and looking like a complete
loser. When she came out William was sitting at a table with a very
pretty black girl, which rattled her considerably at first, until she
realised she must be Georgia. And she stood there, just staring at him,
drinking him in; and she felt a wave of emotion so violent, so charged
with regret and love and intense physical memory, it quite literally
took her breath away.

She must just stay really cool, she thought, refuse to see it as anything but a business arrangement, as William being kind and good
and wanting to help both her and Georgia in a venture that would
clearly seem relevant to him as well as to them.

And then, as she stood there, still watching, he saw her; and he
stood up, with those bloody old-fashioned manners of his, pulled out
a chair, and beckoned to her to join them.

"Hi," she said, walking over, hearing her own voice, calm and
steady, not weak and breathless as she was afraid it might be, smiling
at him, kissing him briefly, coolly on the cheek—how could she do
that when she wanted to kiss him endlessly, desperately?—and then
turned swiftly to Georgia.

"You must be Georgia. Hi. I'm Abi."

"Hi, Abi. It's so good of you to come. William—Mr. Grainger—
has been telling me all about you. How you've done this sort of thing
before, and how you can tell me how to go about it . . ."

"Well . . . I hope so. It's a huge project, Georgia; I hope you realise
just how huge."

"I probably don't. But I'm ready for anything. I'm so, so determined to do it."

Georgia smiled; she was sweet, pretty, rather earnest. It would be
fun working with her. "Good," was all Abi said.

Gradually, the emotional situation eased as they discussed the m of the thing—"I did once suggest a rock festival to William, didn't I? But I think maybe you've got more of a single concert in mind"—possible lead times, possible dates, the vast amount of time and planning it would absorb, how, with the best will in the world, they would need many more people on board—"Don't look so frightened; it's for charity—we can get mostly volunteers. It's a wonderful project, Georgia; I'm really excited about it."

Not about working with William, not about having endless access to William; that was out of the equation. Entirely.

Georgia said they could at least look at a festival.

"Tell us more what it might entail . . ."

Abi told them more: much more. Probably too much more, she thought afterwards. When she started outlining the need for security guards, parking facilities, police involvement, and the infrastructure required, William became visibly worried.

"A road! Abi, I can't start building roads."

"Well, you might have to. The contractors—"

"What contractors?" said Georgia.

"The ones building the stage, setting up the sound systems, all that sort of thing. You've got to think big, or it won't work. Anyway, the contractors and the punters, come to that, need to know they're not going to get stuck in the mud. You do realise it will rain, don't you?"

"No, why?" said William.

"It just always does. Part of the package."

"Oh," said William.

Georgia looked at him and then said rather nervously that maybe they should just stick to the idea of a concert. "An open-air one, in the evening, next summer—it could be lovely."

Abi said a concert would be all right, but it would be hard to make nearly so much of it. "I think a festival would be much more exciting. You'd get far more publicity, for a start, and a much bigger crowd, something where families could come, bring their kids, camp just for one night, have a few bands playing, dance. People really love that sort of thing; it's like a miniholiday, and it's so cool at the moment. That way you'd probably end up with a couple of thousand people . . . and make a fair bit of money. Even quite big bands bring their fee down if they know it's for charity. Anyway, whatever the size of the thing, you have to have a stage and audio equipment, and loos, of course. William, are you really up for all this? And are your parents all right about it?"

William said rather airily that they'd been persuaded to do it: he didn't add that he'd been pretty evasive about the implications, had sold it to them as a charity concert, which sounded rather charming; he knew they'd be totally opposed to the idea of a festival, with all its unfortunate implications of deafening noise, drugs, and general squalor . . .

"No, they're fine about it," he said now.

"Well, that's great," Abi said. "Let's just hope they stay on that side, because they won't be able to switch very easily. Now, you need a sponsor. To make it financially viable. Put up something like a couple of grand, say, in return for publicity. You might start thinking who to approach."

"What, like one of the TV companies or something?"

"Well, more of a commercial concern, some local manufacturing company or other. I'll think too. Anyway . . . what do you think? Now's the time to say no."

Georgia emitted a sort of squeak. Abi looked at her. Her eyes were shining and her hands were clasped together, making a sort of fist. Abi was to get to know that gesture well in the months to come.

"I think it sounds wonderful," she said. "We've absolutely got to do it. If . . . well, that is if William . . . Mr. Grainger's really up for it. It's . . . it's obviously a very big undertaking."

"Please call me William," said William. "Mr. Grainger makes me feel like I'm my dad."

. . .

He looked at the pair of them, two sassy, sexy girls, girls he would never have known a year ago, and thought of spending a lot of time with them over the next six months or so. It made him feel dizzy.

"I'm up for it," he said. "Yeah, course."

. . .

It was just as well, Georgia thought, that she had the concert to distract her. She viewed the inquest with absolute terror. At the thought of having to stand up in a courtroom, in front of a crowd of people, several of whom were still grieving, and describe under oath how she had abandoned Patrick Connell in his cab and disappeared, failing to provide the evidence that only she could and that had been so crucial to him, she felt violently sick.

She knew there was no way out of it—it had to be got through—but it was still there, driving her back into her guilt and remorse.

Moving Away was in the final stages of filming, and the first episode was to be screened in the spring.

It was awful to think she wouldn't be seeing Merlin more or less every day; it had been such an incredibly exciting element in the whole thing, just getting ready in the morning, wondering what to wear, whether he'd be there, what he'd say to her. She was still slightly baffled as to what his feelings about her were: nonexistent, she thought on her bad days, but then she would think, on the good ones . . . Why ask her to go for a drink so often after they'd finished for the day; why spend so much time with her; why make sure she was all right in Jazz's house?

He'd even—once or twice—asked her to the cinema, to see some incredibly intellectual foreign films at what he called his local, the Hampstead Everyman, which she hadn't understood at all, let alone enjoyed—although she'd pretended to, of course—and one wonderful Saturday he'd called her and said he was going to do some Christmas shopping in the Portobello, and if she was around, would she like to join him? She'd loved that, wandering along the stalls, and when they'd finished he asked her if she'd like to have lunch at Camden

Lock—"I can't believe you haven't been there yet, all this time in London"—and she'd said, trying to sound totally cool, that she'd like that, and had sat in one of the bars alongside the canal, convinced this was really it, that he was going to say he really liked her. But he didn't; he said he had to get back quite soon after lunch: "The parents are having a party tonight; I have to go back and help."

"Will it . . . will it be a big party?" she said, trying to sound casual, half wondering if he might be going to ask her.

"About a hundred. Anyone else would have proper help, but Mummy won't—against her principles, like not having a cleaner, so she's run herself ragged cooking for weeks, and Pa just hides in his study and pretends he hasn't noticed."

"And lots of famous people there?" she said.

And, "Yeah, lot of Beeb types, Humphreys, Paxman, Benn, I imagine, the Millibands, possibly Charlie Falconer, but not the Blairs."

"God," she said, "I call that pretty impressive."

"Not really. You're so sweet, Georgia," he added, smiling at her, "so totally unspoilt still. Stay like it, for goodness' sake. Don't get spoilt. I must dash; can you find your own way back?"

"Yes, of course. I want to look in some of those shops anyway," she said quickly.

And that was how their relationship—or rather their non-relationship—proceeded: two steps forward, two steps back. Exasperating, frustrating, baffling.

Most of the time she managed to think it was just luvvie stuff, no more than that, along with the hugs and the brotherly kisses; but she still found grounds for thinking it was more.

She had never talked about him to anyone involved in the production—deliberately. There was no way she was going to risk being laughed at for having an unrequited crush on him. And in any case she wasn't on those sorts of terms with any of them, except for Anna.

She tried to find out a bit about him from Linda, who always knew all the gossip about everybody, but she just said vaguely that she really didn't know much about him except that he was incredibly talented and would soon be a first assistant, probably in the next production he worked on. "You don't fancy him, darling, do you?"

"God, no," said Georgia.

"Good. Because the words *little* and *shit* do come rather to mind."

Georgia ignored this; it was such a typical Linda comment.

And then the mystery was solved—painfully.

The wrap party was taking place just a week before Christmas; Georgia had bought a sequinned dress that was virtually nonexistent, so short and low-cut it was, and some incredibly long, sequinned fake eyelashes to go with it.

The party was at Bryn's house in Putney, a wonderful glass-fronted place on the river. He'd been incredibly generous, provided champagne by the crateful, and Mrs. Bryn, who was a glamorous actress called Jan Lloyd, provided fantastic food. Particularly generous, as she then went out for the evening: "She says no one should be at the wrap parties of other people's productions," Bryn said, laughing, when he made his little speech, and actually, as Anna said to Georgia, it really wasn't very pleasant; you felt like a complete outsider, understood none of the in-jokes, and were deeply wary of discovering any illicit relationships.

Georgia could feel herself going over the top, flirting with everyone, including Bryn—and Merlin, of course—making people dance with her, but it was the last time she'd see most of them, and she was enjoying herself so much.

Merlin was a fantastic dancer, and he was looking absolutely amazing, all in black—black skinny jeans, black T-shirt, black leather jacket. She thought he must be rather hot in the jacket, and suggested he take it off more than once, but he said he liked it, and he liked being hot. She hoped he meant what she thought by that.

And then suddenly the front doorbell went off, and Georgia, who was in the hall, opened it. A girl stood there, a really beautiful girl, tall, with long blond hair and astonishingly blue eyes; she was wearing a short black dress and black knee boots with very high heels. She smiled at Georgia just slightly dismissively and looked her up and down and said, "Hi. Is Merlin here?"

Georgia said he was and that she'd go and find him—the girl was the sort who inspired such behaviour—and had just turned to go into the party when Bryn appeared and said, "Ticky! Darling! What a surprise. Merlin didn't warn us."

The girl kissed Bryn and said, "He didn't know I was flying in today. I promise, Bryn, darling, I haven't come to crash your wrap party. I just thought I might steal him away in a little while."

"You can crash anything of mine, sweetie. Let me go and find the boy."

. . .

Merlin, it seemed, and Ticky—whoever was called Ticky, and what was it short for? Georgia wondered—were an item. Had been since drama school. Only Ticky, who had a very rich daddy, was now attending the New York University film school. And came back to London only for the vacations.

Merlin clearly adored her; so did most of the cast. Davina threw her arms round her and told her she looked divine. Which she did, Georgia thought miserably; she was the sort of girl who was on the cover of *Tatler*, or even *Vogue*. Understated, superconfident, totally classy, she had become, briefly, the centre of the party.

And when she and Merlin left, after half an hour, looking like a Prada ad, Georgia sat down next to Anna and said, trying to sound cool, "What happened to not being at other people's wrap parties?"

"I guess if you look like that, you can be anywhere you damn well like," Anna said, and then, looking rather hard at Georgia: "Listen, sweetie, I've had enough. Want to come home with me? Lila's on her own and she'd love to see you. And catch up on the concert. If there's anything to catch up on . . ."

"That'd be great," said Georgia. "Thank you."

All she felt now was a consuming terror that the whole production had been laughing at her behind her back.

Anna, who had clearly put two and two together, and confronted the issue in the cab home, told her they hadn't.

"I swear to you, nobody ever mentioned it. Listen, even I never guessed. You played it really cool, Georgia. Well done. And good riddance, I'd say. Leading you on like that, never mentioning her. Ticky! What a name."

"No, no, not really," said poor Georgia, the tears beginning to flow now, "and he didn't lead me on; he was just . . . really kind. Oh, I'm sorry, Anna, I think I might change my mind, go home after all."

"All right," said Anna, "of course I understand. But please, please, sweetie, believe me. I never heard a whisper about you and Merlin. Honestly."

It was comfort of a sort.

. . .

Linda had an incredible Christmas. She always enjoyed it; she loved the theatricality of it, spent many hours decorating her flat, went to endless parties, bought a mountain of presents for everyone, and went for the day to the home of Francis and his partner, who was an incredible cook. None of that was altered this year; except that Alex, who had spent the day with the children and his now ex-wife, came up for the evening and, as Linda put it, they fucked their way into Boxing Day.

Linda didn't know quite what she felt about her relationship with Alex. In many ways it was extremely difficult; he was moody and bad tempered and introspective to an absurd degree, and what felt like at least half their dates ended in rows, the less serious resolved in bed, the more serious unresolved for days. Several times, after he had slammed out, she decided that she must finish things, that they just made each other unhappy, and would call him to tell him so and more than once he had agreed. But then, somehow, they would resolve things; one or the other of them would make some approach, without actually apologising, and they would agree to meet and then, having met, found themselves almost against their respective wills quite unable to continue with the hostilities. And then they would start again, amusing, charming, pleasing each other, agreeing that they made each other happier than anyone else had ever done . . . until the next time.

It seemed to Linda quite impossible that it could be a long-term relationship; it was just too uncomfortable and disturbing. On the other hand, she looked into a future without Alex, without the intense colour and interest and drama, and that seemed impossible to contemplate too.

She was perfectly aware what caused the rows: they were both arrogant, opinionated, and for too long had been able to hold on to their opinions and behaviour and not consider anyone else, Linda because she lived alone, with all the self-indulgence that offered, and Alex because his status at the hospital meant that very few people ever confronted him there either.

On her up days—and Linda was an extremely up person—she would think it was fine, that the drama and passion and difficulty of it all were actually part of the pleasure; but when she was down, she could see that it was not at all what she needed, not the warm reassurance and companionship she had been dreaming of. Alex was about as reassuring as a roll of thunder. He also brought with him the burden of teenage children—whom he had not even allowed her to meet, and that in itself had to be significant, and indeed she found it fairly hurtful—and a demanding career entirely out of her orbit.

The only thing she could do—or try to do, and it went against her nature—was enjoy the relationship for as long as she could, and to continue to look for someone more enduringly suitable. The trouble was that Alex, for all his appalling drawbacks, had set the bar rather high . . .

. . .

Laura had hated every moment of Christmas. She had always loved it so much, looked forward to it for months, the planning the shopping, the decorating, the cooking, creating the perfect performance for everyone, had always thought how lucky she was to be able to do it all on such an extravagant scale; and now she discovered that actually it wasn't the present giving, or the family feasts, or the delight of doing the tree with the children, or even the carol concerts and the children's party that she and Jonathan had always given; it was the sense of being at the heart of her perfect, happy family. Her family this Christmas was not only not perfect, it was not even happy; and she was not at the heart of it. At the heart of it this year was a bitter unhappiness: two little girls crying most nights for their daddy and begging her to make sure he came for Christmas, a little boy who said he hated his father, and that he would walk out if he came for Christmas, and a house that was a cold showcase for the lights and the tinsel and the tree and the presents underneath it. She had lavished enormous sums of money on PlayStations and Nintendo games for Charlie, and dolls and clothes for the girls, and iPods for all of them; they had had the tallest tree and the biggest crackers ever, the most perfect Christmas dinner, and even though the girls had expressed delight and told her they loved their presents and loved her, and had sung Christmas carols determinedly as they helped to lay and decorate the dinner table, and even Charlie had tried to be cheerful and said how cool his PlayStation was, and submitted to his grandfather's endless terrible jokes with a good grace, and they had all managed to play a round of charades and a game of Trivial Pursuit after dinner, there had been an emptiness, a greyness over everything, and when they hugged and kissed her good night and settled into bed with their new books, their iPods clamped to their heads, she knew that above anything else, they were relieved it was over and they could stop trying to seem happy.

The compromise reached over Jonathan's visit had been that he would come on Christmas morning and give them presents (during which Charlie glowered from a corner), and then go away, "because I've got to deliver some babies," and then have them on Boxing Day in his flat, and take them to the pantomime at Richmond in the evening. But Charlie had refused to go at the last minute, which had upset the girls, and there had been the hideous empty seat beside them in the theatre, which they could almost hear shouting, "Charlie should be here," and they had cried all the way home after Laura collected them.

And, left alone in his flat without them, contemplating the ugly, empty day that had passed, Jonathan had cried too.

. . .

Barney was literally having nightmares about the inquest. Every time he thought about being asked about the tyres and how he would have to say that Toby hadn't let him check them, he thought he would throw up. The fact that there had been a nail in one of them, initially an immense relief, now seemed of less importance. He should have insisted on doing all he could to ensure the car's safety; that was the whole point.

And he would think about Emma and how happily and quickly they had tumbled into love; and then how much he missed her still. And he would even, in spite of everything, realise how much he missed Toby too, missed having him there to have a laugh with, to send stupid e-mails to, to get drunk with . . . Toby would be back at work after Christmas; he was bound to run into him in bars and so on, and Amanda was bound to ask why they weren't seeing each other. She knew about Tamara, of course, and the broken engagement, and she'd been very upset, her great blue eyes filled with tears. "But I suppose it's for the best; Tamara said they'd just fallen out of love—how awful is that?"

How awful indeed . . .

. . .

Emma spent much of Christmas trying not to wonder what Barney was doing, which large country house he and Amanda would be staying in, and whether there would be discussion with their families—

Christmas being the sort of time such conversations did take place—about their wedding plans.

It was a relief to get back to work.

. . .

Mary and Russell had a perfect Christmas. Tadwick House was absurdly overdecorated, with fairy lights in every room, round every fireplace, and entwined round every stair rail, and strung along every hedge outside as well. A vast Christmas tree stood in the hall, a second in the drawing room, complete with a mountainous pile of presents, mistletoe hung in every doorway, huge log fires burned in every grate, and the house was filled with the irresistible mingling of wood smoke and baking. And it was wonderfully, noisily full.

Not only were Christine and Gerry, Douglas and Maureen and their children, Timothy and the lovely Lorraine there for Christmas Day, together with Lorraine's parents, but to Mary's absolute surprise and delight, Coral and Pearl and their respective spouses asked if they might join them as well, an English Christmas having long been a dream of theirs.

Russell was delighted as well. Christine's initial rejection of him had hurt him badly, and he felt rather proud that his own daughters were more generous-hearted than Mary's. He still found Christine rather hard to embrace—both physically and emotionally. She had failed to say anything to him by way of an apology, and every time he looked at her rather self-satisfied, plump face he wondered at her dissimilarity from her mother.

The weather was most obligingly Christmassy, crisp and sunny; the entire party went to morning service on Christmas Day, came back for a vast lunch (with a break for the Queen's speech), and then went for a short walk before having presents in the drawing room. After that everyone withdrew for a short rest and then reassembled for games and to sing carols round the piano. The piano had been Russell's Christmas present to Mary, who had always longed for one ever since learning to play on her own grandmother's when she was a small girl, and had never been allowed one since. Rusty at first, by sherry time she was sufficiently adept to play "Jingle Bells" and "Away in a Manger." Russell was a superb pianist and took over for the evening performance, finishing with a flamboyant, concert-style rendition of *Rhapsody in Blue* that reduced Lorraine's mother and both Coral and Pearl to tears.

The party broke up at about ten, apart from Timothy and Lorraine and the Canadian cousins, who were watching an old Bond movie; Christine walked to the bottom of the stairs, then turned and went back to Russell and kissed him.

"It's been wonderful," she said. "Thank you very much for having us here today . . . and I'm very sorry about my . . . about . . . well, I can't tell you how pleased I am that you're here. You've made my mother happier than I can ever remember. Since Dad died, that is, of course."

At which Russell kissed her back and said, "Of course," and added that he was proud to have succeeded someone who had clearly been so remarkable a gentleman as Donald.

Later, as they sat in bed, Russell leaned over and kissed Mary and said, "I meant it about Donald. I'm going to have a tough job living up to him."

Mary kissed him back and told him he wasn't doing too badly so far.

CHAPTER 46

She supposed she should have realised, really: if they squabbled as much as they did when they were living in different houses—and different cities, come to that—what hope for them when they were sharing the same room with no escape in any form, even into work?

Actually, and perversely, she had enjoyed the first part of the trip, the conference in Cape Town, a great deal more than she had expected. She had thought it would be tedious in the extreme, and it had actually turned out to be rather fun. Not least because she was quickly established as something of a star, certainly among the men, not just because of what she looked like and how she dressed, but because of what she did: a glossy, entertaining creature from another world altogether.

She had made two friends in particular, one a rather dashing neurosurgeon, who had actually first trained as a barrister; he told her life was too short to spend it in one discipline, as he put it, and asked her, his blue eyes dancing with appreciation at her very low-cut black velvet top, what she was going to do when she grew up. Linda told him she was going to be a lap dancer, and he laughed so much and so loudly that the entire dining room turned round to look.

The other friend was a part-time primary-school teacher called Martin, rather plain but very funny, accompanying his wife; he said he was quite used to coming on the spousal programmes.

"I don't mind a bit, actually. I enjoy it all except the shopping. And the other wives are very nice to me. There's usually more than one of us these days, but I can handle there being just me."

He said he had always looked after the children, ever since his wife, an orthopaedic surgeon, had got her first consultancy. "I mean, why not? She earns squillions more than I ever could. She gets a bit tetchy if dinner isn't ready when she gets home, but I can handle that."

Linda laughed. Maybe that was what she needed—a house husband. It would be great to get home every night to find dinner cooked and the fridge stocked. Not to mention all her dry cleaning and laundry sorted, and the cleaning women organised. Wonderful . . .

But then, house husbands just weren't very sexy.

On the second day the spousal programme took them up Table Mountain via the cable car. Linda walked round the top with Martin; they admired the views, the almost literally intoxicating air, and agreed that they might both duck out of the visit to the township the following day.

"But Alex tells me they don't like that," she said.

"Oh, they don't mind once or twice. I usually say I've got my period."

Linda giggled.

"Your husband come on these things a lot?"

"My partner. We're not married. Well, if you can keep a secret, he's just my boyfriend. I dared him to bring me on this and he did."

"I won't tell a soul. Why should you need to dare him? Any normal red-blooded man would be dying to take you anywhere. Or is his blood a bit pink?"

"No, of course not," said Linda, laughing. "And . . . it's a bit of an in-joke, the dares. Anyway, he doesn't approve of these trips. Says they're thinly disguised bribes."

"Quite right. Fortunately my wife doesn't have such principles."

And all might have been well, had he not brought his wife—a pretty girl with freckles and a Scottish accent, called Fiona—to meet Alex and Linda at predinner drinks and told Alex what Linda had said about the bribery, and how much he agreed with him.

"Frightful racket. Still, who are we to complain?" Martin asked.

"Well, you certainly don't," said Fiona. "I have to work very hard for it. Anyway, it's not exactly true."

"Of course it's not," said Alex. He glared at Linda.

"I call the spousal programme pretty hard work," said Martin. "Linda and I are ducking out tomorrow, aren't we?"

"Yes. Doing a heavy day at the spa," said Linda, and then rather hurriedly, "And how was today's conference session?"

"Very good," said Fiona, "some really interesting ideas, didn't you think, Alex?"

"Yes, not bad."

"Well, if it isn't the lap dancer. Not working tonight?"

It was the neurosurgeon. Linda reached up to kiss him.

"Hi. Not yet. I don't usually start until after dinner."

"I'll look forward to it. Come and rescue my wife, will you? I've told her about you; she's longing to meet you, and she's stuck with some gnome from R and D. Can you spare her, Alex, old chap?"

"Yes, of course," said Alex. He smiled at the neurosurgeon. Linda knew that smile. It came with great difficulty. She winked at him, said she'd soon be back, and followed the neurosurgeon across the room.

Mrs. NS was rather fun: a doctor herself, a GP from Ireland. She was extremely grateful for the rescue—"I really thought I'd pass out with boredom in a minute"—and asked Linda who her husband was.

"Ah, yes," she said, squinting across the room, "very sexy, I thought. Touch of the Heathcliffs."

"That's exactly what I thought the first time I saw him," said Linda. "And the resemblance doesn't end there. Very dark and brooding, he can be. Not that full of sunshine right this minute, actually. I think he's cross because I'm ducking out of the programme tomorrow."

"I might join you in that. Hate the idea of it. What are you doing instead?"

"Beautifying myself in the spa."

"Sounds good. Well, see you there, maybe. We've got to go in to dinner."

Alex scowled at Linda as she sat down beside him.

"Linda, how dare you go round telling people I regard these things as bribery. It's outrageous."

"But you do. You said so."

"That was a private remark. Passing it on here is rather like telling your hostess you don't like her cooking. I can't believe you can be so socially inept. Not to mention rude."

"Sorry," she said, slightly alarmed at his anger. "I really am. You know, I'm truly enjoying it all; it's a bit like being back at school."

"Well, try not to behave as if you actually were."

"Oh, do stop scowling at me, Alex; I've said I'm sorry. And you should be glad I'm enjoying myself."

"I'm afraid not. Or rather, not the way you've chosen."

"Oh, God," she said, putting down her fork, "you really are a miserable bastard, aren't you? First sign of a bit of a laugh, and you're down on everyone like a load of shit. I'm glad I don't work at that hospital of yours."

"Linda, you know perfectly well what I mean. It's very discourteous, setting yourself up in some rebel group like this. You wanted to come and—"

"Oh, fuck off!" she said, and turned her attention to the man the other side of her.

"Shall we go to the bar?" she said, finally turning back to Alex.

"I'd rather not. I'm tired. I'm going upstairs. You can join me if you like."

"I've had more promising invitations," she said. "I'll see you later."

She had one drink with Martin and his wife, and then said good night to everyone and went up to their room. Alex was in bed, reading.

"Good book?"

"Very."

She pulled off her clothes, slid into bed beside him.

"Let me distract you from it."

He turned away slightly; she snatched the book from him.

"Oh, Alex. You're so sexy when you're cross."

Against all the odds he laughed. "I must be sexy a lot of the time, in that case."

"You are. And I'm not the only one who thinks so. Mrs. Neurosurgeon was saying how sexy you were."

"Oh, Linda," he said, switching the light off, taking her in his arms. "I'm sorry. You're a very generous woman."

"I am?"

"Yes. Sam would never have told me some other woman thought I was attractive. Are we friends again?"

"I never wasn't," she said.

She managed to behave after that more as Alex would have wished: went on the obligatory shopping trip—not exactly a hardship in the delicious bounty of Cape Town stores—and went on the other major outing, down the winding coast road to Chapman's Peak, an incredibly beautiful promontory carved out of the cliffs, and then on to Cape Point.

They were heading north after that, to do a few days' safari: travelling on the Blue Train for the first leg to Pretoria, where they were picking up a small private plane to Kruger National Park.

The Blue Train was her idea, and her contribution to the trip.

"If you think I'm going on an ordinary old plane for two hours when we can do the same thing in total luxury in twenty-four, then you've brought the wrong woman."

The Blue Train was sheer indulgence, an excessive, elaborate treat that made her feel, she said, like Lauren Bacall in *Murder on the Orient Express*. She and Alex had their own private suite: a drawing room that converted into a bedroom, complete with immense double bed, and an absurdly elaborate bathroom in which you could take a deep, hot bath and enjoy the landscape at the same time, a peculiarly heady, sexy pleasure. They also had their own butler; all the suites did. Alex didn't approve, was hating most of it: Linda didn't care.

They had the first squabble before lunch, as she tidied up the suite for the third time.

"Linda, do, for God's sake, stop that; I can't stand it."

"Well, I can't stand the mess!"

"Just sit down and watch the scenery!"

She sat there, watching the incredible mountain ranges go past, sipping a glass of very nice Sancerre, and felt better tempered; by the time lunch was served she was feeling very sleek and told Alex so.

"I know what that means," he said, grinning at her.

"You do?"

"Yes. Some considerable activity a little later."

"You're being very presumptuous."

"Sorry. Am I wrong?"

"No, Alex," she said, closing her eyes briefly and smiling at the intense sensation that quite literally swept through her, leaving her almost dizzy, "no, you're not wrong."

"Thank Christ for that. I was beginning to think I'd never say the right thing again."

"I'm not terribly interested in what you say," she said, reaching under the table, gently massaging his thigh, "not just now. More what you do."

"Oh, OK. Linda, do stop that. I can't enjoy my food while I'm having an erection."

"Try," she said. "It's my challenge for the afternoon."

. . .

Much, much later she sat in the bath with yet another glass of champagne; he sat on the edge and smiled down at her.

"That was very lovely."

"Yes, it was. Oh, look, Alex, there's some wildebeest. See, there? God, how amazing to sit in a bath drinking champagne and watching wildebeest. I told you it would be wonderful."

"You were right," he said, reaching out, tracing the outline of one of her nipples with his thumb. "It is very wonderful. All of it."

"Please, please don't do that," she said, reaching down for his hand, kissing it, then replacing it. "You know I can't bear it."

"I thought you liked it."

"I love it. But it makes me feel I'll have to . . . Oh, God, Alex, I'll have to . . . We'll have to . . ."

"Have to what?"

"You know." She stood up, her red hair slicked back. He stood up too, lifted her out, bent his head, and kissed her; very slowly she eased off his bathrobe, and then reached out to pull down the bathroom blind.

"Who do you think's going to see us?" he said, laughing. "The wildebeest?"

. . .

It was their first night at the lodge that the trouble really began. Set unfenced in the middle of the park, their hotel consisted of a main building and then a series of bungalows. Beautifully furnished, colonial style, with its own Jacuzzi in its own small garden, and a huge deck lit only by candles and oil lamps, it was, as Linda happily said, like something out of one of the really posh travel magazines.

Dinner was outside, under the stars, tables set in a horseshoe round a vast fire; afterwards they were escorted back to their room by a guide, complete with rifle.

"Never do this walk alone at night," he said. "It's very dangerous. Remember we're not fenced. The animals can get in and they're not pets. They're wild and they kill. And there are snakes, really nasty pieces of work. Breakfast's at six," he added cheerfully. "I'll knock on the door at five thirty for morning safari."

"Oh, wow," said Linda, wandering into the candlelit room, "this is my idea of true heaven. Such a wonderful idea, Alex. Thank you so, so much. I might not get up at five thirty, though. Give that bit a miss."

"Linda, you have to. It's the reason we're here, to go on safari, see the animals."

"Yeah, OK, but there's another in the afternoon. I can see them then."

"You're expected to go on both each day. They're all different."

"Alex, I don't want to. Not tomorrow. I'm tired."

"Well, I think that's a little pathetic," he said.

"Oh, don't be so stuffy. This is a holiday, not an army workout."

"Yes, and a very expensive holiday. I was expecting you'd participate rather more fully. I'm disappointed."

"Alex, you are joking, aren't you? No, you're not. Expensive indeed! Is that supposed to make me change my mind?"

"I'd have thought it was a factor."

"Well, I'm sorry if I'm a disappointment to you, but I hadn't expected to have to earn my stay here."

"That's a filthy thing to say!"

"It's pretty filthy talking to me about how much it cost. Remind me to write you a cheque when we get back."

"Oh, for fuck's sake. I'm going to bed."

"Good. Because I'm going back to the bar. And don't worry; I'll pay for my own drinks."

She phoned for the escort and slammed the door after her.

. . .

In the morning when she woke, he was gone; she turned over, went back to sleep, and was sitting in the Jacuzzi when he returned.

"Good safari?"

"Very good."

"What did you see?"

"Animals. Wild animals," he said stiffly. "I'm going to have break-fast. I'll see you later."

Linda stuck out her tongue at his back. It spoke of huge hostility, that back. In fact, it was the most expressive back she knew.

Later they made up, lunched by the pool, and went out on the evening safari together. It was very wonderful. Nothing could have prepared Linda for the moment when a pride of lions walked by in a long, sinuous line, so close to the Land Rover they could have touched them. Or when two giraffes stalked languidly past them supermodel-style, heads held high, eyes on some far horizon, totally ignoring them. She'd somehow expected the animals to be about two hundred yards away, not within blinking distance. It was astonishing enough to get her up at five thirty the following day for more.

The highlight of that morning's safari was an elephant and her baby; just a few days old, the baby was being caressed and urged along by its mother's swishing trunk.

"So sweet," Linda said to the ranger, "and so gentle. But elephants always are, aren't they?"

"Until they're threatened. Let her think you might hurt that little chap and you'd have three tons of aggression heaped onto you."

Probably because Linda was tired, they quarrelled dramatically that afternoon, so dramatically indeed that when they emerged from their bungalow for dinner—having missed the safari—they realised from their slightly embarrassed expressions that their fellow guests must have heard them. The initial cause was Linda's getting sunburnt; Alex told her she was a fool to lie out at midday; she told him he was a stuffy old fart; he said he had seen enough skin cancer cases to make him cautious; she accused him of being overdramatic and depressing. Somehow after that they got onto the children, with him informing her it was as well she'd never become a mother, given her total irresponsibility of attitude: which was, she informed him, so far below the belt as to be totally obscene.

He did apologise at that; they had a making up of sorts, and braved dinner; but afterwards, alone in the bungalow, she said, "Just as a matter of interest, Alex, why have you never allowed me to meet your children?"

"What do you mean, never?" he said. "We've known each other only a few weeks."

"Months. Actually."

"All right. But we don't meet very frequently. It just hasn't been practical."

"I hope that is the reason. I'd have thought if you were in the least serious about me, you'd have realised I'd like to meet them. And them me."

"Linda, you know I'm serious about you. Neither of us would be here if I wasn't."

"OK, then. Maybe it's even worse than that; maybe you think they won't like me."

"They probably won't."

"Oh, what? Alex, how can you talk to me like that? You are—"

"I mean, of course, they won't like you because you're not their mother. They're bound to be hostile to any new girlfriend."

"What about her boyfriend?"

"Yes, well, they certainly don't like him."

"I thought they lived with him."

"No, they don't. His house is in Marlow; Sam has her own near Cirencester."

"But they do see him?"

"They have to."

"Well, why don't they have to see me?"

"Linda, this is absurd. Of course they don't have to see you . . . I'm not in a permanent relationship with you."

"Well, thanks for that. I'm glad to have it spelt out."

Whereupon she pulled on a jacket, opened the door, and walked out into the darkness.

Alex waited for a few minutes; he was sure she'd be back. The bar was closed; there was nowhere for her to go. And she'd never dare walk far without an escort. An escort with a gun.

Five minutes later, he was growing anxious; only a few months ago a tourist had been savaged by a lion when he had got out of the Land Rover (totally against instruction) and crept up on a lioness and her cub to take photographs. Both lioness and lion had been shot.

They had all sat soberly in the Land Rover while the scout told them this story, shocked. And now here was Linda, doing something even more insane, out in the darkness, endangering not only her own life but those of the people who must find her. Stupid, bloody-minded, stubborn woman. Arrogant beyond belief. Self-centred, over-dramatic; she deserved all she got.

Alex rang for help.

• • •

There was a track leading away from the lodge; one way it broadened into a wide dirt road, the other into the track the Land Rovers drove along on safari. Linda could see that might be a little dangerous; she simply could not imagine the road could be in any way so. They would exaggerate the dangers to make everything more exciting, and so that people didn't take silly risks. There certainly hadn't been anything more aggressive than an impala as they drove along it on their way.

Fucking Alex; God, she hated him. How dared he talk to her like some patronising father figure, and then tell her his children wouldn't like her. That had been hugely hurtful. Thank God tomorrow it would be over and they would be going home. She realised she was crying—as much as at the disappointment of the trip, which she had so hoped would be happy and fun, as at the hurt he had just slung at her. Thank God they weren't in much of a relationship; they could part at the airport and never meet again. Apart from the toothbrush and razor he kept at her flat, there would be no trace of him left in her life. *Bastard! Bloody arrogant, bad-tempered bastard!* She hated him. She . . .

Linda turned; better not go too far; it was very black, and it was the middle of the night. The park was noisy, sound cutting through the thick darkness, the raw cries of the birds and the chattering of the monkeys mixed with the occasional bellow or roar. Something moved on the ground horribly close to her; she jumped. Couldn't have been a snake. Could it? No, of course not. She heard, from about fifty yards away, a rustling, pushing in the undergrowth; nothing dangerous, she was sure, a bird probably. But still . . . best get back.

She turned and realised that she had actually wandered off the main track, had taken, in the darkness, a minor one; grass brushed at her ankles. *Damn. Bloody silly.* Well, she couldn't be far from the compound; she'd been walking only a few minutes. Actually, looking at her watch, nearly ten. You could walk quite a way in ten minutes. Still, she was fine; it was fine. The hotel lights were . . . shit, where were they? The track sloped slightly; she must just walk back down it, rather than up, and she'd hit the main track. Then she could easily . . .

Fuck. She couldn't easily see anything. It was pitch-black—she hadn't even had the sense to bring the torch. Well, that was Alex's fault; she'd been too upset to think. She walked a few steps tentatively; was that up- or downhill? Hard to tell; the slope was very slight. She could be walking farther into the bush, or out of it. It was impossible to tell. Maybe she should shout . . . shout for help. But if she did, an animal could hear her. A hungry animal. Like the lion that had caught the tourist. Or the mother elephant, startled into defending her baby. What had the ranger said? Three tons of aggression. So . . . no shouting then. *Just keep calm, Linda; walk steadily back.* But . . . she didn't know which way was back.

She stood there, willing herself not to panic, her mouth dry, her heart thudding. What should she do? What the fuck should she do?

. . .

"Several of us will go," the ranger told Alex, "since you have no idea where she went." His voice was calm, but cold. He was obviously very angry: with good reason.

"Yes. Thank you. I'm so . . . so sorry. Should I come with you?"

"Absolutely not. No. Stay here. If she turns up, if you find she's just sitting by the pool or something, tell them at the hotel. And they can radio us."

"Of course," said Alex. He was absolutely confident Linda was not sitting by the pool. Or the bar. Or anywhere. She was out there in all that danger, possibly even now being savaged by something, her lovely body being ripped quite literally apart, and it was his fault for being so harsh with her, so critical, so cruel. Sam had been right: he really wasn't worth having a relationship with.

He stood at the doorway, the light of the room behind him, that gentle, sweet candlelight, so at odds with what he was feeling, what was happening. He strained his eyes into the darkness. He couldn't see or hear anything, except the Land Rovers that the rangers had taken. Jesus, those lions the other day had been only a mile or so away. Several of the other bungalows were lit up; he could see faces at the windows. What stories these people would have to tell when they got home: about this misfit couple who fought endlessly, put the safety of the whole camp and all the rangers at risk . . .

He tensed; he could hear the Land Rover now, drawing nearer. It pulled into the courtyard, its engine silenced. Alex stood, unable to move, more fearful than he could ever remember. They had called off the search; she had been found dead or horribly mutilated; no one could find her, she—

"Right, Alex. Here she is. Safe and sound, although she might not have been much longer; something quite big out there, could have been anything, leopard, lion . . . Please don't do that again, Linda; you're putting us at risk as well as yourself. Good night."

"Good night." Linda's face was drawn and tearstained, distorted by fear and remorse. "I'm so, so sorry."

"That's OK. Night."

He looked pretty cheesed off, Alex thought. He would have been, too. Some silly cow endangering his life, all for a bit of drama. He took Linda's arm, pulled her in, shut the door. He shook her—hard. Again and again. Her eyes were shocked and afraid in her white face.

"I'm sorry, Alex. I'm so sorry."

"You stupid fucking thoughtless bitch. How could you be so selfish, so insanely stupid . . ."

"I don't know. I'm sorry. I . . . well, I'm sorry."

"You'd better be." He stopped shaking her suddenly, set her away from him. "You know, I could . . ."

"What?"

Suddenly he couldn't stand it any longer. Her fear, her misery, his relief. He sat down abruptly on the bed, his legs weak, sat looking at her. She didn't move, just stood there, staring back at him.

"What?" she said again.

"Oh, Linda," he said after a long silence. "I'm afraid I love you. That's what."

CHAPTER 47

It was very odd to be seeing him again. Being with him, talking to him, having a laugh with him, doing everything with him, really . . . except touching him. That seemed to be totally off-limits. And it was all, really, she wanted to do. Well, more or less.

Still . . . it was something even to be working with him.

And Georgia. Georgia was great. Really cool—bit immature, bit spoiled, but funny and clever, and really good to work with, full of ideas, willing to do anything, put in endless hours. A real trouper.

They had formed a committee, which met regularly and then issued properly reported minutes at Abi's instigation: "Formalising it all is the only way to push it forward; otherwise it just turns into a wank, everyone discussing their wonderful ideas and never doing anything."

The committee members were Abi, who was chair—"Only because I've been involved in all this stuff a bit before"—Georgia, and William.

Then there was Emma, representing the hospital, and a friend of Abi's called Fred, who worked for a charity and knew a great deal about the ins and outs of that industry, about fund-raising, about sponsorship, and running events in general. He said he might even be able to find a sponsor for them. He was doing it for nothing.

Fred wasn't too much like anyone would expect a charity worker to be: he looked like a secondhand-car salesman, as Abi said when she introduced him to the group. Fred had taken the implied criticism of this with great good nature and said that selling charities and selling cars were much more similar processes than anyone would think. "You're still getting people to part with more than they want for something. Charities are easier really, in a way, because you can work on their consciences."

Abi knew that William had thought initially that Fred was doing it because he fancied her, but in fact he wasn't; he was a happily unmarried man, as he put it, with a sweet-faced girlfriend called Molly, and a baby on the way. Abi spent a lot of time at the first meeting she brought him to asking Fred about Molly and the baby and when it might be due.

They had a notional date for the festival now, of July eighth and ninth; but as Abi said, it was no use setting anything in stone until they knew they could get some bands.

"There are literally thousands of them," she said, "and they'll all be on MySpace. You'll only get unsigned ones to come, obviously, although it would be great to have one slightly bigger name."

"Would a slightly bigger name come?" asked Georgia, and Fred said they might, if the idea appealed, and there was going to be some good publicity.

"Which there will be, won't there?"

"There certainly will," said Abi coolly. "And quite big bands will bring their fee right down if it's for charity. The smaller ones will probably do it for cost. Just to get the chance to play and be heard. We're just going to have to hit the keyboard, Georgia, e-mail all their agents. Those who have them. We also want quite a good spread of music styles. Like rock, obviously, but also jazz, bit of folk even, for the families . . ."

It was William who came up with the really clever idea: "I was talking to a bloke the other night in the pub, telling him what we were going to do; he was awfully impressed. Anyway, he'd been to a small festival the other side of Bath, and what they did was have a whole load of sort of auditions—play-offs, he called them—called Battle of the Bands, in pubs. Each area fielded a few bands and they played in the pub and the punters voted and the winner was put forward to play. He said it was great because everyone who'd voted wanted to go the festival and hear their band. So they got loads more people than they would have done."

"That is such a good idea," said Georgia, "wonderful local publicity too. You are clever, William. Isn't that clever, Fred?"

Fred said it was a good idea. "Only thing is, what sort of standard would the bands be? Bit of a gamble."

"No worse a gamble than if we chose them from MySpace," said Abi briskly, "and obviously we'd hear them too, and if they were dreadful we wouldn't book them. We should get cracking on this straightaway. William, you give us a list of villages, or small towns I s'pose might be better, not too close together, with really good pubs that you think'd cooperate, and we'll get some flyers done . . . I can run them off at work. Oh, God, if only we had some money. And a name. We've got to have a name. Georgia, you're the creative one; get us a name."

. . .

William felt rather pleased at having made such a large contribution to what he thought of as the theatrical side. Everyone—including him—had seen his role as strictly functional: providing the site, finding the contractors, organising the infrastructure . . . The cost of providing power lines and building the arena was eye-watering, and he hoped his father would never find out. They had settled on a ticket fee of thirty pounds, children half price; it sounded a lot, but not set against the thousands they were going to have to find. In his darker moments, he worried that they wouldn't make any money at all, just a whacking loss, and half wished he had said no in the first place. But then he thought of the heady pleasure of the thing, the sense of purpose it had given them all, and of creating something so original and exciting, and he knew it was worth it.

And besides, it meant he could see so much of Abi.

The hurt of the memories had gone; he just longed now to go back to where they had been. She clearly felt quite differently; and working with her on the festival, seeing her more on her home turf, so to speak, he imagined himself through her eyes: very sound, nice, bit dull, someone she had once undoubtedly been fond of, and had fun with, a good friend, but who really was not in her orbit of consideration for anything more . . .

Laura was sitting in her mother's kitchen, crying. She was in complete despair over Charlie. Jonathan's moving out had made him slightly less tense, but his behaviour was no better. Indeed, his year tutor had said that his work was increasingly erratic, "and quite honestly, Mrs. Gilliatt, he seems to have lost most of his social skills as well."

She had tried everything: persuasion, threats, bribes, even emotional blackmail: "you could do it for me, Charlie, even if you won't for Dad. It upsets me so much, your behaving like this, and life is quite . . . quite difficult just at the moment."

She got little response beyond the now horribly predictable shrug; he clearly felt she must bear some of the blame for his father's behaviour.

Occasionally she thought she had made a breakthrough; one night he had found her crying, after the girls had gone to bed. He had sat down beside her on the sofa, put his arms round her, and asked her if there was anything he could do.

"I'm so sorry, Mum; it must be horrible for you."

Laura told him it would make her feel better if he started working at school again, and told him what his year tutor had said; that had been a mistake.

"Mum, I don't mind helping at home, or trying to cheer the girls up, but I can't go back to being good little Charlie again. He's gone. Dad's sent him packing."

"But, Charlie, that's not fair. To me or to you. You could perfectly well start working again if you wanted to."

"Yeah, but I don't want to. Maybe in time, but not right now. I don't see the point."

"The point is your future, Charlie. Doesn't that matter to you?"

He shrugged. "Not much, no. I couldn't care less about it."

"I don't know what to do, Mummy," Laura said now, blowing her nose. "He's just wrecking his own life and I can't get that through to him."

"I'm no psychologist, darling, but I'd say he was feeling completely disillusioned with everything. He idolised his father and he feels utterly let down. And not just with Jonathan, but Jonathan's way of life. Why should he try to be like him, to emulate him in any way, when he despises him so much?"

"But that doesn't make sense!"

"I think you'd find it did to Charlie He's rejected the way Jonathan brought him up, and that includes working hard and doing well."

"Oh, God," said Laura, "it's all so hideous. Tell me what to do. Mummy, I can't think straight anymore."

"Nothing for now, darling. Give it time. You have no idea how things might turn out."

"Yes, I do. Jonathan's not coming back, because I couldn't bear it if he did. Charlie won't forgive Jonathan, or change his attitude in any way. I can't see how anything could change."

"Laura, just now neither can I. I only know, after living for quite a long time, that things do. Stuff happens, as the horrible expression goes. Try to be patient."

"Oh, Mummy, you know what I often think?"

"No, what do you often think?"

"That if it hadn't been for that bloody car crash, everything would have been all right. I'd never have known about Abi Scott; it would have played itself out; Jonathan would have got sick of her . . ."

"He might not have."

"Well, thanks for that."

"Darling, don't get me wrong. I think what Jonathan's done is dreadful, unforgivable. I can hardly bear to see you so unhappy. And if he wanted to come back, if you did forgive him, I'd find it very hard to accept. All I'm saying is that men do seem to need these . . . relationships sometimes. Well, saying they need them rather overdignifies them. They decide they're going to have them. Especially at Jonathan's age, it's a grab at their lost youth. If it hadn't been Abi Scott, it might have been someone else."

"Daddy didn't do that, did he?" She stared at her mother, suddenly understanding for a brief moment how Charlie felt, the shock of betrayal.

"No, he didn't; he never cheated on me, thank God, but several of my friends had to endure it. Some of the marriages survived. Well, most of them, actually. They did in those days. And there was a lot of turning a blind eye, pretending you didn't know."

"So . . . are you saying I should take him back?"

"No, of course not. Unless you really want to. And as I say, I wouldn't find it easy if you did. I'm simply saying that you're not the first woman to have to endure this."

"No, I know." She hesitated. "He . . . well, he did say he was about to finish the relationship. That it was over."

"Well . . . that's something in his favour."

"You don't believe that, do you?"

"Laura, you know Jonathan a great deal better than I do. If you believe him, then I'd trust your judgment. And maybe you've been too perfect, too good to him. You do—well, you did—spoil him dreadfully."

. . .

"Would you like to go for a walk, Russell, dear?" said Mary, walking into the morning room where Russell was reading the *Financial Times*. He had been persuaded to take it instead of the *Wall Street Journal*; he complained every day about how unsatisfactory it was, and made a great thing of reading the *Journal* online, but Mary had observed he still became totally absorbed in the *FT* for at least an hour and a half each morning. Which was a relief, actually; now that all the excitement of the wedding and Christmas was over, Russell was often restless. He spent a lot of time on the Internet studying the markets and then instructing his broker to buy this or sell that. And he was on the phone for at least an hour a day to Morton discussing the business. Mary had a pretty shrewd idea that Morton didn't welcome these calls, and indeed he had told her over Christmas that it was wonderful to see his father so relaxed and happy.

"He really seems to be letting go of the reins at last."

"The reins?"

"Yeah, of the business. He was supposed to have retired ten years ago; we gave him a dinner, everyone made speeches, we presented him with a wonderful vintage gold watch—that was a kind of a joke, of course—and he even wept a bit, and said good-bye to everyone. Monday morning, nine a.m., he was back at his desk. He's cut down a bit since then, of course, but I'd like to see him taking it really easy."

Mary could see very clearly that what Morton meant was that he'd thank God on bended knees for his father to be taking it really easy, and assured him that she absolutely agreed and that she had all sorts of plans for the coming year: "A bit of travelling, for a start. We haven't had our honeymoon yet, and I'm not letting him get away with that," she said, "and he seems to have plans for making over some of the land here to what he calls a vegetable farm. So that we can be self-sufficient."

Morton grinned at her. "Sounds good to me. He needs new projects. May I warn you, though, he could get tired of the vegetable farm . . ."

Mary said she didn't need the warning. "It's a problem with retirement, Morton. Donald had his bird-watching; it had been a passion all his life; he'd longed for more time to spend on it, and after a few months, he even got bored with that. We started learning bridge just so he could focus on something else."

"Don't play bridge with my father, Mary," said Morton. "He becomes extremely aggressive."

"How do you think he'd be on archaeology? That's always interested me."

Morton considered this. "I can only say the world would hear of some amazing new buried city within months. As for the archaeological outfitters, how are they on bespoke shorts?"

. . .

"Russell, dear, do listen to me. I said, would you like to go for a walk?"

"Not just now, Sparrow. I'm worried about some of my stocks. Thinking of selling them. I'm going to draft a letter to my accountant just as soon as I've finished reading this."

"Well, all right, dear. I'll go on my own."

"Mary, you know I don't like you going out on your own."

"Oh, for goodness' sake," said Mary impatiently, "what on earth do you think might happen to me? Might I meet a herd of wild boar in the lane?"

"Don't mock me, Sparrow," he said, and his eyes were quite hurt. "I want to look after you."

"I know you do. But I need to get out. Can't the stocks wait another day?"

"Possibly. Yes, all right."

"Now, Russell, dear," she said, tucking her arm into his as they walked through the gate at the bottom of the garden and into the wood, "I really would like to start planning our honeymoon. I don't want to be cheated of it. Where would you like to go?"

"Anywhere you like, Sparrow. Italy, maybe—I've always longed to go there, would find all those works of art so wonderful. Or maybe the Seychelles, or even Vietnam . . ."

"Russell, I don't think I want to do anything quite as . . . as adventurous as that," said Mary.

"Well, why on earth not?" he said, looking genuinely puzzled. "We should do these things while we can, Mary, before we get old and stuck in our ways."

"Oh, Russell," she said, reaching up to kiss him, "I love you for so many reasons, but perhaps most because you don't see us as old."

"Well, of course I don't. We're not old. We're certainly quite young enough to enjoy ourselves."

"Yes, of course. But . . . well I would still rather have a quiet honeymoon. I've never been to the lake district. Wonderful scenery, good driving . . . and walking. Would you consider that? Just for now."

"If that's what you want, Sparrow. As long as we can go to Italy in the spring."

"I promise you," she said, "we'll go to Italy in the spring."

. . .

It had gone . . . not badly, but not really very well, Linda thought. They had been polite, but wary, undemonstrative. And Alex had been pretty similar; obviously nervous of appearing in any way foolish, romantically inclined, uncool. He hadn't even touched her, except to kiss her hello and good-bye. And she felt under inspection by him all over again, seeing herself through their eyes.

It had been her idea to take them to a preview. A formal meal would be a minefield: where would they go? Somewhere easy and informal, obviously, but . . . high-profile like Carluccio's or the Blue-bird, or really local and undemanding. And then the former might seem like trying too hard, the latter like selling them short and not bothering much. And then it would be a minefield as well of silences and studied manners. If it had just been Amy, then maybe they could have gone shopping; although what self-respecting fifteen-year-old would want to go shopping with someone of . . . well, knocking on forty, and where on earth could she take her? And would she buy her lots of stuff, which would look like trying too hard, or not anything at all, which would look mean?

Not shopping, then. Anyway, they were all coming together, the three of them.

And then the tickets arrived for a new comedy smash hit, and that seemed too good to be true. She was sent two, asked for two more. The show was for early Friday evening, which was ideal, really; they could just go for a pizza afterwards, the ice broken by laughing—hopefully—and if it was going really badly, just a coffee at Starbucks and then Alex could take them home.

She chose what to wear with as much anguish as if she was going to meet the Queen or Brad Pitt. Both of whom would actually have been easier, she thought. In the end she settled on a short black skirt and polo shirt, and a leather jacket. Any hint of cleavage seemed a bad idea; the skirt was shortish, but that was all right. She initially put on pumps, but they looked wrong and frumpy, so she slightly anxiously changed into some Christian Louboutin high heels. She removed her red nail varnish, and wore much less eye makeup than usual.

Alex brought them to her office, because that seemed safer territory than her flat and a bit more welcoming than the cinema lobby, an acknowledgement that she was a bit more than a casual acquaintance, a bit less than a permanent fixture.

They walked in, smiled, shook her hand, said how do you do; she was pleasantly surprised by that, and by their slightly formal clothes. She had half expected grunting hoods. They were good-looking children, both of them, Amy an incipient beauty, with Alex's dark colouring, all pushed-back hair and posh, languid voice, Adam blond, overall and thin and horribly self-conscious, with spots, braces on his teeth, and a voice perilously close to breaking. Amy wandered round the office, looking at photographs, expressing polite interest when she recognised someone; Adam sat on the sofa, trying not to look at anyone as he sipped his Coke.

The taxi ride was silent; they arrived at the preview cinema in Wardour Street half an hour early. Not good. Linda met a couple of people, introduced them, and then withdrew into the safety of showbiz gossip. Amy looked bored, Adam embarrassed, Alex glowering and Heathcliff-like.

. . .

The film was a success: very funny, very glossy, quite cool. Linda sat next to Amy, then Adam, then Alex. They both laughed a lot, and afterwards Amy turned to her and said, "That was really cool, thank you so much." Adam shuffled out, muttering, "Great, cool, yeah."

"So . . . pizza, anyone? Or shall we just go to Starbucks or some-where for a coffee? You guys choose."

Guys? Should she have said that? More pathetic groping for street cred.

"Pizza?" said Amy.

"Don't mind," said Adam.

They went to Pizza Express in the end, the kids talking and gig-gling between themselves; what were they saying? Linda thought. Were they agreeing that she was gross, or pathetic, or even—just possibly—nice? There was no clue from the subsequent exchanges.

They ordered pizzas, preceded by garlic bread; conversation was strained and mostly about the film and other films they had seen. She longed to ask them what they wanted to do when they grew up, but knew that this above all was what people their age hated. She asked them their plans for the weekend, and they both said they didn't know.

She asked them if their father had told them much about South Africa, and Amy said yes, and it had sounded really cool. Adam said yes, it had sounded great.

She had ordered one small glass of wine, but it was gone in her nervousness before they had even finished the garlic bread; she ordered another—"a large one this time, please"—and then worried they might put her down as an alcoholic.

A very large silence now settled; she almost let it go on, and then, thinking things could hardly be worse, asked them if they had heard about the music festival that Georgia, one of her clients, was putting on "for the victims of the M4 crash last summer; I'm sure your father will have told you about it."

"He tells us about so many awful things," said Amy, smiling sud-denly at her father, then at her, "we wouldn't remember."

"Oh. Right. Well, Georgia—Georgia Linley, she's called—is going to be in a big new thriller series in March. She was involved in the crash and wanted to raise some money for the people who were

hurt, who can't work and so on. But now it's more for your dad's hospital."

"Cool," said Amy. "Was that her, the black girl in the photograph with you?"

"Yes, that's right."

"So . . . when's the festival?"

"Oh . . . July."

"Where?"

"On someone's farm. Nice young guy called William Grainger; his farm borders the M4, and the air ambulance landed on his field."

"Oh, OK."

"Would you like to go?" asked Alex. It was virtually the first time he'd spoken since they got to the restaurant.

"Yeah, maybe. What's it called?"

"I don't think it's got a name yet," said Linda. "They can't seem to get it quite right, the last thing I heard. Got any ideas? All suggestions welcomed."

"God, no," said Amy.

Adam shrugged.

· · ·

Shortly after that they left; Alex was driving them home to their mother. He still hadn't found anywhere decent to live.

"You've been a great help," hissed Linda, as they stood at the edge of the pavement, hailing taxis for her rather fruitlessly.

"Sorry. I thought it was better to let you make the running."

"Hmm. Oh, shit, look, there's one miles down the road, hasn't seen us . . ." She put two fingers in her mouth and whistled loudly. Amy and Adam looked startled, then grinned at her. Or were they laughing at her? How loud, how brash, not the sort of thing a nice, seemly stepmother should be doing.

"Bye, then," she said, holding out her hand, taking theirs one by one. "It's been really fun. I'm glad you liked the film."

"Bye," said Amy. "And thanks."

"Bye," said Adam. "Yeah, thanks."

"Bye, Linda," said Alex.

The last she saw of them was the two children, heads together, laughing . . . at her, no doubt, pathetic, would-be-cool woman, and Alex, looking ferocious.

What a disaster. What a bloody disaster. He'd never want to marry her now.

. . .

She was half-asleep when the phone rang.

"Hi." It was Alex.

"Oh, hi. You OK?"

"Yes, thanks. I'm fine."

"Sorry, Alex."

"What on earth for? Right . . . now, as the kids would say, were you a hit, or were you a hit?"

"What?"

"You, my darling beloved, are just soooo cool. That's Amy's verdict. You are pretty nice. That's Adam's. You have great legs. That was also Adam. You are so not embarrassing. Amy again. She wants to come and see you on her own, maybe—go shopping; your shoes were just uh-may-zing. And ohmigod, the way you whistled for the cab. Oh, Linda. I love you."

"I love you too," she said.

. . .

It felt like any other evening. Not good, not bad, Barney thought, just . . . an evening. For going home, eating dinner—dutifully; smiling—a lot; talking—carefully; listening—even more carefully. Trying not to think too much, not to remember . . . and most of all, not to look forward. Forward into God knew what. More of this? This odd, calm sadness, this pleasant unease, this lie of a life? Lived with someone who loved him so much. Whom he—still—loved too. In a way. In a concerned, tender, guilty way.

It was a horrible night, wet, cold, windy. He was carrying a brown paper bag with a couple of bottles of wine in it, and it was getting dangerously soggy. He'd also got her some flowers. Those Kenyan two-tone roses that she liked so much. It was Wednesday and he always bought her flowers on Wednesday; it was half joke, half tradition. She said if he ever forgot, she'd know there was something terribly wrong. Well, he hadn't forgotten yet.

When he got home, she wasn't there. Which wasn't particularly unusual; she was terminally sociable, always having quick drinks or even supper with girlfriends after work. Although he couldn't remember her saying anything about this evening.

He went in, put the wine in the fridge, the roses in water—without cutting the stems, which would have induced a ticking off if she'd known; she was very strict about such things: "Barney—darling—it doesn't take a minute, and they live so much longer; you're just lazy . . ."

He wondered if Emma fussed over rose stems. He decided it was very unlikely . . . *Don't start thinking about Emma, Fraser, just don't. Doesn't help.*

He wondered if he should do something about supper. He looked in the fridge; there didn't seem to be a lot there. Well, if she was much later, they could go out. Only if she'd eaten—he'd call her. See what she was doing. She'd be amused, not cross, if he'd forgotten some arrangement, would tell him he was hopeless, that she'd be home soon.

Her mobile was switched off.

He sat down, turned on the TV, was watching the end of the seven-o'clock news when he heard her footsteps in the street, heard her key in the lock. She'd be soaked, miserable; he should make her a cup of tea.

He went into the kitchen and was filling the kettle when she came in. He turned to smile at her, and then saw her face. It wasn't quite . . . quite right somehow, her face. It wasn't wearing its usual smile; her eyes weren't warm; in fact, they were staring at him as if she had never seen him before. Barney put the kettle down.

She was taking her coat off, her wet coat; he reached for it, to hang it up.

"It's all right," she said, "I can do it."

He followed her as she walked out of the kitchen, throwing the coat down on a chair—unthinkable, that—went into the sitting room, and sat down. Barney sat opposite her. It seemed the only thing to do.

A silence, then:

"Barney, why didn't you tell me?"

His stomach lurched hideously.

"Tell you what?"

"You know perfectly well what. I saw Tamara today, and she told me all about it."

The cow. The bitch. How dared she? How *dared* she? She'd promised, as he had; that was what came of making a pact with the devil.

"Yes," he said, "yes, I see. Well, she had no right to do that. To tell you. It's nothing to do with her."

"Well, it is a bit, I think. She is my best friend."

"Yes, I know, but . . ."

How had they ever got to be best friends, these two? One so good, so transparently sweet and kind, the other so bad, so devious and cruel.

"Well, she has. Do you want to talk about it?"

"If you do."

"Well, of course I do; it affects us both, doesn't it?"

"Yes, Amanda, it does."

"Well . . . go on."

"I think I . . . might"—he pushed his hair back—"think I might have a beer. You?"

"Not a beer. Maybe a glass of wine."

He poured her her favourite, chardonnay—not very smart, as she often said, but it was so lovely who cared about smart? And poured himself a Beck's.

"Come on, Barney, please. I do need to know."

Oh, God. God, how do I get through this? He looked at her. Her pretty, peaches-and-cream face was very calm, her blue eyes fixed on him intently.

"Well . . ." he said. "Well, it . . . it all happened because of the crash. And while Toby was in hospital."

"Yes, that's what Tamara said. Well, sort of."

"Let's forget about what Tamara might have said. I want you to have the story as it really happened. I . . . never meant it to happen, Amanda. I loved you so much. I do love you so much. It . . . just . . . well, it sort of took me over."

She was silent; he didn't dare look at her. Then she said, "I don't quite see what that's got to do with it."

"Amanda, of course it has."

"Well . . . go on."

"Yes, well, I think it was partly the emotion about Toby, you know. And I was full of guilt about the crash. She . . . well, she helped me over that."

"Who, Tamara?"

"No, of course not Tamara. Her. Emma."

"Emma? Just a minute, Barney, I'm losing it a bit here . . ."

Afterwards, he thought, if he'd looked at her then . . . but he didn't.

"Yes, she's a doctor there. Oh, Amanda, I'm so, so sorry. Anyway, she was just fantastic the day Toby had his operation. I couldn't have got through it without her. Of course, if you'd been there . . . but you weren't."

"No. No, I wasn't."

He did look at her now; she was very pale suddenly, and very still, her eyes darker.

"Go . . . go on," she said. Her voice was strange, rather breathless . . .

"And . . . well, it just went on from there. Our relationship. It developed so quickly. It sounds kind of . . . well, cheesy, I know, but I couldn't seem to help it. Neither of us could. We saw each other a few times, not many at all, but we did decide . . . well, I . . . I was going to tell you that night."

"What night?" she said. Very slowly.

"The night your father died, I was waiting for you, and then while I was waiting your mother phoned, and of course I couldn't . . . then."

"No. Well, that was . . . very good of you." Her voice wasn't breathless now; it was low and very level.

"I know I'm a shit, Amanda. I know I behaved badly. Terribly badly. But . . . well, I did want to take care of you while you were so unhappy."

"Yes, I see. And . . . what about her? Emma. While I was so unhappy?"

"I didn't see her. Of course. We agreed it would be very wrong."

"Nice of you both."

He was silent; then he said, "Anyway, it's over. For what it's worth. Finally, I mean. She . . . finished it. She said it mustn't go on."

"Right. Well, that was very noble of her." There was a silence while she looked round the room, rather wildly, as if she was seeking an escape, her eyes brilliant with tears. Her voice wasn't tearful, though; it was still very level. "Yes, Barney. Very noble. I don't suppose it occurred to her that it shouldn't have gone on while you were engaged to someone else. Or occurred to you . . ."

"Amanda, I know that, obviously. Of course it shouldn't have gone on. I can't justify it or even explain it. I just didn't seem to be able to help it."

"No. So you keep saying. Anyway, it's . . . it's over, is it? Have you seen her since?"

"No. I haven't. And yes, it is over. But . . . well, that doesn't quite alter what I feel for you. Now."

Another silence; he could feel her gathering her courage to go on.

"And what's that?" she said finally.

"It's not the same, Amanda. It just isn't. It doesn't feel right anymore. It used to be so perfect, and now it isn't. I still love you very much, but—"

"Oh, please. So all that time while I was so wretched over Daddy and his funeral and even Christmas, you were thinking about her?"

"Well . . . in a way, yes. I was. But—"

She was crying now. "But it was her who finished it?"

"Yes, it was."

"Well, good for her. At least she has some sense of right and wrong. I suppose you thought you'd just let it go on and on, enjoying both of us . . . or maybe you weren't enjoying me. Just staying with me because you were sorry for me. God, Barney, that's so horrible."

"Amanda, I'm sorry. I can't say it enough. I do still love you. Very much."

"Yes, you keep saying. But . . . you . . . you don't want to marry me, is that it?"

There was a long silence; it was the most difficult thing he had ever done, but he managed it.

"Yes, Amanda," he said. "I'm so sorry, but that is it."

* * *

When he heard the car finally pulling away from the house he picked up the phone and called Tamara.

"You cow," he said. "How dare you, how dare you do that."

"Do what?"

"You know perfectly well fucking what. Tell Amanda about me and Emma."

There was a long silence; then she said, "Barney, I didn't. I really, really didn't."

"But"—now he really was going to throw up—"but she knew. She said you told her."

"I didn't tell her about you and Emma, Barney. I told her about Toby and what he'd done to you. And me. That's all. I swear to you, that's absolutely all."

CHAPTER 48

"Mummy, I want to go and get some sweets and my magazines."

"Daisy, darling, I'm awfully busy. I've got these plans to finish for someone."

"You're always busy now."

This was true; it was the only way she could distract herself.

"I'm sorry, sweetie. Maybe when I've finished . . . Oh, no, Granny's coming to take you all to the science museum."

"Again? Boring." This was Charlie.

"Charlie, don't be rude. If you can't find anything to interest you there, then I'm sorry for you."

He shrugged. "So? It's boring."

"But, Mummy," said Daisy, "I so want my magazines. Especially *Animals and You*; it's got a free necklace. I could wear it to the museum and show Granny."

"Daisy, I just haven't got time."

"It's not fair. You never have time anymore."

"Yes, darling, and I'm sorry. After this job, I won't be so busy. Promise."

"You said that last time," said Charlie.

"Charlie, will you please stop being so difficult."

"I'm not. I'm just telling the truth. And why shouldn't Daisy get her stuff if she wants to?"

"Could Charlie take me?" said Daisy.

"I'm not taking her," he said.

"Charlie, that's not very helpful."

"So? I don't want to; I'm going to go on the computer, look at my Warhammer stuff."

"Charlie, you are not going on the computer."

"Why not?"

"Because I'm about to need it, that's why."

"That is just so mean. Anyway, I'm not taking her to get her stupid comic."

"It's not a comic."

"Daisy, it's a comic."

Laura suddenly lost her temper.

"Charlie, stop being so difficult. Now, get your coat and Daisy's and take her to the shop."

"No."

"I hate you," wailed Daisy. "You're so mean."

"Charlie, I'm not telling you again. If you don't take her you don't get your pocket money, and then you won't be able to buy any more Warhammer stuff."

"That's blackmail."

"I don't care. Go and get the coats. And, Charlie, look after her properly; don't walk miles ahead."

. . .

She'd at least get ten minutes' peace. And maybe if she finished sooner, she could go and meet them all at the science museum for tea.

It was a difficult job, this one: a very dull modern flat that the owner had requested be given "some character. Only not too modern. Maybe a bit pretty, even. Curtains, not blinds, that sort of thing. But still contemporary; I don't want it to look like something out of the seventies."

Such instructions were fairly common.

. . .

Charlie and Daisy walked along the sidewalk, Daisy chattering, Charlie kicking a stone, ignoring her.

"Charlie, if I got a kitten, which I think I might—Mummy said just possibly—what shall I call it?"

He shrugged.

"I thought Paddypaws would be a nice name."

"It's a stupid name."

"It's not. It's sweet. Well, what would you call it?"

"I don't want a stupid kitten."

"Kittens aren't stupid."

"Course they are."

"Well . . . what pet would you like?"

"I don't want a pet."

"Everyone wants pets."

"I don't. Well, maybe a boa constrictor."

"What's that?"

"A snake."

"A snake! You couldn't have a snake; where would you keep it?"

"In my room."

"Charlie, you're so stupid."

"Oh, and you're not, I s'pose. Look, here we are. I'll wait outside. Be quick; don't start looking at all the other comics."

"They're not comics."

He shrugged.

She came out, clutching several magazines and a bag of sweets.

"OK. All done."

He began to walk faster; Daisy had to half run to keep up with him, and dropped one of her magazines.

"Charlie! Wait for me!"

"Well, buck up then."

"I can't buck up. I've dropped one of my magazines."

He stood, arms folded, elaborately patient, while she picked everything up, then set off again.

"Look, here's a picture of a kitten—look, isn't it sweet?"

"No."

"It is. And . . . Charlie, please wait; you're doing it again. I can't keep up . . ."

"Well, walk faster then . . ."

"I am walking faster. Oh, no, now the cover's ripped off; it's got the necklace on it. Charlie, wait, wait . . ."

But he didn't wait; and he didn't see the crumpled cover of the magazine caught by the wind and blown across the road; nor did he see Daisy dashing into the street after it. He only heard things: a car, driving fast, faster than usual down the road, a scream, a screech of brakes, a hideous silence. And then he turned and he did see: the car halted, slewed across the street; a man, not much more than a boy, his face distorted with fear, getting out of it; and Daisy, lying horribly, horribly still where it had flung her, facedown, her long, fair hair splayed out, one small hand still clutching her bag of sweets, and her pastel-coloured magazines filled with pictures of smiling little girls fluttering away down the street.

. . .

They were sitting there in Emergency together when Jonathan arrived: Lily and Charlie. Lily hurled herself at him, crying, "Daddy, Daddy, do something, please, please, make her better, make her better."

Charlie was sitting, arms folded, shoulders hunched, his head somehow sunk down into his body. He didn't look up.

A young man with a shaven head was sitting two chairs away from them; he was a greenish colour.

"Where's Mummy?"

"In there," said Lily. She nodded towards a set of double doors. "With Daisy." Her blue eyes were enormous with fear.

"Charlie, what happened?"

"She . . . she ran into the road."

"Into the road. But . . . how, why . . ."

The young man stood up, came over.

"You the dad?"

"Yes."

"I hit her," he said.

"You hit her. With your car?"

"Yeah. I'm . . . well, I'm sorry. She just . . . ran out. I couldn't help it. I really couldn't; I'm sorry. Really sorry. I . . ." He started to sob himself, like a child.

"Yes, all right, all right." Jonathan could feel a steely professional calm taking over; just as well, they couldn't all be hysterical. "Try to pull yourself together. How . . . how bad is she, what sort of injuries?"

"I don't know. I really don't. I didn't . . . well, I didn't go over her, if that's what you mean. Just hit her."

"The ambulance man said internal injuries," said Charlie. His voice was hoarse, odd. Then he suddenly leaned forward and threw up.

"Poor old chap. Don't worry . . ."

A weary-looking woman came over, looked at the pile of vomit, and sighed. "That'll need clearing up."

"Yes, indeed it will. Maybe you could find someone to do it," said Jonathan. "Look . . . Charlie, go into the toilet; have a wash . . . I must go and find Mummy. And Daisy. Lily, you stay here. I— Oh, look, here's Granny. She'll stay with you. Hello, Stella. Could you get Charlie some water? He's just been sick."

"Yes, of course. How . . . how is she; what's happened?"

"I don't know. I only just got here. I'm going to try to find out."

"You can't go in there," the woman on reception called to him as he pushed open the double doors Daisy had indicated. "That's for medical staff only."

"I am medical staff," said Jonathan, and disappeared.

. . .

Laura was standing outside a curtained cubicle, very pale, very calm. She looked at him and almost smiled.

"Hello."

"Hello. How is she?"

"We don't know. Internal injuries, that's all they'll say. A doctor's with her now."

"Is she conscious?"

"No."

"Has she been? Since it happened?"

"Not . . . not really. Well . . . a bit, in and out. Mostly out."

"Oh, God. Jesus. Laura, how—"

"It was my fault. Really."

"Yours?"

"Yes. She wanted to go to the shop, get some sweets. I didn't have time."

"She didn't go alone?"

"No, no. She went with . . . with Charlie."

"Charlie!"

"Yes. Don't look like that; he's taken her before. And Lily. Several times before . . . Well, you know he has, it was you who said he could in the first place."

It was true. He had. It had been a huge adventure . . . for Charlie. They had watched him from the gateway as he had walked carefully and proudly down the road, never taking his eyes off Lily, calling her back if she went so much as five yards ahead of him. They had had to keep ducking out of sight, in case he saw them; when the kids were nearly back Laura and Jonathan both fled into the house, laughing— Laura to the kitchen, Jonathan to his study—and pretended they hadn't even heard them come in, expressing huge surprise when Charlie called out, "We're back."

Different times. Happy, safe times.

"Anyway, she ran into the road; she'd dropped her comic. Some lad was driving up—much too fast, I imagine."

"Yes, he's out there."

"To give him his due, he stayed with her while Charlie came for me, insisted on coming to the hospital; he's all right, really, nice boy, just desperately frightened . . . Has Mummy come . . . ?"

"Yes, she's there. Charlie's just thrown up."

"I'm not surprised. He's beside himself. He was hysterical; I couldn't stop him crying, screaming, almost, at first. Then he went terribly quiet, sort of disappeared into himself . . ."

"So what actually happened? I mean, why did she run into the road?"

"I told you, to get her comic; it was blowing away."

"She knows better than that."

"I know she does. But Charlie said she was all bothered, as he put it; she kept dropping things."

"Chap must have been going a hell of a lick. Or he'd have seen her."

"I know, I know."

They stood there, staring at each other: she wild eyed, ashen, shaking, he frozen faced, shock-still. Unable to reach each other, comfort each other; each filled with the torment of guilt.

"I'm so, so sorry, Jonathan."

"Laura, it wasn't your fault."

"It was, it was . . . I wasn't there . . ."

"Neither was I," he said, his voice hardly audible, "was I?"

He took a deep breath, stood silent for a moment, then: "What does the lad say? The driver?"

"He says he doesn't know what happened. But he said . . . well . . ."

"Yes?"

"He said Charlie came running back to the car. So it sounds like he'd gone ahead. Not . . . well . . . not with Daisy. Not looking after her. But—"

"Oh, Christ."

"Yes. He didn't want to go, Jonathan; he was arguing with me, saying he wanted to go on the computer, do his wretched Warhammer stuff. I . . . well, I made him. I shouldn't have; I should have seen what might happen . . . Oh, God."

She dropped her face into her hands, began to cry.

"Don't," he said, and his voice was odd, cracked, "Don't cry. It's all right. It was an accident. These things happen."

"They don't have to. They—"

The curtains opened abruptly; a doctor came out. Behind him they could see Daisy, very white and still, a nurse standing by her, checking her pulse.

"I'm her father," said Jonathan quickly, "and a doctor. What's the verdict?"

"Well, it's hard to say with any confidence. We need to do a brain scan. See if there's any real damage to the skull. It could be just the violence of the contact, rather than a direct blow; it's the equivalent of a very hard shaking. She's certainly in shock . . . medical shock, that is. Only half-conscious, very distressed. Her blood pressure's very low, which is worrying; it would indicate some internal bleeding. She has some broken ribs, which could cause liver damage. Or indeed lung damage. One of her legs is broken and one arm as well. And I think possibly her pelvis."

"Oh, God," said Laura, "poor little girl."

"We're setting a drip up immediately. Send her down to X-ray. And we're probably going to intubate her; she's having a bit of trouble breathing. I'm getting my colleague, Dr. Armstrong, down to have a look at her; he's the main chest and lung consultant here. You're lucky; he's often in the country on Saturdays, but he's on call today . . ."

"I know him," said Jonathan. "Tony Armstrong. Good bloke," he added to Laura. "Really excellent."

The young doctor looked at him, and he seemed to be having trouble speaking. Finally: "I'm afraid this child is very sick," he said, "very sick indeed."

CHAPTER 49

It was very quiet on the ward; they called it a ward, ICU, standing for Intensive Care Unit, but actually it was a long corridor, outside some doors. Behind each door was someone very ill indeed, in need of the intensive care. Like Daisy. He hadn't been allowed into the room where she was, but he had got a glimpse once when his father came out: it was a mass of machines and screens. She lay on a high bed, her eyes closed; there was a tube in her nose, which his father said was helping her to breathe. Her hair was spread out over the pillow.

Charlie felt so afraid and so sick that he didn't know what to do with himself. Keeping still was awful, because his head just filled up with what he had done; he saw pictures over and over again, and they seemed to go backwards in time, first of Daisy lying in the road, near the car, then Daisy running along behind him, asking him to wait, then Daisy trying to show him pictures in her magazine, then Daisy skipping out of the gate ahead of him, calling, "bye, Mummy."

She'd been fine then: he hadn't done it then, hadn't killed her. He hadn't argued with her, told her she was stupid, hadn't got crosser and crosser with her, hadn't not seen the car, hadn't not seen her running after the page of her magazine; she'd been safe, held in the past, happy, laughing, alive, alive, alive . . .

At this point he felt so terrible he had to get up and walk down the corridor, away from the pictures; he kept going into the lavatory, thinking he was going to be sick, standing there, bending over the bowl, staring down into it, wondering how he was going to get through the next five minutes even, let alone the rest of his life. He hoped he could find some way of dying too, maybe run under a car himself; that would be right, really; that would make it fair, his death traded for hers; he certainly couldn't contemplate years of this, or even many more hours . . .

His grandmother had gone, taking Lily with her; his parents sat on the chairs in the corridor outside the room. They had been told they could have a parents' room for the night, but they'd both refused, said they wanted to be near Daisy.

It was when they'd said that that he'd known: known that it was so bad that she really was likely to die. Until then, he'd realised it had been terribly serious, that she was very, very badly hurt, in danger of dying; but now he could see from their faces, hear from their voices, that it was actually more likely that she would.

They'd told him to go with Lily, but he refused; he didn't actually argue—he didn't seem to be able to say anything anyway; he couldn't remember speaking since it had happened—he just shook his head and then folded his arms and stood there, daring them to make him go against his will.

"Darling," his mother said, "you'll be better with Granny, and the minute we know anything we'll call you, promise, even if it's the middle of the night . . ."

But he'd shaken his head again, furiously, and his father had said quite gently, "Laura, let him be. He's better here."

His father had been terribly nice to him—they both had; he wished they hadn't. He wished they'd both attack him, shout at him, beat him up, injure him really badly so he'd hurt too, so he might need intensive care too, and then when he was all wired up, he could pull the wires all out so he couldn't breathe or live any longer.

He walked back to them now, after another visit to the lavatory; his mother was holding his father's hand, her head on his shoulder. For a minute he thought she was asleep, but then he saw her eyes were staring down at the floor.

"Hello," his father said. "You OK?"

But still he couldn't speak; just nodded and sat down next to his mother.

His father had explained as much as he could to him; Daisy had had a brain scan, and her skull had what was called a hairline crack in it. She also had some damage to her liver, which had caused it to bleed inside her, and that meant giving her some blood. The most worrying thing, it seemed, was that she had some broken ribs and one of them had punctured her lung, which could lead to an infection. "And you see, as she's very poorly, she'll have trouble fighting that. So they're giving her some antibiotics as well."

The other things, the broken leg and arm, sounded like nothing in comparison.

He wanted, more than anything, to say how sorry he was, but somehow he couldn't. It was such a useless thing to say, because it wouldn't do any good; it wouldn't bring Daisy back or make her better, and anyway, it was too easy; saying sorry was what you did when you'd spilt or broken something or not done your homework. Not when you'd broken your sister, broken her so that she could never be mended again.

The man who'd been driving the car was still downstairs; Charlie felt almost sorry for him. He had been driving a bit fast, but it hadn't been all his fault; Daisy had run into the road in front of him. It had been Charlie's fault for not looking after her, not seeing what she was doing, what she might do. She'd been crying in the end—no one knew that except him—he'd heard the tears in her high little voice as she called, "Charlie, please, please wait," and thought how stupid and annoying she was, and how he wasn't going to give in to her, make her more of a spoilt baby than she was already. It was completely his fault.

Suddenly he really couldn't bear it any longer; he managed to speak, to say, "I'm going for a walk, OK?"

His mother said, "Darling, don't go away, or at least let one of us go with you."

But he'd shaken his head said he'd be OK, and his father had said, "Let him go, Laura; he'll be fine. Charlie, don't go into any of the wards; just go down to the front hall, I would, and if you get lost, just ask anyone where ICU is and they'll show you."

He'd nodded and stood up, and walked rather quickly down the corridor, into the lift. It felt better walking away from it; it felt like he could escape.

He went into the main reception area, and then walked down towards A&E. As he went in through the door, he saw the man, Mick, lying down on three chairs that he'd pushed together; he was all right, Mick was, staying all this time.

He thought he was asleep, but he was awake, like his mother, staring at the ceiling; he saw Charlie and jumped, sat up with a rush, said, "What's happened; has she—"

"Nothing's happened," Charlie said. "She's the same. Just the same."

"Oh, shit," he said, and lay down again; and then: "I'm going out for a fag. I'll be just outside the main door if there's any news, OK?"

Charlie nodded.

He sat down on a chair in A&E for a bit, but then the pictures began to come back and he started pacing up and down, between the front door and the lift, and then when they stayed with him there as well, he went to the front door and looked out into the area where the ambulances came in, and beyond that the high lights of the car park, and thought maybe it would be better if he ran; maybe he could get away from them that way; and he ran round the car park, round and round, weaving his way in between the few cars, until he was breathless and sat down on the wall by the road, staring out at it, and wondering if he had the courage to run into a car himself now, get it over. He looked back at the hospital, up at the third floor, at the lighted window where Daisy lay, probably dying, maybe even dead, and then back across the car park and saw his father walking towards him, waving at him, calling his name. This was it then; he'd come to tell him it was over; he'd not just nearly killed her now: he'd actually killed her, and he closed his eyes and waited, waited for the words.

But, "You all right, Charlie?" his father said.

And he shook his head, and finally managed, "What . . . what's happened?"

"Nothing. She's just the same. I came to find you, make sure you were OK."

He didn't deserve this, this kindness; it was wrong, all wrong. Why couldn't they be cruel, as cruel as he'd been . . . ?

And then his father put his hand on his shoulder and something happened, inside his head, and he started to cry, quite quietly, but desperately, and his father said, "Come on, old chap; let's go inside, see if we can find somewhere a bit nice to sit, shall we?"

They couldn't find anywhere exactly nice, but they did find a corner near a radiator, and his father fetched two chairs from down the corridor, and they sat down, and Charlie felt a bit dizzy and leaned forward and put his head on his knees.

"Poor old boy," his father said, and he felt his hand gently rubbing his back.

And he sat up and pushed him away, saying through his tears, "Don't, don't do that; don't be so . . . so nice to me. Why don't you hit me—go on, hit me, hard, please, please . . ."

But then somehow he was in his father's arms, where he had never thought he would be again, and his face was buried in his chest, and he was sobbing and clutching at him desperately, as if he might go away, and then he stopped suddenly and looked up and said, "Dad, it was my fault."

And instead of saying something stupid and trying to comfort him, as if he was some kind of a retard, his father looked back at him very steadily and said, "Yes, I know it was."

The words hit him like a lash; they were shocking, but they helped, made him calmer, stopped his tears.

"Did . . . did Mum tell you?"

"Sort of. Of course, she didn't see—she wasn't there—but Mick told me as well what happened, and I can put two and two together. Not all your fault, Charlie; these things never are. Mummy and I both played our part, but . . . well, in a way, of course it was, yes. I can see why you feel so bad."

"Not even in a way," he said, and the relief of being able to talk about it, to let the pictures out, made him feel just slightly better. "I . . . I wasn't looking after her. That was why it happened. No other reason."

"Go on. Just hang on a minute . . ." He pulled his mobile out of his pocket and looked at it. "No, it's OK. Just wanted to check that Mummy hadn't called me. Sorry." He pressed a key, said, "Hi. I've got him; he's fine; we're downstairs together having a chat. Any news? No, OK. Ring me if you want me."

"I thought you weren't allowed to use mobiles in hospitals," said Charlie.

"You're not." He smiled at him suddenly, a warm, almost cheerful smile. "They'd better not tell me not to, that's all."

"I'm sure they won't."

"I'm sure too. Now . . . want to go on?"

He nodded, settled back on his chair. The words came slowly, had to be forced out. "She was annoying me. Making me cross. I couldn't help it. I know I shouldn't have felt like that, but . . . Anyway, Mum made me take her to the shop, and I wanted to go on the computer, and I was horrible to her, really horrible, telling her she was stupid when she went on about some kitten she wanted . . ." He stopped, remembering Daisy's face as she talked about the kitten, so serious, so anxious to discuss the kitten's possible name; she'd been all right then, fine . . . He gulped, swallowed some tears.

"It was on the way back. I just walked ahead, faster and faster; she was dropping things, Dad, and I wouldn't help, wouldn't wait. I knew she was getting upset; you know how she does."

"Yes, I do. Go on."

"Well, that was it. I was walking farther and farther ahead, and she called to me to wait, to help her, said the cover had come off her comic, and I still walked on, and then . . . then I heard it. Heard the car . . ."

"You didn't see it?"

"No, and I don't know why, because it all happened really slowly . . ."

"Accidents do. Or seem to."

"I just heard the brakes and I heard her scream and I turned round then and . . . there she was. On the road. Like a . . . a . . ." *Dead person,* he had been going to say, and he couldn't, and then he started crying harder again, and hurled himself at his father, clutching at him, and saying, "I'm sorry, Dad, I'm so, so sorry," over and over again.

Finally he stopped, looked up at him, and waited. Waited for the words, the shocked, shocking, angry words. Or worse, the stupid, rubbish words, saying he couldn't have helped it. They didn't come. Nothing came. Just a silence. His father was staring in front of him, and his eyes were sadder than Charlie had ever seen them; and then finally he looked at him and said, "Charlie, we all make mistakes.

Some don't matter very much; some are terrible. Terrible mistakes that make other people very unhappy. Mistakes we'd give anything, anything at all, to change. To take back. But . . . we can't. I made one, as you know. You've made one. Both serious mistakes that can't be unmade. And that's the thing. They are unchangeable. They won't go away, whatever you do. So . . . the only thing to do is to live with them. Do the best you can. You can't put them right. But you can put them behind you. Which isn't easy, but . . . well, it isn't easy."

He was silent again; Charlie sat looking at him, his sobs quieted, his feelings oddly quieter too. After a while, Jonathan put his arm round him, pulled him closer; Charlie relaxed against him, rested his head on his chest.

And then Jonathan said, "I love you, Charlie. Very much."

And after quite a long time, Charlie heard his own voice, very quiet, almost as if it didn't belong to him: "I love you too, Dad."

. . .

"Oh, God. That's so awful."

"What?" Sylvie looked up from the TV; Abi was sitting at the table, staring at the newspaper, her face very white.

"It's . . . Oh, God, how horrible. I . . . Sylvie, look at this. Look."

Sylvie looked: a small paragraph, next to an item about yet another politician caught taking bribes: "Hero Doctor's Child in Coma," it was headed. "Daisy Gilliatt, seven-year-old daughter of top gynaecologist Jonathan Gilliatt, dubbed the hero of the M4 crash last August, has been knocked down by a car and is in intensive care. Her parents and her elder brother were at her bedside last night. No one from the hospital was available for comment. Our medical correspondent writes . . ."

"God," said Sylvie, "how sad."

"I don't know what to do, Sylvie."

"What do you mean? What could you do?"

"Like I said, I don't know. But I ought to do something, don't you think?"

"No. Like what?"

"Oh . . . I don't know. Call him, maybe, send some flowers to the mother . . ."

"Abi, are you out of your head? Do you really think that poor woman would feel any better if she got some flowers from you? I don't want to be offensive, but it'd probably make her feel much worse."

"Yeah, yeah, I s'pose so. You're right. I just feel . . . well, I don't know. I met those kids, you know . . ."

"Yes, I know. And I can see why you're upset. But I really don't think you can do anything."

"No. No, maybe not."

"Because he really is not going to feel better if he hears from you."

"No. No, you're right. Oh, shit, Sylvie, where is this thing going to end?"

"What do you mean?"

"I mean it just won't let me go. The crash."

"I can't see what the poor kid getting run over has got to do with the crash. Or you, if that's what you're thinking."

"Well . . . maybe it has. Maybe finding out about me stopped the mother from looking after them properly. Don't look at me like that, Sylvie; it's possible."

"Of course it's not possible. Mothers aren't like that. They function whatever. My auntie Cath didn't start letting her kids run around doing what they liked when my uncle ran off with that totty from his firm. She got harder on them, if anything. Stop beating yourself up, Abi."

"Yeah, OK, I'll try. But . . ."

"Abi!"

"Sorry. Look, we've got a committee meeting this afternoon here; you want to go out, or what?"

"No, I'll stay, if you don't mind. I won't get in the way. And I always enjoy the sexy farmer."

"Yeah, well. Anyway, get in the way as much as you like. You might have some ideas. We need them. Oh, shit, and it's the inquest in a fortnight. S'pose the kid . . . well, doesn't get any better—how will Jonathan cope with that?"

Sylvie sighed. "I don't know, Abi. But it's not your problem, honestly. Want a croissant?"

. . .

"It's the first forty-eight hours that are crucial." The paediatrician looked at Jonathan. "She gets through that, then we have reason for optimism."

"And . . . now? It's twenty-four. How's she doing?"

"Well . . . she's holding her own. The BP's gone up, which is good. She's definitely coming out of it a bit. She's woken up several times this morning, sister tells me. Which is excellent. Those fractures are nothing. Apart from the fact that her lung's been punctured. Biggest worry now, to be honest, is infection. She's running a bit of a fever."

"What is it?"

"Oh . . . only thirty-nine."

He spoke overcasually; Jonathan winced.

"Thirty-nine is high."

"Ish."

"No, it's high. She's still on the antibiotics, isn't she?"

"Of course. Look . . . have you been in to see her this morning?"

"Yes, of course."

Well, how does she look to you?"

"Pretty bad," said Jonathan, "to be honest."

. . .

Laura stood, watching her daughter. Her pretty, sweet, merry-hearted little daughter. Reduced to something devoid of personality, a still, white ghost, most of her bodily functions taken over by machines. It was all very well for the doctors to keep saying her vital signs were good, that the concussion was serious but far from fatal, that a few broken limbs were of no great importance. The fact remained that she was extremely badly hurt, her small, slender body knocked about by half a ton of moving metal, her small skull cracked, one of her lungs ruptured, a mounting fever invading her. They were talking now of packing her in ice; Laura knew what that meant. It meant the fever was very serious, very high. She was in pain, too, restless, turning her head constantly; her hair had been getting tangled, and Laura had asked if she might tie it back somehow, but it was difficult; Daisy seemed aware that something was bothering her, tried to push her away with her good arm.

More than anything Laura wanted to hold her, hold her safe, as she had all through all her small troubles, her minor childish illnesses and the more major recent hurts, to be able to say, "There, it's all right, Mummy's here, Mummy will look after you, Mummy loves you." But she couldn't look after her, however much she loved her; her efforts were of absolutely no value; indeed if she held her now, she would die. The only things that could help her were the machines, cold, unfeeling, efficient machines, helping her breathe, hydrating her, dulling her pain, telling them when her pulse rose, her blood pressure dropped.

She hated the machines, even while she knew she must be grateful to them. She wanted Daisy to be able to tell her that she hurt, that she was hot, that she felt sick; she didn't want her function as a mother negated, didn't want to be told that all she must do was stand back, be quiet, wait, not interfere. It was wrong, against the natural order of things: and yet she knew that without the machines, and without the skills of the doctors and the awesome power of the drugs, Daisy would most certainly have died by now.

· · ·

Jonathan came in, stood watching Daisy with her, put his arm round her.

"All right?"

"Yes. I'm all right. Where's Charlie?"

"He's asleep in the parents' room. I mustn't be long; I promised I'd be there when he woke up."

"How is he?"

"Oh . . . you know. Poor little boy."

Jonathan was being amazing: not just sympathetic, not just supportive, but calm, positive, absolutely unreproachful. She had said she was sorry, that she knew she shouldn't have sent Daisy out with Charlie, and he'd said nonsense, that she was right, they'd done it countless times, that children couldn't be wrapped in cotton wool . . . "But they should be," she'd cried, tears coming suddenly. "We should wrap them in cotton wool; that's exactly what we ought to do; then they'd be safe, stay safe . . ."

"And grow up helpless, unable to look after themselves."

"They'd grow up, at least," she'd said, and he was powerless to answer that.

"How's Lily?" she asked then.

"She's all right. Your mother's being so good. She said should she bring her over, did I want her to fetch Charlie, should she bring some food in, all sorts of wonderful things . . ."

"Should she bring Lily? Do you think?"

"No," he said, "not unless she really wants to come. And your mother said she was better at home with her. They're watching movies. Of course, if—"

"Don't. Don't say it."

She knew what he meant. If Daisy got worse, if they had to say good-bye, then Lily must be there too.

· · ·

"Right. Well, I think that's about it. Well done, everybody."

God, this was an effort. It was hard to think the wretched festival mattered. While that poor little girl . . .

"We'll go firm on the date then?"

"Yup. Sure. And the dates for the play-offs. No news on a sponsor, I s'pose, Fred?"

"Nope. Sorry. They like higher-profile causes, most of them."

"Surely not local ones?"

"Well . . . maybe."

"Fred, haven't you tried locally at all? Georgia?"

"Not . . . not really."

"Well, why not, for fuck's sake? Jesus, I thought you were going to take all that off us. I suppose I'll have to do it, like I do everything else."

"Abi . . ." said Georgia, "I'm sure Fred's doing his best; we all are. But everyone's busy . . ."

"You're not."

"Well, thanks for that. I am, actually—got three auditions this week. Look, I know this was all my idea, but it seems to be getting everyone down; it's running away with us. Maybe we should rethink—"

"No," said Abi, "sorry, I shouldn't have lost it. Sorry, Fred."

"That's OK. I should have done more; you're right."

"No, you've got a lot going on. And you're not even personally involved like the rest of us. I'll take that over."

"Well . . . if you can pull a few things out of the bag . . ."

"Sure."

"I might go then, if that's all right. Got a lot going on at home this weekend."

"Sure. Sorry again, I'm . . . well, I'm a bit worried about something."

"I'll see you out," said Sylvie, standing up. "Georgia, William, want a coffee or anything?"

"I should go too," said Georgia. "Promised my mum I'd be back for this evening. Thanks, everyone, so much. Fred, wait for me."

She was going to apologise to him again, on her behalf, Abi thought; perversely, it annoyed her.

"I'll have a coffee, please, Sylvie," said William, smiling at her. He quite clearly fancied her, Abi thought. And she played up to it. Bit annoying.

"I'll have some wine, Sylvie, please," she said tartly. "Oh, dear." She looked at William. "I'm a prize cow, aren't I?"

"I don't think you'd get many prizes," he said. "Not at the shows I go to."

"Don't joke. I am. I shouldn't have said that to Fred."

"Maybe not. What are you worried about?"

"Oh . . . doesn't matter." Of all the things William wouldn't want to hear about, or be reminded of, it was the Gilliatt family.

"It obviously does. Come on, Abi, tell me."

"I . . . That is . . . Oh, God, William, Jonathan Gilliatt's little girl's been run over. She's in the hospital. In intensive care."

"That's very sad."

"I know. It's worse than sad. It's terrible. They don't deserve that, do they?"

"Well . . . no. Life isn't about what you deserve, though, is it? Not always." There was a pause; then he said, obviously with difficulty, "How . . . how do you know?"

Jesus, she thought, *fuck, he thinks I'm still in touch with Jonathan. How awful is that; he mustn't, no, no . . .*

"I read it in the paper," she said, "this morning." She looked at him; his large brown eyes were thoughtful, doubtful even. "William, I swear to you, I have not spoken to Jonathan, not since that night. You really can't think that."

"No. No, of course not. No."

But he didn't sound completely sure.

"Look . . ." she said, reaching for the paper, "it's here. See? William, please believe me."

"I . . . do," he said, "yes, of course I do. Well . . . this was yesterday's news. How is she today?"

"I don't know," she said. "How could I?"

"You could ring the hospital."

"William, it doesn't say what hospital she's in even. And anyway, they wouldn't tell me; they never do unless you're family."

"No, no, I suppose not."

Shock at his clearly still not quite trusting her, combined with anxiety and guilt, suddenly got the better of her, and she started to cry.

"I feel so bad about it," she said, "so bad."

"But why?"

"Why? Because maybe what I did—having the affair with Jonathan, going to the house that night—maybe that contributed in some way. I don't know. Maybe the little girl was upset, maybe her mother was upset, maybe she wasn't looking after her properly . . ."

"Abi, Abi," he said, and he came round the table to where she was sitting, put his arm rather awkwardly round her shoulders. "You can't go on blaming yourself for what you might or might not have done to that family. It's a while ago now . . ."

"Yes, I know, I know," she said, looking up, trying to smile, wiping her nose on the back of her hand. Sylvie had come in with the drinks, and stood looking awkward.

"Thanks," he said, withdrawing his arm. "Here, Abi, have a hankie."

"No, it's OK," she said. "I've got some tissues in the kitchen; excuse me . . ."

"It's all right," he said, grinning suddenly. "It hasn't been up some cow's bottom or anything, if that's what you think. Clean out of my drawer when I left. Where my mother put it."

"Your mother spoils you, obviously," said Sylvie. "Abs, I'm off now. See you later."

"OK. Cheers. William," she said when the door had shut, "you don't really think I'm still in touch with Jonathan, do you?"

"No," he said, and this time he managed to smile back. "No, I suppose not. But I can't help wondering . . . well, you know, sometimes . . ."

"William, I'm not. I swear to you. I still hate him. I just . . . well, I feel bad for the little girl. And Laura."

"Of course. Right . . . well, I'd better go. Milking to do. And the ewes' feeding to sort out."

"The ewes?"

"Yes. About this time of year we scan them. See how many lambs they're having."

"You scan them?"

"Yup."

"What, like you scan pregnant women?"

"Well . . . pretty much. Of course, they don't lie on their backs, but . . ."

"And then what?"

"Well, then we separate out the ones who are having triplets and twins from the singletons."

"Why?"

"Well, to adjust their feeds. So that the ones having more lambs get more food."

"How clever."

"Not really. Just common sense."

"I s'pose so. Well, thanks, William. Thanks for coming. It's such a long way."

. . .

A long way, William thought, starting up the truck. If only she knew.

. . .

"Oh, my God. Abi, are you mental or what?"

"What do you mean?"

"William. God, he's well fit, isn't he?"

"Yeah, OK. What about him?"

"He's still nuts about you. Obviously."

"Sylvie, don't be stupid. He never says or does anything."

"I don't know what's happened to you, Abi. You've got so thick. He might not do anything, but he wants to. Blimey. It shows, all right."

"D'you think so?"

"Yeah, course. I mean, he had his arm round you last night, for God's sake."

"Because I was crying. That's all."

"Why were you crying?"

"Oh . . . about that little girl."

"Must have been nice for William to have you crying over that lot."

"What do you mean?"

"Well, I don't suppose he likes thinking about him too much. About you and him, that is."

"No," said Abi slowly, remembering William's hurt face, "no, I don't think he does. But that doesn't mean he . . . well, he still . . . still fancies me."

"Well, it would make it worse," said Sylvie, "make him mind worse. Don't you think?"

"S'pose so. Yeah. Oh, shit. It's all such a mess. Still."

. . .

"Mr. Gilliatt! Could you come in, please? Quickly."

This was it. She was dying. Or she'd died.

He went in, very quietly, shut the door behind him. She was lying very still, apparently sleeping. Her face was pale, her expression very peaceful. Surely, surely she hadn't . . . not without him saying good-bye, sending her on her way with his love. His special love. It was special. She was his baby; he still thought of her as three or four; it made her—used to make her—cross. "I'm not a baby," she used to say indignantly. "Don't treat me like one. I'm seven." She used to say; she used to say . . .

And now she'd never be eight, never grow up, never change, always stay thus in his memory, Daisy, whom he'd loved so much, who loved him so much . . . "*My* daddy," she used to say, putting the emphasis on the *my*. "My special daddy."

Who'd also, just by the way, betrayed her; her and her sister and her brother and her mother . . . How could he have done that: failed them all, shattered their security, broken the faith?

"Oh, God," he said, and for the first time since it had happened, his calm broke; he felt the tears, hot, fierce tears, filling his eyes, a sob rising in his throat. He stepped forward, took her hand—no longer hot, cool even, smoothed back her hair . . .

"Mr. Gilliatt, she's—"

"Yes, yes, I know . . ." he said, and felt a tear drop onto their hands, their two joined hands. It would never be in his again, that hand, that small, trusting hand, letting him lead her, running with her, skipping with her—she loved him to skip; it made her giggle. He would haul her off the ground as he took great bounds, laughing too . . . "I know. I understand."

"No, you don't know. She's better. Really, she is. Her temperature's down; she's peaceful. I'm just going to call Dr. Armstrong to discuss removing the tube."

"Oh, God. Dear God. I . . ." And then he really started to weep, bent over Daisy, kissed her cheek and then her hand, over and over again, and then said, "Stay there, my darling," as if she could do anything else, and went out to find Laura and Charlie, who were in the parents' room.

. . .

Laura looked up as he went in, saw the tears streaming down his face, and just for a moment thought as he had, what he had; and then saw that he was smiling, laughing even, as he cried, and she said only, "Is she?"

And he said, "Yes, yes, she's better; she's going to be all right; her temperature's right down. Charlie, come here—give me a hug; your sister's better; she's going to be fine." And they stood there, their arms around one another, the three of them, laughing and crying, bound together not only physically but by their relief and joy and their love of the small, precious being they had thought was lost to them forever and who, by some miracle worked by either God or science, or even her small, determined self, and quite possibly all three, had been given back safely to them once more.

CHAPTER 50

Barney was horribly depressed. He might have fallen out of love with Amanda, but he missed her, missed her sweetness and her thoughtfulness, the way she cared for him, the sense of order she had created in their lives. She was so efficient; she ran the house and their life so well, and she was so happy always, so optimistic, distracting him when he was stressed about work, always ready with some new plan or idea for a holiday or a weekend or a dinner party.

He had moved out of the house and into a flat. His life seemed to be disintegrating into a dismal chaos. He didn't want to see anyone; he couldn't be bothered to cook for himself or even get his laundry organised; he spent a fortune on new shirts, as the dirty ones piled up in the bathroom and washing them seemed more difficult than simply buying a whole lot more. It wasn't just Amanda, of course; it was Toby—he had lost both of them, both his best friends; nobody else seemed worth spending time on. It involved too many explanations, too much effort. He just drifted along aimlessly, working absurdly long hours . . . and dreading the inquest. He'd be under oath and therefore surely required to recount what happened over the tyre, and worse, he would obviously have to face Toby across the court. However disillusioned he was about Toby, he had no wish to see his reputation blackened, and possibly for him to face legal redress.

It wasn't the best of times . . .

He spent a lot of time now wondering what Emma was doing.

Back with the boyfriend, maybe, which quite hurt. Or with someone new, which hurt more; or with no one at all, which hurt more than anything. Of course, she didn't know that it was over with Amanda; but somehow, some odd sense of pride kept him from telling her. She had finished it; she had decided it wasn't to be, that she didn't want to wait until Amanda could cope with her engagement being broken off—and he could hardly blame her; it did slightly cast her in the role of understudy—and she had obviously decided she couldn't cope with any of it. What price love then? Barney thought, remembering those fierce few weeks when the world had changed and him with it: when he had looked at a relationship he had thought was forever and found it wanting, and found another that had seemed not to want for anything at all.

. . .

Alex had been called as a witness at the inquest; he and Linda had settled into an uneasy peace, or, as Alex called it, an easy war. Their relationship was never going to be comfortable; they continued to argue, to compete, to fight and reunite, and to enjoy each other physically and emotionally with a passion that still half surprised them. Their latest battleground was where they would live: they had agreed that they wanted to live together; that had been the easy part. Where was proving impossible. Clearly Linda was not going to settle down in Swindon, nor Alex move to NW1. Various compromises like Windsor, Beaconsfield, and even Ealing had been scrutinised and dismissed as too suburban, too far out, and just too horrible. Currently he was looking at Gloucestershire and Wiltshire cottages where they could weekend together, at least; it was a compromise, and like all compromises provided the worst as well as the best of both worlds.

Linda was going to the inquest too, partly as support for Alex, which he said was very nice but hardly essential—he'd attended thousands of the bloody things—but mainly as support for Georgia. Georgia was absolutely terrified at having the whole thing relived, and her own behaviour—and what she saw as her cowardice—publicly recorded. She dreamt about it night after night, couldn't eat, was irritable and tearful. None of which, as Linda remarked to Alex, was unusual.

The only good thing was that she had got a part in another production. It wasn't quite such a good one—in fact, nothing probably ever would be again, she thought, so perfect for her—but it was pretty nice, a comedy about a threesome, two girls and a boy, living together supposedly platonically; both the girls were secretly in love with the boy, and he was meanwhile hopelessly—and also secretly—in love with someone else entirely.

"It's a marvellous script," Linda said to Georgia, "shades of Noel Coward. You're a lucky girl."

It wasn't until she turned up for a preproduction meeting that she discovered the first assistant director was Merlin Gerard . . .

. . .

"Georgia, hi. Lovely to see you. And wonderful to be working with you again."

"Yes. Yes, it's great." Thinking, thank God, thank God she had never let him know how hurt she'd been, how deceived she'd felt. "Er . . . how's Ticky?"

"She's great, thanks. Yeah. Gone back to New York, of course."

"Of course."

"Want to come for a drink tonight?"

"I'm sorry, Merlin, I can't. Not tonight. Another time, maybe." She'd even managed to smile at him.

She'd never felt more proud of herself than she had at that moment.

. . .

"You total star," Lila said, when she told her. Lila had become just about her best friend. They spent a lot of time together, shopping, going to the cinema, and to clubs when they could afford it, sometimes jazz clubs—Lila and Anna had introduced Georgia to jazz, and she was slightly surprised by how much she loved it—but mostly just talking, often late into the night.

"Yeah, I was pretty pleased with myself. He looked pretty . . . pretty surprised."

"Good. He needs to be. And . . . did you still fancy him?"

"Oh, yes. Completely," said Georgia rather sadly.

. . .

Anna had agreed—rather nervously, but with great delight—that she and Lila would play a set at the festival. Abi had said she thought they should have some jazz, and Georgia—who was still a little in awe of Abi—said rather tentatively that she knew someone who had played jazz in quite a big way. Abi had never heard of Sim Foster, but she mentioned his name to a jazz enthusiast at work and had been astonished at his reaction.

"My God, Abi, he was one of the greats, you know. Some of his early stuff, absolute classics. And she was fantastic too, great voice. Anyone who knows anything about jazz'd give a lot to hear her. Even without him. They were an absolute legend."

Abi went back rather humbly to Georgia and told her to ask the legend if she'd be kind enough to consider playing at the festival.

She was totally dreading the inquest; she shrank from having her relationship with Jonathan brought out in court, together with the fact that she had lied when she had first given evidence. She couldn't imagine what the outcome might be; in her darkest hours, she saw herself in jail, or at best with a criminal record.

William had tried rather cursorily to reassure her once, but after that refused to discuss the whole thing. William just wanted it over: for more reasons than one. The thought of being in the same courtroom as Jonathan Gilliatt was not appealing.

. . .

Daisy was home now, frail and very thin, moving around with great difficulty but equal determination; fortunately it was her left leg but her right arm that were broken, so she could use a crutch to hobble from room to room. The family room had been turned into a bedroom for her, and her toys installed, so that she didn't have to cope with the stairs.

With the resilience of children, she seemed fairly unaffected by her trauma emotionally: no nightmares, no display of anxiety. The thing that most worried her was that she had broken the rules, done what was expressly forbidden, and she said over and over again that she was very sorry she had run into the road, and that she would never do such a thing again; Laura had privately resolved that Daisy would never run anywhere unaccompanied again, or not for a very long time.

The person perhaps most adversely affected by the whole thing was Lily, whose pretty little nose had been put distinctly out of joint by all the attention lavished on her sister. Initially delighted when Daisy was pronounced out of danger, and especially when she was allowed home, she now spent a large part of every day quarrelling with her, and demanding that the bounty of new toys pouring into Daisy's possession, supplied not only by her parents and grandparents, but school friends and neighbours, be replicated in her own, and bursting into hysterical tears when she was told they would not.

Charlie, who appeared in some ways to have become at least five years older than he had been before the accident, was alternately to be found telling her to shut up and to be glad she still had a sister to fight with, and patiently playing games with one or the other of them. He had begged not to have to go back to school until Daisy was completely well; after two weeks of acting the perfect brother he suddenly announced that even school was preferable. Laura and Jonathan, who had been a little worried by his newly saintly persona, were secretly relieved.

Jonathan had moved back home. Charlie had begged him to, and so had the girls; Laura could hardly refuse. She didn't exactly want to refuse. But even given the surge of positive emotion towards him that she had experienced in the hospital, she wasn't sure that she was remotely ready to start living with him again. Or indeed if she ever would be. A slow, but savage surge of anger and resentment was filling her once more; in the adrenaline crash after Daisy's initial recovery, it shocked her. She had thought, felt indeed, that if Daisy was given back to her, she would never mind anything again. She was horrified to discover that she still minded about Jonathan and Abi Scott very much indeed.

Once the desperate, clawing fear had subsided, once they had gone home, properly home, faced with the long, long days of sitting at Daisy's bedside, the exhaustion of coping with her querulous demands, her boredom, and her pain, then it began. She would look at him over the table as he laughed and joked with Charlie, teased Lily, as he sat by Daisy reading to her, as he helped her with things like shopping and the school run, for he had taken compassionate leave, would watch him being the perfect husband and the perfect father once more and at times she hated him. And was shocked at herself for it.

She struggled to fight it; she reminded herself constantly of his courage and his tenderness in the dreadful days at the hospital, when Daisy had swung so close to death; she told herself that more than ever now he had earned her generosity and her forgiveness . . . but she was still haunted by the betrayal, the easy lies that he had shown himself to be capable of, and the way he had allowed Abi Scott to cut into the heart of their marriage.

And the thought of sleeping with him was abhorrent; she could not imagine it ever again. There would be a third person in their bed forevermore now, and no longer a shadowy presence, a vague threat, but one she had seen, heard, smelt—she would never forget that rich, cloying perfume—and watched as she sashayed across the room and kissed her husband's mouth.

Jonathan had not suggested that he join her in their bed; he continued to sleep in the spare room without comment, and indeed as if he assumed it was the proper place for him; but one night, quite late, after they had been reading in the drawing room and she said she was tired and thought she would go to bed, he had looked at her and smiled and said, "Do, darling. You look tired. Shall I make you a nightcap?"

He had always done that in the old days, when she was particularly exhausted, brought her a hot toddy; she hardly ever drank spirits, but she loved that; the effect of the whisky in the hot milk never failed to make her sleep. But for some reason tonight, she found the thought of it unbearable, that he was trying to deny the present, to work back into the past, when he had been a source of comfort, not pain, of reassurance, not fear, and she stood up and said, "No, thank you, I can do that for myself," and she could hear the coldness, the rejection in her own voice.

His eyes as he looked at her then were surprised, hurt even. "All right, darling," he said, "but the offer's there."

And suddenly, it happened; she could hold it back no longer, the force of her rage. "Jonathan, don't call me darling, please," was all she said, but her tone was ugly, almost savage, and he could not but react.

"I'm sorry," he said, and his voice in its turn was ice-cold, heavy with anger. "I didn't realise you still felt so strongly against me."

"Is that so?" she said. "You didn't realise? What did you think, then? That I had forgotten about . . . about what you did, your lies, how you betrayed me, betrayed us all?"

"No," he said, "of course not. But I thought . . . perhaps . . . we had moved on. That you could at least start to . . . to accept it, if not forgive."

"Jonathan, how could you even begin to think that? Accept it, you say! Accept the fact that you preferred her to me . . ."

"I did not prefer her," he said wearily. "No comparison came into it. She was . . . well, she was what she was. Nothing to do with you. I love you . . ."

"Oh, please! You love me! So much that you fucked someone else. Not just once—I could endure that—but many times. And not just fucked her—slept with her, really slept with her, lay with her all night, woke up with her beside you. Lied and lied to me so that you could. How could you do that, Jonathan; how could you want to do that?"

"I . . . don't know," he said, "I really don't know. It was some kind of . . . madness. I know, all erring husbands say that, but it's true; it was as if I became someone else. I didn't stop loving you, Laura; I didn't love you any less. It was greed, a grab at something else that I knew I shouldn't have. I can't expect you to understand, but—"

"No," she said, "I don't understand. Of course I don't. Well, I can see that you would want her, but the fact is, you couldn't want her without rejecting me. That's how I see it, a rejection of me, of what I could do for you, what I could offer. It makes me feel so . . . so lacking."

"Lacking in what?" he said, and he looked so bewildered she almost smiled.

"In myself, Jonathan. I know . . ." She faltered, took a breath, started again. "I know I'm not particularly . . . sexy. I know that very well. I mean, I like sex, of course . . ."

"And why do you say 'of course'?" he said. "It's not compulsory, you know, liking it."

"What do you mean?" she said, staring at him in astonishment. "Of course it is; it's part of a marriage, part of loving someone."

"And did you really see it as part of loving me?"

"Of course I did"—and she was shouting now—"of course I saw it as that. It was so precious to me; it was ours, and no one else's, what we shared, only between us. Now it's not anymore; it's hers; she's taken it, or rather you've given it; it's gone; it's gone forever and no one can bring it back."

He was absolutely silent, looking at her with a dreadful sadness in his eyes; then he said, "Well, it seems we are done for, then. We can't be as we were again, can we?"

"No," she said, "no, we can't. Never. Never."

"Well . . . in that case, maybe I should go again. But I want to say a few things first. That really need saying. I did love you. So very, very much. I do love you very, very much. You are the centre of my life and the centre of our family. I can't contemplate life without you, Laura. Oh, that's not some idle suicidal threat; it's true. Of course I'd go on living, but I'd be changed. I'd be lost. I'd be pathetic, useless, dysfunctional."

"Don't be ridiculous. You'd be just fine. Still the successful, attractive, wonderful Jonathan Gilliatt."

"Laura, I wouldn't. I'm only those things because I have you. I'd be anxious; I'd lose confidence, judgment. God in heaven, that happened even when I was living away for those few weeks. I dithered, I took second opinions, I did what others said instead of what I knew was right, I didn't even know what was right anymore. I made one appalling mistake—I didn't tell you about it, and you wouldn't have cared, I should think, given the circumstances—but I missed a cord presentation . . . You know what that is?"

"The baby's head pressing on the cord?"

"Exactly. How often I must have bored you with these technical details. Anyway, the baby nearly died; could so well have been brain damaged. And I missed it, because I was so wretched, so . . . so lost. And deservedly so, no doubt you would say. But . . . well, that is how dependent on you I am. I'm nothing without you, Laura, nothing at all."

She was silent.

"I'm talking professionally, of course, but it extends to everything. The charming, attractive Jonathan Gilliatt, as you call him, is a pathetically different chap on his own . . ."

"Jonathan, this is all very touching, but if I'm so important to you, why risk losing me? Why start an affair with someone else? It doesn't quite add up. Sorry."

"I know that. Of course I do. It was insanity. It was dangerous insanity. And I had never done anything like it before, and I never would again. And I know you don't believe me when I tell you it was over, that I'd finished with her that day, but it's true. But . . . haven't you ever, in your perfectly controlled, beautifully behaved life, Laura, done anything remotely wrong? Or dangerous? Haven't you ever been tempted to kick over the traces? Oh, not to have an affair, but . . . I don't know, spend too much and lie to me about it, or take a day off from cooking and buy a ready meal for the children, or go back to bed or spend the day with your girlfriends and not do any work, or not help with the homework, or . . ."

"No," she said, after a few moments' thought, "no, I haven't."

"Well, then," he said, and he almost smiled, "there you have it, perhaps."

"What do you mean?"

"I mean, it's quite . . . tough being married to you."

"Jonathan, I devote my entire life to you. To doing what you want, going where you want me to be. It's me it's tough for, I'd say. Not you."

"No," he said. "Well, it may be. But that's why—I think—I had this affair with Abi Scott. I'm trying to be honest now. Because she was bad quite a lot of the time. She wasn't perfect. She was certainly less perfect than me. She's greedy and amoral and she tells lies, all the time; I didn't have to live up to her. And I have to say, I treated her very badly."

"Oh, my heart bleeds for her. I'm so sorry."

"I am sorry . . . actually. I should have shown her some consideration, after the crash. It was a trauma for her, as well, a dreadful one. And what did I do? I was so shit scared of you finding out about her that I threatened her . . ."

"You what?" She was shocked by that.

"I threatened her. I told her if the didn't go along with my story that she was a work colleague, I'd tell the police about her drug habit. Not nice behaviour."

"No. Not really. But . . ."

"But it was for you. I was so terrified of you finding out—not because you'd be angry, which you'd have every right to be, but because you'd be desperately hurt—that I bullied her. Harassed her ruthlessly. The irony is that if I'd been a bit nicer to her, she probably wouldn't have turned up here that night. At my party. I was a complete shit. I am a complete shit. Oh, God . . ."

He looked at her, and she could see tears in his eyes. He brushed them away.

"But, Jonathan," she said, "I can't be what I'm not. I'm me. I can't start being lazy or extravagant, or neglecting the children. Just so that you don't have to live up to me, as you put it. It's crazy; you're talking rubbish. Self-indulgent rubbish."

"It may be self-indulgent," he said, "but it isn't rubbish. Everyone's so fucking envious of me. Or was. 'Lucky chap,' they used to say, 'being married to Laura; wish my wife was more like Laura.' God, Mark never stopped going on about it, and how Serena never let him get away with anything, how wonderful you were . . . You remember that song, that music hall song, 'She's Only a Bird in a Gilded Cage'? I felt like a bird in a gilded cage, and I flew out of it . . . just once, once for the hell of it. Or so I thought. Fate trapped me, shut the door behind me, and I'll never be back in it now, and it serves me right."

She said nothing, trying to make sense of what he was saying.

He stood up now, in front of her, staring down into her eyes. "I guess that's it by way of explanation. I have never regretted anything more. I would give everything I have—everything except you and the children—to alter it. But I can't. As I said to Charlie in the hospital, you have to live with what you've done. There's no alternative. It's hardly a justification, I know, but—"

"No," she said, "it isn't."

"Well, that's my swan song. I'll go, Laura. Don't worry. Or if you'd prefer it, I'll stay here, for the sake of the children, carry on pretending. I'm not sure they could face losing me again. That's not meant to be emotional blackmail; it's a fact. But I won't ask anything of you, anything at all. And when they're older, maybe we can get divorced. It's up to you. Whatever you want. It's the least I can do for you. To make amends. I only ask one thing: that you try to believe how much I love you."

"I'll try," she said after a very long time. "I really will try. And . . . don't go, Jonathan. You're right. The children couldn't bear it."

She wasn't sure she would be able to bear it herself. But she really wasn't ready to say that.

CHAPTER 51

Michael Andrews always said the most important quality a coroner should possess was courtesy. And indeed, he had never come across one who didn't. It was important for all concerned: for the relatives of the deceased, of course, still grieving, often disappointed that there was to be no criminal trial, so that they might find retribution for the death of their loved ones, and at least anxious to establish the truth; for the police who had worked so hard to establish that truth and whose evidence, often rather ponderous, must be heard in full, that the hard work might be justified; for the witnesses, often distressed themselves, always nervous; and of course for the coroner's office staff, so at pains to be courteous themselves, to put people at ease, to ensure that proceedings ran smoothly and as swiftly as possible.

The inquest he was to conduct the following week, on the people who had died in the M4 crash the previous August, would be long, possibly running over two days. There were three deceased, and many witnesses; the crash had been complex and high-profile. It would test his skills considerably, and he would need to prepare for it with great care.

Since it was to be so large, and with so many attendees, it was to be held in the council chambers at the county court, rather than in one of the committee rooms; in a way people preferred that; they felt the deaths of the loved ones was being considered a matter of some importance, accorded proper dignity. The other thing about inquests, of course, was that they differed from criminal enquiries in that all the witnesses heard all the evidence. It gave a sense of greater openness and fairness, and it meant those involved could more easily see any concerns laid properly to rest.

There would be lawyers present, of course, because of insurance issues, and several doctors. One of the doctors, Dr. Jonathan Gilliatt, would be giving evidence on two counts: his own involvement in the crash, and his professional observations of the injured and deceased.

It would be wrong, Michael Andrews supposed, to say he was looking forward to the inquest—it would be both gruelling and sad— but it did promise to be what he privately called a yardstick, one by which he would judge and compare others.

His wife, Susan, was prepared for a somewhat solitary weekend.

. . .

"All rise."

Michael Andrews liked this moment, as he walked into the court: not from any delusions of grandeur, but because it was an acknowledgement of his authority and through him the court's.

He sat in the council chamber on a high dais, flanked by his clerk and coroner's officer. The public sat before him, the seats ranged amphitheatre style, and banking up towards the back of the chamber; the witness table—also slightly raised and complete with microphone and Bible—was to his left.

He began as he always did: by welcoming everyone, by explaining the purpose of the inquest. "We are here to answer four questions: who the deceased were, and when, where, and how they came to their deaths. It is not to establish any blame, and no charges will be brought as a result." He paused. "Three of the four answers are straightforward. The fourth, establishing by what means death arose, is the main purpose of this inquest. The families, if they wish, may ask relevant questions."

The families, sitting together in their prescribed area, all looked at one another and then nervously about them. He knew from experience that it was likely at least one of them would ask questions, probably of the pathologist. He also knew what the first question, at least, was likely to be: would the victim have suffered at all?

He named the deceased and described them briefly: their ages, their status, where they lived—the young girl, Sarah Tomkins, the minibus driver, Edward Barnes, the young mother, Jennifer Marks.

He called the pathologist, Dr. Paul Jackson from St. Marks Hospital, who had carried out the postmortems on the deceased and asked him to take the oath. People were very respectful of the oath; they spoke it clearly and audibly, even if they became less so as they gave their evidence. And it reassured the relatives further, he knew: that no one was going to lie, to prevaricate; they were going to hear, finally, exactly what had happened to cause the deaths of those they loved.

Dr. Jackson gave his evidence: the awful bald facts, the exact cause in each case of the deaths. The mother of the young girl began to cry; the husband blew his nose hard and repeatedly. Andrews asked if there were any questions: the wife of the minibus driver, a middle-aged woman, her face pale and etched with strain, said, "I would like to ask a question. In your opinion, Doctor," she said, speaking to the pathologist, "would my husband have suffered at all?"

"I think I can state quite categorically," Dr. Jackson said, "that he would not. It is my professional opinion that all three would have died instantly."

"Thank you," said the woman. The others looked at her and half smiled; Sarah's mother said, her voice shaky with nerves and emotion, "I was going to ask the same thing. But I wondered if whoever found my daughter—I believe it was another doctor—would have agreed."

"We shall come to that evidence a little later," said Andrews, "and you will be free to speak to the gentleman in question—who was indeed a doctor—then."

The police evidence describing the background of the victims, how they had come to be on the road that afternoon, followed: the always tragic accounts of lives ended too soon. They were rich in clichés: "a devoted and selfless mother," "a lively, popular, and clever daughter," "a loving and generous grandfather." He hated the clichés, but they seemed de rigueur; they were what people told the police and, in any case, undoubtedly comforted the families.

He called Dr. Alexander Pritchard, the A&E consultant at St. Marks, to describe what medical procedures, if any, were carried out on the victims. Pritchard, who, like the pathologist, had clearly given evidence at many inquests before this one, spoke straightforwardly and with equal and careful tact: no procedures were carried out, the victims were all dead on arrival, and neither basic nor intensive life-support techniques were indicated. He added that in his opinion also, the deaths would all have been instantaneous.

Nice man, Andrews thought: an old-fashioned doctor of the best kind.

The inquest machinery ground on.

. . .

A large sheaf of photographs of the crash, taken from every angle, with relevant vehicles and trajectories painstakingly marked, were handed out to everyone. A description of the crash was given by Inspector Greg Dixon; he said people were for the most part very calm and helpful and that he would like to pay tribute to the courage of a doctor on the scene, "Mr. Jonathan Gilliatt, who worked tirelessly among the injured for many hours, and cared for a woman who had gone into premature labour, reassuring her and monitoring her condition until the ambulance arrived. He also most courageously climbed up into the lorry to turn the ignition off."

. . .

Andrews asked for the forensic evidence; it was complex and highly technical, as it always was. Clearly the cause of the whole thing had been the wheel nut shattering the lorry's windscreen; there was also considerable detail about a car two behind the lorry, which had apparently had a blowout, and caused considerable further damage, and which had had a large rusty nail in one of its tyres that would certainly have contributed to, if not caused, the blowout.

. . .

Michael Andrews called Sergeant Freeman to present the police evidence. He liked and respected Freeman; he had heard evidence from him many times. He had a certain lack of humour, and he tended to be rather self-important, but was inordinately thorough, incredibly hardworking, and he presented his evidence with great clarity. It took almost half an hour; at the end of it, Andrews was already tired, and it was only eleven. The concentration required by these big cases was exhausting; it never ceased to surprise him. He called a break for fifteen minutes, and sank gratefully into the peace of his own room, a huge mug of strong, sweet coffee supplied by his staff. He worried sometimes that at the age of fifty he was getting a bit old for this game, and then reminded himself that he had found inquests tough at thirty.

. . .

Patrick Connell had obviously once been a big man, Andrews thought, watching him as he came to the witness stand; he was tall, but frail, and walked leaning on two sticks and with a heavy limp. He asked him if he would like to sit down to give his evidence; Connell said he would rather stand, but halfway through what was obviously a gruelling experience, he was forced to give in and sit.

"Now, Mr. Connell, tell us about your recollections, as far as you can remember. We have heard you suffered memory loss, but anything you can tell us will be important."

The evidence was faltering, faulty indeed; Connell had no real memory of the aftermath of the crash before he reached the hospital, and indeed very little of the next few days; memory had begun to return, but only in fragments. "It was a very disturbing time, sir, as you can imagine, I'm sure."

"Indeed. Now . . . you weren't feeling sleepy beforehand? It says in your statement, if I might remind you again, that you had been to see your doctor about this tendency of yours to feel sleepy on the road. Remember you are under oath."

A hesitation; he could feel the lawyers stiffen.

"I had been, sir, yes. About half an hour earlier. But I'd stopped for a coffee, and I was eating sweets, jelly babies—they're my life-savers, odd though it may sound to you, sir—and I was talking to my passenger immediately before the crash; I do remember that very clearly . . ."

He had gained confidence now; he gave a clearly honest description of blame-free driving, within the speed limit, of the other vehicles, of the E-Type ahead of him, "just pulling ahead . . . He was driving very nicely, as a matter of fact."

"I'm pleased to hear it . . . and may I say how pleased I am also that you have made such a good recovery, Mr. Connell, from your injuries. You may step down."

"Thank you, sir."

. . .

Andrews asked for Connell's passenger next: he looked at her as she took the stand, tiny, pretty little thing, clearly absolutely terrified, and asked her very gently to take the oath. Her hand shook as she held the card; he wondered how good a witness she would be.

But she was very good: calm and clear describing how one moment everything had seemed perfectly fine, nobody speeding, nobody cutting across anybody, and then how the windscreen had so suddenly shattered. "It was terrifying. Like being in a thick fog. And then somehow, we stopped and we were in the middle of all this . . . this chaos."

"How long would you say it was before you felt the lorry veer over across the lanes of the motorway?"

"Oh . . . it all happened so slowly. It seemed like hours; I suppose it couldn't have been more than . . . what, ten seconds. And then quite quickly there was this terrible, awful noise and horns going and brakes screaming and then we . . . we stopped."

"Yes. I don't think we need to go over the next few minutes; your statement was very clear, and it must have been very traumatic for you."

He felt bound, driven by personal curiosity as much as professional, to ask her why she left the scene of the crash.

"I don't know," she said simply. "I wish I did, and I'm terribly ashamed of it. But I can't explain it; I really can't. I suppose I panicked. I remember thinking that if I got away, left the accident, it would be all right—no one would know I'd been there. I could just . . . just forget about it. It was so horrible, all the injured people especially—Patrick . . . Mr. Connell—and the wrecked cars, and people shouting and screaming. I felt I . . . well, I had to get away."

"So you walked quite a long way, you say, and then hitched another lift and went home to Cardiff?"

"Yes, that's right. And then I sort of managed to persuade myself that it hadn't happened. Or rather that I hadn't been there. That it was nothing to do with me. And the more time passed, the more impossible it got to admit. Until there were stories in the press, implying that Patrick—Mr. Connell—had gone to sleep."

She started to cry; Michael Andrews waited patiently, then said, "Try not to feel too distressed, Miss Linley. We all make mistakes and do things we can't explain. I'm sure Mr. and Mrs. Connell are most grateful that you told your story when you did."

"Yes. Thank you. And we have become good friends now. But only because they're so good; they've been so forgiving."

Andrews found himself rather taken by her; he thanked her for all her evidence, and then asked her if she had managed to get the part she'd been auditioning for. He did that sometimes, ventured into the personal or lighthearted where he felt it would help the atmosphere. Georgia said she had, and added that it would be shown on Channel Four in the spring.

"I have to tell you, Miss Linley," he said, "commercial advertising is not normally allowed in the courtroom. However, I will make an exception in this case."

. . . .

He heard the evidence of Jack Bryant, the owner of the E-Type. He couldn't think who he reminded him of, and then realised; he was a dead ringer for that Nigel Havers character, the Charmer, the same smooth dress style, the same confident public-school manner. Andrews was about to dislike him, when he said right at the beginning of his evidence, after taking the oath, "I feel absolutely ghastly about this. Terrible. The whole thing could be said to be my fault . . ."

"Mr. Bryant," said Andrews, "as I said at the beginning, we are not here to establish blame. Merely to find out what happened. Now, we have heard it was one of your wheel nuts that flew off and shattered the windscreen of Mr. Connell's lorry; can you tell us how you think this could have happened?"

"No," said Bryant, "I really can't. I checked them all really carefully—my mechanic will second that—before I set out. I was going to Scotland, long way, for a bit of shooting, and I wanted every-thing to be as safe as possible."

"Indeed. And you weren't speeding at all?"

"No, I most definitely was not. Chance'd be a fine thing, in that car. Very beautiful, but not much of a goer these days. She's an old lady, bit past her prime . . ."

Every inquest has its turning point; this one was provided by one of the experts at the police Forensics department.

"Thing is, you can overtighten those old nuts. One turn too far and it can break the thread—in our opinion, and on examining the car when it came into our possession, that's what happened."

Andrews looked at Bryant; he was visibly limp with relief. And then at the families: it was the kind of thing that was in a way most painful, the fatal event that was still an accident, an act that had killed, but made in good faith. He was not surprised to see them all sitting up very straight suddenly, their faces taut, and, in the case of the young girl's mother, already in tears . . .

. . .

The morning moved on. He heard some excellent evidence given by a young man, William Grainger, a farmer whose land bordered the M4: clear, concise, very helpful. Some more, very painful to hear, from the husband of the young mother who had been killed. They broke for lunch after this; Andrews felt he was not the only one who needed it.

. . .

In the afternoon Jonathan Gilliatt took the stand; now here was a smoothie, Andrews thought—even if he was a hero . . . Very self-confident he'd be, his evidence very well presented.

He was wrong; and it was not.

Gilliatt was uncomfortable, nervous, unclear as to exactly what he had seen of the crash, admitted—wiping his forehead repeatedly—that he and his passenger had been having what he called "a rather heated exchange" just beforehand.

"Sufficiently heated to distract you?" Andrews said, and yes, he said, and he was very ashamed that he had allowed it to do so.

"Not a good thing to be distracted on a crowded motorway, I'm afraid. Fortunate you were in the inside lane. You had met your passenger at a business function, I believe?"

"We had met through business, yes."

Cagey answer. Should he press this? Andrews thought. No. It was hardly relevant.

"Now, I believe also that you were on the phone? Which must have added to your distraction."

"I was, yes. Very, very briefly."

"You don't have a hands-free?"

"Not in the car I was driving, no. Well . . . that is to say, I do, but it wasn't working properly. The car was brand-new, and there were teething troubles generally with the communication systems. The

GPS wasn't working properly either. I knew I shouldn't have answered the phone, but I was pretty sure it was my wife; she'd been trying to get through, and she'd have been worried. And I had to get to my clinic in Harley Street . . ."

"I see. But you were obviously driving perhaps unnecessarily slowly, given that you were under pressure. Why was that?"

"Well . . . as I said, there'd been the storm; conditions were nasty. I was tired; I think I must have been feeling generally nervous."

"And then . . . ?"

"Then, as it says in my statement, I realised the lorry was all over the place, that it could be very dangerous. I literally flung the phone into the back and . . . next thing I knew, I was on the hard shoulder. With all the . . . the carnage about a hundred metres behind me."

"And then you walked back to see what you could do?"

"Yes, that's right."

"Which was very commendable. Well done. Now . . . I would like to ask you about the victims, and your undoubtedly splendid work amongst the injured . . . and I think that when I have finished, some of the relatives may want to question you. I hope that's all right."

"Of course."

. . .

"I would like to call Abigail Scott. Miss Scott, please take the oath. But first we shall hear your statement from Sergeant Freeman . . .

Bit of a baggage, this one, Andrews thought. Very attractive, and very, very sexy. Unlikely the relationship with Gilliatt had been purely professional. No doubt he'd considered himself perfectly safe . . . and then found himself skewered by fate.

"Miss Scott. You were in the car with Mr. Gilliatt. I wonder if you can add to his evidence in any way, or rather confirm that, as far as you could see, there was no question of anything cutting in front of Mr. Connell's lorry, from any direction, that might have caused him to swerve."

"No. Nothing. I saw the whole thing, obviously, and everyone seemed to be driving very carefully and well."

"Including Dr. Gilliatt?"

"Yes, he was driving very carefully."

"But he admits himself he was distracted, that you and he were having a . . . a heated discussion?"

"Yes. We were. But it wasn't making him drive badly. He . . . he's a very good and careful driver always."

"You've been driven by Mr. Gilliatt before, I assume from that?"

"Yes. Yes, I had."

"In the course of your mutual professional duties, I presume?"

There was a long silence; the legendary pin dropping would have sounded like thunder.

Then: "Not always, no."

Andrews could feel the entire courtroom tautening.

"Your relationship wasn't entirely professional. Is that what you're telling us? Remember, you are under oath."

"Yes. I mean it wasn't. I . . . liked him a lot. For a while."

"I see. So . . . I want to keep this conversation relevant to the proceedings, Miss Scott."

"Of course."

"So . . . this heated exchange. Was it of a personal nature? I ask only because it seems to me that could have been more distracting for him."

"Well, it was personal. Yes. He had told me that he didn't think we should continue with our . . . our friendship."

"And . . . ?"

"And I was . . . disappointed. So I was arguing with him."

"And . . . did you win this argument?"

"No. No, I didn't. Any ideas I had of continuing with our . . . relationship were futile. He made that very clear."

"Your relationship? I thought you said it was a friendship. Or do you regard the two as the same?"

"Not really," she said, and her eyes meeting his were what Andrews could only describe as bold. "I suppose you could say it was—had been—more than a friendship."

"Well, we need not concern ourselves with the precise nature of it," said Andrews, aware that the entire court longed to concern itself exactly thus. "But you are still quite sure that this conversation didn't distract him in any way from his driving?"

"I'm quite sure."

"Or that you might have failed to notice something untoward or dangerous yourself?"

"I'm sure about that too."

Then: "How did you get home from the crash? Did Mr. Gilliatt drive you?"

"No, of course not. I told you. Our relationship was over. Anyway, I was helping to look after some little boys, the ones from the minibus. I went back to the hospital in the ambulance with one of them, who was having an asthma attack. Shaun, he was called; he was a great little boy. I'd had asthma as a child, so I knew how to help."

"Well . . . thank you for your frankness, Miss Scott. It's been most helpful and much appreciated. Thank you. You may step down."

. . .

Andrews looked round the court; if this was a play, he thought—and inquests so frequently provided wonderful theatre—it would be the obvious point for an interval. He called another break. He desperately wanted to get this over in one day.

. . .

He heard evidence then from the young couple whose baby had been induced prematurely by the accident; he found them mildly irritating without being sure why. And then he said he would like to hear from Toby Weston, the bridegroom who had crashed into the back of them following a blowout.

"But first we should hear your statement, Mr. Weston. Sergeant Freeman . . ."

Weston stood up: good-looking young chap, Andrews thought, seemed pleasant, very conventionally dressed. He'd had a tough time, almost lost his leg. And missed his wedding. Fate again: relentless, unpredictable fate . . .

"Er . . . could I say something, please?" Weston said.

"You may, Mr. Weston. As much as you like. Once you have taken the oath. First we should hear your statement. Sergeant . . ."

"Yes, but—"

"Sergeant Freeman, please go on."

Freeman cleared his throat and began to read the statement; told of the desperate rush to get to the church, the buildup of delays . . . and how Weston had wanted to check the tyre pressures, had been concerned that one of them was soft. " 'However, Mr. Fraser, my best man, persuaded me not to, said it was unnecessary and that we should get on our way again.' "

At which point another young man stood up very suddenly in his seat and said, "But . . . I . . . That's not . . ." His face was scarlet and distorted with some kind of emotion; Andrews held up his hand.

"Your turn will come," he said. "And I will decide when. Please sit down, and be good enough not to interrupt proceedings again. I would remind you this is a court of law, and you are required to show it a proper respect. Sergeant Freeman, continue, please."

Sergeant Freeman continued; and then Weston took the stand and the oath. Andrews watched him with interest. Another emotional revelation, perhaps?

"Now, Mr. Weston, perhaps you would like to start by telling us what you wanted to say."

"Ah. Yes. Well, you see . . . well, that is, my statement wasn't entirely correct."

"Really?" Andrews's voice was full of innocent disbelief.

"No. No, the thing is . . . that bit about the tyres, that's not right. I . . . When I gave my statement to the inspector, I wasn't at all well. I was in a lot of pain: I'd been running a temperature; I had an infection in my leg; they . . . well, they'd thought they might have to amputate. It had all been very traumatic; I was still very upset. And confused."

"I'm sure. Very understandable. I believe your leg is to a large extent recovered now."

"Yes. Yes, it is, thank you. Anyway, it was not correct to say that Barney—Mr. Fraser—had persuaded me . . . not to check the type pressures. It was at my insistence that we left immediately and drove on. I'd had . . . well, I'd had a rather . . . rather pressing call from my father-in-law-to-be. I just felt that we had to get to the wedding no matter what. Mr. Fraser was very anxious to check them, very unhappy at leaving them. I'm extremely sorry about the . . . the confusion. Really very sorry indeed."

"Well, well," said Andrews, "thank you for that, Mr. Weston. Of course, we have heard from Forensics that in their opinion the blowout was caused by the presence of the nail in the tyre, so I don't think you need to worry on that score. But accuracy in statements is, of course, very important, as I'm sure you realise, and mistakes can waste time and indeed change the outcome of an enquiry in certain instances. It's always a pity when it is lacking, and indeed deliberate inaccuracies can be regarded as an offence. Do you have any other corrections?"

"No, no others."

"Good. Then let's go on."

Weston's evidence was without further dramatic input.

. . .

Fraser, his best man, he who had clearly been so distressed earlier, was called; he appeared shocked, strained; his answers were often faltering; then suddenly he spoke of his remorse that he had escaped "literally without a scratch, while everyone around us, it seemed, was horribly hurt. To this day, I feel bad. One of the doctors at the hospital was great; she told me how common that was, helped me to come to terms with it, this survivor-guilt thing."

"I'm glad to hear it, Mr. Fraser. May I say, this kind of remorse is very common. It doesn't mean you should feel you bear any of the blame. And we now know," he added, looking directly at Toby, "that you were keen to do the right thing and check your tyres. I think you will find that gradually you will lose your sense of guilt. I hope so."

More evidence followed: from a rather sleazy-looking chap, the white van driver, whose nail-studded planks had slithered out onto the road; Andrews rather enjoyed questioning him very closely as to how this had happened. It was not for him to apportion blame; it was still possible to make plain where blame lay.

And finally, an old lady gave evidence, a very anxious old lady, who said that she felt responsible in a small way, because she'd made Mr. Weston wait while she paid for her own petrol.

"I feel absolutely awful," she said. "I kept thinking how wrong of me it had been; he asked to go first, he said he was in a terrible hurry, and for some reason, I told him he had to take his turn. Who knows, had I not done that, those young men might not have been caught in the accident, but arrived at the church in time, and . . . Well, I'd like to apologise to them." She looked across at them both rather nervously.

"I really don't think, Mrs. Mackenzie, you should feel too bad," said Michael Andrews gently. "It would have made so little difference to the time and—"

"Yes, yes, but that little difference might have been crucial, don't you think? I'm sure you know the old parable about the horseshoe nail?"

"I'm . . . not sure," said Andrews.

"Oh, yes . . ." And as he waited, clearly expectant, she went on. "Well, it goes like this. 'For the want of a nail a horseshoe was lost; for the want of a shoe the horse was lost; for the want of a horse the rider was lost; for the want of a rider the battle was lost; for the want of a battle, the kingdom was lost. And all for the lack of a horseshoe nail. Who knows? I might have been that nail. If you follow me."

"I . . . think so, yes. But I think even the rather more tangible nail would not alone have kept them from the wedding, you know. Still it's a very interesting thought. Thank you, Mrs. Mackenzie. You may step down now."

. . .

It was five o'clock when Andrews rose to do his summing up. He was surprised by how positive an experience this inquest had been. Long, gruelling, and very sad at times—but uplifting in its own way: the courage displayed by the victims' families, and indeed by some of the witnesses, the general clarity of the evidence. It had also been very satisfying to conduct; there had been no serious confusion, no conflicting evidence, no self-justification . . . except for that ghastly van driver chap.

It had been one of those rare things, this: an accident, pure and simple; nevertheless, for the families of the victims this was little comfort.

He began by speaking to them, saying how sad it was when lives were cut short . . . "any lives, not only young lives; one cannot compare or quantify losses or tragedies. Mr. Barnes had much to look forward to in his retirement; Sarah Tomkins had her whole life ahead of her; and for the Marks family a wife and a mother have both been lost. I am sure I speak for the whole court today when I say our hearts go out to you. Accidents are terrible things: one moment everything is under our control; the next we lose that control, fate takes over, and the world changes. No one can anticipate accidents, and they are in many cases virtually unavoidable. We have heard how the road on the afternoon in question was dangerous because of the recent spell of hot, dry weather and the heavy hailstorm; we have heard that no one was driving in any way dangerously. We have heard that the nut came off the wheel of Mr. Bryant's E-Type not through lack of care, but if anything too much. We have heard that Mr. Connell was driving meticulously and that nothing could have prevented his lorry jack-knifing and his load spilling on the road. We have heard of much courageous and unselfish behaviour, and I would like to pay tribute in particular to Mr. Gilliatt, and of course to the emergency services and the staff at St. Marks Hospital, Swindon. And I would like to thank certain witnesses for their courage in coming forward when they were clearly nervous as to the outcome.

"There is much talk these days of the perfect storm—a confluence of weather patterns that separately would not be fatal or even dangerous, but which combine to be both; I would make an analogy between those perfect storms and this accident—everything conspiring to make it happen as and when it did. Rather as in the old nursery rhyme, as Mrs. Mackenzie reminded us. It is so easy to say if; and yes, if Mr. Weston had left the petrol station a few minutes earlier, if there had not been the queue for petrol, if the thunderstorm had not taken place . . . One can go on ad infinitum: the fact remains that it was not because these things happened in isolation; it was because they happened in a sequence that was tragically fatal. I therefore return the only verdict I can, that of misadventure."

❧ CHAPTER 52 ❧

Abi stalked out of the building. She felt absurdly near to tears. She looked behind her; there was no sign of William. *Shit.* She'd really upset him; he must have felt utterly betrayed. Dragging it all up again, more or less spelling out that she'd been chasing Jonathan Gilliatt, when she'd always sworn he'd done the chasing.

But . . . she knew that she had done the right thing. Her evidence had been, in a strange, subliminal way, a public apology to Laura. Not for having the affair with Jonathan, although she was pretty fucking sorry about that on her own account, but for what she'd done that night, at the party. Testifying had been hard, and it had certainly taken her by surprise; she'd never meant to say any of it, but she'd done it. Without telling a word of a lie either. Not technically, anyway, and certainly not in a way that would pervert the course of justice.

As she had returned to her seat, she'd been aware of two things. One was that William turned his back on her, as far as he was able. And then Laura turned round, and her eyes, meeting Abi's, were very steady, no longer hostile. She didn't smile at her, but there was no hostility in that look. It was almost gratitude. She knew what that meant. She'd got the message. An affirmation that at least Jonathan had had finished the affair that day, the day of the crash. She need feel humiliated no longer.

Abi had made her amends to Laura at last. She could close the book.

. . .

"Abi!" It was William. His face was dark with anger. She hadn't seen him look like that before. He was always so even tempered, so level altogether.

"Yes, William."

"What the fuck was that about?"

He never swore usually either. Not real swearing.

"I can't talk about it here."

"You're going to bloody well have to talk about it somewhere."

"Why?"

"Why? Because I want some answers."

"To what?"

"Oh, for heaven's sake."

"I don't think heaven has much to do with it. William, please leave me alone. You must have something to milk, or scan or something."

He turned then, walked away, over to his mother; she watched them getting into the Land Rover, saw it drive off, saw his bleak, set face. She struggled not to cry.

And then suddenly she knew, with a certainty that took her by surprise, that she had to talk to William, to try to explain and tell him that even while it was clearly hopeless, she did love him. She had to tell him that, in order to be able to wipe the slate clean. She couldn't leave it unsaid. She'd humiliated herself over one man today, in front of a crowded courtroom; she could certainly do it over another in private . . .

* * *

Barney thought he would never forget leaving that courtroom: alone. He thought he had never felt more alone in his life. He looked at Toby, getting into a car with someone who looked like a driver; still avoiding his eyes, he had positively scuttled out of the courtroom, bloody coward he was, as well as a total arsehole. He felt sick just thinking about him. And humiliated and totally stupid. OK, Toby had done the decent thing, in the end, but he had still been prepared to see Barney go to the wall to save his own skin. His best friend. His lifelong best friend. Barney could still hardly believe it.

He saw the Abi girl getting into her car. How extraordinary, saying all that in court. Humiliating herself, in a way. Pretty brave. Dead sexy she looked. Gilliatt must be a pretty cool customer to turn his back on her. The pretty blond wife—bit preppy, bit of an Amanda—must be very good at her job as well. Her job as a wife, that was. As Amanda would have been too. She—

"Hi. Nice to see you. Barney, isn't it? How's it going?"

It was Mark Collins, the surgeon who'd operated on Toby that day. In another time, another life altogether. When he'd had a lot. Instead of nothing.

"Yes. Hello." He didn't really want to talk to him. He didn't want to talk to anybody. Ever again. But he managed to smile, took Collins's outstretched hand.

"And your friend. Toby. I see he's walking pretty well."

"Pretty well, yes," said Barney shortly.

"Has the wedding taken place yet? I was thinking about it the other day, wondering if you'd be here."

"No," said Barney, "no, it hasn't. The wedding's off. Cancelled. Actually."

"I see." He could see Collins was taken aback. "Oh . . . I'm sorry. What about yours? Weren't you getting married too?"

"I was, yes. That's off as well."

"I see." Now he was really embarrassed. Poor sod. Thought he was going to have a quick cheerful chat, and he'd got lumbered with an episode from some kind of a soap opera.

"Er . . . how's Emma?" he said. He was astonished to hear himself asking, so terrified was he of the answer.

"Oh . . . she's fine, yes. Off to pastures new when she can organise it."

"Really? What, you mean to . . . to Milan?"

"What? Oh, no, no, that's history, I think. No, she's applying for new jobs. She's very excited about something up in Scotland; not sure how that's going."

"Great. I mean, well, I hope she gets it. Give her . . . that is, remember me to her, please."

"I will, Barney. Look . . . I'd better go. Dr. Pritchard's waiting. Nice to see you, anyway."

"Yes, sure. And . . . do give my regards to Emma."

"I will. Cheers."

And he was gone.

. . .

So . . . what had that meant? About Milan being history? That the boyfriend was history? Or just . . . no longer in Milan? Maybe he should call her. But . . . supposing she was with Luke again? It would be painful for her. Well . . . he'd made it pretty clear he hadn't . . . forgotten her. Forgotten her. If only. If only you could do that to order, just neatly get rid of something, remove it, throw it away.

Throw away something that had become an intrinsic part of you, grown into you; entwined itself into your memories, tangled into your feelings, changed forever the way you were.

If only.

He got into his car and headed for the M4. The M4, where so much of his life had been changed forever. He would never hear the words again without a sense of absolute despair.

. . .

"Good day, dear?" Susan Andrews had been making marmalade; the house was warm and tangy and welcoming. Michael Andrews felt as he so often did after a day spent hearing sad stories of cutoff lives: that he was inordinately blessed.

"Yes. Yes, pretty good, I think."

"Difficult?"

"No, not really difficult. It's perfectly clear what happened. But . . . surprising in some ways. Extraordinary things, human beings. I'm always saying that, aren't I?"

"Yes, dear, you are."

"Brave and cowardly, foolish and wise, reckless and careful. All at one and the same time. Unbelievable, really."

Susan Andrews looked at her husband. He was looking very drawn, in spite of his positive words.

"Come into the kitchen and have a cup of tea," she said, "and tell me about it."

. . .

Emma had been trying not to think about the inquest all day; but first Alex and then Mark had come in to tell her about it. About the various people they'd been involved with who were there, most notably Patrick Connell and, of course, Toby. "Funny chap, that," Mark had said. "Some confusion over his evidence; he got very aerated. Oh, and your boyfriend was there, of course."

"My . . . boyfriend? What do you mean?" she said.

"You know, the good-looking one, best man, you brought him up to the theatre that day when I operated on Weston's leg."

"Oh," she'd said, "him. Yes, well, I supposed he would have been."

"Nice chap," said Mark, and then proceeded to tell her that not only was Toby's wedding off, but so was Barney's engagement. Adding that Barney had asked to be remembered to her. That had hurt her so much she could hardly bear it; she'd had to say she was in the middle of something and run to the loo, where she cried for a long time.

Barney had finished with Amanda, but he hadn't got in touch with her. As rejections went, that was pretty final. How could it have happened? Where had it gone, that lovely, singing happiness they had found together, that instant closeness, that absolute certainty that they were right for each other? OK, their relationship hadn't lasted long; it hadn't needed to. It had been like a fireworks show: starting from nowhere and suddenly everywhere, explosive, amazing, impossible to ignore. And now . . . what? A poor, damp squib had landed, leaving nothing behind it, a bleak, sorry memento of the blazing display.

She knew now, absolutely certainly, that he didn't want her. If he had, he would have called her; there was no reason on earth left not to. Probably, after all, it had just been a fling for him, fun, good indeed, but no more. The commitment had been fake, the love phony; he was probably even now pursuing some other well-bred, preppy creature more suited to his background, less of a discord in his life.

She would have been outraged had she not been so totally miserable; and maybe that would come. She hoped so. Meanwhile she felt like one of the girls she most despised: feebly clinging to what might have been, unable to break totally away. *He's gone, Emma; get over it.*

But she hadn't; and she couldn't . . .

. . .

Abi drove into the farmyard just after six. The lights were on, and she could see Mrs. Grainger in the kitchen, bending over the kitchen table, making some no doubt wonderful dish or other. William often described what they'd had for lunch or supper; he was very keen on his food. She was clearly the most wonderful cook. Well, fine. William was never going to have to live with her cooking, her spag bol (usually burnt), her lamb chops (always burnt), her pasta salad (not burnt, but pretty tasteless, really). After today, he wasn't going to have to have anything to do with her; he'd probably pull out of the festival, even; they'd have to find a new venue; Georgia would go mental; they'd—

"Yes?"

"Oh. Hello, Mrs. Grainger."

She'd been so absorbed in her thoughts of William, she'd hardly realised she'd got out of the car and banged on the farmhouse door.

"Miss Scott!"

"Yes. It's me. Sorry."

"That's perfectly all right. But if you want to see William I'm afraid you're out of luck. He's out on the farm."

"Oh, right. What, in the dark?"

"Well . . . he's in one of the buildings. He went off with his father."

"Yes, I see. What, the milking parlour? Or the grain store, somewhere like that?"

"I imagine so."

"But you don't know which?"

"No, I couldn't possibly say."

"How long might they be?"

"I have no idea. As even you must realise"—God, she was an offensive woman—"farming is not a nine-to-five occupation. I think the best thing you can do is go home, and I'll tell William you called. Then he can contact you in his own good time."

"Mrs. Grainger, I really want to see him."

"Well, no doubt you will."

She began to close the door; Abi put her foot in the doorway.

"Please tell me where he is. I really won't keep him long."

"Miss Scott, I don't know where he is . . ."

At this point, the old farm truck swung into the yard; Mr. Grainger got out of it.

Abi knew it was Mr. Grainger, not because she had ever been

introduced to him, but because he looked exactly like William, or rather exactly as William might look in thirty-odd years. He looked at her rather uncertainly as she walked towards him.

"Hi. Mr. Grainger?"

"Good evening."

"I'm looking for William. I'm a friend of his. Abi Scott. William might have mentioned me."

"Ah, yes. The young lady involved in the concert. How's it coming along?"

"Oh . . . pretty well. We're so, so pleased to be able to have it here. Um . . . I wonder if you could tell me where William is?"

"Yes. Well, he was in the lambing shed. I left him there, working on the accounts. Would you like me to call him, to find out if he's still there?"

"Um . . . no. No, it's OK, thank you. I know where it is. I'll just go and find him, if that's all right."

"Well . . . I suppose so, yes. You'll drive down there, will you? Won't do that smart car of yours much good." He smiled at her. He seemed rather nice. What on earth was he doing with the old bat?

"Oh, it's fine. Really. Yes. Thank you. Thank you, Mr. Grainger. And Mrs. Grainger, for your help," she called towards the lighted doorway. Mrs. Grainger turned and went inside, followed by her husband.

"She seemed very nice," he said. "Attractive girl, isn't she? Not William's usual type. Is there anything still going on, do you think?"

"I really couldn't say," said Mrs. Grainger. She had been making bread; she was kneading it now, almost viciously, Mr. Grainger thought.

. . .

Abi drove down the track to the lambing shed. Since the time spent in cottage number one, she'd got to know her way round the farm quite well.

It was very dark; she put her lights on full beam. Rabbits ran constantly out onto the track, and she kept stopping, fearful of running over them. William would have found that hugely amusing, she thought; he'd told her how he and his brother had parked the Jeep in the fields at night, turned the lights full on, and then shot the unsuspecting rabbits that were caught petrified in the beam.

It's so cruel—how could you; they're so sweet," she'd said, and he'd said, "Abi, rabbits are total pests; they consume vast quantities of cereal if they're not kept under control. And they make wonderful stew."

Other smaller animals ran across her path as well—God knew what they were—and there was a hedgehog, frozen with terror until she turned the lights off and waited patiently while it scuttled away. A large bird suddenly swooped past her windscreen. An owl, she supposed; the first time William had pointed one out, she'd been amazed by how big its wingspan was.

She'd learnt a lot in her time with him.

She reached the shed; the office was at the far end of it, so he wouldn't have seen her, although he might have heard the car. And probably thought it was his father. She switched the lights off, got out; the quiet was stifling. An owl—maybe the same one—hooted; something scuffled in the hedgerow near her. She reached for her bag—how absurd was that, to take a handbag with her? William was always teasing her about it, but it held her phone and her car keys, easier than carrying them separately. She stepped forward; it was very muddy, and that was—*Oh, what! Gross* . . . She'd stepped in a cowpat. She could see it in the light from the shed. A great, round, liquid pile of shit; and her boot, one of her precious new boots from Office—how very inappropriate—sank deep into it. She stood there, staring down at it, and thought it was rather symbolic—of her, also sunk deep into shit.

She eased her foot out and stepped gingerly forward towards the shed, wary of finding another. The cows didn't usually come this way—it wasn't their territory; maybe they'd got out of whatever field they were meant to be in. They did that, William had told her; they leaned on the fences endlessly, unless they were electric, all together, usually because they could see some better, more lush grass, with their great solid bulk, and every so often they managed to push them over and wander out. Only . . . actually, she'd thought they were usually kept inside this time of year, in the cowshed.

She made the door of the shed without further mishap, opened it, looked inside. It was still empty, no lambing going on yet, and very quiet. She closed the door after her and walked, as quietly as she could, down to the other end of the building, towards the outline of light round the door that had William behind it.

When she got there, she was suddenly rather frightened. Suppose he was abusive, started shouting at her. Suppose he actually hit her. She wouldn't be able to blame him, if he did. Then she thought it would be totally out of his gentle character; and anyway, whatever happened, she couldn't feel worse. Her sense of nobility from her actions in the court had left her; she just felt miserable and rather foolish.

She opened the door carefully; he was sitting at the desk with his back to her; didn't even hear her at first. He was engrossed in a pile of forms; then he suddenly thrust them aside and sighed, very heavily, and pushed his hands through his hair.

"Hello," she said. "Hello, William."

He swung round; he looked extremely shocked. Not just surprised—shocked. Well, more like horrified, if she was truthful.

"Hello," she said again.

"Hi." His voice was dull, flat.

"I . . . came to find you."

"As I see."

"I . . . wanted to talk to you."

"I really don't think there's anything to talk about."

"There is, William."

"Abi, there is not. I'm so tired of hearing your lies and your excuses and your phony concerns. Just go away, would you? I'm very busy."

"No. Not till I've said what I've come to say."

"I don't see any point in your saying it. I won't be able to believe it."

"You could . . . try." She looked down at her boot; it was a hideous sight, the greenish brown cow shit beginning to dry a little, cake round the edges.

"Um . . . do you have any newspaper or anything? Or maybe I could go into the toilet?"

"What for?"

"I stepped in some cow shit. Outside."

"Oh, yes?"

He sounded absolutely disinterested. She felt a pang of panic.

"Yes. Actually, I was surprised; I thought you said you were keeping the cows in this time of year?"

"We're keeping a few out this winter. As an experiment. To see if we can—" He stopped.

"If you can what?"

"Abi, you're not really interested in cows. Or farming. Or me, come to that. Certainly not me. It's all a bloody act. I can't cope with it. Now go and clean up your fucking boot in the lavatory and then go. Please."

Well, that was pretty final. Pretty clear. She really had blown it this time. She couldn't imagine getting past this wall of indifference. And dislike. And mistrust. Better go. She'd tried, at least. Given it a go.

She walked through to the loo, pulled off her boot, sat wiping it with the toilet paper, rather feebly and helplessly. She didn't seem to be able to see properly, and realised that her eyes were filled with tears. God, she was an idiot. Such a stupid, pathetic, hopeless idiot. He must hate her. Really hate her. Well, all she could hope for now was to escape with a bit of dignity. Dignity. Precious little she'd left for herself in the court that day. Saying to them all, "I fancied this man, this married man; I was running after him, actually, and he didn't want me." They must have all found it highly amusing.

She stood up again and walked back into the office. William was apparently absorbed in the forms again. He didn't look round.

"Right," she said, "well, bye, William, then. I'm . . . sorry."

"I'm sure you are," he said, and then suddenly, "Why did you do that today, for Christ's sake? Why? In front of all those people, in front of me, rubbing my nose in it, telling everyone you . . . you'd wanted to go on with it, with that . . . that pile of shit, after what he'd done to you. Are you still in love with him or something? I don't understand . . ."

"Oh, God," she said, "no, of course I'm not in love with him; I loathe him; I'd like to see him strung up by his balls . . ."

"Well, then—"

"William, it's so complicated. But I've always felt so bad—you know I have—about what I did that night. It's not her fault, not Laura's fault. You say I rubbed your nose in it; what did I do to her? And her kids? It was such a ghastly thing to do. And suddenly today, I thought . . . well, I didn't exactly think. I just could see how I could put it a bit right. Let her know that her vile, slimy husband—how she can still be with him I don't know—but anyway, he had wanted to finish it that day. To get rid of me. That it hadn't still been going on. I just . . . just . . . felt I owed it to her. It wasn't easy," she added.

"And how do I know that's true?" he said, and his face was harsh and distorted, a stranger's face, not kind, gentle William's at all. "How do I know it wasn't some kind of a . . . a bid to get him back? To have him thinking well of you again? You've told me so many lies, Abi, about him, about your relationship; how can I be expected to believe anything? And then there was all that shit about how terrible you felt about the child; I had to listen to that, and did I think you should ring him—ring him, for Christ's sake—you ask me that, and then how scared you were of the inquest today. It was fucking endless. Endless. And you seemed to have no idea at all how much it hurt, how horrible it was for me. It was all about you, you, you. You didn't seem very scared, incidentally; you seemed very cool and collected. Almost enjoying it, I'd say. Star of the show."

"That's a horrible thing to say."

"Well, it was a horrible thing to do. Now, please, just go away. Leave me alone."

She walked the length of the shed, her heels clacking on the stone floor. And then stopped. She'd left her bag behind. How stupid was that. She'd have to return, go back into that office, confront him again, confront all that dislike, that sullen, heavy hostility. Horrible. She might have left it there if it hadn't had her car keys in it. But . . . she couldn't get home without them. She turned, walked back as quietly as she could, opened the door.

"Sorry," she said. "Sorry, William, I—"

And then she stopped. Because he wasn't looking at the forms anymore; he was sitting with his head in his arms on the desk; and when he looked round at her, she saw that he was weeping.

"Oh, William," she said, her own tears blurring her vision again, stepping forward, bending over him, putting her arm on his shoulders. "William I . . ."

And, "Don't," he said, turning away, so that she couldn't see his face, "don't touch me."

"But—"

"Don't," he said. "I'll go mad if you do."

"All right," she said, and very slowly, reluctantly almost, she drew back and would have left then; only he suddenly put out his hand and caught hers in it, and held it, and sat looking at it, as if he wasn't sure how it had come to be there at all; and then he turned it, palm upwards, and bent his head and kissed it, kissed the palm, very sweetly and tenderly and then . . .

"Christ," he said, "dear God, Abi, what are you?" And then she pushed his head up and began to kiss him, desperate, hungry for him, her mouth working frantically at his, moaning, almost crying with wanting him, and then suddenly she was astride him on the chair and he had pushed up her sweater and his mouth was on her breasts, licking, teasing, pleasing them, and then she stood up and wrenched off her dress and her pants and then she was astride him again, and he was sinking into her, up her, creating great, searing waves in her of a raw, sweet violence and pleasure that was so close to pain she could hardly bear it, and she came so fast it was shocking, and felt him come too; and they both stayed there for what seemed like a long time, his head on her breast, and she felt him sigh, and then sigh again; then he said, his voice still heavy, "I shouldn't have done that; I'm sorry."

"William, you should, you should; it was wonderful, so, so lovely; I've wanted it for so long."

"For so long?" he said. "You can't have, you—"

And, "I did, I did," she said, "so much I could hardly bear it; every time I saw you I wanted it and—"

"You too," he said, and suddenly it came, his wonderful giggle. "That is just so . . . so stupid . . ."

"What do you mean, me too—you're not saying you wanted it too?" she said.

And, "Yes," he said, "of course I did, you silly cow . . ."

"Don't call me a silly cow."

"Why not? It's a compliment; you know how much I love my girls."

"Oh, all right. Go on."

"Abi, it was driving me insane; I wanted you so much, and I thought you didn't want me, that you just saw me as a . . . a . . . well, I didn't know how you saw me. Some kind of loser, I suppose . . ."

"Loser! William, you can't have thought that . . ."

"Well, I did, of course I did, and then today . . ."

"Oh, God," she said, "oh, William, I'm so, so sorry about today. I really am . . ."

"Don't keep saying that," he said, "please. Let today go. Please. It upsets me, even now; I don't want to . . ."

"All right. But I have something to tell you . . . something rather awful, in a way. I don't know what to do about it, but I have to tell you, just so—"

"Jesus," he said, and his expression had changed—was wary suddenly, almost scared. "Jesus, Abi, there's someone else; is that what you . . ."

"Someone else! William, how can you even think such a thing? There's never going to be someone else, not now, not ever. I love you, William. That's what I have to tell you. I . . . well, I love you."

"You what?" he said, and his tone was so odd, filled with disbelief, and his face too, with something close to shock, and she felt quite scared herself, but she had to go on, had to know he knew, just so they could go forward, in whatever direction that might be.

"I said I love you, and I don't care what you think; I don't care if you don't want to hear it. I love you, William. So, so much, I can't begin to tell you. But if you don't want me—and I wouldn't blame you—I swear I'll never come near you again; I absolutely swear it . . ."

"You'd better bloody not," he said, and her heart literally sank; she felt it, heavy and sad and infinitely disappointed.

"I won't," she said. "I—"

"No," he said, "I mean you'd better bloody not swear it. Do you think I want to lose you, you stupid, stupid girl? Do you think I don't want you . . . ?"

"Well . . . I—"

"Abi. Say it again. Keep saying it. I can't hear it enough."

"All right," she said. "OK, I love you, William. I really love you. I've never said that before, except to my dad—oh, and maybe to that boy I told you about, the one who—"

"Do shut up," he said. "I don't want to hear about any boys."

"No, sorry, I'm just trying to be truthful. Completely truthful. I love you, William. I always have, from that first day, I think, only I—"

"You can't do," he said, staring at her.

"But I do. If you mean because of how I've behaved, well, I'm pretty bloody stupid. As you know. But ignoring that, I do love you. I love everything about you. I love the way you look, and the way you talk, and the way you giggle, and I love having sex with you so, so much; it's just . . . just . . . Oh, don't laugh, William; don't laugh at me; it's not funny; it's pathetic, really, sitting here without any clothes on, telling you all this when you made it pretty clear about half an hour ago that you thoroughly disliked me—"

"Of course I don't dislike you," he said, his tone impatient. "I love you too, Abi. I really, really do love you. I can't imagine life without you now; that was why I was so miserable and . . . and hostile to you. I . . . Oh, hell. Look, do you think we could move? I'm getting a cramp in one of my legs."

"You . . . love me?"

"Yes, I love you too. I just said so, didn't I? I'm a simple sort of chap, you know; I don't go in for anything very complex."

Abi stood up. She felt very odd. Odd and physically feeble.

"OK. Sorry about the cramp. Shall we . . . shall we move over to the couch? And maybe we could . . . could . . . Why are you laughing, William? I don't see what's so funny."

"You are," he said. "If you could see yourself you'd see it."

"Well, thanks."

"No, really. Stark naked from the waist down, except for a pair of boots. One covered in cow shit. Quite appropriate, really."

She looked down at herself and grinned. "No wonder I was getting cold."

"You look cold. Here . . ." He went and pulled a large green sheet off a hook on the door. "Let's put this over us."

"What is it? It looks sort of waterproof."

"It is. We use it for . . . Well, never mind. It might put you off."

"It stinks," she said.

"Yes, well, so do I quite a lot of the time. I'm not always freshly washed and brushed up, you know. You're going to have to get used to smells. If you're going to be a farmer's wife."

"A what?"

"A farmer's wife. Well, I'm not going to change careers. Even for you."

"Did you say wife?"

"Yes, I did. It seems the best thing to me. Don't you want that?"

"William, William, but I can't cook."

"You'll learn."

"And I feel sorry for rabbits."

"You'll get over it."

"And foxes."

"You'll certainly have to get over that."

"And I'm not posh."

"Good."

"Oh, William, I'd love to marry you. Love, love, love it."

"Me too." He looked at her and grinned suddenly. "Really love it. Now, if we could just . . . ah, I think . . . yes, someone's coming through the shed. Um, ah, hallo, Mother."

Mrs. Grainger, clad in Barbour and headscarf and heavy green wellies, looked at Abi—at her naked lower half, her tousled hair, her smudged eye makeup, her high-heeled, shitty boots.

"Yes, hallo, William," she said.

"Mother, I have some really exciting news. Abi has agreed to marry me."

. . .

This is what happiness looks and sounds like, Mary thought, smiling at Russell: a warm room, thick curtains closed against the cold night, a big jug of winter jasmine on the mantelpiece, a log fire, a concert (Haydn) on the wireless—now, Mary, not wireless, but Russell's state-of-the-art sound system; not that it mattered, the music was lovely anyway—new silks for a new tapestry spread out on her sewing table, Russell contentedly sipping at his bourbon and leafing through travel brochures, planning a trip to Italy for them in the spring. And by the hearth, slumbering sweetly, curled up with one another, the latest additions to their household: two Persian blue kittens.

How lucky she was, how lucky they both were, to have found so much so late, and not to have been disappointed by it in any respect.

"You obviously did so well today, Sparrow. I wish I'd come now, I'd have been so proud of you."

"Don't be ridiculous, there was nothing to be proud of . . ."

"Oh now, you say that, but Georgia told me how you recited that nursery rhyme to the judge—"

"The coroner."

"Pardon me, the coroner."

"And what on earth was Georgia telling you that for?"

"She said you'd told her I was tired, and she was worried about me. Really, Sparrow, people will think I'm an invalid or an old man if you keep talking like that."

"How could anyone think you were an old man," said Mary, walking over to him and kissing the top of his head, "when you look so extremely youthful and handsome? Anyway, I didn't recite it exactly . . ."

"She said you did."

"Well, maybe I did. Anyway, it caught his fancy and he quoted it in his summing up at the end. Which was very nice. And I said how anxious I had been about holding up the young man—the bridegroom, you know—and the coroner said—such a courteous, kind man—that I should have no concerns about it, that it would have made no difference. I still think perhaps it might, but . . . he was so very good at his job, Russell; everyone left looking happier, even the poor families of those who died."

"Good. And Georgia was happier at the end of it?"

"So much happier. He was very gentle with her."

"Good. Well, he sounds like a fine chap."

"He is a fine chap."

"Well done anyway. Oh, my Sparrow. You don't have any regrets, do you?"

"Regrets?" she said, surprised at the question. "Of course not. Unless it is that we weren't together sooner. But then, we couldn't have been, could we?"

"Not playing it your way, no. If it had been down to me, we'd have had sixty years together now, instead of six months."

"I know, I know. But . . . we did the right thing."

She sat smiling into the fire, remembering. She had been seventeen at the beginning of the war, Donald nineteen; she had loved him so much, and if anyone had told her she would fall in love with someone else, she would not have believed them; she would have said her heart was far too occupied, her future too settled. But Russell had been irresistible. She told him so now.

"I wasn't, though, Sparrow, was I? You resisted me very well."

"I know. But it was more . . . as you know, keeping faith with Donald. I suppose I might have changed my mind at one stage. But then, you know . . ."

"I know. The letters."

The many letters from Donald, in a prisoner-of-war camp in Italy, all telling her that it was only knowing she was there, waiting for him, that was keeping him going at all.

"Yes. I couldn't have failed him, Russell, could I?"

"I don't believe you could. Being you."

"And I was happy, and so indeed were you. And we have each other now. It's been so perfectly lovely, these past months. At long, long last. Worth waiting for."

"Worth it indeed . . . Now, Mary, do you think Rome and then Florence or the other way round? Remember we'll have just spent a month in New York; I'll have been working, so we'll need a proper break. Maybe we should take a villa in the Tuscan hills and base ourselves there and then we can travel at our leisure; we could hire a driver . . . or we could take the train between the two; that sounds a lovely journey."

"I think either would be very nice. You do have to do this month in New York, do you, working so hard? I'm sure Morton could manage with your being there for a shorter time . . ."

"Mary, we have a very big shareholders' meeting at the beginning of April; it's essential I'm there, and we have to prepare for that."

"Yes, but Russell, dear, perhaps you don't. You've been tired lately, even living down here and—"

"That's purely because I had a touch of flu. I'm never tired normally, as you very well know."

"Of course not, dear. Well . . . I think the villa sounds a wonderful idea. Although . . ."

"Yes?" Russell smiled at her. "I'm getting to know your 'althoughs.' "

"Well, you know, we could just stay here. Spring in England is so very lovely, and I can't imagine anything nicer than sitting in the garden and going for walks and just . . . well . . . just sharing all of it with you, hearing the birds—they sing so beautifully in the spring—oh, and I've been meaning to tell you, I think there's a thrush nesting in the apple tree; I've been watching it, either Mr. or Mrs. Thrush, I'm never sure which, flying in and out, in and out with twigs . . . We'll have to watch our wicked kittens; we don't want any tragedies . . . And then we can see the bulbs come up—we don't know what will grow where; it will be so exciting—and then there'll be the blossoms on the trees in the orchard, and . . . But of course, if you've set your heart on Italy . . ."

"I think I have, dearest Sparrow. We have plenty of years to enjoy the English spring, and I do so want to see Italy with you. I . . ."

Mary was bending over her silks now, sorting out the blues and the greens; she was not looking at Russell, so she did not see his face suddenly change, did not see him momentarily thump at his chest, nor the fright in his eyes; nor did she notice that he was slowly slumping down in his chair; all she was aware of was an odd sound, halfway between a whimper and a gasp, and by the time she did look up, he was losing consciousness fast and she was never to know whether he heard her as she cradled his head in her arms and whispered again and again how much she loved him.

CHAPTER 53

It had been a stroke, they said: a massive haemorrhage in his brain. If he had recovered, he would have been paralysed, probably unable to speak. Or to smile, Mary thought—there would have been no more of that wonderful, quick, loving smile; or indeed of anything else that made him Russell: not just the brilliant blue eyes, the thick white hair, the beautifully kept hands, the proudly erect back; but the fast, almost urgent walk, the swift turn of his head, the way he sat lost to the world, visibly devouring books, the absurdly careful way he folded things—his table napkin, his scarf, the *Wall Street Journal* . . . how often had she teased him about that—the way he laughed, slowly at first, almost reluctantly, then throwing his head back and giving himself up to jokes, to amusement, to fun.

And his voice, not deep, quite light really, but very clear, calling her as he did a hundred times a day, for he liked to know where she was in the house, not so much to be constantly with her as to be able to find her if he needed to. "Where are you, Sparrow?" he would shout from the hall, the kitchen, his study, and she would answer him, quite impatiently sometimes, for she liked to do as she pleased, be where she wished . . . And what would she have given now, she thought, arriving home that first day from the hospital, arriving home to that quiet, dead house, to be summoned, called to account. Now she could wander where she would, from room to room, to the garden and beyond, and no one would care or need to know.

He had died peacefully and apparently happily, twenty-four hours after the stroke, with Mary holding his hand; she hoped above all things that he knew she was there. The nurses assured her he would.

She had sat by him almost all that time. "They don't make them like that anymore," one of the nurses said, looking at her small, upright figure, her eyes fixed on Russell's face, and indeed they did not, the doctor had agreed; they were a special breed, her generation, with the courage to face down for six long years the worst that a savage enemy could do to them and still remain strong, generous, merry hearted.

When she finally became exhausted, they urged her to sleep, but she refused to leave the room, and they brought her a bed so that she could stay with him. She slept fitfully, woke every hour or so to make sure that he had not gone, and was afraid even to go to the bathroom they had made available to her.

"He won't go without you, Mary," the ward sister had said. "He'll wait until you are back with him again; they do, I promise you." But she didn't believe her and each time came scuttling back into the room, fearful of not having properly been with him at this, their darkest hour together.

She had been told that hearing was the last sense to go, and she talked to him from time to time, told him how much she loved him, how happy she had been with him, how wonderful their few months together had been.

"I shall go to Italy, dearest Russell," she said, "even without you. I will see it for you, all those wonders, as I know you would have wished. And I shall watch the spring garden grow and the apple trees blossom in the orchard, and when the baby thrushes fly, I will know you are part of it all."

Every so often his hold on her hand tightened and she would tense, thinking he was coming back to her; once he seemed to try to speak; once he half smiled. But in the end he left her, slipped away with a sigh and a long, long breath, and she knew it was over without having to be told, knew that she was alone now, alone in the room, alone in the world.

. . .

They all came, of course, his children. Shocked, grieving, but saying that it had after all been a blessing, given how much he would have been changed, how poor the quality of his life would have been, and that he could not have suffered; it had been so swift, so mercifully swift. Mary listened, politely patient, nodding, smiling, sometimes weeping, but thinking that he was their father, not their husband; he was not the centre of their worlds anymore. So much easier to see it as a blessing, given all that; so very much harder for her.

Her children came too, Christine remorseful, as well as visibly grieving; Douglas shocked; and Tim and Lorraine both genuinely and horribly upset. All rallying round, loving her, but quite unable to comfort her, to ease the jagged place in her heart.

She kept telling herself that a year ago, Russell had been no more to her than a writer of letters, a happy memory. She had been content then; she would be content again. But it was not quite true, for she had changed; Russell's love and vigour and generosity had brought her back to life, had given her indeed more life, a new, broader, richer one. She had grown accustomed to a voice in the darkness, a presence in the bed, a smile first thing in the morning, a kiss last thing at night; to a face opposite her at the table, an arm to take as she walked. She had come to enjoy ideas, suggestions, to being argued and reasoned with, to being appreciated and loved.

. . .

The funeral was small, family only, apart from the Connells, who had become family. In the same little church where the wedding had been. Maeve found it almost unbearable, looking at Mary standing beside the flower-covered coffin, all alone, when three months earlier she had stood beside Russell, becoming so happily his wife. She was brave, so brave—cried only once, when the coffin was carried in—and after that held her small, strong self together.

Morton spoke of a wise and wonderful father who had been all the world to him; and then Tim, briefly, of a new grandfather in his life whom he had come to love and revere.

"And who made my grandmother absolutely happy. They never seemed old to us, just a wonderful couple who had found each other, and relaunched their lives. We shall remember him always. And we will take care of Grandma for him."

And then Russell left the church again, and was buried in the small churchyard; Mary stood looking down into the grave, quite composed, even when she threw the handful of earth onto the coffin; then she walked quickly away, on Tim's arm. Her flowers went into the coffin, with her simple message: "Russell, thank you, with all my love."

. . .

Morton stayed only a few days, Coral and Pearl for over a week; Mary was glad of their company but more glad when they left. She wanted the house to herself, to grieve and to explore her feelings. It seemed very large, very empty, very silent. But Russell lingered in every room.

One of the hardest things to deal with was his clothes, the vast dressing room in which he stored literally dozens of suits—more than Donald had had in his whole life, she thought: jackets, trousers, shirts, drawers full of ties and sweaters and belts and the silk pyjamas without which he said he would not be able to sleep. She stood there one afternoon, looking at them all, remembering him buying them—or some of them—seeing him wearing them, wondering where to begin sorting them out and getting rid of them . . . and then realised she did not have to begin at all. They could stay there for as long as she wished.

She applied the same principle to his study, to all his absurd gadgets, some of them hardly used, most of them quite useless to her; she called Timothy and told him to come and take what he wanted, and then after that she simply kept it all.

It was all part of Russell, this superabundance of things; and therefore, now, part of her.

. . .

She found routine helpful; she walked in the morning, watched TV in the evenings, in the company of the kittens—another source of comfort—making a great effort to watch at least some of the vast number of DVDs Russell had brought and told her she would enjoy . . . and in the afternoon, she played the piano, his last gift to her. She found this more comforting than anything; she had found a teacher, a sparky sixty-year-old called Genevieve, who came to the house twice a week, saw exactly what Mary needed, and created quite a punishing programme of pieces and practice. Moreover, if Mary hadn't done her practice, she didn't tell her it didn't matter, but that if she hadn't improved by her next lesson, she wouldn't teach her anymore. She also entered Mary for her grade-three piano exam (she had passed one and two as a child) and booked several concerts for them to attend together in Bath, "just so you can hear how it should be done."

Mary was frequently to be found weeping over the piano in the afternoons, partly through frustration, partly through sorrow, but she knew it was helping her more than she would have believed.

. . .

People were very kind: Tim and Lorraine came once a week, sometimes in the evening, sometimes at the weekend, and Christine came twice, once to take her mother to the farmers' market, which she enjoyed, and once to have lunch with her at home. She had ventured quite early on into the realms of apology for her hostility to Russell; Mary told her quite briskly to be quiet.

"You came to the wedding, dear—that was marvellous—and became friends with Russell after that, and I really don't want to discuss it any further."

Everyone told her she was being wonderful; Mary thought they should see her at night, when she had gone to bed, and wept and sometimes howled with misery.

. . .

Other people visited her: Georgia had been terribly upset and wept so long and so copiously after Tim had called her—they had made rather good friends at the wedding, so good indeed that Lorraine had become quite spiky—that her mother thought something dreadful had happened to her.

"It is dreadful," Georgia wailed; "Russell has died, and I was going to visit them the very next week, and now I'll never see him again and I can't bear it."

"You won't see him again, Georgia, no, but neither will Mary. She's the one something dreadful has happened to, and I think she's the one who feels she can't bear it. Go and see her, keep her company, tell her about your life, go for walks with her—that's what you can do for her now.

"Sometimes," Bea said to Jack with a sigh, "I feel Georgia's development was arrested at about the age of six."

Georgia telephoned Mary to arrange a day, and Mary said that if she was coming on the train, then she would send the car to meet her in Bath. Georgia, who felt her visit should be as difficult as possible by way of reparation, said that wouldn't be necessary and arrived therefore an hour and a half late on the twice-daily bus to Tadwick. Mary, who had by then decided she couldn't be coming, was trying to comfort herself by playing the piano, which was in fact rather fortuitous, as Georgia found some old sheet music of Russell's and they spent an extremely happy afternoon together, Georgia singing while Mary accompanied her.

"Right," Georgia said when they were both exhausted and she was hoarse, "that's *Oklahoma* and *My Fair Lady* ticked off; next week we'll do *Annie Get Your Gun* and *Carousel*. And how do you think you'd be with Scott Joplin? This is fun."

"It is indeed," said Mary, "and next week, dear, please do allow yourself to be driven. We'll have more time together; we can even go for a walk as well."

Georgia's visit had cheered Mary immensely; she insisted on hearing all about the festival and said she'd be there.

"Really? Goodness, Mary, that would be . . . well . . . wonderful," said Georgia slightly doubtfully. "But it'll be very noisy and . . . well, very noisy. And a lot of people."

"That's fine; I like noise and lots of people. Tim and Lorraine can look after me, or perhaps the Connells; I presume they'll be there. I may not stay very long, and I certainly won't be camping, but I'd love to see it all."

"You are so cool," said Georgia, giving her a kiss.

. . .

Two days later a letter arrived from Mary, enclosing a cheque for a thousand pounds.

"You said you were hoping to find a sponsor for your festival. Of course, I am not in that league, and I'm sure this won't make a great deal of difference, but it might pay for some posters or something. I know that Russell would have loved to have helped you; he so loved young people—as I do—and even got involved. In fact, he rather fancied himself a song-and-dance man; you might have got more than you bargained for! Please pass this to your committee as a token of my great interest and pleasure in being involved, in a small way."

"Shit!" said Abi, when Georgia told her. "A thousand fucking quid! Shit!"

Georgia felt that this was not quite the response Mary might have expected, but thought that she would have recognised its sincerity all the same.

. . .

The other person who came to visit, to Mary's great delight, was Emma. She was very upset to hear that Russell had died . . . "I shall never forget seeing him in the Dorchester that night," she wrote, "and thinking how handsome he was. And it was such a privilege to come to your wedding. If you'd like a little visit from me, please let me know; if not don't give it a moment's thought."

Mary wrote back and said that the only thought she had given it was how very nice it would be to see her.

"Come and have lunch with me, when you can. I shall look forward to it so much."

Emma arrived with a large bunch of daffodils, and was then mortified to see the drive down from the gate to the house lined with them.

"Talk about coals to Newcastle."

"No," said Mary, taking the daffodils, leading her into the kitchen, where Mrs. Salter found them a huge white jug. "I hate picking them, you see; they die so quickly, and it's wonderful to have yours."

"Well . . . I'm glad," said Emma slightly doubtfully. "Goodness, that is a lovely smell."

"What, dear, the daffodils? I never can find much of a perfume in them, to be honest."

"No, no, it's bread. Baking bread. Isn't it?" she said to Mrs. Salter.

"It is, my dear, yes."

"My mum used to make bread when we were all at home," said Emma. "I've never done it, although I sort of know how. It's hardly worth it for just for me."

"Time enough when you have a family of your own," said Mrs. Salter.

Emma nodded and smiled politely, thinking that while it was clearly ridiculous to completely write off the family of her own, and the bread she might make for it, its likelihood in the near future was so small as to be inconsiderable, given that the only person she would wish to have fathered the family clearly cared for her not in the least, and she had neither the energy nor the inclination to even begin looking for another. *Damn Barney. Damn him.* It was as if he'd cast a spell on her, rendered her incapable of normal sexual and emotional thought. She had to get over him; she had to.

. . .

Mary suggested a walk round the garden after lunch.

"I was half thinking you might be at the inquest," she said, tucking her arm in Emma's.

"Oh . . . no. I had nothing to do with it. No point, really."

"Dr. Pritchard was there. He gave some very good evidence, spoke so well. Such a charming man."

"Yes, he is a sweetheart. And he's very happy with Linda, you know? The lady he brought to your . . . your . . ." She stopped, clearly afraid of stirring up unhappy emotions.

Mary smiled at her, patted her arm.

"My wedding. Nothing makes me happier than thinking about that day, Emma. Nothing. Wonderful things, good memories."

"Yes, indeed," said Emma. She sighed without meaning to, then thought how selfish she was. "Sorry."

"Is anything the matter, dear? You look tired."

"No, no, I'm fine. Really. Well . . . maybe a bit tired. It's hard work, A and E. I was on nights all last week. Takes time to get over that."

"I'm sure. Well, if that's all. Now, I wonder if you heard from Georgia, and those two young men, the bridegroom—Mr. Weston, I think his name was—and his best man, Barnaby someone . . ."

"Fraser?"

"Yes, that's right. They were both there, of course. I was able to apologise to them, rather obliquely. I always felt I'd held them up, you know, wouldn't let Mr. Weston go in front of me in the queue. And then Barnaby paid a tribute to someone I thought might have been you."

"Me!"

"Yes, dear. Not necessarily, of course, but he said how a doctor at the hospital had helped him so much to get over his . . . his guilt at escaping from the whole thing without a scratch. I believe there's some technical phrase for it."

"Oh . . . yes. Yes, there is. Survivor guilt."

"That's it. Yes, and Georgia said you'd been wonderful with her, very kind and patient."

"Goodness." She felt herself blushing. "Um, what . . . what exactly did he say; can you remember?"

"Let me think. Not much more than that, really. But I thought it was you because he said 'she.' 'She helped me so much,' he said."

"Oh. Oh, well, maybe it was me. I don't . . . That is . . . Oh, dear."

And as the memories swept over her—of those early conversations with Barney, of how she tried to comfort him and to reassure him about Toby, and then the day, the fateful day of Toby's operation, when it had all begun between them—she suddenly felt her eyes fill with tears.

"Oh, now, you mustn't cry." Mary looked at her with great concern. "Or rather, cry as much as you like—so helpful, tears, I've always found—but then tell me all about it, what's upsetting you. Shall we go back inside? Mrs. Salter has made some scones; I do know that . . ."

"I'd better not come and see you too often, or I'll be the size of a house," said Emma, smiling through her tears.

"I hardly think so, dear. And if you mean that, I shall give you a glass of water and a dry biscuit next time. Come along, let's go in; here, I've got a hankie you can borrow; it's quite clean . . ."

. . .

". . . and it's just so stupid," said Emma. "I mean, why can't I get over him, just forget about him and move on?"

"I expect because it has never been properly resolved," said Mary gently. "You parted thinking it was only for a few weeks, knowing you loved each other . . ."

"Thinking we loved each other. He clearly doesn't love me."

"And how do you know that?"

"Mary, if he did, then surely he'd have contacted me. He knows I'm not with Luke—that was my boyfriend before, the one at the Dorchester that night—and I know he's not with Amanda. So . . . if he wanted to see me, then surely he would have called me. Or something."

"He might be thinking exactly as you are. Why haven't you contacted him, when you know it's over with Amanda . . ."

"He doesn't know I know."

"I thought you said he told your doctor friend."

"Oh . . . yes. Yes, that's right."

"Well . . . ?"

"Oh, Mary, I'd look such a fool. If there was someone else."

"Does that matter? So much? There are worse things, after all."
She considered this.

"Maybe not. It would be a terrible risk."

"Most worthwhile things are a risk, Emma. It was a risk for me,
you know, meeting Russell again after all those years. It could have
spoilt everything, spoilt all those wonderful memories; it could have
been dreadful. But . . . I decided it was worth it. You ring your Barnaby. The worst that can happen is that you'll know he doesn't love you
anymore—know for certain. And you'll feel a little foolish. And then
at least you can move on."

"Yes, but, Mary, it's been so long now. Months and months since
we met. However much he cared for me, if he did, surely he'd have got
over it by now. Forgotten me."

"My darling," said Mary very gently, "Russell didn't forget me or
get over me, nor I him. We waited more than sixty years for each
other. Love survives, you know. Forever, if need be."

❧ CHAPTER 54 ❧

It was all very astonishing. She still couldn't quite believe it: that she
was actually in a relationship with him, seeing him all the time, sleeping with him even. It just didn't seem possible.

But . . . it was.

It had all begun the day after the inquest; he'd asked her for a
drink—again—and when she'd said she didn't think so, he'd said,

"Please, Georgia. I want to hear about how yesterday went. I was thinking about you all day."

She was touched by that—that he should care.

"Well . . . all right. A quick one," she said. "Thank you."

They were rehearsing in downtown Chiswick; he took her to a bar in the High Road, not the pub, insisted on buying her a cocktail. She was surprised, but tried not to read too much into it. Maybe he had more money, now that he was a first assistant.

She'd told him about the inquest, in some detail. She thought he might be bored, but she didn't care. It was good to talk about it, and she wasn't into impressing Merlin anymore. There was no point.

"It must have been terrifying," he said, "reliving it publicly like that. Such a ghastly experience."

"Yes, it was. Especially having to talk about why I . . . well, ran away. But, you know, it was actually the best thing. I really feel it's over now. I never did before."

"Well . . . good for you," he said, and then added, looking as close to embarrassed as Merlin ever could, "I think you're marvellous, Georgia."

"Oh, for goodness' sake," she said, mildly irritated even by such excess, "of course I'm not. I'm a wimp. You of all people know that. Weeping and wailing all over the set of *Moving Away,* saying everyone hated me, that I couldn't do the part. Honestly, Merlin. Not marvellous at all."

"Well, I'm entitled to my opinion," he said, smiling at her. "Another one of those?"

"Oh . . . why not?"

When he came back, she took a deep breath and said, "How's . . . Ticky?"

"Oh . . . she's fine. Yes. Fine."

"Good." She could hear a *but* somewhere; she didn't even dare think about what it might be.

"Yes. Fine. Doing really well in New York. But"—here it came—"but she . . . I . . . Well, we're not together anymore."

"You're not together. Oh, Merlin, I'm sorry. So sorry."

He looked so wretched, she really was sorry. She didn't feel remotely glad. Well . . . not very remotely . . .

"Yeah, well. You know. It was hard conducting a relationship across two continents. It just wasn't . . . wasn't working anymore."

And if anyone had stopped it working, Georgia thought, it would have been Ticky. Not Merlin. No doubt whatsoever about that.

He sighed. "I miss her, of course. I miss her like hell. But . . . we were never together anyway. Or hardly. So what's new?"

"A lot, I guess," Georgia said. And then said again, "I'm sorry, Merlin."

"You're so sweet," he said, "to be so nice about it. But then you would be. You're such a nice person, Georgia." There was a pause; then he said, " I hope you didn't feel I was . . . well, playing around with you a bit. On *Moving Away.* I mean, I wasn't; I really enjoyed your company and I hoped I was helping. But after the party, I thought that maybe . . ."

"Merlin, of course I didn't," she said, her eyes meeting his in absolute astonishment. "Of *course* not. I just was so glad to have you as a friend. You were marvellous. A sort of wonderful big brother. But . . . heavens, no, it never even crossed my mind."

If I ever get an Oscar, she thought, *I won't have acted any better than that.*

· · ·

The next thing that happened was that he became involved in the festival. He thought it was a wonderful idea; he was clearly and genuinely impressed by how much they had achieved. And it turned out that he knew a lot of bands as friends—"mostly unsigned, but . . ."

"We're looking for unsigned. Although we're hoping to find quite a few through these play-offs we're organising. We've had a pretty big response to our flyers . . ."

"Yeah, that's a very clever idea."

"It is, isn't it? We still need a headliner, though. Do you know anyone remotely famous?"

He thought, then said, "I might. I'll see what I can do."

. . .

Three days later, she rang Abi.

"Abi, Abi, Abi, you'll never believe this. We've got BroadBand. And they can do the eighth. So we can get the Web site up and running . . ."

"Ohmigod. Oh. My. God. BroadBand! How, why—"

"Oh, you know what they say," said Georgia carelessly. "It's not what you know; it's who you know."

. . .

Merlin came to the next committee meeting. Abi was initially deeply suspicious of him—in fact, she'd told Georgia he sounded like a complete wanker. Georgia defended him rather feebly.

"He really isn't, Abi. He's actually very sweet and kind. Honestly."

"Doesn't sound too sweet and kind to me, treating you how he did."

"No, no, you don't understand; he didn't treat me any way, not like that; he really, really wanted to help, he told me, and he apologised if I felt he'd . . . well, you know . . ."

"Played around with you?"

"But he didn't. He behaved like a gentleman, honestly, always; he never tried anything . . ."

"I never did like gentlemen," said Abi.

"But you're marrying one."

Abi was silent for a moment; then she grinned.

"Yeah. S'pose I am. Still can't believe it. God, Georgia, he's bought me the most amazing rock; it's being sized right now, but it's just so . . . so beautiful. Mind you, I'll make the most terrible farmer's wife; I don't understand any of it, and God knows how I'm going to deal with the in-laws. Specially her."

"Abi, I'd back you against any mother-in-law. Against anything on the planet, really. I'm sure you'll do fine."

. . .

In the event, Abi quite liked Merlin; he made her laugh, and he certainly knew a lot about festivals.

"My parents used to take me to Glastonbury every year; I loved it. It's a kid's idea of heaven, all that mud and not having to have a bath. Have you thought about what you should do for the kids?"

"Like what?"

"Well, like face painting and weaving, stuff like that; it'll all add to the atmosphere, and anyway, it'll make more money."

"No, we hadn't thought of that. Good idea."

"And then you should sell tents, the little ones, and those waterproof cape things, and wellies."

"Yeah, and someone suggested blankets to me," Abi said.

"Blankets definitely. And I don't know what you're thinking about food, but I went to Reading last year, and they had some massive paella just bubbling away, and the punters just came and got bowlsful, made a change from burgers, really popular. Oh, now, here's another thought: you could do a CD of the festival. It needn't cost much, honestly; I know a bloke who knocks them out—well, you know him, Georgia, Jazz . . ."

"Oh, really? Jazz's great," she said to Abi. "You'd love him. He's my landlord."

"CD's a brilliant idea," said Abi, scribbling furiously. "You're a real find, Merlin. This is all great stuff."

. . .

"What did you think of Merlin?" she asked William later.

"He was all right. Bit of a poof, I thought. Wasn't too keen on the bracelets."

"Yeah. He probably swings both ways."

"What does that mean?" said William, looking genuinely puzzled.

Abi stared at him, her face blank; then she smiled and leaned forward to kiss him.

"Oh, William," she said, "I love you so much. You're so . . . so wonderful."

William gave up.

. . .

Things escalated fairly fast after that. Merlin drove Georgia back to London, took her out for a meal and then to a club. When the cab stopped outside her house, he kissed her good night, rather chastely, and then said, "Do you really see me as a big brother, Georgia?"

"Course."

"Right. Good. Well, good night."

"Night, Merlin. And thank you again. Not just for the evening, but for coming today."

"It's fine. See you on Monday."

"Yeah, Monday."

This wasn't easy. It so wasn't easy.

. . .

They were rehearsing until really late on Monday; Georgia was depressed, felt she'd done badly.

"It's so hard, doing comedy," she said to Merlin. "So different. I feel I'm right back to square one."

"You're doing great. Come on; let's grab something to eat."

They went to a Pizza Express; she picked at her lasagna rather halfheartedly.

"Come on," he said, "cheer up. You're doing absolutely fine. Honestly."

"You really think so?"

"I really think so. I'll tell you who isn't—Milly."

"Oh, really?" Milly Buchanan was playing the other girl.

"Yeah. She's our problem; she's what's making you feel you're crap."

"Oh. Well . . . maybe. I do find her quite . . . quite over-the-top."

"Exactly. She's playing it like it's *Romeo and Juliet*. Very, very diffi-cult to deal with. But I think Bryn's onto her. I saw him talking to her rather intently as we left."

"Mmm. Maybe. Suddenly I feel hungrier."

"Good. Big brother at work again." He raised his glass to her. "To . . . to stardom. You'll get there."

Georgia looked at him. He was wearing a white T-shirt and blue jeans; his face was tanned still from a family skiing holiday. He looked . . . well, he looked amazing.

"Yeah," she said with great difficulty. "Yeah, you're a really great brother."

Merlin put down his glass and looked at her in silence for a moment. His eyes moved over her face. She sat there, trying to appear cool.

"I have to tell you something," he said. "You can tell me to get lost if you like."

"Yes?"

"I don't exactly see you the same way," he said, "not really as a sis-ter at all."

"No?"

"No. Not in the least. Actually, I think you're utterly gorgeous. Sorry."

Georgia stared at him; then she stood up, went round the table, and put her arms round his neck.

"Oh, Merlin," she said, kissing him repeatedly, first on his cheek, then on his forehead, then finally and rather recklessly on the mouth, "oh, Merlin, don't get lost. Don't say sorry. I . . ."

"Let's get out of here," he said.

. . .

They went to her room. She said she'd rather, although he did offer her his place: "I'm self-contained, and anyway, they won't mind; it's part of their religion . . ."

"No, no, I wouldn't feel . . . happy."

"I want you to feel happy," he said. "Come on."

. . .

She was nervous again, going back. He was probably incredibly experienced—which she wasn't. He'd find her dull, disappointing, and she hadn't made the bed properly that morning; he'd think she was a slut, and she was wearing some really grotty old pants; he must be used to the likes of Ticky in Agent Provocateur . . .

None of it mattered. He clearly didn't find her dull; in fact, he was surprisingly . . . well, straightforward, which was a relief, and there certainly wasn't time to notice the unmade bed; they were on it in seconds after shutting the door behind them, and as for her knickers, well, he just yanked them off completely unceremoniously; anything better would have been a complete waste.

In fact, it was all wonderful; it was as if they had been ready and waiting for each other, perfectly matched, perfectly tuned . . . "That was totally amazing," he said afterwards, lying with his face buried in her hair. "We saw, we conquered, we came."

She hoped he didn't say that to all the girls.

. . .

That was the only thing that worried her: how could he be so suddenly and so totally taken with her, Merlin Gerard, so gorgeous, so sexy, so . . . so sophisticated. Merlin, who was used to girls like Ticky, as gorgeous and sexy and sophisticated as he was; how could he want to be involved with her?

After a few days, a few nights, when she was beginning to feel more confident, she managed to ask him that; he smiled and kissed her and sat up on the pillows.

"I find you totally gorgeous and sexy, Georgia. I always did. You're so special. So unique. So not like anyone else. The first moment I saw you, I felt a catch in my heart . . ."

"Merlin!" That really did sound a bit rehearsed.

"No, I did. But . . ."

"Well, but you had Ticky then."

"Yes, of course. And now I've got you. My own beautiful brown bird. Would you like to sing for me once more? Before we go to sleep?"

Crushing the distaste for this, telling herself he was just . . . wonderfully poetic, that was all . . . she smiled at him ecstatically and climbed onto him, her legs straddling him.

"I love your energy," he said. "It's so amazing." They fell asleep with his head on her breast.

In the morning they met Jazz on his early rounds, as he put it: checking the terminally leaking taps, the blocked lavatories in the house.

"Ah," he said, "very nice. Thought that might be how it was, Merlin, you old bugger. How come you get to pull all the best ones? Georgia, my lovely, any trouble with him, you come straight to me, OK?"

She laughed and said OK; she loved Jazz.

And now, nearly three weeks later, she could hardly imagine life being any different. It was totally, totally wonderful; she was the luckiest, happiest girl in the world.

. . .

Emma hadn't got the job in Glasgow; she went to see Alex, almost in tears.

"That's the second. I'm beginning to feel victimised."

"My dear Emma, you wait till you're trying to get a consultancy. That really does feel like victimisation. Nine jobs I went for before I got this one; it was ghastly. You get there and you see the same old faces each time, with a few variations, and it's always the bloke you least like who gets it, gets called into the boardroom while you all sit waiting like a load of cretins, and then you all shake hands and say you never really wanted it anyway, and crawl back to your hospital with your tail between your legs. I had a special interview shirt; it got quite threadbare towards the end."

"Yes, well, thanks for all that. I can't wait," said Emma. "Meanwhile, it's tail-between-the-legs time for me. Can I stay, Alex?"

"Of course you can. Nothing could please me more. Sorry . . . not what you want to hear."

"It sort of is. Thank you. There are lots more jobs I can apply for in the pipeline, but . . ."

"Emma, the thing about obstetrics is that it's a very popular discipline. There's always going to be lots of jobs, but also lots of people applying for them. You'll get one in the end, promise. Meanwhile, you're a fantastic member of the team here. You can stay as long as you like."

At least she still had a job . . . even if she didn't have anything else.

. . .

"Barney! Hi, darling! How are you?"

"Fine. Yes. Thanks. And you?"

"Oh, pretty good. I called to invite you to my leaving do."

"Your leaving do! That's a bit sudden, isn't it?"

"Not really. It's just that it's so long since we talked. I've done my time. Start at Darwood's in a fortnight. At the French desk there. Taking a bit of a break first."

"Yeah?"

"Yeah. We—Micky and I—are off to Barbados for ten days . . ."

"Micky?"

"Yes, I'm engaged. Again. To Micky Burne Proctor. Getting married in the summer. Slightly déjà vu, but at least I'll be in a different dress. I thought that really would be unlucky, wearing the same. Or could be. But . . . otherwise, same venue, same church, same time of day even. I think. Mummy and I are working on that one. Anyway, Friday evening, sixish, Terminus. Hope you can come."

Well. She didn't let the grass grow under her feet. You had to hand it to her, Barney thought with a sense of grudging admiration: she'd survive an earthquake and hurricane combined, Tamara would. And come up looking immaculate. And sexy. Micky Burne Proctor, eh? In the *Sunday Times* rich list the previous year. Hedge-fund boy. Better prospect than Toby.

He couldn't think why she'd want him at her leaving do. But . . . might be fun. He hadn't had much of that lately. He wondered if Toby knew. Or cared.

. . .

"Order, order. Georgia, you first."

"Right. Well the play-offs are going brilliantly. We've already got three winners from three pubs. One's really fantastic. Called Literate. I don't think they'll be unsigned for much longer. Oh, and a sweet folk band as well. Lots of stalls are coming on board . . . face painting, weaving, a little roundabout, a bouncy castle. Everything we discussed, really. Some guy's got a hat stall . . . says they went really well at Glastonbury."

"What sort of hats?" said Abi.

"Every sort. Baseball hats, sort of trilbies, berets, reggae hats, sun hats for kids. Oh, and some really nice girl's got a sort of beauty stall, does, like, makeovers and massages and all stuff like that. What do you think?"

"Mmm." Abi considered this. "No, don't think so. Doesn't go with the family feel. But quite like hats. Welly stall?"

"Oh, yes, got one of those. Merlin says it's essential, don't you, Merlin?"

"Yup."

"Oh, I do hope it doesn't rain," said Emma.

"It will," said Abi. "Best to accept it. After that anything's a bonus. We might even get some good gear out of it."

"What do you mean?"

"Some guy I met, friend of William's, he had a festival on his land. It rained so hard, two-day festival it was, people were just getting into their cars at the end, stepping out of their filthy, muddy clothes and just leaving them. This guy said lots of it was really good stuff: Fat Face, Abercrombie, all that. His wife washed it about thee times and then they wore it. And their kids, loads of Boden."

"Cool. Best pray for rain then."

"Who's responsible for litter?" asked Merlin.

"Me, I s'pose," said Abi. "Comes under the heading of site management."

"Make sure you've got loads and loads of bins and bags. Twice as much as you think."

"Yes, please do," said William. He had a sudden vision of endless acres of litter and what his father might say or do.

"OK, OK."

"You need people specially briefed to pick it up too," said Merlin. "It's really important. And loos . . . Abi, is that you?"

"Yeah, I'm toilet queen."

"Can we not have those awful urinals in rows where you face the other blokes and try not to look at them, and you all pee into a pit in the middle?"

"Sounds fun. I'll do my best. How are the bookings looking, Georgia?"

"Oh, nothing much yet. But the Web site's only been up and running a couple of weeks. Lots of hits, though."

"Great. Any reactions to the name?"

"Nope. Well, only from my mum. She thinks it's great. She had an LP called *In Good Company* in the seventies."

"Great. Exactly the image we're after. Mum's favourites. Oh, dear. Maybe we should change it."

"We shouldn't," said Merlin firmly. "It's a great name."

"Yeah, well, you would say that," said Georgia. "You thought of it."

"Shut up. Any other objections?"

There weren't.

"OK. Well, I've got everything booked site-wise," said Abi.

"Arena, electrics, sound systems, water. What does everyone think about campfires?"

"We think no campfires," said William firmly.

"Barbecues?"

"Not happy."

"William! People love them. Specially families."

"I'll . . . think about it."

"Bless. We've got the alcohol licence; the police are on-side. Got St. John's for the first-aid tent as well."

"You've done so well," said Georgia, beaming at her. "Security?"

"I've talked to a couple of firms. Both very expensive."

"You have to have security," said Merlin. "And they have to check for drugs."

"Yes, all right. I know that. I just said they were expensive. Now, what are we going to do with our thousand pounds from wonderful Mrs. Mackenzie? Blow the lot on publicity, say, or split it, put it into the various pots?"

"I think split it," said William, "in case we don't get any more."

"William, you are such a ray of sunshine," said Georgia irritably.

. . .

She was very jumpy now; *Moving Away* was going on air in three weeks, and the publicity machine was cranking up. Davina and Bryn Merrick had been the most in demand. Davina's lovely, laughing face had been everywhere, but Georgia had done two interviews already, one for the *Daily News* arts roundup and one for *You* magazine, both of them talking her up as one of the new faces of the summer. She was surprised about it, hadn't thought anyone would take any notice of her. The one in *You* had been a big profile, very personal, had asked her about being adopted—and by white parents, had that been difficult, how had she coped—and had mentioned, inevitably, the crash. She'd hated it, but Linda told her it was fantastic she was getting so much coverage, and she should just be grateful.

"You're getting talked about; most people at your stage would give their eyeteeth for any publicity."

The DVDs of the show hadn't gone out to the critics yet; she was dreading that, everyone seeing how bad she'd been. Although the girl from *You* magazine, who had managed to wangle one out of the press office, said she'd been "stunningly good." Well, what did she know?

. . .

The meeting was over; the others left. Abi looked at William and smiled. "Love you."

"Love you too. You . . . busy now?"

"Not terribly. You?"

"I've got an hour or so."

"Cool."

"Where's Sylvie?"

"Out for the night. With Mr. Perv."

"Right then. Shall we . . ."

"Yeah. I want to show you something first, though."

"That'll be nice."

"No, no," said Abi. "It's what I'm going to wear on Friday."

"Couldn't it be afterwards?"

"No. You might find it exciting; you never know. Although, actually, I hope not. Give me five minutes."

"OK. No more, though."

"No, promise."

She was back in ten.

"How do I look?"

"Blimey," said William.

"Is that it? Don't you like it?"

"Quite . . . you don't look quite yourself."

"That was the idea."

"Abi, you are yourself. That's why I love you."

"I know, but . . ."

She walked out into the hall and looked at herself in the long mirror there. It was true: she didn't look quite herself. She looked good, though, she thought. She was wearing grey trousers and a pink wrap-around sweater. And low-heeled shoes. Her makeup was . . . well, it was rather nice, she thought. Grey eyeshadow, grey eyeliner, not much mascara, pink lip gloss. Her hair was tied back.

She went back to William.

"I think I look great."

"Well . . . you do. But . . . not yourself. Like I said. And why?"

"I thought it would be more suitable this way. More the sort of girl they'd like. Approve of."

"I'm afraid it's a bit late for that."

"It's never too late. That's my motto."

"Abi, my mother's already seen you starkers. Twice."

"Not starkers. I've always worn shoes, at least. Oh, you're so disappointing, William. Here I am trying to be a lady and you tell me there's no point."

"I don't want a lady. I want you."

"This isn't for you. Anyway, this is what I'm wearing on Friday."

"OK. But . . . get it off now. Please."

They were going to have dinner with the Graingers on Friday at the farm. It was not a keenly anticipated evening. Except just possibly by Mr. Grainger.

CHAPTER 55

"So . . . tonight's the night, is it?"

"Yup. I am shit scared."

"Oh, don't be so ridiculous. When were you frightened of anything?"

"I'm frightened of Mrs. Grainger. Or rather, upsetting Mrs. Grainger."

"I'd have thought you'd done that plenty already, Abi."

"Well, OK. But I do want tonight to go well. She's being very good, he said . . ."

"That's big of her."

"Georgia, you're not being very helpful. She's said, apparently, that she's considering letting us have cottage number one, to live in."

"Even bigger . . ."

"No, well, it is a source of income for them."

"So is William."

"I s'pose. Anyway, it would be cool. It's really sweet, or could be. Needs tarting up a bit. But it's got three bedrooms . . ."

"One for you, one for the children, one for her."

"Oh, stop it. No, I could use one as an office. When I start my company. I mean, it doesn't matter these days where you work, does it? I can go and see clients; they don't have to come to me. I'm really excited about it."

"Won't you be living on her doorstep? Literally?"

"Well . . . sort of. But it's about quarter of a mile from the farmhouse. Right at the bottom of a track thing. I don't think we'd have to see much of her. Anyway, listen, what I've really rung to say is, have you seen the *Mail?*"

"No. Why? I've had two missed calls from Linda; could that be a clue? I was just going to call her."

"Could be. It's got a really nice piece in it about *Moving Away.* Saying how great it is."

"Oh, yeah?"

"Yeah. And then it says something about some promising new-comer, Georgia Linley."

"What, like she's crap, lets the whole thing down?"

"Well, obviously But then it says your performance is . . . let's see, oh, yes, extraordinary. And that you're . . . yes, here it is, 'that rare thing, a completely fresh, individual talent. One minute funny, the next heartbreaking, she looks set to steal the show.' "

"Oh. My. God. Oh, *my God.*"

"Yeah, I know. So cool. Georgia, you're not crying, are you? How extremely unusual."

. . .

Friday. Her lucky day. Always used to be. And she'd met Barney on a Friday . . . if you could call it lucky. And Luke, actually, come to that. And got her finals results. And passed her grade-five ballet with distinction.

So . . . this would be the day to do it. She really would. She'd . . . well, that was a good idea: she'd text him; that would be so much less embarrassing for both of them; why hadn't she thought of that before? He could ignore a text, or send her something noncommittal back, like . . . well, like, "Nice to hear from you." He wouldn't have to struggle to find the right words, or to sound pleased to hear from her. And she wouldn't have to act either—at sounding all casual and as if she'd just suddenly thought she might call him, just for old times' sake. Yes, that's what she'd do. When she was on her way out for the evening, not a Billy-no-mates, sitting in her room at the hospital. Mark and some of the others had asked her for a curry. Or even when she'd had a couple of drinks. Nothing like a bit of drink dialling . . .

. . .

Abi had gone to have her hair blow-dried. It was the only way to get it all silky smooth, like those posh girls had. Then she'd go home, change, and set off in enough time to arrive really cool and collected. She'd even bought a much lighter perfume, not her usual heavy stuff.

She had a manicure as well, no colour on her nails, just left them all natural and shiny. She was going to do William really proud . . .

He'd told her to arrive at about seven thirty: "Then we can have a drink; Mother likes to feed everybody at eight sharp."

She resisted the temptation to say, What if everybody didn't want to be fed at eight sharp? Tonight, the world was going to see a new Abi. Or rather, the Graingers were. And actually, who knew? She might even stay that way.

She'd read a *Telegraph* that was lying around the office, so she could converse intelligently, if required, on politics or whatever. Not the foreign stuff; that completely baffled her. And listened to *PM* on Radio 4 as she drove back from the hairdresser. God, it was boring: how could people like that stuff?

She left Bristol at six; that would give her so much time.

. . .

"Barney, hi. Lovely to see you. Come along in. You'll know nearly everyone, I'm sure . . . Micky, darling, have you met Barney Fraser? He's at BKM, on the commodities desk."

"Not sure. Hi, Barney."

Burne Proctor gave Barney an ice-cold smile. What a cliché, Barney thought: the Etonian drawl, the slicked-back blond hair, the blue eyes, the striped pink-and-white shirt, worn tieless under the excruciatingly well-cut dark suit . . . and worth how many millions? Well, it was usually billions now, on that list. A good few anyway. He reputedly took home over a million every year in salary and bonuses alone. *Well done, Tamara.*

"Hi," said Barney. "Congratulations."

"Yeah, great, thanks."

"Off to Barbados, I hear."

"Yah, well, not quite Barbados—one of the little islands off that coast I've bought. Should be fun. And Tam needs a break; she's had a tough time."

"Indeed," said Barney.

"Well, nice to have met you. Hope we'll be seeing you when we're settled."

Yeah, right. He was about as likely to receive an invitation from the Burne Proctors as from the Queen. Probably rather less.

He looked around the bar. It was huge, very, very long, one of the old-fashioned brass-and-glass jobs. With the usual impossible din going on. He must be getting old to notice that. Tamara was right: he did know nearly everyone. Well, they did work for the same firm, so it was hardly surprising. Loads of pretty girls, which was nice. They all looked the same, these girls, with their long hair and their long legs and their dark suits and their high heels. One of the things about Emma was that she didn't look like that. Well, she had long hair and long legs, but she was quirkily pretty, not one of your preppy monotones; her voice was quick and light; she never drawled, and when she smiled . . . God, when she smiled. She'd light up the city of London unaided with that smile. And her nose, and the way it wrinkled up when she giggled. He loved her nose . . .

Shit, Barney, stop thinking about the girl and call her. Go on. Just do it. Lay the ghost if nothing else. Go and . . . Damn. He'd left his phone on his desk. He never did that, ever. Better go and get it. He—

"Barney! Hi! Lovely to see you. You know Sasha, don't you? Yes, I thought you did. Sasha's got the most incredible new job, out in Dubai. How are you, you old bastard? Come and tell us what you've been up to."

The phone would have to wait.

. . .

She'd written the text; she just hadn't sent it. She'd do that bit later. When she'd got her courage up.

She'd written it on the bus: *Hi, Barney. How are you? I was thinking about you and wondering if we could meet sometime. Just for a chat. Call me if you have a minute. Emma.*

She'd added two kisses and then taken them off again about six times. At the moment they were there.

Her phone rang sharply; she jumped. Had she sent it already, by mistake; was he ringing her . . . ? *Don't be ridiculous, Emma; you're getting Alzheimer's.*

"Emma? It's Mark . . . Listen, we're in a different place, not the

Indian; it's a Thai, just by the big shopping arcade; that OK? Got a pen . . . ?"

Emma scribbled down the address and went back to looking at her text. And deleting and reinstating the kisses.

. . .

This was good. She was in really good time. She'd even been able to put her car through the car wash. That would amuse William; he didn't believe in cleaning cars. He treated his cars like shit. Not like his tractors. He tended them as carefully as if they were his animals. One of his cows. One of his girls.

It was a funny thing, their relationship. Everyone was baffled by it; she could see that. Even Sylvie, who was always going on about how fit William was.

"You can't marry him, Abi," she'd said. "You don't have anything in common. What are you going to do in the evenings, talk to the sheep or something?"

As long as it was in the lambing shed, Abi thought, that'd be fine. She really couldn't see the problem with having nothing in common with William. It made life more interesting. Anyway, they did. They found the same things funny; they liked the same people . . . She even liked his farming friends, and they certainly seemed to like her, and he loved people like Georgia . . . And actually she did find the farming genuinely interesting. The pattern of it intrigued her, the progress through the year, the hatching and dispatching of animals, as William called it, the way it all worked: stuff was planted and grew and was harvested and then you started all over again, and it was all rather . . . neat. Neat and satisfying.

She was not particularly fastidious; she didn't mind the mess and the smells—except perhaps the silage; that was quite gross—and she genuinely liked the animals. Especially the cows. They were so sweet, with their big, curious faces and kindly eyes, their swinging walk. She had seen a calf born a couple of weeks earlier, and she had found it wonderful; this little thing slithering out, wet and curly and a bit bewildered, and the mother's great tongue licking it, and the hot, sweet, strong smell. William said it wasn't always like that; they often didn't slither out; they had to be hauled, brutally; she'd been lucky. He'd promised her a night in the lambing shed when the lambs were born: "You'll like that; it's such chaos, and so noisy. They come out one after the other; it's like a sort of conveyor belt; you've hardly delivered one, or rather a set, when there's another one on the go. And they just come out, stagger up on their little legs, make for the milk, and— Don't look at me like that; there'll be no time for us to do anything. Together, that is. You'll have too much to do. You won't be able to just watch."

She was impressed by the rams' performances: "One ram to fifty ewes, thereabouts."

"Not even you could manage that, William, could you?" she said.

And, "Oh, I don't know," he said. "Over a few days, you'd be surprised."

They had discussed the matter of children; they both liked children, wanted several.

"But not yet. I want to get my company up and running first."

"That's fine. I can wait. Although not too long; you're marrying an old man, don't forget."

She did forget how old he was: ten years more than her. It was quite a lot.

He was completely relaxed about her working; he said it was what made her interesting; he didn't want her hanging about, bored.

"You can carry on working when we have kids, if you like. It's fine by me. Just don't expect any help, all right? Farmers are not new men."

Abi said she wasn't too keen on new men; they always seemed a bit suspect to her.

"All that wanting to breast-feed their own babies. Yuck!"

. . .

"Sherry, Abi?"

She was doing it on purpose, Abi thought. She must know that nobody young drank sherry. She'd hardly ever tasted it; she seemed to remember it was absolutely filthy.

Mrs. Grainger had done a double take when Abi had walked in; her disguise as well-bred, well-brought-up girl had certainly worked.

"How nice to see you," she said. "William, take Miss Scott's coat."

"Please call me Abi," she said, thinking how bizarre it was to be addressed as Miss Scott by a woman who had seen her pubes. Twice.

And, "Very well . . . Abi," Mrs. Grainger had said. Mr. Grainger had pumped her hand vigorously and told her it was jolly good to see her; he was a bit of a sweetheart, she'd decided, definitely where William got his charm from.

"Now, I do hope you don't mind," said Mrs. Grainger, "if we eat in the kitchen. It's just scruffy supper, as I'm sure William will have told you." What was scruffy supper, for God's sake? "Do forgive me, but I've been so busy this week. But let's go through to the drawing room and have a drink."

The drawing room was the room where Abi had sat that first day after the crash, waiting for William. It looked rather better, as William had lit a fire in the huge fireplace, but struggle as it did, the fire wasn't making much of a job of heating the room. She made for the chair nearest to it, then drew back, fearing that was not what posh people did. They were used to the cold; for some reason central heating seemed to be regarded—by the older generation, at any rate—as a bit common. Well, cottage number one was going to be dead common; she'd make sure of that.

"Well, congratulations to you both," said Mr. Grainger. "Jolly well done." He smiled, and she could have sworn winked at her; she presumed he'd heard about the encounters between her and Mrs. Grainger.

"Yes, it's very . . . nice," said Mrs. Grainger. *Nice* was clearly the best she could do, but she was definitely trying.

"Any idea when you'll be actually tying the knot?" said Mr. Grainger. "William's been a bit vague about it."

"Oh . . . we're both pretty vague, I think," said Abi. "Probably when William's not too busy."

"I'm afraid there's no such time," said Mrs. Grainger. "Farming is a nonstop process, as you will discover."

"Um . . . yes." She looked at William for help. He smiled at her rather foolishly.

"We don't want to leave it too long, actually," he said. "I can't wait to have Abi here instead of miles down the road."

"Ah, yes," said Mrs. Grainger. "Now, I don't know if William has told you, Abi, but we are proposing you have one of the cottages to live in."

"Yes. Yes, he did; it sounds coo—wonderful. Thank you."

"I hope you'll be comfortable there. Of course, we've had to take it out of the brochures. We have families who come back year after year. They'll be quite distressed, I imagine, to find that their holiday home is no longer available."

Quite distressed. What an extraordinary thing to say. God, she was a strange woman. Was it really going to be worth it? Living next-door to her?

Then she looked at William, grinning at her, lounging back in his chair, dressed up for the occasion in clean jeans and a pair of suspiciously new-looking boots, and knew it was.

"You must tell us about your job," said Mr. Grainger. "I don't really understand it, I'm afraid. I think William said you were involved in photography . . ."

"Well . . . sort of. But I'm hoping to set up my own company."

"Taking photographs?"

"No, no, organising events. You know, like for companies. Conferences and so on."

"Will it be worth it, starting something now?" said Mrs. Grainger. She was looking very determinedly puzzled. "I mean, surely once you're married, you'll be needed by William up here."

"Well . . . I'm not sure . . ." She looked at William helplessly.

"Well, of course you will. You marry a farmer, you marry the farm."

"She could organise some shoots for us," said Mr. Grainger, and this time she knew he winked.

"I . . . don't know anything about shooting. Yet. I'm sure William can teach me."

"You won't be going out with the guns," said Mrs. Grainger. "Wives don't, for the most part. Unless you do some picking up."

Picking up? Picking up what? The farmers? Well, there were a few she could fancy . . .

"It's the lunches, coffees, all that sort of thing. I . . . well, I . . ." She appeared to be struggling to get some words out; finally she managed it: "I shall certainly appreciate some help with it all. It's very hard work, and I'm beginning to find it very tiring." She actually managed a smile. Abi smiled determinedly back.

"I'm not much of a cook," she said carefully, "but of course I'd like to help. You can guide me, I'm sure."

"Indeed. Melanie did wonderful lunches, didn't she, William? I remember once I was ill and she produced lunch for twenty-eight without turning a hair. Melanie was one of William's former girl-friends," she added.

OK, you old witch. So it's to be war. In spite of the low heels. She might as well have saved the money. But: "Still, as I say, I'm sure we'll get along very well."

That was a concession. A big one. She was at least trying.

"More sherry, Abi?" said Mr. Grainger.

"That would be lovely. And then I'm so looking forward to my scruffy supper . . ."

. . .

She couldn't do it. She just couldn't. She'd look so pathetic; he'd be so embarrassed; it was ridiculous. Totally, totally a bad idea. She deleted the text, switched her phone off, and walked into the restaurant.

God, he needed to get out of here. He'd drunk far too much. And stayed far too long. He'd reckoned on half an hour. It was . . . God, nearly nine.

He'd just retrieve his phone and—

"Barney! Oh, Barney, I'm going to miss you!"

Tamara's arms were round his neck, her lips on his cheek, her thick scent everywhere.

"Well . . . I'll miss you too. But Darwood's isn't exactly in another country. I'm sure we'll see each other around."

"Yeah, of course. Isn't Micky sweet? Aren't I lucky?"

"You are, yes," said Barney, adding dutifully, "And he's lucky too."

He suddenly saw himself as he must seem to her: rather pathetic, a none-too-successful relic of their old life. While she . . . she'd got everything perfectly sorted: looked at that life, rejected it, and ordered a new one rather more to her satisfaction. Sleek, sassy, winner-takes-all Tamara.

"Sweet of you to say so. It does all seem terribly meant. Just think, if there hadn't been that crash, Toby and I would have been an old married couple by now."

"Indeed."

"And so might you and Amanda."

"Possibly."

"And . . . Emma? You with her?"

"Oh . . . no, no."

"No! Why not? I thought that was why—"

"You thought wrong," said Barney briskly.

"Barney! So what happened? Come on, you can tell me."

"I . . ." How could he possibly tell her—Tamara, of all people—about his broken heart? That most definitely wasn't a cliché, he thought; his heart did indeed feel as if it was snapped in two. Or, no, more like dead and crumbling to dust. But then . . .

"It was all a terrible mistake," he said finally. "We'd . . . I'd got it wrong."

"In what way?" She looked round, took his hand. "Come on, Barney, let's go outside; I can't hear you in this."

"But—"

"No, I insist. It sounds important."

Outside, in the cold, she listened as he gave her a brief résumé, her dark eyes fixed on his face . . . Then she said, "Barney, you absolutely have to call her."

"Tamara, why? She finished it."

"Only because she thought you were still with Amanda."

"No!"

"Yes!"

"Well . . ." He digested this for a moment; then he said, "Well, she knows I'm not anymore. So she could have rung me."

"Oh, Barney, please! Girls do not make those sorts of phone calls. That's a bloke's prerogative. Is she with anyone else?"

"Don't think so. No. No she's not. At least—"

"Then, for God's sake, what are you doing? Look, you don't have anything to lose. Do you? It's crazy, what you're not doing. Just get out your phone and give her a call. It is so, so obvious. I can't believe it. Anyway, I'd better get back; Micky will think I've run away with you."

"I don't think so," said Barney, "loser like me."

"Barney, you are so not a loser. You're just great. Never tell anyone, but I really, really fancied you for ages. If you'd asked me first, I'd have married you, not Toby. Anyway, just as well; I'd have made your life a complete misery. Bye, darling. And just make that call. Otherwise I will."

"You don't have her number," said Barney. He was smiling now, thinking how wrong he'd been about her. Or partly wrong, anyway.

"I can ring the hospital. I mean it. Promise me."

"I promise," said Barney. He leaned forward, gave her a kiss.

"Thanks, Tamara. And thanks for the party. And have a great wedding."

"I will."

She would. She got everything she wanted. But . . . she knew how to get it.

No possible doubt about that.

. . .

The food was great. She had to admit that. A wonderful chicken pie, and before that, tiny salmon parcels. Followed by a gooseberry mousse. And thick, thick cream. If this was scruffy supper, what would the full-blown dinner party be like? And if this was the sort of food William was used to, he was going to be popping home from cottage number one pretty often.

The wine was very nice too, and Mr. Grainger had made a great thing of letting her taste it, to make sure she liked it, but . . . God! One bottle between the four of them. She finished her two small glasses, made a great thing of lifting it and looking in it, and then at William, but he was studiously ignoring her. In more ways than one; he and his father had started talking about GM crops and whether they might consider a trial.

Finally, as she sipped at her empty glass for about the tenth time, Mrs. Grainger said, "Would you like a soft drink, Abi? I thought, as you were driving . . ."

"Oh, but . . ." She looked at William. "William, I thought . . . well, I thought I was staying here tonight."

"Really? I wish you'd said something to me, William," said Mrs. Grainger. "I would have made up the spare room bed."

Abi waited for William to say something that would indicate she wouldn't be needing the spare room, but he smiled rather awkwardly at her, passed her the bottle of red he was sharing with his father, and returned to the discussion.

Abi poured herself a large glass, smiled at Mrs. Grainger, and wondered what on earth she could find to say to her; in the end she just sat and ate and learnt a lot about GM crops.

. . .

It was very quiet on the trading floor. He didn't often see it like this. It looked and sounded dead, the screens blank, the phones silent.

He went over to his desk; his phone was still there. Well, it would have been; it was hardly state-of-the-art anymore. He was getting one of the new generation of iPhones, but it was taking a time to arrive.

He sat looking at it, hearing Tamara's voice: "It's crazy what you're not doing."

He scrolled down the numbers, found her name, took a deep breath, as if he was about to do something physically difficult, and pressed the button. And listened. Listened for her voice. Her pretty, slightly breathless voice.

It came. "Hi, this is Emma. Sorry I'm not around; just leave a message and I'll get back to you."

Shit. He hadn't expected that. And why not? Had he really thought she'd just be sitting there, waiting patiently for him to call? Of course not. She was probably out somewhere; or maybe she was working. Yes, that'd be it; she was at the hospital. He called the number, asked for the doctor's station in A&E. A female, rather bored voice said, "Accident and Emergency."

"Oh," said Barney. "Ah. Yes. Er . . . is . . . that is, is Dr. King there? Dr. Emma King?"

"No, she's not on duty tonight."

"Ah. Well . . . well, what about tomorrow?"

"Not sure. Do you want me to find out?"

No, thought Barney, *of course not, that's why I asked.*

"That'd be great."

"Just hold on."

She was a long time; when she came back, she said, "Yes, she's on duty from six a.m."

"Right. Fine. OK. Er . . . thank you. Thank you very much."

He felt quite differently now. Charged, up and running.

He sat for a moment thinking. If she was on duty from six, she was unlikely to be anywhere but in that flat of hers. That rather dreary flat, where he had spent those few extremely happy hours. OK, he'd go there. He'd drive down right now . . . No, maybe not, he'd had far too much to drink. Well, never mind. He'd take the train. And then get a cab. Easy. And if . . . well, if she told him to get lost, he could . . . well, he didn't know quite what he'd do then. Best not to think about it. Live for now. As Tamara would have done. Of all the advice from all the people in the world . . . It was very ironic.

He called Emma again; it was still switched off. He left a message this time.

"Emma, it's me. I'm coming down to Swindon."

That was all.

He left the building, hailed a cab.

. . .

"Now, you must tell us about this concert, Abigail." Mr. Grainger clearly felt he and William had been talking about GM crops long enough. "We're looking forward to it, aren't we?" he added to his wife. She gave him one of her pained smiles.

"July, isn't it? July eighth?"

"And ninth," said Abi.

"The ninth as well? There are two?"

"No," said Abi, looking at William in bewilderment, "it's running over two days. It's a . . . well, it's a . . . a music festival. People will be staying, camping . . ."

"Oh, no," said Mrs. Grainger, "that won't be possible."

William looked at her, startled.

"What do you mean, Mother, it won't be possible?"

"I mean exactly that. I . . . we can't have strangers camping on the farm. It's ridiculous. I had no idea. We shall have people breaking into the house, frightening the animals, letting them out onto the roads, quite possibly. Peter, did you realise this was happening?"

"I . . . Not exactly," said Mr. Grainger. He was looking very uncomfortable.

"Dad!" said William. "Come on! I did explain."

"Perhaps you did. I . . . don't remember."

"Well, whether you remember or not, it's not going to happen," said Mrs. Grainger. "It must be cancelled."

"It can't be," said Abi, "not now."

"I beg your pardon?"

"I said it can't be cancelled. Tickets have been sold, bands have been booked, there's a Web site, people will come anyway."

"This is appalling," said Mrs. Grainger, "absolutely appalling. Well, you'll just have to return the tickets, and say on the Web site that it's been cancelled. I've never heard of anything quite so . . . so high-handed. Or so rude," she added.

"Mother!"

"Well, it is."

"Honestly," said Abi, endeavouring to ease the atmosphere a little, "there'll be no trouble with break-ins or letting the cattle out. We've got a very good firm handling the security . . ."

"You've got a very good firm handling the security! With whose permission, may I ask? I'm sorry, but I'm finding this completely incomprehensible. I absolutely refuse to agree to any of it. I was opposed even to what I thought was a small concert in the first place; I was afraid it would get out of hand. But a . . . a campsite. On our land. With bands!" Her tone implied unspeakable connotations. "No doubt there'll be drugs, knives probably, all sorts of undesirables . . ."

"They'll be searched for drugs and knives," said Abi.

"They won't. Because none of it will take place. I'm sorry if you've been under a misapprehension, but I do assure you, so have I. William, I'm astonished at you."

William, William, thought Abi, *stand up to her; fight back.* But he didn't. He just sat there, flushed, wretched, pushing his hands through his hair.

She stood up, pushed her chair back, enjoying the ugly, harsh sound it made on the flagged floor, and left.

. . .

"I . . . think I'll go," said Emma. The evening was turning into hard work; her head ached, and she wanted to be home. Home alone. Again. "Sorry . . . Just feeling a bit . . . tired. Hard week. And I'm on duty at six. In the morning."

"You party pooper!" said Mark. "OK. We understand. Want me to get you a cab?"

"No, it's OK." She stood up. "I'll get the bus."

"Emma, you are not getting the bus. Not the nicest place, Swindon, this time of night. I'll do it. Finish your drink . . ." He looked up at her. "It'll be about half an hour, OK?"

"OK."

She felt the bus might have been quicker, but she was too tired to argue.

. . .

Abi was crying so hard, she could hardly see; she stopped at the end of the road, sat there sobbing for what seemed ages, trying to pull herself together. How could he be so pathetic, so cowardly: how could he? Thank God she'd found out. How awful if she'd gone ahead and married him. Sylvie was right: she'd have married the mother as well. It could never, ever have worked.

God, she was a bitch. But she was allowed to be. That was the worst thing. William and his father just allowed her to get away with everything. They were obviously both terrified of her. All those brave words of William's, and they hadn't meant a thing. He was . . . he was . . .

She suddenly realised a car had pulled up behind her. It was flashing at her. Someone was getting out. It was William. He was running over to her; she wound down the window and put her head out. She realised it was pouring rain.

"Fuck off. Just fuck off. You're a wimp and a coward and I never, ever want to see you again. Ever."

"Abi, I—"

"No, just shut the fuck up. I can't believe how you behaved in there. How you let her behave. It was pitiful. Pathetic. I'm going home, and I never, ever want to see you again. Mummy's boy! Thirty-four-year-old mummy's boy. You make me feel sick."

"Abi, please. Listen. Just for one second. I'm sorry. I'm really sorry. It's my fault and—"

"It's not your fault she's so . . . so rude and vile and snobbish. I know her sort. She thinks I'm common, so she can treat me exactly how she likes. Well, I may be common—I am actually, very common—but that's for me to decide, not her. Please get out of my way, William. I want to go home. At least I won't have to sleep in the guest room."

"No," he said, "you won't."

"Is that all you have to say?"

"No. You'll be sleeping in the cottage. With me. OK?"

"I don't believe you. I'm not sure I want to, anyway."

"Yes, you do. I told her so. And I told her she'd been incredibly rude to you and she was to apologise. And I said there was no question of cancelling the festival, and if she tried to, then I was leaving. Leaving home, leaving the farm . . ."

"You can't do that," said Abi. "You love the farm."

"I know. But not as much as I love you. I meant it; I wasn't just saying it."

"But . . . what would you do?"

"I don't know. Help you with your events company."

"You'd be terrible at that," said Abi. "Really terrible."

"Thanks. OK, well, I'll go and run someone else's farm. Abi, I'm so sorry. I . . . suppose we're so used to her, we just let her . . . let her behave how she does for the sake of peace. When we notice, that is. She's not such a bad old thing underneath. Her bark's so much worse than her bite. But . . . well, that was so awful tonight. I was so ashamed. Of her and myself. I have been feeble—I know I have—but

I just kept hoping she wouldn't find out about the festival until it really was too late."

"William," said Abi, "it would never have been too late. She'd have turfed everyone off when the bands were playing, and I've got to hand it to her: she's very formidable. She should have gone into politics. Mrs. Thatcher rides again."

"Well . . . maybe. But . . . please, Abi, please come back. I'm so sorry. I love you so much. I can't lose you again. Please."

She hesitated, then looked at him and grinned. A wide, happy, glorious grin.

"OK," she said, "you win. Fair enough. I don't suppose it'll be the last battle we have with her. But that's OK. Oh, shit, William, I love you too. You're getting awfully wet."

"Lock your car up," he said. "I'll drive you to the cottage. I've got the key."

"OK."

Inside the door, he looked at her and grinned.

"You know, I told you those clothes weren't a good idea. You'd have done much better if you'd worn your usual stuff. I think you should take them off right now. Starting with those very boring trousers . . ."

And thus it was that when Mrs. Grainger arrived at cottage number one, wearing a most determined smile, her arms full of clean linen, and bearing a flask of hot coffee, she found Abi sitting on the stairs, naked from the waist down, and William tenderly removing her flat shoes, kissing her toes as he did so.

• • •

In the event, the cab was at least forty minutes; they always were, Emma thought. Why did they do that, say they'd be there before it was remotely possible? She had finished her drink long since, and had actually left the table, was waiting in the lobby of the restaurant, amongst the wet coats and umbrellas. She didn't think she'd ever felt so unhappy. Yes. She had. Lots of times lately. God, she was turning into a misery. What had happened to her; where had the bouncy, smiling, always happy Emma gone? Maybe it was just as well; she'd probably been a bit annoying . . .

The taxi seemed to be going a long way round; the fare would be running up into thousands. Well . . . tens, anyway.

"You know I wanted Rosemary Gardens, don't you?" she said finally. "By Rosemary Park."

The driver didn't seem to hear her. He just carried on speaking into his phone, a headset, in Polish. Or Bulgarian. Or Czech . . . Probably didn't understand English anyway, she thought; he was taking her to some completely different place that she didn't know, and the fare would be so stupendous, she wouldn't have enough money, and . . .

"We here. Fifty pounds . . ."

"Fifty!"

"No. Fifty. One five."

"Oh . . . fifteen."

"That's what I said. Fifty."

"OK."

She counted out sixteen pounds, got out. It was absolutely pouring. There was another car parked on the street. It had its interior light on. The person in the back was reading. Must be waiting for someone.

She got out of the cab, ran towards the house, went inside, slammed the door shut. She thought she'd heard footsteps behind her; she didn't want to hang about. She put the chain on the door, turned away.

The bell rang. She ignored it. It rang again. She really didn't want to open it. Not at this time of night. But . . . maybe she'd locked someone for one of the other flats out.

"Who is it?" she called finally.

There was a silence; then: "It's Barney."

This had happened so many times in her imagination, and her dreams, that she more or less assumed he couldn't be real. She waited, unable even to move the chain, to open the door a crack, too afraid that if she did, she would wake up, or he would simply not be there.

"Emma! Please open the door. Please."

It did sound like him. It really did. There was a big mirror in the hall; she looked at herself in it. She looked terrible. She was very pale, and her eye makeup had smudged, and her hair was all lank and wet. She couldn't open the door to Barney looking like that. If it was him.

She rummaged in her bag, pulled out a comb, dragged it through her hair. Wiped a tissue under her eyes, which promptly seemed to smudge more, licked it and tried again, tried desperately to find her makeup bag . . .

"Emma, what on earth are you doing?"

"Sorry. Sorry." She had to do it, had to open the door. Whatever she looked like. She did—very cautiously, leaving it on the chain. She peered through the crack. And . . .

"It is you. Isn't it?"

"Of course it's me. Who else would it be, standing here in the pouring rain, begging you to open the door . . ."

She fumbled at the chain; it seemed to be jammed; it took ages. Finally she pulled it out. Opened the door. And . . .

"Hello, Emma." There was a pause. Then he added—and then she knew it was him—"Hello, the Emma. You all right?" He was staring at her, very intently.

"I'm fine. Yes. Hello, Barney. The Barney. Come . . . come in. Please."

He came in. She stood looking at him, trying to take in the enormity of it, that he was really here, actually standing in front of her, looking a little dishevelled, not smiling.

"I can't believe I'm really here," he said. And put out his hand to touch her arm. She put hers out. And absurdly took his hand and shook it. And giggled.

"Oh, God," she said, snatching her hand back. "I'm sorry. This is so, so stupid. Oh, Barney, Barney, but why are you here?"

"I'm here," he said, "because Tamara told me to."

"Tamara! Now I know I'm dreaming."

"No," he said, "you're not."

"You'll have to explain."

"All right."

"Well . . ." She caught sight of herself again in the mirror. "I'm sorry I look so awful."

"You don't. You look beautiful to me. Absolutely beautiful."

It was still all rather surreal.

And then they were standing inside her flat and he was still staring at her and looking very serious, and not touching her, and he said, "I can't believe this is happening. I really can't."

"Nor can I."

"I've tried so hard to get over you. I couldn't."

"Nor could I."

"I . . . wanted to call you so much, find out what had happened. I just couldn't."

"Nor could I. Even after I knew you'd finished with Amanda."

"I was so afraid you'd . . . you'd . . ."

"I know," she said. "I know what you were afraid of. Same as me. That I was getting over it, had someone else."

"And," he said, moving towards her, reaching out, taking one strand of her hair, winding it just a little round his finger, beginning to smile now, "how stupid was that? How stupid."

"Of both of us," she said, "so, so stupid. As if that would have been possible."

"As if indeed."

"So . . . what happened?"

"Well . . . like I said. Tamara told me to ring you. So I did."

"Since when did you do what Tamara says?"

"Since tonight. She's my new very, very best friend. Yes, she really is."

"Mary told me I should ring you. Only I wasn't so sensible. I went on being too scared."

"Who's Mary, for heaven's sake?"

"Oh, Barney. You know. The old lady who was in the crash. I told you, she was meeting her boyfriend from the war; it was so, so sweet."

"Oh, the one you met in the restaurant. Yes." He was staring at her, absolutely still, looking dazed. "I love you, Emma. I can't bear it, I love you so much. What was so sweet? Did you say?"

"I love you too. I can't believe it. So much. What was so sweet was she told me to call you to get in touch. It's so sad; her Russell's died now. She's been widowed twice."

"Poor Mary. Poor Russell."

"I know."

"Go on telling me what she said."

"She said I should call you. And I said you'd probably have forgotten about me by now, it was such a long time. And she said you wouldn't have. That Russell hadn't forgotten her, not even after more than sixty years. How amazing is that?"

"Well, Emma King," he said, "I'm not being beaten at love by anyone. I couldn't forget you if I didn't see you for . . . for seventy years. How's that?"

"We'd have to be quite old," she said, "for you to remember me for seventy years."

"I'd hang on," he said. "I'd just hang on if I thought I was going to see you again. One day. I'd wait."

"Well . . . you don't have to."

"No, I don't, thank God. I'll have you with me. For all of seventy years, I hope. I love you, Emma. I never, ever want to spend another hour without you."

"You might have to spend an hour. Here and there. While you're banking and I'm doctoring. But after that . . ."

"After that, it'd be OK. So OK. And you know something, my darling, lovely Emma?"

"No. What?"

"You don't look old enough to be a doctor."

Abi woke to the sound of rain. Not just a light shower, but proper, torrential rain. Mud-making, wheel-sticking, tent-soaking, barbecuequenching, spirit-sapping, off-putting rain. Well, she'd said it would. Only she'd kind of thought if she said it enough, allowed for it sufficiently, it wouldn't happen. Wrong. It had happened.

Well, a little rain had never hurt Glastonbury. But then, Glastonbury was . . . well, Glastonbury. People would go if it snowed. Just to say they'd been there. In Good Company wasn't famous. This was its first year. Its only year, if Mrs. Grainger Senior had anything to do with it. Mrs. Grainger Junior had more ambitious plans for it.

There had been a Mrs. Grainger Junior for three months now. Three pretty good months. They had got married, very quietly really, on a brilliantly dappled April day, when the sun had shone one minute, and the clouds had regathered the next; when they had walked into the registry office leaving a doomily dark world behind them and come out an hour later into a radiantly blue-and-gold one. Which, as Georgia said, was an absolutely fitting portent.

They had agreed, William and she, that there was no point waiting for very long at all, since there was absolutely nothing to wait for. No complex family to worry about—none at all, in Abi's case, and while William's was worrying, it wasn't complex—no one's permission to be sought, no need to find somewhere to live. Abi had no desire, she said, for a big wedding; she didn't want to walk down the aisle in a meringue; indeed she didn't want to walk down any aisle in anything. She was a staunch atheist. The only thing she believed in, she said, was William, and how much she loved him . . . which she repeated in her wedding speech—she had insisted on making a speech—and which reduced almost everyone in the room—with a few notable and predictable exceptions—to misty-eyed and foolish laughter.

She said she'd quite like a good party, but not so big she couldn't dance with everyone in the room; she and William had very few friends in common, and she didn't want anyone there who didn't understand what they were doing together.

So there had been about thirty altogether—for a late lunch and then dancing at the Royal Crescent Hotel in Bath, which Mr. Grainger insisted on paying for. Abi had wanted to pay for it herself, and not be any further beholden to the Graingers, but:

"Let him," William said. "It's his way of apologising for my mother's behaviour."

Sylvie was there, of course, with a new boyfriend. He was called Alan Wallis and he worked in the men's department of Marks & Spencer. When Abi first met him, she told Sylvie she must need her hormones examined, that he was bound to be gay, but Sylvie assured her he was most definitely not; he was brilliant at the business, and in fact so demanding that she was quite worn out by it all. Abi, in a spirit of pure mischief, made him go and ask Mrs. Grainger to dance, but in fact, Alan Wallis had the most beautiful formal manners and had done an advanced ballroom dancing course and steered Mrs. Grainger most expertly round the room, and she was later heard to tell William that he was rather a charming young man and that they had had a very interesting discussion about the rise and fall in the Marks & Spencer share price, and the reasons behind it.

Mr. Grainger was in his turn very taken with Sylvie. "Maybe they could set up a *maison à quatre*," Abi remarked cheerfully to William. "That would solve an awful lot of problems."

William's brother and sister and their respective families came; Abi quite liked Martin, who was not unlike William to look at, but a lot smoother, but she thought his sister was frightful and was almost moved to feel pity for Mrs. Grainger when she saw her being snubbed repeatedly by her daughter and even more frequently by her son-in-law.

Georgia was there, of course, and so was Merlin; Georgia was interestingly and rather overtly impatient with Merlin, Abi noticed. He was at his most charming and kept paying everyone very lavish compliments; he told Abi she made his heart stop, she looked so lovely, and William that he was the luckiest man in the universe— that really annoyed Georgia—and Sylvie that she danced like the proverbial angel. In the end, Georgia actually snapped at him and told him to stop behaving as if he was in front of—or behind—the cameras. He looked quite hurt, and Sylvie, bored by now with Mr. Grainger, took it upon herself to comfort him, which made Georgia crosser still.

Emma was there with Barney; they were officially engaged now, and Emma had a rock quite as big as Abi's on her finger. She told Abi privately that she would have given anything to have a quiet wedding too, but her mother had gone into overdrive over the whole thing, and her rating on the nightmare bride's mother scale of nought to ten was about eleven and a half.

"It's a bit like you, in a way: Barney and his family are so posh, and me and my family aren't, and I just can see it all ending in tears." Abi had told her to elope with Barney, or run away and get married on a beach somewhere, but Emma said she couldn't possibly do that to her mother. She also, Abi suspected, wanted very much to walk down the aisle in a meringue.

William had invited a few of his farming friends, and their wives, jolly, horsey girls for the most part, who danced energetically long after everyone else had given up, and Abi invited a small number— three, to be precise—of her better-behaved girlfriends, who would be an adornment to the company and could more or less relied upon not to get so drunk that they were sick or to bring any drugs onto the premises . . . and that was that.

"And you know what?" she said to William as they undressed late that night in their suite of the Radisson Edwardian hotel at Heathrow, prior to a six a.m. flight to Barbados, "it was exactly how I hoped: everyone seemed happy, most people got on with most people, and even your mother smiled quite a lot."

William agreed, rather absently; he was goggle-eyed at the excesses of the hotel, with its vast atrium, its marble floors and pillars, its lush palm trees and gilded mirrors, never having seen anything like it in his life.

"I've only actually been away three times, twice with Nanny to Frinton and once with my dad fishing in Scotland."

Abi told him she thought she could probably improve on that.

The honeymoon had been wonderful; they had stayed at the Glitter Bay Hotel, and done all the touristy things: parasailed, surfed, swum with dolphins, and danced to various wonderful bands night after night on various wonderful beaches. And then returned home to the reality of cottage number one.

Actually, Abi was very happy there. She was absorbed with starting her company, planning the festival, learning to ride—at which she proved rather adept: "We'll have you out with the hounds soon . . . all two of them," Mr. Grainger had said with his usual heavy wink—and struggling to cook. After a few weeks of overambitious failures, she gave up and simply served endless enormous roasts, which were easy and satisfied William's awesome appetite. Mrs. Grainger left her alone for the most part, occasionally arriving at cottage number one with pies and puddings and chutneys and jams—"I know how busy you are; this might help a bit"—which Abi became swiftly grateful for. She knew Mrs. Grainger's motives were not entirely good, being partly to contrast with her own efforts, but on the other hand it all tasted wonderful.

And here they were on the morning of the festival, with three thousand tickets sold. "Three thousand, I can't believe it," Georgia had said. "It's amazing."

Abi told her it wasn't amazing enough—they needed twice that to make any real money; they were way overbudget on the bands. "But we should get loads more on the day . . . as long as it isn't tipping down."

"You said it would be tipping down," said Georgia. "You can't get out of it that easily."

The best thing was that Barney's bank, BKM, had agreed to sponsor it.

"Only a rather modest amount, I'm afraid," Barney had told Abi. "Ten grand, piss in a pot to them, but it should help a bit. And they'll want their pound of flesh or whatever, be credited on all the publicity and so on. They're actually rather tickled by it. My boss said he'd bring a few friends if it's a good day."

Abi told him she didn't see ten grand as either modest or a piss in a pot, and that she'd thank Barney's boss personally in the best way she knew how.

"Best not," said Barney, grinning at her. "He's gay."

. . .

She got up now, pulled on some jeans, her wellies, and her Barbour— "Who'd ever have thought I'd be seen alive in a Barbour?" she said to Georgia. "But they really do keep the water out better than anything"— and drove down to the site.

It was still only seven, but the place was already full of people. She looked at it from the top of the hill, at her creation, at the transformation of the small lush valley into something so unrecognisably different, and felt a mixture of pride and terror in more or less equal proportions. The cows had been moved out, mildly protesting, a week ago, ousted by a rival herd of huge lorries, massive power lines, tall arc lights, neat rows of portaloos and showers; the brilliant red-and-yellow-striped arena stood at the heart of the site, a flag fluttering from the top bearing the words, *In Good Company,* a battery of lights above the stage, a rather random array of mikes and other sound equipment standing on it, together with keyboards and drum kits, waiting to be called to order by their musician masters, and even a rather incongruous-looking piano—that would be for Georgia's friend Anna, the jazz singer, and her daughter—and on either side of it, two huge screens. She parked her car at the site entrance; a couple of portacabins stood just inside the gate. Rosie, the site manager, waved at her and ran over, pulling the hood of her jacket up over her head.

"Hi, Abi. Lovely day."

"Shit, isn't it?"

"Oh, don't worry. I've seen worse. Good thing we persuaded William to put down that stone. You'll need this . . ." She wrapped a brilliant green plastic strap round Abi's wrist. "Being Mrs. Farmer won't get you far today. Green is all areas, for people like us and the bands, yellow for all the stall holders, red for the punters; don't take it off whatever you do. Security doesn't take prisoners. They've arrived too; they're in the other hut."

"OK, thanks. What time did you get here?"

"Four," said Rosie cheerfully. "So much to do."

"Four!" said Abi. "I hope we're not paying you overtime."

"Course you are. No, it's fine. My big worry now is Health and Safety; you know they come to do their final inspection an hour before the first band plays . . ."

"Yeah."

"They called late last night to say they might be late, got another to do the other side of the M4. Which is a total bugger; it could hold us up for hours if they find a cable they're not happy with or something."

"Yeah, William's friend who does one of these every year said they once held them up till ten thirty. Oh, God. You'd think there'd be enough of them to go round, wouldn't you?"

"No," said Rosie. "And . . . oh, look, here comes food. I said they could come anytime after seven. They won't mind the rain; they sell more."

A small armada of trailer-towing vans was moving down the hill, into the site. "I'll have to go, tell them where to park. Still happy with what we agreed?"

"Course," Abi said.

She wondered what on earth Mrs. Grainger might be doing, sent up a small but fervent prayer for a brief, violent, and nonfatal illness, and walked across to a desperate-looking girl at the entrance who said she was in charge of what she called the kiddie roundabouts; one of the trailers had driven into the farmyard by mistake and been unable to turn round, and a very unhelpful woman had refused to move her Land Rover, which would make things much easier. No violent illnesses yet, then, Abi thought, and told the girl to follow her back up the track.

· · ·

Emma and Barney arrived at eleven, just as a very large white van got hopelessly stuck in the mud.

"What are we going to do?" wailed Abi. "It's going to block the way for everyone else; half the stalls aren't here yet and—"

"Abi, I'm no farmer," said Barney, "but a tractor'd sort that out in no time. Where's William?"

"He's trying to sort out some problem with the power leads. The supply isn't enough, apparently; now they tell us— Over there, look . . ."

"I'll go and ask him," said Barney.

He came back grinning.

"He says he can't stop what he's doing, but if I could get his dad or the cowman they'd bring a tractor down. Where do I find either of those people?"

"No idea where his dad is. Strangling his mother, I hope. But the cowman—Ted, he's called—he'll almost certainly be up in the cowshed. There's a cow calving; apparently she's in real trouble; they're getting the vet; he won't be able to leave her just to drive the tractor. Oh, God . . ."

"I can drive a tractor," said Barney unexpectedly, "if it's OK with William."

"God, I don't know. He loves those tractors. Far more than he loves me."

"Do you know where I might find one?"

"Well . . . yes. There's one parked outside the lambing shed. I saw it as I came down."

"Take me to it. I'll risk William's wrath."

"But, Barney . . . Oh, shit. What a nightmare. Can you really drive a tractor? I mean really?"

"I really can. Chap I was at school with, his dad had a farm; we used to drive the tractors all over the place whenever I went to stay with him."

"But—"

"I'm sure he wouldn't say he could drive a tractor if he couldn't, Abi," said Emma. "He's awfully clever."

"Emma, you'd think Barney could drive a rocket into space. I've never known love to make anyone so blind."

"Yes, OK. But—"

"Look, we've got to do something," said Barney. He pointed at the van; the driver had got out and was squaring up to the security guard, calling him an evil nancy boy. The security guard pulled his radio out of his belt and started alternately talking into it and shouting at the van driver.

"Oh, OK. I'll drive you up there. Emma, you stay here and tell William some lie if he comes over."

"OK," said Emma cheerfully.

. . .

She looked around her. It all looked—stuck van aside—extremely organised.

The food trailers were all in place and putting up their shutters, revealing signs that said things like, *Best burgers* and *Finest fries*. A couple of girls were standing by a small children's roundabout, giving a child a ride; two rainbow-coloured tents side by side announced that they were face painting and willow weaving; someone clearly with a sense of humour was hoisting a large hot-air balloon over the loos that read, *In Good Company*. A St. John's ambulance tent was going up; a girl and a man were constructing a large barbecue under a pagoda tent, with a sign that said, *Paella: Biggest portions,* and a small but determined-looking queue was forming across the valley where the punters' entrance was.

Everyone seemed to know exactly what they were supposed to be doing and getting on with it. The air was thick with the crackle of walkie-talkies, the hurdy-gurdy music of the roundabouts, and the occasional burst of rock music as someone checked a sound system. And all the time the picture grew: more vans, more tents, more colour, more stalls. It was astonishing, rather like watching someone doing a giant jigsaw. God, Abi was a wonder. She'd masterminded all of this without any of the histrionics Georgia had brought to it, just got on and done it. William was a lucky chap; she hoped he knew it.

"Oh . . . William!" she said, realising he was behind her. "Hi."

"Hi. Everything all right? Abi gone to find Ted?"

"Yes. I . . . think so."

"Great. Sorry I can't look after you properly, Emma. If you want a coffee, the site manager's cabin's got a kettle and stuff . . ."

"William, I don't need looking after. Did you get the power problem sorted?"

"No, not yet. And that van's causing chaos. God. If only this bloody rain would stop . . ."

"I think it is stopping," said Emma, "actually. Well, it's much lighter, more of a sort of drizzle, don't you think?"

"No," said William, looking up at the lowering sky, "I don't. Oh, good, here comes Ted now. No, it's not . . . it's Barney. What the hell is he doing driving my tractor? Barney, you wanker, get out of that, for God's sake; you'll do the most terrible damage . . ."

"Piss off, William," Abi shouted above the din. "Barney's fine; he can drive this perfectly well, and you'd better get up to the cowshed— that calf's a breach, and the vet needs help."

"Where's Ted?"

"Seeing to another calf. Go on, William, for God's sake."

William roared up the track in the Land Rover, with another agonised yell at Barney of, "You break my tractor, Fraser, I'll have your goolies off."

"You know what they say," Abi said, grinning at Emma. "You wait ages for a calf and then they all come at once."

"You'd think they might have waited another day," said Emma. "So inconsiderate—they must have known what was going on. Abi, would you agree with me that the rain's much lighter? Almost stopped?"

"Mmm. Not sure," said Abi, and then, "God, good old Barney, he's doing wonders with that thing. I hope that cow's all right; we lost one last week; can't afford another."

Emma looked at her, her respect growing by the minute.

"Are you Abi? Security sent me over." It was a girl dressed totally unsuitably in high-heeled red sandals and white trousers. "Tessa Standish, Wiltshire Radio."

"Oh . . . God. Yes. Cool. They said you might be coming. Let's go over to the arena. Have you got any other shoes?"

"No. So stupid, but I wasn't expecting to come this morning."

"Tell you what," said Abi. "We pass the welly stall. You can be our first paying customer. Here, look. Rainbow-coloured, madam? Spotted? Or even a pair of Hunters?"

. . .

Georgia was driving down the M4 just before one when she heard Tessa Standish: "Coming to you from In Good Company, the music festival based at Paget's Farm, just off the M4 near Bridbourne. And I can tell you, if you're thinking of coming you're in for a treat. It looks fantastic, incredible array of stalls, wonderful bands on the programme, lots of them local, great camping area, stuff for the kids to do, and the most amazing setting. It could have been purpose-built for the occasion, a sort of natural amphitheatre . . . and don't be put off by the weather, because the rain's stopping here now, and there's even a bit of sun fighting its way through. Now the headline band is BroadBand, playing at eight, but there are loads of others, starting with a folk band called—what are they called?—oh, yes, Slow-mo. They're on at three. And it's all for charity, in aid of the victims of the

M4 crash last August and St. Marks Hospital, Swindon, so you'll be doing some majorly good work if you come."

It was awful to be so late; she'd wanted to be down first thing, really make herself useful, but the second on the new film had suddenly called her and said they needed rain to film a scene, and here it was, most obligingly; could she get over right away? So she'd had to get over.

Georgia had had a pretty amazing three months since *Moving Away* had gone on to the nation's television screens. She had had rave notices—been proclaimed by various critics as "an incredible new talent," and giving a "near perfect performance" and "exquisitely touching" and "a superbly intuitive actress."

"I don't understand it," she'd said to Linda. "I know I wasn't that good; I just know it. I'm not daft."

"Maybe, but the thing is, darling, the camera loves you. It isn't just models you hear that of; there are certain actors it's true of too. It found more in your performance than you know was there, maybe than actually was there. Frankly, Georgia—and I've always been one of your biggest fans—I didn't see you getting notices like this. You're a one-in-a-million screen actress, and you should thank God fasting for it. And don't come running to me after a bit saying you want to play Juliet at Stratford, you don't feel fulfilled . . ."

"Of course I won't," said Georgia.

"Darling, you'd be surprised how many do. Just enjoy this. It's great."

Georgia's face was everywhere; apart from the arts pages, *Vogue* had used her for a fashion shoot, she'd appeared in the style section of the *Sunday Times,* and in the *Guardian* as their close-up spread in the Monday fashion slot. She'd been interviewed just about everywhere— and wonderfully had been able to plug the festival several times—and most important, had a part in a new BBC series, filming in the autumn, and after that in a main feature film, a screen adaptation of a new novel set against the background of what the publicity called "Thatcher's Britain." Georgia couldn't actually see that it was that different from present-day Britain, although her mother inevitably could, but it was going to be a great movie, and she had a great part.

She had moved out of her room in Jazz's house and bought a minute flat in Clapham; she had bought a ton of clothes from Topshop and TK Maxx and a couple of dresses from Stella McCartney, for special occasions, and one of the new Minis, and she and Merlin were going on holiday to Thailand for a week when the BBC film was finished. Life had changed a bit, as she said to Abi, but she felt exactly the same. "Just as worried about everything, just as insecure, just as—"

"Nuts?" Abi said with a grin.

And yes, Georgia said, she supposed that was right.

"I'd so love to be cool like you, Abi, cool and sorted. I can't see it ever happening. Maybe I need a husband."

Abi said she thought a husband was the last thing Georgia needed. "Who could cope with you anyway, all famous like you are; you'd have to find another luvvie, and anyway, how about Merlin; what's wrong with him?"

Whereupon Georgia sighed and said nothing.

"Yes, there is, I can tell," said Abi. "What's the matter, trouble in paradise?"

"Paradise?"

"Yes. Merlin told me being with you was total paradise. I thought it was sweet."

"Well, it isn't," Georgia said. "I can't bear it when he says things like that."

"I wouldn't mind. The best William could manage was that life's got a lot better since we got married, but he's not so sure about this week."

"Yes, but he means it. Merlin doesn't."

"How do you know?"

"Oh . . . it's all so corny. I swear he practises it in front of a mirror. And he's sooo vain. I don't know, Abi; I'd much rather have someone all lovely and steady like William. I'd love to be a farmer's wife."

"Georgia," said Abi, "you couldn't possibly marry a farmer; you'd be crying all the time—think about the lambs going off to market, or the poor little bull calves . . ."

"Why, what happens to them?"

"I'm not even going to tell you," said Abi; but Georgia was intrigued and asked William, and then, as Abi had predicted, sat with tears rolling down her face at the plight of the poor things, off to market to be turned into veal.

Anyway, the festival looked like it was going to be great; a cautiously optimistic call from Abi at midday had reported a "huge queue" at the gates. "I just drove along the road, saw them from there, a great line of them, straggling between the cornfields, you know, the ones leading across to the end of the farm. Just get here, Linley, you've got work to do. And where's your friend?"

"She should be there," said Georgia. "I spoke to them about an hour ago; they were at Swindon or thereabouts. I hope nothing's happened to them."

"No, not them, they're here and absolutely great. We managed to get them a plug on the radio. And a couple of blokes with beards and prehistoric sandals said they couldn't believe they were going to hear Sim Foster's wife and daughter. They were well pleased. No, I mean the CD guy. No sign of him."

"Oh, Jazz. He's coming down with Merlin; they're only about twenty minutes behind me."

· · ·

Anna and Lila were doing a half-hour set at six: Lila on saxophone, Anna on piano. They'd turned out to be a big draw with both what Abi called the Boden lot as well as the fanatics.

"It adds a bit of class, such a lovely story for the publicity, tying in with you and the TV series and everything. He was huge in his day, her husband; I Googled him, wonderful for us to talk about. And Lila is just totally gorgeous, isn't she?"

· · ·

Georgia arrived just as the sun came out in earnest; she parked at the top of the hill and looked down, smiling. The sky was a rather uncertain blue, but the clouds had gone, and the tents were going up now, hundreds of them, filling the first field—they'd obviously need the second; Abi had been wrong—all different colours, small igloos for the couples, and bigger frame jobs for the families. She could hear the sound of thousands of pegs being hammered into the ground, of children laughing and shrieking as they ran about, of people calling to one another, the hurdy-gurdy music of the little roundabouts; it was all so lovely, their dream almost unbelievably coming true. A few people had already lit barbecues, and she could smell the smoke drifting into the moist air; and across on the other side of the valley, the seemingly endless line of people, queuing in the sunshine.

"Hello, sweetheart. How you doing?"

"Jazz! How lovely. Fine, yes."

"Pretty good, isn't it? Your friend's done a great job."

"Have you seen her? She was worrying about you being late."

"Yeah, I've left Merl talking to her. And some bird in white trousers. Well, they were white. Pretty muddy now. She had a microphone. Well, I mean, show Merlin a microphone and he's off, isn't he. I mean, he's a great guy, but he don't half love the sound of his own voice. You and him a permanent item now, Georgia?"

"No!" said Georgia, and was horrified with the fervour with which her reply came out. "No, we're just . . . well, you know."

"Yeah, think so. Well, you're a big improvement on the last one, I'll give you that."

"I thought you'd have liked Ticky," said Georgia.

"No, not for me, love. All fur coat and no knickers, she was. Not my type at all."

"And what is your type?" said Georgia, genuinely curious.

"Oh . . . it varies. I know it when I see it. Look at old Merl, working the field. He do love a fresh audience."

She looked; it was true. He was moving amongst the tents, talking to people. He looked amazing—of course—wearing jeans and brown riding boots and a white collarless shirt. He was such a sweetheart; she should appreciate him more, stop complaining about him being irritating.

She parked her car and went to find Anna and Lila. Anna was down by the arena, checking everything out.

"Great piano," she said, "Japanese job. Just what I hoped for. And really well wired up. Lila's just been sick for the fourth time. She can do stage fright better than anyone."

"Oh, poor darling." It was Merlin. "Nothing worse. She'll be fine. I'll go and talk to her, see what I can do."

"That won't help," said Georgia tartly to Anna as he hurried off. "Enough to make her sick again, I should think," and then realised she had already broken her resolution to be nicer about him. How could she do this? When six months ago, she would have killed to have Merlin at her side, marked out as her boyfriend. What was the matter with her?

Lila staggered over from behind the arena, where she'd been throwing up. Merlin had obviously been unable to find her.

"Mum, I can't do this."

"Course you can," said Georgia, putting her arm round her. "You've got to, anyway. Come on, let's go and talk to Merlin."

Merlin was now sitting on the ground, sharing a bottle of water with a little girl wearing a long skirt, wellies, and a patchwork hat. Her forehead wore a rainbow.

"Hi, Georgia, Lila. This is Milly. This is her fourth festival this year."

"Goodness," said Georgia. "That's impressive. Hi, Milly. You having fun?"

"So fun, yes."

"I like your hat."

"My mummy bought it for me. From over there." She pointed at the hat stall. "She got one too."

"Very nice." Georgia smiled at Milly's mum, a pretty dark-haired girl who was wearing an identical hat to her daughter's. "I want you to know, that stall was my idea."

"Well, it was a great one," said Milly's mum.

"It's lovely, isn't it?"

"Oh, so lovely. We're great festival people. We always feel they're like miniholidays. No stress, such freedom for the kids, and this is such a wonderful place. We've never been to one here before."

"That's because there hasn't been one here before," said Georgia. "I know what you mean about festivals, though. You're all together, and everyone's sort of the same kind of person; nobody sort of jars; it's really cool."

"Really cool! You look familiar; have I met you somewhere before?"

"Er . . . don't think so," said Georgia. These small sudden signs of her fame, which had initially seemed so exciting, had become swiftly burdensome. She had imagined she would love it, being recognised, feeling important, but it was actually incredibly tedious; everyone asked the same questions: about the production, what various other people in it were like, how she'd got into acting, and—if the questioners were young—how she thought they might get into it.

She looked over at Merlin for help, but he was standing with Lila, talking to her rather intently. For some reason it annoyed her.

"Where's your tent?" she said to Anna. "I might set up near you."

"Oh, darling, do."

"Georgia!" It was Abi. Abi looking sensational in denim shorts, pink wellies, and a pink T-shirt. "How great is this? Listen, I need you to go and talk to that incredibly annoying girl from the local radio. She wants to interview you."

"Do I have to?"

"Yes, you bloody well do. Georgia, you haven't done anything at all yet today. Emma's been here for hours and hours, and so has Barney; I could really have done with you . . ."

"All right, all right. I was actually working, you know."

"Yes, I do know. You've told me at least six times. Go on, she's over there, in those rainbow-coloured wellies. Quickly, the first band's on in ten minutes—at least, I hope they are, if Health and Safety have finished their checks."

· · ·

"Oh, doesn't that look lovely?" said Linda, taking Alex's hand. "So good the rain stopped. Smells so lovely too, the barbecues and . . . what's that other smell? Oh, I know—candy floss. I love the smell of candy floss. In fact, I love the taste of candy floss. Amy, darling, go and buy us all some candy floss, would you?"

"Sure."

"Not all of us," said Alex. "I can't stand the stuff. E numbers on a stick. Terribly bad for you, give you a sugar rush."

"You're such a misery, Dad."

"My sentiments entirely," said Linda. "No, it's all wonderful. Even the music's not too bad."

"All right if you like folk," said Amy. "Still, it's early, isn't it? It'll get better. I still can't believe they've got BroadBand. I think I might go and find my friends. They're all here. And—"

"Hi, Linda." It was Abi. "So lovely of you to come. Not really your thing, I'm sure."

"Now, why should you think that?" said Linda. "I'm a veteran of the Reading festival. I've kept all the wristbands from the very first year."

"Really? That is so cool. You must be Amy, hi. Having a good time?"

"Not yet she's not," said Linda, "but she's about to go and find her friends."

"Yes, I was just saying I couldn't believe you'd got BroadBand."

"Nor can I, Amy. And you know, they're really quite nice."

"Really?"

"Yes, really. Friendly. Chatty, even. Tell you what, if you come and find me about twenty minutes before they play, if I'm still alive, I'll make sure you can be right at the front. You might be able to meet them. They said they wouldn't be rushing off."

"Oh. My. God." Amy's face went bright red. "That would be just sooo cool."

"Sure. And your friends. I'll be inside the arena; we've got a little base behind the bar."

"Wow. Well . . . I'll see you then. God. So cool."

"I think you've impressed her," said Linda, laughing. "Not easy, is it, Alex?"

"Not terribly."

"It's so great you're here, Alex," said Abi. "I'm so glad."

"Abi, this is partly for my hospital; of course I'm here. I'm thrilled. Thrilled and grateful. We won't actually be camping, but—"

"We would have been," said Linda, "if it had been up to me."

"That is a filthy lie," said Alex. "This is the woman, Abi, who said she wouldn't so much as go inside a tent."

"It is not a lie. I love camping. At times like this."

"Well . . . plenty of tents for sale," said Abi.

"Oh, really?"

"Yeah, course. Over there, look. Only fifteen quid."

"Well, we might," said Linda. "You never know."

"Go on. Let your hair down. Lord, I must go. Health and Safety are approaching. Pray they're happy. We've had one hiccup already; they let us start, but said they'd be back to check that we'd done what they said, and if we hadn't they'd pull the plug. We have, obviously, but . . . bye for now."

"Gorgeous girl," said Alex, looking after her appreciatively.

"Gorgeous. Do you think I'd look good in shorts and wellies?"

"Possibly. Then again, possibly not. You're not really going to buy a tent, are you?"

"Yes. I think I might. Why not?"

"You're such a bloody hypocrite. All that fuss insisting on booking into a hotel . . ."

"I'm not a hypocrite. I'm a spontaneous person. That's all. I suddenly realise it'd be really pathetic and . . . and middle-aged to leave all this, go to a hotel."

"Well, we are middle-aged."

"You might be. I'm not. And if I may say so, you're acting more than middle-aged. More like old."

"Thanks. Well, you'll be sleeping in the tent on your own, let me tell you."

"Cool, as your daughter would say."

· · ·

"Oh, this is lovely!"

"Isn't it? You're not cold, are you, Mary?" Maeve looked at her tenderly.

"Why on earth should I be cold? The sun's perfectly beautiful."

They were sitting, well wrapped up, for it was evening now, in picnic chairs, halfway up the hill facing the arena. There was a small metal road dividing the area where they were from the campsite, and the arena was beyond that; it was rather like being in the dress circle of a theatre, as Mary had said.

"Donald would have liked this," Mary added. "He loved folk music."

"And Russell?"

"Oh, now, Russell would have adored those two women. Really very, very good, they were. I heard her husband several times, you know; he was one of the greats. I remember one night he was on at Ronnie Scott's. I so wanted to go, but Donald hadn't been well. He always was inclined to chest trouble, you know. I think it was being in that prisoner-of-war camp in Italy for so long."

"I didn't know he was a prisoner of war."

"Oh, yes, he was. For over a year. Terrible conditions, they didn't get nearly enough to eat, and in the winter they were always cold. When he finally got home, he seemed to have shrunk, skin and bone and somehow shorter and this terrible cough. But . . . we fed him up and the doctor told him he should spend as much time as possible in the fresh air. He got an allotment and it did him so much good. It works a kind of magic, gardening does."

"What a time you all had of it," said Maeve. "My grandparents got off pretty lightly, I think. My grandfather was too old to be called up."

"Yes, it was hard. But you know, it toughened us."

"Indeed it seems to have. And you'd never have met Russell without it."

"Indeed. And missed out on so much happiness. Oh, now, Georgia, dear, how lovely to see you."

"Abi said you were all here." Georgia bent and kissed her. "Enjoying yourself?"

"So much. Aren't we, Maeve?"

"Where are the boys?"

"On that carousel for the fourth or is it the fifth time," said Maeve, "and they've all had their faces painted, and Liam has made a fine willow basket. It's such a success, Georgia. I do congratulate you."

"I didn't do much. It's Abi who's made it happen. Is Tim around?"

"He certainly is," said Mary. "He and Lorraine brought me over. They think it's wonderful."

"You've got a grandstand seat up here, haven't you?"

"We have indeed," said Maeve. "And we're about to open our thermos of tea. Would you join us, Georgia?"

"Oh . . . no. That'd be lovely, but I promised Abi I'd go back down. Some television company has turned up now—we've done so well for publicity—and they want to . . . well to . . ."

"To have you on, I'm sure," said Mary. "Of course. The festival celebrity."

"Mary, hardly. There are masses of celebrities here. Some really well-known musicians. Very small beer, I am."

"Somehow I don't think so," said Mary. "Very few who've been on TV at peak viewing time. I felt so proud of you, dear."

"Well . . . that's very nice. Look . . . I'll be back later. How long do you think you'll stay?"

"Well, certainly for another hour. And then we'll probably set out for home. They're all coming back to Tadwick for the night."

"Patrick has his fine new job now, you know . . ."

"Really? I'm so pleased. I didn't know."

"Yes, he's office manager of a haulage company," said Maeve, "and even better, he's to be based in Reading, so that we can all see one another very much more easily, and Mary comes up most nearly every weekend at the moment, to help and to babysit, so that Patrick and I can go out for an hour or two now and again."

"That sounds lovely. I'm so pleased. Look, I must go, Abi's waving at me. I'll come back later, promise."

"Don't worry too much, dear. You've got a lot on your plate."

"I'm going down to find the boys," said Maeve. "They'll be sick if they have any more rides on that thing, on top of those burgers and the candy floss. Patrick has no idea how to refuse them anything. I won't be long, Mary."

"No hurry," said Mary. "I'm very happy."

And she was. She sat, looking down into the golden evening at the little families wandering about, smiling, holding hands; at the young couples, arms around one another; at the lights of the little round-abouts and the small old-fashioned carousel turning so tirelessly; at the stage with the small figures playing on it, beside their larger selves on the screens; at the hundreds of tents, snuggled down into the grass, barbecues smoking gently; at the lovely evening-blue July sky, a few clouds drifting across it streaked with the sunset; and she felt an immense gratitude all of a sudden, and thought how blessed she had been in her life, her long, mostly uneventful life, to have loved and been loved so much and known so much happiness, in spite of the sadness that she had had to bear. One could not ask more than this, she thought: to be in a beautiful place, on a beautiful evening, surrounded even now by people she loved and who cared for her, and with a head full of memories, wonderful, charmed memories, and not one of them bitter, or angry, or ugly in any way. If her two husbands—both of whom she had loved so much and been so happy with—could be aware of her happiness now, they would be well pleased. And somehow, this evening, looking at the sky and the dusk just beginning to appear above the sunset, she felt it was very possible they were.

. . .

Laura was sitting on the sofa with Daisy, watching the evening news, when the announcer suddenly said, "And now, as some properly seasonal weather seems finally to have arrived, and with more of the same promised for days to come, we take you over to one of those great icons of summer, a music festival. A rather special festival, one created for charity, in aid of the victims of the M4 crash late last summer, and for the hospital that cared for them. The brainchild of two of the people involved, although not hurt, in the crash, Abi Grainger and Georgia Linley—you may remember Georgia from *Moving Away*, the haunting Channel Four drama early this spring—they conceived it, nurtured it, and brought it to life today. It is being held, indeed, on the farm of William Grainger, on whose land the air ambulance landed that day, and who, incidentally, married Abi just three months ago. Isn't that right, Abi?"

And there she was, Laura thought, waiting to feel all the ugly, angry things for this girl, this beautiful, sexy girl, in spite of her generosity towards her in the courtroom, this girl, smiling at the camera, laughing, dressed in shorts and a T-shirt and hugging the arm of her husband and saying, "Yes, that's right, and none of this could have happened without the generosity of William and his parents in allowing it to be held on their land."

"I imagine it could all have been pretty alarming to someone not used to these things," said the interviewer, a rather uneasy-looking young man, dressed for some reason all in black.

"Oh, it was pretty alarming to all of us, used to them or not.

Including William's cows. But it's all turned out brilliantly; we've earned shi—huge loads of money for the charity, and any minute now one of the newest, most exciting bands in the country is going to play. So . . . go, BroadBand, go. And anyone in the vicinity, it's not too late; come on down and join us. Thanks. Thank you so much."

And funnily enough, Laura didn't feel anything ugly at all, just a wave of relief that it was all finally over, the sadness and the bitterness, and a certain admiration for the new young Mrs. Grainger, who could so successfully turn tragedy into at least some kind of triumph.

"That looks fun," said Daisy, looking rather wistfully at the camera, which was weaving now among the crowds, the bizarrely dressed young, fairies, nuns, angels, all dancing in the semidarkness, the children dancing too in circles, in and out of the tents and the barbecues, holding hands, and, "Look, there's a whole family dancing there, and they've got sparklers, see? I wish we could go to a festival, Mummy; I'd really love that."

"We will go, darling. Together. I'd like it too."

It was Jonathan; he had come into the room and was standing beside the sofa, one hand on Laura's shoulder. "If Mummy would like that."

"Mummy would like it," said Laura, not looking at him. "Maybe not that one, but . . ."

"No," he said, "not that one," and bent and kissed the top of her head. "All right?"

"Yes, I'm all right," said Laura. And realised that at last she was.

. . .

"You did a grand job with this, Abi."

Abi turned; it was Jazz, Merlin's hugely sexy friend. How they could be friends, she wasn't sure; she couldn't imagine two people more different, but then, people still kept saying that about her and William . . .

"Thank you. Yes, I'm pretty pleased. It was Georgia's idea in the first place, you know."

"I do know. Now, there's a sweetheart. Too good for Merlin, I keep telling her."

"Really?"

"Well, you know. He's seriously in love with himself. I'm well fond of him—I'd say he's one of my best friends—but a little of him goes a long way; know what I mean?"

"I . . . think so," said Abi carefully. "But he's awfully sweet."

"Course he is. Just . . . knows it, that's all. But he's all right."

"Um . . . is the recording OK?"

"Yeah, it's fine, darling. Sid, me little brother, he's keeping an eye on it. Or rather an ear. Better go and check on him, I s'pose. See you later."

. . .

"Shit. Look at that." It was Georgia, her small face near to tears.

"Now what?"

"Look at that. Merlin and Lila. They've been dancing for ages . . ."

"So?"

"What do you mean, so? He's my boyfriend."

"So?" said Abi again. "You've been complaining about him for weeks. And he's only dancing with her, for God's sake."

"Oh, I know. I'm sorry. I guess I'm just . . . confused. We do squabble an awful lot these days. It's so sad." She sighed. "Abi, what's wrong with me? I can't get it together properly with anyone. Even someone as lovely as Merlin."

"I don't know why you want to," said Abi. "Half the country's in love with you."

"Oh, don't be so ridiculous."

"Yes. They are. You're famous. What you've always wanted. You've got an incredible time ahead of you; you'll probably be in Hollywood next . . ."

"Oh, right . . ."

"You will. You know what it is with you, Georgia? You just want

· 589 ·

so much. Fame, success, all that stuff. And you're beginning to get it. Why don't you just settle for that for a bit? Forget about lurve. You don't have to marry Merlin, for God's sake; you can just enjoy him. And then . . . well, let 'then' take care of itself. I would."

"I s'pose you're right," said Georgia slowly. She sighed. "I do feel I've come rather a long way. Since I first set eyes on Merlin, fell in love with him."

"You have. You've dealt with so much crap, had all this success; make the most of it. It may not last. And then you'll kick yourself that you didn't enjoy it more."

"Yeah. Yeah, you're right. Sorry, Abi. I've been a pain. As usual."

"Well, that's why we love you," said Abi, grinning at her. "We're used to it anyway. Oh, hi, Jazz. Everything OK?"

"Everything's fine, yeah. Sid's doing a good job. This is a great night, Abi. Congratulations are in order. Wondered if you'd like to come down and have a quick dance, Georgia."

"I'd love to."

"Right-o. Mind you, I'm a terrible dancer . . ."

"I'm sure you're not."

"Darlin', I am. Not like our Merl. I know me limitations. Don't mean I don't enjoy it, though. Come on, then."

He was all right, Abi thought, smiling, watching them go off. Dead sexy, funny, cool, with none of Merlin's intense self-regard. Much more suitable for Georgia, really. Now she was doing it, trying to get Georgia settled. She shouldn't be settled; she was a wild card, a loose cannon; she needed to make her own way. And she would. She really would.

• • •

"Right," said Linda. "I've got a tent."

"You haven't."

"Yes, I have. Look, it cost me fifteen quid, just like Abi said. Where shall we put it up?"

"There's no room for it anywhere. You'll be able to hear everybody else breathing, wherever it goes. Linda, do let's leave and go to the hotel."

"I don't want to. I'm having an adventure. We're having an adventure."

"Oh, for God's sake. The music, if you can call it that, is ghastly; it's getting cold; I'm tired . . ."

"OK. You go. That's fine."

"You can't stay here on your own," said Alex irritably.

"Yes, I can. I'll be fine."

"Linda, you are not staying here on your own."

"Well, I'm not leaving."

"Oh, for fuck's sake. Why do you have to be so bloody . . . dramatic?"

"I'm not being dramatic. I'm just entering into the spirit of the thing. Which, considering your hospital is going to benefit so much, I'd have thought you should too. You're such a killjoy, Alex. You really are."

"Well, thanks for that."

He'd been waiting for her, not far from where Mary had been, on the far side of the small valley. He sat down in the grass, glared gloomily down at the arena.

"You know, sometimes I wonder if this is worth it."

"What on earth do you mean?"

"Well . . . we only see each other for two days a week, sometimes less, the occasional evening, and when we do we fight. Where's the joy in that?"

"I . . . don't know. What are you trying to say?"

"That this is hardly an ideal existence, simply being together at the weekends. Maybe we should try again to find somewhere we can live together. Or . . . even . . . call it a day."

"Do you really want to do that? Call it a day?" There was a shake in her voice.

He looked at her, put out his hand, and took hers.

"No, of course not. I love you far too much. But . . . this isn't working terribly well, is it?"

There was a long silence; then she said, "No. Not terribly. Um . . . Alex . . ."

"Yes?"

"I . . . well, actually, I have been thinking maybe I could . . . after all . . . move out a bit. Say to Windsor."

"I hated Windsor. Maidenhead was OK."

"I loathed Maidenhead."

"Well, clearly we'll be settled in no time. But . . . why, suddenly?"

"Well . . . I think I could possibly run my business at least two days a week from farther out. I mean, I can always go in for meetings. And keep the office on. What would you think about that?"

"Well . . . I'd think it would be amazing. Wonderful. But I don't believe it. It's a bit like Cherie Blair or Lady Thatcher suddenly announcing a woman's place was in the home."

"Don't compare me to those awful women."

"Sorry."

"Anyway, I think you might have to. Believe it."

"What do you mean?"

"I was . . . well, I was sick this morning."

"Poor darling. You're obviously run-down."

"And the morning before. And the one before that."

"Oh, dear." He was rummaging in the picnic basket. "I'm sure there was some wine left."

"Alex! God, you medics are all the same. So unsympathetic. Didn't you hear what I said?"

"Yes, of course I did. You said you'd been sick this morning."

"Yes, and the two mornings before that."

"So . . . ?"

"For Christ's sake. So . . . I think I might be pregnant. Well, I'm pretty sure I'm pregnant. Actually."

"You what?"

"Alex, you're not deaf yet. I said I was pregnant."

"Oh, my God," he said, staring at her, his face frozen with shock. "God. Linda. Oh, my Linda." He sat staring at her, then put out his hand and stroked her cheek. Very gently. "How did that happen?"

"Usual way, I suppose."

"Yes, but . . ."

"I had that stomach upset last month, remember? Not good with the pill."

"Oh, my God."

"So, are you pleased?"

"Oh, no," he said, "I'm not pleased."

"Oh. Well . . ."

"I'm ecstatic. Totally, gloriously ecstatic. It's wonderful. Amazing. You?"

"I'm . . . moderately ecstatic. Bit thoughtful . . . I don't know how I'll do at it."

"How you do at everything else, that's how . . . Brilliantly. Oh, Linda, I'm so . . . so—" He stopped. He seemed near to tears. She smiled at him, leaned forward, kissed him.

"I'm glad you're pleased."

"I'm . . . well, I'm much, much more than pleased. How do you feel, though?"

"Fine. Except in the morning. As you'll probably find out tomorrow. Oh, and tired. Bit tired."

"We must get you back to the hotel straightaway."

"Alex, I don't want to go back to the hotel. I want to stay here, in this tent . . . with you."

"Oh, don't be so ridiculous."

"Please," she said, and even in the darkness he could see her eyes shining. "Please. For a little while, anyway. Go on, Alex. I dare you."

. . .

"Well, Abi, what a success, eh?" It was Peter Grainger, smiling at her. "I take my hat off to you. It was quite something, but you've pulled it off. And so far . . . no problems."

"No, not yet," said Abi. "Don't speak too soon."

"Oh, I have total faith in you. You and your arrangements. I must admit I had my doubts, but I was wrong. Where's young William?"

"Oh, I don't know. I haven't seen him for ages. Um . . . where's . . . um, Pauline?"

She still had the utmost difficulty in referring to Mrs. Grainger by her Christian name.

"She's in bed, I'm afraid. Eaten something very nasty. Keeps being sick. And . . . well, never mind. I'm sure she'll be better tomorrow."

"Oh, that's terrible," said Abi. "I'm so sorry." Thinking of her silent prayer of the morning and wondering if the God she so firmly didn't believe in had actually sent Mrs. Grainger's illness as a sign to her of His existence.

"Yes, but you know, I don't think she'd have enjoyed this too much. And she'd have felt bound to come down and have a look. And then she'd have started worrying about everything."

"Yes. Yes, I suppose so. But she must be bothered by the noise."

"Oh . . . no. Funnily enough, you can hardly hear it in the house. Something to do with the sound going over the tops of the trees perhaps. I don't know. Anyway, she'll be fine tomorrow; don't you worry. Now . . . this isn't really my sort of music, but I wonder if we could have a dance."

And William, arriving back at the arena, was met by the astonishing sight of his father and Abi dancing together in the near-darkness, his father doing an approximation of the Twist that his generation still clung to on the dance floor, his arms gyrating like crazed chicken wings, and Abi scarcely moving, swaying and curving with the music, the sparklers she was holding making patterns in the darkness. He really did love her, so very much.

. . .

Later, they climbed the hill behind the arena and sat down, listening to the music, the laughter, the shouting, the occasional child crying; and looking at the little barbecue fires all over the campsite, shining in the darkness, the fairy lights strung across the hill, and above them a full moon, rising most obligingly in the sky, trailing stars in its wake.

"That calf was all right, by the way," he said. "I forgot to tell you. In all the excitement. And a heifer."

"Oh, good. I think you should call her Festival."

"Abi! You sound like a Bambi lover. You know we don't give calves names."

"I am a Bambi lover. And why not? Just this once. It is a very special day. One of the best."

"Oh, all right." There was a silence; then: "You're right," he said, and, "It is one of the best. And, you know, I was just thinking . . ."

"I was thinking the same thing," she said, "that terrible, terrible day then, the awful, awful things that happened. And now . . . well, look at it. Good times, in spite of it. Maybe because of it even. Very good. The best, you could almost say."

"Yes," he said, putting his arm round her, "yes, you could almost say that. Or you could actually say it. Come on, Mrs. Grainger. Let's go down there and dance. And then we might go home and take those shorts off."

✦ ACKNOWLEDGEMENTS ✦

Some very big and heartfelt thank-you's are due over this book.

First, and very, very importantly, to Inspector David Toms-Sheridan of the Traffic Operational Command Unit, who fielded my endless cretinous questions, endured countless plot swerves, and offered his own ingenious take on things to more than one of my dilemmas. And who gave me an enormous amount of valuable police time. I hope no crime went unpunished as a result.

The other person without whom I literally could not have written the book is Aimee Di Marco, who not only instructed me most painstakingly on life in an A&E department, but re-created for me with extraordinary vividness the hour-by-hour progress of a major emergency, the structure of the medical teams, the necessary medical and surgical procedures, and the ongoing care of the victims. Her patients are assuredly very fortunate.

At Headline, my truly wonderful publishers, so many thanks to Harrie Evans for patient, painstaking, and inspiring editing, and for making it all a lot more fun; gratitude in spades to Clare Alexander, my wonderfully imaginative, caring, and calming superagent. In the United States, Alison Callahan, for yet more wise and wonderful editing; Alison Rich, publicist extraordinaire; Steve Rubin; and Bill Thomas.

To my other two daughters, Polly and Sophie, for their astonishingly ongoing interest, encouragement, and support; never taken for granted.

And as always to my husband, Paul, who—on being told in hysterical tones one Sunday morning, when I was about two-thirds of the way through, that I absolutely couldn't finish the book, that it was completely impossible—said kindly, but very firmly "I'm afraid you've got to." It was not the first crisis he has defused; I doubt it will be the last.